LOVE'S AWAKENING

Tamara's eyes widened as Steffan stepped closer, so close that she had to tip her chin up to look at him. He smelled so clean and the overpowering size of him crowded her senses until she could feel a weak trembling in her legs.

"You're very beautiful," he murmured. "Like the first morning sun on a calm sea." His fingers touched the soft curls that framed her face. "You've even caught the sunbeams in your hair."

If Tamara was stilled by his gentleness, it was nothing to the bewitched, bemused feeling that flooded Steffan. He wanted to loosen her hair and run his hands into the thick silken mass. He wanted to rip away the clothes that stood between them and hold her in his arms. He wanted . . .

Tamara stood quietly, her wide green eyes held by his. Slowly, he bent his head and touched her lips lightly with his. Neither of them was prepared for the strength of emotion that lifted them and held them suspended in their own world. Tamara felt his arms as he pulled her against him and suddenly his lips claimed hers and sent her into a world where only Steffan existed . . .

Tamara's Ecstasy

SYLVIE F. SOMMERFIELD

ZEBRA BOOKS
KENSINGTON PUBLISHING CORP.

Dedicated with love to my daughter Kathy, her husband Archie, my son Gary and his wife Linda, and my grandchildren, Shannon, Andy, T.J., and Gary, Jr., one of my main sources of encouragement.

ZEBRA BOOKS

are published by

KENSINGTON PUBLISHING CORP.
475 Park Avenue South
New York, N.Y. 10016

Printed in the United States of America

One

Spring of 1749 in Devon, England was an extraordinarily wet and cold one, but it did nothing to dampen the spirits of Lord and Lady Maxwell Devers. It was the time that heralded the birth of their first and only son, Steffan, for they had only one child after that, a pretty little girl whose entrance into the world put a stop to any ideas Maxwell Devers might have had for another son.

Steffan was a large baby, strong and healthy; and from the time of his birth his father had placed all the hopes of the Devers family and wealth in him. By the time he was ten, it was obvious that his faith had been well-placed. He was a good looking child, his golden brown eyes, inherited from his father, were quick and usually filled with laughter. Again from his father he inherited his mane of thick blue black hair. The build also was the Devers inheritance, for his father stood well over six feet and was broad of shoulder. But from his fair haired beautiful mother he inherited qualities of character that were to carry him through an eventful life. He had an extremely virulent sense of humor which often roused the mischievous side of him and at times brought him close to trouble, and he had a deep sense of honesty and honor and extreme pride in his father and the Devers' name.

The Devers' wealth would open doors to an excellent education for Steffan. It began when a tutor was hired; Steffan was ten, and the gentleman was a man with the infinite patience that teaching required and an excellent mind that ranged from languages and mathematics to history. He found in his pupil a quick mind that absorbed everything he had to offer. Mister Gillis was a tall thin man with dark hair and even darker penetrating eyes, which could render Steffan speechless with guilt when he forgot a lesson, or glow with pride at any praise. At their first meeting, Steffan was determined he was not going to be held captive while "dumb" things were crammed into his brain. He had been told by his mother that a tutor had been hired and was on his way, so, the day he was summoned to his father's study did not come as a surprise. He went with dragging feet, for he felt his days of freedom were over. He had always been an active child and the thought of being pinned to a classroom made him miserable. He also knew that trying to change his father's mind when it was made up was almost impossible. He opened the study door and stepped inside, closing the door after him, then turned to face his father and his teacher.

"Come in, Steffan," his father said. There was no smile on his face, but Steffan did not miss the smile in his father's eyes for they always reflected his own.

"Yes sir," he replied and moved toward his father's desk, watching surreptitiously from under his lashes the man who sat in the large chair in front of it.

"Steffan, I want you to say hello to Mr. Gillis. From today on, he will be your tutor, companion, and I hope, the man who can help me guide that willful spirit in the way it should go."

Steffan turned toward Mr. Gillis and said as politely as he could manage, "Hello, sir." He extended his hand toward the older man and glanced up when his hand was taken in a strong grip and hold. He looked up into eyes that were glittering humorously and filled with gentleness and friendship.

"Good day, Steffan. I'm very pleased to meet you. I'm sure we will become good friends, you and I."

Steffan was doubtful about the last part, for in all his young years, teachers and friends were never put in the same category. Friends were the people with whom one could share his best and worst faults and still have their love and respect. Teachers were the people who forced you to learn what you did not want and punished you when you erred.

"You will begin your formal lessons tomorrow," his father said in his deep authoritative voice. "For today, you will take Mr. Gillis about. Show him the classrooms and the rest of the house, make him acquainted with the rest of the staff."

"Yes, sir."

"Mr. Gillis, you will be expected to dine with us, for I'm sure that my son's education is going to require constant surveillance on your part. Dinner is at seven thirty."

"It will be a pleasure, Lord Devers." Mr. Gillis replied. Steffan's ear was tuned to his voice, for despite his looks, it had a deep rich melodious tone that was almost hypnotically pleasing. "And now, Steffan, if you will wait outside please, I have a few words to say to Mr. Gillis in private."

Steffan left the room, closing the door softly behind him. In the vestibule he waited, watching the bright cloudless sky from the large front window. After almost a half hour, the soft click of the door told him he was no longer alone. He stood with his back toward Mr. Gillis waiting rebelliously for the sharp command to turn around. Instead, the soft voice came from near his shoulder.

" 'Tis truly a lovely day, young Steffan. Too lovely to be marching from room to room being introduced. We could save that for tomorrow and go out and enjoy the sunshine."

Steffan looked up quickly, doubting the words and expecting to see derision on his face. He was surprised again at the warmth of the friendly eyes.

"I'm sure you have a favorite place you'd really rather be?"

"Yes, sir" Steffan replied honestly.

"Do you mind an intruder accompanying you?"

"No, sir" he began hesitantly as he eyed the immaculate suit Mr. Gillis was wearing.

Mr. Gillis laughed. "I take it this is not the appropriate garb to do so in. Well, if you show me to my room, I shall change quickly and we'll be on our way."

Now, for the first time, Steffan realized he was serious, along with the fact that he was not to be confined to a classroom—at least for today. He smiled, and Mr. Gillis cracked open the door to both Steffan's mind and his heart.

Steffan led Mr. Gillis to his quarters which consisted of two rooms, one a bedroom and the other a small sitting room. He waited in the latter while Mr. Gillis changed.

"How old are you, Steffan" Mr. Gillis called from the bedroom. Steffan thought it odd that his father had not informed him, but he answered.

"I shall be eleven in a few weeks, sir."

"How few?"

"Well . . . about twelve, sir."

It was a good thing he did not see the laughter in Mr. Gillis' eyes then. When Mr. Gillis returned to the room he was dressed in a pair of rough corduroy trousers and a heavy wool sweater and to Steffan's delight heavy boots good for walking and climbing.

"I see you approve. I take it we will be doing some walking?"

"Yes, sir."

They left the house and walked slowly down a path that led across a wide lawn and entered a thick stand of trees. Through these Steffan led the way and it was obvious to Mr. Gillis, the boy had been along this path often before. They walked along in silence for quite a while, then Steffan stopped and stood very still in a position of intent listening. Mr. Gillis was going to ask him why, when he noticed the look of sheer pleasure on Steffan's face. It was a sound he got a great deal of pleasure from. Mr. Gillis listened too, and then the sound came to him. The soft rolling sound of the sea against a sandy shore.

"It sounds so pretty from here" Steffan breathed softly, "almost like my mother when she sang to me at night."

"And you love it," Mr. Gillis finished.

"Yes, sir, I do. It always makes me feel like . . . well, like I kind of belong to it . . . like I'm home."

"You want the life of a sailor, young Steffan. I don't think it requires the education your father wants you to have."

"My . . . my father doesn't know," he looked up quickly. "You won't tell him?"

Mr. Gillis put his hand on Steffan's shoulder and smiled down into the apprehensive face. "No, Steffan. If you don't want me to, I shall not. But I would like to discuss it with you. Maybe I can make you see it from another point."

Steffan shrugged. "It's how I feel, sir. If my father won't let me be a sailor, I shall just run away when I'm older."

"Steffan," Mr. Gillis began as they walked along slowly. "Have you ever visited the docks at Newport?"

"No, sir."

"Well, let me tell you what you will see if you ever go. There are men there, begging in the streets. Men who have made their lives as common sailors without any kind of education. Men who had been injured in one way or another and had no place to turn, no other abilities to use. When they were no longer of use to the owners of these ships, they were put ashore to fend for themselves with no pension and no one to turn to. Now they beg for enough coins to keep themselves alive."

Steffan stopped and looked up at Mr. Gillis, his jaw determinedly stiff. "Are you telling me I shouldn't be a sailor?"

"No, I'm telling you you should be more than that. Steffan you are a bright intelligent boy. Look beyond the adventure of being a sailor. Look beyond today. Why be a sailor? Why not be captain of your own vessel? Why not be master of your own fate instead of putting your fate in someone else's hands?"

Steffan watched him closely and the dawning realization grew in his eyes and caused Mr. Gillis to chuckle. "Captain of my own ship" Steffan repeated softly then again came the swift flash of his white smile. Mr. Gillis had widened the doorway between

8

them enough to see the dreams and hopes of the boy within.

"Come, let's see this 'special place' of yours."

"Mr. Gillis, how can I get to be captain of my own ship?"

"Learn, Steffan, learn. Take everything I have to teach you. Go beyond me and learn all you can. When you have grown into a man and you feel you are ready, I shall go to your father with you and stand at your side and help you convince him that the sea is where you belong."

Steffan watched him for a few moments while Martin Gillis waited for the final decision. Then it came, with a few soft words and a smile of trust.

"All right Mr. Gillis. Come on, I want to show you a place I go that's all mine. No one else has ever been there."

Martin nodded and they walked together through the balance of the woods and out along the sandy beach. After they had walked along for quite a while, Martin noticed that the ground to the right of them began to rise and soon they were walking along a narrow strip of beach with the ocean on one side and high rocky cliffs on the other. Suddenly Steffan stopped and pointed to a sharp inverted V in the face of the rocks. As they neared it, Martin saw that it was a narrow entrance to a cave. When they wriggled their way inside, he found a large circular cave that was lit by little threads of light that worked their way through the tiny cracks on the ceiling. It gave him the impression of millions of tiny stars shedding small beams of light. It was remarkably lovely.

"I found it one day when I was wandering about. It's a great place, Mr. Gillis. It has all kinds of little caves running about. You could hide in here and no one would ever find you."

"I should say it's a marvelous find. In here, you could dream of marvelous adventures and make believe that they all come true. You are a lucky boy to have a place all your own."

"You . . . you can use it whenever you like," Steffan replied softly, offering the final gift to a beginning friendship, real trust.

"Why, thank you, Steffan. I shall consider it an honor to share it with you."

They spent the next hour exploring the cave and becoming acquainted with each other. Dinner that night was a much more comfortable affair than Martin thought it would be. Steffan's parents were pleased at the attitude Steffan seemed to have toward his new teacher, for being confined to a classroom had always been the most difficult thing for him. Now he chattered in a friendly way and listened intently to every word his new instructor spoke. When the meal was done, Lord and Lady Devers invited Martin to have brandy with them in the drawing room. Steffan was told it was time for him to go to bed, and Martin knew they wanted to question him. After Steffan had kissed both his parents, he went to Martin and again extended his hand.

"Good night, sir."

"Good night, Steffan."

"Is there a special time that you would like to begin tomorrow, sir?"

"Well, Steffan, what do you say you meet me at the edge of the woods about ten. I think a short instruction walk of a morning is good for both mind and soul."

"Yes, sir," Steffan grinned.

Martin winked at him and saw the immediate reaction of laughter in his eyes.

When Steffan had left the room, his father poured three glasses of brandy, then sat with his wife by his side, opposite Martin.

"Well," Ellen Devers smiled. "What do you think of our son?"

"Ellen, Martin has only had a day with Steffan; how can he tell so soon?"

"Oh, I think I can tell you exactly what I think at this moment, Lord Devers, and I don't believe my opinion shall change over the years."

"Over the years?" Maxwell questioned. "Then you intend to take my offer and stay?"

"Lord Devers, I think you have an extraordinarily intelligent and strong son and I shall consider it a pleasure to open as many doors for him as I can."

"Excellent," Maxwell replied with a broad smile. "You know I consider you the best England has to offer. I want Steffan to be able to take my place one day at the head of my business and you are most capable of preparing him for it."

Martin was about to answer when Ellen caught his eye and gave a small negative shake of her head. He changed his words.

"I shall consider it an honor to prepare him for whatever the future has to offer." He watched Ellen's satisfied smile. "Why, she knows," he thought. "She knows exactly what her son wants to do with his life and she agrees to it. Steffan will be delighted to know he has another ally."

The days passed rapidly, and Martin found Steffan to be exactly what he expected. He was like a sponge, soaking up every drop of learning Martin had to offer. Classroom lessons were held in-

10

side for three hours a day from lunch until four. In the morning, they would walk and talk. Martin was sure that Steffan got more from their discussions than from the classroom. From dinner on, Martin's time was his own and he had Sundays to do with as he chose. Often he found Steffan at his door on Sunday asking for or returning a book and suggesting that they spend the day either riding or sailing the small sailboat that was always tied to the docks a few miles from Devers Hall. It didn't take Martin long to see that he was being used to get access to the sailboat whereupon Steffan would take over and sail it expertly up and down the coast.

A few months later, Steffan and Martin were on more solid ground in their friendship when Steffan asked him about himself.

"Did you always want to be a teacher, Mr. Gillis?"

"When I was a young man like you, Steffan, I was blessed with a father who had a great respect for learning. I thank him every day of my life for it, although I was not wise enough to enjoy it at the time. No, I was a rather rebellious boy. Since we were quite wealthy, I wanted just to be free and roam the earth. He, for the most part pushed the education down my throat; although learning was easy for me, it is still quite difficult to teach someone something he is not willing to learn. I travelled every summer and by the time I was twenty, I had seen every part of the world there was to see. Then, when I, in all my conceit, had thought I had seen everything, life handed me an experience I shall never forget. It took away my mother, father and all our wealth in one fell swoop. It was only then that I discovered the real value of the education I had. I realized that without a good education a man is merely a slave, but that with it, he is the master of his life. I had many hard blows in the next few years. I saw a side of life I had never known existed. I spoke to you of the sailors at Newport. I lived among them, and among others of even poorer existence. Then, when I was desperate, lonely, hungry, I realized that I had a tool in my hands to make my life better. I took a position as instructor at a school and got along reasonably well. I wrote and had published several books. I was beginning to feel better about myself when I met your father. We developed a very good friendship. Then, he offered me this position. I was to decide whether I wanted it or not after I met you." He laughed at Steffan's surprised look when he found that the teacher did not have the responsibility forced on him but had the right to choose if he wanted to teach him or not. The look of surprise was replaced immediately by one of deep respect and sincere affection. Mr. Gillis

11

had stepped across the final barrier into Steffan's heart and was now prepared to teach the boy to be a man.

Steffan was to find, in the years that followed, that no matter what kind of problems he had, Mr. Gillis seemed to have the answer, and the answer was always given to him from two directions so that the choice was always his. He had taken to weighing the choices he made by whether or not Mr. Gillis would be pleased or disappointed.

On the fifth of April in 1764, Steffan celebrated two things in their own individual way: his fifteenth birthday, and acquiring his first true friend his own age. For his birthday, his parents presented him with a horse of his own and a new saddle. Among all his other attributes, Mr. Gillis was an accomplished rider and took it upon himself to teach Steffan to ride properly. By the end of the day, Steffan was sore and stiff but overjoyed that he had received Mr. Gillis' nod of approval in establishing a rapport with the horse he had named 'Starlight'.

It was early the next morning when Steffan, groaning over his stiff, sore body, climbed into the saddle again. He was going to ride for a half hour alone before he met Mr. Gillis at their usual place for their morning walk. He urged the horse forward and down the path through the woods. Once on the beach, he let the horse have its head and they ran freely down the sand, splashing the surf about them. He felt exuberant. Catching the wind in his face and feeling the power of the animal he was astride, he wanted to shout for sheer joy. It was only when his horse faltered slightly and his flesh was lathered that Steffan pulled him to a halt. He dismounted and walked the horse while he cooled then he took a cloth from his saddlebag and wiped him clean.

He was about to remount when he heard the sound of voices on the opposite side of a large pile of rocks. The voices were taunting and cruel and occasionally there came a small muffled sound of pain. He dropped the horse's reins to the ground and climbed over the boulders to see what was happening on the other side. The sight he faced made him cry out in anger. Three boys about his own age had another boy pinned against the rocks and were proceeding to give him a beating. The boy was trying his best to defend himself but the odds were too much for him. With a loud shout, Steffan leapt from the rocks and landed in the midst of the battle. Taken completely by surprise, the three boys momentarily backed away and for the first time, Steffan recognized who they were. The largest boy was the same age as Steffan. His name was Jaspar Sinclair, and he lived not too far from Steffan. The boys knew each other well, but no friendship had developed because Steffan did not like or trust Jaspar.

Jaspar was a very good looking boy with blond hair and blue eyes. But about his face lingered the look of the spoiled, arrogant only child of wealthy parents. Steffan knew Jaspar to be vicious to those under him, although he could be charming when he chose. The other two boys were followers of Jaspar, mostly because they were afraid of him. One was the Sinclairs' stable boy, Ralph Walters, a young man of limited intelligence but strong of back and arm. The other boy was a surprise to Steffan. His name was Mackenzie Davidson and he was the local clergyman's son. He was the only one who looked away in shame at being caught at what they were doing. He was a slender boy with large dark eyes and rather gentle features.

"Well, well" sneered Jaspar. He was well aware that the odds were still three to two. "Look who's playing knight. Steff, old boy, why don't you get away before you get your wings clipped?"

"I would if it were one on one" Steffan answered coldly. "But don't you think three to one is a little unbalanced?" He was aware that the boy behind him had pushed himself away from the wall and had come to stand beside him. He threw a quick glance to see who he was. He discovered he knew him also. His name was Thomas Braydon. His father was a shipbuilder in the town of Hampton only a few miles away. Steffan did not know much else about him. He was only two or three inches shorter than Steffan and slender of build. He had a thick mane of straw blond hair and deep green intelligent eyes. There was a small trickle of blood from his cut lip and his eye was already turning black.

"Yes, come at me one at a time and I'll lick you all" he said angrily.

Steffan had been watching both Jaspar and Mackenzie for he knew instinctively, Ralph would do nothing unless Jaspar told him. Mackenzie's eyes refused to meet Steffan's directly and Steffan felt he would take advantage of a way out of the situation.

"Mackenzie" Steffan said quietly. "You back away and keep Ralph off of him and I'll do the same. Let's leave this between Jaspar and Thomas."

"Mack, Ralph!" Jaspar snapped authoritatively. "Stomp on him. Show him it's not polite to interfere in someone else's business."

Ralph began to move forward but Mack's arm stopped him.

"That kind of sounds more fair to me; after all, Ralph, this fight is between Jaspar and Tom."

Ralph stopped, unsure of which way to go. He looked at Steffan then back at Mack.

"Get him, Ralph" Jaspar ordered. But it was soon evident that Ralph was in this more for Mack than for Jaspar, as he silently turned his back and walked away. Jaspar glared at Steffan with hatred plain on his face, and Steffan did what would always anger his opponents through life. He laughed.

"He's all yours, Tom," he said softly.

No more needed to be said to Tom as he threw himself at Jaspar. Tom's white hot anger seemed to give him maddening strength, which eventually got the best of Jaspar. Both boys were bloody and filthy from the sand and water they were rolling about in. But Tom finally straddled Jaspar and gave him the finishing blow that made him cry enough. Mack and Steffan pulled Tom away from Jaspar's half conscious form.

"C'mon, Tom, he's had enough, and you need some looking after. Mack, let's get him on my horse and take him home."

The two boys half dragged, half carried Tom around the rocks. They did not notice that Jaspar, raised on one elbow, was glaring after them, his eyes alive with a virulent, deadly hatred; and the hatred now centered upon Steffan. Once they had Tom on the horse, Mack walked beside it to steady Tom's weaving form and Steffan led the horse back up the beach and through the path in the woods to the edge of the lawn. There, he was stopped in his tracks by the quiet voice of Martin Gillis.

"I thought you would have a good reason for being late, Steffan. From what war did you rescue this gladiator?" he said with a half amused smile.

"He's a friend of mine" Steffan said. "He . . . he fell from the rocks on the beach and got hurt. I thought it best to bring him here before he went home so we could clean him up and put something on those cuts."

"Maybe it would be best if you took him to my room. We can clean him up there and there will be fewer questions asked," he replied and was rewarded by a quick look of gratitude from Steffan. They got Tom safely to Martin's room where he washed away the dirt and treated the cuts on his face, none of which had been caused by a fall. He watched Steffan and realized he was going to get no answers there, for whatever was the cause of Tom's battle, the reasons and the outcome were safe with Steffan.

"Steffan, go down and have cook brew you a pot of very strong tea. Tell her it's for me."

Steffan left and Martin drew Mack into his sitting room. He

14

looked at the boy who met his eyes. "Tom didn't fall" he stated firmly.

"No, sir."

"How did he get hurt?"

"He was in a fight."

"With Steffan?" he asked, surprise heavy in his voice.

"Oh, no, sir. Steffan . . . well, Steffan just kind of made it even."

"Tell me, Mack." Mack poured out the whole story.

"What was the fight over?"

"Jaspar. Because he's always had everything he wants, he thought just because Tom's family was poor, he could get his sister. He tried, and Martha got frightened and told her parents. They went to Jaspar's father, who punished him. After that, Jaspar started rumors about Martha. When Tom heard, he told Jaspar to be quiet or he'd beat him black and blue."

"How did you get mixed up in this, Mack? I know you and your family. You're not that kind of boy."

For the first time since they had begun to talk, Mack's eyes fell and his face flushed.

"I . . . really don't know, sir. Jaspar has a way when he really wants something. When we found Tom on the beach, one thing led to another. I guess I sort of got caught up on the wrong side. I'm ashamed, sir. I really am, and worse, my father will be ashamed for me."

"He need never know" Martin said softly.

"Sir, my father always seems to have a way of knowing when I've done something I shouldn't have. He has a way of looking through me, like a window. I'd rather tell him than have him find out somewhere else. He may be ashamed and he may punish me, but he'll understand, and I'll feel a lot better."

Martin smiled and was about to reply when Steffan returned with the tea. Martin took it and told both boys to wait in his sitting room while he took the tea to Tom. After Tom had drunk some tea into which Martin put a few drops of laudanum, he drifted off to sleep, and Martin was about to rejoin the boys when their quiet voices drifted to him.

"We'll just keep our mouths shut, Mack, and if we hear anything else about Martha, we'll tell the person we heard it from the truth. Maybe we can stop Jaspar's bad mouth."

"One of these days, Jaspar is going to try to get even with you, Steff. You know his kind. He never forgets what anyone does to him. One way or another, he'll try to get back at you. Maybe you

15

should have stayed out of it."

"Mack, one of the things my parents have taught me, and Mr. Gillis, is that a man's name is one of the most valuable things he's got. He should never let anyone—even himself—dishonor it. I guess that goes for a girl too. Martha can't fight Jaspar herself. So it's up to us to see that he doesn't do that to her again. What kind of life would she lead if her name was blackened like that. I'll watch for Jaspar, and I can take care of myself. Let's just keep this a secret between you, me, and Tom. All right?"

"Sure, Steff. My lips are sealed."

"Ahh," Martin thought with a deep sense of satisfaction, "If I've been responsible in any way for that sense of honor, my young gladiator, then I am deeply proud. Hold on to it forever, Steff. There will be no end to the mountains you can climb or the battles you will win."

Two

Tom spent the night at Devers Hall. When he awoke in the morning, he found both Martin and Steffan waiting in the next room. The hours of sleep washed away the soreness in his body but his face showed severe signs of the battle. Both eyes were blackened, his lower lip was swollen and there was a jagged cut on his left cheek, that would eventually leave a scar. Martin smiled and offered him a cup of strong tea, which Tom accepted gratefully.

"I had imagined your parents would be quite worried about you, so I took the liberty to send a message to them last night that you would be spending a few days with Steffan."

"A few days!" Tom said aghast. "Me? Spend a few days at Devers Hall. My parents will be wondering where I got the nerve to come here at all."

"Why should it take nerve?" questioned Steffan.

Tom laughed. "Steff, you and I don't exactly move in the same circles. You're Steffan Devers, son of Lord Maxwell Devers, heir to great wealth. Me, I'm plain Tom Braydon, son of a poor shipbuilder and heir to a lot of work and no money."

Steffan looked at him levelly. "I don't see where that makes a difference; either you want to be my friend or you don't."

"You know I'm your friend" Tom said quickly. "But don't you think your parents will disapprove?"

"You've misjudged my parents, Tom. Neither of them judge a man by the money in his pockets. Stay for a few days . . . see for yourself."

"Thanks, Steff, I'd like that."

"Good, then we can all go down for breakfast," Steffan laughed. "Guest or no guest, I'm sure Mr. Gillis won't allow me to get out of my lessons today. If you struggle through them with me, we can go riding afterwards, then maybe go for a swim."

"You're right, young man," Martin laughed. "Your last Latin translation was atrocious. Classes as usual. Now I'm famished; let us retire to the breakfast room where I shall have the pleasure

17

of watching you two healthy animals stuff yourselves."

They went downstairs and found Steffan's parents and his sister Cecile already at the table. Cecile was younger than Steffan by one year. She resembled her brother so much that people often thought they were twins with the exception that where Steffan was extremely large, Cecile was very tiny. She had the same humorous glint in her golden brown eyes and the same thick raven black hair. Steffan often referred to her as 'brat' or 'mouse,' but the names were given in sincere affection. After being with them for a few moments, it was obvious to everyone that she adored her brother.

Although Tom's presence was a surprise, no one said anything. Steffan introduced Tom to his parents. "Mother, Father. This is a good friend of mine, Tom Braydon. I've invited him to stay a few days. Tom, this is my mother and father and my 'baby' sister, Cecile."

"Good morning Lady Devers, Lord Devers and Miss Devers," Tom said, unsure of whether the greeting was proper or not. If it was not, no one gave a sign.

"Good morning, Tom," Ellen Devers smiled.

"Good morning," Maxwell said. "Braydon? Is your father Josiah Braydon? The one who builds ships?"

"Yes, sir," Tom answered. 'Here it comes' he thought. The arrogant what-are-you-doing-in-my-house type of attitude would make it clear to him that his visit should be short and final.

"I know Josiah well. He builds the best ships in England and is one of the most honest businessmen I've ever dealt with. I'm surprised I haven't seen you before. I've been in business with your father for years."

"Father has me working as a laborer in the shipyard. He insists that I have to learn the business from the ground up before he'll let me run it. I even had to make a trip to the Macmillan forest to find out what kind of trees we grow for the lumber and how they cut, season and ship it. Father is very thorough."

Maxwell's eyes took on a light tinge of respect. "I'm sure your father must be proud of you and consider you an able man to follow him. You have large shoes to fill."

"Yes, sir. I only hope I don't disappoint him."

"I'm sure you won't. Sit down; enjoy your breakfast."

Tom sat beside Cecile who had been watching him from under lowered lashes from the moment he came into the room. Tom watched as the conversation flowed easily about him. He was included as though he had spent many mornings in their home.

He never enjoyed anything more than the three days he spent at Devers Hall. The signs of the fight were fading from his face when he finally went home. He was allowed to leave only with the promise to Steffan's mother that he would come again soon. Over the next three years, he did so, often accompanied by Mackenzie Davidson who made up a threesome which was to remain together for many years to come.

When Steffan was eighteen, Cecile was seventeen and about to be presented formally to society. It was to be her first big party, her first long gown, and the first time she was allowed to wear her hair up. She was beside herself with anxiety, and Steffan did not understand the reason why, until a week before the party. Steffan had just risen and dressed and was preparing to go down for breakfast when he heard the light rap on his door. Before he could answer it, Cecile opened the door and came in closing it quickly behind her.

"Well" he grinned. "To what do I owe the honor of this early morning visit, brat?"

"Steffan, I've got to talk to you, please" she replied urgently.

His smile faded when he saw how serious she was. "What's the matter, Cecile?" he said quietly, then he walked to her and put both hands on her shoulders. "C'mon, brat, tell me what's wrong."

"Steff . . . do you know for sure if mother invited T . . . the Braydons to the ball?"

"Of course. Josiah is one of father's friends, Tom is my best friend and" he laughed, "I think Tom is more than that to you."

She blushed prettily but did not smile which caused Steffan to frown.

"Cecile . . . there's something you want to tell me and you might as well tell me now."

"Steff . . . I . . . I want you to tell Tom not to come."

"Not! . . . why?"

"Be . . . Because I don't want him to."

"Now, brat," he said gently, "we've never lied to each other in our whole lives, let's not start now."

"Oh, Steff," she sobbed as she threw herself into his arms. "Jaspar is going to kill him."

"Kill him! Jaspar Sinclair! I know the Sinclairs are invited just for protocol, but what does Jaspar have to do with Tom? They've managed to stay out of each other's hair for the last three years."

"It . . . it's me, Steff. At the last social, Jaspar asked me if he

19

could talk to Mama and Papa . . . so that some day we could be married. I was angry. I . . . I told him some day I was going to marry Tom. Oh, Steff, he got so angry. He told me if I had anything more to do with Tom he would create an incident and fight with Tom. You know what an accomplished swordsman he is. Steff, he'll kill Tom. Tom is such a gentle man . . . he's a builder, Steff. He can't fight Jaspar!''

Steffan had become so angry his teeth were clenched to keep the words from slipping out. ''Has he ever . . . ever tried to touch you, brat?'' he shook her slightly as she tried to turn away. ''This isn't the first time something like this has happened is it . . . is it! Why didn't you tell me?''

She looked up at him, her eyes filled with tears. ''Because I love you more than my own life, Steff. I couldn't stand it if something happened to you because of me.''

He pulled her back into his arms and held her. His face was a frozen mask of anger. Slowly, he controlled himself until a cold core of anger burned deep within. He held her a little away from him and smiled. She had no idea how much control it took.

''Now, you trust me, don't you, brat?'' he smiled. She nodded.

''Then don't worry about a thing, I'll see to it that there's no argument or fight the night of your big party.''

''Steff, I don't want you hurt, you won't . . .''

''I won't do anything foolish, brat, I'll just make sure Tom and Jaspar don't tangle at your party, all right?''

She smiled, her golden eyes glowing with affection for the tall handsome brother she loved.

''Thank you, Steff.''

''You're welcome,'' he grinned. ''I'm sure Tom will be pleased to know you care for him as much as he does you. I'm tired of watching him moon about when you don't smile at him.''

Her eyes widened. ''Steff! You wouldn't tell him! I would die of embarrassment. Promise me, Steff, you won't say anything to him. He . . . he's never said . . . I mean . . .''

Steffan laughed, ''No wonder, he's scared silly of you. Why did you tell Jaspar you were going to marry Tom if you don't want him to know?''

She looked up into the mirror of her own laughing eyes. ''Because I intend to, just as soon as Tom discovers that even if father has a little money, I'm no different than any other girl he knows.''

''That's been a hard thing for Tom right from the beginning. Have you ever given him a sign that you might be interested?''

"I'm not like Mary Carter! The way she throws herself at you is disgraceful," Cecile snapped, but she began to giggle as Steffan laughed heartily.

"Never mind me," he grinned. "You'd better give Tom a little nudge or you might grow up to the old age of eighteen without a proposal of marriage."

"Smarty! I've told you Jaspar Sinclair has already proposed."

Steffan's smile faded. "You wouldn't give him any real serious thought, would you, brat?"

"Oh, Steffan," her eyes grew gentle. "You know I wouldn't! I know how he hates you and Tom, and I know you don't trust or like him. You know I wouldn't marry someone like that. I don't know what caused it, but I know you and Jaspar have tangled before. That would be one of the most important things about the man I marry; you would have to approve because I know you love me and want me to have the best."

Steffan was silent, for he was a little overcome with the deep love his sister had so openly shown him. He held her close for another moment.

"I love you, brat, and I want you to know that you would have to look a long time to find a better man than Tom, if you can get past that silly pride of his about father's wealth."

"Well," she said with a bright smile, "I'm going to stun him. My gown is so beautiful, Tom Braydon won't stand a chance."

"I don't know whether to feel sorry for Tom or not," Steffan added mischievously.

"Don't, because I'm going to make him the best wife in the world."

"Well, you go on and make your plans, little spider; I've got some errands to run for father and Mr. Gillis wants to talk to me this afternoon so I've got to be on my way."

"What's he want to talk to you about? Since he came back from his vacation, you and he have had your heads together like a couple of thieves."

Steffan shrugged, but turned away from her so her questioning eyes could not read the suppressed excitement on his face. He knew that Martin Gillis had a close friend in the naval academy and had gone to London to see if Steffan could take the entrance exam. If the answer was affirmative, he and Steffan were going to present the idea to Steffan's father. Martin had kept his word to Steffan. He had held secret the fact that Steffan's one ambition was to captain his own vessel. In return, Steffan had concentrated on learning everything Martin had to offer. Steffan could barely wait to hear what Martin had to say. He only hoped his father would understand.

"I guess Mr. Gillis will tell me if he thinks I should know. In the meantime, run along, brat. I've got to be on my way."

"Well," she replied with a smile, "thanks again, Steff. You always seem to be the shoulder I cry on when anything in my life goes wrong."

"What else are big brothers for?" he replied.

She reached up on tip-toe and kissed him. "Well, anyway, I'm grateful. Maybe someday I can do something for you."

Steffan watched her as she left, closing the door quietly behind her, but his mind was on Jaspar Sinclair. Since the first time they had tangled, Steffan had purposely tried to stay out of his way, not because he was afraid, but because he didn't want any trouble that might interfere with his future plans. Staying in his father's and Mr. Gillis' good graces had been a consistent battle on his part. But this time, Jaspar had touched him in one of his most vulnerable spots. There was no way he would let this kind of thing pass and somehow he had a feeling Jaspar knew this. He left his room and went to the stable where his own horse was waiting to be saddled. In a little over two hours, he found himself on the edge of Sinclair property. He made his way to an area of riding trails that he knew Jaspar rode often, usually in the morning. He dismounted and loosened the cinch on his saddle to let his horse breathe; then he leaned against a tree and waited. Soon he heard the sound of an approaching horse. He pushed himself away from the tree and watched the bridle path intently, then gave a little satisfied sound when he saw the approaching rider was Jaspar Sinclair.

He stepped out onto the path just as Jaspar was a few feet away. Jaspar reined up sharply, surprised to find someone there. Jaspar's arrogant face twisted into a malicious grin when he saw Steffan.

Slowly he stepped down from his horse, his eyes on Steffan's face. "I take it since you saw fit to waylay me on my own property, there's something important you feel you have to say to me." He was tapping his riding crop against his boot top methodically, punctuating each word as he walked toward Steffan.

"Yes, I have something to say to you, Jaspar. Believe me, I wouldn't take the time to come here if it wasn't important. I'm making every effort to stay out of your way, Jaspar, but you seem determined to push it; so let's have it out right now. You don't like me and I don't like you and that's fine. But I want to give you a warning. Stay away from Cecile. She told me what you said to her. I know you hate me and Tom, but I won't stand by and let you use my little sister as a weapon. She's sweet and innocent and I intend to see that she doesn't mix with people like you if I can help it. If anything happens the night of her party between you and Tom, you can be sure, you'll have to face Tom and me together. Just stay away from Cecile. She loves Tom.''

Jaspar's face became mottled red from his anger. ''Just who the hell do you think you Devers are? You think your sister is too good for me. The Sinclair name is as old and as distinguished and wealthy as yours.''

''It has nothing to do with money. If we were as poor as church mice and you as rich as Croesus I wouldn't let her marry you.''

''You damned, conceited bastard! You and that teasing bitch of a sister . . .''

Whatever else he was going to say was cut short as Steffan, in a brilliant flash of pure rage, struck him with every ounce of strength he had. Jaspar's knees buckled and he dropped to the ground. Steffan stood for a moment glaring at the inert form, then slowly he turned from Jaspar and walked to his horse, mounted and rode back to Devers Hall. Deep inside, he knew that the problem that existed between himself and Jaspar was far from over, but at least now he felt Jaspar would not cause any problem with Tom. For with one blow, he had centered all Jaspar's hatred on himself.

At the moment of Steffan's confrontation with Jaspar, Maxwell Devers and Martin Gillis were seated together in Maxwell's study.

''What was it you wanted to talk to me about, Martin? Has my son been shirking his studies?''

''On the contrary, Steffan is doing quite well; in fact, I really think that I am not equipped to teach him any more.''

''Are you suggesting he should be sent to school elsewhere? I want him prepared to handle all my business enterprises.''

''That is what I wanted to talk to you about. I know Steffan might be angry with me for going behind his back, but I really felt it was something I should discuss with you first.''

Maxwell and Martin had been friends for over twenty years. They respected each other completely. Maxwell knew that Martin was preparing to broach a very touchy subject, for he could tell by the look in the other's eyes that what he was going to say was serious and probably of great import to himself and Steffan.

What concerned Steffan was of the highest importance to Maxwell, for he had placed all his hopes and dreams and pride in his one and only son.

Maxwell sat back in his chair and watched Martin intently. "Why do I have this feeling, Martin, that what you are about to say is something I don't want to hear?" Martin stood up and walked to the large french doors that overlooked the garden. He looked out without seeing the loveliness there.

"Maxwell," he said gently. "If you will have the patience I should like to tell you a little story."

"A story?" Maxwell smiled. "All right, Martin, let's hear this story."

"Once upon a time" Martin began, then he laughed and turned to Maxwell "I guess I should say 'once upon many many times.' There was a gentleman who captured a very rare and beautiful bird. Its plumage was beyond description and he wanted to keep it all to himself. But the bird was a wild, free kind of spirit that could not be held in captivity. The man was warned that the bird, if set free, would return to him often of its own volition, but if held a captive, it would slowly die. He was so selfish and so afraid that the bird would never return, he refused it its freedom. Often the bird would batter against the cage that held it, but it could not fight itself free. It loved the man, but could not bear the cage. And then one day, it died and the man was left to grieve alone." Martin's voice died to a soft whisper and for several minutes there was a deep and poignant silence in the room. Then he heard Maxwell get up from his chair and walk to the small table on which he kept a bottle of brandy. He poured two drinks and crossed the room to stand by Martin. Silently, he handed Martin a drink. They sipped and stood together at the window.

"I love him, Martin" he said softly. "He and Cecile are our whole life."

"I know that, and I'm sure they do also."

"Why should he want to leave us?"

"Maxwell, it isn't that he wants to leave you. Don't you see the kind of man you've raised? You have created a brilliant honorable, courageous independent man who wants to bear the responsibility for what he can make out of himself. Give him the chance to carve out his place in life, as you have. You started with nothing and built. Let him do the same. Don't cage him, Maxwell, or as surely as there is a God, his independence and self respect will die and you shall be left with the shell of a man whose spirit is dead.''

"Martin, I would be the last person in the world to cause Steffan any deliberate harm. Is it wrong to want your only son near you, to want to give him the best life has to offer?''

"What is the best? Is it best to choose his life's path for him, to show him every step to take, to cushion every fall he might have? Or is it best to open the cage door and tell him to fly, but to remember that he has a haven to return to? To let him know you love him and that you respect his abilities. He will love you in return, Maxwell, by never really leaving you.''

Maxwell sighed deeply. "And I suppose you know what it is he really wants to do?''

"I am breaking his confidence for the first time in eight years, but yes, I know what he has had his heart set on since he was a child.''

"May I ask what?''

"To be captain of his own sailing ship. To travel the world. To be part of the adventurous future.''

"My God, Martin, I could buy him his own ship.''

"Yes, and give it to him as a toy. Then he would never really know if he had the ability to earn it or not. Don't make that foolish mistake, Maxwell.''

"Damn you, Martin. What do you expect me to do?''

"I went to London recently to speak to an old friend of mine. He is an admiral in His Majesty's Navy. If Steffan can pass the examination, to be given in two weeks, he will be taken aboard the H.M.S. Godspeed. There he will be trained from the rank of common sailor as far up as his abilities can take him. I have asked for no special favors on his part; I'm sure Steffan would resent it if I did.''

"A common sailor! My son! He would never be able to stand the pressures. He is too used to everything our money can give him.''

"I think you're wrong, Maxwell. In fact, he's eighteen now; I think by the time he is twenty-six, he'll have his own command. I have that much faith in him.''

"Are you suggesting I don't?''

"Do you?''

Their eyes met and held for a few moments; then Maxwell said gently "Yes, yes Martin, I do.''

"Then, when Steffan comes to you, will you give him your blessing? Will you . . . open the cage door?''

"When?''

"As soon as I inform him the exam is possible."

"And when will that be?"

"This afternoon. I told him I wanted to talk to him. I shall present him with the facts, then he will come to you. I would appreciate it if you did not tell him I have intervened on his behalf."

"Meaning it will look better for me if he thinks it is an agreement between us. Thanks," Maxwell said dryly. Martin smiled in response and extended his hand to Maxwell, who took it firmly with an answering glitter of humor in his brown eyes. Martin returned to his room, and waited for the inevitable visit by an impatient Steffan. It was not long before he heard the rap on his door. "Come in, Steffan."

Steffan stepped inside. Martin could have laughed aloud at the control Steffan was trying to hold over his curiosity.

"You wanted to talk to me, sir?"

"Yes, Steffan, sit down, please."

Steffan obediently sat, but it was on the edge of the seat with his eyes pinned on Martin, who slowly took the seat opposite him.

"Steffan, my trip to London was quite rewarding on your behalf. There is an exam you can take to enter the Naval Academy. If you can pass it, you will be accepted only as the lowest recruit. It is possible with diligence and hard work that you could one day command your own ship. What you do now is up to you."

Steffan bounced to his feet, his excitement too much to let him remain seated.

"Wonderful! Do I know enough to pass the exam? Mr. Gillis, are there books I should study, something I could do to . . ."

"Wait, Steffan, I think the first thing you should do is go to your father."

Steffan stood still, then he gulped. "Father?"

"Yes."

"I . . . I guess I do have to ask my parents first."

"Steffan," laughed Martin. "I think your mother has known for as long as you have. She loves you and understands you. Go to your father. If you need friends, your mother and I are here."

Martin knew he had said the right thing when he saw Steffan's shoulders straighten at the thought of having to hide behind either his mother or Mr. Gillis.

"No, sir. I'll talk to him myself. I'll try to make him understand."

"Give him the benefit of a doubt, Steffan; it might not be as hard as you think."

After he left Martin's room, he walked down the stairs slowly forming and discarding words in his mind. He stood outside his father's study door for several moments before he raised courage to poise his hands to knock.

"Come in," came the muffled reply. He stepped inside the room and looked across at a father who had never looked as imposing as he did at the moment.

"Father, may I have a few minutes of your time? There is something important I would like to ask you."

"Of course, Steffan."

Steffan walked across the room and stood in front of his father's large oak desk.

"Do sit down, son," his father smiled.

"Yes, sir."

"What is it you have to say, Steffan?"

Steffan took a deep breath, then rapidly the words tumbled out of his mouth as though he could no longer control them. He explained exactly how he felt, that he wanted to join the navy, and why. Then he sat back in his seat and waited for the thunderstorm he was sure was about to erupt. He was quite shocked when his father smiled at him and nodded slowly.

"I see. I take it you prefer this to taking over as head of my enterprises?"

"Father, I feel I'm not ready or suited for that at the moment. Your managers are most capable men and really sir, at forty, you are not really old enough to retire."

Maxwell had to turn his back to regain control of his laughter. "Old," he thought. "This boy thinks I'm ancient." Steffan waited, almost holding his breath, then his father turned back to him.

"Well, Steffan, I understand how you feel, and after taking everything you said under consideration, I shall think it over and give you my answer by the night of the ball. Agreeable?"

It was almost more than Steffan could bear. Just the idea that his father had even agreed to consider it was beyond his wildest dreams. "Yes, sir, that is quite agreeable."

"Good!"

Steffan walked to the door, but there he paused for a moment, then turned back to his father. "Father, I want you to know that I will do whatever you think best, but . . . well, sir, I've dreamed of this all my life and I would appreciate it if you would give me the chance to try."

"Steffan," his father said slowly. "I take back what I said about thinking it over. I don't see why I should let you worry about this for a week. Except for your references to my advanced age, I agree, Steffan, you should have the chance to find your own direction in life. If you feel this is what you want I shall put forth every effort to give you all the support you need."

Steffan gazed at his father momentarily speechless. Maxwell walked to Steffan's side and put both hands on his shoulders. He realized then that Steffan was already taller than his own six feet, and he could feel the hard muscle under his hand. Maxwell also realized for the first time that his son was no longer a child, but a man.

"Steffan, I've never told you how very proud I am of you. In the short years your mother and I have had you, you have never given me anything but reason to be proud of you. I love you, son, and if this is what you want to do with your life, then I want you to try. In whatever you do, do your best, Steffan. You carry with you a name I have guarded for forty years. Wear it with pride, handle it carefully, Steffan, it is the most precious possession I can give you."

The two men looked at each other for a moment, then Steffan said quietly: "Thank you, father. I shall do my best, sir."

Maxwell's eyes twinkled. "I think it best you don't tell your mother or your sister until after her party else you will spoil it for them. I'm sure Cecile will be upset at your leaving."

Steffan grinned in response. It was plain for Maxwell to see that he was containing his happiness with superhuman effort. When the study door closed behind him, Maxwell could hear Steffan's exuberant shout of pure joy as he took the steps two at a time in his haste to tell Martin the good news.

Maxwell stared for a few moments at the closed door and tried to control the sudden sense of loss. "Where have the years gone?" he wondered. Just yesterday Steffan was a boy safely under his wing and now . . . now he was leaving. Maxwell smiled. "Go, my beautiful bird, fly. But dear God, remember the cage and the captor who loves you."

Three

At the same time as ten year old Steffan Devers was first making the acquaintance of Martin Gillis, a seven year old girl was romping in the surf of Marriott Island. Tamara was pleased with the world. Her world consisted at the time of an island that carried her family name and a tall handsome father whom she worshipped. She did not know the circumstances under which they moved to the island; all she could remember was how desperately ill her mother had been before they came here and how well she was now.

As for Tamara, she was an exuberant child who was much more at home climbing the rocks and crags along the shore or swimming in the surf on her father's private beach than in her mother's drawing room.

She had an oval-shaped face dominated by large, slanted crystal green eyes. Her mouth was pronounced determined by her father and stubborn by her mother. The chin could be lifted in arrogance, determination or pride. But it was her hair that caught everyone's notice. Glossy auburn curls captured the sunlight in their thick mass. At seven, it fell well below her hips and her father refused to let her mother have it cut one inch. At the moment it hung in two thick, long braids. She was forced to wear skirts although her preference was pants. Often she had tried to sneak away wearing the pants she had borrowed from her very best friend Mikel Robbins, only to be caught and punished by her mother.

Today she wore a dress but she had, as usual, made do with what she had. She had reached down between her legs and caught the back hem of her dress, pulling it up to tuck into her belt. Thus, she instantly created a pair of baggy pants that left her slender bare legs free. She had tossed aside her shoes, and was splashing through the surf. She felt the warm water splash against her ankles and the wet grainy sand beneath her feet, and her bubbly spirit rose. If she hurried to her favorite spot of huge gray rocks she would be the first to see her father's ship as it rounded the tip of the island and headed toward home. She reached the pile of rocks that extended out into the water for about fifty feet, and scampered up them like an agile young monkey. At the top she stood, legs apart and her hand shading her eyes. Her heart leapt as she spotted the white sails of the ship she was searching for coming around the tip of the island. She breathed deeply, her eyes watched every motion of the ship.

"Hey, Tamara! What are you looking at?" a voice shouted above the waves. Tamara looked down from her perch at the boy who was standing on the sand below, his hands on his hips and the wind whipping his sandy brown hair in front of his eyes. He cocked his head to one side and watched her as she turned her attention back to the ocean.

"What is it?" he insisted.

"The *Sea Borne*, Papa's ship. He'll be home in an hour or so." She climbed down from the rocks with an abandoned agility. She landed at the boy's side on both feet.

"Hi, Mikel. It's Papa's ship. I've got to get home."

"I thought we were supposed to go and fly the new kite I got. The wind is high; she should sail beautifully."

"We'll have to go tomorrow, Mikel. Papa will be home soon and I want to be there when he arrives."

Mikel Robbins looked at Tamara, disappointment in his blue eyes, but he knew from past experience it was useless to argue with the girl when her mind was set on something, and especially if that something was her father.

Mikel was soon to be twelve. He was a tall boy for his age and rather skinny. His father, a fisherman in the small village on the opposite end of the island, had worked for Andrew Marriott since the day the latter had purchased the island. Mikel had been cautioned by his parents over and over again that Tamara was the owner's daughter and he should always remember his place, but despite these admonitions he and Tamara had become the closest of friends. When Tamara had begun her lessons at five, she had insisted Mikel accompany her to the classroom. By now, it was an accepted fact that he would be educated with her. He felt as protective toward her as an older brother would for a wayward younger sister, and he joined the ranks of people who spoiled her atrociously.

"I came over to tell you somethin' special, Tam."

"What!" she said excitedly. "A secret? . . . tell me!"

"You know the sailboat father made for me? Well, it's finished. If you want, I can take you for a sail tomorrow. My father says I'm as good a sailor as he.''

"Oh, Mikel, that would be great, some day," she said proudly, "Papa is going to give me a ship of my own . . . he promised."

Mikel made a sharp sound between his teeth. "What's a girl going to do with a ship?"

"Why is sailing supposed to be just for boys?"

"Cause, it is, that's all. Girls are supposed to grow up to be ladies and take care of the house and cook."

"I don't care," Tamara said stubbornly. "I don't like to cook and take care of a house. I want to sail all over the world like Papa does. Papa always keeps his promises. Someday, Mikel . . . you watch . . . someday, I'll have my own ship."

Mikel laughed. "You probably will, Tam. Your father gives you everything you want."

They were nearing a flight of wooden steps that led from the beach to a gazebo on the back lawn of the Marriott home. Mikel stopped.

"Do you want to go?"

Tamara squinted up at him and smiled. "If you'll teach me to sail it."

"You're too small yet."

"You're not much bigger than me, Mikel Robbins, and if you won't teach me to sail you can keep your old sailboat."

"All right, all right, I'll teach you. But if you get dumped in the ocean it will be your own fault."

Tamara smiled, happy again that she had gotten her own way. "I'll meet you on the beach tomorrow."

"You'll have to come down to the dock, stupid. The boat will be tied up there. I sure can't drag it up on the sand just to pick you up."

"Oh."

"I'll meet you just after lunch, okay?"

"Okay . . . Mikel?"

"What?"

She smiled up at him with the extra special smile she saved for people who were special to her. The smile began in her pretty green eyes long before it touched her lips. "I'm glad you got a sailboat. I know you always wanted one, and I know you'll be the best sailor in the world . . . next to Papa, of course."

Mikel smiled back. It was impossible to be angry with Tamara when she decided to turn on the charm.

"Thanks, Tam, I'll see you tomorrow. You'd better hurry or you won't make it to the docks before your father gets there."

Tamara ran for the steps and climbed as fast as she could. She had planned to sneak back into the house before her mother saw the condition she was in. She pushed open the kitchen door slowly and looked about. The room was empty. Quickly, she went inside and closed the door behind her without a sound. On silent feet, she tiptoed across the kitchen and peered around the door into the dining room. Luck was with her; it was empty also. Now came the big test. She crossed the dining room. The stairway that led upstairs was directly across from her but just on the opposite side was the door to the huge drawing room and she had no way of knowing whether or not it was empty.

Forgotten completely were the shoes she had discarded by the rocks. Her hair, moist from the spray of the surf was curling waywardly about her face, the wet braids hung heavily on her shoulders. The hem of her dress, still tucked between her legs, was wet and dirty. She tiptoed across the floor, her eyes intent on the bottom of the steps, unaware of the wet grainy marks she left in her wake.

One step, two, three, four, then a pleased smile began to grow on her face. A smile that came just a little too soon.

"Tamara Marriott."

She froze for a minute, then turned slowly to see her mother standing in the doorway of the drawing room.

"Yes, Mama," she said in a choked quiet voice.

Joanna Marriott was as much opposite Tamara as the day was from the night, yet she loved deeply the one child she had been able to bear her beloved Andrew. She was a tiny woman with dark hair and eyes. Her skin, a pale porcelain color, gave her a translucent look as though she were fragile enough to break.

"I came to your room to wake you for breakfast. I can tell by your disheveled condition where you've been. I thought I expressly told you not to roam those rocks and that beach like a little hooligan."

"Yes, Mama," Tamara's head dipped and her eyes fell to the floor. She was wise enough now to know not to debate with her mother. The storm clouds often passed faster if she pretended regret. A regret she never felt for she knew she would be back on the beach at the first opportunity.

Joanna smiled; she knew Tamara too well. There was no regret in her daughter for what she had done, only for the fact that she had been caught. She lifted her skirt and walked up the few steps to stand beside Tamara. She looked down on the tousled, bowed head. Gently, she lifted her chin. "Tamara, child," she said softly, "when shall I ever be able to make a lady out of you?"

"I don't want to be a lady, Mama."

"Why?"

"Because, Mikel says a lady has to stay home and clean and cook, and I'd have to wear skirts all the time and . . ."

"Tamara, whether you like it or not, you were born a girl, and whether you like it or not, you will grow to be a lady. Can't you take my word for it now that there is also a good side to being a woman?"

"I don't know what it is. Boys have all the fun in the world. They can do whatever they want and go wherever they please. I should like to do that."

Joanna reached out both her arms and pulled her daughter close. "My little gypsy," she murmured.

Tamara hugged her mother for she knew the anger had passed and she loved her mother with her whole heart. Then she lifted her sparkling green eyes.

"Papa's home, Mama. I saw his ship round the point." She said the words in excited expectancy, hoping the enthusiasm would catch and she and her mother would go to meet him. She was rewarded by the bright glow in her mother's dark eyes and the pink in her cheeks.

"Then, if you can be changed to a little girl in five minutes we shall go and meet him."

Tamara gave a small yelp of joy and flew up the stairs, unbuttoning her dress as she did. By the time she reached her room, she was completely undressed. She grabbed for petticoats, pantaloons and shoes and whipped them on in record time. Going to her closet, she grabbed the first gown she came to and slipped it over her head fumbling with the buttons. She came flying down the stairs to join her mother, who was laughing.

"Tamara, if I could just get you to react like that when it was time for lessons or for chapel I would be much happier."

Joanna took a handkerchief from her dress pocket and wiped the smudges of dirt from Tamara's face. Gently, she smoothed her hair as best she could.

"Come along, the carriage is waiting."

The ride to the docks seemed an interminable time to the impatient Tamara, but they arrived before the ship. To Tamara, it seemed to fill the entrance to the harbor the way her father had always filled her life.

They stood on the docks and watched the expert way her father brought the ship in. Tamara stood, literally bouncing up and down, at the bottom of the lowered gangplank until Andrew Marriott appeared. He came down the gangplank with long strides and swung a delighted Tamara up into his arms. Her slim arms clung to his neck and she kissed him again and again.

"Papa, oh, Papa. I'm so glad you're home."

She could feel the rumble of laughter deep in his big chest. "Have you been a good girl while I've been gone, little one?"

She looked into his eyes, hers wide and solemn. "I've tried Papa, honest I've tried."

Again he laughed and she felt his strong arms tighter about her as he carried her back to her mother's side. He slid her to the ground and reached for Joanna who made a soft sound and opened her arms to him.

Tamara watched closely for it always made her feel warm and glad all over when she saw her father and mother together. She had no way to put words to it, but she welcomed the warm feeling that spread through her when they looked at each other.

"Oh, Andrew, I'm so glad you're back. I have missed you dreadfully."

"And I you, my love," he held her close and kissed her, deeply sensing the warm welcome feel of the only woman he would ever love.

Tamara chattered all the way back to the house. Her questions seemed to have no end, and her eyes grew wide with wonder as her father spun stories of all the places he had been and had seen.

"Andrew, I do wish you would not always be filling the child's head with all these romantic tales. It is difficult enough trying to turn your little tomboy into a lady."

"Don't try to change her, Joanna. Don't you see what a rare beauty she is. Let her be. She's a spirit that will never be tamed."

"But one day, she'll marry, Andrew, and just what kind of a wife will she be?"

"As good a wife as her mother is," he said softly. "The man she will marry will have to realize what she is and not want to control the rare qualities that Tamara has, but that is a long time away. Let's just enjoy her day by day, and not worry about tomorrow."

"And of course," Joanna's mouth curved in a half smile, "you realize in her all the qualities I have?"

"Every one," he chuckled. "No man realizes just how very lucky he is better than I."

They laughed together and Tamara felt pleased with the sound. Slipping her hand in his, Joanna rested her head on her husband's broad shoulder while they looked at the daughter they had created and listened to the flow of her happy chatter.

Andrew came awake early the next morning when a small body nestled itself gently against him. Tiny arms circled half way around his large body. He kept his eyes closed for several minutes while he enjoyed the soft curves of Joanna's body on one side and the gentle touch of Tamara's small arms on the other, then he whispered in her ear to keep from waking Joanna. They had kept a late night after they had put Tamara to bed, for Andrew could not seem to get enough of the passionate love of the wife he had missed for so many nights.

"What are you doing here so early, little one?"

"I just wanted to make sure you were really here, Papa," she whispered back as she lay her head against his chest and listened to the strong steady beat of his heart. "I love you, Papa. I shall love you more than anyone else all my life. I will never get married." Again she heard the deep rolling laughter.

"I think I will remind you of those words one day, my sweet, when you bring some tall handsome man home and declare your undying love for him and beg my permission to let you marry." He squeezed her close to him. "I'm not sure I'll be able to give it. He will have to be a very special man."

Joanna came awake at the sound of their voices and the three of them had a joyous romp before a light rap on the door put an end to it. They shooed Tamara back to her room to dress for breakfast while Joanna's maid came in to help her mistress dress.

At breakfast, Tamara's wide-eyed request of her father to be allowed to wear pants like a boy caused him to almost choke with the laughter he tried to suppress. "Tamara," he said gently, "if I had wanted a boy so badly I would find one. I like you just the way your mother has you . . . in dresses . . . would you do a special favor to me and stay my pretty little girl?"

"Yes, Papa," she replied. "Can I go down to the dock and see Mikel's new sailboat?"

"Of course . . . you're not planning on sailing away are you?"

"No, Papa, of course not, just around the harbor. Mikel is a good sailor, his father says so, and he's so proud of his own boat."

"Tamara . . ." her mother began, a worried frown on her face.

"I'm sure Mikel is an excellent sailor; he's been sailing in the harbor for his father the past two years," he interrupted Joanna.

"You mind what Mikel tells you to do and you may go once around the harbor."

"Thank you, Papa." She bounced from her chair, and ran first to her mother, then to her father, kissing each soundly. Then in a few minutes, she was gone like a breath of summer wind.

"Andrew, you spoil that child terribly."

"I know," he laughed. "The two most precious flowers in my life deserve all the spoiling I can give them."

"Andrew," she began; her gentle eyes held his. "What will become of her when I'm gone?"

"Joanna!" he said harshly, then his voice softened. "We promised never to speak of that again."

Quick tears filled her eyes when she answered. "Whether we speak of it or not, Andrew, you and I both know the future. You remember the doctor's words the same as I do."

Andrew rose from his seat and walked around to her chair. He knelt beside it and took both her hands in his. There was emotion in his voice as he spoke. "Joanna, I will never let you go. There is no future without you. All I have, all I ever expect to have is built around you. When the doctors told us of your condition in England you were much worse. You have to admit," he said, hope in his voice, "you are so much better now. Don't you see, love, I can't go on without you . . . I will not let you go."

Joanna leaned forward in her chair and gently touched the side of his face with her hand. "Oh, Andrew, we've had so much, you and I. We've had a love so very few people know. Between us, we've created a being to help you. We've been given a lifetime in our few years. We must be strong enough, each of us separately, to be strong enough for the other. I have never been happier, and I am not afraid. There is only one thing I want you to remember. I will be with you always. But memories are supposed to be good things and I want you to remember only the best so that you can give your memories of me to our daughter when she's older. You have to be strong so that Tamara can grow, you have to be there so she need not walk alone. I place all my love for you and all I hope for her in your hands. Never, in our lifetime, have you ever disappointed me, Andrew Marriott, from the first time I saw you to this minute. Despite what you feel now, I know you will never disappoint me in the future."

"God, can you ever know how much I love you, Joanna, how much I need you?"

Joanna slid her arms about his neck and brought her warm tear-moistened lips to his in a kiss so tender, so full of love that he could hardly bear it.

"I need you, Andrew, to hold me, to make love to me. I would so have loved to have given you a son. If God were willing maybe . . ." Her voice died away as he kissed her again and drew her into his arms, but he vowed silently there would be no child to drain the strength and the time from Joanna. He was going to hold her as long as God would permit.

Tamara ran down the dock to the very edge when she saw Mikel seated in the small sailboat moored there.

"Hi, Mikel, Papa says I can go around the harbor once with you." Tamara called, neglecting to inform him of her father's orders to be obedient and listen to what Mikel said.

"Hi, Tam, come aboard," he laughed in pride. Tamara took the short jump from the dock to the sailboat without a qualm. Mikel looked at her silently and wondered if there was anything in the world Tamara was afraid of. Maybe that was one of the reasons he liked her so much; while most girls he knew seemed to walk through life quietly with their hands folded, Tamara seemed to run at it, completely unafraid and with both arms outstretched to grasp it to her.

Feeling quite proud of his small boat, and his ability to sail it, Mikel hoisted the small sail and the craft glided across the water.

Tamara refused to let Mikel dock the boat after the first time around and insisted they do it again. In her mind she had stored every move Mikel had made and was sure she could do it too, although she knew Mikel would adamantly refuse her until they had gone out more often.

The balance of their summer was spent more in Mikel's boat than in their homes. By the time the summer was over, Tamara acquired two things, the age of eight, and a phenomenal ability to sail the sailboat Mikel had named *Tamara*.

Andrew fell victim from that day on to constant pressure from Tamara for a sailboat of her own. She suddenly became so obedient to the rules and regulations that everyone down to the stable boy was amazed and waited for the explosion to come. She had taken to wearing her shoes and stockings, except of course when she had an opportunity to slip alone to the narrow strip of beach. There, she would throw them aside and blissfully enjoy a brief moment of freedom. The thought of pants seemed to disappear and she wore the frilly petticoats and dresses she hated so much. It was her mother who watched with smiling eyes, and knew right from the beginning what Tamara was up to.

Joanna had to admire the single-minded perseverance with which Tamara attacked the problem of acquiring her boat. When she was sure she could handle the sailboat efficiently she went to Mikel and asked him for a favor.

"Let you borrow my boat!" Mikel almost shouted. "You're crazy, Tam. I'd never let you go out in that boat by yourself. If anything ever happened to you, your father would skin me alive."

"I didn't say anything about going out alone, Mikel," she replied coolly.

It was then Mikel was bitten by the green eyed monster. Jealousy was new to him and he wasn't quite sure how to handle it.

"Who . . ." he gulped, then continued, "who are you taking?"

"Why," she said in wide eyed surprise, "Father, of course."

"Oh."

"Who did you think I would share our boat with, Mikel?" she questioned innocently.

"Nobody . . . I just wanted to know for sure."

"You and I are good friends, Mikel. Papa says good friends should always be treated like they were family. I would never share our boat with anyone else cause you're almost my brother."

"I know, Tam, I'm sorry. Sure you can have it, but do you think your father will come?"

Up came the stubborn little chin and the eyes glinted with determination.

"Papa will come."

"Okay, it's yours," he said.

Tamara laughed and ran toward home. Tonight at dinner would be the best time to approach her father. It always seemed better to ask for something when her mother was around for her father always seemed more contented and more susceptible then. She could hardly contain herself while the dinner seemed to drag on and on. Joanna had only to take one look at Tamara to know something serious was brewing in her head. She also knew it concerned Andrew so Joanna sat back as an interested spectator and watched as Tamara worked her charms on her father. "Papa," she smiled brightly, "Could you come down to the docks for a few minutes tomorrow? I have something special I would like to show you."

"What is it, pigeon?"

"It's a secret, Papa . . . would you please? It will only be for a minute?"

"I have a lot of work to do tomorrow, pigeon. The *Halifax* made port today and I've a lot of manifest to go over."

Tamara rose and went to her father's side. Taking his huge hand in hers, she pleaded, "Papa, it is the most important surprise I've ever had and it means so much to me. Couldn't you come just for a few minutes?"

Andrew's eyes met Joanna's over the table. He could see the sparkle of laughter in hers and knew that he faced one of his only two weaknesses.

"All right, pigeon, but just for a few minutes."

"Thank you, Papa," she said as she threw her arms about him. "First thing in the morning, Papa?"

"All right," he laughed. "First thing in the morning." But he groaned as with the first rays of the morning sun, Tamara was at his bedside, fully dressed, and shaking his arm to urge him awake.

"Go downstairs quietly, pet," he said sleepily. "I'll be down as soon as I'm dressed."

They made their way to the docks walking hand in hand. When they stopped, Tamara pointed. "That's Mikel's boat," Andrew said quickly. "That's certainly not your secret Tam, you've been in it all summer."

"No, that's not it, Papa . . . get in please." Andrew realized at that moment just what Tamara was about; words of refusal were on his lips until he looked down into her pleading eyes. Without another word, he slipped into the boat.

From the first hoist of the sail until the moment Tamara brought the boat safely back to the dock, Andrew sat in silence and watched with fascination as his slender eight year old daughter handled the small boat with ease.

When they stepped ashore, Tamara took his hand again and they began the slow walk home.

"Tamara, my love, I'm very proud of you. I could not have handled it any better. But remember, a calm harbor is quite different than the ocean." He turned to look at her, "and when you get your sailboat, next summer, you must promise me never to go near the harbor inlet."

Tamara looked up at her father and quick happy tears rolled down her cheeks, that he knew her so very well.

"I love you, Papa."

Four

For the next four years, Andrew watched her with pride. She was a completely contented girl. She spent her summer days in laughing competition with Mikel in races back and forth across the harbor, and it did his ego no good when a twelve year old girl beat him.

Mikel turned sixteen. His figure, still slender, had begun to take on the hard muscle of manhood. And that year, to Tamara's distress, he began to notice girls. More and more often, Mikel was taking this girl or that out on his boat and leaving a fuming Tamara to shift for herself. No matter how hard she tried, she could not understand why Mikel wanted to be with any of those 'pretty little fluffs' who did not know the bow from the stern of a ship and were contented to sit and smile while Mikel did all the sailing. Of course, she did not know of the hidden strips of beach where Mikel would go to taste another part of life.

He had become quite handsome, his tan skin a perfect foil for his bright blue eyes and sun blond hair. Girls found him completely irresistible. But Tamara vowed revenge for all the neglect she was suffering and it was only another few years before she achieved it.

It happened on her fifteenth birthday. Her mother had planned a party for her against Tamara's wishes. She had only kept silent because it seemed to have a bad effect on her mother whenever there was any kind of argument.

Tamara sat in her room cross-legged on her bed. She had loosened her braids and brushed the red gold hair until it shone like the morning sun. There was a knock on her door, and she expected her mother to come in when she answered. Instead, her father came in and closed the door behind him.

"Tamara, I've come to wish you goodnight, child. Your mother . . . isn't feeling well."

He sat down beside her on the bed. In his hand he held a small black velvet box.

"I've also brought you a birthday present. This is a special gift, just from me to you." He handed the box to her. Quickly, Tamara opened it. Inside, on black velvet, lay a thin gold chain small enough to fit her wrist. Dangling from the chain was a small charm carved in the shape of a schooner under full sail.

"Oh, Papa," she breathed. "It's beautiful. I shall wear it forever."

She took the chain from the box and handed it to him, then held out her wrist for him to put it on. As he fumbled with the clasp, Tamara noticed for the first time the fine lines of worry on his brow and the tense look about his eyes. It was the first time in a long time that she began to realize there had been a subtle change not only in her father, but her mother as well. Then she began to realize how often lately it had been her father who had come to wish her goodnight, and how often her mother was . . . tired . . . not feeling well. She made a quiet promise to herself to pay closer attention to her mother from now on. If something was wrong, she wanted to know about it.

"You don't go sailing with Mikel too often any more. Have you two had an argument?"

"No, Papa . . . I guess Mikel doesn't have time for me anymore. He thinks I'm a baby. He's always chasing Nancy Berkly or Ramona Alexander. I don't know why; they're so useless, neither of them can do anything but stand around and giggle every time Mikel comes near her. It makes me sick."

Andrew chuckled. "I wouldn't worry about it, pet. You're prettier than both of them put together, and I don't want young men underfoot too soon."

Tamara looked up quickly into her father's eyes. It was the first time anyone had ever referred to her as pretty. She was tall for her age, and since she was not really interested, she took no special care in how she looked. She wore her hair carelessly braided and the oldest and shabbiest dresses she could find that would not restrict her roaming. "Do you really think I'm pretty, Papa?"

"You're more than pretty, little one. You are going to be a beauty with those lovely green eyes and that hair that looks like sunlight captured in a gold bottle."

Tamara contemplated his words and in the way of woman since the beginning of time, she instinctively knew how to get her revenge on Mikel Robbins.

The next morning, she went to her mother's room. To Joanna's surprise, she broached the question of how she would wear her hair for her party and exactly what color dress she would look her best in. "Why, Tamara," her mother smiled, "am I really going to see my little tomboy finally turn into my pretty daughter?"

"I just want to be pretty for this party, Mama. What do you think I should do?"

They put their heads together. Laughing and talking and deciding how she would wear her hair and talking of perfumes and dresses for the entire morning. She tried on and discarded several dresses before her mother nodded approval. The dress was a dove gray-silver and was cut just a little bit lower than Joanna wanted, but Tamara's figure carried it well. It was suddenly obvious to Joanna that Tamara had the full rounded body of a woman.

They were in front of Tamara's mirror, she seated and her mother brushing her hair, then trying it in assorted styles. It was then that Tamara took the time to study her mother's face. She became alarmed at the pale white of her mother's complexion, and the deep blue shadows under her eyes. She noticed also that her mother had lost a lot of weight. She was slender almost to the point of thinness. Her hand trembled under the slight weight of the hairbrush.

A sudden feeling of terror choked the breath in Tamara's throat. Her mother was ill—desperately ill—and the sudden overwhelming thought almost stopped her breathing. Their eyes caught and held for one long moment in the mirror and Tamara knew. The pain of it was almost too much for her to bear. She had no words to put to the emotion that held her speechless and motionless but she promised herself to find her father and talk to him. Ask him if her terrible suspicions were true and if they were, why she was not told and just how badly ailing her mother really was. The idea that she could lose her mother was something she could not accept, could not even think about.

As if to confirm Tamara's fears, her mother returned to her bed for an afternoon nap. Tamara walked slowly to the offices her father had on the docks. There, another stone was added to the anxiety she carried when her father hurried over to her, worried lines on his face. "Tamara, is something wrong? Is your mother all right?"

"Father, do you have time to take a short walk with me? I must talk to you about something."

"Of course," he said gently. He gave orders to his secretary telling him he would be gone the balance of the day, then he and Tamara walked together.

They strolled down the beach in silence for a long time while Tamara formed in her mind the words she wanted to say and prepared herself for the words she knew she didn't really want to hear. It was her father who stopped and taking hold of her shoulders, he turned her to face him and said gently, "What is it, Tamara?"

"Papa," the voice came out in a despairing whisper, "what's the matter with Mother?"

Andrew's face looked as though he had been stricken by an unbearable pain. His eyes clouded with suspicious moisture and she could feel his hands on her shoulders in an iron grip.

"What do you mean? I . . ."

"Papa," she interrupted gently. "I'm not a child any more. You must tell me. I am not a baby who still believes in fairy tales; I know there are many sad things to be faced. How ill is she? Can we not take her to England to a good doctor?"

Slowly Andrew regained control of himself. He motioned to several large flat rocks.

"Sit down, Tamara; you and I must have a long talk." His voice was quiet and controlled as he touched her elbow to guide her to the rocks. She sat down and looked up at him. Andrew looked out to sea, his eyes seeing something other than the rolling water and cloud filled sky. "Tamara, eighteen years ago, I met your mother in England. I loved her from the minute I saw her, but she refused every overture I made. One day I could stand it no longer. She was coming out of church and I persuaded her to sit for a moment in my carriage until her parents arrived. She was such a tiny fragile thing she stood no chance against my superior strength. Once inside the carriage I held her while I drove to a secluded spot I had chosen before." His voice went on and Tamara could picture the scene in her mind.

"What are you doing, Andrew Marriott," Joanna had demanded. "You take me home this instant."

"Joanna, I have to talk to you and since you gave me no chance anywhere else, I find I had to kidnap you to get you to listen."

"This is insane," Joanna had said, but she sat back in her seat, her trembling hands clasped in her lap.

"Yes, it is insane. I've been so close to you at all the balls and parties. Spoken to you so often and yet I can't get you to even look at me. In fact, Joanna Millard, you are a snob. I see that you do not have the time or disposition to speak to any of the young men who have the uncommon bad judgment to throw themselves at your feet. Just what do you think you are, some virginal goddess on a white pedestal that no man is good enough to even look at. You don't dance, you don't smile, in fact, you act as though you don't even see the rest of us mortals." Andrew's voice was harsh with his frustration and anger, but suddenly he stopped when he saw Joanna trembling and her eyes filled with tears, tears more of anger than any other emotion.

"Andrew," she choked, "you want the truth. You drag me out here and shout at me. I'm doing you the best favor that's ever been done you. Don't you think I want to laugh, to dance, to have fun like every other girl my age?" Her hands clenched and she leaned forward and pounded her small fists against his huge chest. "I can't, damn you, I can't."

He caught her hands and effortlessly held her as she collapsed against him in tears that tore at his conscience.

"Joanna . . ." he began.

"Let me alone, Andrew. Take me home and forget you ever saw me. It would be the best thing you could do."

He slid one arm about her and with his free hand he tipped up her face and slowly bent his head to touch her tear-washed lips with his. When he released her lips she was quiet and he caressed the side of her face with his fingertips.

"I want you, Joanna Millard. I want you more than I've ever wanted a woman in my life. Will you marry me?"

For a moment her eyes closed as though the pain was something she could no longer bear.

"No, Andrew," came her faint whisper. "No."

"Why? Tell me why. Don't you think I know by the way you kissed me that you love me too. Tell me why, Joanna, for I will not free you unless you do. I shall drag you to the *Sea Borne* and sail away with you. I will keep you locked in my cabin if need be."

"A man should have a strong wife, Andrew, especially a man like you. You're so vital, so alive. You need a woman who can give you everything, a woman who can give you sons. I cannot," she cried, hard choking tears as her head fell against his chest. "I cannot, Andrew for I am slowly dying."

The shock of what she said went through him like a bolt of lightning.

"Dying?"

"Yes, dying; now will you take me home and let me alone . . . please?"

"Tell me, Joanna," he said gently, "but first, tell me that you love me. I want to hear you say it."

"Don't torment me, Andrew," she begged.

"Tell me!"

"I dare not!" she sobbed.

"Tell me," he said again gently, but she felt his arms tighter about her and his lips hovered dangerously close to hers. So close that it disrupted her senses.

"I love you, Andrew," she said softly. "I've loved you for so many months, and that is why I will never marry you."

"That, my sweet darling, is what you think," he said with a happy laugh. "With or without your permission, I'm taking you to the *Sea Borne* and when I've thoroughly ruined your reputation, you will be forced to marry me just to save the Millard name."

Shock registered on her face as she realized he intended to do exactly what he said. She fought, but Andrew was more than twice her size. As they neared the dock, she threatened to scream.

"Go ahead," he laughed. "I want everyone to know I've dragged you aboard. Then you will have to come home married or live forever in dismal disgrace." He dragged her aboard struggling in his arms and walked to his cabin while he shouted orders to his men to set sail. When he got to his cabin, he dropped her lightly to her feet then turned and locked the door behind them.

Andrew smiled at her and she stared back in rage and disbelief. "Andrew, this is insanity. You cannot do this!"

"Of course I can," he said, "I just did."

"Take me home this instant." She tried to sound brave and full of fury but Andrew was slowly walking toward her and her courage and will power fled before him.

"Andrew," she began. He reached out and put his hands about her slender waist and slowly drew her into his arms. His mouth swept down and took complete command of hers, forcing her lips apart, his tongue touched hers in a searching kiss that sent sparks of flame to the center of her being. His lips moved to her hair, her neck. Her hands sought the hard muscular body that held her as though trying to memorize every inch of him. She felt his hands in her hair and did not know how it had been loosened. She felt his fingers caress her soft round breasts and could not remember how or where their clothes had gone. Her world was filled with him as he caressed her letting his hands familiarize themselves with every inch of her and when he felt her body

45

tremble in expectant surrender, he lifted her and carried her to his bunk.

Now he was gentle as he kissed her and his huge magical hands drew from her a passion and a need for him she thought had existed only in her dreams.

"Joanna, Joanna," he whispered. "Love me."

"I do," she moaned softly. "I do." Her hands clung to him pulling him closer until he was within her, filling her. Their bodies, slicked with perspiration moved together in flowing urgency. They blended, separated, blended until she cried out his name. He felt her body quiver with release, and it was only then he allowed himself the pleasure of sinking deeply within her and lying so.

They lay still, holding each other, too content to even detach their bodies and lie apart. Very gently he kissed her eyelids, her cheeks, and brushing a gentle kiss across her lips. "I love you, Joanna."

"I love you also, Andrew."

He rolled over on his side and drew her with him, her head on his chest, then, bodies entwined he spoke softly.

"Now I believe you have something to tell me."

"I have tried to tell you, Andrew, but you have refused to listen. It seems I have something very rare and . . . incurable. In the old days, they referred to it as 'the white sickness.' There is nothing that can be done about it."

"How long . . .?"

"I don't know, neither do the doctors. It may be months, it may be years, but it will be. That is why I cannot marry you. How could I put the man I love through such a tragedy?"

Andrew leaned upon one elbow and looked down into her eyes. Gently, he touched the side of her face then let his fingers drift through her hair. "Joanna . . . give me those years. Don't let us waste a single minute of them. Marry me and let us be happy for however long we have. Why would you separate us and let each of us live alone, knowing we want each other, need each other? Whatever time we have should be ours. We can make it a whole lifetime if we try . . . Joanna, I love you, give me those years."

Joanna's heart swelled with love for this tender, passionate man, and she cried hot salty tears as she said softly, "There will be no children, Andrew."

"I want you, Joanna. Whether or not we have children is God's will, not ours. Let's just be happy together."

"Oh, you are a stubborn, stubborn man."

"Only when I'm fighting for my life."

The rhythmic rocking of the ship told her they were already at sea, and the glint in Andrew's eyes told her he would never release her willingly.

"I've been kidnapped," she smiled.

"That's right."

"You've ruined my reputation."

"That's right."

"No other respectable family will have me."

"Right again."

She sighed and slid her arms about his neck. "Then what else can I do but accept your offer."

Andrew laughed and drew her body tightly against him.

They had stopped at the first port and been married. There they also sent a message to her parents that she was safe and was now the wife of Captain Andrew Marriott. It was only after they were married that Joanna found out how wealthy Andrew really was.

A few months after they were married, Joanna was overjoyed to find she was carrying Andrew's child. She was happy but Andrew was frightened to death.

"Andrew" she begged. "Don't you see? We will have this one remembrance of our love even after I am gone."

Tamara was born seven months later and she was so very beautiful that Joanna and Andrew felt they were blessed by Heaven.

A little over a year later, Joanna fell desperately ill. The doctors told Andrew it was the damp English climate. In a furious battle against the forces that would take his beloved Joanna away from him, Andrew bought the island and built the mansion on it.

Andrew turned to look at Tamara's tear-stained face. "We vowed to each other that we would never speak of what was happening."

"Oh, Papa," Tamara cried and threw herself into his arms. He let her cry, and held her while he allowed her to shed the tears he could not.

"Do you see how strong you and I must be, child. We must make it as easy as we can. Your mother lives for you and me. She wants us to be happy. So we shall be happy. We will smile and sing and make her life beautiful, and if we cry we will cry together so that no one else knows."

Tamara looked up into her father's misery filled eyes and at the moment she loved him more than she ever had before. Slowly she nodded her head.

"I understand, Papa. I will do my best, but oh, Papa, how can we bear to lose her?" she sobbed.

"As long as I have you, Tamara, I have never lost her for you are the best part of us both, and as long as you live, Tamara, remember, that you carry her hopes and her love with you. That is the only way we will be able to stand the loss."

"I will do the best I can, Papa."

"That will be enough I'm sure." He smiled.

"I can't go home right now, Papa. If I do, I will surely cry and mother will know. I'm going to take my boat out for a while."

Again he nodded his understanding. Sliding his arm about her shoulders, she rested her head on his and they walked back to the dock.

The girl of fifteen who took her small boat on the water that day left as a child and returned as a woman. A woman who had made herself several promises. One, that she would share her mother's love with silence for as long as she had her. That she would turn herself into the woman her mother wanted her to be, and second, that she would never belong to any man until she could find the kind of love, rare and beautiful, that her mother and father shared.

The change in Tamara was quickly observed by Joanna and her quick intuition when she saw Andrew and their daughter together, told her that Tamara knew. She said nothing; she let them keep their little secret and enjoyed the bond that was forged between them, for in the years to come, she knew they would need each other.

Tamara's fifteenth birthday ball was a combination success and failure. If attracting Mikel's undivided attention, not to mention that of every eligible young man present was her goal it would have been a tremendous success. To Mikel, who stared at her in wide-eyed wonder, she was like a beautiful butterfly just emerging from her drab cocoon. He was the first person at her side when she entered the room. "Tamara . . . you're so . . . pretty" he stammered.

"Thank you, Mikel," Tamara smiled. "But I'm still the same girl you were too busy to go sailing with yesterday."

Mikel's face flushed when he realized Tamara was calling attention to the fact he had chosen to go sailing with Nancy yesterday rather than go with Tamara. Mikel's success with other girls made him wonder just how Tamara's soft red lips would taste or how that suddenly miraculously beautiful body would feel.

The failure lay in the fact that Tamara realized the difference in what she was looking for and what Mikel and all the others were looking for. She was aware that though she and Mikel were the very closest and dearest of friends, the relationship would go no further than that.

She made many conquests that night; she laughed, danced and thoroughly enjoyed herself. But her heart remained intact.

When she went upstairs that night and began to prepare for bed, she smiled to herself. Mikel had asked her several times to go sailing tomorrow; finally she had agreed knowing there was a disappointment in store for Mikel. For Tamara had made another discovery that wonderful evening—that she could read people easily by watching their eyes and that she had the unconscious ability to influence the emotions of people around her.

Mikel arrived early to pick her up and they rode to the docks in silence. Once there, Mikel insisted they take his boat. Tamara agreed because it really didn't matter to her which they took. Her mind still dwelt painfully on her mother. She had tiptoed into her room as she had so often done as a child and her eyes misted with tears as she looked at the two people she loved so dearly. They slept, as they always had, with her father's huge tanned arm protectively holding Joanna near. Her head rested on his shoulder and her small frail hand lay gently across his massive chest. She knew the loss of her mother would be the most painful thing she would ever know, but as she looked at them she became frightened of what it was going to do to her father when his beloved Joanna was gone.

She bent and lightly touched her mother's arm. "Tamara," her mother whispered. "What is the matter?"

"Nothing, Mother. I'm going sailing with Mikel. We're taking a picnic so we probably won't be back until dinner. I just didn't want you to be worried about me."

"All right, child. Take care."

"I will, Mother," she said, then she impulsively bent forward and kissed her mother's cheek. "I love you, Mother."

Joanna watched her leave the room, then she lay her head on Andrew's chest and clung to him. For the first time, the fear and pain of her illness clutched at her and she clung desperately to the only rock of strength she had. She was not surprised when she felt Andrew's arm tighten about her for he always seemed to sense when she needed him most. Slowly, his arm lifted her gently until she was lying across his body and his crystal green eyes probed deeply into hers. He saw there the pain and the loneliness she felt.

"I'm here, Joanna," he said softly. "Hold on to me. You're not alone, you'll never be alone."

"Oh, Andrew," she said in a soft whisper, then she kissed him and as the softness of her lips parted, he sensed her deep need for him, for their love to chase away the black dragon that they both knew hovered near. His hands caressed her slender body, gently touching, gently rousing her. She closed her eyes and let the feel of his strength surround her. Their bodies entwined and he slid his hands under her hips and lifted her as he gently joined their bodies. Their lovemaking had become a thing of such fragility and gentleness that she felt swept along in a warm stream of love as he moved their bodies together. She felt his strong arms about her and her hand caressed the heavy muscles of his back and slid down his narrow waist to his hips to urge him more deeply within her as though drawing all her strength from his body. She heard the soft murmured words of love and knew the deep peace and contentment that only Andrew gave.

They lay together afterward as he gently caressed her and eased the trembling weakness that overcame her often now. There were times now when she had to spend many hours of the day in bed just to have enough strength to have dinner and a short evening with him and Tamara. Andrew's eyes were always on her and at the first sign of weakness, he would lift her in his arms and carry her to their room. There, he would undress her with infinite care and put her in the big four poster bed they had shared for eighteen short years.

Both of them knew the brave battle was being lost. Andrew could not deny what his eyes could so plainly see, but they did not speak of it.

Now he held her and wished fervently that he could go with her in a moment such as this. His mind was drifting when she spoke. "Our child has become a woman, Andrew."

"Yes, almost overnight, it seems," he laughed. "I think young Mikel has discovered that also."

"Do you worry about her and Mikel?"

"No, Joanna. Mikel is in for a disappointment. Tamara has grown past him in the last few weeks. She's so much like you, Joanna. There is a great and beautiful love within her. And I think she will know when and to whom she wants to give it. I think she was at one time romantically inclined toward Mikel, but something has shown her that there should be much more to love than that."

Joanna looked up at him, her wide dark eyes filled with laughter. "I don't believe, Andrew, that you really know what that something was."

"No, what?"

"Oh, my love," she laughed. "You wonderful man. Can't you see she's looking for another you. You are her ideal man. Can't you see that she senses what we've got between us and she's looking for that elusive thing we found long ago."

Andrew was silent, stunned by the enormity of what Joanna had said. Then he began to chuckle.

"What is so funny?"

"I was worrying about losing my daughter to the first handsome face that came around. Now I can see I've nothing to worry about."

"Why?"

He looked at her very seriously, but his eyes twinkled suspiciously. "Now, where in the world is she going to find another me?"

Joanna collapsed against him laughing and he rocked her in his arms, laughing with her and enjoying the sound he was going to commit to memory.

Five

Cecile stood in front of her mirror and surveyed herself critically. As far as she could see, everything was in place, but she was so anxious to look perfect that she searched for flaws. Her black hair was coiled atop her head in large smooth shiny curls. Small curls fringed her face. Her honey brown eyes looked wide and luminous. Her cheeks, flushed with excitement, glowed a bright pink.

Her gown was a pale ivory satin, its scoop neck cut out much lower than her mother had wanted, but she had coaxed the seamstress into the change. The sleeves were short and puffed at the shoulder and held by small bows of green ribbon. A pale green velvet sash encircled her tiny waist, tied in a bow at the back with trailing ribbons that fell to the hem of her full skirted gown. She wore wrist length ivory lace gloves and had her dance program encircling one wrist with a slender green ribbon. In her free hand, she carried a silver and green lace fan which she had practiced using for days before the ball. She chuckled to herself as she flipped the fan open and waved it gently in front of her face. It made her look demure and shy. Looking up coyly from under her lashes at her reflection, she was pleased to see it created the impression she wanted. "Heaven help you, Tom," she giggled.

"I wholeheartedly agree with that."

Cecile whirled about, surprised and a little flustered that someone had caught her practicing flirting.

"Oh, Steff, you startled me."

Steffan stood in the doorway and smiled at his sister. Cecile appraised him. He had reached his full height at six foot three, his broad shoulders tapering down to slender hips and long muscular legs. He was immaculately dressed in fawn colored pants that hugged his body like a second skin and a rust colored jacket. The front of his shirt and his cuffs were a froth of white lace. His thick unruly black hair was, for one of the few times Cecile could remember, under control. His skin was very tan and his teeth square and white, flashed in an affectionate smile. He pushed himself away from the door frame and walked toward her. It was only then she saw the black box he carried in his hand. He came and stood behind her and with both hands, he turned her again toward the mirror. Their eyes met in the glass. Slowly, he unfastened the box and withdrew a slender gold chain from which hung a little gold cross encircled by tiny diamonds. He put it about her neck and fastened the clasp.

"Oh, Steffan, how very beautiful," she said, her eyes aglow.

"This is a very special night for you, brat; it called for a very special gift. I hope you appreciate the hours I spent in town shopping for the right thing."

"I do, Steffan, I really do." She whirled about and laughed in delight. "It's the absolute perfect thing. Oh, Steff, I'm so excited I could burst."

"Well, if you do, Tom will be a very disappointed man. He and his family arrived about a half an hour ago. I imagine he's waiting at the bottom of the stairs for his goddess to appear," Steff replied, a teasing twinkle in his eye.

"Do I look all right?"

"You're getting no compliments from me, brat, your head will be big enough before the night is over."

Cecile laughed and faced her mirror again. "Steff, why don't you do me a big favor?"

"A favor?" he asked suspiciously.

"You go down and make sure Tom is waiting, I want to make a grand entrance and sweep him off his feet."

"You are a conniving little thing, aren't you?"

"Please, Steff. I want Tom to be there; it will be so perfect."

"All right," he said, but his eyes glittered humorously as he left. "Just make sure you don't make a misstep and come tumbling down into his lap," he laughed in satisfaction as he heard her worried gasp and quickly closed the door behind him.

The soft strains of music reached him at the top of the large spiral staircase that circled its way through the center of the house to all three floors. The ballroom itself led off the foyer through large doorways that had huge doors which folded back to make the foyer a part of the ballroom when necessary. Both Mack and Tom were standing in the doorway watching the dancers, their backs to Steffan.

"Eying all the pretty ladies, I take it," he said as he came up behind them. They both laughed and nodded. "There are certainly enough of them here," Mack responded. "Did you have something to do with the guest list, Steff?"

"Gentlemen, there is nothing but the cream of the crop here; I took it upon myself to make sure each of you would have a harem to choose from tonight."

"Well," Mack said with a wry grin, "that might be all right for me, but I think Tom has eyes only for one beauty lately and she's not here yet."

Tom cast a quick look at Steffan to see the effect of Mack's words. After all the years it still annoyed Steffan that Tom still felt some intangible difference between himself and the Devers family.

Tom, though an inch or so shorter than Steffan, was broad shouldered and muscularly built. His brown-blond hair, worn a little long, curled with a will of its own. His green eyes had a tendency to look deeply into others with a controlled gaze that gave the object of his view the feeling he was being read like a book. He had a quick, shy grin and the calm air of a solid man who could surmount any problem.

Mack, almost the same height as Tom, was several pounds lighter. He was slender with large soulful dark eyes that faced a world with complete honesty. His straight dark hair drooped continuously over a wide intelligent brow.

"Tom, Mack, let's get a little away from the music. I have something important to tell you." Steffan drew both of them to the bottom of the stairs, both to tell them his news and to aid Cecile in her grand appearance.

"What's going on, Steff?" Tom questioned. "You've been jumpy all week."

"Yes, what are you up to, old boy?" Mack queried.

"Next month I'm going to London to take the entrance examination for the Naval Academy, and believe it or not, it's with my family's blessings."

"Steff," Mack smiled. "That's wonderful. Why man, it's what you've wanted all your life. Congratulations!"

"Great, Steff! My congratulations also," Tom said, but Steffan noticed a little hesitant sadness in his eyes, and he suddenly realized that Tom was envious of his chance and doing his best to hide it. Then the sudden idea flashed in his mind. Maybe Tom and Mack didn't have quite the education he did, but maybe they had enough to get them into the Academy also. It would be great, he thought if the three of them could remain together as they had always been in the past three years. He made up his mind to talk to Martin Gillis the next day. He was about to mention the idea to

Tom when a sudden shocked look came over Tom's face and Steffan heard him murmur softly, "Oh, my God." Steffan looked up and suppressing his laughter he held back, with great control, a few amusing remarks that might have upset Cecile's majestic descent of the stairs.

Tom's stricken look followed Cecile as she seemed to float down the stairway. Both Steffan's and Mack's eyes met over Tom's head and by silent mutual agreement they faded away and left Tom and Cecile alone.

When Cecile reached the bottom step, she held out her hand to Tom and he took it without even knowing what he was doing, for he was so lost in the golden brown eyes that looked up at him, and enveloped in the sweet scent she wore. He couldn't believe that this was the gamin who rode with him and her brother and walked the sandy beaches barefoot with her hair blowing free about her. He stood so speechless that it was Cecile who spoke first.

"Good evening, Tom. It's nice that you are the first person I've seen tonight."

"Cecile," Tom replied gently, "you look absolutely beautiful."

He spoke in such a subdued voice that Cecile's eyes glowed with devilment and she replied coolly. "My goodness, is it such a shock to you that I can look presentable?"

"Oh no!" he said quickly. "Cecile you're always beautiful," he blurted " . . . I . . . I mean," he was at a loss for words and Cecile was too happy to let him be upset.

"Am I pretty enough to dance with?" she tilted her head to the side and smiled up at him with a smile she had been practicing for over two weeks. The effect was just what she wanted. Tom was thoroughly captivated. He held out his arm and smiled.

"It would be my pleasure tonight to dance every dance with you, but since I can't, I'm happy to be the first, and Cecile . . .?"

"Yes, Tom?"

"I would like the last dance also if you would . . ."

"It would please me very much, Tom." He led her to the dance floor. On their way, they passed Steffan and Mack. Steffan bent close to her just for a second and whispered "spider" in her ear. He was pleased with the effort it took her to control her features.

It was over an hour later, an hour filled with good food, good liquor, excellent music to which dancing was a pleasure, that Steffan looked toward the doorway to find Mr. and Mrs. Marshall Sinclair—alone. He watched as his parents greeted the Sinclairs;

then his attention was drawn again to the pretty girl he had been talking with.

"Oh, Steffan, what are you planning on doing now that your studies here are over? Are you going away to college?"

"No, no, Mary. I really haven't made any plans for the future; I guess it's something I have to talk over with my father."

"Well, I hope you stay here," she smiled. "I would really miss you if you were gone."

He smiled down into her eyes. Mary was a very pretty girl, with blonde curls and soft gentle eyes. She looked delicate, which fooled everyone but Steffan and possibly Steffan's sister. The gentle exterior covered a warm blooded woman who enjoyed Steffan as much as he enjoyed her.

"Well, if you're so anxious to keep me home, why don't we go out on the terrace and discuss the reasons for me to stay," he whispered. He was rewarded by her low throaty laugh as she tucked her arm through his. Out on the terrace he took her hand and pulled her into the shadows and in a moment she was in his arms, her mouth searching hungrily for his. When he finally held her a little away from him, his blood was pounding furiously through his veins and his body ached with the wanting of her.

"Damn you, Steffan," she murmured softly. "Why didn't you come to me after the musical last week? I waited for you for over an hour in the garden."

"After the way you were flirting with Jaspar Sinclair all evening, I thought I wasn't welcome."

"Oh, Steffan!" she said angrily as she turned from him. She would have been even angrier if she had seen the glint of laughter in his eyes. "You know damn well I was only trying to make you jealous." She turned to face him again and a shadow of sorrow fleetingly crossed her face before she regained control. "But I can't, can I," she said softly. "I can't make you jealous because you really don't love me, do you Steffan?"

"Mary, we never talked about love," he said gently, the smile fading from his face. "I thought everything was always to be kept honest between us. I thought that was a mutual agreement."

She laughed a short broken laugh. "I was a fool to believe I could ever make you really love me, but I did, Steffan, I'm sorry, but I did."

"Mary . . ." he began.

"No," she held out her hand toward him, "no, don't say anything else, let's let it die here." She turned to walk back into the ballroom. In the light of the doorway, she turned to face him again. She was a pale golden haloed shadow. He could hear the tears in her voice as she whispered. "I love you, Steffan, I guess I always shall. But unless you can say the same . . . don't come to me again."

Then suddenly he was alone with the scent of the garden flowers and the soft strains of music about him. He turned and placed both hands against the marble banister looking out over the dark garden.

"Now, what's a young man like you doing out here alone, with all those pretty girls and beautiful music inside?" Steffan turned.

"Hello, Mr. Gillis. I don't feel like dancing at the moment."

Martin walked out and stood beside Steffan and remained silent for a while, then he said gently, "Want to talk about it?"

"No, sir."

Martin sighed, this was one time Steffan's sense of honor was a brick wall. He knew about Steffan and Mary and he wanted desperately to tell him that this was not a mountain to climb, that there were many bigger ones ahead. "Is it your relationship with young Mary Carter?"

Steffan looked at him in surprise, but kept his mouth resolutely closed.

"Steffan, I'm too old and experienced a man not to recognize your strong enjoyment of feminine company. I know of you and your friends' occasional visits to another part of town. Don't be so alarmed, Steffan. It's certainly not a thing I would tell your parents, although your father would understand quite well. Before he met and married your mother, there were many women in his life. He, like you, was a man of strong appetites. It's what I'm trying to tell you, Steffan. That one day a woman will come along who will capture your whole heart. In the meantime, enjoy what life has to offer. As for Mary . . . what do you regret, not loving her? You have nothing in the world to say about it. Love either exists or it does not. Nothing is worse than trying to live with someone you do not love. You cannot control it, Steffan, and you have to learn to be wise enough to walk away from it a little older and a little wiser."

Steffan remained silent for a few minutes then his smile gleamed in the pale half light. "Thank you, Mr. Gillis."

"You're welcome, son," Martin smiled in return. "By the way, there's something I want to talk to you about."

"What, sir?"

"I've just been speaking to Mr. and Mrs. Sinclair."

"Oh?"

"You know Jaspar did not come tonight?"

"I can't exactly say I missed him," Steffan replied shortly.

"Well, the thing that aroused my curiosity is the reason the Sinclairs gave."

"What was it?"

"It seems young Sinclair had an accident."

"Really?"

"Yes, it seems he fell from his horse and broke his jaw."

"That's too bad."

"Yes," mused Martin. "I had always thought young Sinclair an excellent rider, hadn't you?"

"That's what I've heard."

"Does seem strange that an excellent rider should fall from his horse and break nothing but his jaw."

"Yes, doesn't it?"

Martin chuckled and Steffan grinned in response. "You're not going to tell me a thing, are you?"

A quick negative shake of his head was all that Steffan offered and Martin knew there would be no other information given so he allowed it to pass.

"Mr. Gillis?"

"Yes."

"I know over the years you've done a lot for me and I want you to know it is appreciated. I hate to ask you for another favor."

"Another favor? Steffan, is there something I can do for you, speak up."

"It's Tom and Mack. If they agree, do you think it possible they could take the exam also?"

"I could ask Admiral Track, I'm sure it's quite feasible."

"I'd be grateful sir, especially for Tom."

"Why Tom in particular?"

"Well, sir, I know it's obvious how Tom feels about Cecile and she feels the same toward him, but Tom has the idea that he's a nobody and Cecile is princess of the castle. If Tom could cut out a place for himself, sort of make his mark in the world, it might make it easier for both of them."

"I see; well, I'll do my best. I'll contact him tomorrow; by the time you're ready to leave, we should have word one way or the other."

"Thank you."

Martin nodded his welcome and the conversation drifted to other subjects until Mack appeared with a young girl on his arm.

They talked for a few minutes then Martin and Steffan drifted away to give the young people some privacy.

Steffan enjoyed dancing with every pretty single girl in the room, while keeping one eye on Tom and Cecile. He could see Steffan's disappointment because despite her smile and gaiety, he knew her too well. They were dancing together, the one obligatory dance; Steffan smiled at her. "They're falling all over you, brat; looks like your party is quite a success."

"Yes, it does, doesn't it?" she replied solemnly.

"But you're unhappy . . . Tom?"

"Oh, Steff, I could throttle him," she declared angrily. "When is he going to stop feeling sorry for himself because he's not as rich as we are. I almost wish Papa was a poor fisherman. That way, Tom would at least look at me."

"Listen, brat, I've got something important to tell you."

"What, Steff?"

"I know how Tom feels about you; that will never change. Give him a little time to establish himself."

"Establish himself . . . how?"

"Well, Mr. Gillis has arranged for me to take the exam to enter the Naval Academy. If all goes well, I could have my commission in four years. Some day I hope to have a ship of my own."

"You . . . you're going away, Steff?" she asked with a worried frown.

"Well, brat," he said gently, "I have to go sometime."

She gulped, but her eyes glistened with unshed tears. "I . . . I know, I just didn't think about it."

"Don't worry, brat, I won't ever go so far that we can't still reach each other."

"What does this have to do with Tom?"

"Well, I thought if Tom could get in, get himself a commission, sort of be his own man, he might feel differently about things."

"You mean you want Tom to go, too! Steff, he'll find somebody else. In all those big towns, there are so many girls, prettier than me, and Tom would look so . . . so inviting in uniform."

"Let me tell you something. If a thing is meant to be, it will be. If Tom loves you, he would go to the ends of the earth and still come back."

"And if he doesn't!"

"If he doesn't then it wasn't meant to be from the beginning."

"Have you told him yet?"

"No, I was going to wait until I knew for sure he could get in."

"How long will it be?"

"Oh about a week, maybe two."

"So soon?"

He was about to answer when the music stopped. Steffan tucked his sister's arm in his and turned to walk off the dance floor when they found Tom beside them. His eyes never left Cecile's face. "It's the last dance, Cecile. You promised."

"Of course, Tom," she answered quietly. Steffan gave a slight curt bow to Tom, then left the two of them together. Tom took Cecile's hand as though she were made of very fragile porcelain.

"Cecile, would you mind if we didn't dance? I . . . I would like to talk to you for a minute."

"Of course, Tom, I'm a little tired of dancing anyway."

"Shall we walk in the garden?"

"Yes," she said softly as she tucked her hand under his arm. Her heart was pounding and she could feel her cheeks flush. "Maybe," she thought excitedly, "just maybe he'll finally say something."

If Cecile was excited, it was nothing compared to how Tom felt. He had watched Cecile all evening. She sparkled like a beautiful diamond and he found himself unable to bear the thought that she would never belong to him. What he had in mind at the time was just to ask if she would wait. Wait until he could care for her on his own, then some day they could marry. He felt he was asking the impossible, that a wealthy beauty such as she would even give Tom Braydon a single thought. They walked out through the french doors and down a stone walk that led through the garden. They walked in silence for so long Cecile wanted to scream. When they finally stopped Cecile turned to face Tom. "There was something you wanted to say to me, Tom?"

To Tom, it sounded so imperious he almost lost his nerve completely. Resolutely, he gathered his nerve together. "It's now or never," he thought wildly. "Cecile, I've . . . I've known you for over three years."

"Yes, I'll never forget the first time I saw you, your face all bruised and your eyes blackened. You really looked so terrible."

"What I'm trying to say, Cecile, is . . . well . . . I've more of a feeling toward you than friendship. I . . . I just want you to know . . . to understand . . . well . . ."

Cecile's nerves and her patience had finally come to an abrupt end. She knew now what he was trying to say and she could no longer bear his hesitation. She reached out both hands and placed them on his chest, her eyes asparkle; she said softly, "Are you trying to tell me you care for me, Tom? I do hope so, for I've cared for you from the moment we met."

Tom's eyes went from shyness to doubt, then to happy amazement and for a moment, he stood still, too stunned to do anything else. Then slowly, he put his hands about her slender waist and drew her into his arms. Gently, he touched his lips to hers and cradled her against him. Her mouth was soft and innocent under his and Tom knew she had never been kissed so before. He felt a sense of wonder and joy that she could feel the way she did. He held himself under control, holding back the desire to crush her against him and devour her sweetness until she cried out for him in as deep a need as his own.

With more control than even he thought he possessed, he held her a little away from him.

"Cecile, will you wait? Wait until I have something I can offer you. Will you say that one day in the future you will marry me?"

"Tom," she said quietly. "I must tell you something. When I first met you I was fourteen. You were so hurt and so shy. I loved you then. I wanted to nurse you, to care for you. All the times we've been together, I've prayed you felt the same as I, that some day you would ask for me. I think I have loved you more every day."

"I . . . I just don't believe one man can have such luck. I feel this is a dream and I'll wake up and find that you are gone."

"Then?" she said with a mischievous smile, "why don't you kiss me again just to prove to both of us that it is not a dream."

Tom needed no more encouragement than that; with a murmur of her name he drew her back into his arms. This time, he held her tight and searched her parted lips with his until he heard the soft sighing sound and felt her quiver in his arms.

Tom knew if they spent another moment, as close as they were, in this dark garden he would not be able to stop himself from possessing her. What made him stop was the knowledge that she wanted him as much as he did her and that she would give herself to him willingly and freely. He loved her too much to let it happen like that.

"Come, Cecile," he said softly. "Let's go in and tell your family. I'd like to tell the world, to shout from the rooftops 'Cecile is mine! Cecile is mine!'"

They laughed together and arm in arm they walked back into the ballroom. Many of the guests had already left, and Tom waited until the house was empty of everyone but family. He made the request for Cecile so formally and so stiffly and obviously full of fear that Steffan laughed to himself. He had seen Tom with other girls and at some of the better 'houses' they had visited; in fact Tom had the reputation of being an excellent partner. It amused Steffan that when Tom did look in his direction his face flushed and he looked away quickly.

"So," Maxwell said firmly. "You want to marry my daughter. She's only a child, barely seventeen."

"Oh, I didn't mean right now, sir," Tom interrupted quickly. "In fact I'm afraid it will be a while before I can support a wife. I'm only asking Cecile to wait. I . . . I want to do the best for her, sir. I want her to have everything."

Steffan cast a surreptitious look at his sister who had been sitting like a demure lady, her eyes downcast and her hands folded in her lap. At that moment, Cecile looked up and their eyes met. She smiled and winked at him and Steffan was almost unable to control his laughter.

"And you, Cecile, how do you feel about this?" Maxwell asked.

"Father," Cecile said gently. "I care very deeply for Tom, and I would like to be his wife. I would be content to wait . . . a short time, for Tom to acquire . . . whatever it is he thinks he has to have to marry me."

"Ellen?" questioned Maxwell. "Do you have any objection to this match?"

Ellen Devers had been her daughter's confidante all her life. She had known Cecile loved Tom for years.

"I think Maxwell, that Cecile has made an excellent choice and I agree they should be allowed to become engaged. But I concur with you, it should be a long engagement. At least until Cecile is twenty."

"Twenty!" Cecile gasped. "Mother!"

"Cecile, I'll hear no more about it. If your mother says twenty, then twenty it shall be," Maxwell said firmly.

"But Mother, twenty—that's three years. Why . . . I'll be old."

"Hardly, child," her mother replied with a slight smile.

"It's understood then, young Braydon?" Maxwell said. "You can become engaged but she cannot marry until she turns twenty."

"Of course, sir," Tom smiled. He walked over and took Cecile's hand in his. His eyes held hers and her anger faded at the intense, loving look on his face. "Cecile, we'll wait. It will take me that long to make a life to share with you. But just to know you're here, that you'll belong to me some day . . . that's enough for now."

If her parents and her brother were taken by surprise by her subdued acceptance of Tom's words, they hid it well.

"All right, Tom," she said gently. "If that is the way it has to be. I'll walk you to the door."

Tom said his good nights and left with Cecile. After a few minutes his parents went to bed, but Steffan waited for his sister's return. At the door, Tom kissed Cecile very hungrily and possessively then he reluctantly held her away from him.

"Do you know how hard the next three years are going to be for me. Help me along a little. I don't want to mess things up and take the chance of losing you."

"All right, Tom," she smiled. "Good night."

"Night, Cecile."

When the door closed behind him, Cecile whirled about in a circle her arms outstretched and bubbling laughter on her lips. Steffan stood leaning against the doorway smiling at her.

"Happy, brat?"

"Delirious," she laughed.

"Boy, I feel sorry for Tom."

"Sorry? Why?"

"Can you imagine having someone you love right under your nose and then having a time limit put on being with her."

Cecile walked slowly toward her brother, sly laughter in her eyes.

"Don't," she said softly, "count on my waiting three years to marry Tom Braydon. I'm too much like my brother and my parents. What I want, I generally go out to get and," she giggled, "I generally get it."

Standing up on her toes, she kissed him lightly, then her soft laughter trailed behind her as she went up the stairs. Steffan watched her and made himself a promise. If and when he ever found the one woman he wanted, he would take her no matter what. Nothing would stop him and nothing would make him wait for the one he wanted.

Slowly, he walked up the steps to his room and closed the door silently behind him.

Six

Mikel was a constant visitor to the Marriott household. He escorted Tamara everywhere on every occasion that gave him an opportunity. There were many parties held at the naval training base and Mikel did his best to keep Tamara at his side during these, but it was impossible. Her unusual beauty drew men like bees to a honey pot.

No matter how many swarmed over the mansion, Tamara took the time every afternoon to sit with her mother who was confined to her bed for most of the day. She had become more and more frail until it was an effort for her to even lift a book to read.

Tamara read to her occasionally, but most of the time they talked. Joanna told her many stories of her father that thrilled her. In every way, she tried to strengthen the bond that had developed between the two. Tamara knew this, but they kept up the facade of secrecy.

Joanna slowly worsened, and Andrew spent more and more time sitting by her bed and holding her hand. Tamara watched his silent suffering as he told Joanna amusing stories and clung to her as though he could keep the black shadow of death away. And then the day came when Joanna quietly closed her eyes and slipped into a deep coma from which she never again wakened. Both Tamara and her father were numb with grief. They stood side by side at the grave holding each other.

The house became quiet. So quiet that Tamara was frightened. Her father seemed to have retreated into a world she suddenly could not reach.

It was a rainy morning, too wet to ride or sail, and too soon after her mother's death to go visiting. Andrew was locked in his study where he had been every afternoon since the funeral. Tamara knew he drank a great deal for often she heard him stumble up the stairs in the gray hours of the morning. She also knew that her father had never lain again on the bed he had shared with her mother. He seemed to be locked in a shell, a shell Tamara could not seem to break.

Tamara walked down the quiet hall and stopped in front of her mother's door. Slowly, she opened it. From first glance, Tamara knew the room had not been touched by human hand since Joanna was there. She walked slowly into the room. She could feel her mother's gentle presence all around her, it was as though she were beckoning her. She walked about the room touching things, each with a memory. The last book she had read to her mother lay on the small stand beside her bed. Tamara ran her fingers over the soft leather cover. It was then she saw the white edge of paper protruding slightly. She opened the book. For a moment she froze as she looked at the letter that bore her name in her mother's fine handwriting. With trembling fingers, she unfolded it and read.

My beloved daughter,

When you read this, I know I shall no longer be with you. I must write to you so many things I have never been able to say. I am so proud of you, Tamara, the beautiful person you have become. I know your strength and that is why I am going to tell you of what you must do.

Your father and I have shared a deep and abiding love for many years. He is a strong and courageous man in all things with the exception of me. I have watched his face these last few weeks and it has frightened me more than the thought of death. I am afraid that your father wants to make this last journey with me if not in body then in spirit. He will lock himself away and mourn. Tamara, I want him to remember me with love, but I want him to live. He is a strong and giving man; you must help him seek a direction for the love he has or it will shrivel in him and die. My soul would never rest if I knew that Andrew walked alone the balance of his days.

Tamara wiped the misty tears that clouded her eyes and thought of her father locked away in that room too hurt even to cry. She continued to read.

You are a woman, Tamara, and I know you understand. Your father must realize that I am gone and that his life must continue. You are the only one I have who can reach in to that broken heart and help mend it. No matter what he says, help him day by day until he regains his balance. I am very grateful to God that I bore a child as beautiful as you have become and I pray for the very best for you. I hope one day you find a man as good and loving as your father, and that you know, as I do, the joy of having a child. My only regret is that I will not be with you the balance of your life, but I walk beside you in memory and in love.

All I can hope for you, Tamara is that you know all the beauty I have known, that you find the happiness I have had.

All my love always,
Your mother

Tamara crumpled the letter against her heart and for the first time she cried all the pent up tears she had never released. Slowly, she sagged to the floor and lay her head against the soft coverlet of her mother's bed and washed herself clean of all the agony that had been lying below the quiet surface.

After a while, when the tears would come no more, she began to think of her father, alone and grieving in that lonely room. Slowly, she rose to her feet and walked to the door. She turned and took one last look about the room and then she left it, closing the door firmly after her. She went to the study door and found it locked. After she had rapped a few times, and called her father gently, she realized he had no intention of letting her in. She summoned her father's valet and personal secretary, a man who had been in her father's personal service for longer than she could remember.

"Thomas, you have a key to this room?"

"Yes, Miss Tamara."

"Get it please."

"But, Miss Tamara . . ." he began.

"Thomas, if you do not want us to lose my father also, you will get the key for me."

"Yes, Miss Tamara," he said quietly, marvelling at the sudden change that had come over her. She seemed to be suddenly a mature woman. He went to his room and returned with the key, handing it to her.

"Thank you, Thomas . . . and Thomas?"

"Yes, Miss Tamara?"

"One day, my father will thank you, also."

He looked at her clear crystal green eyes and the determined lift of her head.

"Yes, Miss Tamara," he said. "I believe he will."

He watched her as she unlocked the door, stepped inside and

closed it gently behind her.

"God bless you, Miss Tamara," he said gently. "I hope you help him find his way."

Tamara stood still gazing in horrified shock as her eyes met her father's across the room. He sat at his desk, his face a frozen mask, but what made her blood run cold were the two objects that sat on the desk in front of him. One was an almost empty bottle of whiskey . . . the other a pistol.

"Will I have the words," she thought wildly. "Will I be able to offer what he needs to pull him away from this insanity?" Suddenly her thoughts blended and became clear. She knew what had to be said and she had the courage to say them. If Tamara had begged or pleaded the words would never have reached the black well in which Andrew's soul dwelt. She did neither, but in a voice as cold and hard as ice, she said: "How very selfish you are, Father, to want to leave me alone to face this tragedy. You must not care what happens to me. You are so involved in your own grief. Has there never really been any room in your heart for me?" Andrew's red rimmed eyes blinked as though she had struck him.

"Tamara," he said hoarsely. "I can't . . ."

She walked slowly to his side and knelt in front of his chair. Taking both his hands in hers, she said gently. "I know you can't, alone. Neither can I . . . alone. But Father, maybe together we will have the strength to bear what we must. Oh, Father, don't shut me out—I need you so desperately."

Andrew's hands trembled and tears filled his eyes. The first tears he had shed for Joanna. The dam broke and with an agonizing sob he pulled Tamara into his arms. She held him against her feeling his big body shake with the uncontrollable grief he had never been able to release until now.

It was several hours before a weary Tamara sent for Thomas.

"Make some strong coffee, Thomas, then prepare my father's room. I think he may be able to sleep now."

Thomas looked at Tamara in deep respect and admiration, then he smiled. "Yes, Miss Tamara."

Tamara urged the coffee on her father until she could see he was beginning to recover from the effects of the liquor: then she and Thomas helped him to his bedroom where he fell into a deep sleep that lasted forty-eight hours. Tamara herself sought her bed and let healing sleep restore her body and mind.

The days passed slowly, turning to weeks and then to months, but the ghost of Joanna Marriott walked yet in the halls of the mansion.

Tamara and Andrew were seated at the dinner table one evening when he first brought up the subject of a small vacation. Tamara grasped at the idea immediately. It would give them both a chance to get under control.

"Where would we go Father, to England?"

"No, Tamara, England has too many memories for me. I thought, since I have some friends in the Colonies we might take a trip there. You will like it in America," he laughed. "A girl with your free and independent spirit should feel quite at home there."

"The Colonies? Have you been there often, Father?"

"Yes, quite often. I've a few good friends there who would make your stay interesting."

"Good. I shall begin to pack tomorrow. Are we taking the *Sea Borne*."

Andrew still shied away from seeking things which made Joanna's memory too alive. The *Sea Borne* was one of them.

"No, I thought we would take the *Adventurer*. She's new and quite a bit smaller. In fact," his eyes gleamed, "I would be glad to give you some lessons. I would wager by the time we sighted the coast of America, you would be able to handle her. In fact, I would even wager you would be as good at it as I am."

"Oh! How wonderful! You know I have been gathering my courage to ask that very thing."

"Well," he laughed, "I thought I would offer before you started to wage another campaign."

She laughed, but if Andrew had known her thoughts then even he, with his knowledge of her, might have been surprised. For, at that moment, another campaign was beginning. She knew that one day, not too far away, she would ask her father for the *Adventurer* as her own.

Tamara excitedly prepared for the trip, although it was several weeks before her father pronounced his time free.

Mikel had been very upset at the thought of their leaving. He could picture Tamara in the arms of some colonial and the picture did not ease his moods any. Tamara sensed his anger but there was nothing she could do about it. In fact, she wasn't too sure but time apart might do them both some good. The whole picture changed when Andrew casually asked Mikel if he would care to go along as part of his crew. He smiled at Mikel's enthusiasm but could not read the downcast eyes and strange silence in Tamara.

They left with the early morning tide on a bright Sunday morning.

"Tamara, I feel the need to wander for a while, do you mind if we don't go directly to America? There are a lot of fascinating places to see and if you are interested, we could see a few." Andrew questioned her on the evening of their first day out. The sea was calm and a light breeze propelled the ship in a slow steady movement. Tamara fell in love, first with the beautiful little brig *Adventurer* then with the magic of the sea. It was as if she had suddenly come home from a long journey.

"Father, it would not bother me if we sailed on and on forever, stopping here and there to see everything new."

"Well, I'm afraid it can't be forever, but we could stretch it into several months."

Andrew was surprised and unprepared when Tamara presented herself at his elbow at dawn the following day. She smiled up at him, her eyes filled with mischief and delight.

"Your new recruit, sir. Ready and willing to begin training whenever the captain is ready."

"Well," he sighed in mock helplessness. "I guess this is as good a time to begin as any."

They laughed together and Tamara felt again the warm glow of protective love she had come so near to losing. An excellent teacher combined with an enthusiastic student made the trip memorable for both of them. Tamara absorbed everything Andrew had to offer. He was not surprised at the inexhaustible hours she devoted to learning. He had felt this deep love of the sea and his ship and he knew what she was feeling. He felt a moment's pang that she was not a son to carry on his empire when he was gone, and then he realized Tamara had more to offer than a son for she combined a sweet gentleness with brilliant intelligence. "One day," he thought, "she will marry and if her choice is the kind I think it will be, I will have a son and grandsons."

The trip was the most pleasant time Andrew could remember in a long while.

Tamara celebrated her seventeenth birthday aboard ship. Her father gave her the oddest birthday party any girl ever had. The cook aboard ship made the best cake possible with the ship's limited supplies. Musical instruments were found and as Tamara sat on the hatch clapping her hands in rhythm, songs were sung from each country to which the entertainer of the moment belonged. Tamara had never had such a sense of belonging in her life as she did aboard the confines of this miniature island. Hand made gifts were given her with the accompaniment of deep affection. Small carved wooden boxes, necklaces of small sea shells, and other things that must have been gleaned from ever corner of the world. Mikel had presented her with a beautiful scarf of red silk. But it was her father's gift that brought tears to her eyes. It was a thin strand of perfectly matched pearls. Her eyes glowed with love as he clasped them about her neck. "I've also something else for you."

"What, Papa?"

"I see you wear the chain on your arm."

"Always."

"Well, I'm going to add to it another charm," he held out his large hand in the center of which lay a small gold butterfly. "It reminded me of you," he said gently. "So I had to buy it for my little golden butterfly."

She threw her arms about his neck and kissed him with laughing tears in her eyes.

When she went to sleep that night, it was in a state of glowing happiness. The slow steady rise and fall of the ship lulled her to sleep accompanied by faint singing voices of the crew.

At their first port of call Andrew took her ashore and let her run wild in the dress shops. Tamara had her first taste of the extent of her father's influence and reputation abroad. To her, he had always been the world, but it was the first time she realized how much of the world he knew.

After a day of shopping they ate a leisurely dinner and he took her out for the evening to celebrate. The next morning, Tamara stood at the rail and watched the city diminish behind them.

There were many more cities to follow, many more nights and days that enlarged Tamara's viewpoint not only of her father's astounding circle of friends and acquaintances but the charm he held for beautiful women. Wherever they went Tamara was the one who noticed how their eyes followed her father's tall handsome figure across a room. When it was found that Tamara was his daughter, instead of his woman, the contemplating looks turned predatory. She also noticed another thing . . . that her father was used to these looks and paid them no heed. His love for Joanna had held him faithful for eighteen years and his beautiful memories would hold him faithful even longer . . . unless . . . Tamara remembered her mother's letter. Joanna had not wanted Andrew to be alone. Tamara began to look at each woman with an appraising air of her own until her father brought it to a stop.

They stood at the ship's rail, having just left the port of a week before, where they were guests of one of the wealthiest families. The eldest daughter in the family had reached the age of twenty-seven and was unmarried, an unheard of situation in these times. Tamara had used every maneuver she could imagine to throw the two together. She smugly believed what she was doing went unnoticed by her father, but it was only a few days before her father called the visit over and, despite her protestations, hustled her aboard ship. Now they stood together.

"Tamara?"

"Yes, Papa?"

"We'll have no more of the shenanigans you've just tried to pull this past week."

"Shenanigans, Papa?" she blinked in wide-eyed innocence.

"Don't bat your pretty eyes at me and pretend you don't know what I'm talking about," he said firmly, then he took hold of her shoulders and looked deeply into her surprised eyes.

"Tamara, listen to me. Love is not a thing that you can put on and take off like an old coat. I want you to understand something here and now. I loved your mother very much, and I know she is gone, but what we had is not so easily replaced, and I will not have you matchmaking in my life. You will see, one day, that love either exists or it does not and you cannot have a lifetime relationship on anything less. No matter whether you understand now or not, I don't want that to happen again. If and when the time comes, I will choose the woman. Is that understood?"

"Yes, Papa," she said meekly.

He drew her into his arms gently and held her. "Tamara, I want you to understand that I appreciate the fact that you don't want me to be lonely, but for now, the memories and you are all I need to sustain me. Let us just enjoy ourselves on this trip and let the balance of our lives work out as God wills . . . all right?"

"Yes, Papa, I guess you're right. I'm sorry to have been such a child to try to do something like that. I promise you it won't happen again. From now on, I will be good and not meddle in your private affairs."

"Good," he said with a smile. "Well, I'm going to retire. I'll see you at breakfast. Good night."

"Good night, Papa," she smiled and rose on tiptoe to kiss him, then she watched his broad back disappear through the companionway door. She turned back to the rail, leaning both arms against it as she stared out over the moon-kissed waves. She closed her eyes and lifted her face to catch the softness of the breeze. She jumped in fright as a voice spoke from her elbow.

"Tamara?"

She turned and found Mikel standing behind her. A feeling of deep sadness enveloped her as the truth of her father's words came through to her. "Love either exists or it doesn't." It hurt her to realize that no matter how very close they had been all their lives, the love that Mikel wanted did not exist in her heart. She loved him, yes, as a sister would love a brother. But she knew she could never spend the rest of her life married to Mikel. She wanted . . . what? The magical look that appeared in her mother's eyes when she looked at her father. The way they seemed to be able to speak to each other across rooms. The gentleness, the tenderness, the . . . love.

"Can't you sleep, Mikel?"

"I've been waiting for a few minutes to talk to you alone. You and your father were busy so I didn't interrupt."

"Papa's a little put out with me," she grinned and watched the white of his smile answer her in the dark.

"What kind of mischief have you been up to?"

"Nothing," she laughed. "It's all over now and it really wasn't too important anyway. What did you want to talk to me about, Mikel?"

Mikel stood beside her and folded both arms on the ship's rail. For a few minutes, he stood in silence and watched the rise and fall of the waves. Then he said softly, so softly she wasn't sure she really heard him.

"I love you, Tamara."

"Mikel . . ."

"No, don't say anything. You see, I know how you feel about me, but I had to say it. I just wanted you to know how I felt. I'll be around, Tam, if you ever need me for anything."

"Mikel, I'm sorry, so very sorry," she said, her voice choked with the sincere misery she felt.

"You're not half as sorry as I am. But you see, Tam, I love you enough to want you happy, so no matter what happens, consider me the closest friend you will ever have, all right?"

"Mikel, I do love you, in a way."

"I know," he grinned. "I'm the big brother you never had."

"Yes, I guess that's how I really feel."

"Okay, little sister, from now on, it's you and me. I guess you could say I'm your first mate."

They laughed together then suddenly Tamara's face became serious.

"Mikel?"

"What?"

"Would you really be?"

"Be what?"

"My first mate."

"Tam, what are you talking about?"

"You know I can navigate, read the maps and sail the *Adventurer* as well as Father."

"Well . . . close anyway," he grinned.

"When we come back from the Colonies, Mikel, I'm going to ask Father to give her to me."

"Give . . . are you crazy? He'll never give the *Adventurer* to you."

"Bet me?" she laughed.

He looked down into her laughing green eyes, then his mild chuckle joined hers.

"Nope, I guess I wouldn't be surprised if he did."

"Well, will you?"

"Will I what?" he laughed again.

"Mikel!"

"All right, all right. Yes," he said as though he were surprised himself. "Yes I guess I'd like that."

"Oh, Mikel, thank you," she squealed, then she threw her arms about his neck. Mikel's arms closed about her and he enjoyed for a few minutes the chance to hold her close. She looked up into his smiling blue eyes.

"Kiss me goodbye?" he asked softly.

For a moment she was hesitant then she smiled. "Yes."

His mouth touched hers gently, then he was caught in a softness of the creature he held so close but could never have. His lips parted hers with sudden demanding pressure. He could feel her stir in his arms, then she backed away from him a step. He looked down into her crystal green eyes and felt a deep envy for the man who would reach her heart for he sensed now the hot passionate woman that lingered just below the surface.

"Goodnight, Mikel," she whispered.

"Goodnight, Tam . . . Tam?"

"Yes."

"Nothing is ever going to change the way I feel. I want you to remember that. If you need me, I'm here."

"Thank you, Mikel. I'll remember."

He reached out a hand as though to draw her back into his arms, hesitated, then dropped his arm and turned to walk away.

Tamara watched him leave then turned back to the star-filled sky.

"Am I asking too much? Maybe what Father and Mother had was that rare thing that happens once in a lifetime. But I can't settle for less. I've got to try."

She stood for a long time thinking over her life and trying to form some kind of plan for her future. Then she went below deck to the captain's cabin. Her father and Mikel shared the first mate's quarters, giving her the cabin to herself. She undressed and climbed into the bunk.

No matter what else he was, she thought as sleep began to over-take her, the man I will love will have to have the deep affection for the sea and my ship that I do. I don't think I could love a man who wanted to stay tied to the land all his life.

She drifted off into dream clouded sleep, and when the sun rose, the next day she stood with her father and watched the nearing coast of the American Colonies.

Seven

Steffan spent the next week and a half watching for mail from London. It was twelve days before the expected letter for Martin came, and he was away the day it arrived. Steffan waited impatiently for him to return. When he arrived, it was dinner time and Steffan was forced to wait until the meal was over before he could get Martin alone. He watched in avid curiosity as Martin read the letter. When finally Martin looked up, his eyes glittered with amusement.

"I won't keep you in suspense any longer Steffan. I really don't think you can bear it. If Tom and Mack pass the exam, they will be accepted at the Academy. The exam will be given the third of April which is . . ah, let me see . . . about three weeks from tomorrow."

"That's the best news I've heard in a long time. I can't wait to tell Tom and Mack. Do you approve if I go and tell them now?"

"I'm sure you wouldn't be able to sleep tonight if you didn't."

Steffan laughed and left the room in a rush. Once his horse was saddled, he rode as rapidly as possible into town and toward the Braydon shipyard.

The elder Braydons, starting from nothing, had begun their shipyard when Tom was a child. Tom's father, his uncle and two friends had worked together to build two ships of extremely good quality. From then on, they had received commissions to build on a regular basis, for their work was always well done. Josiah Braydon would not allow a ship to leave his yard without the stamp of final approval from him. Josiah and his wife Jennifer had built a small house on the edge of the shipyard so that it was more convenient. From the time Tom could remember, his home was noisy, affectionate, and filled with love. He had three brothers and three sisters, and he stood directly between the six. He was watched over by three brothers and mothered affectionately by three sisters. There was never much money and yet there never seemed to be a lack of the necessities in their home.

Tom had come home from a demanding day of work with his

father and was preparing for bed when Steffan knocked on the door. For days, there were thoughts running about in his head as he searched for a way to make enough money to ask Cecile to marry him. The knock found him tired and not in the best of humor. He swore mildly to himself and went to open the door. He was not surprised to see Steffan there; Steffan had spent many nights in the Braydon home when he had paid a late night visit to some girl or had drunk more than he wanted his parents to see. He was so excited at the moment that Tom got the first impression that he had been drinking.

"Steff," he grinned, "where have you been?"

"No place . . . home, like a good boy, waiting for news that is going to change your life, old man."

"My life? Steff, are you drunk?"

"If I'm drunk, it's with happiness. Listen, Tom, in about two weeks, I'm taking that exam I told you about."

"Yes."

"Well, it's been arranged that if you and Mack want to take it, you can. We can go to the Academy together."

"Me," Tom gasped in shock.

"You! You and Mack," Steffan laughed joyously as he clapped Tom on the back, but Tom did not return the smile, instead, his face had turned pale.

"What's the matter, Tom? Don't you want it?"

"Want it?" Tom groaned. "Steff, it's the one thing that could be the answer to everything I've ever wanted, but . . ."

"But what?"

"Christ, Steff, I'll never pass that exam. It's been a year of hard work at the yard since I've been in school. I can't even pretend I'm ready."

"I thought of that. Maybe you're not ready now, but I'll guarantee Mack and I will have you ready in time."

"Oh, God, Steff, I'd give my life . . ."

"Tom, say you want it," Steff laughed. "Then come home with me. We'll pick up Mack along the way and between the two of us and Mr. Gillis, we'll pound you day and night until we're sure you'll pass the exam."

Tom looked into Steffan's expectant eyes, then he grinned. "I'll give it my best try."

Steffan shouted from the top of his lungs from pure unrestrained joy, which quickly brought the Braydons from every corner of the house to see what was happening. By the time a laughing Tom and Steffan had explained and gotten themselves free of the well-wishing family, it was nearly midnight. "Do you think we ought to wait until tomorrow to tell Mack; it's awfully late," Tom suggested.

"Would you have wanted me to wait until tomorrow to tell you?"

"Not on your life."

"Well, then let's go roust him out of bed and tell him the good news."

They went straight to Mack's home which they found completely dark. Mack's parents lived in the small cottage which stood next to the church. It was another place Tom and Steffan had spent a great deal of time. They knew which room was Mack's so they went to the back of the cottage and rapped several times upon his window. It was only a few minutes before the window was open and Mack's head appeared.

"What are you two doing here, don't you know what time it is? Have you two been drinking?" he asked suspiciously. Mack, always the more cautious of the three had taken it upon himself to act as their conscience.

"Come out, Mack, we've got something to tell you that just won't wait until tomorrow."

"All right, just be quiet, Steff. You're talking loud enough to wake the dead. I'll be right out." He closed the window. Steff and Tom had waited almost ten minutes when Mack appeared in the back garden.

"Okay," he sighed. "Now just which of you has just met the most beautiful girl in the world, or found a new place to enjoy an evening?"

"Neither, Mack," Steffan laughed. Then quickly he told Mack the situation and watched Mack's face brighten with each word and finally break into a wide smile. In no uncertain terms, he told them how delighted he was with the idea and how anxious he was to help Tom prepare.

"Why don't we go down to Madam Sophie's first and have just a couple of drinks to celebrate," suggested Steffan. They both agreed immediately and the three of them went off together toward the small town about two miles away.

It was well past five in the morning when Martin Gillis came awake suddenly. He lay still in the half light of early dawn trying to place the noise that had wakened him. Then it came again—the sound of something tapping against his window. Someone below was obviously throwing pebbles at it. He rose and went to the window. Pushing it open he looked down and held back his

77

laughter with some effort. Below stood Steffan, Tom and Mack, a little worse for drink and very much afraid to go in the front door of the house at that time of the morning for fear someone was up.

"Shhh," he cautioned. "Wait, don't move, I'll be right down."

Martin went down the back stairs that led from his apartment to the side door of the house. He opened the door and dragged in the three weaving, glassy-eyed young men. He tried to get them to his rooms quietly, but they stumbled on the stairs and laughed until Martin was almost beside himself with frustration. Finally, he closed his door with them safely inside and turned to look at Steffan.

"You are disgraceful, young man," he said firmly keeping his mouth from answering Steffan's broad grin.

"We . . . we waz ony gonna have one drink," Steffan mumbled. "Bu' every one wan'ed to celebrate."

"And so you got drunk, you young scalawag."

Steffan tried to stand straight and look sober and succeeded in almost falling backwards. "I'm not drunk," he said aloofly. "I'm just having a li'l trouble finding my way about in the dark."

"It's past daylight young sir, and I'm going to put you to bed and pray that tomorrow you pay very dearly for tonight."

He succeeded after another hour in getting all three quietly bedded down.

Just after noon, he opened the door to the room in which they slept, walked to the window and drew the drapes open to the bright afternoon sun. He smiled as he was rewarded by agonized moans from all three young men who shielded their eyes from the sun's glare.

"Well, good morning," he boomed heartily and laughed uproariously as Steffan sat on the edge of the bed and cradled his head in his hands. "I've taken the liberty of having a nice warm lunch brought up."

Tom groaned and threw himself back onto the bed, covering his eyes with his arms as though defending himself from attack. Mack lay still, his eyes closed and his face a sickly green color. It was Steffan who made a mad dash for the chamber pot and relieved himself violently to the sound of Martin's delighted laughter.

When they had feebly gotten themselves together, Martin was asked if he would help them set up a schedule for study. Martin suggested, to their relief, that the rest of the day be spent in recuperation.

Tom spent the most difficult three weeks in his young life in preparation for the examination. When Cecile was told the situation, she offered to help but was gently dissuaded by Steffan and Martin, who found soon enough that when Cecile was in the room, Tom's thoughts strayed from studies to other more pleasant things.

There were short breaks and rest periods that Tom took advantage of. Being in the same house with Cecile gave them some time to be alone. They rode together occasionally and walked in the garden talking, as young lovers do, of the day that would one day come when they could be together.

"Think of it, Cecile," Tom said enthusiastically, "if I can get through the Academy, I could come out in four years with a commission. I could be second mate on a ship, maybe even one day make captain. There would be no reason for us to stay apart. After that we could marry."

Cecile stood and looked up at him, her eyes wide and unfathomable. "Do . . . do you really want to wait that long to marry me, Tom!" she asked quietly.

"Cecile," Tom said gently. "Do you think I want to wait at all to marry you? Don't you think I would ask for you tomorrow—no, today, if it were possible."

"Tom, it is possible."

"No, Cecile, I couldn't offer you a thing."

"What do you think I want! You, only you!"

"Cecile, where would we live?"

"Here!"

Cecile had made a mistake. She had touched Tom where he was most vulnerable, his pride, and as soon as the words were out of her mouth, she regretted them when she felt Tom stiffen.

"When I marry you, Cecile, I'll take care of my own family. I'll never live on charity of any other man . . . not even your father."

"I'm sorry, Tom," she said softly, tears forming in the corners of her eyes and her lips trembled. Tom drew her into his arms and held her.

"I love you, Cecile, possibly more than you will ever know. Help me, Cecile, I need you. Make it easier for me to do what I have to do."

"All right, Tom," she sighed. "Please don't be angry with me, I couldn't bear it if you were."

"Angry with you?" Tom said in surprise. "How could any rational man be angry when the most beautiful girl in the world is

79

anxious to marry him? He would have to be an imbecile to be angry, and I'll have you know, madam, that I am so brilliant I may one day be admiral of His Majesty's Navy."

They laughed together. Tom put his arm about her waist and they walked back toward the house.

The three weeks came to an end with Tom groaning protest that he would never be able to pass and everyone else's hearty assurance that he was quite capable of doing so.

Then the day of departure came. Farewells were said to three pale faced young men who were about to face the unknown. Accompanied by Martin Gillis, they boarded the coach that would carry them to London and a two day examination that would decide their careers and their lives. The trip took them two days; they reached London in the early morning of the third day. The bustle and size of London fascinated all three boys, and they were even more amazed to find that Martin Gillis not only knew his way about, he knew the history and background of every important spot in the city. He pointed them out and captured the boys' imaginations with stories about each. By the time they were to be finished with London, all three boys were to have an even greater respect for their teacher and friend Martin Gillis.

The exam was to begin early the next morning and Martin insisted that they have a relaxing evening in a local playhouse, a late supper, and then a long quiet night's rest. It was just so—a quiet relaxing evening. By the time midnight appeared, all three boys were in bed. Martin sat in the small sitting room of the lodgings they had acquired, reading. Sleep seemed to be an elusive thing. He, of course, realized that he was extremely tense and nervous also. Martin wanted desperately for Steffan to pass this exam for he knew how deeply his heart was set on the sea. He also knew that by pulling a few strings, he could have gotten commissions for all three boys without their having to take the exam at all. One day he promised himself he was going to tell that to Steffan. He wanted Steffan to reach his goals on his own for he knew Steffan would not appreciate his interference. He heard the creak of the floorboard and sensed a presence long before he looked up from the book.

"Well," he said softly. "You are the last of the three I suspected wouldn't be able to sleep."

Mack stepped out from the shadows of the doorway with a half smile on his face.

"Do you mind if I sit out here and talk to you a while, Mr. Gillis?"

Of course, not, son. Come, sit down."

Mack eased himself down in a soft chair opposite Martin. He was quiet for so long, Martin thought he might not speak at all.

"Something bothering you?"

"Not really, sir . . . I . . . I guess I don't know. I'm not really worried or upset about the exam. Maybe that's the reason why I keep wondering why I don't really seem to care if I pass it or not. Maybe I'm not cut out to be officer material. I'm no hero, just a plodder, really, I have to reason things out, prepare, sort of have a good cause for what I do."

"You've just stated three of the best qualities an officer can have. What's really bothering you?"

"I guess it's lack of a purpose. Steffan, well he's independent. He belongs on the sea the way the sun belongs in the sky, and Tom, well he wants to build a career so he can marry . . . but me . . . I don't seem to know what I really want or where I'm going."

"Mack, sometimes it takes a man a while to find the path God intends for him. Because you haven't found it, don't discontinue the search. I will say one thing—don't do something just because you think others expect it of you. When it comes down to it, each man has to live his own life with as much happiness and as little pain as he can find."

"You know my father wanted me to go into the ministry?"

"I surmised he might. How do you feel about it?" Again Mack remained silent for a while, then he looked at Martin and smiled.

"Would you understand, sir, if I said I'd like to do both, or would you think me a foolish child reaching for the moon?"

Martin chuckled, then leaned forward placing both elbows on his knees.

"What's to stop you?"

"Are you serious, sir, how can I handle two careers at a time?"

"Mack, the only thing that stops a man from doing anything he wants to do are the limitations he puts on himself, and I do believe," he said humorously, "His Majesty's Navy is in dire need of a man of God. If you are determined, you could have it both ways. It would of course take a tremendous amount of work on your part."

"I've never been been afraid of work, I just don't know how to go about it."

"Take the exam tomorrow. If you pass, enter the Academy. In the meantime, I shall arrange for you to study in every spare moment you have under Reverend McDonnell. He can guide you better than any other man I know. He is an excellent teacher and a more deeply devoted man of God cannot be found. If he finds you have the . . . what does he call it . . the 'inner glow' then you will be taught by an expert. But mark me, if he feels you are inadequate, he will waste no words in telling you so.'' Martin laughed again. ''David will not let his sheep be led by anyone but the best shepherd.''

Mack was listening intently, his large intelligent eyes studying Martin.

''I would be grateful, sir, if you would speak to Reverend McDonnell, and I promise you, sir, I shall work hard. I won't disappoint you.''

''Don't ever worry about disappointing another, Mack, that will always happen occasionally; just don't disappoint yourself. Set your goals with honesty, then work to achieve them. I shall speak to Reverend McDonnell while you take the exam tomorrow and we'll make arrangements for you to meet him when the exam is over and before we return home. Now, young man, if you want to keep your eyes open tomorrow, you had best get some sleep.''

Mack rose, stood in front of Martin and looked down on him with a half smile on his lips. ''I wonder if Steffan knows just how very lucky he is to have had you for a teacher all his life?''

''Thank you, son,'' Martin said gently.

''No, thank you. I'll never forget this. Good night.''

''Good night.''

Mack closed the bedroom door behind him gently and left Martin to sit alone for an hour or so enjoying a deep contentment and peace of mind.

Morning found them hustling with nervous energy to prepare for the exam. There was a lot of aimless chatter on the ride to Brighton Hall where the test was to be held. When the carriage stopped in front of the Hall, Steffan stepped out and looked up at the huge gray stone edifice that would be the turning point in his life. Once inside, they were ushered into a long hall that contained over two hundred desks with accompanying stools. The instructor told them to find a seat. Within a half hour the hall was almost filled. The instructor, a small erect man with thin black hair and deep piercing brown eyes, stood in front of the young men.

''Gentlemen, may I have your attention, please?''

Immediately the hall became quiet. ''On each desk is a quill and ink. I shall have one of you assist me in passing out the exam. It is over forty pages. There will be a break for lunch, a half hour, then we will resume until three. Take your time and answer each question carefully. You are on an honor system here. The rules are that you are not to discuss the exam outside this room. Anyone caught cheating will be expelled immediately. If there are any questions, ask them now for there will be no more speaking until lunch." He waited, but no one said a word. "All right, gentlemen . . . you may begin."

Absolute silence fell as two hundred heads bent over their desks. Time ticked slowly by. Steffan was concentrating so deeply he was surprised when a voice cut into his thoughts.

"Gentlemen, you may put down your quills, it is time for lunch." Steffan did not believe the time had passed so quickly until he tried to sit erect and found himself stiff and cramped.

"There are a few quick refreshments being served in the room opposite this one, for any of you who care to partake." The instructor said, "If not, you have a half hour to be back in your seats."

Tom waited for Steffan and Mack by the door. "Are either of you hungry?"

"Not me," Mack replied. "I guess I'm still too nervous to eat. Why don't we just take a walk outside."

"Good idea," Tom replied. "I could use the fresh air too."

"Tom, how are you doing?" Steffan questioned.

"I don't know, Steff. The test is a lot harder than I thought it was going to be. If I make it, it will be by the skin of my teeth."

"You'll make it," Steffan laughed. "You have no choice."

"What?"

"Now just how would you go home and face Cecile and tell her she has to wait? Besides that we don't want Mr. Gillis to think all his teaching has been in vain."

They laughed together and walked out into the bright April sunshine. Small groups of young men gathered together and there was the steady buzz of conversation.

"I guess we can't talk about the test," Tom said.

"We're on our honor," Steffan replied. "We don't want to compare notes anyway. Whatever we do, we'll each do it on our own; that way," he finished with the gleam of laughter in his eyes, "when we become the great naval heroes we're destined to be no one will be able to say it was because we cheated on our test. It will be all our own indomitable brilliance."

"Oh, God," groaned Mack.

Tom leaned back against the stone front of the building and chuckled. "Somehow I just can't picture me as a great naval hero. I'll probably get seasick.''

Steffan stood facing the front of the building and Tom and Mack stood with their backs to it. It was impossible then for Steffan to see anyone approaching. Any further remarks then were stilled on his lips as he saw Tom and Mack's faces register shock. He turned to see what they were looking at and came almost face to face with Jaspar Sinclair. All four people were too surprised for a moment to say anything. Jaspar's cold gaze appraised Steffan then drifted arrogantly to Tom and Mack.

"I thought the Navy was more particular just who it let into its ranks. Now I see she's accepting . . . anything," he said, looking pointedly at Tom, whose anger was quickly apparent as he began to move toward Jaspar. Steffan's arm held him back. "Don't Tom," he said softly. "He's trying to get you mad enough to do something foolish and ruin all your chances. Besides," Steffan grinned. "He's after me," he turned back toward Jaspar. "Any time after this test is over, Jaspar, I'll be glad to accommodate you. Maybe," he chuckled infuriating Jaspar by his cool humor, "I'll get the opportunity to close your mouth more permanently this time."

Jaspar's face reddened with his suppressed anger while Steffan's smile glimmered infuriatingly in front of him.

"The last time was unexpected," he said softly, "but you will pay for that one day."

"Don't worry, Jaspar," Steffan replied calmly, "I'll never turn my back so that you can do me any harm. If you want satisfaction choose a time and place," Steffan's gaze had turned cold and hard and his words could only be heard by the four of them. It was Jaspar's eyes that dropped away first.

"You are right. I shall choose the time and place and I guarantee you it will not be where you have your friends to help."

"I don't need anyone to help me," Steffan answered. Jaspar was about to answer again when he looked up to see the instructor standing in the shadows watching the confrontation with deep interest. Jaspar's face became expressionless, he laughed and moved past Steffan toward the door. "Later," he said quickly, as he passed Steffan. The instructor stood for a while contemplating Steffan with an appraising air, then he stepped out onto the front walkway and said loudly. "Your lunch is over, gentlemen, will you please return to the classroom." He did not wait for an answer but turned about and went inside, the crowd of young men following him.

If the morning's test was difficult, the balance of the afternoon proved to be even more so. By the time they were dismissed for the day, they were all three so exhausted that they wolfed down their supper and found their beds early to drop in weary sleep.

The next day was a repetition of the day before with the exception, Tom thought, that the exam was even harder than the day before. It was an intensely difficult day and at one time, just for the moment, Tom was thinking of putting down his quill and walking out of the room. Then he remembered Cecile. Her face came between him and the paper, her bright smile and trusting honey gold eyes, and he knew he could never quit.

They all breathed a deep sigh of relief when the instructor tapped the desk lightly. "Your time is up, gentlemen. The results of the exam will be forwarded to your homes as soon as possible. Good luck."

They all rose and stood still as the instructor left, then they broke up into small groups and slowly drifted away.

Steffan, Tom and Mack went outside to find Martin Gillis sitting in his carriage waiting for them. "Come, gentlemen," he said. "I'm going to treat you all to a large supper and a musical evening, and this is for the last time. On the salaries of young officers, you will be able to afford to take me to supper more often than I can afford you."

They all laughed. The evening was a very enjoyable one, for all four of them became a trifle mellow.

"How long will it take before we know the results?" Tom inquired.

"Ah, I imagine about a month," Martin replied.

"A month!" both Tom and Steffan groaned.

"Now, come now," Martin laughed. "You don't think you're the only three involved do you? They've got to evaluate the exams and choose those they think capable."

"It's not done just with grading then?" Tom asked.

"No, no my boy. You've been watched and every word you wrote will be evaluated. By the time they are through with that test, they will probably know you better than you know yourselves."

"Watched?"

"The instructor who gave the exam was probably the best judge of men that the Navy can find. He will add his opinion to the results of the test. You were under surveillance by him from the first moment you entered that room, and especially while you were gathered together talking and thinking you were unobserved."

"Great," Tom said with a laugh, then he lifted his glass of wine. "I should like to propose a toast gentlemen. 'To our instructor, I hope he has a pleasant month, that he stays in good humor and good health and' " he laughed again, "I hope he found us the most intelligent and charming men in the class."

They laughed, drank and enjoyed the final night in London. The morning sun found them on the road toward home.

Eight

If the three weeks before the exam had been difficult ones, the month that followed was almost unbearable. The three boys, unable to contain their nervous tensions, were swarming all over the area in bursts of wild enthusiasm and mischief that caused even Martin to shake his head and pray that word would come soon. Even Mack, who was the most reserved of the three, joined forces with the other two.

Steffan had invited Tom and Mack to spend the night. They had had a joyous laughing late evening. At breakfast the next day, they were quiet, a little subdued at the presence of Cecile, Steffan's mother and father and Martin. The conversation was rather desultory. They were about to leave the breakfast table when the butler came in bearing a small silver tray upon which lay an oblong white envelope.

"This just arrived for you, Mr. Gillis," he said.

"Thank you," Martin said. He took the envelope and slowly opened it, conscientiously ignoring the bated breath and intense looks that followed his every move. He read slowly, allowing no expression on his face.

"Mr. Gillis, please," Steffan laughed, "I just can't stand it any more. Is the letter from London or not?"

Martin grinned. "It is my boy, it is."

"Well?"

"It seems you all three have been accepted."

Steffan jumped erect and gave a wild shout of pure joy. Suddenly everyone was laughing and hugging one another.

"Maxwell, there is one added note in here which I think will please you immensely."

"What is it, Martin?"

"Steffan has not only been accepted, the letter came with a personal endorsement by the instructor and telling us that Steffan has placed in the upper third of his class. They are 'pleased to acquire a young man of such character and obvious intelligence combined with the ability to make a fine officer.' "

Maxwell turned to face his son, his eyes aglow with pride. Steffan smiled and stood erect, straightening his shoulders and seeming to stand an inch or so taller than usual. Maxwell extended his hand and Steffan took it.

"I'm proud of you, my son, and I'm not surprised. I've always known the quality was there."

"Thank you, Father."

Steffan's mother came to him and he held her against him, then Cecile threw herself into his arms with a delighted laugh. Even Tom took advantage of holding Cecile for a moment when she hugged him in delight.

"I think this calls for some kind of celebration." Maxwell laughed, "Do we have enough time to plan a party before they leave, Martin?"

"Oh, quite, Maxwell. They do not have to report to the Academy for another thirty days."

"Good," Ellen said. "I shall plan a big farewell party."

Steffan was the only one who noticed that his mother's eyes glistened suspiciously of tears and there was a controlled volume to her voice. At the first opportunity, he drew her a little aside.

"What's the matter, Mother? Aren't you happy about the Academy?"

"Oh, Steffan," she half laughed, half cried. "I'm very very happy for you. It's just that . . . well, it is so difficult to watch the child who was your baby yesterday, suddenly in front of your eyes turn into a tall handsome young man who's going to break your heart by leaving you. It's very selfish and I'm sorry but I find it very hard to imagine this house without you."

She had placed both hands on his chest as she spoke to him. Steffan drew her into his arms and held her for a moment until her tears were under control. "I do love you, Mother, you and Father and Cecile are an inseparable part of me, I could never forget or leave entirely. I'll be back sooner than you think. Why, I'll bet you won't even have time to miss me before I'm under foot again." He put his arm about her shoulders and they rejoined the others.

The days flew. The party was planned. Tom tried his best to spend as much time with Cecile as he possibly could. Steffan and Mack did their best to romance and enjoy the company of every available girl in the area. Both Martin and Maxwell turned their eyes away from this, letting the boys enjoy their last fling before the hard hand of military discipline descended on them.

The party was to be held the day before they were to leave. The day of the party, Tom and Cecile were walking together along the sandy beach about a mile from Devers Hall. They walked hand in hand in contented silence.

"Tom, why have you avoided being alone with me for the past three weeks? It always seems to me that you arrange to have someone around when we have a chance to be together," she stopped and looked up at him. "Are you having misgivings about proposing to me? Would you rather be free?" she said the words softly, her eyes watching him closely for his reaction. Tom stood stunned by her question. Then he put both his hands on her shoulders and gave her a gentle little shake.

"Cecile, that is the most unbelievable thing I've ever heard you say. I'd rather die than lose you, don't you know that?"

"How could I possibly?" she pouted. "You've made such a point of staying at arm's length."

"And," he said softly, "don't you know the reason for that?"

Cecile stepped closer to him and slid her arms about his waist and tilted her face up looking at him from under her thick eyelashes.

"Tell me," she whispered her eyes a melting glow of invitation and her lips soft and tremulously waiting.

"Cecile," Tom murmured as he bent his head and captured her willing mouth with his, then suddenly he held her away from him. "And that is the reason," he said. "Cecile, just how strong do you think I am? Are you child enough to believe I can be so near you, touch you, hold you and not want you? God, woman, don't do this to me, I love you too much."

"And I love you, Tom," Cecile said, her face serious. "I love you, I want you. I can't bear the thought of your going away for months without seeing you. If you really love me, if you really want me to wait for you . . . then I want you to let me know. Show me that you care. Don't set me on a shelf like a little china doll to take down and play with when you come home. I'm a woman, Tom. You are the man I love, the only one to whom I ever want to belong. I want to know today just whether you want me enough."

"Oh, God," Tom groaned almost to himself. He drew her back into his arms and held her. Then slowly he tipped up her chin and took possession of her mouth in a deep kiss that moved the ground from beneath her feet and left her weak and clinging to him, in a wildly spinning void. Her lips parted under the demanding pressure of his. Feeling the warm softness of her body pressed against his and the seeking urgency of her kiss, Tom lost any idea he might have had of denying himself the luxury of holding her for a few stolen moments. At least that was the idea in his mind. Where it got lost he didn't know. He only knew she was vibrantly alive in his arms and every nerve in his body screamed out his need for her. They parted for a moment and he looked deeply into her honey gold eyes that told him everything he was feeling was mirrored in her.

"Tom," she whispered, "between us is a love that is beautiful and good. We want to be together unashamed and unafraid. I cannot lie to myself or to the world. Why should I push you away with both hands when I want only to hold you, to belong to you."

Tom put his hands on each side of her face, holding her gently. "Cecile," he said, his eyes warm with the wanting of her, "I want you now and always. There is a place near here where we can go, but first . . . do you know what you're doing? Do you . . .?"

"Yes, Tom," she smiled. "Yes, I've always known, since the first time I saw you that I would one day belong to you. Oh, Tom, I've waited so long for you to see . . . to know."

Tom took her hand and they walked down the beach until they came to an outcropping of trees that extended to the water's edge. Deep within it, Cecile could make out the outlines of a small deserted fisherman's cottage. They walked toward it and Tom pushed the door open, drew her inside, and closed it gently behind them. Cecile walked a few steps ahead of him. In the center of the room, she stopped and turned to look at him. It was dusky in the room with thin strands of sunlight coming through the one window. Tom surveyed the cabin. It had been deserted for some time. He knew, because he had used it as a fishing cabin for years. He also knew there was a large bed in the next room. He looked again toward Cecile who had been watching him. Then he walked to her. Tentatively, with gentle fingers, he touched the side of her face and ran his fingers lightly down her cheeks to her throat. Slowly, his hand slid to the back of her neck and he drew her toward him. Her lips parted gently as his mouth covered hers. The kiss began gently, but soon his arms cradled her tightly against him and she was lost in the wonder of the pulsing flame that began somewhere in the depth of her being and burst forth like a brilliant blooming flower. Every nerve in her body was vibrantly aware of the hands that caressed her and gently removed the clothes she wore until she stood in front of him proud of her beauty and aware of the desire and love in his eyes as he devoured her.

"God, Cecile, you are so very beautiful," he said softly. He took the two steps that separated them and with one swift movement he bent and lifted her in his arms and carried her to the bed. He put her down against the pillows and removed his clothes. Then he was beside her and her arms lifted to accept him, to hold him close to her, to share with him, the burning need that consumed her.

Now the hunger for her that had built in him for years overcame every rational thought he might have had. His mouth ravaged her willing one and his hands discovered vulnerable spots that awakened her to an urgency that bordered on wildness. That he was the first man for her was unquestionable; he knew by the inexperienced way she fumbled for him, yet he was exuberantly happy to know she wanted him as deeply and completely as he did her.

They were the center of the world for those few sweet minutes, the beginning and ending of all beauty. She heard his whispered words of love with a deep pleasure, for she knew beyond doubt that Tom was hers now and would be for all time. They lay still together, both silent, both experiencing an emotion completely opposite from the other. Cecile felt a deep sense of inner peace and contentment such as she had never felt before . . . and Tom . . . Tom was frightened to death. Words refused to come to his mind that would be able to convey to her what he felt.

"Tom?" she whispered as she lay close to him, her hands caressed his bare chest with a gentle possessiveness. Tom rolled over on his side and looked down into her eyes.

"I wonder if I'll ever be able to make you understand how grateful I am and how very much I love you, Cecile."

"You needn't," she murmured. "You've shown me."

"Oh, Cecile," he whispered as he pulled her even closer to him. "You are the most beautiful part of my life. If I felt so before it is stronger now. Maybe . . . maybe we ought to be married this fall when I am home on my first leave."

"Why?" she asked wide-eyed. "You're supposed to wait until you graduate."

"Wait! What if something happens. I wouldn't let you go through something like that, you are too perfect for anyone to say anything about."

"Maybe nothing will happen this one time."

His eyes glittered with laughter. "Do you think I could stay away from you from now until Christmas? If you do, you're crazy. It took all I could do to keep from touching you before, now that I've tasted what a miracle our love is, I would have to be superhuman not to reach out and experience it again and again. No, you've got to be mine as soon as possible."

"But . . . Mother . . . Father."

"There's not a mountain too big to climb. I'll try to find a way to make your parents agree. If I can, will you marry me soon, Cecile?"

"Yes, oh, yes, Tom." She laughed and threw her arms about his neck drawing his head down to hers.

If it wasn't noticed by anyone else it was noticed immediately by Steffan, the glowing change in Cecile. She and Tom danced together as if no one else in the room existed. Steffan sensed something had happened between them but he was not sure what. Not for a minute did he give thought to the idea that Tom had taken advantage of his sister. If, he thought, anyone had taken advantage of anyone, it was Cecile taking advantage of Tom's deep love for her.

Nevertheless, when the celebration was over, a nervous Tom requested permission to talk to Cecile's parents. Steffan made sure he was present because he was sure the young lovers would need his support.

They sat together in the large drawing room sipping brandy. Maxwell and Ellen sat on the small sofa in front of the fireplace, Tom and Cecile sat on a matching one directly opposite them. Steffan stood with one shoulder leaning against the carved mantel. He caught his mother's eye, she smiled and winked at him and Steffan was stunned with the realization that his mother knew exactly what was happening and was going to support Cecile completely. For a moment, he felt a little sorry for his father.

"Father, Mother," Cecile began, her voice deep with respect. "Tom and I have something very important to discuss with you."

"Something that is so important it can't wait until tomorrow? It's quite late and I'm sure everyone is tired."

"Max, we should listen," Ellen said. "I'm sure it is very important to them or they wouldn't have wanted to talk tonight." Warmly smiling at Tom, Ellen added, "What is it you have to say, Tom?"

Tom recognized immediately he had a friend in Steffan and Ellen. It completely slipped his mind that it was Ellen who had suggested the wait in the first place. He felt Cecile's hand slip into his and he held it tightly. Clearing the imaginary lump in his throat, he began. "Cecile and I would like to change our plans.

Since I've been accepted at the Academy and I'm twenty, soon to be twenty-one, I feel I can care for Cecile. There will be a small income, I know, but it will be enough for us to manage on. I love her, sir, and I don't want to leave her here for someone to steal from me. I'd like to get a small house near the Academy, we could manage . . ." Tom knew he was rambling but he couldn't seem to stop himself.

"Tom," Maxwell said. "Cecile is only seventeen."

"I know that, sir," Tom said miserably. "But that does not change the way we feel about each other. If we waited for years or married now, nothing would change. It would only mean that two people who should be together would be separated for wasted years."

"Mother?" Cecile questioned, "how old were you when you married Father?"

Ellen smiled, "I was sixteen, Cecile, as you well know."

Cecile smiled, "And would you change one day of your marriage, would you have waited while Father left you?"

Ellen tucked her hand through Maxwell's arm and he turned to smile down into her eyes.

"Answer your daughter, I'd like to hear myself." Ellen laughed.

"I wouldn't trade a single minute I've shared with you, and I think we'd better give in, Maxwell, we've no solid ground to stand on."

"I quite agree. I'm sure if we plan well, we could have the marriage arranged by the time you come home for Christmas leave," Maxwell said.

Cecile jumped to her feet and ran to her parents' side. She knelt in front of them. "Thank you, I'm so very glad I have the wonderfully understanding parents I've got. I only hope I have the same marriage that you do and can give my children the love and kindness you've given Steffan and me."

She rose and threw her arms about her mother while Tom who had followed her to her feet stood by beaming with happiness.

"Speaking of Steffan," Steffan said. "I'd like to contribute to the happiness. I'd like to give Cecile and Tom half the money Grandfather left to me for a wedding present."

Again Cecile squealed with delight and ran to her brother giving him several resounding kisses. He held her and bent his head close to her ear. "Good work, spider. Some time you have to tell me just how you got around Tom's stiff-necked pride." She giggled.

"Never, that's a secret between Tom and me."

Tom and Cecile did not get a chance to meet alone again before the day of departure arrived. It was a very disappointed Tom who held and kissed Cecile goodbye. It was a pleasant trip back to London, and all three boys were so filled with nervous excitement that they could barely control it.

At the time their carriage left Devers Hall another was arriving at the same Naval Academy in London. From it descended two men who were obviously father and son. They entered the registration building and remained for quite some time. They left with self satisfied smiles on both their arrogant faces and went to a local tavern where they sat over a luxurious meal and drinks. It was the older man who spoke first in a gloating voice.

"I told you how very simple it is to get what you want when you have the right leverage."

"So I see," the younger man answered. "I would say knowing someone's darkest and deepest secrets is more than just leverage. It was amusing, the look on his face when you informed him of what you knew."

The older man chuckled maliciously. "I know a great deal about a lot of people."

"Then why the hell don't we dig out something on the Devers? I'd like nothing better than to make Steffan Devers crawl on his hands and knees to me."

The older man's face took on an introspective look and his eyes clouded with an emotion the younger man could not fathom.

"Maxwell Devers," he mused. "That is a completely different matter. I've tried for twenty years to get some kind of hold over him. Always, he has eluded me, always he's had the upper hand. Maybe now his son will not be so lucky. Maybe now the Devers will taste the other end of the stick. Give it time, with our friend's help, young Devers might not find his stay in the Naval Academy as rewarding as he expects."

"Rewarding! He'll never graduate, never receive his captaincy from this Academy. He's going to find the course twice as difficult for him as any other. And I intend to make his life here as miserable as possible. You're sure of my position?"

"Of course, you will be one rank ahead of Devers when he joins. I expect you to stay so. Then you will have it in your power to see the young man succeeds at . . . nothing."

"Good! Now, I've got to move along. I want to be settled and prepared to meet my friend—sort of give him a friendly welcome when he arrives."

They laughed together as they left the tavern.

When Steffan, Mack and Tom arrived, they were met at the registration hall by three cadets who were in their second year of training. They were welcomed and helped with their luggage. The three who met them were only a year or two older, but to Steffan and his friends, they seemed so much more mature that they tended to speak and act around them with a great deal of respect . . . until one of them laughed.

"I'm Langley Miles, I'm a second year cadet and you don't have to treat me like I'm an admiral. We're all in the same leaky boat here. You'll have your quarters with us and we're supposed to help you get indoctrinated to the routine around here."

"And I'm Brighton Claire," the second offered, and motioned to the third young man. "This is Jeffery Sables; he's the brains who will probably pull us all through."

"I'm pleased to meet you," Steffan smiled as he extended his hand first to Langley then the others. "I'm Steffan Devers, this is Tom Braydon and Mackenzie Davidson."

"Well, come along," Langley said as he lifted one suitcase. "We'd better get you settled as soon as possible; there'll be an inspection tonight so they can lay down the law for the new cadets. You'll get to meet some of the brass and our new barracks master."

"Barracks master?" Tom questioned.

"Yes, we're to get a new one. It's sort of an honorary title, but he is one rank ahead of you. He's responsible for our behavior. It's best to stay on the good side of him or he can cause you a lot of grief."

"What kind of grief?" Tom questioned.

"Probably things not enough to get you thrown out, but enough to make your life here miserable. Small things, like . . . well demerits for being out after hours, not having your room ship-shape, disrespect to anyone of rank higher than yours, you understand the barracks master has been responsible for the resignation of more future officers than anyone else or anything else for that matter."

"Remind me," Tom said in mock seriousness, "to kiss his boots when he comes around."

They all laughed together. The walk from the registration hall to their quarters took fifteen minutes. They chatted amicably together, Langley filling them in on procedures they would have to follow, letting them know exactly what was expected of them.

"When will we be on board a ship?" Mack asked.

"You won't see any active service for at least the first year. The book work is the hardest. I'll bet I know every great naval battle ever fought, who lost and why."

"Doesn't sound very easy," Steffan said.

"If you are looking for an easy career," Jeffery replied, "I'd suggest you try something else."

"I'm not afraid of hard work," Steffan laughed. "If you'd had a tutor like mine, you'd understand. Mr. Gillis thought hard study should be my one aim in life."

"How about the officers—how are they?" Mack questioned.

"Well, there's Commander Crawford. He's strict as hell, but he's fair. Then there's Lieutenant Commander Gilpatrick. I guess he's all right. I personally think he's a little odd, but he's a good instructor and if you keep your nose clean, he'll treat you right. Then there's Captain Kyle . . ."

"I take it you're not too fond of Captain Kyle."

"I have nothing against him . . . I just wouldn't want to serve under him."

"Why?"

Jeffery was silent for a few minutes then he said gently, "The gentleman has a wife quite a few years younger than him. She, in turn, has a taste for young officers. It doesn't make him exactly sympathetic to any of their problems." He turned to look at Steffan. "And you're just the type she likes. She devours your kind whole."

"My kind?"

"Young, damn good looking and big. If you want some friendly advice, stay away from Morgana Kyle. She's pure poison for a man who wants a career in the Navy. You mess with her and he finds out you'll be in and out of the Navy before you can blink an eye."

"I'll just stay out of her sight. I'm only one of many, she'll never notice me."

"Don't ever count on that my friend. In the first place you stand out like a sore thumb, and in the second place, Morgana looks over every new cadet that comes in one way or another. Either they get summoned to the Kyles for a small party or she spots them at the first opening ball which is held to welcome all the newcomers in about six weeks."

"Well, I'll cross that bridge if I ever get to it. I'm sure it takes two."

"Okay, dreamer," Jeffery laughed. "Here we are, gentlemen, this is your home away from home for the next four years."

Before them stood a two story building that rose among several duplicates.

"Each barracks contains eight rooms upstairs. There are two or three cadets to each room. Downstairs are facilities for eating, studying and believe me a limited amount of entertaining. The barracks master's room is downstairs in the front. He has access to everything and everyone. He'll know who comes and goes and why. Come, I'll show you to your rooms. They come in two sizes. Do you three want to stay together?"

"If possible," Tom answered.

"Okay, I think one of the bigger rooms is still empty."

He took them in the front door and up a flight of stairs that was about fifteen feet away across a square foyer. Opposite the staircase was a door.

"That's the barracks master's quarters. The door on the other side leads to the eating hall and the door next to the entrance is the combination study room and entertainment room."

He led them down a hall with closed doors on either side. At the end of the hall he stopped in front of the last door.

"Here we go." He swung the door open and let the three of them view the room they would be sharing for the next four years.

The room was oblong in shape, about eighteen feet in length and about twelve feet wide with a large window at the far end. There were three narrow beds against one wall; beside each was a small stand with two drawers. Against the wall were three dressers that had four drawers apiece. The floor was bare wood and the walls empty of adornment. The color was an atrocious cream color. It was a rather drab and unimpressive looking room. "You can add a personal touch here and there to help brighten it up," Brighton chuckled. "Believe me any little thing could help."

"I can see that," Mack replied dryly. They set their luggage down and each put a few of his belongings on the bed of his choice. "What do we do with our days exactly?" Steffan asked.

"Well, the schedule of your individual classes will be posted in the main hall. After you find out just where and when each class is held, the rest is easy."

Langley laughed. "Easy? Sure, if you find getting up at five in the morning easy. If you find that you have to run at full speed from class to class to get there on time easy. If you find there's not enough time in a day to get all your work done and still have time to care for your room and your personal belongings the way they expect them to be cared for, then I guess you'd say it's all very easy."

"Sounds like a lot of pressure," Mack said.

"It's the way they weed out the men from the boys, I guess, or so I've been told. I imagine they're right. If you receive your captaincy and are responsible for your crew and your ship, I guess you'd have to be able to operate well under pressure."

"For the balance of today, we'll show you around. Let you get a good idea of where everything is. We'll find your schedule of classes and get you acquainted with the barracks master. Tomorrow you're on your own. Oh, by the way, tonight there'll be a welcoming speech by Commander Crawford, and you'll be issued your uniforms. We'll take you out to a few spots and have a good supper, but I suggest you get to bed early because five in the morning comes entirely too soon."

"Good, let's get started, I'm hungry enough to eat a horse," Tom said.

They left the room and went directly to the main hall where the schedules of classes were posted. After finding out where their classes would be held, they were taken to each classroom and made acquainted with the time it would take them to get from one place to another.

After the tour, they were taken to a small tavern that served as a meeting place for all the underclassmen, as a place to eat, drink and find amiable companionship and relief from the daily pressures. They were introduced to several other cadets, newcomers and established alike. The supper was excellent, and about eight, Langley suggested they get back.

"You have to make up your beds and get your clothes put away. There's regulations for everything, and believe me, if you deviate even an inch, Captain Kyle and the barracks master will be down on you fast and heavy."

When they returned, they were given all instructions on the proper way to do everything, and when every inch of the room had been thoroughly examined and had passed Jeff's inspections, he smiled.

"You three should be all right, you learn quick. Make sure everything is done the same way. We should go down now. The barracks master should be in his quarters. He'll go with us to hear the Commander's speech and then . . . the day is over. Tomorrow starts a whole new life."

This sobered the six of them for a few minutes, then Jeffery laughed.

"Come on, let's go. We'll beard the first lion in his den. Makes us look good to be on time. We'll knock on his door and let him meet the six best cadets he'll find in the Academy.''

They clattered down the stairs noisily and in a short time, all the occupants were assembled in the hall. The conversation was hushed as the door to the barracks master's quarters slowly opened. Steffan was momentarily stunned and his heart thudded heavily. His emotions mirrored Tom and Mack's as they turned to face the gloating, smiling face of Jaspar Sinclair.

Nine

They watched Jaspar in silence, all three of them too surprised to speak.

"Good evening, gentlemen," Jaspar said smoothly, but his eyes wre on Steffan when he spoke. "My name is B.M. Jaspar Sinclair. I would like to be the first to welcome you to the Academy. I hope your stay here is rewarding. I'm sure for some of you, it will be an experience you will never forget." Casually, he took a large gold watch from his vest pocket and looked at it. "Uniforms are to be distributed in ten minutes, after which we will assemble in Gayton Hall for a few words of welcome from our Commander. Then we return here. Lights are out at ten. I want you to know, gentlemen, that I am an easy man to get along with, only," he grinned at Steffan, "there are rules and regulations we must abide by and I am here to see that none are broken. Along with rules, there are also punishments for willfully breaking them. I," he said gently, "am also here to see that any misdemeanors are properly disciplined. Now, I suggest you get your uniforms quickly for the Commander's speech is in an hour and at this Academy, there is no excuse for being late. I shall meet you at Gayton Hall in one hour." He said the words to everyone but the three of them knew the silent threat that would be hanging over them for the next few years. It took a lot of their exuberance away. Steffan watched Jaspar leave in silence wondering just how he had gotten his rank and just how bad Jaspar could make it for him.

"How the hell did that happen," Tom said quietly. Steffan shook his head negatively.

"I don't know."

"Somebody pulled some strings somewhere," Mack supplied. "You know he's going to be all over us, Steff. I've got a feeling our stay here, especially yours, is not going to be as pleasant as we thought."

"He can't do anything to us if we don't step out of line," Steffan said grimly, "and I don't intend to give him a chance to do anything. If there are rules and regulations, we'll abide by them better than any cadet has done before. Jaspar Sinclair is not going to ruin my chance for the one thing I've wanted all my life."

"Then let's get going and get our uniforms. We should be the first in the assembly hall. That ought to make Jaspar twitch a little," Tom said humorously. They laughed, but it was restrained laughter, each wondering just how far Jaspar would go.

They were among the first to receive their uniforms which consisted of two pairs of pants, one black and the other light brown. A striped blue and white shirt and two waist length double breasted jackets both of deep navy blue with two rows of gold buttons up the front.

"The light pants," Lang told him, "and one jacket are dress uniforms. For church and public wear. The striped shirt and dark pants are everyday wear. The other jacket is only worn when we serve ship board duty. It's up to us to see they're cared for, as it's the only issue you'll get for six months, then anything worn is reissued. If you're smart, Steff, you'll do what I did. I had another set made up. That way I can always look presentable even when I get a little lazy."

"Good idea, where do you find a tailor?"

"On our first leave, which will be in about eight weeks, we'll go into town and I'll take you to mine."

"Thanks, Lang."

"Let's get going," Bright said. "If we hurry, we can drop the clothes off and be at the assembly hall in plenty of time."

They were among the first cadets in the assembly hall and found seats near the front. It didn't take long for the hall to fill with the two hundred new cadets, and very shortly attention was called for and Commander Crawford was introduced.

He was an imposing figure. He had a mane of thick, wavy, snow white hair, a full moustache and short beard to match. Steffan estimated his age at about fifty-five. He could only guess for Commander Crawford kept the physical build and strength of a much younger man. He looked to Steffan and the others like a man who had the ability to do himself what he expected from his men. He stood in silence, his hands clasped behind his back, and just his air of complete authority brought the entire hall to silence.

"Gentlemen," he said, his voice deep and resonant. "Welcome to the Royal Naval Academy. You have been chosen by our instructors as the best qualified men to train and become the backbone of His Majesty's Navy. Great things are expected of you here and if you succeed, great reward will be returned. Many of you will go on to gain captaincy of your own vessels, and others will attain the status of ranking officers. What you accomplish depends solely on you. You will be offered every opportunity. The four years will be difficult, but I am assured that with diligence and work, you will find a great future in store for you.

"England is the naval power in the world today, and you have a great reputation to live up to. Always be proud of the fact that you are the best our country has to offer. You are the cream of our youth and the life blood of our country. When you leave this Academy, you carry with you the hopes and dreams of a great nation; you are an example to all the world of the type of men our country produces.

"As Commander of this Academy, my doors are always open. I and my staff are not only here to train you, but to assist you in every way necessary to achieve your goals. I want to wish you all the very best for the years to come. Tomorrow, your classes begin. Good night, gentlemen . . . or should I say officers?"

He gave a slight bow toward them then turned and left the room amid cheers and loud applause from the men.

The six of them walked slowly back to the barracks.

"They were right about one thing," Steffan thought as he groaned himself awake at five the next morning, "Morning comes entirely too early around here."

It took each of them only half an hour to dress and put their room in order for inspection. Steffan took special care in making his bed and the proper order of his things for he knew that it was Jaspar who held the early morning inspection and if one thing was out of place, he would soon find it. He was right; it began that morning and continued daily until Steffan had to control the urge to do what Jaspar wanted him to do, to attack him openly and in front of witnesses. It was the one thing Steffan was determined he would never do. Instead, he used the best weapons he had against Jaspar's tyranny . . . patience and humor.

Just after inspection in the morning, the three of them separated for the day. Their schedules were completely different. There were classes in the morning in navigation and naval history, then military strategy and great naval battles. After lunch, there were classes in mathematics, astronomy and knowledge of each type of ship and the arms she would carry. Another on types of arms and their uses. It was Commander Crawford who held the classes in naval strategy and history and Steffan quickly recognized the military genius of the man and his astounding ability to make the class come alive. Commander Gilpatrick held the classes in mathematics and navigation and Captain Preston taught astronomy. Steffan received his first acquaintance with the husband of the notorious Morgana Kyle. Captain Kyle held a class on ships and arms. He was knowledgeable and, Steffan thought, a decent man. He was tall and extremely thin. His hair was dark brown with streaks of gray at each temple that gave him a distinguished look. He had deep brown eyes that were clear and penetrating. Steffan instinctively felt that he was not only an extremely intelligent man, he was also a very unhappy one.

It was three weeks later, when Steffan was rushing at full speed toward class that he heard his name called. He turned to see a man walking rapidly toward him. For a moment, he did not recognize him, then suddenly he remembered. It was the instructor who had given the entrance exam. Steffan jerked to attention and saluted sharply then waited to find out why this officer was taking an interest in him.

"Good afternoon, Cadet Devers."

"Good afternoon, sir."

"In a hurry to get to class?"

"Yes, sir."

"I'll walk along with you, that way you won't be late."

Steffan was surprised, but he said nothing as he fell into step beside the officer. He waited for the man to enlighten him on why he was stopped.

"How are you coming along here, Devers? Do you like it?"

"Yes, sir," Steffan smiled. "I believe I'm doing all right, sir, but I guess it's a little too early to tell."

The officer chuckled. "Don't believe that. I've been picking out the best officers since I came here fifteen years ago. I've yet to be wrong. I've had my eye on you since the day of the exam."

Again Steffan kept a surprised silence.

"I'm Commander Pierce. When the time comes, in about a year, it is my duty to pick the candidates for active sea duty. I command His Majesty's ship, *Good Hope*." He stopped and turned to Steffan. "I'm prepared to choose you among the first group if you maintain your studies."

"Sir!" Steffan smiled. "Thank you, Commander Pierce."

"Don't thank me. Believe me, it's a hard journey from where you stand to the bridge of the *Good Hope*. But I firmly believe you will stand there one day."

"I appreciate your faith in me, sir, but . . ."

"But how do I know?"

"Yes, sir."

"I know more about you than you imagine. I've made it a point to find out all about you. I know and admire quality when I see it. It is my job to give His Majesty's Navy the best officers I can find. We are going to need you soon."

"Why, sir?"

"There's the sound of thunder from across the sea. The Colonies are growing, they're beginning to flex their muscles. I admit their Navy is small, in fact practically nonexistent, but I sense a growing storm."

"War, sir?" Steffan said in deep surprise. "Why, sir, the Colonies are so small, so . . . so infantile. What could they possibly expect to do to a strong country like England?"

"Steffan, never underestimate what the combined will of men will do if they believe in a cause."

"But, sir, the English Navy is the strongest in the world, and her Army is," he chuckled, "almost as good." Pierce laughed with him at Steffan's obvious slight to the Army.

"I'm a man much older than you, and I can tell you from experience that nothing stays the same, everything and everyone changes. They don't want to believe my words, but I've been there, I've sensed the patriotism of these people, the strong will they have. I tell you that one day soon, they will be a threat to the stability of England in the New World. At the same time, she will need the strong young men she is training here." He turned to Steffan. "Would you be interested in training under me on the *Good Hope?*" Steffan felt a sudden sense of pride, both in his country and in the fact that Pierce thought he was a prospect for something as exciting as this.

"I would like nothing better, sir."

"Good. There is no need for me to tell you how very important your studies are; I can see by your attitude, you already know. I'm going to say one thing I hope you remember."

"Sir?"

"Don't let a personal problem interfere in what you want. Don't let anything . . . or anyone . . . lead you away from the path you should be on. I will warn you that I know of a strong influence here that opposes you in every way. I just want you to know you have a friend if the need arises."

They had reached Steffan's classroom door. Steffan was speechless when he realized that someone besides Mack and Tom knew about Jaspar's personal vendetta. It gave him a sense of relief to find a friend in Commander Pierce's position. It also formed a million questions in his mind, first how Commander Pierce knew and why he was singled out for such attention. Neither question was to be answered as Commander Pierce interrupted before Steffan could begin.

"Get to class, Cadet Devers. In less than twenty seconds, you will be late and not allowed to enter the classroom."

"Yes, sir," Steffan saluted again, went inside and closed the door behind him.

Commander Pierce walked out of the building and across the Academy's green lawn. He entered another building, climbed two flights of stairs and walked to a door that had his name in small square black letters. Inside, he closed the door behind him and turned to smile at the man who was seated in the leather chair in front of his desk.

"I've planted my seeds, Martin," he smiled. "The Colonies could use a man the caliber your young hero is going to be."

Martin Gillis rose from his chair. "You did not mention the fact I was here, or that we know each other."

"No."

"The boy will do well in his studies. I know, I've been training him for years. Under you, he will learn all there is to know about commanding a ship. When the time is right, I will take him to America, show him firsthand why she will need him so desperately. The only barrier we will have to cross is his deep loyalty to his country and his friends. Both young men close to him would be very welcome additions and I might just try to acquire all three. Once their young souls have been stirred by this new country's desire for freedom, then we need only sit back and allow their fiery spirits to join the others."

"Do you suppose he will think us disloyal?"

"For a time, but young Steffan is learning just how it feels to be oppressed. I know Jaspar Sinclair doesn't have an idea of how much he is helping our cause but he is. We have time. The ingredients have been thrown into the pot. Now we must wait for it to come to a boil. Let him receive his training, then, when the time is ripe, I will show Steffan the truth. From that day on, all the choices are his. The best we can hope for is that he understands the real value of freedom."

"And the worst?"

"The worst," Martin sighed. "Is that he will be blind to everything but his own achievements and glory."

"And you, Martin," Pierce smiled, "just how do you think the dice will fall?"

"I will tell you at the proper time, I will put my life in Steffan Devers hands. That is how much faith I have in him. Since the boy was ten, I have watched him grow. Whether he does yet or not, I know his heart. I know how he thinks and in all honesty, I believe he will understand and we will be richer in our endeavor by one excellent sea captain . . . maybe even three."

"I hope you're right, Martin, we will need him. We are pitifully small. Sometimes, I'm amazed at our audacity."

"Ah, but Leon, old friend. Where would the world be today without audacity? Where would we be without the courage of men who fight tyranny, who are not afraid to break away from the old corrupt way and begin a whole new future? It is in the hands of young men such as Steffan. We can merely serve as beacons to light the way, they must sail their ships into the bright new harbors of the future."

"How are you going to reach him?"

"I don't know yet, I think I will recognize the opportunity when it appears. For now, I am going to let Jaspar Sinclair help us mold Steffan. You will see how well Steffan reacts to pressure."

"I wonder if Steffan is going to appreciate our putting him at Jaspar's negligible mercy."

"I really don't believe it will last that long. Watch, Leon, you will see Steffan's friends rally and follow him in whatever he does. He is a natural born leader of men."

Leon Pierce poured two drinks of brandy and handed one to Martin. Wordlessly, they touched their glasses in a silent toast to their hopes for Steffan Devers' future.

A few miles away, two men sat alone in another room. One was an older man of approximately sixty. There was some familial resemblance that would have told any viewer that the two men were related. The older man sat behind a desk and watched the younger who stood at the window looking out without seeing for he was seriously contemplating the words that had just been spoken.

The man at the window gave the deceiving appearance of a boy. He had on a full laced uniform. His lank unpowdered hair was tied in a stiff hessian tail of extraordinary length. The old fashioned flaps of his waistcoat added to the general quaintness of his figure, and produced an appearance that would always immediately attract notice. Few had seen anyone like him before, yet there was something in his stance and attitude that showed quickly that he was no ordinary being. The slight oddity of appearance, the power to arouse affection, and the glow indicating a fire within, were always felt by people who met Horatio Nelson face to face. "Am I right in what I am doing, Uncle?" he said softly. Captain Maurice Suckling rose slowly from his chair and came to stand at the young man's side.

"Horatio, I feel in my own heart the depth of passion for freedom these people must have. I also believe that such an opportunity reaches out and touches a man rarely. What choice you make can only be yours. The country is building a Navy, small I agree, but with the help and influence of men like you, it will grow. You could be the catalyst about which her naval strength is built; why just the mention of your name would influence the young men who train at the Academy to serve under you."

The younger man shrugged as though his shoulders had suddenly accepted an unwelcome weight. "And what about the country that trained me, Uncle? It is disloyalty to take what she has to offer and use it against her."

"It isn't only England that has trained you. Haven't you also studied the subject of naval warfare in France? Have you not also fought a battle or two under the flag of Spain? Listen to me, Horatio, you know I love you as a son. I believe in this new America. I believe in the freedom she has to offer, and I also believe that without you, her chances grow slimmer. You are the grand hero of the Navy. They look up to you . . . they will follow you, the ones we choose. I'm sure of it."

Captain Horatio Nelson was indeed the hero to the Naval Academy. He had attended school there at seventeen, seen battle by the time he was nineteen and was placed in the rank of Post Captain at twenty. Now, against his will, they wanted to use him in the Academy as an instructor of naval tactics. It irritated him for he felt they were suddenly casting him aside. It wasn't until he turned to face his uncle that one could see the empty right sleeve of his jacket. He would never believe it was not the reason for them to take him from the command of his ship *Worchester* and ask him instead to teach.

"Yes," he said bitterly, "I remember my own words well. I will be a hero, and confiding in Providence, I will brave every danger. The words rang well to their ears then. Suddenly they do not hear the words; they only want the reputation of Horatio Nelson to hold men to the classrooms and build new heroes for the future. Well, Uncle, I am not to be a forgotten hero. Yes, I will join your young Navy and yes, at the right time, I will speak to the men your friends have chosen, and if the name and reputation of

Horatio Nelson still has the power to influence them, we will all stand under this new red, white and blue banner of theirs."

"Good, good," the older man exclaimed. "I have with me the names and the backgrounds of the men chosen. You can study them. By next year, they should be ready for active duty. We will see to it that you meet them and you can judge for yourself those you want to accept."

"How many have you chosen?"

"Well . . . here," he handed a paper to Nelson. "Here are the names."

"Jeffrey Sables, Michael Dewberry, Brighton Claire, Langley Miles, Steffan Devers," he read. "Why are these other two names bracketed with Devers, Tom Braydon, Mackenzie Davidson?"

"We want Steffan Devers, probably more than any of the others with the exception of Sables. But the man is extraordinarily loyal to his two friends. I don't believe he will come without them. I thought we might even reach him through them. One of them, Davidson, is inclined toward the ministry also. They have allowed him to begin study when he's in the second year at the Academy. Braydon is Devers' future brother-in-law, the two have been very close for years. It also might prove difficult for us to reach Braydon since he plans on marrying Devers' sister this Christmas leave. It goes without saying that his heart will be firmly planted in England."

Horatio laughed. "Maybe, Uncle, you should consider transplanting the whole family, then you would have no trouble getting the son."

"Don't think we have not considered that avenue. It will be tried . . . everything will be tried. This is one war the Americans must win . . . or die."

"All right, Uncle, we will meet with these men from America and discuss this further. There is ample time to begin working on these men. It is still three years before they graduate, and none of them has seen any active duty yet. Who are the commanders these men will serve under?"

"We've arranged for Devers and his friends to serve under Commander Pierce. There are very few better captains, outside yourself, and very few men as loyal to the American cause as he. The others will be under Commander Weber and Commander St. Thomas. Both excellent men. Eventually," his uncle interjected humorously, "we hope they'll be serving under you . . . on the right side of the ocean."

Horatio laughed again and his brown eyes gleamed with the undisguisable urgency to be aboard ship and on the sea again as an active captain.

They put on their coats and left the house. A carriage waiting outside for them carried the two men half way across London to another house that sat on the outskirts of the city and was walled in by a three foot high stone wall that gave it an air of seclusion. A quick rap on the door by Maurice Suckling and it was immediately opened. Inside a small fire burned in the hearth and one lamp was lit casting a soft red-gold glow of light over the small group of men who were gathered there. They rose as a man when the two were ushered into the room for they had waited long and impatiently for this meeting. They desired more than anything else the influence this boyish looking man had to offer. From his earliest years, Horatio Nelson was endowed with a daring spirit of adventure which, one day, would establish his memory for all time as one of the most illustrious men who have filled the ranks in national contests. Courageous to the degree of rashness, of sound judgment, self possessed, confident, full of resources, he combined to an extraordinary degree all the qualities whose influence would lead the men who had unknowingly been chosen for a great endeavor and would change the course of world history.

He was introduced to all men in the room, but he noticed one young man who stood a little apart as though he were afraid to meet him.

"Good evening, sir," he said with a half smile.

"Good evening, Captain Nelson," the man replied. He was obviously deeply impressed.

"Your name, sir?"

"Jones, sir . . . John Paul Jones."

"And you are to be one of our captains?" Horatio inquired.

"I hope to have the pleasure. I have been at sea since I was twelve, sir, and although I have tried other things, I have come to the realization that my heart is on the sea."

"And what do you think of the endeavor of the Colonies we are about to defend?"

"I offer her my services, sir. I do not do so lightly. I believe she is right in her desire to gain her independence and I offer her my life if necessary to see that she achieves it."

Nelson nodded, but remained silent as the others about him began to discuss the situation. He noticed that Jones stayed unobtrusively in the background but listened intently.

John Paul Jones was born in Scotland, the son of a humble gardener. Without encouragement and lacking the advantage of even a meager education, but possessed of an indomitable spirit and a constant and passionate desire for fame, he had a singularly acute and conceptive mind which, like Nelson, possessed the power to frame great projects and convey the inspiration to others. His was a calm enthusiasm. With cool deliberation he always estimated every chance for his success or failure and having once concluded to act, he entered upon the undertaking with a dash and persistence which only death could have dismayed.

He had been impressed into the British Navy from which he had at the moment full intentions of deserting. The most important reason being that his spirit of independence could not submit to tyranny, and the other that he believed in the American struggle to throw off the yoke of despotism.

At the conclusion of the meeting, Jones found himself offered the position of first lieutenant on the ship *Alfred*. He accepted this quietly, but Nelson laughed to himself for he knew, like he knew himself, that this would never be enough for a man such as Jones. He also knew that one day, Jones should command his own ship. Suddenly, he felt the swift current of inevitability, and as the group began to break up, he found himself next to Jones. With a smile, he held out his left hand to Jones who took it with the same knowing glow in his eyes. It was unnecessary to say anything. Both knew they were going to fight together for a common cause and one in which they had believed all their lives—that each man should be master of his own heart and soul. America, at the moment acquired two of her strongest patriots. In the near future, she was to acquire another small group who were to come to believe as deeply as the men who guided them.

Ten

The harbor in Boston teemed with activity. Tamara was fascinated by the number of ships in the harbor, but even more so when her father pointed out each and named it and the country from which it came. When they finally went ashore, she was delighted that her father seemed to be as well known here as in every other place.

She was more surprised when a handsome young man presented himself, hat in hand and a warm welcoming smile on his face. Andrew suspected the smile was more for Tamara than him. He extended his hand.

"David . . . how are you?"

"Fine, sir, and I hope I find you the same. Where is Mrs. Marriott, hasn't she come ashore yet?"

"Joanna died a few months ago, David."

"Oh, God . . . I'm sorry, sir."

"It's all right, David. I want you to meet my daughter Tamara. Darling, this is David Perry. His father and I have been friends for many years."

Tamara extended her hand to him accompanied by her brightest smile. He took it and bent over it for a moment. When his eyes rose to hers, he smiled. "It is a pleasure to meet you, Miss Marriott. We have heard a great deal about you, but your father never told us how very beautiful you are."

"Thank you, Mr. Perry."

"David," he corrected.

"David," she laughed. "And I'm Tamara, not Miss Marriott."

"It would be my pleasure, Tamara, to show you about Boston, or rather to show Boston you."

"Thank you, David," she replied, and gently pulled away the hand he was still holding.

David escorted them to the carriage and when they were seated, Andrew was amused to find himself opposite David and Tamara.

David was a handsome young man, tall, but yet several inches

111

shorter than Andrew. He had pale blond hair and deep blue eyes. He laughed easily, and his enthusiasm bubbled as he pointed out places of interest to Tamara on their way to the Perry house.

The Perry house was one of the first built in Boston. It was a large two story frame house. Over the years as Randolph Perry slowly acquired a fortune, he added two wings to the house, each one attached to each side but extending far beyond the original building. It was now shaped like a box with one end open. To all of this, Randolph had added a beautiful young wife who had an eye for creating a delicate air of splendor in the house. The walls in the house were painted a soft shade of ivory, with the solid oak woodwork and large glass windows Roseann had insisted upon. It was a fresh and airy home. To this she added bright carpeting and green plants. The furniture, imported from France, was delicate yet well built.

David was his first born son; he was followed by two girls and another boy. When they arrived and David was handing Tamara from the carriage, they were suddenly bombarded by a whirlwind who resembled David remarkably. He was followed by two laughing girls in fluttering white petticoats.

"David," the young boy shouted. "Papa says when you get back to come right into the library."

He was a boy of about ten years and as soon as Tamara had a moment to watch him, it was obvious that his hero was David.

The two girls stood apart a little shyly until David motioned them forward.

"Tamara, these are my sisters, Martha and Jennifer. This rather rambunctious young man is my brother, Joshua."

Joshua grinned. "Hello, Miss Tamara," he looked toward Andrew. "I know who you are."

"Do you, young man?" Andrew laughed. "And just who am I?"

"You're Mr. Marriott; Papa says you're probably the very best friend he has and if I'm not good, he's going to warm my seat. Have you really been all over the world, Mr. Marriott, and do you really own hundreds and hundreds of ships and . . ."

"Joshua," David said firmly. "That is not a very polite way to make a friend welcome. No more questions until our guests are made comfortable and have a chance to see Mother and Father."

David turned back to Andrew and Tamara. "Come in, Father and Mother will be waiting." He led the way and Andrew followed. Tamara walked beside Martha and Jennifer.

Martha, at age sixteen was not really a pretty girl, but she had

112

striking blue eyes almost the color of violets. Her blonde hair was pulled back in a long plait that did nothing for her rather sharp features. Jennifer was fourteen, her heart shaped face was fringed in blonde wayward curls and her hair was tied back by a blue ribbon. She showed promise of being rather pretty when she was older.

They were escorted into the house where they were greeted warmly by Randolph and Roseann Perry. David had obviously acquired his blond good looks from his mother. She was a tall slender woman with his deep blue eyes and a ready smile. Randolph was tall and remarkably slender. He had dark brown hair and a matching moustache and beard. He crossed the floor immediately to meet Andrew, his hand outstretched. "Andrew, Lord man, it is good to see you again." His eyes fell on Tamara. "And can this be the child you have spoken of so often? She is lovely, Andrew."

"Yes, Randolph. This is Tamara, my daughter."

Tamara curtsied and smiled. "I'm pleased to meet you Mr. Perry."

"And I you, my dear. We have heard so much about you, I'm afraid we feel you're as much our daughter as you are Andrew's."

Tamara smiled in pleasure at the warm considerate way they were welcomed into the Perry home.

Their stay in the Perry home was to be memorable for Tamara in more ways than one. It was a bright and happy household who included her in their family life as though she had always been a part of it.

Martha, only two years younger than Tamara, took her to meet her friends, took her shopping and shared her room with her. But it was David who seemed, as the weeks passed on, to be more and more at her side.

They were seated at the dinner table one evening when a subject arose that was to eventually change Tamara's life.

"Randolph," Andrew began. "What is the rumbling I hear from this side of the ocean?"

"It's not rumbling yet, Andrew. It is more the birth cries of a new nation severing the umbilical cord."

"Is it possible?"

"Not only possible, Andrew, quite probable. There is a spirit here in this country you will not believe. It is warm and vital, and it is growing in strength."

"Strength? . . . you worry me. I've heard rumors of war."

113

"I for one would hate to see it come to that, but I am afraid if England keeps making the same mistakes and continues to underestimate the people here, it might just come to be."

"But man, a war! That is senseless. This country is not big enough or strong enough to wage one."

"Not so," Randolph replied. "It takes faith too, to win wars."

"Yes," Andrew said quietly. "Faith . . . and guns."

"That too. There are ways to acquire arms and ammunition. The faith is already here."

"I don't see how you expect to win," Andrew insisted.

"I cannot explain as well as some friends I have can. Will you be upset if I invite them for dinner tomorrow? I would like you of all people to understand what is happening."

"Why me of all people?"

"Because, I intend to ask for your help."

"Help with what?"

"Have patience, Andrew. Talk to my friends. If you do not agree, I will say no more. If you do . . . then I shall ask."

Andrew had a million questions he would like to have asked, but he swallowed them and decided to wait and meet Randolph's friends. "And just who are these friends?"

"Well, one is Tom Jefferson. I want you to meet him especially. He is the most brilliant young man I've ever met, and he has some definite and strong ideas on the freedom of men."

"Randolph . . .?"

"Andrew, just listen. If you do not agree I will not mention the subject to you again, agreed?"

"All right." Andrew smiled. "I agree."

They laughed together and the conversation turned to other matters. Neither man paid close attention to the wide intelligent green eyes of Tamara as she sat quietly and absorbed with rising excitement what she had heard. She also vowed she would hear this Tom Jefferson's ideas if her life depended on it.

The next day, Tamara and David were taking a late afternoon buggy ride. "David, this Tom Jefferson, do you know him well?"

"Mr. Jefferson? Oh, yes. He's a marvelous man," David's eyes lit with a glow Tamara had not understood. "You should hear him speak. He makes you want to go out and fight for all men to be free."

"You keep saying free, David? Aren't you free? I don't understand what you are talking about."

"No man is free, Tamara, unless he has control over his own

home, his possessions and his future. We don't; we are in constant subservience to England. Our taxes, which are not only exorbitant now but are becoming worse, are sent to England in whose parliament we have no representation. We are nothing more than slave labor with the profits going to a country that does not know or care about any of our grievances." He turned to Tamara and grinned. "And I did not bring you out on a buggy ride on such a beautiful day to talk of such things."

"And just what ulterior motive did you have, sir?" she demanded with a teasing smile.

"Well, I'm not too sure. I think I had something in mind like getting you away from my nosy sisters and brother to talk with you for a while."

"What did you want to talk to me about, David?"

"I heard our fathers talking. You might be going home within the next two weeks."

"Yes, I know, Father told me."

"Tamara . . . I wish you could persuade your father to stay a while longer."

"Why?"

He pulled the buggy to a halt under the shade of a tree and tied the reins firmly, then turned to face Tamara. "Because, I can't stand the thought of not seeing you every day. I . . . guess I've grown attracted to you."

"Like another sister?" she laughed.

David took hold of her shoulders and looked into her eyes. Her smile faded as she realized how deadly serious he was. "The last thing I feel for you is brotherly, Tamara, I'm in love with you."

"David, don't."

"Don't . . . just like that. Tamara, I've a good future in my father's bank. I'm reasonably intelligent, I've got a great disposition," he laughed, "and I'm not the ugliest man in the town. What I'm trying to do is ask you to marry me."

"David . . . I don't want to hurt you. I like you, I really do, but . . ."

"But, what? What are you looking for, Tamara?"

"I don't know, David. I just know that when it happens, when I really fall in love, he won't have to tell me or ask me. I'll know . . . somehow, I'll know."

"And you don't love me?"

"No, David, but I do care for you enough not to want to cheat you out of the kind of wife you should have. I'm not the kind of girl to be married to a banker. You don't know me, David; I'm

115

really a wild little gypsy who would rather be out in a sailboat than anywhere else. I like to run free on our own island. I would die here, cooped up, restrained, never to be able to breathe the cool sea breeze. No, David, I wish it were otherwise, but if I married you, we both would end up being unhappy and some day hating each other."

"You'll be going home soon. I'll miss you, Tamara. Will you keep in touch with us?"

"Of course, I will."

"And Tamara?"

"Yes?"

"If you change your mind, if you ever decide this is what you want, will you write me?"

"I know my heart, David, what I want is still out there somewhere in my future."

"You're lovely . . . God, I wish I were the lucky man who is going to get you."

He had taken both of her hands in his while he spoke. Now, he bent forward and gently touched her lips with his. But when he looked into her eyes, he knew the worst defeat he'd ever known. Without another word, he lifted the reins and turned the horses back toward home.

When they arrived home another buggy stood by the front gate. David helped her down and they went into the house. Voices from the library could be heard. David excused himself and went to join the men gathered there. Tamara stood still for a few minutes as her boiling resentment grew at the age old custom that women were too delicate to be included in discussions that controlled their own futures. Slowly, she walked to the door that stood open several inches. She stood quietly in the hall and listened to the deep resonant voice that held her attention and made her heart beat faster at his words. When the words he said came to her, it was as if he were speaking to her very soul. He spoke of the independence of men, of the rights each person should have. He spoke of spirit, of loyalty, of all the very things that made up the girl who stood and listened.

Tamara wanted to talk to this man, to see him. She sat on the last step of the stairs until the meeting was over. When she heard them moving about in preparation for leaving she stood up and slowly walked toward the door. When it did open, she was only two feet from it. She stood face to face with a man whose stirring words would help mold her own future.

Thomas Jefferson stood tall and erect as an arrow, with

116

angular features. His skin was delicate, yet he had a ruddy complexion. He had full deep set hazel eyes, and a quick smile that lit his eyes with an intelligent questioning look when he saw Tamara before him. She curtsied low then stood erect and looked at him with eyes that were as filled with questions as his.

"Good afternoon," he smiled. "And I imagine a lovely vision such as you has an even lovelier name."

"Tamara Marriott," she answered quickly.

"Andrew's daughter?"

"Yes."

Andrew and the Perrys appeared in the doorway behind him.

"Tamara," her father held out a hand to her and she went to his side. "I want to introduce you to Mr. Jefferson. Tom, this is my daughter, Tamara, and this," he motioned toward Tom, "is Thomas Jefferson from Virginia." He looked down on Tamara as Tom and Tamara exchanged polite amenities.

"Were you looking for me, my dear?"

"No, father," she laughed. "David and I just returned from a buggy ride and we heard you talking," she looked up at her father, unashamed wickedness in her bright green eyes. "I was listening."

Tom Jefferson joined in their laughter. "And were you interested in what you heard?"

"Yes, very much so," she replied. He raised an eyebrow of interest as he looked from father to daughter. Andrew read his look and again his hearty laughter was heard.

"Tom, you were speaking unknowingly to the most independent heart that exists in the Colonies today."

Tom Jefferson was about to make a mistake when he looked at Tamara again. "If she were not so very beautiful, I could almost wish she were a man. We need every patriot we can get."

Tamara's face blushed in the quick anger she felt. "And why is it that you gentlemen believe that because a person is female she has nothing to offer to the cause of freedom? We women have as much to offer as any man. Our hearts beat with the same emotions as yours. We seek the same freedoms as you. Why do you always feel that we are only the shadows of your loves and hates?"

"Tamara!" her father said quickly.

"No, Andrew," Tom interjected; then he looked again into Tamara's wide, angry green eyes. "I'm sorry if I offended you, Tamara. What I said was not properly worded. Of course being man or woman makes no difference in the way we feel. I simply

117

meant that . . . one day, there will be war and we need hands to carry guns, and I would not be surprised in your desire to lift one. I would only hope that it would not be necessary. No country should demand the blood of its women, they are too desperately needed to form the minds of the children who will one day inherit this country. Please accept my apology.''

Tamara's anger subsided at his word and the apologetic sound of his voice. She nodded her head in agreement.

"I have just invited your father to come to Monticello for a few days before you return to your island. Now, I find myself even more anxious to open my home to you and show you the better part of my world.'' He turned to look at Andrew. "Will you come, Andrew?''

Tamara looked expectantly at her father who, grinning, said, "Do you think I dare refuse, Tom? If you think you have seen her angry, believe me you have not, and I do not want to be the cause of a violent eruption or you might think twice about putting a gun in her hand, and directing her toward the enemy.''

They laughed again at Tamara's quick blush. "Of course we will come, but only for a few days. It is time I returned to work.''

The conversation continued for a few minutes, then Tom left with the urging that they come to Monticello soon. For Tamara it could not be soon enough.

It was over a week before final preparations were made and they began their journey to Monticello. Tamara stepped down from the carriage and stared in open-mouthed wonder at the beautiful home Thomas Jefferson had built.

They were welcomed by Tom and his wife Martha who, at Andrew's request, conducted them on a tour of the lovely estate.

The Monticello plantation that Jefferson had created was unique. Unlike any previous one, it was built on a level plateau on the top of a mountain eight hundred fifty-seven feet above sea level. To make all parts of the mountain accessible, Tom had constructed on its slopes at four different levels, paths, or as he called them roundabouts. These were connected by oblique roads.

Before Tom built Monticello, there was on every plantation a series of small outbuildings, such as the laundry, smoke house, dairy, stable, weaving house and sometimes a schoolhouse and always a kitchen. These things Tom sought to render as inconspicuous as possible by locating them beneath two long terraces terminating in two balanced outchambers. Connecting these terraces was the all-weather passageway in which were strategically placed the wine room, ware room, beer cellar, cider room, and rum cellar. Beneath the south terrace were to be found the kitchen, cook's room, servants' rooms, rooms for smoking meat and the dairy.

The small pavilions on the end of each terrace attracted Tamara's attention, for each one was fully equipped with fireplace, bed and other furniture. Martha blushed as Tom told the story of the night they were married. On the trip home, the weather became so bad that no one believed they would arrive. The supposition that they would stay elsewhere caused the servants to lock the house for the night and retire. When Martha and Tom did arrive, on horseback, because they could no longer travel by carriage, and half frozen, they found the entire house dark and locked. The only door that had accidentally been left unlocked was one of the small pavilions where he and Martha had spent a cozy wedding night. Martha's shy smile appeared as Tom lovingly referred to it as his favorite room in the house and laughingly named it the honeymoon suite.

The house was a three story building of thirty-five rooms including twelve in the basement. The dominating feature was a huge dome with an octagonal roof under which the Jeffersons placed a ballroom.

The gardens held long gravel walks with beautiful shrubs and trees and well planned flower beds. There was a huge oval fish pond in which Tom kept a supply of fish for dinners.

The home was a rare beauty but it was not the thing that held Tamara's attention. It was Tom Jefferson himself. She was held spellbound by the philosophy and beliefs of the man. During the two weeks they spent at Monticello both Andrew and Tamara were fascinated by the brilliance of the man who had built it.

Tamara took advantage of any excuse to be present when Tom and Andrew spoke together. In his efforts to swing Andrew to his cause, Tom was only half successful, but without even knowing it, he acquired one of the best patriots the cause could ever have in Tamara Marriott.

When they left Monticello regretfully, Tamara carried with her a silent determination that in some way, she would do something to support the cause Tom Jefferson had given her such belief in.

The trip home was long and uneventful. If Andrew wondered at Tamara's quietness, he said nothing. He knew she was bound up in the books Tom had given her, but he never seriously gave a thought that she was harboring the plan in her mind that would have changed his complexion to red and his hair to white had he known.

Mikel too, noticed Tamara's reticence, but he, like all men, did not credit the thoughts Tamara was thinking to her. It also never entered his mind that he would one day become an accomplice in an escapade that would nearly cost them their lives.

Tamara's campaign for possession of the *Adventurer* began slowly, so slowly and subtly that neither Mikel nor Andrew gave it any notice. She was always at their elbows, with gently asked questions. She urged her father to let her maneuver the ship through difficult drills until he agreed she could handle the *Adventurer* under any situation.

Just before they reached home, Tamara celebrated her eighteenth birthday.

"Tamara," her father said. "It is impossible for me to get you a gift now, but tell me what you would like and when we get home, I will purchase it for you."

"Father, let's not worry about a gift now. One day I will want something. You can get it for me then."

Andrew was pleased with her attitude and compounded his problem by making a promise. "You can have anything that pleases you."

"Anything, Father?" she questioned seriously.

"Anything that is in my power to give is yours," he replied.

"You are a man of honor, father; one day I will remind you of that promise."

Andrew laughed and hugged her to him. Not for a minute did it occur to him that a woman would ask to own one of his ships.

Mikel too, fell into the same trap. Captivated heart and soul by the calm beauty she had become he made a fateful promise also. "Mikel, it's not necessary for you to give me a gift," she said.

"But I want to, Tam. You're important to me and I hate to see your birthday go by without giving you something."

They were standing together at the rail on a calm sea in the early morning. Tamara's smile glistened in the half light. She leaned forward and took one of Mikel's large hands in both of hers.

"You can give me a promise, Mikel."

"A promise?"

"Yes, it's all I want."

"Sure, if it's something I'm free to give you need only to name it."

"I want your loyalty Mikel and reassurance that the promise you made me long ago is still good."

"What promise was that?"

"That if I ever had a ship of my own you would be my first mate."

"I remember, of course I would. I don't usually go back on my promises to anyone, especially you."

"Thank you, Mikel . . . it is all I want for now."

She rose on tiptoe and kissed him quickly, it was then that some sense of fear, some strange thing touched him. He wondered if he was going to regret the promise he had just made.

Once back on the island, Andrew resumed working eight to nine hours a day and Mikel was kept busy between helping Andrew and assisting his father. This left Tamara much to herself and she was pleased to be so, for now she had a plan that she slowly began to put into motion. She developed a regularity in some habits so that when she repeated them they would go unnoticed by the servants. She took to riding over the island both in the morning and again in the afternoon. She often spent a day or two with young friends she knew at the military village, so that if she claimed that was where she was going she could be gone two or three days. Now she realized she had to have a confidante, someone she could trust, someone she could get to cover for her if she were gone occasionally. She found this in two friends she had for many years. One was Mary St. Claire, whose brother had permanent duty at the training fort. He had at one time tried for Tamara's hand. They had become friends when she made him understand that friendship was all they would ever have. Then there was Barbara McBright. Her father had been in the employ of Tamara's father since she could remember and she and Barbara had been close friends from the days of their childhood.

Without telling them exactly what she was planning, she allowed them to believe that she was interested in someone special. Both being romantically inclined, they vowed eternal secrecy and assured her they would do everything in their power to help her. If they had known exactly what Tamara had in mind, they would have been shocked. They did not know and Tamara wisely neglected to tell them.

As the months rolled along, both Mikel and Andrew were pleased with the calm new Tamara. She was receiving letters often from the Colonies. Andrew thought they were from David and relaxed with the idea that one day, Tamara might choose to marry David Perry. They were not from David, they were from a shipbuilder in Boston who was building a swift new ship to astounding specifications he had received through the mail. The ship would be the fastest on the open sea, he assured her, and mounted with twenty cannon and enough sail to make her fly. Tamara had been slowly sending money month by month hoping her father would not notice the absence of some of her jewelry.

The last letter she had received told her the ship was nearing completion and would she send instructions on the color she was to be painted, the name to be put on her, and the destination to which she would be delivered.

This was the one problem that was always uppermost in her mind. There was no place about the island that her father didn't know like the palm of his hand. Where she was going to hide a ship was a problem to which she gave her undivided attention for weeks. But it was an unforeseeable accident that gave her what she wanted, and it happened when she was at her wits end for a place to anchor her ship.

Mikel and Tamara were talking together; he was telling her of a huge rock that jutted out of the ocean a few miles away from their island. "Tam, you should see the monster. It's about six hundred feet of solid rock. There's not an inch of beach on it. You can hear the waves crash against it for miles. The tide is so strong against it, it could pull your boat in and smash you against the rocks and no one would ever find the pieces."

"Mikel!" she said, excitement bubbling in her eyes. "Take me to see!"

"It's too dangerous, Tam. If the tide caught our boat, you might get hurt, and if you did, and I had the luck to survive, I'd never be able to face your father."

"Mikel, if you don't take me," she said with the devil glittering in her green eyes, "you know I will go alone. Which would be the most dangerous do you think?"

"Tam," he said miserably, "why do you put me in such damnable situations?"

"Situations?"

"You on one side and your father on the other."

Tamara laughed. "Father need never know, Mikel; we've gone sailing so often, one more time won't make any difference."

"Unless he has to pick up your broken body out of the wreckage."

"He won't," she replied with assurance. "You are the best sailor on the sea," she giggled. "And I'm second. What do we have to be afraid of?"

Mikel smiled down into her excitement filled eyes. How I wish she would look at me like that, he thought. "Tam, you're so damn full of life and always looking forward to everything being so interesting and exciting. Don't you know you cán get so hurt that way?" he said gently.

"But Mikel," she said softly. "How do you find all the beautiful things in life if you don't have the courage to look? Sometimes getting hurt is small price to pay for all the good things life has to offer."

"You run into things too fast for me, Tam, maybe that's why God never meant you for me. I kind of feel sorry for any man who tries to tame you. He'll have to be something really special."

"Why does someone have to tame me? Why can't he be like me? That's what I expect from the man I will love. He'll want me to feel the same freedom as I, love the sea as much as I. Not want to be pinned to the land."

"That kind of man doesn't exist."

"Why?"

"Because a man wants his woman to have his children, to ease all the troubles he finds in life, to make his home some safe haven for him."

"I've not met a man who makes me feel so," she admitted.

"When he comes along, I hope to be around to see the fireworks. In fact, I hope to find out just what kind of man can reach that wild heart of yours."

"I'm not going to worry about it, Mikel. I have other plans for my life right now and they don't include a husband. The last thing I'm looking for is a romantic entanglement with anyone."

"Sometimes, you don't have anything to say about it," he replied.

"I have no intention of falling in this so called love you talk about. I just haven't the time right now, and I don't want to talk about it. Are you going to take me to see this . . ."

"Corvet's Rock," he answered.

"Corvet's Rock," she repeated. "Are you going to take me, or do I go alone?"

"I'll take you," said he resignedly. "But we have to be more careful than we've ever been. If that Rock with its tides draws us into it, it will be all over."

"I'll be at my best," she laughed. She tucked her arm through his and they walked to the docks, she with a light heart and laughter on her lips and he with a dread in his heart that was weighted with the feeling of impending disaster.

Eleven

At the docks it took them no time to unfurl the sail of Mikel's boat, and in a few minutes, they were on their way. A bright, crisp breeze carried the small boat along at a rapid rate of speed. Still, it was almost an hour before they neared their destination.

"Listen, Tam," Mikel shouted above the wind. The sound of waves crashing against some unseen shoreline came and Tamara turned her head in the direction from which the sound came.

Suddenly she spotted the rock which Mikel had told her about. Even from the distance she could tell how immense it was. As they grew nearer, the thunder of the roaring waves that crashed against the high granite rocks drowned out every other sound.

Mikel began to ease the boat away from the rock.

"Mikel," she shouted, "just a few minutes, just a little bit closer," she screamed to make her voice heard above the roaring ocean.

"We can't get too close," he shouted back. "The tide's going in and if it catches us, we're not strong enough to fight it."

Tamara turned again to look at the huge gray monster that towered above them. She could feel the strong tug of the tide that tried to grip the small boat. The boat was controlled only by the expert handling of Mikel, but this was to be brought to a sudden soul shattering end, as to both Mikel and Tamara's horror, the strain on the small mast became too great. With a loud cracking noise, it split in two and the remnants of the sail collapsed at their feet.

Mikel's face became gray with fear as the surging tide lifted the small boat and with tremendous force pulled it toward the huge gray rock.

Tamara shook with the first real fear of her life. They were helpless and she felt the painful guilt for having drawn Mikel to what seemed to be his obvious death. She turned to look at him, her eyes wide and filled with regret and fear. Mikel worked his way to her side and drew her against him, trying to give her some of his strength to bear what he knew was inevitable.

The rock was like a huge gray mountain above them; the thunder of the crashing waves made it impossible for them to even console each other by words for it was not possible to be heard above them.

Tamara trembled in Mikel's arms and he buried his face in her hair and held her as tight as he could. He would like to have put himself between her and the harsh gray rocks.

Suddenly complete blackness enveloped them. Mikel looked up in surprise and suddenly gave a wild shout that echoed in the huge black cave that they had entered. Tamara too, blinked her eyes open in surprise. The rapid movement of the boat told them they were still rushing inward at a tremendous rate of speed. Then suddenly the boat surged out into the bright open sun that glittered beautifully on a calm peaceful lagoon.

Both of them were entirely too shocked for a few minutes to even move. They stared in wide-eyed wonder at the calm beauty surrounding them. The whole center of the rock was hollow somewhat like a volcano. The center area, about two miles wide was a calm, deep lagoon surrounded by an area of white sandy beach. Beyond the beach was a heavily wooded area that extended another two miles and touched against the high walls that were perforated with caves.

"Mikel," Tamara gasped in wonder.

"I don't believe this," he said in a rasping voice.

"What a beautiful place," she replied in a hushed voice. "I bet there has been no one here since the beginning of time."

"No, I imagine they haven't."

"How do we get out?"

Mikel turned to look at the huge open mouth of the cave they had just come through. "When the tide goes out, we can ride out with it, but we have to fix the mast and pray we can escape the pull of the island."

"Mikel," Tamara said softly with a calculating look in her green eyes, "that cave is so huge why hasn't anyone seen it before?"

"No one," Mikel responded firmly, "is stupid enough to come that close to the rocks."

"Why, Mikel," she answered, but he frowned deeply as he saw the wicked glitter in her eyes, "I bet you could bring a ship through that cave with no trouble."

"Sure a ship . . ." he stopped as she began to smile broadly. "Tamara, what the hell are you up to?"

"Mikel, I'm up to several things at the moment. One is to help you fix the mast, two is explain to you all I've been doing the past few months and three," she grinned wickedly, "is to remind you of a promise you made me quite some time ago."

"A promise? What promise?"

"All things in good time, first we explore. How long before the tide goes out?"

Mikel looked up at the sun. "We have about five hours."

"Good, while we work, I'll talk."

"Then I guess the only way to get you to talk is to start working."

Together they dragged the boat up on the sand. It took three hours of hard work and Tamara told him all that had been happening without anyone knowing. She calmed his first burst of anger and tried to explain her feelings. Then she told him that she already had the ship she wanted and now the secret place to hide it.

"You can't do this alone, Tamara," he objected.

"I have no intention of doing so."

"Who will your crew be?"

"Picked men who are loyal to the right cause."

"Who will captain it?"

"Me."

"You! Impossible!"

"Why, Mikel? Because I'm a woman? Without lying, tell me if you think I can sail it or not?"

"Damn it, Tamara, you know you can sail it, but you just can't do this without help."

"Oh," she said softly, "I intend to have help."

"From whom?"

"One of the best sailors on Marriott Island."

Now he looked close and saw the laughter deep in her eyes, and her final idea hit him. "Me?"

"Yes."

"I won't do it!"

"Doesn't your word mean anything to you?"

"You know my word is sacred; what are you getting at?"

"You made me a promise," she said firmly. "That if I ever got my ship, you would be the first mate. Did you lie, Mikel?"

"Oh, God," he mourned gently. "I think I've been trapped."

Her laughter burst and she threw her arms about his neck and kissed him several times.

"You honorable lovable man." She laughed, "I knew if I told you how much I needed you that you would help me. Look

126

around, Mikel. No one will ever find us here."

"What are you going to do?"

"Relieve the English government of some arms and ammunition that are badly needed elsewhere."

"How are you going to know which ships?"

"I already have a contact sending me word on all ships sailing from England with arms. We simply capture them, store the ammunition here until our other contacts can pick them up."

"What of the men on those ships. They'll tell right where we are as soon as they get home."

"No, the ships and men will be held here until a prize crew comes. Then ships and men will be taken to America. The ships will be renamed and the men," she shrugged, "I think some will join us and others will be held until this is over."

"You have everything covered," he chuckled. "Except one or two little things."

"Such as?"

"How you're going to get out from under your father's eye for one or two days at a time."

"Oh, Mikel," she giggled. "That was the easiest thing of all."

He was resigned to it now and threw up his hands in despair. He walked away from her on the pretext of looking about, but really to catch his breath at the wild plan she had. Try as he would, he could find no fault in it. They explored several caves together, some of which went clear through the mountain and from which they could clearly see any passing ship that would come within miles of Corvet Rock.

The tide was beginning to ebb when Mikel hoisted the sail and they began to float toward the tunnel. This time as they were swept rapidly through, he kept his eyes open and could see that the tunnel was so huge he could barely make out the roof above them. A ship would have no problem getting through.

"You've got to remember the times of the tide or you'll either be trapped in or out."

She nodded and then they both concentrated on handling the boat as they were rapidly swept through the tunnel and into the open sea.

When they arrived home, Mikel joined Andrew and Tamara for dinner. He watched in silent admiration as Tamara put on another performance of the contented, docile sweet young lady.

Later that night in the seclusion of her room, Tamara smiled to herself at the thought of what her shipbuilder would do when he was asked to turn over the ship to a pirate. Jack Teel, often known as 'Black Jack' was a pirate of wide repute in the waters near the English coast. No one but a chosen few knew that he was in reality a combination spy, courier and supplier of the Revolution. He would bring the ship and the chosen men to the rendezvous point she had mapped out for him in explicit detail.

After she had sealed the letter she sat back in contentment and let her mind stray to what she would name the ship. She thought of several but they were hastily discarded. Then her eye happened to fall on the thin gold chain about her wrist. The thought suddenly flooded her mind. How appropriate that her father should have given her two charms, one, a ship . . . and the other—a butterfly. She smiled to herself. She would paint the ship bright red from top to bottom. What an excellent way to slap the arrogant English in the face. And of course she would name it . . . *The Scarlet Butterfly*.

It was only three months later that the ship *Eastern Star* made the mistake of crossing the path of *The Scarlet Butterfly*. Tamara had chosen to strike whenever a ship would pass in the early part of the day. That way, her escape to Corvet's Rock would be in time for the tide to carry them in. She came from the direction of the morning sun so that they did not see her until she was almost upon them. Warning shots across the *Star*'s bow brought her around. Tamara stayed on board ship the first time because she did not want to be recognized, but this did not sit well with her. She wanted to be a part of the boarding party. By the time they were prepared to strike again, she had devised the disguise she wore which stunned Mikel and the crew, and no less the captain of the second ship that had the misfortune to be in the wrong place at the wrong time.

Tamara was so pleased with herself that Mikel had to laugh, but it would be several weeks before another ship would cross their path. The ruse was just as effective as the first two times. Arms and ships fell to the well pleased Tamara. But the fourth time was not to be so fortunate. They came so close to falling into a trap that Mikel was in a cold sweat for days at the terrible thought of what they would do to Tamara should they catch her. Not once did he give thought to the idea that he also could be hung for piracy. They raced back to their hideaway to lick their wounds and repair their ship. She would be idle for a time so Tamara spent more time at home with her father.

It was only three weeks later that she was to celebrate her

nineteenth birthday, and she knew exactly the gift she was going to ask for. But before she had the birthday party her father had planned, she was to meet an adversary that was to be the most difficult challenge she would ever face in her lifetime.

She held the small folded piece of paper in her hand and read quickly then she held the edge to the candle light and watched it burn with a satisfied look on her face. The following morning, she rose early. She saddled her own horse and rode quickly to the docks where she found Mikel.

"There's a ship coming through, called *Cecile*, carrying arms. From what my letter says, she's not too heavily protected."

"Tam, I've been thinking about this since the last time when you almost got blown out of the water."

"About what, Mikel?"

"Listen," he said as he drew her aside and sketched out his plan for using two ships instead of one. "They're expecting you to strike somewhere, sometime. They're prepared for you, but they're not prepared for you to have a back-up ship. We'll follow the same plans with with one exception. I'll be there to help you if it turns into a trap like it did before. You keep them busy and I'll come up on the blind side. That way if there are any more tricks, we have them in a cross fire."

"What do we use for another ship?"

He grinned. "Why not use one of their own against them. Teel hasn't picked up the last one yet. She's big and we can mount a few more guns on her. Won't they get a shock when the report comes in that one of their own has been used against them? It won't take long for me to get a few more cannon mounted. In fact, I was going to suggest this idea to you a long time ago. I'm sure we could make this more profitable for America if there were two of us working these waters instead of one."

"It sounds like a good idea. I should have thought of it at the beginning. I came close to losing the *Butterfly* once; I don't want to ever do that again. I love her too much to see her sent to the bottom."

"Don't worry, you'll have all the protection you need. I'll scare the hell out of them when I come up on their blind side so suddenly. They won't have time to turn their guns on me. Since they're carrying ammunition, they won't want me planting a cannonball right in the middle of them."

"Oh, Mikel," she giggled. "You're getting downright wicked in your ways."

"Only by association with you," he laughed in response.

"When does she come?"

"In about a week."

"Good, I'll have all the arms from the other ship stored in the caves at the rock. We'll plan this out and give them another surprise. Soon, they'll be thinking that *The Scarlet Butterfly* has a whole fleet of ships."

"I'll bet it's driving them insane wondering where a bright red ship can disappear."

"Now, they can begin to wonder where we moor two ships."

The week passed quickly. Tamara rose long before the sun, for she wanted to use the bright rays of the early morning sun for camouflage. She crept from the house leaving a note for her father that she rode early to Mary St. Claire's house and would not return for two days.

At the docks, Mikel was waiting with the small boat and they did not speak or make any unnecessary noise as they left the harbor. Soon, they were again making the breathless entrance to the rock. No matter how many times they did it, it still had the power to scare them both.

Inside the calm beauty of the place struck Tamara again. If it hadn't been necessary for the cause, she would have kept it as her own secret place.

The bright red ship rocked gently in the water; beside it, another larger ship stood. They made their preparations without words for they had been done often enough and now time was of the essence, if they wanted to catch the rising sun.

Slowly, the sails on both ships were unfurled and they moved with majestic beauty toward the dark entrance of the cave. Tamara's breath caught in her throat as the strong current lifted them and pulled them through the dark channel and thrust them out into the ocean.

It was still dark and she had to time everything perfectly to be in the right place at the right time. It was imperative that she kept the rising sun at her back. That gave her the element of surprise and let her get a lot closer before she was spotted. There were just a few streaks of sunlight touching the horizon when the lookout shouted. "Sail ho!"

Tamara laughed, as usual caught up in the excitement. The new maneuver that Mikel had devised would work well. Tamara was to realize just how well when she tried to capture the *Cecile*.

Twelve

Three months, Steffan thought miserably. Three more months and he would be going home for Christmas vacation. Home had never looked better to him than it did now. The past six months had been the most difficult of his life. He was alone in the room he shared with Tom and Mack because he was studying for an exam he had been forced to miss. Jaspar had held him, maliciously, in their quarters until he, despite running at full speed, had been ten minutes late for the class and the instructor had refused him entry.

He had gone to the instructor after class, and received permission to take the exam the following week. He realized that what Jaspar had done was deliberate, along with other things he had done to make Steffan's life miserable. Small things that had made Steffan's first six months enough to make a less stubborn young man quit and go home to the easy life. Determined as Jaspar was to get him to run, Steffan was just as stubbornly determined he would not be forced out.

It was obvious to all the cadets who shared the barracks that Jaspar was deliberately goading Steffan, but, because of Steffan's stubbornness, none of them knew why.

While Steffan sat laboring over his books, Tom and Mack, Langley, Brighton and Jeffery sat in the community room and shared a bottle Brighton had smuggled in. They sat in silence for a while, but each of them shared the same thoughts. It was Brighton who spoke first. "Damn it! Someone should be able to get that bastard off Steff's back. He's determined to push Steff into doing something stupid and get thrown out of here." Bright was the most volatile of all of them. He found it extremely difficult to control something when he truly felt it needed saying or doing. He was of average height and slender of build. He had a quick smile. His hair was sandy blond and his eyes a deep glittering blue.

"Just what do you have in mind, old sport," questioned Lang. "Should we grab him some dark night and beat him bloody?"

"Sounds like a good idea to me," Bright retorted.

"Sure, then as rotten as that fellow is," Jeff said, "he'd turn everybody in and we'd all be out on our ears."

Jeff, the serious one, was also the unspoken leader of the group. He was six feet in height with thick dark brown hair that continually fell over his wide intelligent forehead almost concealing the calm gray eyes that studied every situation coolly and levelly.

"I wish we could get to him somehow," Lang replied. Lang was a tall broad shouldered young man with curly blond hair and a full moustache of which he was inordinately proud. His gray green eyes were gentle yet he was a strong and formidable foe when angry. "We can't even figure out why he's got it in for Steff so badly."

Tom and Mack exchanged looks. From the very first Steffan had forbidden them to say anything to anyone about the problems between him and Jaspar. He was determined to handle his problems by himself. Up until now, they had honored that request. Now, both of them realized, even though Steffan did not, that because he couldn't reach Steffan, Jaspar was getting more and more determined to get him discharged from the Academy.

"Mack?" Tom questioned gently.

"Yes, I think we should tell them no matter what Steff says."

"Tell us what?" Jeff questioned.

"Yes, if you know what's behind all this, you should fill us in. Maybe there's a way we can put a stop to it," Lang replied.

"All right," Tom said. "I'm going to tell you, but I'd prefer you all did not mention it to Steff. He's kind of touchy. He'd be angry with us if he thought we were trying to fight his battles for him."

"It's a secret as far as I'm concerned," Bright interjected. "The rest of you?"

"I'll never say a word," Jeff said.

"Neither will I," Lang said quickly.

Tom told them of the small hatred that had begun when they were boys. He continued the story up to the day they entered the Academy.

Bright whistled lightly through his teeth. "Then it isn't just a personality conflict. He's really out to get Steff bounced out of here completely."

"There must be something we can do," Jeff offered.

"I don't know what," Mack said dejectedly. "Steff would

never speak to any of us again if we went over his head and reported this to someone higher up."

"Well, then," Jeff said thoughtfully. "We've got to go at this problem from another direction. What if . . . what if Sinclair was a recruit the same as us, instead of B.M. What if he lost his little title of seniority? Then he and Steff would be on equal ground."

"You have a plan, Jeff?" Tom said quickly.

"Sort of. Give me a couple of days to think about it and talk to a friend of mine. Maybe, just maybe there might be a way out of this yet."

"It would sure suit me," Tom said. "Whatever Jaspar gets, he's certainly asked for it."

"Steff has to take the exam in the morning. We've got to arrange it so he gets there with no interruptions from our B.M." Mack answered. "One of us will keep Jaspar busy until Steff is gone."

"I will," Tom offered.

"No, not you, Tom," Jeff answered. "You're second on his list. He'd like a reason to cause you some problems too. No, I think it's up to me."

"All right," Tom agreed. "I've got to get to bed too. I'm tired. You coming, Mack?"

"I'll be up in a little while."

Tom rose, stretched then left the room and climbed the stairs. When he went inside, the room was quiet. He looked at the desk to see Steffan, his arms folded on his books and his head down on them in a sound sleep. He felt a tug of anger at Jaspar for pushing Steffan so hard. Of all of them, he knew, Steffan was the finest prospect for officer material the Academy had. His grades, despite Jaspar, were consistently high, and everyone respected his ability and trusted him as a man. No one knew of the battle he was fighting as well as Tom did, and Tom admired him for his determination to fight alone, but he was just as determined that the brother of the woman he expected to marry would never stand alone as long as Tom had a breath in his body. He went to Steffan's side and shook him gently.

"Come on, Steff, get some sleep or you won't be able to accomplish anything tomorrow."

Steffan stirred awake and sat up looking wearily at Tom. "Yes, you're right. I'm so tired I'm seeing double." He rose and went to his bed; throwing himself down across it he was immediately asleep again. Tom threw a blanket over him them went to his own bed where he lay awake for a while allowing himself the luxury of remembering a small cabin on the beach and the lovely vision that shared it with him.

Steffan found himself being shaken awake over an hour before normal rising.

"Tom, what's the matter?"

"Steff, would you mind leaving a bit early this morning and accompanying me to Grover Hall? I have to drop off some papers; then I thought I'd wait for you and we could have lunch together before the afternoon classes."

"Okay, Tom, just give me time to get dressed." Tom waited, pleased that Jaspar would already find them gone just in case he had thought up another way to delay Steffan. Just before Tom and Steffan left, Jeff knocked on Jaspar's door. When he heard the words 'come in' he opened the door and went inside. One glance told him they were right about Jaspar's intentions. He was dressed and prepared to leave the room with obvious intent of stopping Steffan on his way out, delaying him long enough to be late for class, for which he could then be expelled. Missing a test a second time would be enough to give him a low mark. "B.M. Sinclair, sir, would you happen to have a copy of the information schedules for next term?"

"Next term?" Jaspar questioned peevishly. "Why are you worried about next term when this one is barely half over? Maybe," he sneered, "you may not have need of it at all, at least some of you."

"My father has written me, sir. It seems Father has found that Commander Crawford is an old childhood friend he has not seen for a long time and he wants to see what kind of curriculum he has prepared for next term when Father visits us. He's preparing to donate a substantial sum to the Academy and he wants to find out in just what area it would be most useful." Jeff laughed to himself when he saw Jaspar's face change at the mention of the friendship between the Crawfords and the Sables families.

"I see; well, I'm sure I have some extra copies here you can have." He rummaged about in his desk drawer and pulled forth some papers. He was just about to hand them to Jeff when they heard the clatter of footsteps on the stairs and then the slam of the front door. Jaspar caught immediately the gleam in Jeff's eyes and his face became stiff with anger.

"Very clever," he said vehemently.

"Sir?" Jeff said his eyes wide with innocence.

"You're dismissed, Sables," he snapped angrily and without another word, Jeff turned to open the door. "Sables?"

134

"Yes, sir?"

"Don't you want the papers you came for," he asked contemptuously.

"Well, sir, on second thought, I'm sure Commander Crawford can explain everything to Father better than the schedules can."

"Then," Jaspar said malevolently, "you got exactly what you came here for?"

"Oh," Jeff smiled broadly. "Yes, sir, I got exactly what I was after." Again he turned to the door.

"Sables!"

"Yes, sir."

"Be careful."

"Of what, sir?"

"Of interfering in something not your concern."

"Thank you, sir, I'll remember that."

"See that you do," came Jaspar's ominous reply. Jeff closed the door with a pleased grin on his face. He went off to a class of his own feeling good that at least Steffan would have no problem with Jaspar for that day. It was a Friday, and since there were no classes on Saturday, the cadets were allowed to go to the village to purchase necessities and to have a drink or two at the local tavern. Again, Jeff smiled to himself, for a sudden hilarious plan had presented itself to him. It required the aid of the pretty young barmaid, who was a prostitute. Jeff knew her well. He could barely wait to put his devious plan into motion.

When Saturday came, Jeff was up and gone early. By the time the others had eaten a leisurely breakfast and finished all the studying that needed to be prepared for Monday, it was well after noon. Jeff returned whistling tunelessly and with a pleasant smile on his face. The mischievous look in his eyes did not go unnoticed by the others and that included Steffan himself.

"Jeff, are you up to something?" he asked with a smile.

"Me?" Jeff asked, all innocence and surprise. "Now, Steff, what ever gave you that idea? Besides what in heaven's name could I be up to?"

"I don't know," Steffan laughed. "That's what's worrying me. You know our B.M., he's not too tolerant of our stepping across the line. It doesn't take much to upset him. I wouldn't want him on your back."

"The way he is on yours?" Jeff asked softly.

Steffan chuckled. "It'll take more than Jaspar Sinclair to stop me. I'll stay out of his way and keep from doing anything to give him the chance to do me any harm. After a while, he'll get the point."

Jeff stared at Steffan in surprise. "Do you honestly believe that you just trying to stay out of his way is going to matter? Christ, Steffan, you're not that foolish are you? It's as plain as the nose on your face and no matter how you try to keep it a secret there isn't a man in this barracks that doesn't know Jaspar Sinclair hates you and would go to any lengths to get you bounced out of here."

"It's a personal thing between Jaspar and me," Steffan said. "I don't want anyone else getting involved. I can handle Jaspar."

"The only way you can handle Jaspar is if he were the same rank as you, then he couldn't sabotage every move you made."

"Well, it isn't like that, so I'll just have to make do with the situation. At least until graduation, then we'll go our separate ways."

"He won't let it go like that, Steff. You give him enough time . . . he'll get you."

"Jeff, you listen to me. This is my fight. I don't want you getting involved with Jaspar Sinclair. Do you understand?"

"Sure, when you go down . . . you go alone. You don't want to drag anybody with you, especially your friends."

"For one thing, I don't intend to go down, but you are right. If anything happens I'm not taking any of you with me. Especially you, Jeff. If anybody has a bright future around here, it's you. So stay out of this."

"All right, Steff, all right," he grinned. "Let's go into town and have something to drink."

They walked to town and joined the others in the tavern. They were all seated about a table, laughing and talking and enjoying a cup of ale when a young woman came from the kitchen. Jeff was the first to see her and he motioned to her with a smile. "Brandy, come over here, I want you to meet some friends of mine."

She worked her way through the tables of laughing men, all of whom had a few words to say to her. She went directly to Jeff's side and he put his arm about her waist and pulled her against him.

"Brandy, this is Steffan Devers, Tom Braydon, and . . ." he went on to introduce the rest of the men in their group.

Brandy was well-named; her hair was the color of wine and so were the pouting red lips that parted in a smile as she contemplated Steffan's huge frame. But it was not from her coloring that Brandy had received her name. She was a foundling of the Maguires who owned the tavern. They had found her one morning in an empty brandy cask that they had put in the back alley to be gotten rid of. She was promptly named Brandy Maguire by Jenny Maguire who took her in and helped raise her.

Brandy was a basically honest young woman of twenty who was the first to admit to herself that she liked the boys as well as they liked her. She was particular whom she slept with, and the ones she chose knew without doubt the wild pleasure she enjoyed. She was not the least bit hesitant in accepting money, or what other favors the men had to offer, but the ones she spent time with would always swear they had the best of the bargain. Another peculiar thing about her, was that unlike any other prostitute, she shared her time with only one man at a time. For now, and for the past months it was Jeff Sables. He bent down and whispered something in Brandy's ear. She nodded and jerked her head in a quick motion toward the kitchen door, then she left his side with the excuse she was going for more ale. Jeff met her a few minutes later, but before he told her what he wanted he took the advantage of her willingness and held her, kissing her warmly and letting his hands roam where they would.

"Jeff, love, not here," she panted. "Come up to my room tonight . . . I've missed you."

"I'll be there," he whispered, but still it was with a great deal of reluctance that he moved her away from him. "Brandy, I have to ask you a great favor."

"What, love, you know I'd do anything for you." He told her then of the situation between Jaspar and Steffan.

"What can I do about it?" she questioned.

"You know . . . you were friends with . . . a certain young man who works for Commander Crawford."

"Lieutenant Morris?"

"Yes."

"What can I get from him that would do you any good?"

Jeff went on to tell her his plans and in a few minutes, they were laughing together as Brandy agreed to his plans.

"You'll be coming back tonight, Jeff?"

"Don't I grab every opportunity I'm allowed to spend time with you? I'll be here."

He kissed her again, then rejoined the party which became a little boisterous and didn't break up until the wee hours of the morning. The others made their way back to the barracks with the exception of Jeff who headed for Brandy's room.

She was awaiting him in the way she knew he enjoyed most. There were two candles lit in the room and Brandy sat on the bed with her legs curled under her and without a stitch on. Jeff smiled at the beautiful amber vision she made and Brandy returned his smile, proud of the effect her unusual beauty had on this tall handsome man. Jeff, so far, was the favorite man in her life. He was tender, yet deeply passionate. They had made it very clear to each other from the beginning, neither of them wanted any permanent entanglements. They met and made love for the sheer joy of being together and each knowing they satisfied the other's needs completely. If there were others in the life of each neither questioned, for they were not only compatible physically, they were also a very rare thing . . . friends. He walked to her side without saying a word. Gently, he ran the tips of his fingers up her bare arm and across her shoulder letting them slide down to cup one breast and caressed it. She half closed her eyes as her body trembled under his touch. He bent forward and lightly touched her lips again and again until she murmured a deep throaty sound. He rose from the bed and removed his clothes. This time, it was Brandy's turn to admire the physical qualities Jeff possessed. She watched his sun bronzed body as he discarded his clothes carelessly and knew, despite what she told Jeff, that this was the one man who possessed every part of her. Passionately, she reached out for him as he joined her on the bed and drew her body into his arms.

"Brandy" he whispered against her throat, "you're so very beautiful, I want you so badly. I dream of you at night, holding you like this, feeling your soft warm skin against mine."

Theirs was a need now that flamed into white hot passion as he felt her body move against him, as urgently wanting him as he did her. She drew him within her and moved with him to a completion that left them both shaken and still.

"God" she gasped, "with you, it's like dying."

"The French call it la petite morte, the small death. I can see why," he chuckled. "I wish I could put you in my pocket and carry you along with me for all those long lonely nights I dream about you."

"I'm sure the friends who share your barracks, especially that big beautiful one you introduced me to tonight, would have something to say about that," Brandy laughed.

The sudden tingle of jealousy that swept through Jeff took him completely by surprise. There was no room for permanent attachments between a wealthy young cadet destined for a great career and the young girl from the streets. It was the same for him as it would be for Steffan. Society would never accept it, this he knew, but his body and his heart were telling him a different story, and it suddenly shook him to the core that he could actually be falling in love with Brandy and not being able to face the fact that one day he would be out of her life and she would be sharing what he now possessed with another. He knew, if he were wise, he would break the relationship now. But he used Steffan as an excuse, that he needed Brandy's help in his little plan for Jaspar. It would be necessary for him to see her again. On his way back to the barracks, Jeff found himself wondering if there was a place in the world that he could take Brandy and they could be happy together without outside influence destroying his career and her life. He knew it was impossible . . . society, as it stood, would never allow it. But once his mind had the idea, it stored it away to be thought about at some future time.

Sundays at the Academy were spent mostly in study and quiet relaxed conversations. First, the morning was begun by church services at seven. There were games on the fields bordering the Academy, and some held indoors. Steffan found himself drawn to the fencing and shooting. Most Sunday afternoons he joined the Academy's fencing master and soon found himself developing a skill both with the sword and the pistol. Sundays were brought to a quiet end by another church service at eight, and by nine thirty, most of the cadets were abed for classes began again early the next morning.

Jeff went quietly about his business waiting for word from Brandy. It was almost three weeks later. Jeff and Steffan had just returned from their last class. When they opened the door of their room, Jeff's eye fell on the white envelope that lay on his bed with his name written across the front. He knew it was from Brandy because his name was spelled Jef. He had taken it upon himself, out of sympathy, to teach Brandy to read and write. In her position, it was something she never would have had an opportunity to do, but she had a tendency to spell every word exactly as it sounded to her, which was sometimes quite humorous. Jeff tore the envelope open and read:

"Der, Jef, I went to see him. What you want is all rit for him. It will tak a little mony if that all rite with you. Meet me sunday and give me the mony and by Munday you wil hav what you want.
                                                                        B."

Jeff grinned and folding the envelope, he put it back in his pocket. Steffan watched him, but when Jeff ignored the fact he thought maybe the letter was from a woman and none of his business so he put the matter out of his mind and in a little while, it was forgotten.

Sunday, Jeff could hardly wait to see Brandy. He went after morning church service, and he went alone. The less people involved in this the better it would be when questions were asked, and he was quite sure Steffan would ask a lot of questions.

It was a beautiful day, the sun was bright and warm. On days like this, Brandy and Jeff had a special meeting place. An old stone bridge about a mile out of the city that was surrounded by woods. When Jeff came to the edge of the woods, he saw Brandy standing on the bridge looking pensively down into the water. He wondered what she was thinking, and would have been quite shocked if he had known. He walked toward her slowly so that she didn't hear him approach. It was only when he was quite close that he saw she was lost in some dream . . . and that she was crying. He was only a few paces from her when he said "Brandy?" Quickly she brushed the tears from her cheeks and turned to him with a smile brightening her face. She ran to him and he opened his arms and caught her to him. He held her for a few minutes, then kissed her gently, but very very thoroughly. They walked under the bridge and sat together on a blanket she had brought. The shade was cool and they sat for a few minutes in silence and enjoyed the beauty about them. Jeff lay back on the blanket with his hands folded behind his head and watched Brandy who seemed so still and quiet.

"Brandy, why were you crying?"

"Crying? I wasn't crying, Jeff, something got in my eye," she replied, but she refused to look at him as she spoke pretending an interest in a small yellow flower she had reached out and plucked. Jeff reached out and gently took the flower from her and laid it aside. Then, he reached up and caught her thick hair in his hands and held her face immobile while studying her. "You don't lie well, Brandy, maybe it's because you're not used to doing it."

"Jeff," she said. Her face had become frozen and her words trembled slightly. "When you go back to your barracks, today, I don't ever want you to come back to me again. I . . . I just can't see you anymore." She could see the sudden hurt look in his eyes, but he controlled himself.

"Why, Brandy? Is there someone else?"

Brandy pulled herself away from him and stood up. Turning away she walked to the water's edge.

"Well, Brandy?" he said softly, "is there?" Again she could not answer for Jeff was right about one thing, lying was something Brandy did not do well. He rose and came to stand beside her, but did not touch her for he could see she was visibly

140

trembling and close to tears again.

"At least don't you owe me a reason?" he asked surprised at the pain in her eyes.

"Jeff, before you came into my life, I was happy. Nobody cared what happened to me and I didn't care for anyone else. I knew where I stood in life, what I would always be. And then you came along with all your gentleness, your books, your trying to teach me things I never should have known. You opened doors to a world I must look at and never touch. I love you and I hate you Jeff Sables. I love your kindness, and the knowledge that you wanted something better for me. And I hate you. I hate you for letting me see w I can never have, never be. You and I both know that there is no mixing of your sort and mine in the world, so one day you will go on with your life as you should, but you could have let me be in my world so I wouldn't hurt so bad when you had to go."

Jeff did not try to control the elation he felt when she said I love you. He recognized their past lies when they each claimed no involvement. "You said you love me. What would you say if I told you I love you, too."

"I would say it was like one of the books you gave me to read . . . a tragedy."

"Why? We can find some way . . ."

"No, Jeff! If you think for one minute I'll let you ruin your career, you're crazy. Be honest! You and I both know it would be the end of your career and the end of your family, for they could never accept me."

"And if you think I'll just drop you and walk away just like that, you're crazy, too. There has to be a way we could be together and I'll find it." He pulled her into his arms and sought her lips in a frantic possessive kiss. It was the deep wanting feeling in her when he kissed her that made her realize she was right in what she had done before she had come to meet Jeff.

They made love on the blanket in the warmth of the late summer sun, and it was the finest most sensitive moments they had ever shared for he thought she had surrendered . . . and she knew it was the final time.

Afterward, she let him talk, let him make fairy tale plans she knew could never come true, and when the time came to leave, she let him believe she would meet him at the tavern the following Saturday. He gave her the money to pay Lieutenant Morris for what he planned for Steffan, then they walked toward town together.

Jeff went back to the Academy and told all the others what he had arranged. Brandy went back to the tavern and packed what few belongings she had in a small valise. With what money her foster parents could give her and amid a great deal of tears, she let them accompany her to the docks, where she boarded the ship that stood in the harbor.

The week before her final meeting with Jeff, she had discovered she was carrying his child. She knew what Jeff would do should he find out. Nothing would stop him from throwing away his whole life to marry her. She cared too much to let that happen. She had gone to the docks and indentured herself for three years in return for passage to America. There, she would work until her debt was paid off and from what she heard, she could disappear and no one would ever know her past. Jeff's child was the one thing she would have to keep from their love and she intended to keep it, care for it, love it as she had never been loved.

She watched the shores of England through a cloud of tears, standing at the rail until land could no longer be seen. Then she wrapped her shawl tightly about her and turned her back on the heartbreak of her past and toward the uncertain future.

Jeff had been thinking of Brandy all week and had come to the decision that he was going to force her to marry him and to hell with what everyone else in the world thought. He left the Academy as soon as he could and went straight to the tavern. There were very few people there and he searched for Brandy. When he could not find her, he asked her foster parents where she was.

"She's gone, boy" Maguire said sympathetically.

"Gone . . . gone where?"

"She left you this note, son, that's all we know."

Jeff tore open the note with trembling fingers and read.

Der Jef,

This is the onli way. I will be gon wen you reed this. Don't look for me or ask for me becuz no one noes wher I went. I love you Jef. I want you to kno that now. What Im doin is the bes thin I can do for you. someday you will understand. I could not let you give up your whol liv for me. I hope god blezes you and gives you all the thing you deserv for you are so good.

Goodby
All my luv always
Brandy.

With a small cry, Jeff crumpled the paper and stuck it in his jacket pocket. The rest of the weekend was spent in a fruitless search for her. No one seemed to know where she went. It was as if the ground had opened up and swallowed her.

It was a disbelieving group of friends who sobered him up and kept him steady for the next few anguished weeks. Then, he seemed to get himself under control and regain the balance of his life. It was only his closest friends who knew of the letter he kept in his shirt that was read and reread, and of the name he called in his sleep in a soft mournful sound.

Thirteen

It was several more agonizing weeks before the fruit of Jeff's well placed money and Brandy's sacrifice became evident. Agonizing weeks for Steffan, and for Jeff, who found himself missing Brandy more and more each week. Each weekend, he carried on his search for anyone who might have seen her, or might know where she had gone, and each weekend he returned, drunk, and more miserable than the week before.

Steffan and the others were deeply worried about him, so Steffan and Tom invited him, Lang and Bright home for Christmas vacations and to attend the wedding. Since most of their families were much further away than Steffan's, they all agreed to come.

It was quite a trip home. All the boys who had gone away were coming home men. Steffan was well pleased with the look of pride in the eyes of his parents when he leapt down from the carriage and swung his mother into his arms in a bear hug that took her breath away. But it was Cecile's delighted laughter when she threw herself into his arms that warmed his welcome.

"Steff," she cried, as he held her at arm's length. "You are beautiful."

He laughed, a little embarrassed yet pleased. Then Cecile and Tom faced each other.

"Hello, Tom," she said softly. Tom seemed suddenly so much larger, so very masculine that she could hardly move. It was Tom who took the two steps that separated them and bent to touch her lips lightly. "Cecile," he murmured.

But that was not enough for Cecile, who had been living in remembered warmth of him for six months. He found two soft arms about his neck and the gentle touch of his mouth on hers suddenly changed as his lips sought hers. His arms caught her to him for one moment, then he held her away from him.

"Beauty is obviously in the eye of the beholder. I certainly think the feminine side of the Devers family has a lot more to offer."

Steffan introduced his friends to his family and their month

144

long vacation began in earnest. Preparation for the wedding had begun weeks before and the house seemed to be in a perpetual uproar. Amid this, Steffan and his friends thoroughly enjoyed their days . . . and nights, with the exception of Tom who could not seem to get enough time with Cecile. Every waking moment they spent with each other, but there were only a few times they were able to meet at the small cottage. These rare times, they savored and enjoyed with a frantic leisure.

The day of the wedding, Steffan and his friends dressed in their best uniforms. Added to each was a thin band of gold about each cuff that told the world they were no longer beginners at the Academy. About the waist of each was a gold fringed belt made of a soft material and over this they buckled their swords. Swords they would unsheathe and form into an arch for the newly wedded couple to pass under as they left the chapel.

It was a perfectly planned wedding and Tom's eyes as Cecile walked toward him on her father's arm, told her he thought she was the perfect bride.

It was only the misery Steffan saw in Jeff's eyes that took some of the glow away. Again, as he had once before, Steffan vowed that when he found the one woman he wanted to marry, nothing and nobody was going to stop him from having her.

Cecile and Tom laughed and danced at the reception with almost every guest present, and it was late in the evening that Steffan got a chance to dance with Cecile. "Happy, brat?" he said affectionately.

"Oh, I'm delirious, Steff. I never thought it was possible for anyone to be this happy."

"I'm glad. I hope you stay that way the rest of your lives."

Cecile laughed, then suddenly she stood on tiptoe and kissed him.

"What was that for?"

"For bringing Tom home so long ago."

Their laughter mingled, and at the close of the dance, Tom was at Steffan's shoulder and retrieved his bride. "Cecile, it's time for us to leave. You've only a few minutes to change, the carriage is waiting."

After Cecile had left them, Tom spoke to Steffan, his voice low, meant only for their benefit.

"Steff, have you noticed anything?"

"In all this confusion it's hard to tell what you have in mind. What's on your mind Tom?"

"The Sinclairs are here."

"What's important about that?"

"Jaspar's not here."

Steffan was quiet for a moment. He had not noticed that Jaspar was not present, but now that Tom called it to his attention, he wondered why.

"He probably stayed at the Academy to think up new ways to get at me when I get back."

"Nope, he came home the day after we did. I saw him out riding one day."

"Well, I'm not going to worry about him. We only have a few more days at home and the less I have to see Sinclair, the better."

"Yes, I guess you're right."

"Did you find a place for you and Cecile when you get back from your honeymoon?"

"I took one of the small cottages on Braker Road, just off the campus. It's close enough for me to get to school and," he grinned, "close enough for you fellows to find your way over once in a while."

"Don't worry, you'll probably spend a lot of time throwing us out."

They were joined at this time by Martin Gillis and Steffan's father.

"Well, Maxwell," Martin said. "I must say these gentlemen do look well in their uniforms."

"Thank you, kind sir," Steffan laughed. "Now we only have to work like the devil three and a half more years to earn the right to wear them."

"Seriously, Steffan," Martin questioned; "How do you like the Academy?"

"I like it. The studies are hard, I admit."

"Hard!" Tom interjected. "If it wasn't for Steff pulling me through by the teeth, I would have been home by now. He and Jeff Sables can take the credit for at least four commissions that I know of."

"You'll be taking active duty training next year?" Martin asked.

"Yes, if we get past this one. I meant to ask you, sir. Do you know a Commander Pierce?"

"Pierce? Well, I know quite a few people in London; offhand, I can't remember a Pierce, but I might know him, Why?"

"I checked up on him. He's got the reputation of being one of the best in the Navy."

"Why the interest?"

"He approached me and said if I could keep my grades up, he would arrange for me to train under him at sea. It's a great honor, but I can't help asking myself, why me? Why not Jeff, who's ahead of me in brains or Lang who's probably one of the best around."

"Maybe," Martin said quietly, "he intends something for their future also."

Steffan shrugged as though some elusive thought annoyed him and Martin changed the subject. Cecile reappeared and there was a great deal of confusion as she and Tom prepared to leave.

The next morning, Steffan decided to go riding alone to explore his old sanctuary as he did when he was a boy. He saddled his horse himself to keep from waking anyone else and as the sun crested the horizon, he was thundering down the beach sending up a spray of water and enjoying every moment of it. He tied his horse and climbed to his well remembered secret place. He stood in the cave and smiled to himself for suddenly it seemed so much smaller than he remembered. When he walked out of the cave, Steffan knew it was goodbye to the childhood he remembered fondly and hello to the future and the man he hoped to become. He walked a little further and found the spot where he had first joined forces with Tom. He sat on the rocks and enjoyed the view for only a few minutes for despite the fact he wore a warm coat and scarf the cold December wind bit through. He walked to his horse and mounted, just as he was about to turn around, he heard his name called. He looked about and there, just in the shadows of the rocks sat Jaspar Sinclair. Slowly, Jaspar edged his horse forward until they faced each other.

"You think you're very clever, don't you, Steffan? That little trick you just pulled off must have taken a lot of influential string pulling."

Steffan had no idea what he was talking about. "What's on your mind Jaspar?"

"As if you don't know," Jaspar sneered. "I received my transfer papers yesterday. For some unaccountable reason, I've been transferred from your barracks to another . . . on the other side of the campus."

"I don't really care if you believe it or not, Jaspar, but I've no idea how or why that happened."

"Why?" Jaspar laughed. "Because you're afraid you can't handle the problem yourself. You had to get Papa to pull some strings and get it done for you."

Steffan was angry at the implication of his fear. He nudged his horse forward until he and Jaspar were only inches apart. For the first time, Jaspar was to see the dangerous man Steffan could become when his fury was aroused.

"I'll tell you only once, Jaspar. I knew nothing about this. I need no help from my father or anyone else. I can fight my own battles and that includes you. If you ever call me a coward again be prepared to defend yourself."

Steffan said the words calmly, but the effect was like striking steel against steel. It was the first time Jaspar was to realize what a formidable foe Steffan could be if aroused. Steffan, his white hot anger barely under control pulled his horse about and rode home. Once there, he went to see his father. Before Maxwell could speak, Steffan asked him in a cold harsh voice.

"Father, did you pull any strings, ask any favors for me at the Academy, and worst of all, did you have Jaspar transferred?"

If Steffan was angry, Maxwell was angrier. "First off, young man, don't you talk to me in that tone of voice, and second, although I don't have to answer to you for anything I've done, no, I've not raised a finger for you. Does that answer your rude and insufferable questions?"

Steffan swallowed his anger immediately, and lowered his voice to a more calm speaking level. "I'm sorry, Father. I certainly did not mean any disrespect. I've just come from a meeting with Jaspar Sinclair who accused me of letting you use your influence at school. For one minute, I was afraid you had."

"No, Steffan, I've more confidence in you than that. I know your abilities. Whatever you do, you're doing on your own."

Steffan was relieved, and he and his friends packed to return to school. It never occurred to Steffan to ask Martin Gillis the same questions he had asked his father. Martin heard of the incident and wisely kept his mouth shut as he and Steffan's parents watched the carriage until it was out of sight.

Once back at the Academy, life rolled along at a much easier pace. With the threat of Jaspar's constant harassment gone, Steffan found less strain and therefore not only did his grades improve but he became more at ease and outgoing. Making friends had always been easy for Steffan, mostly because of his exuberant and sometimes wicked sense of humor. He had a way of laughing at the difficult things and leading others about him to believe the difficult things were not so hard after all.

Tom and Cecile returned from their honeymoon and opened the doors of their small home to all of Steffan's friends who immediately became constant visitors there.

The first year came to a close and for the first time in months they were to go their separate ways until the beginning of the next school term. While everyone else was packing to go home, Steffan noticed Jeff was not.

"Jeff, aren't you going home?"

"No, Steff, I'm staying in London for a while."

"Jeff, what good is it going to do. You know in your heart Brandy isn't in London any longer," Steffan said in sympathy.

"Damn it, Steff! A person just can't disappear without someone knowing. There's someone somewhere that knows either where she was going or at least how she was traveling. I can't explain this to you Steff, but I've got the feeling she needs me. I also have the feeling I'm going to find her somewhere somehow and this time, I won't let myself be a fool and let her get away again."

"Jeff . . ."

"Don't say it, Steff. I've said it to myself a million times. 'Be smart, Jeff. What Brandy did, she did because she cared what happened in your future.' But when you compare, Steff, someone who loves you and you love with an uncertain future, somehow, I feel I've lost the most important of the two."

"Even if you find her, it won't work, Jeff. There's no place you and Brandy could live together in peace. Society just wouldn't let you rest. Brandy's life would be hell."

"I know . . . I know all the things you're saying are sensible and true, but," he looked at Steffan, "but it doesn't matter, Steff. I've got to try. You go on home, maybe I'll even pay you a visit over the summer," he laughed shakily. "I'll be back in school come September, but for now, no matter what the odds . . . I've got to try."

"All right, but Jeff, if you need us, me, Tom, Mack, you only have to send word and we'll come."

"I know . . . thanks."

Steffan spent the summer relaxing, enjoying the company of the pretty girls in the area and letting himself be pampered and spoiled by everyone . . . everyone except Martin Gillis who insisted on both mental and physical activity to keep him prepared for his return to school.

Jeff spent the summer in a fruitless search for any trace of Brandy. The few who knew her, refused to tell him anything. But the one man who was to open this hidden door was docked in a small harbor off the coast of America. After depositing his cargo and the indentured people he had brought, he was acquiring a cargo for the return trip to England.

Brandy found herself working as an upstairs maid for Mr. and Mrs. Jeremy Whitticer who proved to be considerate people. She was to work for them for a very small salary for three years to pay off the price of her ticket over. When they found she was pregnant, they gave her easy jobs to work at. Sewing was her specialty, so soon she found herself designing and making clothes for Mrs. Whitticer and her young daughter Margaret. As the months passed, Brandy grew heavy with the child and in the first week of February, she gave birth to a large eight pound baby boy. She had definitely decided that she would keep the child at all cost and when she informed Mr. and Mrs. Whitticer, they agreed to have the baby cared for and live in their house at the cost of one more year of Brandy's servitude to which she readily agreed.

Brandy named the baby Jeff because he was her one reminder of him and because daily, the baby looked more and more like the father with calm gray eyes and unruly dark hair.

The situation worked well for Brandy and her son. They lived in an attic room which, though small, Brandy kept clean and comfortable. The work she did was appreciated by Mrs. Whitticer who became the best dressed lady in the backward area's society. Brandy made her plans. When her indentured time was up, she would open a small dressmaking shop and raise her son with everything she had never had. The small amount of money her foster parents had given her slowly began to grow as laboriously, she added to it one small coin at a time.

The Whitticers were pleased that Brandy was such an obedient and pleasing girl who took her little boy to church on Sunday, worked hard and kept herself away from outside influence. In Brandy's heart now there was room only for two. The child she loved and the man she could never have.

September came, and the Academy reopened its doors for the new fall term. There was a happy reunion for the ones in Steffan's barracks and the life of training and hard work began again. Most of the time, Jeff and Steffan were at the top of the list when the grades appeared. With grim determination, they pulled their friends along in their wake, too stubborn to let any of them slip backwards. Tom and Cecile were so very happy and Tom's life so pleasant at home that he found studying much easier. Consequently, his grades took an amazing jump from the year before. Tom was trying harder than ever for he wanted to at least be able to qualify for a second position on a ship if Steffan received a captaincy.

Mack began his evening studies in the small church not far from the Academy. He was so immersed in both sets of studies he had no time for social affairs at all.

It seemed to be a year that was to be filled with nothing but success . . . it seemed to be.

All the second year cadets, at one time or another were invited to small parties that were held by the instructors and their wives. The annual mid term party held by Commander and Mrs. Wade Kyle was usually one of the brightest affairs of the year.

Commander Kyle and his wife occupied a large home about two miles away from the Academy. It had the reputation of being one of the most beautiful homes in the area. It was decorated by a woman who also had the reputation of being the most beautiful in the area.

All the cadets who had been invited were anxiously preparing to go. Steffan, as nervous and excited as the rest, looked at himself in the mirror and fussed over an appearance that was already perfect. The ill-fitting uniforms that had been supplied them had given way to well tailored uniforms that accentuated Steffan's large frame. He looked every bit the supremely masculine warrior. His white pants, tailored to hug his long slender legs like a second skin were topped by a blue jacket with the high necked close fitting collar. There was the addition of a second stripe about the sleeve of his jacket that gave him the negligible authority of a second year student. Gold epaulets and the bright gleam of polished gold buttons made the uniform complete. His high black boots were polished until he could see himself reflected in them. To this magnificent ensemble, he added his dress cloak and was finally prepared to go. He glanced up and saw Jeff standing in the doorway as resplendent as he and he grinned. "We look like a group of blue and gold peacocks."

"Speak for yourself, sir," Jeff said arrogantly. "I think I look absolutely magnificent."

"Hmmm," Steffan said seriously. "It must have taken you hours to get that pretty."

Jeff laughed. "Come on, the carriage, overrun by impatient fellows, is waiting for us. Now, we don't want to keep all those pretty girls waiting, do we? After all the time they've already been waiting, I do believe the poor things deserve a look at His Majesty's finest."

They went down to the carriage. It was a boisterous, happy group that arrived at Commander Kyle's home, but outside the door, Jeff settled them to some semblance of order and they entered. Even Steffan and Jeff who had been used to the finest of everything in life were stunned to absolute awe at the beauty surrounding them. Crystal chandeliers reflected hundreds of candles. The polished wood floor also gleamed like a mirror of the reflecting light. The walls were a pale ivory color, the only other color to contrast was gleaming black furniture. It was the most unusual room they had ever been in. They were to find out soon the purpose for which the decorator worked. It was to reflect also the rare beauty of the woman who obviously reigned there.

The music came from some hidden source that took Steffan a few minutes to locate. The orchestra was seated in an alcove in front of which sheer curtains had been hung. "Where are our host and hostess?" he inquired of Jeff.

"On the other side of the floor. Come along, let us pay our respects, then browse around and see just what this party has to offer in the way of . . . refreshments."

They crossed the room and found Commander Kyle standing alone welcoming his guests.

"Good evening Commander Kyle," Jeff said.

"Good evening Cadet Sables, Cadet Devers," he went on to welcome each by name and Steffan wondered just how he managed to remember the names of every cadet who approached him, especially when they almost all looked alike to him.

"Is Mrs. Kyle here, sir? We would like to pay our respects," Jeff said.

"Morgana will be down soon. She likes to make a grand entrance," he laughed, but again Steffan noticed the tightness about his mouth and the strange aura of sadness that always seemed to hang over him.

"I'm anxious to meet her, sir," Steffan smiled. "I've been told she is the most beautiful woman in London. You are a very lucky man."

"Yes," Commander Kyle said restrainedly, "very lucky."

There was an uncomfortable moment of silence, then Commander Kyle looked over their heads. The glimmer of something in his eyes which came close to resembling hatred caused Steffan to turn and follow his gaze toward the stairway that led to the second floor.

It was as though someone had struck him violently in the chest and he could barely get his breath. She glided down the steps as though she were walking an inch off the floor. From where Steffan stood, her beauty was breathtaking. But as she grew closer he could see its absolute perfection.

Morgana Kyle was flawless, her beauty absolute. She was very small in comparison to Steffan—the top of her head would barely reach his shoulder. Her skin a soft pink and her hair was a pale blonde. It had been pulled severely back from her face and coiled atop her head, threaded with thin black velvet ribbon. The dress she wore was black and off her creamy white shoulders. It was cut so daringly low that Steffan expected any moment to see it fall away from her. He was alarmed at the fact that his heart was beating furiously; he could not draw his eyes away from her. When she reached their side, she smiled at her husband and put her arm through his. Her smile was warm and inviting. When she spoke, her voice was deep and throaty.

"Good evening, gentlemen."

Commander Kyle introduced her to each of the group and she said a few words to each. When they reached Steffan she held out her hand to him and he automatically took it. It was cool and soft in his, but at the moment Steffan was deeply immersed in eyes that were large and the color of violets. He knew he said something to her, but he didn't know what it was. He heard the light melody of her laughter as she was swept away by her husband. Morgana and Kyle danced the first dance together. "He is a charming young man, that Steffan Devers," she said.

"Morgana," Wade's voice was heavy and filled with the touch of warning. "He's one of the brightest young cadets at the Academy, an intelligent and sensitive young man. His career should be most fulfilling if it follows the path it is on and there's nothing to interfere with it."

Her deep laughter sounded again. "Good heavens, Wade, you make him sound like a paragon of virtue. Has no one disrupted that virtue before?"

Wade's voice echoed with a sound of deeply buried anguish. "For Christs sake, Morgana, leave him alone. Haven't you made enough conquests? I would hate to see his future die here."

"And you could kill it, couldn't you, Wade?" her eyes glimmered with excitement. "I wonder if the gentleman knows enough to be afraid of you?"

"Yes," Wade said wearily. "He's afraid of me because I can control his future for the next few years. But it's a different kind of fear. I just hope he has enough sense to be afraid of you."

"I don't think," she said softly, "that he's afraid of anything or anyone, but it might be amusing to find out."

"And you need to be amused, Morgana . . . even at the expense of someone else's life."

Morgana smiled up at her husband again and to every onlooker, it was a smile of warmth and admiration for her distinguished husband, but Wade knew better. It was a smile filled with challenge and contempt.

"Someday, I may kill you, Morgana," he said in a hoarse whisper. She laughed, and people turned to look at the lovely couple they seemed to be.

"You won't," she said in soft derision. "You and I both know you won't . . . but you'd like to, Wade. We know why you won't. No matter how much you hate me, you still want me. What would you do if I decided to leave you, Wade?"

He said nothing to her taunting question but she saw the swift look of fear that fluttered in his eyes and felt the sudden tightening of his hand on hers. Again, the soft sound of her laughter floated on the air.

Fourteen

Every cadet was obliged to dance one dance with the hostess. In this case the rule took no enforcement, for they battled each other for the privilege of being next to dance with Morgana Kyle. When Steffan finally got his opportunity, he thoroughly enjoyed himself. He was so thoroughly caught in Morgana's web of beauty, he could see nothing else but her. Jeff, who kept one eye on him, saw what was happening but was helpless to do anything about it. He had warned Steffan once about her power and he knew from this moment on, Steffan would not welcome any other words about her. He was going to have to learn for himself. Jeff only hoped the lesson he felt Steffan was about to receive would not be fatal.

There was no doubt Steffan's senses were filled with her. For weeks after the ball, he kept his eyes open for any glimpse of her and a few times he was rewarded by her quick smile of recognition when their paths did cross. He had no idea that their paths crossed often by her well-laid plans.

It was a few weeks later that their inevitable meeting came about. Steffan was so bewitched by her he did not suspect that their meeting was anything but accidental.

Steffan rode often, mostly in the early morning just before dawn. During this time, he found a few secluded places that in some way were reminiscent of home—quiet places where he had time to be alone, to think. He always had to be back before seven o'clock, in time for his first class.

He was returning one morning when he crested a small rise and saw a riderless horse grazing contentedly in a patch of grass. He noticed immediately that it carried a lady's side-saddle. He looked about him, worried that some one had been thrown and might be badly injured. He could see no one so he dismounted, tied his horse and walked off the bridle path into a deeply shaded wood. He could hear the ripple of a small stream somewhere near. Slowly, he walked toward it. As he neared it, he could make out a lone figure seated on a fallen tree beside it. Her back was to him, so he deliberately made as much noise as he could to warn her of his approach. When he was only a few feet from her, she turned and he looked into the wide purple eyes that had been haunting his dreams.

"Mrs. Kyle, I saw your horse on the path, are you all right?"

She laughed, that deep throaty laugh. "I'm fine, Mr. Devers, with the exception that when that nasty beast unseated me, I seemed to have twisted my ankle. I'm glad he did not wander too far away. If you could catch him for me and help me back into the saddle, I'm sure I can get home all right."

Steffan stood beside her and looked down into wide violet eyes that played havoc with his heart. "Is your ankle badly hurt?"

"I'm afraid I can't put any weight on it."

"I'll go retrieve your horse." He moved away from her reluctantly and walked back to the bridle path, but when he stepped out of the trees, he saw that indeed her horse had wandered out of sight. Possibly he returned to where he had been stabled, Steffan thought, and where he knew food and water would be. He took his horse's reins and led him back to where Morgana was seated. "I'm afraid, Mrs. Kyle, your horse is gone. I can take you back if you care to ride double or I could go back and bring some help."

Morgana patted the log beside her and laughed. "Do come and sit down a moment and we will discuss what is best for us. And do stop calling me Mrs. Kyle as though I'm a century older than you. I'm not much older than you, you know!"

It was the first time that Steffan had noticed that Morgana was indeed much younger than her husband. In years, they were near the same age, but something more than time separated them. Morgana Kyle had never been young. She was a sensuous woman who never had refused herself anything she wanted . . . or anyone. There had been many men before Wade, and there had been many men after, for she was a voracious woman who reached out and took whatever she wanted. She knew her power over men, had known it from childhood, and had never hesitated to use it. Sometimes, it had even destroyed the dreamers who had reached out for the Morgana they thought existed in her beautiful face, only to find their arms filled with the taunting laughter and remains of the ashes of their dreams. Steffan sat beside her breathing the scent of her perfume.

"Would you like me to see if your ankle is swollen?" he suggested.

"No, I've already loosened the laces on my shoe. I'm sure it will be fine once I get home.''

She turned to face him and he felt that she was as much aware of him as he was of her. Morgana watched in deep satisfaction as his eyes darkened with a look she knew and understood so very well. It excited her, for Steffan was a very masculine man. He was so large, and large men always had an effect on her. She reached out and laid her hand gently on his arm. It pleased her immensely when she felt the tremor in his muscles.

''Tell me about yourself. I am curious why a wealthy young man such as yourself would choose the life of a naval cadet. Aren't there much easier ways you could live?''

It was the opening of a door, and without realizing it, Steffan found himself pouring out his life, his plans for the future, his dreams. He was flattered that she seemed to be very interested in what he was saying. But what she was doing was contemplating his handsome features and thinking of the plans to enjoy him that she had made.

It was over an hour later that Steffan realized how long they had been sitting together. ''You must be tired and that ankle must be very painful. With your permission, I'll put you on my horse and take you home.''

''Thank you,'' she said. ''You're right, I am a little tired. If you will help me, I can get to your horse.''

Steffan was going to take her hand, but Morgana stepped close to him and he found his arm about her slender waist as they moved slowly to his horse. Once there, she faced him, and her eyes held his as he took her waist in both hands to lift her. She placed both hands on his shoulders as slowly he lifted her from the ground and placed her in the saddle. Not for a minute did Morgana doubt that he wanted to pull her into his arms and kiss her but, she smiled to herself, it was not the time or the place . . . yet. He swung himself up behind her and turned the horse toward home.

''Do you ride often?'' he asked quietly.

''Yes, every morning.''

''On this same trail?''

''Yes, why?''

''Maybe . . . maybe we could ride together. It is much more pleasant to ride with a friend.''

''I think that would be wonderful. Wade hates to ride. I would certainly appreciate the company. Especially,'' she laughed, ''if there is a repetition of things like this. I can't really expect to be so lucky as to have you rescue me every time, can I?''

Steffan and Morgana were both silent for the remainder of the ride, he enjoying the feel of her near him and she, planning the next occasion when she would only settle for much more than this.

Jeff knew, with a sinking heart, that Morgana and Steffan had met again. He watched as every morning Steffan rose early and left, to return just before morning class, his eyes aglow. Jeff realized there was nothing he could say or do about it for Steffan was still deluding himself that no one, not even Morgana, knew of his deep infatuation.

He dreamed of her at night, turbulent wild dreams that woke him with a hunger for her that was almost a pain.

Occasionally, they met elsewhere, which Steffan was sure was accidental, and they would look at each other across a room and each sensed in the other the magnetic pull.

Morgana laid her plans well. It pleased her to whet Steffan's desire until she knew he was almost crazy with the need for her. She stood in her room early one morning preparing to meet Steffan. This time, she smiled at her reflection; this time, she was going to taste the pleasure she had wanted for so long.

As she walked toward the stable, she noticed the gathering of dark clouds on the horizon. They too, were part of her plans. She had waited for this kind of day. If she were right, and she usually was, the storm should overtake them in exactly the spot she wanted. There was a place she intended to wait out the storm . . . in Steffan Devers' arms.

They met where the bridle path joined the edge of the woods. The breeze had picked up and even the horses sensed the storm and were skittish.

"Maybe we should forget riding today. If that storm catches us, it might be bad," he suggested.

"Nonsense," she laughed. "We'll be back long before the storm hits." She kicked her heels into her horse's sides before Steffan could answer, and he urged his horse up beside hers. They rode together while a few miles away the storm gathered force. When Morgana reached the spot she wanted, she pulled her horse to a stop. Steffan reined in his horse, and when his eyes met hers, he read them clearly. His heart made a mad leap within him as he dismounted and walked to her side. He said nothing, just reached his hands up and put them about her waist. She bent down and put both hands on his shoulders. Slowly, he lifted her and let her slide slowly down the length of his body until her feet barely touched the ground.

The wind whipped about them, but neither of them noticed for each of them was caught up in the violent storm within.

Her arms crept up about his neck and his enclosed her in an iron grip that made her tremble with expectancy. There was not a rational thought in Steffan's mind now, all he knew was the need for her that thundered through his veins. His mouth sought hers in a wildly demanding kiss that was matched by the urgency her parted lips displayed. Black rolling clouds and roaring thunder went unnoticed as they clung to one another in a stormy and violent need. Steffan looked about him for a place they could find sanctuary, for he was determined to possess Morgana if he had to die for it. The thought that she was married to a man who had the power of life and death over his future, was pushed aside. He wanted her. Now!

As she had hoped his eyes spotted the small shack that had once been used as the falconer's cottage for the estate on whose land it was situated. Morgana had known of its location and planned on its usefulness. Quickly, Steffan took the reins of both horses. Sliding his arm about her waist and drawing the horses after him, he walked with her to the cottage door. He tied the horses and taking her hand, he pushed the door open and drew her into a room that was almost as dark as the thundering clouds overhead. Inside he drew her into his arms again and possessed her mouth with a fury of passion.

"God," he whispered against her throat, "I love you, Morgana."

Morgana smiled as she twined her fingers through his hair and drew his mouth to hers. I love you, were not words Morgana cared to use. She wanted to hear them for they meant to her another heart she had captured. Morgana did not love. She lusted. She wanted to enjoy him and slowly she moved out of his arms and stood a little away from him. The cottage contained a small table and chairs that stood in front of a fireplace and a few blankets that the previous owner had thrown in front of the fireplace upon which he had obviously slept.

"Light the candle on the table, Steffan," she said softly. Steffan found the flint and struck it, lighting the candle. He turned again to look at Morgana.

Slowly, she reached up and loosened the pins in her hair, allowing the golden mass to fall about her. Then she began to unbutton her jacket and shrugged it from her shoulders. Steffan stood fascinated as one piece of clothing followed another until his golden goddess stood before him bathed in the glow of the

159

candlelight, an absolute perfection of soft pale beauty. Slowly and sensuously, she moved toward him until her body and his barely touched. Steffan felt as though he were drowning. He slid his fingers through her hair capturing her head between his hands, he kissed her forehead, her closed eyes, her cheeks and finally his seeking lips found hers in a kiss that devastated the foundations of Steffan's world.

It took him only moments to rid himself of the clothes that restricted him. Morgana smiled in satisfaction that she had chosen well. Steffan stood six foot three and weighed over one hundred eighty pounds. They were hard muscular pounds. She also saw clearly that nature had endowed him with size in every way. She breathed deeply in anticipation of the moment he would take her as he reached for her again and drew her down on the blanket with him. Steffan had been with many girls, but never had he even dreamed of a woman such as this. One who met his every touch, his every move with a fiery passion that matched, no, surpassed his.

If they were fighting the eternal battle of the male and female, it was a battle he could not even hope to win. He was dazzled by her fiery possession and held spellbound with the flowing warmth of the body that seemed to surround him. As he entered her and felt her warm moist body sheathe him, he knew the wonder of loving such as he had never experienced before. He whispered the words of love as their bodies blended and she smiled again in the deepest sense of fulfillment and satisfaction.

It was afterward, when his reeling senses came tumbling back into reality, that he realized she was a fever he could not cure himself of. He knew, from the way she still felt in his arms that he would have to possess her again and again, and even then, he felt he would never have enough.

"Morgana," he whispered against her hair.

"Yes?"

"I love you."

She looked up into his eyes and smiled a smile he would never be able to fathom. "I know" she said gently. "I think I've known that from the moment you took my hand at the ball. I've wanted you since then. It's you who have been slow in realizing it."

He touched her lips lightly again and again. "Morgana, I must have you. Not like this, but for always."

"What are you saying, Steffan?"

"That you've got to divorce him."

"Divorce! You know that is impossible. I or no other woman

can get a divorce without slander being applied to her name. And you! You cannot marry a divorced woman. It would ruin any chance you had of a career. No, it is an impossibility."

"Morgana," he said miserably, "I cannot bear the thought of you going home to him. I cannot bear the thought of him touching you, holding you."

"Steffan, we cannot do anything now. We need time to think, to plan."

He rose on one elbow and looked down at her pale gold body against the dark blanket. He caressed her gently, enjoying the smooth silken touch of her skin.

"Plan what?"

"You must graduate first, then, maybe, there is something we can do about us."

"Graduate! That is a year away."

"Steffan, a year is not so very long."

"To me, it is a lifetime. How can I be near you so long and know you belong to another?"

"I belong to no one, Steffan. And we can spend our time together. No one need know. We will meet here as often as we can and when the right time comes, we will be together."

A normal rational thinking Steffan would never have allowed his deep sense of honor to be discarded so easily, but he was so deeply in love and so sure of it being returned that he ignored the cry of his conscience. There was nothing of more importance in his life now but this golden haired goddess, and the deep emotion he labeled love that he felt for her.

In the weeks that followed, Steffan's world was changed completely. He met Morgana as often as he could and stayed in a state of emotional suspension when they were apart. She had complete control of his heart and his thoughts. Steffan suffered, Morgana gloried, Jeff worried . . . and Wade Kyle hated.

Wade knew from the very first the moment Morgana and Steffan had finally been together. He knew better than anyone that Steffan was just another toy for Morgana to play with. But that didn't stop him from burning with jealousy when he knew Morgana had slipped out to meet him.

He was seated in her bedroom one night when Morgana returned home. She opened her bedroom door, and the smile on her face faded. "What are you doing in my room, Wade? You have certainly not been invited."

He got up slowly and walked toward her. "Damn you!" he said with quiet fury. "You are a bitch from the farthest spot in hell, Morgana.''

"You're drunk, Wade. Get out of here'' she said disdainfully.

"Yes, I'm drunk. I've been waiting for you to get home from your little rendezvous with your latest lover. Cadet Devers, or should I say ex-cadet Devers . . . for I'm going to destroy him, Morgana.''

At any other time, Morgana would have laughed and let Wade do what he wanted, for no other man had meant that much to her. But with Steffan, she had found a man who could meet her passions on her own ground. She enjoyed him more than she had any other and was not ready yet to free him. Instead, another plan crept across her mind. She needed time to examine it and find a way. Morgana was not the least bit afraid of Wade for no one knew better than she the power she held over him. They had fought this battle before and Morgana had stepped aside to allow Wade to do whatever he wanted with the unfortunate man involved.

"Wade," she said softly. The quietness of her voice held him in his tracks. "Look at me, Wade.''

He lifted his agonized eyes to her.

"If you touch Steffan Devers, I will be gone.''

"Morgana," he cried hoarsely.

"Listen to me well, Wade," her voice was musical and she walked toward him. "You want me to stay with you, to be here when you need me . . . and you need me, Wade.'' Her hands reached up and caressed the sides of his face, she rose on tiptoe and put her mouth close to his. "I'm here, Wade," she whispered. "I will always be here.''

"Damn you, Morgana," he almost sobbed as his arms came around her and his hungry mouth sought hers. When he released her for a moment she walked to her bed and removed her clothes then she turned to face him again. She watched him for a moment and knew the insatiable hunger for her that ate at his soul day and night.

"You can choose now, Wade. Your revenge on Steffan Devers . . . or me. You cannot have both.''

Wade stood and stared at her for a moment. She was so fragile looking, so breathtakingly beautiful and the need for her that gnawed at him day and night screamed aloud in his mind. Slowly, he walked to her. With one tentative hand, he reached out and put it on her slender hip. Morgana stood still, a small half smile on her lips. He slid his hand over the softness of her skin.

"Morgana," he moaned gently. "I should kill you. You are an

evil that needs to be killed.''

"Then do so now, Wade," she reached out for both of his hands and raised them to her throat. "You could kill me so easily, all you have to do is squeeze. But then," she whispered, "I will not be here when you want me.''

His hands jerked away from her throat as though they were burnt. Morgana ran her tongue over her parted lips as she gazed at Wade. It was an expectant gaze for she knew Wade's passions when he was aroused. With gentle fingers, she began to loosen the robe he wore. Then she moved her body against his and with a bitter cry of absolute defeat, Wade lifted her in his arms, and they fell onto the bed together. Morgana's successful laughter rang out and Steffan Devers was still her possession for as long as she wanted him.

Morgana was enjoying the balance of the school year. She met Steffan only when the need for him filled her and Steffan lived in misery the rest of the time, picturing her in Wade's arms. His studies suffered and if Jeff had not been there he might have lost everything. It came as a relief when he and Steffan were on the list for active sea duty under Commander Pierce and were at sea for the final four months of the year.

None of his family could understand the change in the Steffan that came home that summer. He was often moody and depressed. They knew nothing of the sleepless nights when the craving for Morgana almost drove him mad.

He greeted the final school year with enthusiasm. For him, it meant graduation and Morgana could safely leave Wade and they could be married. He celebrated his twenty-fourth birthday just before the summer vacation and felt he was man enough and capable enough to care for Morgana. It never occurred to him that there would never be one man who could take care of her needs and that she had intentions that were completely different from his.

If Steffan's summer was a disaster, Jeff's was the most amazing in his life. He had kept up his continued search for Brandy every summer. Captain James Daugherty, the man who had made the arrangements for Brandy's transportation had been in the London harbor often, but his and Jeff's paths never crossed. It was the day before he was to return to school that Jeff checked the harbor once again for any ships he had not seen before. He found the *Mary D.* in port. He asked for the captain and a few minutes later, he was shown to his quarters where he explained his situation. He explained Brandy as his runaway sister, which

163

Captain Daugherty did not believe for a minute. But he felt sorry for the young man as Jeff almost pleaded for any information he had.

"How long ago was this?" he questioned Jeff.

"In '71, over two years ago."

"Well, I'll have to check through my log books and find the lists," he grunted as he bent down and slid open a deep drawer in his desk. From it he removed several large books.

"71" he said and he chose one of the large volumes. "Here we are." He opened the book. "What month was it?"

"The end of July, sir," Jeff said hopefully.

"July . . . I took a group of indentured people to America then."

"Indentured?"

"Yes. Someone over there pays the ticket and the persons work off the price when they arrive."

"Is her name on the list?"

Captain Daugherty looked down the list slowly, so slowly Jeff wanted to grab it from him and look for himself.

"Ah, here we go."

"You found her?" Jeff almost shouted at the wild surge of hope that flooded through him.

"Brandy Maguire?"

"That's it, sir. Can you tell me, do you remember anything about the trip?"

"I remember not only the trip but the young lady as well. She helped me nurse a sick group of people on the way over. She's a lovely young woman."

"Yes, sir," Jeff smiled. "She is."

"Did you know," the captain asked gently, watching Jeff's face, "that your sister was pregnant?"

Jeff stared at him in stunned silence. "Pregnant?"

"Yes, I imagine that's another reason I admired her so, even when she was deathly ill herself, she helped me with the sick." His eyes held Jeff's. "I hope the bastard who left her with child and let her take that perilous journey alone, roasts in hell."

Jeff looked at the captain, his eyes straight and proud. "Did it ever occur to you, sir," he said, "that the man didn't know she was carrying his child?"

"And do you think, if he knew, that he had plans to remedy the situation?"

"I assure you, sir, that is exactly what I intend. You know Brandy's not my sister."

"Of course," the captain smiled. "She's much prettier than you."

"Let me tell you the story, sir. I need your help to find exactly where Brandy is now. Then I intend to go to her as quickly as I can and bring my wife and child back with me."

He told the captain all that had happened between him and Brandy. The captain did not interrupt until he had finished, but he looked at the situation much differently than Jeff who was ready to drop all he had worked for and go immediately to Brandy.

"Are you going to make all she has sacrificed in vain? She gave up a lot to make sure you received your commission. Is that all to be for nothing?"

"Do you expect me to know where Brandy is, that I have a child I've never seen, and do nothing about it but worry about my own life?"

"If you're wise, young man, you'll listen to me. I'm going to America again this trip. I will find where she is and see that everything is well with her and the babe. In the meantime, you finish your education. Then, you can go to her, commission in hand, and she will have succeeded in giving you what she wanted to give."

Jeff knew he was right, but it was painful to be so close to Brandy and his . . . what? . . . son or daughter, and not do anything about it.

"I've plenty of money, sir, will you see she gets it. I want her comfortable until I get there."

"Now, where do I tell her the money came from? No, I will see all is well, you can repay me later."

"When do you leave, sir?"

"Tomorrow."

"And when will you be back?"

"In about four and half months. You should be near graduation then."

"Four and a half months, that's a lifetime."

"To one as young as you, maybe. But it's really not, you will have a lot of happy years to spend together."

"If I can convince Brandy to come back here and be an officer's wife."

"I can see how afraid she would be to do that with all the spiteful people who would desire to pull her down because of her past. But, don't worry, sometimes fate has its own way of working things out."

Neither of them knew just how true his words were, for soon, fate was going to offer him the opportunity that would change not only his life, but Brandy's and his friends as well.

Fifteen

Jeff, Langley and Bright graduated eight months before Steffan and his friends. Jeff spent the summer afterwards in London again impatiently awaiting word from Captain Daugherty.

He had acquired a full commission, and both Langley and Bright had received commissions. They were trying to get themselves stationed as second officers on Jeff's ship when he acquired it. That was the reason all three of them were still in London when Steffan, Jeff and Mack began the last months of their schooling.

Steffan's life outside the classroom and his occasional ship board service was spent with Morgana. Every moment that he could get free, they spent together in the small cottage. He lived for the moments he could be with her. He talked long and often of the future they would share together. Although she hid it well, Morgana planned another kind of future. She would never tire of Steffan physically, this she knew because he was an apt pupil of her far greater knowledge of lovemaking. But she decided to rid herself of Wade and yet keep the wealth and position that Wade carried and she intended to use Steffan to accomplish that.

It was late in November when Jeff received a message that he was wanted in the harbor by the captain of a ship newly arrived from America. Jeff knew immediately who wanted him and why and he wasted no time in getting to the docks and to Captain Daugherty's door.

Captain Daugherty welcomed him with a smile and offered him a seat and a drink. Jeff took the seat but refused the drink. He was too impatient to hear what he had to say.

"Did you find her, sir? Is she all right? The baby, what . . ."

"Whoa, just a minute, young man. One question at a time is all I can handle. Yes, I found her. She's still in service to Mr. and Mrs. Whitticer. She has a good bit of time left to serve, and that is only her repayment for their accepting the child into their home. She is dressmaker for Mrs. Whitticer and they treat her very well. When I spoke to her . . ."

"You talked to her, sir?"

"Yes. I made the acquaintance of the Whitticers and met her on one of my visits to their home."

"How is she, really?"

"She's as pretty as I remember her."

"And the baby, what . . . what was it?"

"A boy."

Jeff felt a thick lump rise in his throat and for a minute he thought he was going to break and cry. He rose and went to the porthole looking out with unseeing eyes until he regained control of himself.

"My son," he whispered. "Do you know, sir . . . what she named him?"

"Yes, the boy's name is Jeff Maguire, the same as his father's with the exception of the last name, and that is a situation I expect you'll be changing as soon as you can."

"You're right. I'm asking for an extended leave, at least six months. I'll go for her personally, if you'll take me there."

"My pleasure. I've almost a full cargo. If you can make the arrangements, we'll be on our way in less than two weeks."

Jeff left the ship in a mild state of euphoria. He felt he'd never been as happy in his life.

It was a weekend and the six friends had decided to get together to talk, have a few drinks and enjoy the evening. But each of them, when they returned, found an envelope addressed to them. Each message, when they compared them later, said the same thing. They were requested to meet Commander Pierce, at his home, at exactly eight thirty.

"I wonder what he wants," Steffan said. "I'm sure Tom, Mack and I aren't in any difficulty, and you three certainly can't be. I wonder if there's something going on, we don't know about."

"Like what?" Jeff questioned.

"Well, some time ago, Commander Pierce voiced a suspicion that there might be some kind of conflict between England and America."

The rest of them began to laugh before Steffan could finish.

"Come on, Steffan, not really, a war between England and the Colonies. That's well nigh impossible. Why, they have no Navy at all as far as I know."

Steffan shrugged. "I'm just telling you what Pierce said. It might be something completely different."

"Well, whatever it is, we'd best go and find out," Mack said.

168

"Let's walk over, it's not far," Tom grinned. "And besides, I need the exercise. With Cecile's good cooking and the comfortable life at home, I've started to gain weight."

It was obvious, after a short while, that Tom had suggested the walk so that he could talk to Jeff. As they drifted toward Commander Pierce's home, Tom touched Jeff lightly on the arm and motioned silently to him. They dropped back a few steps from the others.

"What's the matter, Tom?"

"Jeff, what's happening with Steff these days? Cecile is worried to death about him. He used to come over at least once a week. It's been months since she's seen him, and I don't like the way he looks. There's something wrong."

"Why don't you ask him?"

"I did."

"And?"

"He says everything is fine, but . . . he's losing something, Jeff, and I don't know what's happening. Steff always had a . . . sort of . . . drive about him. Now it seems that everything runs second to something else."

"Well, you're right about that. Look, Tom, I hate to talk behind Steff's back, but dammit, I've been worried about him for a long time."

"What is it? I think Cecile and I should know if Steff has a problem. Maybe we can help."

"There's no one who can help Steff out of this mess. He has to see for himself and he's blind."

"For God's sake, Jeff, tell me what's going on."

Jeff sighed deeply. If Steff ever knew he was discussing Morgana like this he would be angry, but he was thinking, in desperation, that Tom and Steffan's beloved sister just might be the ones to help.

He began explaining things to Tom about Morgana that Steff never knew, then he told how entangled with her Steff really was.

"Tom, I know that Wade Kyle is not a stupid man. I also know that one day something's going to happen to make him find out about Steff and . . . her, and he's going to ruin Steff for the rest of his life."

"Who knows about this?"

Jeff made a sharp disgusted sound. "Just about everyone it seems, except Wade Kyle."

"Do you think that's possible?"

They stopped for a moment and looked at each other.

"No . . . no, I guess I don't. I guess I've been wondering all along just how soon Steff's world is going to explode. What is really making me worry is what is going to happen to Steff when Morgana decides she's finished with him and just laughs and walks away."

"Steff's a hell of a lot stronger than that," Tom said, but a worried frown wrinkled his brow.

Jeff was about to reply when they reached Commander Pierce's house. The others were too close now for them to discuss it any further.

"Jeff, come over to the house soon. We've got to talk to Cecile. She and Steff are very close. Maybe she can reach him before it's too late."

"All right. First chance I get, I'll be there."

When the group arrived at Commander Pierce's door, they saw immediately that there were other guests already there. Two carriages sat in front of the house, and the house itself was bright with light. They knocked, and were taken to Commander Pierce's library. There, they found four men, two of whom they already knew and two they did not. No one was more surprised than Steffan to find Martin Gillis in the group.

"Mr. Gillis, I didn't even know you knew Commander Pierce."

"I met Commander Pierce two years ago; you remember Steffan, the summer I took an extended vacation? I went," he said quietly, watching Steffan's face closely, "to the new American Colonies. I had been curious about them for some time, so I thought it well that I satisfy my curiosity by a first hand look."

Steffan was immediately filled, not only with suspicion, but with a million questions he wanted to ask. Before he began, he was interrupted by Commander Pierce who urged them to come in and poured them each a drink.

"I wanted you gentlemen here tonight because I've been honored by two distinguished guests and I was sure you gentlemen would like to meet them."

Jeff Sables had been looking closely at the one guest who stood quietly in front of the fireplace studying the newcomers intently. His heart beat a little more rapidly when he felt he knew the slender quiet man.

"Captain Sables, Mr. Langley, Mr. Claire, Cadets Devers, Braydon, and Davidson, I would like you to meet," he extended his hand toward the stranger, "Captain Horatio Nelson."

All of them stood for a moment in frozen respectful silence, because all of them were completely overcome with the honor of meeting a man with such an illustrious reputation. It was Jeff who reacted first by taking the few steps that separated them and extended his hand which Nelson, with a half smile accepted.

"It is a great honor to meet you, sir."

"Thank you, Captain Sables."

It took the others only a second to follow Jeff's lead. "And now gentlemen, my other guest, Captain John Paul Jones . . . at the moment he is serving under Captain Nelson but I suspect he will soon command a vessel of his own."

Again it was Jeff who extended his hand first.

"I called you gentlemen here because it is not often one has such illustrious guests and I felt sure you would want to meet them. Now, come, let us sit by the fire and discuss great and noble endeavors." He laughed, but Steffan, who had been watching Martin Gillis and Commander Pierce had a deep feeling there was more to this than a chance meeting. The conversation during the evening held the deep interest of the younger men. They questioned and listened to Captain Nelson's exploits. All the time they were talking Steffan had the feeling that much was being left unsaid; he also had the instinctive feeling they were brought here for a definite reason and that they were being studied closely by the sharp eyes of Horatio Nelson.

Reluctantly, the younger men left at the close of the evening. After he closed the door, Pierce turned to face the men whose opinion he wanted.

"Well, what do you gentlemen think of my choices?"

Nelson laughed. "Excellent, most excellent. But you will play merry hell in getting those men to change sides. Every ounce of their conversation dripped with honor and a deep sense of duty, not to mention love of country. Just how do you go about changing the lives of men such as that?"

"Oh, I don't know exactly, I only know that some way, somehow I'll change them."

"May I make a suggestion, sir?" Jones spoke quietly.

"Of course, I'm prepared to accept anything you have to offer that might be of help."

"You only have two minds to really change."

"Two?"

"Captain Sables, and the other young man . . . Devers."

"Why only these two?"

"It was obvious to me, and I'm sure, to Captain Nelson that these two are the unspoken leaders. I feel sure if Sables goes then

171

Miles and Claire will go also, and if Devers should choose to join us, I think Davidson and Braydon would stand with him for I sensed above all their loyalty to country comes the loyalty to each other. They are a close knit group with that rare quality between them . . . true and genuine friendship."

"Then," Pierce said humorously, "all we have to do is convince two strong minded, loyal and honorable men to change sides in a conflict and fight against the country that bred them and trained them. Small endeavor."

They all laughed and settled to discuss feasible plans they might use to accomplish their end.

Jeff could not understand, in the following two weeks, why his request for an extended leave received no answer. Captain Daugherty had a full cargo and had been waiting daily for word from Jeff.

The papers Jeff waited for sat upon the desk of Commander Pierce. They had been there for two weeks while he checked into the reasons. His inquiries bore fruit, and for the first time he felt he had the one thing that would change Jeff's mind.

It was impossible for Jeff to believe what he read when his request finally was answered. His request was denied; Jeff stared at the paper in profound surprise. He went immediately to see Commander Pierce who faced him with unreadable eyes and told him that due to the fact that they were building heavily, they could not let Jeff go for an unlimited time.

"If you want a few days' leave, I'm sure it can be arranged, but any extended length of time is out of the question."

"But sir, I haven't even received an assignment yet. Surely, there is time . . ."

"Captain Sables," Commander Pierce said firmly. "You are not expendable at the moment. There is no point in arguing with me. We cannot give you an extended leave at this time, so further discussion is useless."

Jeff was furiously, murderously angry. He left Commander Pierce's office and went to the docks where Captain Daughterty watched him pace the floor in angry frustration and curse the system he was bound to from His Majesty down to the smallest clerk.

"How much longer was Brandy indentured for?" he questioned Captain Daugherty.

"It was one year when I left there. It's been almost five months since. She's another seven months to go."

"God!" Jeff groaned as he threw himself down in a chair.

"Her time will be up soon. She could take the baby and be gone, be almost anywhere before I could get there. I might never find them. I've got to find some way to get there."

"Do you want me to go to her and tell her the situation? That way maybe she will wait until you get the freedom to come."

"Wait! Brandy left here with the thought in her head that my career and position in life should come first. Do you think she would wait? No, she'd take the baby and disappear, and this time would cover her tracks so that I would never find them."

"Maybe she's right," Captain Daugherty said slowly, "you know things would be quite different for you both should you start life together. English aristocracy has no room in it for the Brandy Maguires of the world, and when you take her as a wife, it will probably feel the same for you."

"Who cares what the aristocracy thinks?"

"After a while, you both will, when it begins to affect your son."

Jeff remained silent. In his mind, he pictured the child. What could they do to him with a mother branded as a whore and a father who had broken all the rules by loving the wrong woman. Jeff rose and walked to the door, than he turned and looked at Captain Daugherty. The look in his eyes was determined and completely resolved.

"I'll find some way to get to Brandy and my son. When I do, I'll find some place that accepts a man for what he is, not who he is. But I guarantee you, Captain, nothing is going to keep me from finding my son and Brandy. Nothing and nobody."

The door clicked behind him, and not for a minute did Captain Daugherty doubt that Jeff Sables meant every word he spoke.

Jeff went back toward London, but he felt too much at odds with himself and the rest of the unforgiving world in which he lived. He went out for a walk, then quickly decided what he was going to do. He hired a carriage and in about an hour, he stepped down in front of Tom Braydon's small cottage. He knew Tom wouldn't be home yet, but he felt he had to talk to someone so he decided he would wait for him. The door was opened by a smiling Cecile.

"Hello, Jeff. I saw you coming up the walk. Tom's not home yet, but he should be soon. Won't you come in and wait? I'll get you something to drink. Are you hungry?"

"No, Cecile," he laughed at the bubbling chatter. "I'm not hungry and I don't really care for anything to drink. What I really need is a friend I can talk to."

"Well," she said firmly as she tucked her arm through his and drew him inside. "You've come to the right place. What better friends do you have than Tom and me?"

When Jeff was comfortably seated and holding the drink Cecile had pressed on him, she seated herself across from him.

"Jeff, Tom told me that the both of you were quite worried about some problem Steff is involved in. Is that what you came to talk about?"

"I'll explain to you all I know about that too, Cecile, but the reason I came was more selfish than that. Cecile, being a woman, you would probably understand what has happened better than anyone. I need some kind of advice, some kind of help."

Cecile's face became serious when she saw that Jeff's expression was one of despair. "Tell me, Jeff," she said quietly. She sat back and listened to Jeff's whole story of all that had happened between himself and Brandy, how he'd found her, and how difficult things were becoming.

"She must have loved you very deeply, Jeff, to do what she did for you."

"Yes, but I want her back, Cecile, I want her and I want my son. I just don't know what I can do about it. They won't give me an extended leave so that I can go and get her; if I send someone else you know what will happen. She'll disappear . . . she'll take my son and I'll never see either of them again."

"Oh, Jeff, there must be something. Maybe through Mr. Gillis, or my father, they could use some influence to get you a leave. Father and Mr. Gillis seem to know an awful lot of people here. Commander Crawford and, well, most of the others. I'm sure Father would do everything he could."

"That would be wonderful, Cecile. Maybe if I go to him, explain to him, he'll . . ."

Cecile reached out and touched his arm.

"He'll do everything he can."

"Thank you, Cecile."

"Thank me by telling me just what trouble my brother is in. Steff hasn't been the same person for a long time. I've known something is wrong, but I just didn't know what. Do you know?"

"I know, I just wish I didn't because I know no one can do anything about it but Steff himself. He's blind to an evil so strong that it's tapping all his mental strength. He's got to see for himself. He's got to realize the evil for what it is and no-body . . . nobody can do it but Steff himself."

"Will you tell me what it is, Jeff? At least, I think I have a

174

right to know if something is hurting one of the people who is dearest in my life.''

"Yes, you've a right to know.'' He sat back in his chair with a deep sigh and told Cecile all about Morgana's background, of the others who had been loved and destroyed by her. He told her of Morgana's fabulous beauty and how she used it to get whatever and whomever she wanted. "Steff can't see, Cecile. He believes, because he is so honest and so honorable, that others are too. One day soon, Morgana is going to tire of him and she'll shatter his life without giving it a second thought.''

Cecile's face was pale but her voice was steady. "Has anyone tried to tell him about her?''

"I told him once when he arrived here, then a few weeks ago, Mack and I tried to tell him again. Cecile, it was the first time I've ever seen Steff react so. He told us, not exactly in these words, to mind our own business, that we didn't understand Morgana. That she was going to divorce her husband and marry Steff.''

"And they would live happily ever after in their own world,'' Cecile added bitterly.

"That's about it. It makes Steff sound like a dreamer and he's not. He's just under some kind of spell Morgana is capable of weaving and the only way it can be broken is for Steff to see Morgana as she really is and not how he thinks she is.''

Cecile was about to speak again when the sound of footsteps sounded on the porch. Jeff smiled at the sudden glow on Cecile's face as she rose quickly from her chair and went to the door. Tom opened the door and in a second, Cecile was in his arms and he was holding her tightly and kissing her. He put his arm about her waist and held her against him as they walked back into the room.

"Hello, Jeff.''

"Tom,'' Jeff smiled. "I just came over to cry on your shoulder, but your lovely wife played listener instead.''

Tom looked down at Cecile, the look on his face was as close to adoration as it could get. "Cecile's good at listening. She listens to my complaints all the time. But of course, Cecile's good at everything she does.''

"And that,'' she smiled at Jeff, "is a completely unbiased opinion.''

They laughed together; Cecile and Tom urged Jeff to stay for supper which he accepted. It was a very pleasant meal and when he left, with both Cecile and Tom telling him they would do everything they could to help, he felt a little better.

Tom closed the door behind Jeff and turned back to Cecile.

"Now, how about a proper welcome home kiss," he grinned as he reached for her. He heard her light laugh as her arms came up about his neck and she lifted willing lips to his.

"Oh Tom," she whispered. "I'm so glad I have you. My life is so good, so full when you're here. I miss you terribly when you're away."

"No more than I miss you, love. But Cecile, graduation is only a few weeks away. Then I'll be home for a while because I want to try to get second officer's position on Steff's ship if I can. It will probably mean I'll be home every day for weeks until Steff's orders come through."

"Weeks, that would be wonderful. Maybe we could even go home for a while. I would love to see my parents again, it's been so long since we've been home."

"I know how much you miss home, Cecile."

"It isn't just that," she smiled up at him. "I just want to talk to my mother and father. I . . . I want to tell them they'd better prepare the nursery since they're going to become grandparents one day soon."

Tom stood in silence for a moment looking down into the eyes that always reminded him of melted honey. His heart swelled with love for the tiny woman he held against him. Gently he bent and captured her lips again in a tender kiss. "I never thought anyone would be able to do or say anything in the world that would make me happier than I've been for the past two years, but you just did. Cecile, I love you, I love you so much sometimes it hurts."

She clung to him as he kissed her again in deepening passion.

"Cecile," he whispered against her throat, "would it hurt if you . . ."

"No, oh, Tom, I want you to hold me, love me." He gently lifted her from the floor as though she were fragile. She laughed a little as he carried her to the room they had shared in love so often before.

"You know it just isn't done."

"What isn't?"

"Making love in the afternoon, in broad daylight. Most of the matrons around would be shocked."

Tom laughed with her. "Maybe what most of those matrons need is love in the afternoon. Maybe then, they'd learn how gloriously beautiful it really is." He stood her on the floor beside their bed. She began to remove the clothes she wore.

"No," he said gently. "Let me." Her hands paused and very

176

slowly, Tom removed her clothes, tossing them aside as his eyes held hers. "I want to see you."

Very gently he touched the flat plane of her belly where, he knew, his child lay.

"Our daughter," he whispered.

"Or son," she replied.

"Or both," he laughed with a wicked smile in his eyes.

"You're greedy," she chuckled. "Tom, hasn't anyone told you you can't have everything you want?"

"Shhh—I already have, I just don't want anyone else to know. It would be too hard for anyone else to accept that I've got all the best things life has to offer and the rest of the world has to make do on what little is left."

He removed his clothes and gently pulled her cool slender body close to his, running his hands possessively over her.

"I've got you, Cecile, and all the beauty you have to offer. That's enough for me."

"Tom," she whispered as his hungry mouth silenced hers and he pulled her down on the bed with him.

The white hot passion of their earlier days had grown to a beautiful gentle thing. As he eased himself within her he felt as he always did when they made love together. That he was suddenly all of one piece, whole, while all other times, he was half, waiting for this one miraculous thing that happened when he was joined with her. It was a blending of all the deep emotions that each of them felt but could not put into words.

Jeff made his way back home. When he arrived, he found a note from Captain Daugherty telling him that it was no longer possible for him to wait any longer. He was under direct orders to leave port in three days, and would Jeff please come and inform him of his plans. Jeff sat down and wrote an answer. He told Captain Daugherty he was not free to leave at this time but there was a great possibility he would be able to get leave soon. He would find other passage to America. He also asked him not to mention his name to Brandy if he saw her again. He said he could not come and see him off because it was too painful to watch the ship leave and know it was heading where he wanted to go, where his heart was, and he could not go along.

He hired a young boy to carry the message, then went out and got himself rousingly drunk and wound up Sunday morning with a miserable hangover in the bed of a young barmaid who left him as empty as he had felt since Brandy had gone. His grim determination grew greater and greater from that moment. "Somewhere, somehow, there's a way, Brandy, and I'll find it. Wait for me, love. Whatever you do, wait for me," he whispered.

It was only four weeks before graduation. But many things were to evolve in those four weeks that were going to abruptly change the lives of all involved.

Storm clouds gathered over the Colonies of America. Her strong and loyal people sought all the trained men they could find to help organize a people who were seeking independence, yet seemed as vulnerable as children against the mighty strength of mother England.

The days Steffan, Tom and Mack had waited and worked for so long and so hard finally came. Tom and Mack did well, much better than either of them had thought they would do, but Steffan graduated with the highest marks in the class.

The speeches were long and to the new officers, rather boring, especially since they wanted to add the gold stripes to their sleeves and exchange the hat of the cadet for the blue and gold visored hat of ranking officers.

There was a huge celebration that night to which the families of the new officers had been invited. It was then that Mack announced the plans for his ordination into the clergy. He would serve on whatever ship he was assigned to as chaplain. Of course, he voiced his hope that the ship would be one commanded by the man he considered his best friend, Captain Steffan Devers.

Tom and Cecile told their families and close friends of the expected addition to their home.

There was much laughter, dancing and drinking. It did not escape the notice of the people close to them that neither Jeff Sables nor Steffan Devers seemed to be as happy as they should be.

Steffan watched with intense jealousy as Morgana danced, mostly with her husband, but often with others. The jealousy ate at him and Morgana knew it. She also knew it whetted Steffan's passion for her and she grew excited at the thought of their meeting planned some time later, for she knew his lovemaking would be demanding and breathtakingly violent.

Cecile watched, from across the room, her brother's intense and unhappy face. She looked at the woman who was hurting her beloved brother so and immediately a deep and burning hatred filled her. She prayed silently that the time would come soon when Steffan would see the evilness in Morgana unveiled.

The party was almost at its close when Commander Crawford called for everyone's attention. "I wish to extend my congratulations to the men who have graduated today. I wish you all the very best. There are two announcements I have to make tonight. Of course, in due time each of you will be given your assignments, but tonight I want to announce the first two. His Majesty's ship *Bremington* will be commanded by Captain Jeffery Sables with Lieutenant Brighton Claire and Lieutenant Langley Miles as her second officers.''

There was a rousing cheer, for the three officers were well admired.

Commander Crawford held up his hand for momentary silence. ''His Majesty's ship *Godolphin* will be commanded by Captain Steffan Devers with Lieutenant Tom Braydon second officer.''

Now there was another loud cheer; both Steffan and Tom were delighted. For Tom, it meant their friendship would remain unbroken. For Steffan, it meant that Morgana could get free of the terrible, brutal man who held her against her will. Free to marry him.

Morgana stood by Wade Kyle's side. To all outward appearances, they were both happy, but no one heard Wade say softly and maliciously, ''He's slipping away, Morgana. Soon you'll have no hold on him. When he's away, out from under your spell, he'll come to his senses. I almost envy him. I need to rid myself of your poison.''

Morgana smiled at Steffan across the room. A smile that to him promised everything, but the words to her husband were soft and quiet.

''I wouldn't be too sure, Wade. Maybe soon, all of us will get what we want.''

From that night on, things seemed to happen in rapid succession. Things that were to set many new lives on different courses and change others in ways they could never imagine.

They were to look back on this time in their future and wonder at the suddenness of all that came about.

Sixteen

It began when they all received another message from Commander Pierce asking again for their presence in his home. Of course, there was no question, they all arrived. Jeff's motives were to try again to get permission for his leave. Again, as before, Captain Nelson and Captain Jones were both present along with Martin Gillis.

It was Captain Nelson who stood in front of the fireplace, hands clasped behind his back, and began the discussion they were all brought together for.

"Now that you gentlemen have graduated, you find yourselves facing a challenging future."

"Both Steff and I have received our commissions and our ships, sir," Jeff replied. "And we're fortunate enough to have Tom, Lang, and Bright as our second officers. I would say that the future is well marked for us."

"That depends upon a lot of things, Captain Sables," Nelson answered. "Do you want to face a life that is laid out for you like a blueprint . . . by someone else . . . or, would you like something a little more challenging and a little more exciting?"

Steffan looked at the faces about him, and suddenly, as though someone had opened a door to a brightly lit room, he knew why these men had gathered here and he knew what Nelson was about to say. His eyes met Martin's across the room and Martin also knew that Steffan was aware.

"Steffan," he said, "listen . . . just listen for a few minutes."

There was too much inbred respect, too much love for this man for Steffan to argue. He nodded and waited for Captain Nelson to continue.

If there was anything at which Horatio Nelson excelled, it was creating enthusiasm in others with word pictures. He had the ability to capture men's minds and spirits both during the heat of great battles and in the quieter atmosphere of the drawing room. He brought into use every ounce of his deep magnetic appeal as he began his story with the first seeds for the desire of independence that had grown in the bosom of young America. He told of a fabulous breadth of land that harbored and nurtured all types of people from the very lowest to the very highest in complete freedom and more, complete equality. It was at this moment that he caught and held Jeff Sables' undivided attention.

He spoke of the pressures and taxes the people in America lived under, almost in a state of abject slavery to England. "I love her, this England of ours, I love her and yet I know that this time she is wrong in what she is doing. It is not right for her to hold in oppression a people who could be our friends instead of our slaves. This new country offers an opportunity to all men despite their wealth or lack of it, despite their positions in life or lack of it. She is going to face a severe struggle. Although at the moment she seems weak, believe me gentlemen, there is an indomitable spirit here that will not be crushed."

"Are you telling us that one day there will be conflict between our two countries?" Tom questioned.

"Not conflict," Nelson replied, "war."

There was silence for a moment, then Steffan said, "What are you saying to us, Captain Nelson?"

"I am telling you that I have resigned my commission in His Majesty's Navy and will lead the Navy of the American Colonies. I am telling you that I want you to join me, and I am telling you, before God, that I firmly believe that what I am doing is right because the injustices of the world should be righted and even though England is my homeland, what she is doing is an injustice both in the eyes of God and of man."

"How dare we, sir!" Steffan replied. "Do you not think that we owe a debt to our country? She has given us all the best things life has to offer. She has trained us and given us every opportunity. In all honor, sir, how dare we?"

"In all of history, young man, great and impossible things have been done only by those who dare. In all of history we must realize that all great powers tend one day to trample the downtrodden in the world. You do not love or honor your country any more than I. Haven't I fought battles for her, and I would again if she were right. I would be the first to rise to her call of arms if she were right. Let this small country rise to her feet. Let us treat her, not as slaves, but equals. If I had a child, and that child lived in error, no matter how much I loved it, I would do my best to correct this error if only for fear of the safety of its own soul. So I feel about my country. I must do my best to help correct a most serious error she is making for I tell you, my friends, she lives in

181

danger of the loss of her own honor."

Martin could see quite clearly that all the young officers were moved by the words they were hearing. Jeff Sables was watching Commander Pierce intently. Then a slow smile formed on his lips. He suddenly knew that no extended leave would ever be granted him and now he was going to be faced with a choice: either he stayed in England and served his own pride and honor or he did what Captain Nelson wanted and had Brandy and his son as a reward.

"We need time to think over what you have said to us, sir. Just how much time have we got?" Jeff asked.

"A few months at most. I know that the *Godolphin* is to be sent on a mission soon that will probably take about four months. After that, I will be prepared to leave and I pray you will accompany me. I also trust you gentlemen to keep what you have heard here in utmost confidence."

"Of course," they agreed. As they made preparations to leave, Steffan asked Martin Gillis if he would walk with them, saying he urgently needed to talk with him. Martin agreed and they left together. At the same time, Jeff was talking to Commander Pierce.

"Commander Pierce, what are your plans?"

"I'm prepared to train young recruits," he said with a smile. "I hope with as much success as I've had with you."

"Thank you, sir. Oh, by the way," their eyes met, "is there any news on my request for leave," he asked casually, yet he knew before Pierce could answer what he was going to say.

"Your request has been denied," Pierce replied. He did not drop his eyes away from Jeff for he was not ashamed of what he was doing. He believed he was right and he stood firmly on that belief.

"I see," Jeff said quietly. "Do you think it's fair to make a man choose between two such things?"

"Life is always filled with choices. Each of us must do what he thinks is right. I am doing what I feel is right, now the choice is up to you. Knowing you as well as I do, whether you realize it or not, I know the way you will choose for I know the kind of man you are."

Jeff sighed deeply. "I'm confused, I need time to think."

Pierce watched him leave the house and closed the door behind him.

Steffan, as much upset as Jeff, walked beside Martin Gillis in silence. Martin did not interrupt his deep thought, for he knew the mental confusion Steffan's mind was in.

"Mr. Gillis . . . what is the right thing to do?"

"Steffan, I can't tell you that, no one can tell you what's in your heart."

"My parents, my sister, Tom, my friends, everything in the world I have is here. You know I respect the way you feel. Tell me what is right or wrong."

"There is no right or wrong, my boy. This is one time you will have to make a decision without anyone's aid."

"Would . . . would you be disappointed in me if I were to refuse Captain Nelson?"

"I have never been disappointed in you, Steffan. If you were my own son I could not be prouder or love you more. Whatever you do, I am now and always will be your friend."

"I . . . I am not sure."

"Take your time, Steffan. Go on this mission they intend to offer you. Maybe when you're away from all the . . . outside influences, you will find your way easier."

Steffan caught the reference to outside influences and for the first time guilt about his affair with Morgana hit him. He was to meet her later that night and he was determined to make her understand how important it was for her to leave Wade and marry him now. He and Martin walked the balance of the way home in silence.

It was the same for Tom, Lang and Bright. Each of them had been too stunned by what they had just heard to talk much.

"What are you going to do, Tom?" Bright asked.

"I don't know. I'm going to talk it over with Steff and Cecile before I make any decisions. How about you, Lang?"

"Well, I'll tell you, I'm proud of my country and what she's given me, but . . . if Jeff goes, I go with him."

"You feel that Jeff will go?"

"I don't know. In fact, I can only tell you how I feel. I've been with Jeff a long time and I know he will be the best captain any navy has to offer. He's also the best friend outside of you three and Steff that I've ever had. I have enough faith in Jeff that I'll stand on what he thinks is right. Again I say, if Jeff goes, I go with him."

Again there was silence as they each became deeply engrossed in his own thoughts. They said a quiet goodbye to Tom in front of his house. He went inside quietly thinking Cecile might be asleep. Instead, he found her curled up in his favorite chair waiting for him. Tom dragged a small stool in front of the chair and sat upon it. Taking both Cecile's hands in his, he began to explain to her all that was happening.

In the Kyle house, another situation was fomenting. Wade Kyle sat in a large chair in front of his cold fireplace. The fire had gone out hours before. He had beside him on the floor two bottles of whiskey, one empty and the other nearly so. He looked upward at the light sound of footsteps that moved back and forth across the floor above him.

She's getting ready to go to him again, he thought. The knife of tormenting jealousy twisted within him. Why, he thought desperately. Why did he desire her so? Why didn't he just leave her? He questioned himself, but they were the same questions he had asked himself a million times and no matter what he tried to do, he knew the answers would always be the same. Morgana was an illness of his mind and body from which he would never recover. How often had he cried out against it, tried to break the hold she had on him but it was useless. In spite of the fact that she taunted and tormented him and flaunted the lovers she had taken in his face, still one touch, one kiss and the feel of that magically intoxicating body beneath his hands drove him to the brink of insanity. He needed her like a drunkard needed his whiskey amd worse, he knew she knew it.

At the moment he was deep in black, death-filled thoughts. He liked Steffan Devers, admired him for the intelligent, basically good and far too honorable a man that he was. He knew that Morgana could, and on any provocation would destroy him without a second thought.

He knew Morgana was preparing to meet Steffan. He not only knew they met, he knew where and when. Only this time, Morgana, he thought venomously, this time it will end differently.

He sat, like a spider, waiting for the moment she would leave. He planned on giving them enough time to put them in a compromising position. Then he intended to act. At that moment, he did not know if he intended to kill Morgana or Steffan. Maybe, he thought, maybe both.

He was so deep in his thoughts, he did not hear Morgana come down the stairs and leave. He was only roused from his lethargy when he heard the sound of retreating hoofbeats. He waited, slowly sipping the whiskey until the second bottle was also empty. Then he rose from his chair. For a man who had drunk so much, he was surprisingly steady on his feet. About his waist he buckled his sword. From a small table, he took a pistol. Then he went out, saddled his horse and rode toward the two unsuspecting people whose fate he intended to seal.

Steffan paced the floor waiting for Morgana. He could hardly wait to hold her, to tell her that there might be a way they could both be free. If he accepted what Captain Nelson had to offer, they could go to this new country together. She could divorce Wade and no one in America would question who or what they had been. All the way to their meeting place Steffan had turned the matter over and over in his mind. It was their one way out, their one way to be together for always. He was tense with barely controlled nervous energy when he heard the approaching horse. He went to the door and pulled it open at the same time Morgana reached it. Without a word, he pulled her into his arms and kissed her deeply.

"Morgana," he whispered, "God, I want you more every time I see you."

"And I you, my love," she said in her husky voice.

"I must talk to you, Morgana, it's important."

"Later, Steffan, please, it's been days since I've been with you. Don't talk to me now . . . love me."

There was always a wild abandon with Morgana. A sensual passion that bubbled like a flood of molten lead through him. As usual it overcame his senses and all other rational thought. It still, after all the time they had been together, never came to Steffan that he and Morgana shared nothing but passion.

They lay together, so engrossed with one another that they did not hear the door creak open slowly. They did not see the rage-filled, wild eyes of Wade Kyle. He walked toward them slowly. A combination of emotions gripped him and even he was surprised at the direction they took.

His beautiful Morgana, his sensual and passionate wife. He could not, would not lose her . . . even if he had to kill to keep her.

Morgana Kyle smiled to herself. Everything was going as she had planned it. She knew the condition Wade was in when she came home earlier in the evening. She had laughed at his fumbling efforts at bedding her. Morgana wanted Steffan and only Steffan now. She had pushed Wade away and gone to her room where she had made the deliberate noises of preparation. Wade knew she was going to meet another man. Morgana had counted on his being drunk enough and angry enough to follow her. Despite the passion she was pretending, she had kept her ears open for sounds of Wade's approach. She would warn Steffan in time and they would battle, but she had every intention of seeing that the battle ended only one way. Wade Kyle's death. His death at the hands of Steffan Devers would keep Steffan forever in her power. "Steffan," she whispered in his ear, "don't move for a moment. Wade is here. He's by the door watching us and he has a pistol." She could feel Steffan grow tense and still in her arms. "There is a pistol by the bed. If you reach down you could get it. He's drunk, Steffan."

If Steffan had performed as Morgana had thought he would, if he had reached down and taken the pistol she had planted, Wade Kyle would have been dead in a few moments. But Morgana had underestimated Steffan and overestimated her hold on him.

Slowly, so that he would not shock Wade enough to make him fire the pistol he held in his hand, Steffan turned to face Wade Kyle.

"You have to listen to us, give us an opportunity to explain. Morgana and I . . . we're in love and we want to be married."

Steffan was the one to register absolute shock when Wade Kyle threw back his head and laughed. "Married!" he choked out. "Good God, you hopeless bastard, do you really think she would marry you? You're a toy. I must say one toy among many. Morgana will never divorce me. I know too much about her black and sordid past." He looked at Morgana again and his voice became cold.

"Tell him, Morgana. For once in your rotten life, tell him."

Steffan turned to look at Morgana. In her half dressed condition, Morgana's beauty was breathtaking. Her face remained blank as she looked past Steffan at Wade.

"Tell him of the young cadet who killed himself over you, Morgana. Tell him of the boy who put a pistol to his head and shot himself for love of you. Tell him of the long line of other lovers there have been, other lives you have shattered."

"Wade," Morgana's voice was soft as velvet, "why do you have to lie about me? Do you hate me so very much for loving another man instead of you?"

Wade's face became suffused with rage and he took two steps toward Morgana, forgetting for the moment that Steffan was there. At that moment, Steffan leapt for his arm.

Wade Kyle was a much stronger man than Steffan had thought he would be. They fought for possession of the pistol. Wade gave a violent jerk that unbalanced Steffan. He held onto the hand holding the pistol because he knew now, if Wade could get free, one or both of them would be killed. They tumbled to the floor battling silently for possession of the gun. If Steffan had seen

Morgana's face at that moment the fight would have been over. She was on her knees watching them intently, her eyes aglow with a malicious gleam and her lips half parted in a vicious smile. She was sure that Steffan would win, but the idea that they were fighting over her and that one would soon kill the other excited her beyond what any man could hope to do.

Slowly, Steffan's superior strength won out. With a violent jerk, the gun flew from Wade's hand and they both scrambled for it. Wade was on his hands and knees when Steffan retrieved the gun and turned to face Wade. They stood in that one position for a quick moment of frozen silence as Wade looked up at Steffan, who held the pistol a few inches from Wade's face.

"Kill him!" Morgana said in a harsh grating voice, "Kill him!"

Steffan turned his stunned eyes to look at her. Her face was twisted in a violent mask of hatred. Her wide eyes filled with contempt as she stared at Wade. It was only at that moment that Steffan realized Wade had been telling the truth and all that he had shared with his imaginary goddess of beauty had been a lie.

"Yes, Steffan, kill me," Wade said hoarsely. Steffan turned back to see Wade Kyle's eyes filled with anguished tears. "Kill me, and she will twine herself about you like a huge snake and when she has crushed you and there is nothing left but your soul, she will drain it of all happiness and all life until you will be grateful to die. I . . . I almost feel sorry for you."

Morgana leapt from the bed and struck Wade violently across the face, then she turned and threw herself into Steffan's arms. "Kill him, Steffan and the world will be open for us. With all his wealth we can go where we want, do what we want. Just you and me, Steffan. Kill him! Kill him!"

Steffan was speechless. He could not believe what his eyes were telling him was true. In place of the love he thought he had felt for Morgana, grew a feeling even he could not recognize at the moment. All he wanted to do was to be away from this unbearable pain that seemed to be seeping into all of his pores. Without saying a word, he threw the gun directly to Wade and, gathering his clothes quickly, he walked to to door.

"Steffan!" Morgana shouted. "Come back here! What he said was lies, all lies. He just wanted to hurt us. Steffan! Please?"

Steffan could not bear to look back. He almost ran to his horse and, once he was in the saddle, he let the horse have his head and run until he could run no further.

He sat still, frozen immobile like a carved granite statue. He refused to think, refused to open the dam of emotions that were bottled up. Words crowded his mind. I feel sorry for you . . . Kill him! . . . she'll crush you until you have no soul . . . Kill him! . . . She will drain you of all happiness . . . Kill him! . . . Kill him! . . . Kill him!

Steffan cried out against the knowledge that all he had been told about Morgana had been true. All the warnings of her fatal touch had been true. He realized he had to get some control of himself, but he seemed to be flying apart, to be disappearing in all directions. He nudged his horse forward, knowing in the back of his mind that he desperately needed someone to talk to, someone who could help him put the pieces together. He thought then of the one person near who had loved him completely, understood him always, and would listen with sympathy and understanding. He needed a friend more than he had ever needed one in his life.

Martin Gillis had been such a consistent visitor to London that he had finally taken a small house where he alternated his time between London and the Devers estate. It was a blessing that when an exhausted Steffan stumbled to his door, he was there to welcome him. Martin needed only a glance to tell that Steffan was completely distraught. He let him in, then went about preparing a drink . . . a strong drink.

"I . . . I almost killed a man tonight," Steffan said in a hoarse, cracked whisper. "I came within a heartbeat of killing a man who had done me no wrong."

Martin sat down opposite Steffan after he had handed him the drink. Steffan gulped it down as though he were dying of thirst. Martin's face did not register the surprise he felt for he was sure Steffan did not realize he had drunk at all. When the drink finally began to hit him, Martin could see the visible trembling of his hands.

"Steffan, if you tried to kill a man, at the time you must have thought you had a reason. It would be better if you began with the reason and tell me what happened."

Steffan buried his face in his hands and for a few minutes, Martin did not think he was going to say anything. Then slowly, the hands dropped and in a quiet, restrained voice Steffan began to speak. When the words began he could not stop them. He babbled on and on of Morgana, of Wade Kyle and of the nearness of tragedy.

It was almost dawn when Steffan's voice finally died and he sat immobile and silent. "Steffan, what has happened to you is an age-old story. You are not the first man nor will you be the last to

188

love something evil, for evil often has a face that is extremely beautiful. Because you have seen it for what it is, do not feel you are lost, and do not believe that there is no beauty in the world, for there is. Evil cannot love, Steffan. There was no love between you and Morgana Kyle, there was only lust. What happened was the best for you, for Wade Kyle was right. The kind of man you are would have lived in hell with that woman.

"Now you have come to a point in your life where you can only do one of two things. You can let this ruin you and your future or you can accept what happened just for what it was and become a stronger, better man. There is only one person who can make the choice . . . you."

"But I almost killed him."

"No, Steffan, you are not a man who kills. You would not have killed him."

"How do you know?" Steffan asked, his eyes searching Martin's face for some ray of hope and strength he could cling to.

"Because I know the kind of man I helped to raise. You would not have killed him."

"I . . . I can't believe . . . all this time . . . The times I planned what our future would be. She must have been laughing at me all the time. What a fool I must have looked to everyone," Steffan said miserably. "What a damned fool I was."

Martin chuckled lightly and Steffan looked up at him in surprise. "If you expect me to deny that you made a fool of yourself, you're wrong. I agree, you made a fool of yourself, but we all learn our lessons in just such a way. Do you remember Steffan, when I was teaching you to ride?"

"Yes."

"Remember the black stallion Midnight who dumped you in the dust repeatedly making you look like a presumptuous child?"

Even Steffan chuckled in remembrance. "Yes, I never did master him until I was grown. But what has that to do with this?"

"You were wiser then, as a child, than you are now, it seems. You were grown up when the horse finally allowed you to ride. You faced him as a man with strength and purpose and he sensed it. That is the way you must face this problem, too. Either you are going to lie in the dust like a child, or you are going to grow up and face your friends and the rest of your life like a man."

Steffan stood up and walked to the window. Drawing aside the curtains, he stood for quite a while watching the first rays of the early morning sun. Martin could almost hear his thoughts as they began and he saw the straightening of the shoulders, the lift of the chin and heard the deep intake of breath as Steffan accepted what he said and made his choice.

They went out for a walk in the bright early morning sun, then went to Cecile's to rouse them from bed for breakfast.

Tom didn't know what had happened, but he and Cecile sensed the change in Steffan. "Tom, Cecile," he said at the close of the meal, "I know I'm being given some sort of assignment soon. There are a lot of things I want to think over. Let's all go home for a while."

"Sounds wonderful to me," Tom said quickly.

"Marvelous, Steff, Mother has been writing and asking when we're going to come home for a vacation. It will be good for all of us."

Martin and Steffan informed their friends they were going home for a few days. They all agreed that independent thought was a good thing for them all, for one day soon, Horatio Nelson's request would have to answered. Martin knew it was a thing that Steffan wanted to discuss with his parents also.

They packed and made the journey home. Once there, Steffan seemed to relax. He walked the beaches of his childhood, and sat in contemplative silence in his cave of a million stars. He rode, slept, ate and thoroughly absorbed the contentment he always felt here. It was weeks later when Martin noticed the laughter return to Steffan's eyes.

They were walking along the beach one sunny afternoon. "I see you've been taking the young Bradley girl riding occasionally," Martin said.

"Yes, Martha's a nice girl, good company."

"Is that all?"

"It's nothing serious if that's what you're hoping. I think I'll be a little more careful who I give my heart to, next time. It got a little bruised the last time."

"You'll be amazed at the punishment it can take and still go on beating."

"I don't expect to get serious about anyone. I'm going to concentrate on my career. Right now, I don't have time for anything else."

"Ah! I see you've got it all planned out."

Steffan grinned and Martin was delighted to see the old glow of devilment in his eyes.

"I have. I intend to do a magnificent job of whatever this assignment is going to be, and when I stun the Admiralty with my inestimable worth, I'll get a grand promotion. Why who knows, I may one day be admiral.''

Martin laughed, then his face became serious. ''Steffan, have you given thought to Nelson's offer?''

''Yes, some. Jeff is going to accept, you and I both know why. I'm sure Lang and Bright will go with him.''

''And you?''

''I don't know, I honestly don't know. When Nelson talks it all sounds so right and so exciting, but when I'm alone, I remember that I am a son of England amd I owe her a great deal. That is not a thing that is easily forgotten, and then there are Tom and Mack. I'd hate to break up a friendship as good as ours has been and be fighting against each other on different sides of the ocean.''

''Have you talked to your parents about it?''

''Only one of them,'' Steffan laughed. ''I'll speak to the other as soon as I have my own thoughts straight in my mind.''

''When do you have to report back to London?''

''I've another week I can spend at home. This duty they are assigning me should only take at the most a couple of months. We are all meeting in London to make a final commitment one way or another.''

''You're back on an even keel, Steffan.''

''I've a mentor who always seems to have all the right answers to my problems.'' Steffan chuckled. ''I think I've gotten hold of myself.'' His smile faded. ''I've put Morgana out of my mind. There will be no more foolish mistakes like that. I will never see her again and I will never be put in a position to be used to injure another. I've even put all the memories aside. It is a thing that will be forgotten and buried.''

They walked along in quiet conversation, but Steffan was wrong in his thoughts.

Wade Kyle had vanished, simply disappeared from the world that knew him. Only one person knew exactly what had happened to him.

Morgana, the night that Steffan had left her had been in a black and violent rage. Her corrupt mind had turned its evil on Wade. She had again as she always could, seduced Wade into thinking she regretted what she had done, then, coldly and without mercy, she had shot and killed him with his own pistol. She had buried the body in the soft earth behind the cottage where she and Steffan had met so often, and had gone back to their home. She slowly began to accumulate money while she enjoyed the sympathy of well-meaning friends who could not understand why a man would leave a wife as beautiful as she.

Deep inside her burned only one black hate-filled thought; somehow, somewhere, Steffan Devers would pay for leaving her. One day, she would reach out and kill him, kill him with any means she could and make him suffer as much as she could in the process.

Seventeen

The days at home were drawing to a close before Steffan spoke to his father about the choice he needed to make, and again, Maxwell was faced with the same problem. Trying to let Steffan make whatever decisions were best for him, no matter where the decision took him.

"Steffan, if I were to tell you what I really desire, it would be to hold you here as long as possible, to transfer your naval duties to a close port and spend all your time here. I'm sure your mother would be pleased also. But we know we're being selfish, so I will tell you what you should do. You should return to London, take this tour of duty, question everyone about their opinions in this situation between the Colonies and England. Talk to your friends about their plans, and in the end . . . follow your heart, follow your judgment and know that your mother and I stand behind you in whatever you do or wherever you go."

It was a relief for Steffan to know how his parents felt but it did nothing to help him decide what course to take. Tom, Cecile, and Steffan returned to London to await further orders and to be shown, for the first time, the ship they were to command. One of the problems facing Steffan on his return was the possibility of facing Wade Kyle again. He was shocked when he was told the news upon his return that Wade Kyle had deserted both his post at the Academy and his wife. He found himself unable to believe it, and asking discreet questions, found that Wade's disappearance dated back to the fatal night he had almost died at Steffan's hand.

Morgana had also left the house she and Wade had shared near the Academy. In fact, where she was at the moment no one seemed to know. Steffan had a deep suspicion that something more tragic than he realized had happened that fateful night, but there was nothing he could do to prove it. He would have given anything to disprove the words that were said against Wade Kyle. To the surprise of all his friends, he took it upon himself to defend Wade's name whenever it was mentioned. The ones closest

193

to him also knew that the name Morgana Kyle never crossed his lips and wherever and whenever she was mentioned, Steffan had a way of ignoring the conversation that left no doubt in anyone's mind that it was a subject he refused to discuss.

It was only a week later that the small group of them were invited to Tom's and Cecile's home to celebrate their third year of marriage. It was then that Steffan and Jeff took the opportunity to discuss their plans.

"Have you given it a lot of thought, Jeff?"

"Yes, I've thought of nothing else since that night at Commander Pierce's home. Bright, Lang and I have talked it over a million times. There is only one way for me, Steffan. When Nelson leaves for America, I'm going with him. I'm not sure but I think Lang and Bright will be going also. I intend to find Brandy and my son before her indenture is up and she's gone. I'll build my future in the Navy there, win or lose, but either way, the way I see it, I have nothing to gain and everything to lose if I stay. What about you, Steff, have you made any decisions yet?"

"I've talked to everyone whose thoughts mean anything to me, and I find I get the same answers from all of them. The decisions are mine . . . so, I'm going to take Mr. Gillis' advice. I'm putting the decision aside until this tour of duty is over. By then, maybe my thoughts will be clearer or I'll have found some reasoning to help me decide."

"What about Tom?"

"Tom's life is here, Cecile would never leave home to go to a strange land and start a new life, especially with their first baby due."

"It's strange isn't it, all the new paths our lives are taking since the first day we came to the Academy?"

"I guess, as Mr. Gillis puts it, that's the only thing that never changes, the fact that everything changes. Anyway, I'm not going to think about it any more. Maybe if I'm lucky by the time this tour of duty is over, the whole argument will be peacefully settled and there will be no need for decisions. In the meantime, let's just enjoy the party."

"Good idea," Jeff laughed as he retrieved two glasses of champagne from a passing maid. "Here's to the settling of all arguments."

"I'll drink to that," Steffan grinned in return. They were joined by Cecile and Tom, who raised their glasses in quick agreement to the hope that no conflict was going to separate them.

"Steffan, have you gotten word about our ship yet, or when

194

we're leaving?'' Tom questioned.

"Got some papers this morning. We're to be at the dock entrance at seven sharp tomorrow. We're to get a tour plus a personal introduction to the *Godolphin*. After that we'll go to Commander Pierce's office where he'll fill us in on where we're going, for how long, and most important, why.''

"I'm getting excited,'' Tom laughed.

"Getting excited,'' Cecile said teasingly, "he's been dreaming of this at night. I swear if that ship had a woman's name I would have some cause for jealousy. He's been mumbling about the *Godolphin*. Can you imagine if she were called Jezebel or some such?''

"Yes, it's a good thing we didn't get the *Margaret* or I might have had a lot of explaining to do,'' Tom agreed. The laughter was contagious and the party warmed with enthusiasm. It was some time later when Steffan and Cecile found themselves alone together.

"Steff, Tom has told me about the offer Captain Nelson has made you. I know that Jeff is going. What are you going to do?''

"I'm not sure, brat,'' he smiled down into her golden eyes that so clearly mirrored his own. "All I love is here in England. If I go, I'll be leaving home, Mother and Father, you, Tom and my nephew. I think it's just too much to give up no matter how much I'm beginning to sympathize with the cause.''

"Steff, I just wanted to tell you. You know how much Tom admires you and how anxious he is to sail as your second in command.''

"Tom's the best there is. It will be good to know I have someone like him on my first tour.''

"What I'm trying to say is . . . when you make up your mind what you're going to do, would you let Tom be the first to know?''

"Why, Cecile?''

"Because,'' she said coyly, "I'll need time to pack and get everything ready to go.''

"To go . . . you mean you would go too, . . . you and the baby to a strange country and start all over?''

"I know that Tom would rather die than leave me just as I know it would kill him a little to have you sail without him and know you might be fighting against each other tomorrow. I love Tom, and I want him happy. That's the most important thing in my life and if it means crossing the world with him, I'll do it.''

"I'm so proud of you, Cecile; have I ever told you that before?

Tom's a lucky man. I appreciate the way you both feel and when I make my decision, I promise you'll be the first to know."

Steffan walked home alone that night. He wanted time to think. The wilder spirit in him, usually kept under tight control, was given free rein. To go to a new country, to carve out a career for himself independent of everything he'd known before was exciting. Comparing this with what he would leave behind, left him as confused by the time he reached his quarters as he was when he had left them earlier.

Steffan arrived on the dock at six-thirty only to find Tom already there. To Tom, who had been raised around ships all his life, this was like being home. He knew everything about each ship berthed here and just about all her particulars. To keep their nerves settled, Steff listened while Tom rattled off information about each.

"Look at that one, Steff," he said, pointing to the closest. "Do you know the name?"

"Nope, but I bet you could tell me."

"She's the *L'Abenakise*. She was built in Quebec. They built her for the French Navy but our *Unicorn* captured her for us."

"Sorry, old boy, you're wrong," Steffan grinned. "She is the *Aurora*. Her name is on the side."

"I'm never wrong, Steff. They must have renamed her."

Their conversation was interrupted by the arrival of Commander Pierce. Just to soothe his own ruffled feathers, Tom pointed to the ship under discussion. "Do you know her background, sir?"

"Yes, she's the *Aurora*," Commander Pierce said and Steffan grinned broadly, but his grin was cut short as Commander Pierce went on. "She was the *L'Abenakise* out of Quebec but we renamed her. We took her in and mounted thirty-six guns. She's about one hundred forty-six feet of deck, has a fifteen foot depth of hold and goes about nine hundred and forty-six in tonnage. Any other questions?"

"No, sir," Tom laughed. "I'm sure we're both satisfied."

"You were going to take us on a tour of our ship, sir," Steffan said pointedly ignoring Tom's silent laughter.

"Yes, come along. We'll make this a hasty visit, for I want to go over your duties with you. This is a rather unusual task we want you to undertake. It requires some explanation."

He motioned them to follow him; they did rapidly for he was already walking ahead of them. He stopped in front of the ship they were to command and both Steffan and Tom gazed at her in open-mouthed wonder. She was a twenty-eight gun frigate whose construction had been completed only the year before. She was armed with a mixture of twelve pounders and eighteen pounders which made her one of the most powerful frigates of her rate in the port. She carried a crew of 170 men. Her length overall was one hundred forty-four feet and the length of the deck was one hundred twenty-seven feet.

As a class, the frigate was one of the very best. They were fast, maneuverable and good fighters in bad weather. They were at their best when speed and independence were required.

Steffan could hear his heart thud as Commander Pierce escorted them aboard, and Tom, who knew ships better than the others, was almost licking his lips in anticipation. A few minutes after they were aboard, Tom requested permission to go below deck. When it was granted, Steffan smiled to himself. Tom would go over every inch of the ship and by the time they were ready to leave, he would know just how well built she was, of what materials she was built and exactly what she could and could not do in any situation. He was right, Tom did not appear until an hour later with a definite gleam in his eye and a smile of pure pleasure on his lips. They went to Commander Pierce's office to be told exactly what their mission would be. Once there, he motioned them to a seat and took a large rolled map that stood in a corner near his desk and unrolled it. Bracing both sides with a weight to keep it stationary, he stood and looked at the two young men seated before him.

"There are a lot of extenuating circumstances surrounding the task we're sending you on. I feel I must explain them so you will understand completely the situation you will be involved in and exactly what is expected of you. First, since no war has been declared between the Colonies and England, it is difficult for us to send you there in an official capacity. In fact . . . you will not be in uniform nor will you fly Britain's colors until you return. In short . . . you will be going as a privateer."

Stefan and Tom exchanged looks of surprise.

"Just what are we after, sir?" Tom queried.

"A smuggler."

"A smuggler," Steffan answered quickly. "Isn't smuggling a problem for local authorities?"

"Not when what they are smuggling are arms and ammunition meant for British troops and ships in America but somehow find their way into the wrong hands. They are lifted from under our noses and we don't know how or by whom."

"Maybe you'd best start at the beginning, sir," Steffan suggested.

"Good idea . . . well, let's see. It began about six months ago when the third ship to leave here carrying arms disappeared."

"Disappeared?"

"Vanished off the face of the earth as far as we knew then."

"Then what happened?"

"We sent out another . . . a well-armed vessel disguised as a merchant ship. We sent her along the same route. She was attacked, so the captain said, by the fastest damn frigate he's ever seen. What will really take you by surprise is that the entire ship was bright red, sails and all and she flew a bright red flag with a golden butterfly imprinted on it. When they were hailed to heave to the captain swears it was a woman who hailed them. Whoever the captain was . . . man or woman . . . was wearing red also. It was highly insulting, as though they thought that even if they were bright red we couldn't follow or catch them on the open sea. The captain was so angry he opened fire too soon. The frigate, once she realized it was a trap, turned about, . . . and though he tried to follow her, the captain swears she just simply . . . vanished."

"Commander Pierce," Steffan laughed. "A frigate just can't disappear."

"I know that, damn it! But that's what the captain said she did."

"Where is the nearest place to there, she could have run to?"

"That's the rub of it. The nearest place is an island. An island owned by a very wealthy man who is one hundred percent loyal to England. Captain Brady went directly there and searched thoroughly. There was no sign of her and I'm sure it would be quite difficult to hide a ship painted bright red."

"What island is it?"

"Here," Commander Pierce pointed on the map. They both rose and bent over the map. An island marked on the map had a small 'x' on it. It was the only land area marked for miles. There was obviously no other land in the area.

"Marriott Island," Tom read.

"Yes, owned by Andrew Marriott. An extremely wealthy man who decided he liked the privacy of his own island. He built on the northern end of it the most beautiful mansion you could imagine. He has granted the Navy a small portion of the southern tip for a training area. There has sprung up about the naval base a small village where naval personnel are housed. Not far from this is another small village where the workers and their families employed by Andrew Marriott are housed. The balance of the island is strictly Marriott property and very few trespass unless specifically invited.''

"What exactly do you want us to do, sir?''

"The way we think is this. Someone, somewhere on the island knows who the scarlet ship belongs to, where they're storing the arms once they've taken them, and where the hell three ships and almost four hundred men have gone. Not only that, but where that ship hides. It can't deliver the arms to America; it has to transfer the cargo to another ship . . . when, where, how, and most important of all . . . who.''

"That's all you want us to find out?'' Tom laughed.

Pierce smiled. "I know it's a rather large order but we've got to find out. I for one, would like to know just how secure their operation is.''

Steffan looked closely at Commander Pierce who was frowning deeply as he studied the map. Again the touch of instinct nudged him. Did Pierce want to know about this organization to stop it, or to use the British Navy to find out just how vulnerable they were. He knew that eventually Pierce was going to resign his position and go to America. Was this a future plan or did he already work for the American cause?

"We're painting out the name *Godolphin* temporarily, for her name is known. Feel free to name her whatever you want for this journey. I also leave it up to you to devise an excuse to be stopping at Marriott Island.''

"When and if we discover what you want to know, just how do we report our findings? Do we come back here?''

"No, if you find the answers to our questions, you will go to the naval base. We will have the Brig *Stewart* anchored there. She'll report your findings to us while you stay on top of the situation.''

Steffan was curious about the frowning look on Tom's face at the mention of the *Stewart,* but he held his questioning until later. If Tom said nothing about what upset him in front of Commander Pierce, it was because he didn't want him to know.

"When do we leave, sir?''

"Tomorrow at dawn.'' He held his hand out to Steffan and to Tom. "Good luck to you both.''

"Thank you, sir.''

They left the commander's office and walked together slowly back to Tom's home.

"Well, what shall we name her?" Tom said.

"Let's see" Steffan grinned. "We could call her *Searcher* or *Surprise* or . . ."

"Or . . . *Entrappe*" Tom laughed.

"Why don't we just call her *Cecile*. I think it would please her."

"The name might but the mission sure won't."

"Why did the mention of the *Stewart* upset you, Tom?"

"I take it you have no idea who captains the *Stewart*?"

"No, who?"

"Captain Jaspar Sinclair."

"Great," Steffan replied. "That was just about all I needed to complete a perfect day. Given a mission that is almost impossible. Given a problem like changing countries to think over then given the added blessing of Jaspar Sinclair to report to."

"I wouldn't put it past Jaspar to inform on you and get you killed somewhere near that island."

"We'll have to keep an eye on him. I agree with you, I don't believe I could trust him any further than I could toss him."

"You watch what we're doing and I'll report to Jaspar . . . and keep an eye on him."

"I know you're dying to tell me about our ship. I suppose I should put you out of your misery and let you extol all her virtues."

Tom chuckled. "She's from home, Steff."

"What?"

"Just what I said. She's off my father's line. I know his work anywhere. Only, Steff, this ship is going to be a miracle of speed if I know my ships. First things, she's got a round tuck stern, no drag. She's got an oak frame, her keel is one huge oak. They used locust wood trunnels, and my father had been toying with a new idea when I left. Usually, the planks are cut from naturally curved wood, but my father heard of this new invention, a steam box that impregnates the wood with steam then bent to the shape they wanted. None of her timber is green so she's not likely to rot too soon. And Steff, did you notice the amount of sail she can carry?"

"No."

"First off, she's got studding sails and royals. God, Steff, she's got enough canvas to make her the fastest thing in the water today. Talk about virtues, Steff, she'll be the prettiest virgin that ever got seduced by a couple of lucky sailors. If I'm any judge, Steff, Pierce gave us the swiftest ship he could find. He must mean for us to chase down this scarlet shadow one way or another even if we have to take the chance of splitting the masts with all the canvas she's got. She's even rigged to mount staysails between the masts. She's got perfect balance and she ought to steer like a gem. It's going to be a pleasure to serve on her and an even greater one to tell my father about it.''

"Well, with all this enthusiasm, I can hardly wait to take hold of the wheel.''

"You've got a real treat in store for you, and I think the days of our scarlet shadow are numbered. Pierce is going to be happy when you come back with that red ship as a trophy.''

"I wonder?''

"What do you mean, you wonder?''

"We both know Pierce is planning on going with Nelson. I'm wondering if he doesn't know just a little more about this than he will admit. After all, he's not quite sure yet just where we stand.''

"I don't understand, Steff. If he knew why would he send us to find it?''

"Think about it, Tom. If you had an operation like this going on and the Admiralty was down on your back for not stopping it, what would you do?''

"I guess it's pretty obvious, isn't it? I should have known when a couple of fresh graduates like us are given a task like this. He expects us to fail and fall flat on our face. Then the operation goes on and he can tell the Admiralty he's done all he could to stop it.''

"And?''

"And what?''

"And if we decide to join Nelson, we're right there where we can do the most good.''

"Damn!''

"Yes,'' Steffan agreed. "I think he hopes we'll find some reason while we're there to join forces with them.''

"He mentioned Andrew Marriott, the man who owns the island, is completely loyal to England. You think that's not true?''

"Any man who becomes a millionaire and owns his own island, who can run a business from some mansion on a cliff, and successfully, can't be the kind of man who doesn't know what's going on either on his own island or around it. We'll have to be very careful and find out just where Andrew Marriott's loyalties really lie. But I've a feeling there's a whole lot more to this situation than we know and I'm damn angry at being used like a boy.

If Pierce really wants to see what we can find, then, by damn, we're going to do our best to really find it. I won't have my choices made for me and I won't be pushed into doing something unless I believe in it.''

"There's only one thing wrong with that logic, Steff."

"What?"

"Maybe Pierce wanted to see what we could find, but if he didn't really want us to catch them . . . why did he give us what I consider the fastest thing that could sail?"

"Because, he either didn't have any control of what we got, or he remembered that you and your father built ships all your life and if anyone knew ships, you would. There really was no way of fooling you, now was there?"

"No, I guess not. Boy, he must think we're really naive."

"I don't know what he thinks and I really don't care. From tomorrow morning on, we're going to do our own thinking and make our own decisions. We'll find his scarlet ship and when we do, we'll ask some questions of our own."

Steffan's voice faded to a whisper as they walked up the steps of Tom's house.

They were welcomed by Cecile who had kept a warm meal waiting for them. While they ate, Tom told her all that he was allowed to tell.

James Pierce made his way to Martin Gillis' small house. There he drew a chair close to the table around which sat Horatio Nelson, Jones, and Gillis.

"Well, they will be on their way tomorrow at dawn. We will find out for sure, gentlemen, just how secure our operation is. We've sent a message to our friend to stay away from this particular ship."

"Do you think your message will be obeyed?" Martin questioned worriedly. "You know just how unpredictable our friend can be."

"Our friend! Our friend! Damn it, I hate this negotiating with a third party as though they cannot trust us. I've been keeping the Navy's nose out of this little action for over six months. I also hate dealing with these fanatical patriots. Don't they know we have the same cause in mind?"

"Rest easy, James," Martin said. "Our friend is not a fanatical patriot. Merely a patriot who wants to do the best for the cause. You must admit we have done well so far."

"Yes, dealing with someone we've never even seen. I almost wish war would finally be declared. At least then, everything is fought in the open, not shady behind-the-back type of things. I chose where I would stand a long time ago."

"As have I," Nelson replied quietly. "But we all must do our part in this. Soon, we will all go where we rightfully belong. In the meantime, it is of the utmost importance that those arms get where they are needed most."

"I know," sighed James. "But still, it goes against the grain to be involved in smuggling."

"The ship you gave Steffan and Tom," Martin said. "Just what was it?"

"I know what you're getting at," James laughed. "Young Tom knows his vessels well. Believe me, Martin, neither Tom nor Steffan will have anything against the *Godolphin*. She's a beauty, I don't know if Tom will recognize it or not, but it was built in the Braydon Shipyard. As soon as I saw it nearly finished, I knew it would be perfect for this mission. I commissioned it personally. You and I both have pride in the training we've given these men. I wouldn't trust the *Godolphin* to anyone more than I would Tom and Steffan. Nor would I put these two in any kind of danger without the very best we have to offer. If our message gets through, then they will search in vain for that phantom ship and those lost arms. I will be able to say I have given our best in the search. Within four months, the arms should be delivered. Tom and Steffan will return a little more experienced and maybe with the help of young Sables and his friends, we will be able to convince them to join us. The results of this trip should only prove that all our timing and work are done to perfection."

"I hope you're right," Martin replied.

"Do you think I would have sent two excellent men and one remarkable ship out if the Admiralty hadn't forced me to? Do you think I really want them to find out what's going on before the right time?"

"Of course not, James. We only have to wait now and see what happens."

None of the men present were too contented with the events that had just come to pass. If they had seen another event that was happening they would have been less contented. A small ship tossing in a wildly tumultuous storm. Her masts cracking and her planking splitting under the tremendous force of an enraged ocean. After fighting valiantly for her life, she was forced to surrender to the strength of the mighty waves. She sank, and with her sank the message to the mysterious captain of the red ship. The captain would never know that the *Godolphin* which would be heading her way soon, was not to be touched.

Eighteen

Cecile was delighted that their first ship was to be named after her. "It's almost as if I were going along," she said.

"Have you made all the arrangements for going home, Cecile?" Steffan questioned.

"Yes, Papa's coming for me tomorrow. I wanted to be here to say goodbye to Tom."

"I wanted to take her home last week, but she refused to go. I don't know who's more stubborn, you or Cecile."

"I'll be here," Cecile said with finality,"when you leave, and I'll be here when you get home."

Tom's eyes glowed with love as he looked at Cecile and for a minute Steffan was filled with an acute sense of jealousy at the emotion that seemed to connect Tom and Cecile with an invisible chain.

"Well, since I'm stuffed with good food, I think I'll go home," Steffan said as he stood up slowly and stretched. "Morning's going to come pretty early."

Tom watched Steffan kiss his sister a quick goodnight and close the door behind him. When Cecile turned toward him, he could see the sparkle of unshed tears in her eyes and he knew they felt the same about Steffan. They wished he could find the happiness that could soothe the injury he had received and make him the way he used to be.

"Oh, Tom, how I wish he had never met Morgana Kyle. She's hurt him and nobody can reach in and touch the wound."

"Give him time, Cecile," Tom said gently as he slid his arms about her and held her close. "One day someone will come along to make Steff forget everyone who came before. There's nothing we can do except be around if he needs us. In the meantime, have a little faith in him, Cecile; Steff will find his way."

Cecile slid her arms about his waist and smiled up at him.

"I do love you, Mr. Braydon, and I shall miss you desperately while you're gone."

"Not nearly as much as I shall miss you, my sweet," he said.

He gently touched her lips several times with his, pleased with the warmth that kindled in her eyes. "We should be back in about three months," his eyes twinkled mischievously, "your figure should change somewhat while I'm gone. I expect to come home and find you round and ripe like a pear."

Cecile's laughter matched his. "Then you'd best take all the advantage you have tonight. I'm afraid you'll be a hungry man by the time you get your next opportunity." They laughed together, but it was in truth the most memorable night they would ever spend together. It was the sweetest memory Tom would carry with him in the days to come.

Tom and Steffan met at the gangplank of the *Cecile* before the sun rimmed the horizon. In the half gray light of early dawn, the docks were a quiet, deserted place. All that could be heard was the light sound of the lapping of water against the side of the ship and the echo of their footsteps as they came aboard.

The rising sun found her sails unfurled and the *Cecile* moving with the light breeze toward the neck of the harbor and into the open sea. The rising curl of foam beneath the bow told them of the touch of the ocean's heavy tide. Steffan spun the wheel and felt the solid lift beneath his feet as the rudder rode deeply into the sea and moved the *Cecile* like a gentle feather on the crest.

Steffan's first desire was to test the *Cecile's* speed. The mainsail up, he ordered on all sails except the extension sails, royals and studding sails. He felt the *Cecile* leap ahead and even Steffan was amazed at the speed she acquired. His eye caught Tom's grin of complete satisfaction and pride in the Braydon ships.

The weather favored them for the next few days with a fair breeze and calm sea. Steffan made himself acquainted, with Tom's help, with the *Cecile*. They went over her from bow to stern and found nothing to criticize in any way. In the meantime, he also made himself acquainted with the men who served under him and had begun to have a good bit of admiration for his sailing ability and his pride in them. He and Tom were sitting in his cabin sharing a late meal and a drink when they were six nights out of port.

"Have you checked our location in the last few hours, Tom?"

"Yes, we're about three days away from Marriott Island."

"Good."

"Have you come up with any good reason for us to stop there?"

"No, but I'll think of something before we sight land. I was thinking of some repairs on the ship but I don't have the heart to damage any part of her just to make my claim legitimate."

"Mmmm, I agree. I don't think I could do her any harm either."

"Maybe a good night's sleep will help me think of something."

"I've got to make my rounds and check the maps, then I guess I'll go to bed, too."

Tom rose and left the cabin. For a few minutes, Steffan sat motionless at the table. The slow rise and fall of the ship created a lulling atmosphere and for an unguarded moment, he let his mind slip into the past. To the beauty of her face and the warmth of her willing body. Then, catching himself, he shook off the unwanted memories. Slowly, he undressed for bed. Dreams came to him. Disconnected dreams. Faces blended together, then suddenly in his deepest dreams, she came, a soft wraith that blended into his arms and gave him a deep sense of peace and contentment as he had never felt before. But as suddenly as she had come, she was gone. Before he could see her face, she was pulled from him and disappeared into the mist-shrouded dream.

He felt someone roughly shaking his arm as he came up slowly from the depths of his dreaming. Pale rays of the early morning sun told him he had passed the entire night, yet he felt tired and the need to slip back into that more pleasing world.

"Cap'n, sir . . . Cap'n Devers, sir," came the insistent voice accompanying the again urgent shaking of his arm. He blinked his eyes open and and looked up at the bearded face that bent over him.

"Mr. Potter, what is the matter?"

"Mr. Braydon, sir. He says will you come up on deck as fast as you can."

"What's happening?"

"We've sighted a ship coming in at us from out of the rising sun. We can't make her out, sir, but if I didn't know better and know it was the reflection of the sun . . . why, sir, I'd swear that ship was red from topsail to keel."

Now Steffan jerked himself completely awake and grabbed for his clothes. Within five minutes, he was on the quarterdeck beside Tom. "Where is she Tom?"

"Coming directly against us from the sun. I expect she doesn't think we see her yet. There's no doubt about it, Steff. She's as red as blood . . . and, from the way she's bearing down, she's the fastest thing I've ever seen."

"She can't be mounting much cannon if she's moving that fast. She must think we're another plum carrying arms."

"Shall I man all the guns?"

"No . . . no, in fact keep them pulled back and hidden, let her come a little closer. Let's get a good look at her and find out what she wants. I'd like to have a few words with this . . . scarlet butterfly." He laughed in expectation of having the good luck to run across his adversary so soon and have the element of surprise more on his side than on hers.

They stood in silence watching the red menace bear down upon them with a speed that surprised them both.

"He's a damn good sailor, whoever he is," Steff said softly.

"This amazes me," Tom replied.

"What?"

"Where the hell you could hide a ship painted blood red? The fellow's got a lot of nerve. It's like being slapped in the face then daring you to come after her. Kind of insulting isn't it?"

"Well, this time, he's in for a big surprise."

The ship was getting close enough now for them to no longer be able to ignore her presence. Steff shortened sail and ran up his colors as though he were an innocent merchant. He allowed the red ship to come within hailing distance. Then, he got his second shock of the day. For it was definitely a woman's voice that called to them. He shaded his eyes and saw her standing on the quarterdeck. She was tall and very slender, yet her form shouted female even across the span of water. She wore a man's red shirt and black pants that clung to her like a second skin. Knee boots and a wide black sash about her waist accentuated the lithe figure. Her hair was bound in some kind of scarf that hid it completely and shading her eyes was a black mask.

"My God," Tom whispered in amazement, "I don't believe this."

"Ahoy, the *Cecile*!" came the laughing feminine voice across the water.

"Who are you and what do you want," Steffan shouted back.

He heard her deep throaty laughter and had the urge to grab her and rip that mask away and beat her soundly.

"You've got ten guns pointed directly amidships. We could hardly miss at this range. Haul down your sails and prepare to be boarded. You've a cargo of arms I need. I'm sure you're wise enough not to want a cannonball dropped among them."

"We're on the King's business. What you are doing is high treason," Steffan shouted back. "They'll hang you when they catch you."

"First they have to catch me," came back the reply accompanied by muffled laughter aboard. "And I don't think your country has anything afloat nor a captain who can."

Tom muttered a mild curse and even Steffan could feel the rise of anger.

"Nervy witch, isn't she?" Tom said

"Let's see how nervy she is when she's looking down the barrel of our cannon and finds out we have no arms aboard to be afraid of."

"We're a ship carrying messages for His Majesty," he shouted. "What you are doing is treason."

No reply came for a few minutes and they could see her say something to the man who stood by her side. Then her cannon spoke for her. She had aimed at masts and sails. Steffan could hear the cannonballs rip through the rigging, tearing at the sails and splitting the foremast. Now he became truly angry.

"This is His Majesty's ship. We have no arms, but we do have cannon that are pointed down your throat. Now it is your turn to decide how quickly you can surrender."

The laughter on the ship was cut short as Steffan gave the order to uncover the gun ports. They were frozen when they heard her next shouted words. "Before you do anything foolish, look behind you, captain."

Steffan and Tom whirled about to see the large ship that had come up behind them. Everyone had been concentrating so hard on their one point of danger they had let the larger ship come up on them completely unaware. Caught between them, Steffan knew his ship would not stand a chance nor the men aboard her. If he was angry before it was nothing to the cold hard fury he felt now.

He looked at Tom, whose face was white. His clenched jaw spoke of his anger. Anger at their own stupidity for thinking she was the only danger they faced.

"I'm going to let her come aboard. She'll have to have proof that we carry no arms. When she finds none, we'll have at least met. There's no way she can pull the same trick twice and if she stays in these waters, by Christ, I'll find her and run those cannon down her throat."

He ordered the sails furled and though it only stoked the fires of his anger he hauled down his colors. One ship came up on each side of them, grappling hooks were tossed and the red ship was pulled close alongside. The woman was the first aboard. Despite his anger, Steffan had to admire her physical beauty. The white flash of her smile made him wonder what she looked like. He vowed he would one day rip that mask from her face. Her first order sent men scrambling below decks. They came back to affirm his claim. There were no arms aboard. She stood in front of Steffan and he could read the mischievous glitter in her eyes. "You're a privateer. What made you believe I would swallow your story about being on the King's business?"

"I thought you might have sense enough not to harm one of His Majesty's ships, but," Steffan said coolly, "I see you are either not intelligent enough to know how foolish you would be, or foolhardy enough to not realize what it would cost you." The smile on her face faded and bright anger glittered in her eyes. Steffan grinned, then added another broadside, "Of course, now, I find that you're both."

Then the smile returned again.

"I could sink you now, captain, and no one would be the wiser. You'd best hold your tongue and not try my anger any further."

"I guess I was right. You're not very intelligent, are you?" he said coldly and was pleased again to see bright hard fury. "You're not going to sink me without a fight. You'll have to back off to use your cannon and when you do, don't think for a minute I shall sit here and let you sink us."

She contemplated his words in silence. Then suddenly she smiled again.

"I've really no use for you, captain, but to sink this beauty would be a shame. I'm going to release you, but get out of these waters. The next time I will know you and you will not be as lucky." She knew he intended to follow her if possible. She turned quickly and gave an order to her men. They immediately herded all his men below decks and locked them in. Steffan's and Tom's hands were bound and then tied to the rail. When all her men were gone, she walked over to Steffan. With a quick move she took a slender knife from her belt and plunged it into the rail between his hands. "By the time you get free and release your men, captain, we will be gone. Mark my words and put these waters behind you."

"If and when I find you," Steffan growled, "you will regret this."

Her laughter tinkled again and Steffan's face flushed with the urge to get his hands about her throat.

"Now, now, captain," she chided. "Such evil thoughts. Is that the way a gentleman treats a lady?"

"An opponent, yes . . . I see no ladies present here."

She stiffened, then the smile reappeared. Slowly, deliberately, she came so close that they almost touched. He could smell the soft faint perfume she wore and his masculine body sensed her soft femininity. She reached up and took hold of his face and drew it down to hers. The kiss she gave him could have burnt his ship to a cinder. He was stunned for a moment, then he heard her whisper. "Goodbye, captain. May we never meet again. I should hate to kill a man as handsome as you."

"Our paths will cross again. That I swear," he replied. For another moment she was there, then just as suddenly she was gone. Immediately Steffan began to scrape his bonds against the sharp blade. In about fifteen minutes, he was free. He released Tom and they unlocked the doors, freeing their men. He gave swift orders to use whatever sails were usable. Then he set their course for Marriott Island.

Tom watched him pace the deck in cold hard anger. He did not know that Steffan could still feel the soft fiery brand of her lips against his. It had awakened in him a feeling he refused to acknowledge or put a name to. It also made him renew his vow to find her and remove that mask. "What are we going to do now, Steff?"

"Exactly what we started out to do. Our lady friend has just given us the excuse we need to stop at Marriott Island. She's somewhere very near. I don't know how you hide a ship like that, but by damn, I'll find her and when I do, she'll regret ever stepping foot on my ship."

Steffan went to his cabin, and Tom's smile did not break through until Steffan was gone. No matter what had happened to his ship, Tom was delighted at what had happened to her captain. He had seen a glint in Steffan's eyes he had not seen for a very long time and he was filled with jubilation at its return. The gauntlet had been thrown in his face and Steffan had accepted the battle. He was the old Steffan again, and Tom knew it was the exciting, seductive kiss she had so casually given him that whetted his appetite for challenge. He turned to look out over the open sea in the direction the ship had disappeared. He raised his hand and saluted silently in her direction.

"Thank you, my lady, for giving us back a friend. I almost hope you get away with whatever it is you're doing."

It took them better than three days to limp into the private harbor of Andrew Marriott. Safely anchored, Steffan and Tom rowed ashore and requested permission to see Andrew Marriott.

Andrew had offices on the dock and chance had it that he was there at the time. When word was brought to him, he came out immediately to meet them. His handclasp was firm and strong. Andrew was a tall, heavily built man and Steffan soon realized the weight was mostly muscle. He had hard-chiseled features that looked as if they had been carved from granite. A hawk-like nose above which he saw a pair of intelligent green eyes. He looked over their shoulders at the ship in the harbor.

"Gentlemen, did you run afoul a storm?"

"Yes, sir," Steffan replied, "a rather bad storm. We are requesting permission to dock here until repairs can be made to make us seaworthy again."

"Of course, of course. Feel free to use my harbor as long as necessary. Come to my home tonight, gentlemen. We will have dinner together and you can tell me about your recent adventure." They agreed but when dinnertime arrived, Tom was deeply involved in the ship's repairs.

"You go on, Steff. I think I'll stay here tonight and work."

Steffan hired a carriage and was driven to the mansion of Andrew Marriott. Steffan had been used to luxury all his life, but the mansion of Andrew Marriott took his breath away by its beauty. The man had obviously spent a small fortune to create this little bit of heaven and Steffan found himself wondering why.

He was greeted by his host and made welcome. Andrew poured Steffan a drink and waved him to a seat in front of a large, cosily burning fireplace while they awaited dinner.

They talked aimlessly for a while about the conditions in England: trade, politics. And after a while, Steffan realized that Andrew was waiting for someone else. "Most likely his wife" Steffan thought.

"Tell me" Andrew said, "what happened to your ship?" It was not a storm?"

"It wasn't a storm of nature, sir, it was more the interference of man . . . or should I say woman."

"Woman?"

"We were waylaid by pirates, sir, headed by a woman in a ship of scarlet and dressed in scarlet."

"Why, there hasn't been a woman pirate since Anne Bonney."

"Well, there is now, sir, and if I ever cross her path again, she will regret the day she damaged the *Cecile*."

Tamara took . . . an exceptional amount of time in preparation for dinner that night.

She had chosen a gown of black lace over green satin, a green that was almost the same shade as her eyes. Her deep golden-red hair was caught up on her head in a mass of thick shiny curls bound with matching green ribbon. Fringes of curls framed her face and her slender neck. About her throat, she wore the pearls her father had given her. A dab of perfume at her throat, ears and wrist and she stood and surveyed herself.

"Mellie?"

"Yes, Miss Tamara?"

"Go down and see if father's guest has arrived."

"Yes, Miss Tamara," she dimpled. "If you want to make a grand entrance, you sure did pick a good dress to do it in. I swear Miss Tamara, if you breathe too deep, you're going to pop right out of it. I think you're Papa's going to have fits when he see it."

"Scoot, Mellie," she replied in mock sternness and heard Mellie's laughter as she closed the door behind her. Tamara regarded herself in the mirror, wondering herself at the flush of color in her cheeks and the strange fluttery feeling in the pit of her stomach. The gown was revealing; hardly covering the soft roundness of her breasts, it made her look distinctly feminine. "That is my purpose," she told herself, complete contrast to the last time he had seen her. But her mind told her differently. She wanted to see the look in his eyes she had so often seen in Mikel's and David's. The closest Tamara had ever come to love was a soft, gentle inexperienced kiss. She was playing with fire and she knew it. Every day that he spent here, her chances of being discovered were greater, yet she didn't want him to go.

Mellie returned, her eyes aglow and her cheeks pink from running up the stairs. "He's here, Miss Tamara, my goodness he is beautiful. They're waiting for you in the drawing room." Mellie's eyes twinkled, "If he were waiting for me, he wouldn't have to wait long. I bet there's a string of broken hearts from here to England."

"Mellie," Tamara said in exasperation, "he's a man like any other man."

"Miss Tamara, I have six brothers and tons of cousins who drag all their friends home; I've seen my share of men and I'm telling you he ain't like all the others. You ain't going to be able to tease and play with him like you do all the boys at the fort, and he ain't the kind of man you can lead around by the nose. If I were you, I'd be careful, he's dangerous."

Mellie realized her mistake the moment the words left her lips. Telling Miss Tamara to be careful or that something was dangerous was like waving a red flag in front of a bull. She groaned inwardly when she saw the wicked glitter in Tamara's eyes.

"Would you care to make a wager, Mellie?" Tamara asked.

"No, Ma'am I wouldn't," Mellie said firmly. "I am not goin' to be no more party to you gettin' into trouble than I already am. Ain't it enough I cover for you when you go off on one of those trips you take. I don't know what you're up to, but I am not goin' to get in any deeper. I have to face your father."

Tamara's laughter sounded at Mellie's distress. "Don't worry so much, Mellie. He's no danger to me. He'll be leaving the island in a few days and we'll never see him again. What's the harm in a little flirting?"

"Miss Tamara!" she said, frowning. How could she warn Tamara of what she didn't know. "I'm tellin' you, you can't flirt and play with that kind of man. He's got rules of his own and all you can get is hurt."

"Hurt, how?" Tamara laughed. "Do you think he's going to attack me in front of my father?"

"No, Ma'am worse. He won't attack you at all, he'll make you come around to seein' things his way, and before you know it, you'll get caught in something you might not be able to get out of."

"Oh, Mellie, really," Tamara snapped. "I've never been in a position in my life that I couldn't get out of. You make him sound like some evil monster with fangs who will swoop down and devour me. He's just another man."

Mellie's mouth opened to reply but before she could say anything else, Tamara interrupted. "I don't want to hear any more about this ogre capturing his prey. I'm nobody's prey and I'll not be captured by anyone unless I want to be and I have no intention of being caught by him or any other man for a long time. I've things I want to do and I'm not going to let him or any other man interfere in my plans."

Mellie could not resist one more remark before she closed the door. "Sometimes intentions ain't enough. Sometimes things get out of control and we can't do anything to stop it. What we want in this world ain't always what we get. There's things that happen to us that we can't control. With that kind of man, Miss Tamara, things can get out of control easy. I just want you to be careful. I care a lot about you and I don't want to see you hurt."

Tamara smiled contritely. "I'm sorry Mellie. I didn't mean to snap at you. I know you have my best interests at heart and I do appreciate it. Believe me, I have no intention of getting too near your 'dangerous' captain. I'll play no games with him, and in a few days, he'll be on his way and we can forget him."

Mellie smiled, then left closing the door after her, but her mind was still troubled at the first wary look she had ever seen in Tamara's eyes. "Whether she knew it yet or not" she muttered to herself, "Tamara can be caught in the male magnetism I felt when I saw him."

Tamara left her room and walked down the stairs quietly. She stood just outside the drawing room door listening to her father and the captain talk. She found she liked the sound of his voice, deep and resonant. Another step and she could see them without their noticing her.

"God, he's a handsome man," she thought wickedly. He was dressed in fawn colored pants that hugged his long muscular legs, and high black boots. The coat he wore was a deep wine color which enhanced the strange golden brown of his eyes. She watched as he gestured to her father and noticed again the immense size of his hands. A shiver of some emotion she could not fathom held her for a moment. She was amused at the way he angrily described the attack on his ship on the way to the island. She was even more amused at her father's sympathetic reply. Actually, she was frightened to death of what would happen if her father ever found out what she was doing.

"There hasn't been a woman pirate in these waters since Anne Bonney," her father exclaimed.

"Well, there is now, sir, and if I ever cross her path again, she'll regret the day she ever damaged the *Cecile*."

"My, my," Tamara said to herself, such vehemence. Both her father and the captain turned to look at her, but while she only sensed her father's gaze, she was caught in the liquid gold of Steffan's eyes as he beheld her. The look told her in no uncertain terms that all the effort she had put into her appearance was rewarded. He rose slowly, a half smile on his sensuous lips.

"Captain, let me introduce you to my daughter. This is Captain Steffan Devers of the ship *Cecile*. Captain, this is my daughter, Tamara."

Steffan stood erect and Tamara was surprised that he seemed to tower over her. She had always considered herself tall, but now she suddenly felt overpowered by his height. He took her extended hand in his and held it just a little longer than she thought necessary.

"Miss Marriott," he murmured. "My pleasure I assure you. I never expected there would really be a lovely Eve in this Eden."

Flowery compliments she was used to, but the warmth and the unreadable look in his eyes caught her completely unprepared.

She could feel her cheeks redden under his gaze and she became angry more at herself than at him. She tried for coolness in her voice.

"Thank you, Captain Devers. Welcome to Marriott Island and to our home. How did you come about finding our little . . . Eden?"

"Strictly by accident. My ship was attacked by pirates and I was fortunate to find refuge here to make some badly needed repairs."

His words told her a reason, but his steady gaze told her quite another.

"How long will you be incapacitated?"

"I really don't know. There was extensive damage and it may take us quite a while to make all the repairs we need."

Now Tamara became suddenly aware of the fact that he was deliberately lying. She, above all, knew that the damage had not been that severe.

"Be careful" her mind warned, but her senses were not so easily convinced.

"We'll do everything we can to help you," her father offered. "But until your ship is repaired, please consider yourself our guest and our island your home."

"I thank you, sir," he smiled and bowed politely to her father, but then his gaze returned to her as he said, "I'm sure the repairs will take quite a while, just as I'm sure I will enjoy the beauty of the island. One can only enjoy heaven when he sees that it is really blessed with angels."

Nineteen

The dinner would have been much more enjoyable for Tamara if she had been able to control the reaction of her body and her mind when Steffan caught her eyes with his. She was aware of a man for the first time in her life and it was an emotion that unbalanced her thinking. The conversation held her interest as he created, unknown to father and daughter, a fictitious background and reasons he had turned to privateering for a livelihood instead of a more respectable career.

If Tamara was disconcerted, Steffan was even more so. His honor was floundering nervously in the sea of lies he was telling and he found himself hating each one, but once the chain was started, he found he was unable to stop. By the time the dinner was over, he was immersed in a fabric of lies he would never be able to get out of. He was also disconcerted by the green gaze he felt was looking straight through him. He could not shake the strange feeling of deja vu that he had seen her somewhere before, but he knew he never could have forgotten a girl as remarkably beautiful as she was. When he was asked questions, questions by Tamara especially, he felt uncomfortable. Lying was a thing he found very hard to handle and he made the mistake of handling it in the one way that touched fire to the explosive temperament that existed in Tamara . . . humor.

"Your father tells me you love ships, Miss Marriott."

"Tamara," she corrected with a smile.

"Tamara," he said slowly, as though his voice was caressing her name. "Perhaps you would like to see my ship when she is repaired. She is very beautiful."

He was speaking of ships, but his eyes were speaking a language she did not understand.

"Yes, I would, Captain Devers."

"Steffan," he laughed. She could see the fine lines around his eyes and the glow of that unnameable thing that lay there.

"Steffan, I doubt if any other ship could compare to the *Adventurer* either in beauty or in speed."

216

"Ah, the *Adventurer* is yours." What he felt as admiration came through as amusement and Tamara stiffened at the idea that he was laughing at her.

"Well, she is my father's, but I can sail her as well as he."

"My daughter is an excellent sailor, captain," replied her father.

"You sail your own ship?" he questioned and again Tamara misinterpreted his question as one of a slight on both her ability and her femininity.

"You find that hard to understand? I love the sea and my ship. Is that an emotion reserved only for man?"

"No," he said seriously, "I do not believe love could ever be an emotion reserved only for men, any kind of love, but especially a love of the sea and ships. They are two things dearest to my heart; I can certainly see and understand how someone else could share the feeling. I was only surprised that you sail your own ship. You must admit it is an unusual occupation for a woman."

"Unusual only when a woman is too cowardly to do what she really wants to do."

His eyes sparkled with swift amusement. "I would never call you a coward."

She flushed with anger. Why, she thought, did he make her feel less than a woman and so defensive. She was not going to be laughed at by a . . . a pirate.

Andrew knew the signs of Tamara's anger and did not want it to explode on his unsuspecting guest.

"Captain Devers . . . Steffan," he corrected before Steffan could get a chance, "we are having a party tomorrow evening to celebrate Tamara's birthday. We would like to extend an invitation to you."

"Why, thank you, sir," he looked at Tamara and again she thought she saw the same glimmer of laughter. "I would be delighted to come."

"Of course, you may bring friends with you if you choose."

"Thank you."

Tamara was struck by conflicting emotions; she did want him to come, yet she didn't. He created a feeling in her she could not name and she knew she would feel much more secure if Captain Steffan Devers were on the other side of the world. Nevertheless, she added her invitation to her father's.

No one was happier than Tamara when the dinner came to a close and Steffan took an obviously reluctant farewell. She needed to collect her thoughts before she saw him again. She did not believe the damage to his ship was extensive and she was not fool enough to believe he would linger at the island for an extended length of time for a girl he had only just met. Some sixth sense nudged her, but she could not find a flaw in what he said or did, but she promised herself to be more alert from this minute on.

When Steffan returned to his ship he was met by a curious Tom who wanted to know everything about the Marriotts, their mansion and most of all, what Steffan had learned about the island.

"What are they like, Steffan?"

"Well, for one thing, the father is nobody's fool. When I mentioned our lady friend, you would really believe he knew absolutely nothing about her."

"Well, maybe he didn't."

"Tom, for God's sake. Where on earth could that ship have disappeared to except somewhere on this island, and believe me, nothing happens on their island that astute man doesn't know about."

"What about the girl?"

Steffan was silent for a moment longer than necessary. Just enough time for Tom to realize Steffan had been deeply impressed.

"She's beautiful . . . no, more than that, she's . . . I don't know exactly how to describe her. She is certainly different from any girl I've met before."

"How?"

"Well," Steffan laughed. "She is an accomplished captain of her own ship."

"You're joking."

"Nope, and don't ever dare say anything derogatory about it. If you want to see storm clouds gather just mention the fact that a lady belongs in the kitchen."

"I take it you already made that mistake?"

"That's right, but I won't make it twice. I want to keep good relations with both father and daughter. I've a feeling they both know a lot more than they are saying and I don't want to take the chance of being told to leave before I find out what I want to know."

"What are our plans now, Steff?"

"Have you checked what kind of repairs we need and how long they will take?"

"Yes, the damage isn't really bad. I could have her back in perfect condition in a week."

Steffan chuckled. "I think you are wrong Tom."

"Oh?"

"I think the damage is very bad."

"Oh?"

"I think it will take you quite a while to make repairs."

"Uh, huh . . . weeks?"

"Weeks," Steffan replied. Tom grinned in return.

"Of course, there must be some damage I've not noticed."

"Of course."

"And while I'm doing all this backbreaking work, what is her captain going to be doing?"

"Oh, I don't know," Steffan replied. "Since I've been so overworked and under such strain, I might require some rest and relaxation. I might just drift about the island enjoying its natural beauties."

"All its natural beauties?"

"I'm not a man to overlook beauty wherever it can be found."

"After meeting that granite rock she calls a father, I'd be very careful if I were you."

"I will. I don't want any animosity, but what better way to examine this island than to be guided by someone who knows it as well as she must."

"Well, she's certainly not going to lead you to any evidence."

"I know. But I can certainly pay attention to all the places she doesn't show me."

"Very clever."

"By the way, we're invited to a party."

"A party?"

"Yes. It is Tamara's birthday and they are having a party tomorrow night. We're invited."

"Tamara?" Tom smiled. "Pretty name."

"Different . . . but then it suits her. I'd say everything about her was different from any other woman I've known."

"God," Tom replied in mock horror, "I hope not."

"Oh, no," Steffan replied with a deep laugh. "All the parts are in the right places, and very well placed I might add. It's just that despite the firm way she shouts her independence and abilities, she's kind of like a little girl all wide-eyed wonder and innocence."

"She's charming, beautiful, sweet," Tom said, his eyes becoming serious. "But don't make the mistake of getting too close, Steffan, because she might also be a traitor and you might find yourself in the position of having to arrest her. English law is not very gentle on traitors no matter if they are male or female.

219

They'd hang her just as fast as they'd hang her father."

Steffan stood immobile. The realization of what could happen froze his thoughts. He had put the idea from his mind when he thought of Tamara, but now he realized what Tom said was true. He would have to be very careful. He had made one foolish mistake before and he certainly did not intend to repeat that painful episode.

"Don't worry, Tom," he said quietly. "I don't intend to get burnt twice. We'll do the job we came here to do."

No matter what words he said, the realization was deep in Steffan's mind that he was desperately wanting to find these people innocent. In fact, Tom was sure that Steffan would be looking more for evidence of innocence than of guilt.

Tamara climbed the stairs slowly, deep in thought. She would have to be very careful, and she would also have to warn Mikel as soon as possible. She would go early tomorrow morning and find Mikel, let him know what was going on. She stepped into her room. It was dark and the french doors to her terraced balcony stood open to the sea breeze as usual. Mellie knew to leave them open, for Tamara enjoyed the sound of the sea to lull her to sleep at night.

She loosened her hair, then removed her clothes and put on a thin white robe. Then she drifted out onto the terrace and stood leaning against the stone rail and closed her eyes breathing deeply of the cool night breeze. She allowed her thoughts to drift free, and found they conjured up laughing honey gold eyes, and strong hands that reached out and touched her gently in a way she had never been touched before. She felt a warm unwelcome stirring deep within her, and rapidly smothered it. It was possible to smother it when she was awake, but when she slept, the dreams came and she was helpless against them.

Steffan rose early the next morning and after a quick breakfast, he decided to walk along the docks to see if it were possible to engage anyone in careless conversation. The fishermen, for the most part, were already gone and few boats remained tied to the docks. As he walked he tried to take notice of every boat remaining. His attention was quickly drawn to a trim, well cared-for craft that rocked gently against the dock. He walked closer, then stopped as the name of the boat became clear . . . *Tamara*. He wondered if the boat were hers or belonged to her father. The question was soon to be answered as a tall, good looking young man appeared. He walked directly toward the *Tamara* but appraised Steffan with quick knowing blue eyes. That Steffan was a stranger, he knew immediately, for on this island most every man was his friend. Mikel, on board the ship which had assisted Tamara had never seen Steffan, but he quickly associated the two in his mind and came to the obvious conclusion. His alert and clever mind prepared him for the subtle questions he knew would be coming. What he didn't understand was the deep frown lines and clenched jaw as Steffan read the name on his boat.

"Morning," Mikel called brightly.

"Good morning."

Mikel knelt by the ropes that secured the boat to the docks and called nonchalantly back over his shoulder.

"You're a stranger here," he stated.

"Yes, we docked last night for repairs. I'm Captain Steffan Devers from the *Cecile.*"

Mikel rose and extended his hand. Steffan's hand was firm and authoritative and Mikel was aware of the scrutiny of the gold brown eyes.

"I'm Mikel Robbins."

"This is your boat?" Steffan asked as he gestured toward the *Tamara.*"

"Yes, she's beautiful, isn't she? Fast and trim. My father built it for me. I can guarantee it's the best built boat of her type you'll find around."

"Yes, she is pretty . . . pretty name, too."

"Pretty girl she's named after," Mikel replied introspectively.

"You've lived on this island all of your life?"

"That's right."

"Ever hear any rumors of pirates in these waters?"

"Pirates?" Mikel shrugged. "I'm sure if there were any pirates in these waters, I'd know about it. I can't say anyone's mentioned them before. There's no place on this coastline they could dock without everybody on the island knowing about it. No, I think, if you're looking for pirates, you're looking on the wrong island."

Mikel had strayed no further from the truth than he absolutely had to. Somehow, Steffan sensed this, yet he could not put his finger on anything suspicious Mikel had said.

"You work for Andrew Marriott?"

"Yes, have you met him?"

"Last night, when we docked. He's generously offered to give us all the help we need repairing our ship."

"Andrew's a good man. He and my father have been friends for more years than I can remember. Right from the first day Andrew came here."

"Is his daughter the *Tamara* your boat is named after?"

Mikel laughed. "If you've met her, you must realize there certainly couldn't be two of her."

Steffan chuckled his agreement.

"You've been friends a long time too, I take it?"

"We grew up together." Steffan was strangely disturbed by the glow in Mikel's eye. "Tamara and I are like brother and sister."

Steffan's raised eyebrow was all Mikel needed to make him bristle. He spoke through a smile but his blue eyes gleamed dangerously.

"Tamara is a beautiful lady, and whether you believe it or not, that's exactly what our relationship is. She is a sister I care deeply for and would do my best to protect from harm . . . any type of harm."

Steffan was about to answer when the sound of approaching hoof beats reached their ears. He also was not blind to the effect they had on Mikel who lifted his head quickly and gazed expectantly toward their source. "He is in love with her," Steffan thought quickly, and just as quickly followed a swift pang of jealousy toward the handsome young man who had shared the years with her.

Tamara had risen long before the rest of the household was astir. She slipped out and saddled her horse. The urgency in her to warn Mikel was combined with the need to do something, something strenuous and exhilarating, anything to relieve the tenseness in her body and mind. She rode like the wind down along the sandy beach splashing the surf about her. She had tied her hair back carelessly, but the wind had somehow loosened the ribbon. Strands of it blew across her face. She had seen Mikel by the boat, but did not yet suspect that he was already in conversation with Steffan. Her horse clattered to a stop and she slid lightly to the ground only slightly feeling the hand that came out to steady her, then she turned and came face to face with Steffan. He stood so close to her she could feel the warmth of his body and smell the clean masculine scent. For an unguarded moment, she stood looking up into his eyes. Her cheeks flushed from the ride and her bright hair falling free about her, held Steffan speechless too. It was Mikel who read the look as well as he could read the weather and, whether Tamara knew it or not, that there was a magnetic attraction between these two that anyone but a fool could see. Steffan regained his composure first and his eyes sparkled with laughter.

"Do you always arrive everywhere like a bright gold whirlwind?"

I'm sorry I . . . I didn't know it was you." The words were so childish that she immediately was again reduced to contained anger.

"You're up early."

"Yes, it's a habit of mine. I've found a lot of truth in the old axim 'the early bird gets the worm'."

Tamara caught Mikel's warning look and his slight negative shake of the head; she knew that although Steffan had been fishing for information he had gotten nowhere. She ignored his words and looked at Mikel with her warmest smile.

"Mikel, I've just come to make sure you will be at the party tonight. You know I would miss you terribly if you didn't come." She caught Steffan from the corner of her eye and was further enraged by the disinterested glimmer in his eyes. He was, or so it seemed, completely unconcerned with whatever existed between her and Mikel. She stepped closer to Mikel who slid his arm protectively about her. Although he smiled at both of them and his eyes glowed with amusement, Steffan felt the distinct urge to push Mikel into the ocean.

"Well, I must get back and see that my men are about the repairs. I shall see you both this evening." He spoke to them both, but Mikel knew that for all intents and purposes, Steffan and Tamara might have been the only two people in the world. He gave a curt half-bow and turned away. They stood and watched his tall retreating figure.

"He's dangerous," Mikel said quietly.

"I know," Tamara answered in a half whisper.

"Why do you think he's here?" Mikel asked.

"I really don't know, but it's not for repairs. You know as well as I the damage to his ship was not that bad. I believe he's a privateer who has somehow gotten wind of what we're doing and wants in on what he considers a profit-making scheme. Well, he's not going to find any profit here."

Tamara was surprised and unsure of Mikel's quiet answer as he turned away. "I'm not very sure of that."

"What do you mean by that?"

"Forget it, Tam."

"Mikel!"

223

Mikel turned back to her, his blue eyes gentle; he reached out and cupped her angry face in his hand. "I love you, Tam, but you, you're always excited by danger. He's just the kind of man who could reach you. God," he whispered, "I wish it wasn't so, but it is the truth. You're both the same kind of people—all thunderstorms and lightning."

Tamara slapped his hand away and now she was blazingly angry.

"I hate his arrogance, his assurance."

"And hate, Tam," Mikel replied, "is just the reverse side of the coin. Love is on the other."

"Love!" she almost sputtered. "Oh, Mikel you are impossible." She turned from him in anger and mounted her horse. In another moment she was gone.

"Maybe so, Tam," he said miserably as he watched her leaving, "but you can't hide from one who knows you as well as I what I just saw in your eyes, and . . . it wasn't hate."

Steffan returned to his ship and took Tom aside. "Leave some orders for repairs and we'll take the small boat and explore a little bit. I'm sure there are some coves about that could hold a ship of that size. There are also some caves on the high cliffs near the point where arms and ammunition could be stored. We'll give these a quick look and be back before it's time to dress for the party."

Tom agreed. He quickly gave his orders and he and Steffan took out the small boat. They explored for the balance of the day without finding a clue to the whereabouts of the mystery ship and completely unaware that a pair of slanted green eyes watched their every move from the mansion on the hill.

Tamara walked to the door of her father's study and rapped lightly.

"Come in."

She entered and walked across the gleaming hardwood floor, her feet making a soft tapping sound in the still room. Above Andrew's seated form was a large portrait of her mother. Joanna smiled down on her with the calm serenity she always had. For a moment it made Tamara want to run. Run away from an emotion she was feeling and did not understand. Run away from those golden eyes that looked at her . . . how? . . . and it came to her. She had seen her father look at her mother so often with that intense warm look. When she was a child she had felt bathed in the intensity of the love that existed, but now she was a woman, and for the first time in her life, she was afraid.

"Tamara, are you all ready for the party?"

"Yes, Papa, everything's ready."

"You don't sound overly enthusiastic."

"I am Papa, . . . it's just . . . I don't know."

For the first time Andrew noticed the tremulous mouth and the wide green eyes.

"What's the matter child?"

"I . . . I guess I miss Mother," she whispered. Her eyes filled with tears and Andrew held out his arms in unspoken understanding. Joanna's shadow would always live on Marriott Island.

"She would be ashamed of us," Andrew whispered against her silken hair. "Mourning and weeping on a day that would have made her so happy." He tilted Tamara's tear stained face up. "I like to think she sees you, Tamara and is as pleased and proud of you as I am. Come, we'll not spend any more time with tears."

"Papa . . . I don't know what is always right or wrong. I never want to do anything that would make either of you ashamed of me. If I ever do, Papa, it is because I felt in my heart at the time it was the right thing to do."

"And haven't I always taught you to do just so? Tamara, I have never been ashamed of anything you have ever done. A little annoyed, perhaps," he grinned, "but never ashamed. If you feel in your heart that what you are doing is always the best for you, then do it, and know that I will always try my best to understand."

"Thank you, Papa."

"Come, let's talk of something a little happier. It is your birthday and if I am not mistaken, I owe you two birthday gifts."

"You are right," she replied. "And I have the Andrew Marriott word of honor that I can have anything in his power to give that I want."

"The promise is good."

"I do hope so, Papa" her eyes glittered mischievously.

"Why?" he laughed.

"For I am going to ask you for something very dear to you, and something you might not want to give away."

"There's nothing dearer to me than you. What is it you want? Say it, and it is yours."

Tamara took a deep breath then said quickly. "I want the *Adventurer*."

"You what!"

"I want the *Adventurer*."

"But Tamara . . . a ship?"

225

"It is all I want, Papa. It is something I've dreamed of since I was a child. You've taught me and taught me well. Mikel has promised, reluctantly, he would be my first mate."

"I'll bet he would really be pleased if I gave it to you," Andrew said dryly.

"Not really, but he is as honorable a man as you are and won't go back on his word. The only way Mikel can get out of it is if you go back on your word." She looked up at him expectantly and held her breath waiting for his reply.

Andrew laughed uproariously and pulled her into his arms to give her a ferocious bear hug. "Why should I let that scalawag off the hook so easily? After all, he started it with that sailboat of his. He deserves whatever he gets. It's yours with all my love."

Tamara squealed in delight and threw her arms about his neck. She kissed him over and over between bubbling words of thanks. "Oh, I can't wait to see his face when I tell him," she cried.

"I don't really think Mikel will be that surprised," her father said. Tamara remained silent for the hasty words she had just said were not spoken about Mikel, but about Steffan Devers. She did not even know why she had said them, it was just the first thing that had popped into her mind.

She sat in her scented warm bath water later and actually licked her lips in anticipation of his shock when she told him the *Adventurer* was completely hers.

Her maid Mellie fussed about gathering the clothes Tamara would wear. She kept one eye on Tamara for she had never seen her mistress in this state before. "Everything's ready, Miss Tamara," Mellie said. She picked up the large towel as Tamara rose from the tub and wrapped her in it.

The gown she wore was silver gray silk. The sleeves were long and clung to her slender arms but extended only from wrist to curved creamy shoulders. To this she added a necklace her father had given her that was made of a series of slender gold chains held to each other by tiny green emeralds. Her hair, pulled up on her head in a cluster of wayward curls with soft fringes of curls about her face and down the back of her slender neck. She added a few drops of perfume and turned to look at Mellie.

"Well, Mellie?"

"Oh, Miss Tamara, you are so beautiful. I think you look prettier than you've ever looked before. Your cheeks are so pink and your eyes so shiny. There won't be a man with a whole heart left when this night is over."

To Mellie's surprise, Tamara said nothing. She turned back to her mirror but Mellie sensed she really was not seeing herself. She wasn't. She saw instead a tall golden eyed man and her heart began to beat furiously. She turned from the mirror refusing to acknowledge how the insistent thought of him made her feel.

"Well, I'm ready, Mellie. I'd best go down before Father comes to get me."

Mellie laughed as Tamara closed the door, for Andrew's impatience was a well-known fact. Tamara walked to the top of the stairs. She arrived there at the same moment Tom and Steffan were handing their coats to the butler. They were unaware of her standing above them. "He looks so wickedly handsome," she thought. "He almost frightens me."

She took two or three steps down and said, "Good evening, Steffan."

Twenty

Steffan looked up at the sound of her voice as did Tom. Both of them were held silent by the beauty that stood above them. Then for some unaccountable reason, Steffan recalled a night several years ago when Cecile had desired to make a impression on Tom. Tamara walked down the stairs with the same aloof dignity Cecile had used. He held himself immobile, but nothing could disguise the humor in his eyes, and at the moment, it was the only thing Tamara could see and her sudden anger brightened her eyes to brilliant emeralds. It almost choked her with fury to sense that he was actually laughing at her. She could not wait to throw the information in his face that the *Adventurer* was hers.

"Tamara," he said, and again his voice was almost a caress, a sound she overlooked. Steffan held out his hand and she placed hers in it with a smile that would have frozen a lesser hearted man. Steffan's lips curved in a surprise smile.

"Tom, this is our lovely hostess, Tamara Marriott. Tamara, this is my second in command, Tom Braydon."

"Hello, Miss Marriott," Tom smiled, "I would like to thank you for your invitation. It has been quite a while since we've been in such a beautiful home and," he added, "in the company of such a beautiful lady."

"Thank you, Mr. Braydon." The smile she turned on Tom was certainly warmer than the one she had given Steffan.

"It is my pleasure to welcome you to our home. My father will, I'm sure, be anxious to welcome you also."

"Do come in and enjoy yourself, Mr. Braydon," she gestured towards the ballroom where the sound of music could be heard.

It had taken about two minutes, after being married to a lively woman like Cecile, for Tom to feel the current that flowed between Steffan and Tamara. Being the best friend Steffan had, he knew he could resort to a little fun without Steffan becoming angry . . . at least he thought he could. He lifted Tamara's hand in his and touched her cool fingers with his lips.

"You have no idea what a pleasure it is just to see such a lovely face as yours, and in such a beautiful setting.'' He gave her his warmest smile and was about to add a few more flowery compliments when over Tamara's shoulder, she saw Steffan, his brows drawn together and his eyes darkened with an emotion he obviously did not know he was showing.

''Hallelujah,'' Tom thought. ''There is more to this than even Steffan knows. He's jealous, and jealousy doesn't happen without other feelings first.''

Instead of the words he was going to say, Tom offered her his arm. She took it and turned to face Steffan who offered her his arm also with a swift return of his smile. She slipped her other hand through his arm and the three of them entered the ballroom.

The party was a gay affair. Both Steffan and Tom were thoroughly enjoying themselves. It did not take long for the girls who were Tamara's friends to wangle an introduction to him. When he wanted to turn on his charm, Steffan was irresistible to women, and he turned on every ounce he had, but it still amused Tom to see that while he charmed the other blushing, laughing girls, he kept one eye on Tamara who seemed oblivious to his attentions. Tom made a wager to himself on just how long it would take for Steffan to find a way to get her undivided attention. It didn't take long.

There was a small group of them gathered at the edge of the dance floor watching the slow movements of the dance. Steffan looked directly at Tamara as he spoke, but she stubbornly ignored his eyes.

''It's too bad you haven't visited London lately,'' he said.

''Oh, really, Captain Devers?'' Barbara McBright said.

''Yes, there's a new dance now that's taking everyone by storm. It's referred to as 'round dancing'.''

Mary St. Clair smiled brightly. '' 'Round dancing.' It sounds like fun. Do tell us about it, Captain. Do you know how it is done? What is it like?''

Steffan smiled directly at Tamara. ''If Tamara would allow me, and be my partner, I would be delighted to show you how it is done.''

Tamara hesitated but at the insistence of both her friends she reluctantly agreed. ''After all,'' she thought the dances of today allowed a man to come no closer to his partner than occasionally touching her hand.

''Listen everyone,'' Barbara called brightly, ''Captain Devers is going to show us the latest dance.''

Steffan spoke for a second to the orchestra leader, then he returned to Tamara's side. The music was different than any she had danced to before. He stood close to her, his gold eyes holding hers as he said softly, "It's easy, it's like this, one, two, three, one two, three." She held up her hand for him to take as she quickly memorized the step, but she gasped in surprise as a strong arm came about her waist and he pulled her against him until their bodies touched. Her gasp of shock was echoed through the room. No one had ever held a woman to dance before. Their bodies began to sway gently as he whispered, "one, two, three." The strains of the waltz flowed through her and they began to move about the floor as one.

Tamara lifted her eyes to him; they held, both filled with the excitement that flowed between them. Excitement that could not be credited all to the dance.

They whirled about the floor now as Tamara relaxed in his arms and began to enjoy the new whirling dance called 'the waltz'.

Enthusiasm filled the room as everybody, laughing with a new excitement, joined the two on the floor. Their bodies molded to each other. Tamara felt the long hard muscles of his tall body. He was large yet he moved with grace and ease. He held her so tight she could barely breathe, yet she didn't want him to let her go. She lost control of everything except the invisible hand that seemed to link them together. Everyone so caught up in the fun of the new type of dancing did not notice when Steffan swept Tamara through the large french doors and out onto the stone terrace. In the pale reflected light from the ballroom, Steffan slowed his steps until they were barely moving, yet he did not relax the arm that held her close to him. He bent his head until his lips lightly brushed the softness of her hair, and without a sound they moved slowly to the beat of the music until the music stopped. He did not release her, instead he slid his other arm about her until he was holding her close in a silent firm embrace.

It was then that some semblance of reason entered Tamara's mind. She shook herself free of the warm feeling of belonging that pervaded her. Taking a step back from him, she felt his arms drop away and she looked up into his eyes. There was a look in their golden depths she had never seen before. It sent trembling warmth through her body and with it followed confusion.

"Steffan, that was very exciting, but don't you think this new dance is rather . . ."

"Rather what?"

"Well . . . No one has ever . . . I mean."

"No one has ever held you like that," he supplied. "I'm glad it was I who taught you. It's an exciting dance but with someone as lovely as you it is even more so."

The music that had stilled began a new waltz for the fun of the new dance had created enthusiasm in all the young people present. Steffan held out his arms to Tamara.

"Shall we?" he asked softly.

Tamara sensed that if she stepped back into the arms he held out she would be lost. What she was afraid of she didn't know, but she only knew she did not want to lose control again. "Let's wait for the next one, and take a walk in the garden." She wanted her voice to sound cool and untouched but succeeded only in sounding like a frightened little girl.

"Good idea, it is a little warm inside." He took her hand and pulled it through his arm lacing his fingers with hers. At his touch, Tamara became unsure if dancing would not have been better than a walk through a dark garden with this handsome and very dangerous man, but it was too late for he was already leading her down the terrace steps and out into the rose scented night.

They walked along in silence for a while, both of them enjoying the light, cool sea breeze and the close proximity of the other.

"Your island is a lovely place," Steffan remarked. "Do you think your father would mind if we looked about it? There's not much leisure time for us and we would certainly enjoy the few days we have here."

"Certainly you may, I'm sure Father would have no objection to you enjoying the island."

"You've lived here all your life?"

"I was born in England, but we moved here when I was just a child."

"Not that I blame you for moving here, this is an Eden on earth; but why would your parents bring a child to a place like this, especially a girl child?"

"Why 'especially a girl child?' "

"Well, I thought girls liked . . ." he shrugged, "parties, society, fun. This seems like a kind of Godforsaken place for a pretty girl such as you."

They stopped and he turned to face her. "I'm perfectly happy here. I don't think there is another place on earth I would rather be. I like being . . . free. Society is too inhibited. One has to always be careful of what one says or does, how one dresses. Here

I can just be me. I can ride if I choose, swim, sail. It's the kind of life I enjoy most.''

"Don't you want to travel . . . see things?"

"I haven't been exactly a prisoner here, Steffan. My father and I have travelled a great deal."

"Oh?"

"Yes. We've been to most of the large cities in most of the other countries at one time or the other. We've even visited the Colonies, but I still prefer my island."

"You have friends in the Colonies?"

"My father has many; of course, Father has friends all over the world."

Steffan did not want to push the questions about her father's friends in the Colonies, but he stored the thought for later. "Tell me," he smiled, "would you be able to spare a little time occasionally to show us about? It's easier to see the place through the eyes of someone who loves it than to wander about by ourselves."

She wanted to refuse, but with his intent gaze holding hers, she could not think of any logical reason. "Yes."

"Tomorrow?" he asked tentatively.

"Yes."

"Good; shall we begin with a ride to give us a general idea of the island?"

"All right. Tomorrow morning."

Steffan kept saying 'us', but he certainly had no intention of bringing Tom along. The 'us' he kept referring to was just Tamara and himself for as long as he could keep it that way.

The strains of another waltz crept out the windows. They stood in a frozen moment of silence. Steffan reached out and gently touched the side of her cheek. Her eyes widened as he stepped closer, so close that she had to tip her chin up to look at him. He smelled so clean and the overpowering size of him crowded her senses until she could feel a weak trembling in her legs. "You're very beautiful," he murmured. "Like the first morning sun on a calm sea." His fingers touched the soft curls that framed her face. "You've even caught the sunbeams in your hair." If Tamara was stilled by his gentleness, it was nothing to the bewitched, bemused feeling that flooded Steffan. He wanted to loosen her hair and run his hands into the thick silken mass. He wanted to rip away the clothes that stood between them and hold her in his arms. He wanted . . . Tamara stood quietly, her wide green eyes held by his. Slowly, he bent his head and touched her lips lightly

232

with his. Neither of them was prepared for the strength of the emotion that lifted them and held them suspended in their own world. Tamara felt his arms as he pulled her against him and suddenly his lips claimed hers in a kiss that loosened all the controls she held and sent her into a world where only he existed.

The sound of approaching footsteps remained unheard by both of them. They only realized some one else was there when, after he had seen them, Mikel coughed with a loud enough sound to warn them of his approach. Tamara almost leapt out of Steffan's arms, her face flushed with sudden guilt at the way she had fallen so easily into his spell. She was angry with herself, after knowing so well just how dangerous he might be to their safety, for allowing him within her guard so easily.

"Mikel."

"I'm sorry to interrupt," Mikel replied, but Steffan knew he meant exactly the opposite, "your father has been looking for you and I thought I saw you go in this direction."

His eyes held Tamara's, as he spoke and Steffan could feel the unspoken words of warning. He wondered exactly what Mikel was warning her against him . . . or what he might be able to learn from her. Outside of the fact that he knew Mikel was in love with Tamara, he felt she was not receptive to it and that there was much more between the two than what he saw on the surface.

He watched Tamara's face as she regained her composure and silently cursed Mikel for his untimely interruption.

"I'd best go and see what Father wants," Tamara murmured, and before Steffan could say anything to stop her, she slipped by him and fled. Mikel stood looking in the direction Tamara had gone for a few moments, then he turned back to Steffan and his eyes were two blue chips of ice. "I'm sure you've been to a lot of places and tumbled a girl in every one, but Tamara's not a conquest. She's a sweet trusting girl. Don't make the mistake of hurting her. There are many on this island who wouldn't take kindly to it. You might find it's a mistake you'd pay for dearly. Leave Tamara alone." His words were spoken calmly but with the depth of tone that was like steel encased in a velvet glove. Before Steffan could reply, Mikel turned and walked away.

"Conquest," Steffan muttered, then he came to the sudden realization that what he had started out to accomplish was just that, a conquest, a way to gather information, but somehow, somewhere, that idea had gotten lost in the soft scent and softer lips of Tamara. He jerked his conscience awake. To take advantage of a girl as obviously inexperienced as Tamara, and to use her as a way to get the information he wanted was a degrading thing to do. When he thought of her so soft and vulnerable in his arms, he knew that a deeper feeling stirred awake. He had loved before and had been hurt; he had no intention of letting himself in for the same pain again. He did not want to be the one who would ever hurt Tamara either. "Of course," he lied valiantly to himself, "it was just a kiss in a dark garden on a moonlit night. It meant nothing to either of us." He walked back to the ballroom doing his best to ignore the small voice in the back of his mind that whispered, "you lie, . . . you lie."

Tamara stood on the opposite side of the room in conversation with Tom. Instead of following his first desire and going to her side, he deliberately looked away. Soon, he found a willing partner and danced again, but no matter how hard he tried to control it, his mind drifted back to Tamara and he found he could also not keep his eyes from straying in her direction. If he could have heard the conversation in progress, he might have made it a point to interrupt as soon as possible.

"You've been a friend of Steffan's a long time?" she asked Tom.

"Yes, Steff and I go back to childhood days."

"What was he like . . . as a boy, I mean?"

"What was he like? . . . Steff has always been the same as he is now, a dependable friend; he's always been the one who was leader and he's always been honest."

"He sounds as though he has a lot of good qualities," she murmured.

"Oh, I guess he has as many faults as the rest of us. For one thing, he's tenacious and as stubborn as an ox. If he sets his mind to something, he'll do it, and if he wants something . . . he usually gets it."

She looked up quickly into Tom's eyes for some double meaning, but his eyes were expressionless. "He's very attractive . . . I imagine there's someone special at home?"

Tom looked at her a moment questioningly. "His ship," she stammered, "it's named *Cecile*, I thought it was named after someone . . . close to him."

Tom's sense of humor caught him and he replied wishing he could see Steffan's face when he found out. "Yes, I guess you might say Cecile is someone he's cared for a long time."

"Oh . . . is . . . is she pretty?"

Tom was in his element now, describing Cecile's beauty was easy for him. "Pretty is not quite the word I'd use to describe

Cecile. There are a lot more like . . . exquisite . . . beautiful. She's got hair as black as midnight and skin so soft it's like velvet.''

"Are Steffan and Cecile . . . married?''

"No, they are not.''

"But he named his ship after her. She must mean a great deal to him.''

"Yes. There's nothing in the world Cecile could ask for that Steffan wouldn't try to give her.''

Tamara was about to ask another question when Mikel appeared at her elbow. She would have died before she would have let either of the men know just what she was feeling at the moment. Making a quick excuse, she slipped away from the two and went upstairs where she paced the floor of her bedroom in growing fury. "How dare he! Who did he think he was playing with?'' Her anger grew the more she thought about the casual way Steffan had taken her kiss. She paid no attention to the fact that she had enjoyed it more than any other man's. Slowly she got her anger under control and it was a calm Tamara who opened the door of her bedroom and went back down the stairs. She had made up her mind to allow Steffan to play his little game for as long as he was here. But methods of revenge would be found and when they were, she would not hesitate to use them.

Tom and Steffan were invited to share a last glass of brandy when the party was over and before they returned to their ship. They were in Andrew's study with Tamara and Mikel. Andrew poured each of them a drink. He sat beside Tamara on the large sofa with Mikel seated directly across from them. Tom stood just to the left of Mikel's chair and Steffan stood by the huge fireplace.

"It was quite a successful party, my dear,'' Andrew smiled down on Tamara.

"Yes, Papa, it was and I thank you, both for the party and for the wonderful gift you have given me.'' She kissed him lightly on the cheek, then turned her radiant smile on Mikel, "and Mikel, I want to tell you how much I appreciate your gift also. I shall wear it always.''

"You're welcome, Tamara. I'm glad you like it.'' She showed the small gold cross that dangled from a thin chain that she wore about her neck.

"Isn't it beautiful?''

They all agreed. Steffan smiled. "If you will excuse me for a moment, in all the excitement, I forgot the gift Tom and I brought.''

No one was more surprised than Tom at the mention of a gift he knew nothing about. He watched Steffan leave the room and return with a package under his arm that Tom had never seen until that very moment. Steffan handed the package to Tamara who took it with just as much surprise in her eyes as in Tom's. "Happy Birthday, Tamara."

"Thank you," Tamara said in a faint voice. "I really didn't expect a gift Steffan; after all, you had no way of knowing when you came here that you would be invited to a birthday party."

"I bought that at the last port we were in. I saw it and liked it. I'm glad I found someone as lovely as you to give it to. I remembered it the first time I saw you, it kind of reminds me of you."

Tamara opened the package with trembling fingers and could not contain the gasp of pleasure when she lifted the contents.

It was a small mahogany music box twelve inches wide and about six inches high. The lid was exquisitely carved with twining roses. Slowly she opened the lid and the soft sound of a lovely melody filled the room. The inside was lined with red velvet.

"It is very beautiful," Tamara said excitedly. Tom looked at a pleased Steffan with amusement. "I don't know how he does it," Tom thought, "but he surely has a way about him."

"I thank you both. It is an exceptionally lovely gift and I shall remember you both always for such thoughtfulness."

"Tell me," Steffan said. "What was the gift your father gave you?"

Tamara's eyes glowed. *"The Adventurer"* she replied.

"A ship?"

"Yes."

"For a birthday gift . . . for . . ."

"Don't say for a girl, Steffan," Andrew laughed. "I wouldn't want violence to end our evening."

"I wasn't going to sir," Steffan chuckled, "but you both must admit it is an unusual gift."

Tamara looked up at Steffan, her eyes expressionless. Mikel became instantly alert. He had seen that look too often not to know it meant some kind of trouble for the hopeless person it was cast upon.

"You simply cannot believe can you, Steffan, that a girl can love the sea, love her ship, and be just as good a sailor as you."

"I didn't say that."

"But you implied it."

Steffan shrugged. "All right. If you want me to admit it, no, I don't think you can handle a ship as well as I."

"How are your repairs going?"

Steffan looked at Tom who raised his eyebrows negatively, he had no idea what she was up to.

"They're going well. I imagine in a week or so, she should be in excellent condition."

Tamara rose slowly and stood facing Steffan with a faint smile on her lips and a glow in her eyes that made even Steffan uncomfortable.

"I challenge you, Steffan, to defend what you believe," she said ominously.

"What?"

"I said, if you do not want to admit that you are just another conceited man who thinks the world and everything in it was created just for him, you will stand behind what you believe. I challenge you to a race. Then we will see who can and cannot sail."

For once in their lives, all four men were struck completely speechless and Steffan realized with a mental groan, he had pushed Tamara one step too far. To back down would be impossible, but to race her, he thought, was just as impossible. He did not know of any graceful way to get out of it and the smile on Tamara's face told him she knew it also.

"Tamara . . ." Andrew began.

"Father, you gave *The Adventurer* to me."

"Yes, but . . ."

"It is my ship."

"Yes," he said resignedly.

"Then I repeat. I will race you, captain, and prove to you just what I can and cannot do." Mikel smiled to himself. Tamara had unleashed her claws and Steffan's tender flesh was what she was going to sharpen them on. For one quick moment, he felt a little sorry for Steffan. "This is impossible," Steffan said, and for the first time, he allowed anger to creep into his voice.

"Why?" Tamara taunted, "Are you afraid I will beat you?"

"Of course not."

"Then . . ."

"All right," as soon as my ship is repaired, I will take up your challenge."

"Good."

"But there is one thing I must add."

"What?"

"A race really isn't interesting unless you can make a wager on

237

the outcome."

"I agree," she replied quickly. "What do you want to wager?"

"Well, I'll have to think it over for a bit," Steffan's eyes sparkled with mischief. "I'm sure I can come up with something suitable."

"Whatever you have in mind, Steffan," she laughed, "I'll accept whatever it is you intend to lose."

"I wouldn't," he said drily, "be so sure of yourself if I were you. If you lose I might ask for something you might not care to pay."

"I do not," she replied coldly, "back down on anything I have given my word on."

"Then you agree to whatever wager we decide on?"

"Tamara!" her father said, but before he could say another word, Tamara replied, "Yes, I do."

There was a moment of silence as all of them realized just what had happened. Steffan's sparkling eyes did not leave Tamara's angry ones for a minute. "I too would like to make a wager then," Andrew said to Steffan.

"Good" Steffan replied, "What do you wish to wager, Mr. Marriott, and . . . on whom?"

"Really!" Tamara said in fury.

"Tamara, child," Andrew laughed, "he is only teasing you. Of course, I will bet on my daughter, Steffan. I have seen her handle my ship and I feel she is quite capable of beating you. How about three hundred pounds?"

"Very well, sir," Steffan grinned. "I would hate to take your money, but," he shrugged expressively. Two pink spots on each cheek and the brilliant green fire in her eyes spoke just as eloquently of Tamara's anger. Without another word, she swept from the room slamming the door behind her.

Mikel was the first to leave, and was followed by Tom and Steffan who refused Andrew's offer of a carriage and walked through the warm night toward their ship.

"What are you trying to prove, Steff?"

"Nothing; you saw what happened. She pushed me into it."

"Oh, come on, Steff, you could have backed down like a gentleman and this never would have happened."

Steffan laughed. "Yes, I suppose I could, but now I find I'm kind of looking forward to showing Miss Marriott a thing or two. She's a spoiled little girl who needs to be beaten at her own game."

"And what are you going to do if she wins?"

"She won't."

"But, if she does?"

"Well, I guess I'll pay my wager like a gentleman, apologize deeply and profoundly and enjoy her unbearable attitude for the balance of our stay."

"And just what kind of terms are you thinking up for this wager?"

"That," Steffan replied with a chuckle that made Tom frown, "is something that will be between Tamara and me, but I guarantee you," he added, "it will be a rewarding adventure."

"Steff, we're here for a purpose, remember?"

"Of course, I remember, and I don't intend to shirk my duties one bit; but there has to be a free moment or two, now doesn't there? We're making a good search of the island and now we're going to take some time for a little amusement."

"Amusement?" Tom muttered. "I know you too well my friend, and you've got something up your sleeve that's going to cause us some trouble. I can just feel it coming."

"Tsk, tsk," Steffan replied. "You're getting like a worried old woman, Tom, my friend; now what kind of trouble can a little race cause?"

They arrived at the ship and made their beds. Tom lay unable to sleep; worrying about what he had said in a teasing way to Tamara about Cecile was one of the reasons for her challenge and what Steffan would really do now if he found out how Tom had misled her.

Steffan lay awake, but he was enjoying the remembrance of a soft pair of lips and the warm curvaceous body he had held so close to him for such a short time. His smile flashed in the dark room as he made the plans for the wager he and Tamara were about to make. The idea had come to him when she had arrogantly flung her challenge at him, and now he knew. If he had won, he would make certain he collected all that was due him.

Combined with the creaking sound of the ship's timbers and the lapping water against her sides came the muffled laughter from the captain's bed as he thoroughly enjoyed the plans he was making.

Twenty-one

Tamara disengaged her long slender legs from the covers and stood up. She stretched her arms above her head and yawned. With the grace of a cat, she walked to the large windows that stood open to the refreshing morning breeze. She stood gazing out over the shifting blue-green ocean for a long time. She felt so confined this morning, almost as though something important in her life was about to happen and she didn't know, was completely unprepared for whatever it was. It left her both mentally and emotionally unsettled.

She turned from the window when Mellie entered. Once Mellie had prepared her bath, a bath she usually sat in and enjoyed for a long time, she bathed quickly and dressed even faster. The clothes she took from her closet made Mellie groan mentally. "Tamara is going off on one of her rambling days," Mellie thought.

The dress was a faded blue and Tamara wore it with no petticoats at all. Her hair was tied carelessly back with a piece of blue ribbon. The shoes she donned on stockingless feet were worn and comfortable for walking and climbing. Mellie said nothing, for she had seen this wild unsettled look in her mistress's eyes before and knew she had to be free to get it out of her system.

The house was still quiet as Tamara slipped from the back door and ran across the lawn to the stables. She saddled her horse herself without waking Jamie, the stable man, for she was in no mood for his startled looks and his underbreath mutterings about the training of young people. Once she had him saddled she bent and grasped the back hem of her dress and tucked it into her belt creating the pants she needed for riding. Quickly, she was up on the horse's back and clattering across the stable yard away from the house. She allowed the horse to run as fast as he could for a short time and when its breathing became heavy, she pulled on the reins and slowed him to a walk; then she let him walk where he would while she allowed herself to drift mentally.

On the cliffs, she stopped the horse and slid off his back. Loosening the cinch of the saddle, so he could breathe, she

240

hobbled him and let him graze in the high grass. She wandered to the cliff edge and sat looking out across the ocean. The days of her life were so exciting and uncomplicated before Steffan's arrival. Why did his taunting laughter and casual manner upset her? In fact, why did he bother her at all? "After all" she thought, "I have met men much more handsome than he." But before the thought was even finished, denial followed. She could picture him in her mind's eye and try as she did, there was no way to convince herself that he was not the most handsome, most masculine man she had ever met. In her mind, she stood him beside each of the others and found them lacking one or many of his qualities. She pictured the laughing gold brown eyes, the dark winged brows that shadowed them, the square strong chin. The smile that made her heart do strange things within her as she remembered again the strong feel of his arms about her and his insistent demanding mouth that had claimed hers. "Am I falling in love with him? . . . . . No!" her mind shrieked before the thought was finished. "I cannot. There are too many things I have to do. Too many obligations for me to let myself be caught up in his charm. He's a pirate, nothing more, and I imagine he has a girl in every port. What I am doing is necessary to a great and ugent cause and I will not let myself be led astray by some traveling pirate's charm . . . but," her inner mind suggested slyly, "what is the harm in enjoying his company while he is here. There need be no strings attached. He would be fun to be with for a time and when he chose to leave . . . then let him go."

Tamara shrugged off the thoughts and rose to her feet. Slipping off her shoes, she walked down a narrow well worn path to the sandy beach. She unbuttoned the neck of her dress and lifted her face to catch the coolness of the breeze. She walked barefoot through the edge of the water, deep in thought, and did not notice the man who sat in the shadows of the rocks ahead of her and watched her walk toward him.

Steffan woke early and, unable to go back to sleep, had taken a small boat and drifted down the coast of the island until he found a small secluded cove. There, he had pulled the boat ashore in the shade of the rocks and stripping away his clothes, he had taken an early morning swim. Afterwards, he had sat in the cool shade of the rocks and enjoyed the peacefulness of this quiet beautiful place.

He watched Tamara walk toward him unaware of his presence. "She is so amazingly beautiful," he thought. Among the lily white ladies of London society, Tamara would have been a wild flower. Her golden tan skin spoke of days in the sun. She was so unaffected, so unaware of her startling beauty. The sun sparkled on her red gold hair and she walked with a relaxed easy grace. He observed, with a chuckle, the bare feet and legs and the way she was obviously enjoying herself completely. He knew, without having been told, that she had done this often before and found himself wishing he had known her all those years.

She stopped when she saw him, and it gave him the sudden impression she was a wild bird poised for flight and if he did not find a way to hold her, she would be gone.

"Good morning," he called and walked toward her. His condition did nothing to ease the unrest in her. Dressed only in a rough pair of pants that had been cut off just above the knees, his shirt had been thrown aside so he could feel the warmth of the sun. His hair, still wet from the water curled thickly about his face and the broad white smile that was still fresh from her dreams the night before caused her to frown. He saw the frown and couldn't for the life of him think of what he could have done to set her on edge merely by saying good morning. When he reached her side he said, "I'm sorry if I've intruded on your private beach. It's such a beautiful morning, I thought I would go for a swim. Do you swim here?"

"Yes, occasionally." She was angry at herself for letting him disturb her so. His near nakedness made her heart beat a little faster and the way those honey gold eyes were taking in everything about her set her nerves on edge. "It's all right, you may feel free to use it whenever you choose."

She was going to pass him, for at the moment she wanted to get away from him as fast as she could before those eyes noticed her emotional state.

"Tamara?"

"Yes?"

"About last night."

"What about last night?"

"I'm sorry I upset you. This race is a silly thing to do. Why don't we just call it off?"

For the first time, the teasing laughter was gone from his eyes, they were serious and warm. Much too warm for Tamara's comfort. She desperately felt she had, for some reason, to keep him at a distance.

"No" she said quickly. "I challenged you and you have accepted. We will race if only to prove myself that I am as good as I claim to be. There are times when spoken words will not clear up unspoken thoughts." She smiled up at him. "I've even thought of several things I could wager."

He returned her smile. "Again I must say I'm sorry."

"For what?"

"You challenged me. I think I have the right to say what the wager will be."

"Of course. Name the wager."

"If you win, I will apologize formally and in public for anything I might have said to slight your abilities."

"And?"

"And if I win, you spend a day with me from morning until midnight . . . alone." He expected her to refuse. He saw the refusal glittering in her eyes so he added the words calmly that he knew would change her mind. ". . . unless of course, you're afraid to. In that case, we could just call it off for those are the only terms I will accept."

"Afraid!" she said sharply. "I'm certainly not afraid of you, why should I be?"

He shrugged silently, but the laughter was back in his eyes and her anger exploded.

"I accept your wager, Steffan," she said coldly, her chin up, "and I expect your apology to be long and loud. I hope your ship is ready soon for I find myself impatient to hear your humble words of apology."

She pushed past him and walked on down the beach. He watched the sway of her hips with a wicked glitter in his eyes. When Steffan returned to the *Cecile*, he found Tom engrossed in repairs. "How is she coming?" he questioned.

"Fine; I could have her finished in a day or two. Steff, we've searched this island from top to bottom, there is no sign of that ship. We must be in the wrong place. How much longer do we keep up this pretense at repairs?"

"No longer, by day after tomorrow, I want you to claim her finished. We've a race to run and I can't wait to get to it."

"That race, Steff, you're joking. Surely you don't intend to really go through with that?"

"Tom, my friend," Steffan chuckled, "if I never do anything else in my life I surely intend to race the *Adventurer* and her captain. There's more at stake here than you know. I not only intend to run the race, I fully intend to win it with your help."

"Steff," Tom began hesitantly, "you and I are about as close as friends can be, so I'm going to stick my neck out and say something you might not like to hear."

243

"Go ahead."

"I like her—Tamara, I mean. She's a sweet girl. I don't want to see her get hurt. Whatever is going on around here, the Marriotts certainly aren't involved. I think we ought to get out of here before she begins to think you're serious. I don't think Tamara is the love 'em, leave 'em with a smile type of girl. I think she's the kind that puts her whole heart into a commitment. I don't want to see it broken."

"It's only a race, Tom. Just a little fun."

"Is it?" Tom replied pointedly.

"All right, maybe there is more to it than that." Steffan admitted, then he smiled, "Okay, Grandma Braydon, after the race we leave; you're right, there is no evidence here to involve Tamara or her father, though I admit I'm suspicious of that Robbins fellow."

"Why, because he has free access to everything on the island . . . or because he's in love with Tamara? Why don't we just go and leave the two lovebirds to share this Eden together?"

Steffan ignored the question. "You take the sailboat and go down the coast after dark. Meet Jaspar and tell him there's nothing going on here." He turned to meet Tom's eyes. "*After* the race, we'll leave." The words were so final that Tom decided not to push the matter any further. He turned back to his work and Steffan went below to his cabin. He sat down at his desk with the idea of completing the written report of their findings but found he was unable to concentrate on it. Tom's words annoyed him mostly because somewhere deep inside he knew they were true.

They were invited again to Andrew's table for supper which, for Steffan, turned into a rather difficult affair. Tamara did her best to pretend Steffan did not exist. She laughed and talked animatedly with Tom who was seated next to her. Steffan and Andrew talked of things that afterwards he could barely remember. He was in a foul mood by the time he and Tom made their way back to the ship. To his great aggravation, Tom took no little delight in some mild teasing on the ride home.

Tamara went to her room in no better a mood than she had been that morning. She prepared for bed and after extinguishing the last candle, she climbed into her bed and lay wide awake. Suddenly there was a rattling sound against her window that brought her upright, followed by another almost immediately. She slid out of bed, donned her robe and went to the window. Mikel stood below in the shadows and motioned her silently to come down. There were a set of stone stops that ran from her balcony to the garden below; she ran down these silently.

"Mikel, what is the matter?"

"I've just received a message. In five days they're sending another ship through. It will be loaded with arms and ammunition. It is the *Peacock*."

"Good."

"Tamara, how can we do anything with these strangers in port? They're most likely pirates who would like nothing better than to get their hands on us. You know there is quite a reward for any information about us."

"I don't believe either Steffan or Tom are the kind that would turn us in for a reward, Mikel, and neither do you. Anyway, there's no way they can find out what we're doing. I will just go visit my best friend Barbara when she's so very ill. I'll return in a day or two and no one will be the wiser."

"I don't know, Tamara. I've got a funny premonition that some of the things you get away with won't go over so well with Steffan. He's the kind to ask questions then check out the answers."

"He won't be here to ask any."

"Why?"

"He's anxious to repair his ship for our race, good; but when the race is over and his ship is repaired, what excuse does he have then to remain?"

"Tam . . . Do you really believe his ship is the only thing that keeps him here?"

"What else?"

"You."

"Me! Nonsense Mikel. He's nothing but a pirate with a lot of charm who thinks he can add me to his string of conquests. Once he's shown the impossibility he'll be on his way to calmer seas."

"I think we ought to let this ship go through safely."

"And let those arms reach the English soldiers so that they can kill our friends? No, Mikel, it is in our power to stop it and stop it we will."

"Tam . . ."

"No, Mikel, I will not let one man stand between me and what has to be done. He'll never know, he'll be gone before that ship comes through, I promise you, Mikel. Now don't argue with me. You have to leave before someone finds us out here. Go to our contact and send word to our men to ready the ship. That *Peacock* is going to have its feathers plucked."

245

"All right, Tam," Mikel sighed, "but I still feel there is more to Captain Steffan Devers than we know."

Tamara laughed and gave Mikel a little shove towards the back gate; then Tamara ran lightly up the steps to her room and soon was contentedly asleep. If she had seen the folded message that was handed to Steffan at the moment she might not have slept so easily.

"What is it, Tom?"

"I just recieved this from Jaspar. I think you'll be interested."

Steffan unfolded the message and read it quickly.

"Well?" Tom questioned.

"In a few days, there's a ship coming through called the *Peacock*. She's carrying arms for the colonies. They think maybe our *Scarlet Butterfly* might try to grab it. Well, now we just might find out something definite. We'll keep a close eye on Andrew Marriott. If he knows about this ship, and he is guilty, it will certainly be too much temptation for him to let it go by."

"What are our plans?"

"First things first," Steffan grinned. "Repairs done, we run a race, then we put our minds on an excuse to stay here for another two days. You go and see Jaspar, tell him we'll take care of our lady pirate."

Tom nodded, but he wasn't too happy with Steffan's still obvious concentration on this race. Tom wondered just what it was about the race that held Steffan.

Tom guided the small boat down the coast in the light of the moon where the ship he was looking for stood at anchor about a half mile away from the docks. Jaspar had come to the military base with orders to lie in waiting for any word from Steffan about the pirate that plagued the arms ships from England. It was not enough for Jaspar just to wait. He felt there was some chance of advancement and glory in this little endeavor and he did not want either to go to Steffan. From the first day he had arrived, Jaspar had set about developing contacts throughout the village and the base. It did not take long to find the malcontents, troublemakers, and in general the type of men who would not hesitate to spy or do any other deed for the right amount of money. Slowly, rumors filtered through to him and after a while, he noticed that no matter how many different directions they came from, all the rumors seemed to center around a young man named Mikel Robbins. Some had told him that every time the pirates struck, Mikel was nowhere about. Now, Jaspar had taken one of his best men and set him one task alone . . . to watch every move Mikel Robbins made. When the boat touched the side of the ship a rope ladder was lowered. Tom climbed aboard and went directly to Jaspar's cabin. At his knock, he was told to enter. He pushed the door shut behind him and turned to face Jaspar.

Jaspar stood up from behind his desk. He had grown into an extremely handsome man, yet there was a coldness in his blue eyes that when he left it unveiled would show the real man beneath the exterior. They were, at the moment, two frigid orbs. His arrogant manner always had the ability to raise Tom's hackles. It was no less so tonight.

"Well, well," Jaspar said derisively. "Steffan's errand boy. What accomplishments has our friend come up with? Has he captured our pirate single handed and ready to turn the culprit over to the Crown?"

"Captain Sinclair," Tom said, in a voice just as cold as Jaspar's "Steffan and I have conducted a thorough search of this island as we were instructed to do. There is no place on this island where that ship could be docked and Steffan is sure Andrew Marriott knows nothing at all about any of this. If he thought for one minute the man was guilty, he would find evidence and bring him in."

"And I say the man is guilty as hell. He knows where that ship is and there are men here on this island that help him. If Steffan hasn't the guts to call the man out, I will. There are ways to find out things without using velvet gloves."

"What are we supposed to do, charge into the man's house on his own island and accuse him of things for which we have no proof? He has no idea we belong to the British Navy. He thinks we're privateers. There would be no reason to keep it a secret from us; in fact he needs, if he's guilty, privateers to carry the contraband to the Colonies. We would be the first he would ask."

"Steffan's message is that there is no sign of any activity so far. We'll be here at least another week. In that time, we'll find out everything we can, but if Andrew Marriott is innocent, he deserves to be treated like the gentleman he is."

"This woman, the one who is working with the pirates. Do you think she is someone who lives on the island?"

"No, both Steff and I have met most of the women who live here. Steff thinks it is the lady love of one of the pirates. No matter, if she stays in these waters or attacks the next ship, we'll be right there to catch her."

"What are Steffan's plans for guarding that ship that is coming through in a few days?"

"That's the last thing he wants to do, guard her. Leave her wide open like a ripe plum to be plucked, then wait for our red ship to come out of hiding. What he wants to do is find where they're hiding the arms, how they transfer them and where that red ship is kept between strikes. If there is a way to get all those answers, we will."

"If we don't have any of those answers and that ship gets taken, I'm moving in on Andrew Marriott. With the right persuasion, he'll tell us everything we need to know."

"You were given orders to remain here. Steffan was given orders to find the pirates. I don't think the Admiralty will look favorably on your taking matters into your own hands."

"You just tell Steffan what I said. If he can't handle the job the way it should be handled, I will do it for him. Once the pirates are caught and brought back I don't think the Admiralty will question the way it was done."

Tom was so angry he thought of several things to say, all of which might have gotten him in serious trouble. Slowly, he regained control of his anger. "I'll tell Steffan exactly what you said, word for word."

"You do that" Jaspar smiled. "Steffan is a sentimental fool. He gets too involved in other people's troubles instead of taking care of himself. It leaves him wide open for everything he gets."

Tom smiled and opened the door. As he went to close it behind him he looked again at Jaspar and there was a humorous glitter in his eyes. "You know," he said, "I believe for the first time I agree with every word you said." Jaspar stared at the door for a moment after it closed behind Tom.

"Bastard," he muttered. "Watch yourself, Tom Braydon when you friend goes down you go with him." His malevolence was lost on Tom who whistled softly to himself as he guided the small boat through the moonlit night.

"God" he whispered to himself, "I wish Cecile was here to see how beautiful this is." His thoughts, once occupied with Cecile remained so until he was back aboard her namesake. He informed Steffan of what Jaspar had to say and the threats he had made. "I wouldn't take him too seriously, Tom, Jaspar has always been more talk than action."

"That's your problem, Steffan. You're a completely honorable man. It's a blind spot. You can see everyone in the same light."

"For example?"

"The Marriotts."

"They're both innocent of this Tom, I'd stake my life on it. Andrew is an honest man. I've questioned so many people about the island, most of them would die for him if need be. If he were doing this, he's the type of man who would stand up and shout his loyalties to the sky whether we were English or American."

"And Tamara?"

"How could she be involved without her father knowing? Where is God's name could she get a ship and the crew to man it. She's a beautiful and charming girl, but I don't think she's capable of doing all that without her father knowing it."

"Are you getting more attached to her than you should, Steff?"

"You've said that before, Tom. I'll tell you again, I have no intention of developing any deep or permanent relationship with anyone. Of course, I'm not blind, I know how beautiful she is. But right now, I've a career and a job to do and I intend to do both. I've fallen into that perfumed trap before, Tom," he added ruefully. "I don't intend to fall into it again. The race is just fun; the time she and I might spend together is just a passing amusement for both of us. If I need a woman that badly, there are plenty around that are easier to get. Quit worrying about me. When we leave here, I go intact, ship, crew, captain and heart."

"I don't mean to pry, Steffan, I just . . . well, I don't know. I've had an uneasy feeling for a long time that this little episode is going to turn into more than we've bargained for."

"In what way?"

"Now you are really going to think I'm an old lady. I don't know. I just don't know. Sometimes things happen you just don't count on or plan on. Sometimes fate has your path in life chosen a little differently than you've chosen."

"Boy, you are getting philosophical in your old age. I'm a stubborn man. I've got my life all planned out and I'm going to see everything goes the way I want it."

"I hope your right," Tom laughed and held up his hand as if to ward off the words Steffan was about to speak. "All right, all right, no more premonitions. Life goes as we plan it. Our repairs, our race, a trip home and organized careers from then on."

Steffan grinned. "Go to bed, Tom. I want all those repairs done tomorrow. Then we'll put in our order for a bright breezy sun-lit day for the race."

Tom walked to the door; then he stopped as if a sudden thought came to him. He turned to face Steffan again.

"Steff?"

"What now?"

"I never did find out what the wager on the race was. What did you two decide on?"

"If I lose, I have to make a loud elaborate apology, I imagine in front of every guest Tamara can gather for the occasion."

Tom laughed. "It would serve you right for insulting the lady's ability. And if she loses, just what is the other side of the bet?"

"A personal tour around the island." Steffan replied quietly, his eyes challenging Tom to make any further comment. Tom was entirely too clever for that. He merely grinned and left the room without another word.

Tom walked on deck a few minutes before he decided to go to bed, his thoughts on Steffan and Tamara. The two are drawn to each other, he thought of both of them too stubborn to admit it even to themselves. He knew of the damage Morgana had done but he felt that Tamara was just the medicine Steffan needed to cure him of the poison. He hoped that Tamara would lose the race. He knew it would disappoint her, but before they left the island forever, he wanted to see Steffan and Tamara spend some time together alone. Maybe then they would find something that would shake them and open their eyes to that very special thing he and Cecile shared.

Steffan was just as deep in his own thoughts. He was sure there was no involvement between Andrew Marriott and the red ship that hid somewhere in these waters, but he intended to find out for sure the night the arms ship came. He had planned exactly what he was going to do. After that night, there would be no questions about Andrew's innocence or guilt. That the leader of the red ship was Tamara never entered his mind. That the capture of his ghost pirate would cause him more grief than he'd known did not occur to him or that the mission he was on now would change the direction of his life.

He went to bed and slipped immediately into a deep restful sleep.

All was quiet now in the Marriott home. Tamara had made her plans to sail once again, to capture more arms for the American cause, and to tempt the fates again. The thrill of the chase coursed through her. She had also made plans for her future to be just exactly what she wanted, and what she thought she had the ability to achieve.

All the plans were made, all the lives were planned and everyone rested easily with the arrogant assurance that they were

250

really in control of their own futures.

And fate chuckled heartily at the impudence of man and with the touch of its finger it stirred the waves of life and created a storm that would tumble them all from their safe little harbors into the open sea of life.

Twenty-two

The morning of the race dawned with every sign of being the perfect day they prayed for. The sky, lightened by rays of the morning sun was a clear crystal blue, and the breeze pushed along the white billowing clouds with an unseen hand.

Both Steffan and Tamara stood on the docks waiting for the two people her father had chosen as impartial judges. One of them would board each ship to guarantee that all the rules of the race were strictly adhered to, the rules that Andrew was now explaining to them.

"You will circle the island, but only a half mile from the coast line," he touched the map of the island in several places. "There are reefs here, and here. There is also a narrow channel between these two reefs which you will have to go through single file. The water is not deep enough for you to go side by side, so the first there is obviously the first through and stands a good chance of winning. Watch for the violent tide at the tip of the island, it's quite dangerous and has tried to throw me against the rocks many times. You will board your ship now and at my signal, you will start. You should be back here by late tonight. We'll all be waiting here. Good luck."

Steffan turned to Tamara and held out his hand. She put hers in his for a brief moment before she pulled it away. They both boarded their ships and stood awaiting the signal. Her father raised a pistol in the air and fired. The race began.

White sails puffed out their chests and inhaled the crisp breeze. Both ships reached the neck of the harbor at the same time and so close together that Tamara could see the white flash of Steffan's smile as he waved to her. She smiled and waved back; once on the open sea, the deep current of the ocean combined with the wind-filled sails drove them along at an astounding rate of speed.

The first obstacle that loomed in their paths were the huge rocky reefs that lined the first curve around the island. There was no way to go around them for it would have put them beyond the limits of the race. It was obvious that they would have to shorten sail and ease through the rocks, but, neither Tamara or Steffan gave such an order.

"Steff," Tom shouted, "we'd better shorten sail. If we hit those rocks at this speed they'll never find pieces of us."

"Look at her, Tom, is she shortening sail?"

"No."

"Then she knows the way through those reefs and she's going to lead us through. Hug her as close as you can and let her be our guide."

"She's probably going to expect you to slow down and feel your way through."

"Sure, while she shows us her heels. Won't she get a surprise."

Tom chuckled and maneuvered the *Cecile* as close to the *Adventurer* as he could. So close that Tamara was afraid for a minute they were going to ram her. Then it dawned on her that Steffan had read her maneuver accurately and she saw what he was going to do. She laughed and Mikel watched her. She was in her element now. The excitement of the race made her eyes sparkle and the sound of her laughter encouraged the men of the crew who watched her with pride. She was their lady and for her they would put every effort of their combined minds and bodies to winning this race.

Tamara maneuvered the tricky area of the reefs with amazing agility and though Steffan kept the *Cecile* as close to her as possible they still came out of the reefs with Tamara holding the lead. Now that they were clear of the reefs, there were several miles of clear deep water before they met their next challenge.

"Tom," Steffan shouted, "get up every piece of canvas the *Cecile* has. Use your shirt if you have to."

Tom shouted the orders necessary and within minutes, every piece of canvas that was on board the *Cecile* was feeling the pressure of the wind. Slowly, Steffan narrowed the lead Tamara had to less than half the length of her ship. She watched him come with grudging admiration not only for the beauty and maneuverability of the *Cecile* but the expertise of her captain.

The canvas that Steffan had put on placed the *Cecile* in the greatest danger of plowing herself into the ocean. Tom watched Steffan in hopes that the studsails and royals could be brought down at least before this happened. Steffan gave no sign that he had any intention of doing so. Instead, he held her steady and slowly he came bow to bow with the *Adventurer*. Their bows cut the ocean like huge sharp blades and left a white froth in their wake. Masts quivered under the strain of excessive canvas. Timbers groaned under unaccustomed strain. Mikel and Tom watched as the will and determination of the people they cared for the most refused to bend. Minutes turned to hours as they ran ahead of the wind, bow to bow toward a spot that they both knew only one ship could go through at a time. It was well past noon; Steffan paced the deck, one eye watching the straining mast with its overload of sails and the other on the *Adventurer* who held her own beside him. Whether he liked to admit it or not, he was forced to acknowledge Tamara was an exceptional captain and by rights deserved a public apology for anything he might have said to slight her abilities. He even had to admit to himself that the only reason he wanted to win was the thought of her spending the whole day and evening with him. If it had been any other wager, he might have taken the overload of canvas down and run the race under standard sail. After studying his map, he knew that within an hour or so, they were going to reach the narrow channel. Who would be the first through? Steffan knew that with the extra canvas he carried, he had the advantage; given enough time, he would be able to pick up any lost time that might occur should he let her go through the channel first. At least that was the logical excuse he found, any other thoughts that slipped into his mind were pushed firmly aside without recognition. Huge sentinel rocks protruding from the ocean marked the entrance to the narrow channel. When they came in sight, Steffan, to Tom's complete surprise ordered the studding sails and the royals down. The small, almost imperceptible slowing was enough for Tamara to enter the channel first. Steffan was so close behind her that there was hardly a breath between the stern of her ship and the bow of his.

For a few minutes, Tamara could not believe she had reached the entrance to the channel before Steffan. She turned to look at the *Cecile* and saw the lowering of the extra sails. Anger choked her at what she thought was a direct and deliberate insult. That he had gracefully stepped aside and allowed her first passage was like a cold slap in the face, reminding her he still considered her an inferior woman and needed some advantage to compete with him.

They came out of the narrow channel, and now it was Tamara's turn to show her disdain for Steffan. She deliberately slowed just enough to let Steffan come almost even with her, to show him she did not need his gallantry to let her win. Steffan and Tom exchanged glances and Tom laughed. "Fair minded lady. She's letting you know in no uncertain terms that she needs no help from you to win. I'm almost beginning to wonder if I shouldn't have placed a wager on her."

Steffan chuckled, "Don't count your money until the race is over. I think the *Cecile* still has a few tricks up her sleeve yet. She's a proud lady. I don't think she'll let an *Adventurer* beat her."

They raced before the wind, every sail puffed with pride. By the time they rounded the tip of the island they were side by side. Both captains could feel the strain on their ships but neither would give an order that would slow them one bit. Both second mates watched with fascination and no little trepidation as the ships leapt through the waves and drove themselves forward.

The rounded tip of the island, for an area of over ten miles, held a deep and treacherous current. Here, there was no sandy beach, but cave filled cliffs upon which the thundering ocean crashed.

Tamara refused to let Mikel or any of the others help her control the *Adventurer* through this, but determinedly held the wheel and guided her ship through the current and away from that deadly shore. Steffan, having all he could do to keep *Cecile* under control was caught again in deep admiration for the woman who a few hours ago, he had considered a fragile female. "No matter if I win or lose," he thought, "she will receive an apology for my uncharitable thoughts."

And now, as they left the last of their obstacles behind them came the mad dash for home. Nothing stood between them and their goal but clear open sea.

Timbers groaned in agony, yet gave their strength. Sails filled and strained at the masts that held them. The spars and masts themselves quivered from the tremendous pressure upon them. Both ships rose and fell in the troughs of the ocean's waves.

They rode alongside each other, so close that a man on one ship could have hailed a man on the other. The sun dipped low toward the horizon before the map told both captains that before its fading light was gone one of them would be victor.

Tension tightened as both ships moved together as though they were bound to one another. It looked, by the time the lights of the harbor blinked into view, as if the race would end up a tie, then disaster struck.

The tip of the foremast on the *Adventurer*, unable to bear the strain any longer, snapped. Only the tip of it, about four feet, broke away, and it would have done no damage to the

Adventurer's speed if, on its descent it had not ripped through one of the topsails flattening it against the mast. The imperceptible loss of speed was not much, just enough to let the *Cecile* bound ahead and enter the neck of the harbor, which was the finish line, a half a ship's length ahead of the *Adventurer*.

Everyone involved in the race and all the onlookers were amazed at the outcome.

Mikel, who had actually prayed silently that the race would turn out to be a tie, looked from the broken mast and torn sail to Tamara's misery filled face. She stared in absolute disbelief at the small piece of bad fortune that shook her emotions to the core.

Her father, who had been watching their approach through a telescope, knew at the moment what his daughter was feeling. He stood and watched both ships until they were safely docked then went immediately to the *Adventurer's* gangplank. He wanted to be the first to talk to Tamara.

No one was any more surprised than Steffan and Tom, both of whom, although they would not have admitted it to the other, had silently hoped for either one of two finishes . . . either a tie or that the *Adventurer* would win.

Tamara and Mikel walked down the gangplank to face her father together. Andrew could see the effort it took her to keep herself under control. There was the suspicious glitter of unshed tears in her eyes. Mikel could still hear the hollow sound of her voice as she had thanked her crew for the tremendous effort they had put forth and laid the fault where it had belonged—on uncertain fate.

"Tamara" Andrew said, "that was a well run race, and if a treacherous piece of bad luck hadn't occurred, you might have won, but either way, I'm very proud of the way you handled the *Adventurer*."

"Thank you, Papa. It's not the losing, it's just that I hate to see her beaten by an accident. It's not fair."

"No matter, we must pay our wager to Captain Devers."

He was surprised at the paleness of Tamara's face and the way her hands trembled. "Was the wager so much, child, is it too difficult to pay?"

Tamara looked past him, her eyes caught by Steffan's walking purposefully in her direction. "I will pay my debt, Papa," she said sorrowfully, but it was the first time in her life her father had seen uncertainty in her eyes and something else that hovered close to fear. Steffan took Andrew's hand and accepted his congratulations but his eyes found Tamara's and held them.

Soon, Tamara and Steffan were left together as the other three drifted away as rapidly as they could.

"Tamara?" Steffan said gently, but his brows furrowed in a frown. The very last thing he wanted from Tamara was the cold uncompromising look in her eyes.

"Congratulations, Steffan. The race was excellent competition. Your ship truly is a beautiful lady."

"Thank you. I must say I have never admired such ability in my life as yours. I'm glad fate was on my side for you came within a hair of beating me."

"Nevertheless, you are the winner and I owe you my wager."

"Tamara . . . not like this . . . not in competition. Can't we call a truce between us and have a nice day to spend together?" His eyes were serious and intent upon her as he stepped so close they were almost touching.

"Why," she whispered, "why do you want to spend so much time with me?"

"Because, I want to know you, really know you. You're such a combination of people, yet I feel there's a Tamara I've never met yet and one I would sincerely like to know. I think that other Tamara and I would enjoy ourselves if the others are left behind and can't interfere. Will you compromise and let me and that elusive Tamara share a day together?" He had reached down and taken her hand while he spoke and held it. She was aware of him with every fiber of her being and felt suddenly as though she were standing on the edge of a cliff above a sea of emotions she could not understand. He pulled her hand up close to his chest, so close she could feel the solid thud of his heart beat.

"Say yes," he whispered insistently.

"Yes."

His quick smile appeared as he tucked her hand under his arm and they moved toward Andrew, Mikel and Tom who had been standing apart watching them. Andrew and Mikel had been observing the two closely, but not as closely as Tom. He could sense the interest Andrew showed in their conversation, but not as much as he felt the awareness of Mikel's attention. He saw the drawing together of his brows and the narrowing of his lips as he pressed them together. "Here," he thought "was the danger in himself and Steff being discovered. Mikel Robbins would bear watching." That he was obviously jealous, Tom noticed immediately, but he sensed something much deeper than that.

"Come," Andrew said. "We'll go back to the house. I have a late meal arranged and we'll drink a toast to two excellent ships and two excellent captains."

Andrew had brought along two buggies that would hold four, but with some expert maneuvering on Steffan's part, Andrew, Mikel and Tom found themselves headed home in one, while Steffan and Tamara shared the other. As they rode along slowly, as slowly as Steffan could manage without stopping, Tamara remained silent. "I thought," Steffan began, "that we could go for a ride in the morning, then take a small boat and go down the coast. Our cook prepares the best lunch you can imagine. After that we'll just let the day take care of itself."

"It sounds very nice, Steffan."

"Yes."

"Our wager was from dawn until midnight."

"That's right."

"After midnight, the agreement is completed."

He pulled the reins and the horses came to a stop. Although he could barely make out her form in the dark, he could feel she was watching him. He tied the reins and turned to face her.

"Tamara, will it be so very difficult or," his voice became slightly amused, "are you a little afraid?"

"Afraid! Afraid of what?"

"Afraid of letting someone too close, maybe afraid that you might really enjoy sharing. That the beautiful ice princess is really a warm blooded woman who is not really happy in her castle away from the rest of the world."

"Do you really believe that? That I feel so very safe here I shut out the rest of the world?"

"Only what you think might be a threat."

"Neither you nor anyone else is a threat to me, Steffan. I am in control of my life now as I expect to always be."

Steffan reached out and touched her face with his fingertips. "You're trembling," he said softly.

"It's become cold."

Gently he let his fingers trace a line from her cheek down the smooth column of her throat. He could feel the pulse beating rapidly. She did not make a sound as he slowly drew her toward him and his mouth found hers.

It was a gentle kiss, meant for no purpose than to touch, yet he could sense the quivering response in her.

Without another word, he picked up the reins and slapped them against the horse's rump to set him in motion.

They ate an excellently prepared supper and later sat in the comfort of Andrew's study awaiting the drinks that Andrew had ordered. When they arrived, Andrew raised his glass and smiled at Steffan. "My toast to your so excellent ship and to the expertise of her master."

"Sir," Steffan replied before he drank, "I would, if you would permit, like to say a few words."

"Of course."

Steffan turned to Tamara and raised his glass to her.

"To one of the most accomplished captains it has ever been my good fortune to know, and to the *Adventurer*, a ship worthy of her. I apologize sincerely for any doubts I had of the abilities of either."

Tamara's eyes sparkled with surprise and delight and another emotion a little warmer that brought a smile to Steffan's lips. This was what he would want, that unguarded, relaxed smile, the look of flushed pleasure and the sparkle of laughter in her eyes that had replaced that cold guarded look.

"Thank you," she said lightheartedly, "both for myself and for my crew. That was unnecessary, Steffan. The wager was lost by me. You had no need to apologize."

"Of course, I did," he disagreed. "It was not a need, it was the truth. I meant every word I said."

"And I certainly agree with him," Tom added. "I have never seen a more outstanding piece of seamanship than I witnessed today." He too raised his glass towards Tamara. "To Tamara and the *Adventurer*."

Steffan's eyes held Tamara's across the room as he drank from his glass. They told her in no uncertain terms that he meant all he had said and even more that he left unsaid.

"Tell me, Andrew," Steffan said. "Tamara tells me you have friends in the Colonies. What do you think of the situation that is fomenting there?"

Andrew sat down in his chair with a sigh.

"I have many friends there, and I do sympathize a little with their cause. I can see without doubt they have the spirit and the valor to win a war . . ."

"War!" Mikel exclaimed. "That is still a foolish thing. They haven't the Army, Navy or weapons to wage a war against England."

Steffan looked at Mikel, something in the tone of his voice told Steffan there was more than he was saying.

"Do you think that's why these pirates are waylaying ships, to get the arms for the Colonies?"

"Of course," Tamara said quietly. "What better way to defeat a tyrant than to use their own weapons against themselves."

"Tyrant?" he questioned in surprise.

"What else would you call a country that keeps another chained in servitude?"

"I don't believe that."

"Have you ever been there?"

"No, but . . ."

"I have. I have seen first hand a country that has the potential to be great, held down by the iron hand of despotism. I have heard the voices of brilliant patriots shout their desire to be free. Because they are young and ill equipped now, don't believe for a moment they will not be victorious. In time they will grow in strength for they have the most important ingredients it takes."

"And that is?"

"Determination, pride, loyalty and most of all, love of country. They will defeat England in time."

Mikel was desperately trying to catch Tamara's attention. He knew she was angry and consequently saying things she wouldn't have said under normal circumstances. He grasped the first words that came to mind. "Of course, no matter which way the winds blow, it will have no effect on us here at Marriott Island. We have nothing to do with either side; we are neutral and will obligingly trade or do business with either."

"Is that true, Andrew?" Steffan asked.

"Yes, in essence it is. We have friends in almost every country in the world. We trade and do business with them all."

"But," Steffan said, "if war were to break out . . . then where would you stand?"

"To tell you the truth Steffan, I don't really know what I would do. England was my home, but for the past twenty years, this island has been the only real home I've known. I suspect I should try to remain neutral and stay out of it. In that case I would hesitate to deal with either country until the hostilities ceased."

"I see," Steffan turned to Tamara. "And do you feel you would do the same?"

No one was watching Tamara more intently than Steffan and Mikel. Both, for different reasons, awaiting her answer.

"I am my father's daughter, captain," she replied thoughtfully. "I hope I possess the same sense of honor as he and would defend what belongs to me the same as he."

Mikel hid his satisfied grin in his glass. Tamara was in control of herself now. There would be no more outbreaks to arouse suspicion.

"If you all would excuse me," Tamara said demurely, "the day has been exhausting."

"Yes," Steffan said with the flicker of laughter again in his eyes, "and I have to be up early in the morning."

"Yes, very early," Tamara replied. "Just after dawn."

"Agreed," Steffan grinned and bowed slightly toward her. "Just after dawn," he repeated, meaningfully. "Good night, Tamara, sleep well and have pleasant dreams."

"Would you like me to have my coach brought around?" Andrew asked.

"No, it's a beautiful night," Steffan answered. "Tom and I will walk back to the *Cecile*."

"If you go around the house and through the back garden, there is a gazebo there; on the other side of it are a flight of steps leading to the beach. It is a lovely walk along the beach at this time of night."

Tom and Steffan thanked Andrew and left, followed by Mikel who said a quick good night to them outside and disappeared quickly into the dark night. Steffan and Tom made their way around the house and stood for a minute in the garden. Expertly, Steffan absorbed the area for future use. They crossed the garden and walked across the green expanse of lawn to the octagonal shaped gazebo that sat several feet from the cliff's edge. Steffan went inside for a few moments. The gazebo was about eight feet across and had open lattice work windows. There were cushioned benches that ran around the entire building. From where they stood, they could see miles to sea.

"What a beautiful view!" Tom said.

"Yes" Steffan answered. "There would be no surprising anyone in this mansion. From here you can see up and down the coast for miles. Why," he pointed "I'll bet those dim lights there are the *Cecile*."

"That's right." Tom said. Very convenient. With a telescope you could see every move we made from here."

"Umm," Steffan murmured. "Let's go find those steps."

They went to the edge of the cliff and found the flight of steps that led to the beach. They walked down in silence, then along the beach.

"Kind of convenient to have a private beach in your back yard," Tom suggested.

"Yes, that way no one at the docks can see your comings and goings."

"What do you think is going on, Steff? Do you think Andrew is our pirate?"

"No; I don't think he's the pirate. I think he would have been honest enough tonight to tell us where his sentiments lie."

"Then what do you think is going on?"

"I think they might know or deal with the pirate, whoever he, or she is. I think they might be able to lead us to our pirate friend."

"What do we do about it if they do?"

"I don't want to rest Andrew," Steffan said firmly, "or Tamara?"

"Especially Tamara," Steffan laughed. "I just want to get hold of our pirate friend and put a halt to all this gun running. When we catch them, Andrew can be warned about any such dealing in the future."

"Steff?"

"What?"

"What are you going to do when the day comes that you have to admit just who you are and what you are?"

Steffan walked along for a while longer in silence then said quietly "I guess I'll cross that bridge when I get to it. In the meantime, I'll make it as easy on them as possible."

"Think that will carry any weight with her? When she finds out who you are and why you really came here, she'll be so angry, she'll probably shoot you."

"Maybe she'll understand. Clearing the waters of a few pirates shouldn't upset her that much."

"You and I both know it's not the pirates, it's finding out how we lied to them that might cause the explosion."

"It can't be helped, now, Tom." Steffan said with an uncomfortable shrug of his shoulders. "We're stuck with the lies. Much as I hate it, we have to play the game to the finish. When it's all over, I'll explain to Tamara and her father. I'm sure they'll both understand. They'll have to see that as officers under orders, we had no other alternative. The little inconvenience it is causing them won't be such a problem."

Tom remained quiet as they walked along, but Steffan could feel the words he was not saying.

"Speak up, Tom, no use keeping it to yourself."

"All right, at the risk of making you angry, I'll play a little

262

game with you called 'what if'."

"What if?"

"Yes, it's an easy game. I'll just say 'what if' something and you supply the answer."

Steffan chuckled.

"What if," Tom said. He stopped and he and Steffan faced each other, "she's falling in love with you?"

"Tom!"

"What if, she believes you're really who you say you are and accepts you so?"

"Stop it, Tom."

"What if her father is guilty?"

"Tom, I said stop it."

"Worse yet, what if they are both guilty?"

"Impossible!"

"Is it? Play along, Steff. What if they are, and it falls on Captain Steffan Devers, newly appointed captain in His Majesty's Navy, to arrest them both and take them back to England to hang?"

"Damn it!"

"All right Steff. I just wanted you to see something clearly, to admit it to yourself."

"What?"

"No, you say it. You tell me the truth. You've never lied to me in all the years I've known you."

"All right, Tom. You know it's been a heavy load for me to carry. You know I didn't want this to happen but . . ."

"But you love her."

"Yes, and I know she isn't guilty. I'd stake my life on it."

"That may be exactly what you're doing."

Steffan was silent as Tom went on. "If she is guilty and you have to arrest her, would you be able to do it, Steff?"

"It won't come to that. She may be a little angry with me for lying about who I am, but that's the worst that can happen. It's a chance I have to take. I'll explain everything to her and she'll understand."

"Will she?"

"Yes."

"What if . . ."

"Don't start that game again. I don't care to play."

"No matter what, the questions still remain."

"What do you suggest I do?"

"Tell her the truth. I think she's the kind of girl who would accept that better than finding out you could have told her and chose to keep on lying."

Steffan again remained silent.

"I know what you're thinking Steff."

"You do?" Steffan replied shortly.

"You're wondering if there is just a slight chance that her father is guilty. You're wondering if you tell her the truth and he is, she'll warn him to protect him or worse yet . . ."

"No, I'll never accept the fact that either of them know anything about this and just to prove the point, Tom, I'm going to call your bluff. Tomorrow, we spend the day together, Tamara and I. I'm going to tell her not only who and what I am and why I'm here, but I'm going to tell her how I feel about her. Then you'll find out that I was right all along and the both of them are innocent, and if you say 'what if' one more time, I'm going to knock your head off your shoulders. We've searched this island from top to bottom, into every cove or place you could put a ship. The fact that blood red ship isn't here proves one thing, someone else captains her. The fact that Andrew Marriott is an honest man, respected almost all over the world should prove to you that he's above these shoddy dealings. Tamara could not buy, man and sail a ship without her father's knowledge. Not only am I going to tell her all about me . . ." Steffan paused, then grinned. "I'm going to ask her if she'll consider me eligible husband material."

Tom laughed with him. "If the lady has any sense," he said wickedly, "she'll see what an obnoxious temper you've got and throw you off the cliff."

"Either way, I'll find out tomorrow. Let's get back to the ship. I need some sleep." He walked ahead of Tom who was suddenly thinking again of the way he had led Tamara to believe Cecile was a special woman in Steffan's life.

"God" he muttered, "I hope the lady has a sense of humor and doesn't throw me off the cliff." He trudged silently back to the ship. Both of them became quiet now and deep in their own private thoughts.

Twenty-three

It was a long and frustrating evening for both Tamara and Steffan. Both of them were caught up in the tide of deep emotion. For Tamara sleep came hard, and when it finally did, dreams followed. Her mind was determined that she would see through the results of her careless wager with as little emotional involvement as she possibly could, but her body, completely insensitive to her mind's logic, refused to cooperate. She could still feel the light touch of his hand on hers, and the gentle brush of his lips on her mouth. Giving up the idea of trying to sleep she lay and contemplated the events that had led to her insomnia. Steffan Devers, mysterious puzzle. She knew what he was, a privateer, a captain who was a wanderer who would do just about anything for profit. She knew he had lied about his reasons both for being on the island and for staying. She could not attribute all his reasons to his attraction to her although she knew he was. No, it was some other reason that held him here. Was he really suspicious of what she was doing? Did he see some financial gain in it for himself or did he know of the possibility of betraying her for a much easier profit? Somehow the idea of betrayal and Steffan did not seem to fit together. No, he may be a privateer, but she felt he had some sense of honor even toward this precarious profession. As her thoughts drifted on, she began to wonder just how deep his loyalties to England ran. As a privateer, he was technically without a country. "Maybe, just maybe," she mused, "he might be able to be enlisted to help our cause." As the day went along, she would tentatively feel him out. It would be interesting to see if she could gain his help. Another ship to acquire the arms for her adopted country's cause excited her. Of course, she mentally denied the fact that to do so would keep him on or near the island for a longer time. "No." It was not that, it was America's need to which she credited her enthusiasm. She would find a way to bring their conversation around to what she wanted she was confident. Of course, she laughed to herself, his memories of the pirate lady had not left him in a receptive mood to her, but she was sure she could overcome any anger he had left. If she could get close enough to him to convince him to help her she wondered just what effect it would have on, as Tom said, the oh so beautiful Cecile. Another wave of emotion washed over her and she firmly refused to recognize it for what it was. She was not jealous of the beautiful Cecile; after all, there was nothing serious between herself and Steffan. She needed him to help her, what he did with his private life was his concern and did not really interest her. Yet the warm feeling that fluttered somewhere deep within her belied her thoughts.

Sleep continued to elude her so she rose from the bed, slipped on a thin white robe and went out the large windows to the balcony. The night was clear, washing in bright white moonlight. She looked out over the garden to the white gazebo that sat on the edge of the cliff. Then beyond that, to the calm deep sea. Slowly, she walked down the steps from her balcony to the garden below. She drifted past the quietly murmuring fountain in its center and walked toward the gazebo. Climbing the five steps she stood within the confines of the small octagonal room. All the latticed windows had been pulled shut for the night. She walked across the small room and pushed one window open. She sat on the cushioned bench and laid her arms on the window edge, resting her chin on her folded arms she looked out over an old familiar and loved scene. The pleasurable drug of soft breeze and the sound of the water brushing against the sand lulled her and after a few minutes, she could feel her heavy eyelids begin to close. In a little while, she drifted off into a light relaxing sleep.

Steffan lay on his bunk with his hands folded behind his head and his thoughts on a pair of deep green eyes and a soft rounded form in his arms. The delicate scent she wore was as fresh in his senses as though she lay beside him, and that thought sent a million others after it. Tamara, soft and warm in his arms, in his bed. The feel of her lips against his and the trembling surrender he had felt. It was too much to allow him to sleep. He pushed himself up from his bunk and slipped on the ragged pants cut off above the knees he wore the day he met Tamara on the beach. Without adding any more clothes, he went on deck. Leaning against the ship's rail, he looked toward where he knew Tamara must lie sleeping. Pictures conjured up in his mind of her beautiful hair across a pillow, of arms that reached to draw him to her aggravated the restlessness in him. In a quick decision, he decided to go for a late swim to perhaps cool off his overheated body.

He took the small sailboat and guided it silently down the coast until he found the small secluded harbor below Marriott Mansion. He pulled the boat up on the sand and discarding the pants, he ran toward the water and dove in. He pushed himself down until the need for air overcame him. Then kicked himself upward breaking to the surface gasping for air. The water was cool and exhilarating. He swam until he was mildly tired then headed toward shore. He walked from the water shaking his hair free of moisture and stood for a moment letting the warm breeze dry his skin.

Tamara did not know how long she slept or what had wakened her. She blinked her eyes open, then began to rise. Suddenly, her attention was drawn to the small boat that had just entered the harbor. She thought for a minute it might be Mikel bringing her some added news about the arms ship. Then she realized the boat was not the *Tamara*, but a strange one. She sat motionless watching it until it neared the beach, then it was out of sight. Curious, she left the gazebo and walked to the top of the cliff. She kept herself unseen from whoever was below. When the man leapt from the boat and pulled it ashore, he turned in her direction. The bright moonlight left his identity unquestionable . . . Steffan.

The moonlight washed over his tall muscular body. It was as clear as the bright day. So clear she could see the ripple of muscles as he moved about securing the boat. Her heart thudded heavily and she was aware of a deep feeling of warmth that seemed to urge her toward him. She stood still watching him in breathless expectant admiration. That he was handsome beyond endurance, she silently admitted; his body glistening tan in the moonlight reminded her suddenly of the description of the Greek gods she had read about in mythology. She froze as he discarded the ragged pants, and this time she gasped in amazed shock at her first look at a naked man.

She watched his lithe body as he dove gracefully, then when he came to the surface, she kept her eyes on him as he swam. Then, he walked up from the water shaking his hair free of it and enjoying the feel of the breeze. He stood like a bronzed Adonis and Tamara's eyes devoured him. Emotions she had never felt before coursed through her. She felt her body react in a way she could not control. Sensitive prickling of her skin and the deep sweet pain of need seeped through her like molten fire. She slowly dropped to her knees and a small sound escaped her lips. She wanted to go to his side, to touch with her hands that glistening wet skin, to feel the strength of those arms about her and the touch of his demanding mouth on hers. For the first time in her life, she wanted a man to make love to her, to possess her as she desired him. Tears of awareness filled her eyes and it took all the control she had to remain motionless. She watched him retrieve his clothes and don them, then he pushed the boat back into the water. She watched until the boat disappeared, then slowly she rose and walked back across the garden to a bed that she knew would never give her ease again until it was shared.

A red-gold sun was just peeking over the rim of the horizon, lighting the sky with fingers of light that began to push away the night sky, when Mellie shook Tamara awake.

"Miss Tamara, Miss Tamara," she whispered.

"Yes, Mellie," Tamara replied, her voice still heavy with sleep and her eyes closed.

"You told me to wake you at daybreak," Mellie answered. For a minute, Tamara remained quiet and motionless then suddenly remembrance flooded her mind and she sat up, startling Mellie with abruptness.

"Fetch me some water, Mellie. I have to bathe quickly if I want to be ready. I have a feeling our Captain Devers is very prompt."

"Yes, ma'am" Mellie answered and left the room.

Tamara sat still and thought back over last night. Was it some erotic dream? she thought. No, it was real for the tingle of the same deep unknown emotion washed over her again. That mysterious sense of belonging, as if they had somehow touched and blended together. What would this day bring? The bubbling excitement coursed through her. She rose from the bed and gathered together what she would wear, keeping his words in mind.

I want to know you, the inner Tamara. Well, today she would be Tamara, herself, unhampered by all the people she had to be for others. Mellie returned with the water and eyed silently the old clothes Tamara had chosen. She did not say a word for she felt her mistress was in no mood for warnings. She watched as Tamara bathed quickly and donned the green cotton dress.

"Only one petticoat, Miss Tamara!"

"Only one, Mellie," Tamara said firmly. "Today I will be free

268

to move as I choose without being tied down by all the extra clothing. I want to ride, to sail and I can't do it dressed like a lady going to tea."

Again Mellie clamped her mouth against the warnings. She watched as Tamara drew her long hair over her shoulders and braided it, letting the long thick braid hang carelessly down her back. The end of the braid she tied with a piece of green ribbon. She slipped on her old shoes then smiled at Mellie.

"I won't be back until midnight, Mellie. Keep a candle burning for me, will you?"

"What shall I tell your father?"

"The truth, that I'm spending the day with Steffan and I shan't be home until late."

"What are you going to do alone with that man until midnight?" Mellie questioned worriedly.

Tamara laughed. "To tell you the truth, Mellie, I really don't know. I lost my wager and I must pay my debt. The day has been planned by him. I'm sure he's thought of something to do that will be fun for both of us. See you later, Mellie," she smiled as she closed the door after her.

"I'm sure he has something in mind," Mellie said to herself. "But I'm just as sure you're going to be surprised by what it is. Don't let him hurt you, Miss Tamara . . . don't."

Tamara went downstairs and started toward the kitchen where she planned to get something quick to eat, when she heard the knock on the door. To keep anyone else from being wakened by it, she ran quickly to the door and pulled it open. Steffan was a little surprised to find Tamara opening the door, but he smiled.

"Good morning. It's surprising to find a woman who's ready to go when she say she'll be."

"I'm always an early riser, I enjoy the dawn. It's very beautiful. I was about to get something for breakfast, would you like to join me?"

"I brought along something. I thought we might go up to the high cliffs and have a sort of picnic breakfast and both enjoy the dawn."

"Yes, that does sound wonderful."

"Ready?"

"Yes."

"Then come along, Madam" Steffan laughed. "Breakfast and dawn are awaiting."

Securing two horses, they rode to the crest of the cliffs. There, they sat on a blanket, Steffan had provided and ate the food he had brought. Still warm rolls filled with butter and wrapped securely were unfolded accompanied, to Tamara's surprise, by a flask of hot tea. Unfolding another small bundle, Tamara found several small crisply fried pieces of ham. She exclaimed delightedly over the value of the ship's cook who could provide as well as this.

"Don't believe," Steffan chuckled, "that we get this kind of food at sea. Jocko just wanted to impress the lovely lady with his abilities. At one time, Jocko was an excellent chef in France."

"Good heavens, why is he a cook aboard a privateer ship?"

"One does not always question a man's past, my dear; there may be some things in it that he'd rather not have known."

"Of course," Tamara murmured. She turned her face to the almost risen sun. It was sending its rays through clusters of blue white clouds and dancing them off the crests of the ocean waves. The sight, though Tamara had been there before, was always different . . . always beautiful. They watched individual beauties in silence, Tamara, the sunrise and Steffan, Tamara. She sat in profile to him, her wide green eyes rapt with the beauty of nature, her lips slightly parted, her hands folded in her lap, and her slender body still as though she awaited something. The soft clinging dress brought into relief every rounded curve of her body and Steffan restrained himself from reaching out to touch the soft curve of her breast that pressed against the cotton dress and rose and fell gently with her breathing. He did reach out a hand, and she was unaware that he gently slipped the green ribbon from the end of her hair in hopes that it would loosen the confining braid. He slipped it into his pocket just as she turned to him.

"Breakfast is over, captain," she laughed. "The sun has risen and the day is yours. What is next?"

"Well, I thought since this was your home, you could give me a guided tour, then, just to please Jocko, I promised to bring you to the *Cecile* for lunch. After that . . ." he shrugged. "Suppose I keep the balance of the day a surprise?"

"All right. Whatever you say, sir," she stood up and he rose beside her. "Your every wish is my command." She laughed, but in a frozen instant, the laughter was stilled on her lips as gold brown eyes pierced hers with a look so deep and intense she found herself almost unable to breath. "Steffan" she whispered.

"I thought you were beautiful that night in the garden, but you're even more beautiful with the early morning sunlight dancing in your hair." He said as he reached out and brushed a stray wisp of hair that had been caught by the breeze. His touch seemed to awaken her and she stepped back from him.

"Your guide awaits. Shall we go?"

He nodded and followed her as she walked toward her horse, his eyes raking over her gently swaying hips as she walked ahead of him.

She guided him to all her more favored spots and enjoyed the fact that he seemed to appreciate her island's beauty as much as she did. Then she became aware that as they enjoyed the island, he was also enjoying her. He asked her questions about herself and listened with avid attention as she told him all about her childhood. He laughed with her over some of her escapades, became silent and sympathetic when she stumbled through the loss of her mother. He was silent when the subject of Mikel came up and she was completely unaware of the swift touch of jealousy that burned in him at the knowledge that Mikel had shared all the good and bad memories of her life. He was also aware of her deep profound love and admiration of her father. In fact, he was so often on her lips, that Steffan began to wonder if any man would have the power or courage to try to take his place in her life. Suddenly her capacity for love swept over him. He remembered well the selfish love of Morgana who had no room in her life for anyone other than herself. That she surrounded herself only with people who gave to her. Suddenly, he felt only sympathy for Morgana and all the old feelings for her seemed to melt away in the glow of Tamara's smile. Tamara had a place in her life, in her heart for all those dear to her and each received a full measure of love. He was overwhelmed with wonder at what the man she would love would receive. A deep burning need to reach that spot began to burn within him and by the time they arrived at the *Cecile* for lunch, it was a flame that consumed him completely and left him aching with the desire to drag her away to a quiet spot and make love to her until she cried out her need for him. The lunch was a gay affair. Jocko had outdone himself and Tom kept Tamara smiling at his teasing and brilliant jokes that were quite often directed at Steffan's boyhood escapades. It was only when Tamara began to ask questions about their lives when they were grown that Steffan laughingly declared the lunch was over and by rights the rest of the day was his.

Jocko was a small man of an unguessable age. He beamed in pleasure as Tamara smiled and complimented him on the excellence of the meal.

"We have an excellent cook, but I know he could not have done any better than you. It was one of the best meals I've had the pleasure of eating."

"Thank you, Ma'am. I'm very pleased you enjoyed it."

Both Steffan and Tom froze at his next words.

"The Navy doesn't give me much to work with, but I do the best I can."

There was a breathless silence while both Tom and Steffan wondered if she would realize what he had said. To their relief, Tamara believed he was referring to the French Navy.

"I'm sure your meals would be excellent no matter what the circumstances. Thank you."

"Shall we go, Tamara?" Steffan said. One look at his pale face told Tom that as yet, Steffan had told her nothing about himself or their reasons for being on the island. Tamara nodded and accompanied Steffan to the deck of the *Cecile*.

"Your ship is beautiful, Steffan. You must be very proud of her," Tamara said gently. "And the lovely lady for whom she's named," she added meaningfully.

Another misunderstanding of words would compound a feeling Tamara already had toward Cecile, for Steffan took it for granted Tom had told her Cecile was his sister. He was surprised and taken aback by the sudden look of anger that flashed into her eyes for a moment before she could disguise it as he said: "Yes, I'm proud of both Ceciles. they're both very beautiful ladies."

With a toss of her head, Tamara walked ahead of him down the gangplank and Steffan followed wondering what he could have said or done to upset her. At the bottom of the gangplank, she turned to face him, but her emotions were completely contained now. She smiled up at him, but he realized he had somehow lost the warmth he had gained during the morning. He didn't know what he had said or done to have her react that way but he was determined not only to find out but to change her again into the warm happy woman she had been a few short hours before.

"Where to, now, captain?"

"Let's take the boat and sail to the other side of the island. We could find a nice quiet cove there and swim."

"Swim? I brought nothing to swim in."

"You could borrow something from our cabin boy." His eyes challenged her to refuse, the sparkling laughter in their depths

272

told her so.

"Then would you mind asking him, captain? I would love to swim on such a lovely day."

He chuckled as he took her arm and they returned to the *Cecile*.

Steffan called his cabin boy and told him what she wanted and the boy led her to his quarters. When he showed her what he could supply, a mischievous glitter came to her eyes and she laughed. "Do you have a pair of scissors?"

"Scissors, Ma'am?"

"Yes, scissors."

"Yes, Ma'am, I'm sure I can get you some."

"Good, run along and get them." "I'm sure it's time Steffan Devers has a surprise, maybe one he won't be able to handle for a change." she told herself.

He left the cabin and in a few minutes, he returned with the scissors and Tamara chuckling to herself, set to work on the clothes while the wide-eyed cabin boy watched.

Tamara returned to Steffan's side with the small bundle in her arms and a glowing smile on her face. "I'm ready."

"Good," he grinned and escorted her to the boat. Within a few minutes, they were riding before a crisp breeze toward the mouth of the harbor. Tamara sat cross legged on the deck of the small boat and watched as Steffan guided the boat expertly out of the harbor and headed it along the coast of the island.

"You handle a sailboat well."

"I should, I've been doing it since I was a boy."

"I know a lot about you as a boy, but not much as a man. What happened?"

Steffan grinned broadly, "I went astray, Ma'am, and I found myself captain of a privateer ship and in the company of one of the most lovely ladies I've ever seen. Such phenomenal luck is almost too much to believe."

Tamara laughed, but was aware that he had deftly dodged her question. It made her wonder just what Captain Steffan Devers had to hide. "Maybe," she mused, "he's a wanted man." Her mind dismissed the thought. He would not have to be a criminal to acquire what he wanted, he was a man of ability and wit. He would do well honestly.

Steffan was angry with himself. Why couldn't he tell her about himself? He wanted to; why didn't he take the opportunity when she had asked him?, he asked himself. But he knew the answer.

He wanted this day first, he wanted to share this time with her for as long as he possibly could before he took the chance of making her angry with him. He changed the subject as quickly as he could and for the balance of the trip, they talked of her. Combined with all she had told him in the morning and the questions she answered now, he felt he knew all she would tell him.

Tamara pointed to a small cove as they rounded the tip of the island and Steffan expertly maneuvered the boat ashore. Without his help, she leapt ashore as soon as the boat touched the sand and helped him pull the boat further up on the sand.

"It looks like a beautiful place to swim."

"It is, I've come here often. Mikel and I have swum here since we were children. We even dive off the rocks," she laughed as she pointed to an outcropping of rocks that extended out into the water. Steffan looked at the huge rocks in sincere amazement.

"You . . . you actually jump from there?"

"Of course," she said lightly, her eyes aglow with mischief. "You're not afraid are you?"

"You'd best change," he chuckled. "Then we'll see who's afraid of what."

She sensed a double meaning but ignored it. Retrieving her bundle from the boat, she said, "I'll change behind those rocks, and be out in a minute."

She ran behind the shelter of the rocks. Steffan donned the ragged cut-off-pants, and put the rest of his clothes safely in the boat, then he turned toward the rocks. His eyes widened in surprise and he was speechless at the vision that presented itself. Tamara had taken the cabin boy's shirt and pants and trimmed them down amazingly. The pants hugged her slim hips, but were cut off just below leaving her long tanned legs free. She had removed the sleeves from the shirt, then cut it to her waist and tied the ends together in the front. It was obvious to him, she had nothing on under it.

"Do you like it," she smiled as she turned in a circle for him to see.

"I admire your taste in clothes," he chuckled, "more than you can imagine. My cabin boy never looked that good in them, I assure you."

"Let's swim over to the rocks; we can dive from there," she shouted back over her shoulder as she ran for the water.

Steffan laughed as he ran after her and they dove into the water together. She swam well, so well that Steffan was pressed to stay abreast of her. When they reached the rocks, she climbed up as agile as a monkey and he followed. They stood together on the top of the rocks.

"I used to stand here as a child and watch the dolphins play out there. I used to think it would be nice to leap in and swim with them, they're so graceful and beautiful."

Steffan looked down at the churning waters below them.

"Good God, you mean you dive from here?"

"Yes, it's a fantastic experience."

Steffan looked at her. She stood, smiling, fine wisps of hair blowing across her emerald eyes. Her tanned body glistening in the sunlight. The wet shirt, pressed against her skin, outlined her body. "She's as much a part of this as the sun and the water," he thought. "A beautiful child of nature at home in her element."

"You're not a bit afraid are you?" he asked.

"No, there are too many things in that other world to be afraid of, but nothing in mine."

"Things . . . like what?"

"Pretense, dishonesty, acting out what you don't believe, don't feel."

"What do you feel, Tamara?" he said his eyes holding hers and searching for what he needed.

"I don't know. I only know what I feel is so . . . different. You stepped into my life Steffan Devers and upset it. I'm unsure and I don't like to feel that way."

Steffan stepped so close their bodies almost touched, he put both hands on her slender hips. "Don't be unsure. Let me tell you how I feel. I'm in love with you, Tamara Marriott, and I want you. There has never been anything so sweet and clear in my life as that is." He slowly pulled her into his arms and bent his head to gently take possession of her soft half parted lips. He felt the soft breasts that pressed against his chest and the slender arms that encircled his neck. He felt an exuberant joy that she was no longer afraid of him, that her body trembled with the same emotion as his. Her mouth opened under his and his tongue explored, met with the same seeking as hers and the strength of his arms increased as he held her closer. When he released her lips, she looked up into his eyes and her heart thudded wildly at what she saw there. This was what she had been searching for. This was the look of deep and abiding love, of wild and tempestuous desire that she had seen so often exchanged between her parents. She stepped from him, a half smile on her face and a warm inviting glow in her eyes.

"Shall we go back to the beach, Steffan?" she said, temptingly. He nodded, unable to speak at the open invitation. She turned from him and walked to the edge of the rocks. There she stood poised for a moment, then she sprang forward. Her body arched up and out from the rocks and shot downward as straight as an arrow.

He stood for a moment until he saw her reappear and laugh as she gazed upward in challenge, then he leapt outward praying silently his body would clear the rocks. When he surfaced, he looked about for her and saw she was almost at the shore. He swam toward her. When he stood up in the shallow water, he saw her standing at the edge of the trees. Slowly, he walked toward her; she stood silently waiting. When he was less than three feet away, she put out one hand, palm outward, as if to stop him. He stopped. Slowly she reached up and began to untie the shirt she wore. Without her eyes leaving his, she shrugged it from her shoulders. The cut off pants followed and she kicked them away from her and stood proud of her extraordinary beauty and knowing that he was the one she had awaited all those years. He walked the few steps that separated them. With one hand he reached behind her head and drew the long braid of her hair over her shoulder. With trembling fingers, he worked the hair free of the braid and let it fall about her. She was a goddess of slender golden beauty and he could not stand another moment of waiting.

"Tamara," he whispered.

Suddenly, she was in his arms, her cool wet body against his and her parted lips searching for his. Her fingers twined in his thick hair as she claimed him. Bending down he put one arm behind her legs and lifted her, hearing with joy, her deep throaty laugh of possession.

Twenty-four

He carried her to the shade of a tree and lay her on the soft grass, kneeling beside her.

"You are the loveliest woman in the world, and I love you beyond hope, beyond reason," he said as he lay beside her and pulled her into his arms. She trembled, aware of him, wanting him, yet a little frightened of the unknown. "Don't be frightened of me, love," he whispered as their eyes met. "Never of me."

The words were said muffled by her hair as he held her against him. She could feel the deep strong beat of his heart as he held her tight. It matched the insistent throbbing of her own. She pulled her head away from his chest and looked up at him. They lay, bodies molded together, their eyes speaking expressively and silently to each other. Then he lowered his head and took her mouth with his. Tamara was unprepared for the wild flood of heat that began somewhere in the depths of her and exploded through her body. She only knew that she wanted to drown in his kiss. Her body became soft as she melted against him. To her it was suddenly as if this was something that had always been meant to be, as if she had always belonged to this man, to this place, to this time. Her breath came in short sobbing gasps as his hands, gentle and seeking, discovered and drew forward the desire and passion she felt. The world faded into nothingness, a brilliant void that contained only Steffan and his gentle exploration of her.

Within her blossomed the need to know him as he did her. Her hands sought him, the broad muscular back, arms of iron that held her, his broad chest with the mat of soft hair. Down to the lean ribs and heavily muscled hips, her hands sought, touched and burned his flesh like an iron, branding him hers now and forever.

He caressed her, cupping her breast gently in his hands, seeking the erect nipple with his mouth and hearing her soft moaning sobs of pleasure. Her body was consumed by an unquenchable, demanding flame, and it sought his in an unconscious knowledge that he held the release for this demanding fire. He moved his hands down her body finding the center of the blinding need. Gently separating her legs, he drew her to him and as he entered, he caught her mouth with his. The murmur of pain was drowned in his kiss. He moved deeply within her, lifting her body to his. The pain disappeared and suddenly she was engulfed with an urgency, a wanting that blinded her to every other thought. She clung to him whispering his name over and over as his body and the slow deep movements drove her to a frantic edge of passion. There was no beginning, no end. Just this moment of deep and abiding love that blended them together with a heat so intense that they were completely consumed, each of them losing one to the other, yet each of them gaining the other's greatest depths of love and belonging.

They lay still, their bodies still joined, clinging to each other in the wonder of the emotion they had just shared. He kissed her now, a soft lingering gentle kiss, his hand gently cupping her face as he looked down into her eyes.

"I always promised myself that if and when I ever found the woman I wanted beyond all others, I would make her mine, keep her bound to me forever and never let her go. I've found her, and I've possessed her, now I will say to her the words that bind us as the love we have shared has bound us. I love you, Tamara, and I want you to be mine from now to eternity . . . for always . . . will you?"

"Oh, Steffan," she whispered. "I've been looking for you for so long. I'm so happy to have found you and know you want me also. I should have died had you left me after this beauty we have shared." She put both hands against his face and drew him down to her. "For the first time in my life, I can say I love you without reservation. I can know what 'I love you' means—this deep need for you to want me, to hold me, to possess me as no other has or ever will. I love you, Steffan Devers, no matter what or who you are or what you have been. To me you are the world in which I live. Stay with me always, don't leave me."

"You will be with me, belong to me, no matter where I go. That I promise."

She sighed, completely happy, completely contented. In silence he held her against him wondering how to acquire the courage to tell her about himself. He wanted no lies between them. He wanted to take her to England, bring her to his family in pride and love, but to do all this first he must begin with the truth.

"Tamara," he began, gently touching the side of her face with his fingers. "There are many things about me you don't know . . . things you should know. I will tell you . . ."

She placed her fingers over his lips to stop his words. "No, Steffan, not today, not now. This day is ours for now, not for past or future. One day soon, we will talk of other things, but I have just found you and I don't want to share you today with any past memories."

"But Tamara . . ."

"Shhh, love," she whispered, as she drew his lips to hers. "Tell me only that you love me. Tell me again for I cannot seem to get enough."

"First tell me that you will always remember that I love you. No matter what happens or what anyone says or does." His eyes were intent on hers, glowing with an intense inner light she could not understand.

"Steffan?"

"Will you, Tamara? Will you always keep it in your heart, in your mind, that I do love you, that I would give my past, my present and my future for you. That I would never hurt you . . . ever!"

Suddenly it occurred to Tamara that Steffan might be talking about the beautiful Cecile, and a sudden shiver of fright went through her.

"Steffan . . . is there someone . . . someone you left behind, someone you care for?"

Morgana appeared in Steffan's mind, her face twisted by hate . . . by murder. "There was someone once," he said, "but when I see you, know you, I know again how very wrong I was. No, there is nothing in my life to compare to you."

"But, you must have loved her?"

"Why?"

"A man who loves the sea loves his ship. He does not name it after a woman for whom he feels nothing."

Steffan looked at her blankly, the sudden switch from Morgana to Cecile was too quick, and he didn't understand why Tamara would be jealous of his sister. "Tamara, what does Cecile have to do with anything?"

"You named your ship Cecile, surely you must care for her very deeply?" Her voice shook and her eyes fled from his. It was then that it came to Steffan that Tamara really did not know the relationship between him and Cecile. He chuckled, desiring to see just how far her jealousy went.

"Yes, I do care for Cecile a great deal."

Her eyes snapped back to his and he could see the anger beginning to grow.

"She's very pretty?"

"Oh, Cecile is not pretty . . . she's beautiful. She's a lovely lady with long black hair and eyes . . . well, about the color of mine. My feeling for her goes back a lot of years."

Tamara turned her head against his shoulder. He could feel the trembling in her body and her voice cracked as she whispered in anguish, "Tell me, Steffan, tell me if you intend to go back to her, tell me . . . do you love her more than me."

Steffan laughed, his arms about her he rocked her against him. He was startled when she thrust him away and leapt to her feet. She ran toward the ocean, and once the shock was over, he jumped up and ran after her. He caught her just at the edge of the surf. He grasped her arm and spun her towards him and enjoyed the picture of her beauty in anger. Her hair that he had unbraided, hung about her golden body in wild profusion blown by the wind. Her fists clenched she glared at him her emerald eyes blazing. Unaware now of her naked beauty she spat at him.

"Don't touch me! How dare you make love to me, then tell me of your love for another. How dare you take me so lightly. I am not a whore you can tumble on a beach with then walk away from. Go back to your beautiful Cecile, but do not look at me again. I am second in no one's life and I do not play the harlot for your pleasure, captain priate!"

With her last words, she slapped him with all the strength she had. Steffan grabbed her in his arms dodging the blows she threw and laughing at the undesirable names she called him as she slowly gained control. That her strength was no match for his, Tamara knew; but she fought until he held her pinned so tightly against him she could hardly breathe. Tears were new to Tamara, but in sheer frustration she lay her head against his chest and sobbed her anger.

"Tamara?" Steffan said gently. She refused to answer.

"Whether you speak or not, I know you hear. I told you less than an hour ago that I loved you. I asked you then if you would remember. Are your promises so easily forgotten, can you turn your love away from me so easily?"

Still she refused to answer. He held her arms pinned against him by crushing her close with one arm. With the other hand, he tipped up her face. Slowly, he lowered his head and took her mouth with his. She held herself stiff and unresponsive. Ignoring it, he continued to savor the soft feel of her lips. Slowly, gently, they warmed under his as he forced them apart and drank deeply of their honeyed sweetness. He felt her quiver in his arms. Still his storming of her fortress continued. He nibbled gently at the corners of her mouth. Then he kissed her cheeks, her eyes, and again took her mouth in a kiss that was becoming more heated, more demanding. Suddenly, with a soft whimpering sound, she relaxed against him. Her body, soft and warm pressed against his. He released the pressure of his arm and sighed in pleasure as two slender arms crept up about his neck and her mouth opened to his like the petals of a rose to the warm morning sun. Now, his hands found more delightful pleasures than merely holding her immobile. They softly caressed the gentle curves of the woman who had just told him she was his now and for always.

He lifted his mouth from hers and looked down into emerald eyes blinded in tears. "Do you really think I could hurt you like that? After what we've known. After the truth you just felt can you really believe I don't love you more than my life. Can you not feel the force that draws us to each other?"

"Yes, I will ask you no more, Steffan. I will tell you, despite my pride or any other emotion I know that I want to belong to you; that I want you to love me. I cannot deny it no matter what you do."

"Tamara" he whispered as he gently brushed his lips over hers again. She was surprised when he wrapped both arms about her and again pinned her arms securely. She looked up into his laughing gold brown eyes. Then her eyes glowed with suspicion.

"Steffan?"

"I'm holding on to you to save my skin for I have something to tell you."

"What?"

"Cecile . . . the beautiful Cecile. She is all the things I said, she is also my sister."

Tamara's mouth opened in surprised shock. "Your sister?"

"Cecile Devers, my young sister, and I might add, wife to Tom Braydon, my first mate."

"Wife to . . . oh! That despicable man! He led me to believe she was something special in your life."

"He didn't lie, did he? She is."

"No . . . I thought, oh, that wretched man will pay for all the nights I suffered."

"Did you, Tam?" he asked gently. Her eyes raised to him, this time with a glow of love so intense it made him catch his breath.

"I did," she said gently. "I thought of you in the arms of another woman, one more beautiful than I and I wanted to kill her. I wanted to tear out her hair and make her ugly so you would never desire her again."

"There is no one more beautiful than you, just as there is no one I love as I do you. Tam," he whispered as her arms slid about him and she raised her mouth to his kiss. They held each other, drawing from each other the depths of their love. Slowly, he drew her down to the soft ocean washed sand. There, with the warm water washing over them, they blended their bodies together and rose to the heights in a passion that would mold them into one with its blazing fire.

Later they retrieved their clothes. As they dressed, Steffan reminded Tamara, "The rest of the day is still mine, love. You promised until midnight."

"And what plans do you have for the rest of the night?" She asked as she was dressing. Her eyes met his and saw the devil's laughter there. She laughed helplessly as she went to him. "Are you insatiable, sir?"

"I am, with you. You're like no wine I have ever drunk before and I want to become completely intoxicated."

Her eyes met his challenging ones and he saw that she too would drink from the same nectar as he, with the same deep pleasure as he.

The sun was just setting and they stood for a few quiet moments and watched it disappear below the horizon. Silently, he took her hand in his and they walked down the beach. The warm water swished about their ankles. The night was black and millions of stars lit their path. They spoke in whispers to each other, although there was no one around to hear them. Occasionally, they stopped to taste and to touch.

Later that night, under the light of the moon, they lit a fire on the beach and cooked food that Steffan had brought. Much later their soft warm laughter mingled as again they recreated the beauty of their mutual love. The fire burned low before she laid in his arms and slept.

A huge white moon had risen high in the sky when he reluctantly wakened her with soft kisses and gentle caresses.

"Tamara?"

"Ummm" she murmured as she moved closer to his warmth.

"Believe me, darling," he whispered, "I hate to waken you, but it's long after midnight."

She looked up at the shadowed outline of him as his form came between her and the moon.

"I wish time would stand still," she murmured. "I wish we could stay here always."

"I too, but if I don't have you home soon, your father may come looking for us. I don't think I care to have him angry with me when I'm about to ask him to give me his most valuable possession."

"Oh, Steffan," she sighed as she raised her arms and put them about his neck. He lifted her body and cradled her in his arms while he found her lips in a deep tender kiss. Then he got to his feet pulling her with him. "There's no help for it, love, I've got to get you home."

They gathered their belongings and climbed into the boat. Within minutes, the sail was full and they were leaving the harbor.

"Steffan, take me to the beach below the house. I can go up the steps and through the garden." A little over an hour later, he was pulling the boat ashore and walking with her to the steps. At the bottom of the steps, she turned to look at him. The sound of her soft laughter touched the breeze.

"What is so amusing?" he asked.

"I've a confession to make," she replied.

"Oh?"

"Yes."

"What is it?"

"Last night, you went swimming here."

He looked at her in surprise.

"I was here also," she turned and pointed. "Up there, watching you."

"Why didn't you join me?" he laughed.

Her eyes glittered wickedly as she ran one hand up his chest to twine in his hair. "Would you believe me if I told you I wanted you? I watched you, and I thought 'he is so handsome and I want him desperately' and then I thought 'what would he think of me if I walked down these steps and let him know how I felt?' "

Steffan chuckled, "you would have saved me a bad night of restless dreams. Dreams of a beauty I wanted so desperately to have."

"I should have come," she whispered, "for it was a long night I spent in a very lonely bed."

"Tam . . . tomorrow . . ."

"What about tomorrow?"

"It's another day we could spend together, and there are a lot of things I have to tell you. Tomorrow you will listen, for I want no secrets between us."

"Tomorrow is tomorrow. We will see what it brings. I'm too happy tonight to care."

"I'll be here before lunch. I think I should talk to your father as soon as possible. I will have to leave soon, and I don't want to go without you."

"Steffan, must we go? There are a lot of opportunities in these waters for a good captain to make a profit." She put her arms about him and looked up into his face her eyes very serious now. "It would be so wonderful if you could stay here always. We could be happy, Steffan, there is more here than you know."

Tam, we'll talk about that tomorrow, but will you think about this. You are proud of your father. He made his way in life by himself. He took care of your mother and you to the best of his ability. And without help from anyone. I have my way mapped in my heart, it is the only way I can go. I want my woman to walk with me. I want us to carve out our own place in this world without depending on anyone. You and I, Tam. Together, we can conquer anything. Could you feel the same toward me over the years, if I just coasted through life allowing your father's wealth to care for us? You couldn't and neither could I. You would love me, respect me less and less every year of our lives, until our love dwindled to nothing. I love you too much to take the chance of losing you like that. Come with me, walk with me in my world, Tam. I need you, it would be a hard dark place without you, now that I've found you."

"Where is your world, Steffan?" she whispered.

"Shall we sail the seas together in search of fortune? Shall we find a new place you and I and make it our own?" Her lips pressed against his neck; she clung to him, somehow fear crept into her heart. Some tingle of knowledge that the rare and beautiful love she had found could be lost.

"Is it important where we are as long as we are together?"

"No, no, it isn't." She sighed and felt his arms tighten possessively about her.

"We'll find our way, my darling," he said soothingly. "As

long as I know you are here, that I can reach out and hold you when the way gets rocky. As long as I know you believe in me, trust me, we'll find our way.''

She closed her eyes and rested her body against him, feeling the strength of his love surround and hold her and fill her with a deep sense of peace.

"Tam," Steffan chuckled, "if you don't go up those stairs and find your bed, you will find yourself in mine.''

"Such a dangerous threat," she murmured gleefully. He held her a little away from him and smiled down at her, then he swiftly brushed a quick kiss across her lips, turned her about and gently headed her up the steps.

"Goodnight, love," he laughed. "Don't tempt me too far.''

He heard her answering laugh as she ran up the steps and disappeared into the garden. He turned and went back to the boat. In less than a half hour, he was tying the boat at the dock and walking toward where the *Cecile* was berthed. A soft laugh caught his attention as he stepped aboard and he looked up at the quarterdeck to find Tom smiling down at him.

"What are you doing up?" Steffan growled.

"It's my watch," Tom answered innocently.

"Uh-huh," Steffan said doubtfully. "and if I had come home later would that be your watch too?''

"Of course," Tom said happily, "and if you hadn't come home until morning that would have been my watch too. I want to know everything is out in the open, if they understand our reasons for being here and if I can quit being on my guard all the time and relax.''

"Well . . . not exactly.''

"Not exactly what?''

"I didn't tell her who or what we are.''

"Steff, for God's sake . . .''

"I know, I know, Tom, but I couldn't, I just couldn't. The right time just didn't come about. I'm to go up tomorrow for lunch. We'll talk then." He put his hand up to ward off Tom's words. "I swear, Tom, tomorrow. I'll tell her the truth.''

"Did it ever occur to you, Steff, that you're making matters worse by putting it off?''

"Of course it did. Tomorrow there will be no more secrets. I'll tell her the truth, and with any kind of luck, we'll be able to trap our scarlet butterfly. Then, my friend, I intend to take them both back to England with me.''

"I hope you can snap the trap shut on our red phantom tomorrow night. I'm anxious to get home. I'm worried about Cecile."

"Speaking of Cecile," Steffan said firmly.

"Oh God," Tom laughed. "The subject of the two Cecile's came up between you and Tamara."

"It surely did. She was furious with me. Said I was trying to take advantage of her while I had someone waiting at home, and you, you idiot, you led her to believe all kinds of things. I played along in my ignorance. I thought you had told her you were married to Cecile. I was telling her how pretty Cecile is, how sweet, going on and on until a volcano exploded."

"Get your feathers singed?" Tom laughed.

"Not as much as you're in store for when the lady gets hold of you."

"Is she angry with me?"

"I wouldn't be surprised to see her come up with some evil form of revenge to get back at you. Better walk carefully, Tom, the lady is very formidable when she's angry."

Tom grinned. "I'd best be apologizing to her tomorrow, I want to be best man at the wedding."

"Well, I hope we catch this phantom. I can hardly wait to take Tamara home and introduce her to Cecile, just to prove it's all true. The red phantom is the only thing that stands between me and Tamara and I intend to eliminate it as soon as possible. We'd best get some sleep if we're going to be up all night tomorrow night."

They both went to their respective bunks, Tom to sleep, and Steffan to the land where dreamers abide, a land filled with Tamara and the magic of her love.

Tamara passed the white gazebo and made her way across the garden toward the flight of stone steps that led to the balcony outside her room. She was just about half way up the stairs when a small noise startled her. She spun around and Mikel stepped out of the shadows.

"Mikel!" she gasped. "You frightened me to death. What are you doing here?"

"Waiting for you. The plans for tomorrow night are all made. You'll receive a message from *Barbara* and you'll know that everything is ready."

"Good."

"Tam, do you still want to go through with this while the *Cecile* is still in the harbor? If he's a privateer and he finds out what we're doing it would be easy for him to slip down the coast and turn us in.''

"He won't," she said positively.

"Just how sure of that are you? You know nothing about him. Who he is, where he came from, or why he's really here."

"Mikel, I know nothing about him, and yet I know everything. My heart has told me all there is to be known."

"You love him?"

"Yes, Mikel, I do."

"Is that enough Tam? What if he turns out to be more than you think he is."

"Tomorrow we are going to talk, both of our pasts and our future. After he has told me all that he is, I intend to tell him about our cause and what we're doing. I intend to ask him to join us, to adopt America as his country too. You'll see, Mikel, he will join us, and we'll be stronger by one more ship and crew. Together, we can do so much to strengthen our cause."

"I hope you are right, Tam, but I can't fight this feeling that we should let the *Peacock* go. I still think something we haven't planned on is going to happen. I've not told you, but someone has been following me pretty closely lately."

"Who?"

"I don't know. I only know, he's a stranger on this part of the island and that could only mean one thing, he's either from Steffan's ship, or he's from the navy base. Either way, it could spell trouble for us."

"He's not from Steffan's ship," she said firmly.

"Then worse yet, someone at the naval base is suspicious of us."

"There's no way they can find the entrance to Corvet's Rock. The only other way they could stop us is to catch us red-handed and we're too fast for that. Mikel, I'll take my own boat tomorrow night to Corvet's Rock. You go another way. That way you can spot whoever is following you and lead them a merry chase."

"What will you be doing while I'm leading them off?"

"Relieving the *Peacock* of some arms."

"Alone?"

"With the crew of the *Butterfly*, I'm hardly alone," she laughed. "If they think it is you, and they follow you, no one will be expecting me."

"I'll lead him around for a while, but I'll lose him and bring the big ship to protect your back."

"All right, but make sure you lose them completely. If they trace us back to the rocks and find what we've got stored there, all our work will have been for nothing."

"What would we do then?"

"I would rather blow up the rock and everything with her before it falls into English hands and is used to kill our friends."

"All right, Tam," he sighed.

"Mikel?"

"What?"

"Don't be angry with me," she whispered. It was the same little girl who he had taught to swim and to sail that pleaded with him, and he could resist her no more now than he could then. He put his arms about her and held her against him.

"Do you really love him, Tam?"

"Yes, yes, Mikel, I do."

"Then everything will be all right. You know I want you to be happy."

"Thank you, Mikel."

He held her for another moment then she was gone. The door clicked shut behind her.

"But if he hurts you, Tam," Mikel said in a low voice. "I will see he never hurts anyone again. Steffan Devers had better be what he says he is or he will regret it for a long time."

Twenty-five

Mikel, unable to sleep, crossed the island to the small village near the military encampment and went to a tavern. He was well aware of the shadowy figure who followed him. Inside, he joined some friends for a drink, keeping one eye on the door. He saw, and stored away in his memory, the face of the man who slipped in a little later, and sat at a table alone watching him.

He was a small man with a round, moon-like face. His eyes, narrow and beady watched Mikel's every move surreptitiously. Mikel chuckled to himself as he tilted his chair back and sipped his drink. It was then that he and the little man became aware, at the same time, that the conversation at the next table was becoming loud and boisterous.

Mikel would have ignored it, but he noticed his shadowy friend was paying closer attention to the disturbance than to him. He began to listen himself and a prickle of fear followed by a swift surge of anger almost overcame him. He recognized the loudest speaker in the group as a man who had sailed with him on all four trips when he had helped Tamara. The man knew a lot . . . in fact . . . too much, and he was rousingly drunk and making sly innuendos about activities he knew of that were supposed to be kept secret.

Slowly Mikel rose, picked up his drink, and walked to the table where the drunken, laughing group were talking. He was a step or so away when they noticed him. The man Mikel wanted to silence rose weavingly to his feet.

"Mr. Robbins," he said, his bleary eyes barely making out Mikel's face. "We wuz jus talkin', sir," he winked "about that last trip."

"Dundee," Mikel said. "Why don't you let me buy you another drink?"

"Sure sir," Dundee grinned and sat solidly down in his seat. "Then you can tell 'em sir. The bozos don't believe me. They don't believe we sent those scurvy English . . ."

"Dundee," Mikel interrupted, "better than having another drink here why don't we go to Maybelle's. There's a couple of pretty girls there. I'm sure one of them would be happy to listen to your stories."

"Yeah?" Dundee said, his interest aroused.

"Very pretty girls; come on, I'll take you over."

Dundee staggered to his feet spurred by the tormenting jeers of his friends.

"Go on, Dundee, tell them pretty babes some of your tales; just might be they'll believe 'em."

The men's laughter followed them as Mikel drew Dundee with him and moved toward the door. He could see from the corner of his eye the moon-faced man watching him. With the arms ship coming the following night and Tamara's life in the balance, he could not afford Dundee's loose mouth to be heard by the wrong people.

As they staggered along the dark street, Mikel had all he could do to keep Dundee on his feet and moving in the right direction. It was a good while before Dundee realized he was not headed toward Maybelle's, but toward the docks.

"Hey!" he slurred. "This ain't the way to Maybelle's."

"No," Mikel laughed. "You're going with me, Dundee."

"Where . . . where we goin'?"

"To a safe place where you can sleep it off."

"I ain't goin' no place but Maybelle's," Dundee said belligerently. "I ain't goin' with you."

He stopped and turned to face a Mikel who was also beginning to get angry. He grabbed a surprised Dundee by the front of his shirt and shook him violently as a dog would shake a rabbit. "Dundee, if you were sober, I'd kill you. You're going with me. I'm going to sober you up, then get you off this island before you hang us all."

Dundee gulped, for this was the first moment he actually realized who he was talking to and what he had been talking about. His eyes filled with tears of self pity.

"Mr. Robbins, I ain't said nothin' to nobody. All the boys at the table wuz friends of ours. They all knew what's been goin' on."

"Sure, the friends at the table, but how about the not too friendly ears that were listening elsewhere in the room."

"Huh?"

"Others were listening, Dundee," Mikel said patiently.

"There were no strangers there."

"You were in no condition to recognize a stranger if you fell over him. He came in right after I did. In fact, he's been following me. I could have led him a merry chase, but your mouth got him quite interested in you. I've got to keep you hidden for a while."

"Ain't I goin' with you tomorrow night? Miss Tamara's goin' to need our help. You ain't lettin' her go alone are you?"

"No, I ain't lettin' her go alone, and yes you'll be with us tomorrow. I've just got to find a way to put you out of sight for tonight. Tomorrow night we'll be out to sea and you'll be safe abourd my ship."

"Why don't I just sleep aboard the *Golden Star* or the *Sea Lady*, both of them would give me a berth for the night."

"Good idea . . . can you make it there on your own?"

"Yeah, I can make it. Mr. Robbins? . . ."

"What?"

"You ain't goin' to tell Miss Tamara that I was drunk and talkin' too much. I sure wouldn't want her to think she couldn't trust me. It won't happen again."

"All right, I'll keep my mouth shut; you get to the *Star* and stay low. I'll be by tomorrow night to pick you up."

"Yes, sir, goodnight, sir, and thanks."

"Goodnight, Dundee."

Mikel watched as Dundee moved slowly away and on very unsteady feet. After he had disappeared, Mikel moved slowly toward his home, grateful v.nen he heard the soft footfalls that followed him.

Once he was home, he satisfied himself that the man who was following him still stood in the shadows of the building across the road. He then went blissfully to bed, hoping, wickedly, that it would rain during the night to add to the discomfort of the man who waited.

He would have remained sleepless had he known that the man who stood across the street was just there to ease Mikel's suspicion. He was not the moon-faced man. That man, and another had followed Dundee to the *Star* and before he could board her, he was silently attacked in the dark shadows of the dock and dragged quietly away.

Dundee woke over an hour later to find himself tied to a chair and sitting across from a man who at first glance he took to be young and friendly. Then his eyes lifted to Jaspar Sinclair's and saw the cold, merciless gaze. His heart leapt to his throat for without a word he knew Jaspar was a man of little emotion except self preservation and a cold hard determination . . . and Dundee realized that both he and Jaspar knew exactly what he was determined to find out.

Mikel rose the next morning refreshed and prepared to handle the shadow that he knew would be waiting. He had no doubt that he could elude him when the time came. After he dressed and had breakfast, he went outside. It surprised him, after his very clumsy efforts from the day before, that his shadow was nowhere in sight. "Maybe he's getting more careful now," he muttered to himself. He walked leisurely toward the docks and by the time he arrived, he was sure he was no longer being followed. Mikel went about his daily work and kept his eyes open for the moon-faced man, but saw no sign of him. It created a small nagging worry in the back of his mind. His worrisome thoughts were interrupted by someone urgently calling him.

"Mr. Robbins!"

"Yes, what?" he called to get the attention of the man who was walking down the dock calling for him. Once Mikel was spotted the man came to him quickly. "They need you down at the far side of the docks."

"Need me? Why?"

"There's been an accident."

"An accident, what kind?"

"A man, he must have been drunk last night, at least that's what his friends say. He fell off the docks, down between the docks and the *Star*. He drowned, but his body is badly beaten by gettin' caught between the *Star* and the dock. We've been told he was one of your men."

Mikel felt a tingle of indefinable fear, but he put aside what he was doing and went with the man. They found a small group of men gathered around a blanket covered form. When Mikel had pushed his way through the crowd, the blanket was drawn back for him and he looked down on the badly mutilated body of Dundee. "Of course," he thought, "the body would be terribly beaten by the ship that rocked against the dock, but did Dundee fall in, or was he pushed?" There was no way Mikel could prove it, in fact no one he could point to as guilty. No reason for Dundee to be dead except for a few careless words he had spoken the night before. Had they been enough to cause his death? Why would he be killed? . . . for what reason?

"He was one of your men?" someone questioned.

"Yes, his name was Dundee, Jon Dundee."

"He must have fallen in. Some friends said he was very drunk last night and you yanked him out of the tavern. Is this true?"

"Yes, he was one of my best men. I told him to go sleep it off. Christ, I should have gone with him, seen that he got safely on the *Star*."

"Well," the man sighed. "It's too late now. Does he have any family hereabouts?"

"No . . . nobody. I'll see he gets a proper burial."

"Good. I'll have the body taken care of and you can see to the details later."

"Yes, thank you," Mikel said. He walked away. There was no way he could prove that Dundee's death was not an accident, yet he knew it wasn't. The only thought that clamored in his mind was 'why . . .' and 'who . . .'?"

There was no way he would go to Tamara now, frighten her, and maybe lead the murderer to her. What could he say if he did, that a sailor was killed because . . . because of what? She would laugh it away, and nothing would stop her from doing what she wanted. He vowed he would keep a close eye on her at the next dawn. He would not let the *Scarlet Butterfly* be captured if he had to sacrifice his life and his ship to prevent it.

Tamara rose early, too glad to see the new day to sleep any longer. "Steffan," she thought as she stretched luxuriously. "Steffan would come soon." They would ask her father's permission to marry. "Oh, Steffan," she murmured, "I love you, I love you, I love you."

She could barely wait for time to pass. For the moment when he would come. She wanted to feast again on that warm and possessive look that could make her bones melt within her, feel again the gentle strength of his arms that held her and turned her world into a golden flame. She could still feel the hard muscular body she had thrilled to last night. He had given her a magical new world to enjoy and she intended to enjoy it completely and thoroughly for the rest of her life. She understood, for the first time, the depth of love and devotion her parents had shared. She understood now why her father's grief had been so deep and lasting. Could she ever forget Steffan if he were gone . . . no, it would be impossible. But it would never be. Steffan knew her, loved her. He would listen to her and share her adventure.

Together there were no barriers to stop them. Together they would work for the same goals. After this silent mission, she would tell him what she had been doing and the next arms ship that came through would be met by her and Steffan together. This one last time, she would be alone, but tomorrow and all the rest of tomorrows would be theirs to share.

Mellie enjoyed her bright and laughing enthusiasm and knew without words that Tamara was, for the first time, truly in love.

Breakfast was a bright and laughing affair and Andrew questioned her about it. "You seem to be in exceptionally good spirits today. Any special reason?"

"Yes, Papa," she said, "but I would like to tell you about it a little later if you don't mind. I have a special surprise for you at lunch. Will you be here?" she asked hopefully.

"If you have a special surprise for me," he chuckled, "how could I miss it. I'll be here, and probably dying of curiosity. I haven't seen you so happy in a long time. Am I safe in saying some young sea captain is the reason for all this happiness?"

Tamara rose and went to her father's side. She knelt by his chair and took one of his huge hands in both of hers. Could she tell him how she felt? Would he understand? "Papa," she began shyly, "all my life I lived in a warm and beautiful place that was made so by the love you and Mama shared. All my life I have promised myself to settle for nothing less than the kind of man and the kind of love that you shared with her. Oh, Papa, I've waited for Steffan, I think, all my life. I feel for him what Mama must have felt for you. It is such a warm and beautiful thing that I can hardly contain it. I want to shout it to the world. He loves me Papa . . . he wants to marry me."

"And you pet?" Andrew asked hoarsely. He was, after all those years, still unprepared to give her to another man. As far as he was concerned, she was still his little girl.

"I want to marry Steffan more than I have ever wanted anything in my life." She said, aware of her father's intense love.

"You don't know him very well, Tamara; are you very, very sure?"

"I feel as if I have known him all the days of my life. I want to be with him, I want to share the rest of my days with him."

"Tamara, it is hard for me to lose you; this island will be empty and lonely without you."

"It need not be, Father," she laughed. "There is room on Marriott Island for another small house, or maybe Steffan would

294

be happy to settle here. After all, as a privateer he has no country."

"Surely, whether he has a country to be loyal to or not, he must have some family somewhere to which he feels loyalty . . . love. There are others in his life he must think about and long to return to now and again."

"Can they not share him with me?"

"Providing you are willing to share," he replied.

"I want him happy, Papa. Whatever it takes to make him so, that I will offer."

He touched her face lightly and smiled down into her eyes. "You are so like her, even though you look like me. You have that inner beauty that your mother had. If you make Steffan as happy as your mother made me, he will consider himself blessed. If you are so sure, my child, then you have my blessing."

She held his hands close to her heart and smiled through her tears. Andrew drew her into his arms and held her for a moment, then he kissed the top of her head and held her away from him. "I must be about my work if I'm going to be back here for lunch."

"Thank you, Papa."

"For what, child?"

"For understanding, for knowing always how I feel, and most of all for loving and trusting me. I hope I will never disappoint you."

Andrew kissed her again and left the room before he let his emotions control him for he wanted nothing more than to keep his child close to him for a few more years. Giving her up was going to be very difficult.

Tamara walked from the breakfast room to her father's study. There she stood before the portrait of her mother who seemed to be smiling down on her in compassionate understanding.

"Mother," she whispered. "You always told me that there were many good things about being a woman. For the first time I understand what you meant. I know you are here, that you've never left us. Please help me to make this marriage as complete and beautiful as yours. Guide me as you always did. Help me to know and to give to Steffan the happiness he gives to me."

In her mind and her heart, she felt Joanna's presence and a warm touch of comfort. Leaving the study, she walked to the foot of the stairs. Just as she started to ascend, someone rapped on the door. Steffan was not due to arrive until lunch time and she wondered, as she went to the door, just who could be on the other side. Pulling the door open, she smiled as she looked up into a pair of warm honey-gold eyes that swept her up in the love that glowed there.

"Sorry love," he grinned, "but waiting until lunch was just too long for me."

Without words, as he closed the door behind him, she stepped into the warm circle of his arms and felt him lift her almost from her feet in a fierce possessive embrace. His hungry mouth found hers and she clung to him and let the fire of his love seep through her, turning her body to liquid flame. She returned his kiss with the same urgent need.

"Oh, Steffan," she whispered when he finally released her lips. He kept his arms about her, holding her close to him.

"God," he replied, "it seems like forever since I've held you. I can't stand the hours we're apart. I want to wake in the mornings to find you safe beside me and close my eyes at night with you in my arms."

"Our thoughts are the same Steffan. For the first time I realize how lonely I was. I know now how much I have needed you, how empty my life would be without you." Again he tasted the sweetness of her willing lips before he spoke.

"Where is your father? I want to speak to him as soon as I can."

"He's at his office, Steffan, but he will be back here for lunch. We'll talk to him then, but I'm sure there will be no problem with my father. All his life, he has made my life happy and beautiful. He won't deny me now when the one thing I've searched for all my life has finally come into it."

Steffan chuckled lightly as he tightened his arms about her. Passionately he kissed her cheeks, letting his mouth drift slowly and gently across her parted lips. He heard her soft murmur of complaint and felt the warmth that flooded his body at her soft nearness.

"And what," he grinned, "are we supposed to do with the morning? I really hate to waste hours." The glowing eyes were decidedly wicked and she could not help responding with laughter.

"Steffan, you beast, are you suggesting that we slip away?"

"Um-hum," he replied.

"To some quiet secluded place."

"Good idea."

"I fear, sir, you plan to take advantage of me."

His smile faded and he leered evilly at her. "You are so right. My intentions are strictly dishonorable, but exciting. I want to get you away from anyone's eyes but mine so I can enjoy your rare beauty properly. Someplace where there is no one for miles who can rescue you from my clutches. There," he laughed, "I intend to devour you . . . whole . . . like a lump of sugar." He made a smacking sound with his lips to emphasize his words and she lay against him laughing. "Seriously, Tamara, have you told your father anything about us . . . I mean that we want to marry?"

"Not exactly, I merely told him that I was madly in love with you, and that I could never be happy anywhere or with anyone else than you. That you were the one person I have been dreaming of, waiting for all my life."

"Merely?" he questioned, his eyes dancing with pleasure at her declaration of love.

"Well," she said thoughtfully, "I could have told him that you took advantage of my sweet innocent nature and made mad passionate love to me all night. That I was swept up in your charm so thoroughly, I could no longer fight it and in my weakened condition, I succumbed to your voracious lust."

Steffan laughed. "If your father knows you as well as I'm beginning to, he won't believe a word of it. He's more likely to believe it's the other way around."

"Your innocent nature," she scoffed. "Why I'll bet it hasn't been in existence since you were sixteen."

"Well, maybe you should tell him that. Then he would force us to get married right away before my 'voracious lust' becomes obvious. I would see to your honor, madam, like the gentleman I am and make an honest woman of you."

"You'd like that," she said aghast.

"Tam," he chuckled. "I'd take you under any circumstances I could get you. Whatever it takes to make you mine is fine with me. If he wants me on both knees, that's where I'll be for I won't let the best and most beautiful thing in my life get away. And I'm warning you."

"Of what?"

"If he should refuse, I'll steal you from him, because neither heaven nor hell will keep us apart. I love you too much to be able to live without you now. You," he whispered, as his lips hovered near hers "are the sweetest thing in my world. It would indeed be a black void without you. I love you . . . with my whole being I

297

love you." His voice faded as his mouth again took possession of hers and with a soft sigh, she clung to him and gave in to the boiling urgency of his love.

It was the sound of approaching footsteps that separated them. Mellie came half way down the steps before she noticed them, then her cheeks blushed furiously as she realized what she had interrupted. "Oh . . . I'm . . . I'm sorry, Miss Tamara. I . . . I didn't mean . . . oh . . ."

"It's all right Mellie," Tamara laughed, then she turned to Steffan. "Have you had breakfast, Steffan?"

"I've had coffee. I was in too much of a hurry to get here to stop and eat."

"Good, come in and sit down and we'll get you something to eat."

Tamara took his hand and with Mellie leading the way, they walked toward the breakfast room. Mellie heard a small light laugh from Tamara, but she did not hear the words Steffan had whispered in Tamara's ear.

"It's certainly isn't the kind of food I had in mind. My stomach is running second to an appetite I'd rather feed."

"Glutton," she whispered and was rewarded by his huge hand slipping down from her waist and gently caressing the roundness of her hips.

"I'm undernourished, madam, but I promise you I won't remain so for very long."

The soft whispered words sent a tingle of expectant joy up her spine and she found that whatever his urges were, she shared them completely.

They sat at the table while Mellie served Steffan a huge plate of crisply fried ham and eggs; this was followed by warm rolls and hot coffee which were devoured by Steffan who found he really was hungry. Steffan sighed contentedly as he put the last piece of roll in his mouth and sat back in his chair with a contented sigh.

"Ah," Tamara said with a mournful expression on her face. "I suppose it is the same with all men. They make extravagant promises, but when their stomachs grumble, one finds out where their true priorities lie."

Steffan stood up and walked around the table to her side. Without a word, he took her hand and drew her up and into his arms. He kissed her so deeply and thoroughly, that she was silenced completely, stunned by the urgent possessiveness in the kiss. He held her, and neither of them knew that at that particular moment both of them were thinking the same thoughts.

"I'll tell him later," she thought. "I can't spoil all this happiness I've found. Someday soon, I'll tell him . . . but not today."

"I'll tell her tomorrow," he thought. "When we have her father's permission to marry. Today I'll just enjoy the happiness I've found. Someday soon, I'll tell her . . . but not today . . . not today."

"Why don't we go for a ride, Steffan. It would keep you from getting fat with all that breakfast you ate."

"Sounds good to me."

"If we go now, we can cross the island and come back along the beach. We could be back by the time my father arrives. I've still several beautiful places to show you."

"I'll go happily, but I doubt if there's anything out there that could touch the beauty I've got in my arms right now."

They spent the morning together, riding for a while; then, leaving their horses to graze, they walked along the beach with their arms about each other, laughing and talking of the future and the days they planned to spend together. Each of them, carefully avoiding any words that might open doors they were not prepared yet to open.

By the time they arrived home, windblown and laughing, Andrew was already there. His eyes took in quickly Tamara'a flushed cheeks, her soft glowing eyes, when she looked at Steffan, and the aura of complete happiness that seemed to surround her.

"You two seem to have had an enjoyable morning?"

"Oh, Father, it is a beautiful day," Tamara laughed. "We went riding for a while and the ocean is so smooth and peaceful today we decided to walk. It is truly lovely."

"I'm sure Steffan will agree with me, it's not half as beautiful as you are at this moment."

"I can't offer a comparison, sir," Steffan replied. "I'm afraid I didn't get a good look at the ocean. My attention was too busy enjoying the real beauty near me."

"My goodness," Tamara exclaimed, "with you two about, I'm going to get spoiled atrociously; you'll have me becoming very conceited."

"Absolute truth, love," Steffan grinned, "absolute truth."

"Steffan, you wanted to talk to me?" Andrew offered.

Steffan laughed. "I'm sure there's not much need for words,

sir. Tamara and I would like your permission to marry. You may be upset, sir, but I want to take your daughter away from you. I love her very much, and I intend to make the balance of her life as comfortable and happy as you've made the first. I'll do everything in my power to keep her happy.''

Andrew laughed. ''Why is it I get the feeling you wouldn't take no for an answer?''

''Because, I most likely wouldn't. I would not want Tamara to be unhappy, and parting from you is going to be hard enough as it is, but I'll persevere until she belongs to me.''

''Determined young man.''

''If a man is lucky enough in his life to find a woman like Tamara, wouldn't you consider him a fool not to do anything in his power to get and keep her?''

''I know exactly how you feel, Steffan. I can remember the difficulty I had in capturing her mother. If Tamara wants you, I certainly will put no obstacles in your path.''

Steffan turned to Tamara. He reached out his hand and with a smile she put her hand in his.

''If you'll accept, my love,'' he said gently, ''I would like to marry you as soon as possible.''

''Yes, Steffan'' she replied. He drew her into his arms and brushed her lips with his. Andrew watched them reaching for one another and a swift painful pang of loneliness struck him. When Tamara as gone he would only have the ghosts of Marriott Hall to live with. Then with determination, he pushed the thought aside as he rose to kiss his daughter and congratulate Steffan.

Twenty-six

The nagging worry in the back of Mikel's mind about the death of Dundee was compounded by his knowledge that Tamara would not put a stop to their plans over his suspicious intuition. He went about his day reluctantly making the plans for their attack at dawn the next morning, keeping one eye open for anyone who might be spying on him. It only made his uneasiness worse when he could spot no one. It seemed his shadow was no longer interested in his comings and goings.

He had to get away unobserved just after nightfall, but just before he left he had to send a message to Tamara so that she would know that everything was ready. He would word it as usual, a request by one of her good friends to come because she was ill. Tamara would then know that he had already left for Corvet's Rock.

He walked from his home to the docks signalling the few of his men that were there that they were to meet at the *Tamara*, as soon as night covered their movements. Once aboard the *Tamara* himself, he stripped to the waist and began what looked like a repair job on the boat. He worked away diligently all afternoon, but to his distress, no one watched who was unknown to him.

"Why?" he wondered. Why would he be followed for days, then suddenly the night they were to move he was left unobserved. There was no way anyone would know about the entrance to Corvet's Rock unless they followed him, and he had not visited there since the night he and Tamara had taken the *Cecile*.

Night shadows began to lengthen and no matter how he felt, Mikel knew it was time to send the message. He wrote it out swiftly and then signalled to the man who was to carry it.

"Jamie," he cautioned, "make extra sure you are not followed."

"Aye, sir," Jamie grinned. "Nobody will be followin' me, I'll see to that. You want me to come back here or go with Miss Tamara?"

"I'd feel safer if you stayed with Tamara. She won't listen to my warnings and she's too happy to believe anything's going to happen so I'm trusting you to protect her from no matter what or who, and that includes Captain Steffan Devers from the *Cecile*. I still have a feeling there's more to him than we know."

"Is he goin' to be at Miss Tamara's?"

"I wouldn't be surprised. If he is, make your story good."

"You don't trust him?"

"Not for a minute."

"Want me to . . . ah . . . see that he don't cause no trouble?"

"No, Tamara would have our heads on a plate if we did something like that, then found we were wrong about him. She'll be able to get away from him, but you'll be with her to see he doesn't follow you. All right?"

"Right. He won't get a chance to cause any problems; we'll disappear into the night just like ghosts."

Mikel nodded. Jamie left and Mikel went back to his non-existent work on the *Tamara*.

The moon had crested the horizon, a bright huge golden moon that caused Mikel even more trepidation. The time had finally come. Mikel climbed up to the dock and bent to release the ropes that held the *Tamara* when a low cold voice caused him to freeze in his tracks and a film of perspiration to appear on his forehead.

"Well, well, well. Our pirate lady's second in command. All prepared for another foray against the Crown. We must see that you and your lady love no longer harass His Majesty's ships."

Mikel stood up and slowly turned around. His eyes met Jaspar's cold ones and he knew that no guarantee would be given there.

"I beg your pardon, sir," he said coolly. "Were you addressing me?"

"Nervy bastard, ain't he?" one of the men accompanying Jaspar said.

"Don't worry, friend," Jaspar chuckled. "He won't be so nervy when we're through with him." He looked at Mikel with a smug grin on his face. "Have you sent your message to Steffan's little trollop?"

Mikel stiffened and his brows furrowed in a deep glare not only at Jaspar's slight of Tamara, but to the reference to the message. "I don't know what you're talking about."

"Oh, come now," Jaspar laughed outright. "Captain Devers has spent enough of our precious time trying to trap the lady.

302

With his charm, he should have bedded her by now and found out all we want to know. She must be quite good for him to dally so long instead of tending to our business."

"Our business . . .?"

"Yes . . . oh," Jaspar said in mocking surprise. "You don't know Captain Devers in his real capacity, do you? Captain Steffan Devers, captain of His Majesty's ship *Godolphin*, sent here on special mission to ferret out the lady pirate who's been causing such a disturbance. He's to capture her . . . and bring her back to hang. Of course," he chuckled evilly, "no one told him he couldn't thoroughly enjoy the lady's . . . charms before he did."

Mikel felt a red haze of fury almost overcome him. He had been right about Steffan. A naval officer sent here to capture Tamara. With the cold deliberate plan to seduce Tamara. "God!" He thought to himself in agony, "to hurt her like this was unforgivable." Somehow he had to get to her in time to stop her. If she did not sail they would never be able to catch her. He would try to explain everything as gently as possible, if he could get away from this arrogant officer and to Corvet's Rock in time.

"I don't believe a word you say about Captain Devers, and I don't understand anything else you're talking about."

Jaspar stood quietly for a moment, then slowly he walked toward Mikel. Stopping just a few inches away. "I have known Captain Devers since he was born. I went to the Naval Academy with him. I am part of this assignment he's been sent on. Believe me, I know just what he has done," Jaspar smiled a cold hard smile. "He's irresistible to women, especially sweet innocent women like your friend Tamara. He's charmed her until she believes everything he says, then . . . when she is completely unprepared, he will snap the trap shut."

"I still don't know what you're talking about."

Jaspar chuckled, for his observing eye took in the clenched fist, the anger filled eyes. "Oh," he said softly, "you understand my friend, and you think that somehow you are going to rescue her. Well, you're not. No, your little friend will be gobbled up by Steffan, and until then, we are going to hold you. Then we are going to take you both back to England . . . and hang you both."

Mikel's mind was spinning frantically. Jaspar faced him and the two men who accompanied him and the two men who only a few feet behind him, but both men were armed with rifles primed to fire, and were watching him closely. He mentally crossed his

303

fingers and hoped his ruse would work.

"Hang?" he said, his voice breaking with fear at the thought, "why should you want to hang me? I haven't done anything." He allowed himself to tremble, but it was more with anger than fear.

"It's quite possible, if you tell us the truth, that we might be able to save you."

Mikel gave all appearances of being relieved and anxious to do just that.

"I . . . I don't want to hang," he mumbled. "I had no part in this, it was all their fault. I told them it was foolish . . . crazy to try to fight a force so big, but no, they wouldn't listen to me. No, they had to be stupid and try to fight England."

"You come along with us. Tell us all we need to know, and when we put an end to this charade, we'll see you're left here unharmed. Of course, we'll have to take our lady pirate back with us. In fact, that might make the journey home much more interesting." Jaspar laughed smugly and the two men behind him snickered suggestively. Mikel's rage almost choked him and the urge to get his hands on Jaspar's throat almost overcame him. He let his voice become hopeful.

"I can tell you everything. You'll guarantee I'll be left here?"

"I give you my word," Jaspar said coolly, but Mikel was sure just how good that word would be.

Dejectedly, he hung his head. "All right, I'll tell you everything you need to know, but . . . I'll only talk to you . . . alone."

Jaspar motioned the two men to move out of range of hearing, then he turned to Mikel.

"Well" he said impatiently. "What do you have to tell me?"

Mikel hoped he was fast enough to do what he wanted before the two men could get their rifles up and fire. The end of the dock was only a few feet away. "I'll tell you what I want to say," he said grimly, his head lowered. Jaspar leaned a little closer and Mikel's body uncurled with a tremendous blow to his exposed chin. "You can go to hell!" he said. Jaspar staggered backward and Mikel ran for the edge of the dock. As he neared the edge, he leapt forward. His body arched outward just as both men fired. His body jerked as the bullets found a mark. He hit the water and dove downward. Both men ran to the edge of the dock with Jaspar right behind them. But Mikel did not surface.

"Bastard," Jaspar muttered. "If you're not dead, now, I shall see to it you hang, my friend, right next to your lady love."

They watched the dark waters for several minutes, but there was no sign of Mikel. "I hit him, sir," one of the men said. "I saw the blood before he hit the water. I'm sure I got him. If he wasn't dead, he would have had to surface by now."

"No matter. If he's wounded, we'll find him. There's no place he can go on this island for help except to the Marriotts. If he does, we'll pluck him like a ripe plum and he will regret putting a hand on me."

"Yes, sir."

"Come, we can't stay here all night. She probably has received the letter and is on her way to the *Peacock*," Jaspar said.

"Expecting him to come help."

"Well, let's not keep the lady waiting. Get back to the steward and give orders to Mr. Ramsey to take her out and collect our unsuspecting lady pirate."

"And you, sir?"

"It's about time I visited Andrew Marriott and let him know that we're in on his game. It will be a pleasure to see Steffan's face when he finds out we've done his job for him." Jaspar chuckled and they walked down the docks toward the steward and the capture of the *Scarlet Butterfly*.

Mikel clung weakly to the bottom of the dock that stood only five or six inches from the water. Pain and the dark cloud of unconsciousness hovered near, and he knew if he surrendered to it, not only would he die, but Tamara and her father would die as well. Waiting until he heard the receding footsteps, he tentatively worked his way out from the close pilings of the dock, but he felt his strength ebbing and could not pull himself up on the dock. He knew that men would already be sent to search for him. He had to get to Tamara—but how? The *Tamara* would be under surveillance. There was no way he would be able to get it free from the harbor. He gasped in agony as he again reached for the dock. The wave of black pain almost engulfed him. Only with grim determination did he cling to it. Somehow, he had to get a boat and make his way to Corvet's Rock. He prayed silently. Tamara's safety, Tamara's life depended on him. Time was flying and he knew within a few more minutes, men would be back to search the area for him. Slowly, painfully, he allowed the tide to push him toward the sandy strip of beach between the docks. Then he crawled ashore. Black waves of unconsciousness washed over him and it took all the strength he had not to surrender to it and lie on the cool sandy beach allowing the black void to ease the tearing pain that ripped through him and left him trembling. He forced himself to his feet. The pain of it brought a gasping groan from him. Then he began to stagger forward. He had to get away from this area before they found him. Uppermost in his mind was the one pounding thought that drove him on. Tamara . . . He had to get to Tamara in time. Keeping himself to the shadows, he worked his way laboriously around the village. Once he had gotten around it, he thought of the distance between himself and the cove where Tamara kept the small boat that would carry her to Corvet's Rock. He had to get to it before she did. His dizziness told him he was losing a lot of blood. Quickly, he slid out of his jacket, then removed his shirt. Tearing some strips off his shirt, he bundled the rest into a heavy pad and pressed it against the wound just under his right arm. He tied the strips about him holding the pad firmly against his body. It would not stop all the bleeding, but it might give him enough time to get to Tamara. He put his jacket back on, panting with the agonizing effort. His body trembled and he could not stop his teeth from chattering. Gathering all the strength he had left, he began to stagger on. Two thoughts kept him going, the first to protect Tamara . . . the second, to get his hands on Steffan Devers. "Just for a moment," he prayed silently, "if I have one ounce of strength left, I shall kill that treacherous bastard if it is the last thing I ever do."

He was oblivious now to anything but the determined need to go on and on. Pain blurred his eyes and every time he staggered and fell, he didn't know if he would have the strength to get up and go on. He knew it would be a much shorter distance if he could go along the beach. The private beach of Andrew Marriott would be safe temporarily so he made his way to it. It was quite a while before Mikel realized that he was weakening too rapidly to make it. He clenched his teeth and drove himself on. Falling, rising, falling again, leaving drops of bright crimson blood on the sand as he did. In the distance, he could see the steps that led to the Marriott garden. "I have to make it," he thought frantically, "I have to!" Just beyond the steps and over the small cluster of rocks a small boat would be at anchor. If he could get there before Tamara he could warn her to stay away from Corvet's Rock and the *Scarlet Butterfly* . . . and the man who had betrayed her.

Both Steffan and Tamara were seeking a way to separate for the night without causing the other any alarm. They had spent a joyous afternoon talking and making plans for the future; now both of them knew that the time was slipping away fast and that each of them had to find some logical excuse to absent himself.

After a leisurely and relaxing supper they were seated with Andrew in the comfort of his study, Tamara nervously watching the clock tick away the minutes, and Steffan just as nervously watching Andrew beat him soundly at chess. It was a game at which he was usually quite proficient, but tonight, he was completely unable to concentrate.

"Caught you again," Andrew chuckled.

"That you have, sir."

"You aren't by any chance letting me win, are you?" Andrew asked suspiciously.

"I assure you, sir, I have no such intention, it's just that," he grinned, looking toward Tamara, "I find it very difficult to concentrate. Maybe some time in the near future I'll be a better match for you, for tonight, I find my mind wandering."

Andrew was about to answer when a light rap on the study door interrupted him. "Come in."

Mellie opened the door and took one step into the room. No one but Tamara realized the real reason that Mellie's face was so pale and that she was trembling . . . Mikel's message had come.

"Yes Mellie?" she queried, holding Mellie's eyes with hers and mentally commanding her to control.

"There's a message for you, Miss Tamara. It's from Miss Barbara. She is ill, and wants to know if you will come to her."

"Is Jamie here, Mellie?"

"Yes, Ma'am."

"Tell him I'll be with him in a few minutes."

"Yes Ma'am," Mellie said quickly, then she fled the room as rapidly as she could.

At any other time, Steffan's observant eye would have caught the subtle messages of Mellie's nervousness and Tamara's quick acceptance, but he was relieved that there was now a way for him to get away. He knew Tom would have the *Cecile* ready for sea and that he only awaited Steffan's appearance. Tamara turned to Steffan. "Steffan, do you mind terribly? Barbara is my very dearest friend. She would not send for me unless it was terribly urgent. I shall be back early in the morning and we can spend some time together."

"Of course, Tam. It's quite all right."

"Steffan can stay and accept my challenge for another game,"

Andrew laughed. "Now that all his distractions are gone, he might be able to concentrate better. Might even beat me," Andrew looked doubting.

Tamara joined in their laughter for a minute then she went to her father and brushed her lips across his cheek. "Goodnight, Papa. I'll be home bright and early in the morning."

She went to Steffan, but before she could say goodnight he took her hand and said, "I'll walk you to the door. I have to get back to the *Cecile* anyway."

Andrew's eyes sparkled with the knowledge that Steffan preferred to say goodnight to Tamara when they were completely alone.

"Goodnight, sir."

"Goodnight, Steffan, but don't forget my challenge still stands."

"I won't sir," Steffan laughed. Steffan and Tamara left the room together. Outside the door, he drew her into his arms and kissed her slowly and passionately.

"Where does this Barbara live?"

"In the village, why?"

"I don't know if I trust someone else to take you there. Maybe I should take you myself."

"No! Steffan . . . I'm perfectly safe. I've traveled this island many times before with Jamie as protection. He won't let anything happen to me. He would have to answer to my father."

"No, love," Steffan said gently. "He would have to answer to me. You belong to me now, and I would kill anyone who touched you. I'm a possessive man . . . it's a warning, love. No one takes or harms what is mine. I love you, Tam."

For a moment Tamara was surprised at his words, but when his lips took possession of hers again, they were brushed aside for the fiery feeling that flooded her body and her mind. Reluctantly, she drew away from him.

"Goodnight, love," she whispered, but she was vowing to herself that this was the last time they would separate like this. "The next time" she thought, "he will be with me."

Steffan went to the door with her and eyed Jamie thoroughly. He watched Tamara and Jamie walk toward the stables together and suddenly he couldn't shake the feeling that he should follow her . . . stop her . . . keep her with him, that somehow he might lose her. For just a second, the temptation was so great that he even took a step or two in their direction. Then he stopped. He

308

had a job to do, once it was done, he would take Tamara and keep her with him. He turned and walked around the house and across the garden toward the steps that led to the beach.

"Miss Tamara," Jamie whispered.

"What?"

"We'd best not cut across the garden and go down the steps. He might be goin' back to his ship that way. Best we go to the other side of the house and down over the cliff path."

"Yes, that's a good idea, Jamie. Come, let's hurry. Mikel is probably there already."

They cut across the side lawn and walked through a small stand of trees. On the other side they came to the cliff edge. A small path led down to the beach and they went down it quickly, knowing the way well, having used it many times before. They found the small boat Tamara kept hidden there and soon, they were skimming across the water toward Corvet's Rock. When they made the perilous entrance to Corvet's Rock, Tamara was again amazed at the silent breathless beauty both of the lagoon and the crimson ship that rocked in its waters. Pulling the boat ashore with Jamie's help, she ran to the small dock they had built to which the *Scarlet Butterfly* was moored. She went quickly up the gangplank.

"Where is Mikel?" she asked the closest men to her.

"Don't know, Miss Tamara. He ain't come yet." Tamara frowned. It wasn't like Mikel to be late.

"Get the ship ready. We leave as soon as the entrance is clear. That should only be in a few hours."

"What about Mr. Robbins?"

"He'll be here soon," she answered. "He has to be. In an hour or so he won't be able to make the entrance at all."

"What if he don't make it in time?"

"Then," she said firmly, "we go alone."

The man eyed her silent determined face for a few moments, then he turned and went about his duties while Tamara stood at the rail and watched the cave entrance slowly fill with water. The tide was coming in. If Mikel did not come soon, it would turn, then entering the cave would be impossible.

Steffan walked across the garden to the top of the steps that led to the beach. He stood and looked out to sea for a few minutes. The view was extraordinarily beautiful and he wished he could have shared it with Tamara. "Soon," he thought, "all this would be over and they could start a happy life together." Whistling lightly, he went down the steps unaware of the cold blue, hate filled gaze that watched him from the shadows of the gazebo.

One step after another, slowly, Mikel had climbed the steps on his hands and knees. "Only a little further," he promised himself after each step. He would be in time to catch Tamara before she left the house. He staggered at the top and made his way to the gazebo where he leaned against it to gather enough strength to cross the lawn and climb the stairs to Tamara's room. He was just about to push himself away and start across the lawn when he heard someone approaching. As quickly as he could, he got inside the gazebo. He watched through the closed shutters and almost cried when he saw Steffan's huge shadow stand between him and the moon. If Steffan were here, on his way back to his ship, then Tamara was . . . gone. Too late! He was too late, and the man who stood there relaxed, enjoying the beauty was the man who had betrayed her, had condemned her to death. He knew, in his weak and bleeding condition, he could not do anything now. Steffan could handle him easily. He watched, hot violent hatred coursing through his veins and vowed he would find Steffan as soon as his body would let him, and he would kill him, to revenge the pain he was in now and the pain Tamara would feel when she found out the truth.

Steffan walked away whistling which made Mikel grind his teeth in sheer murderous hate. When he was gone, Mikel made his way across the garden and up the steps to Tamara's room praying that Mellie had left the doors unlocked. They were! He pushed one slowly open. Mellie stood with her back to him, hanging a gown in the closet. Quietly, he crept up close to her. "Mellie," he said hoarsely.

"Oh!" Mellie spun around fear and shock on her face. Mikel's bloodied hands covered her mouth.

"Shhh, for God's sake woman, do you want the whole island down on me?"

"Mikel," she whispered. Her eyes grew wide with renewed fear when she saw his bloody exhausted condition. "Holy Mother, what happened to you? Oh, God," she moaned, "I knew this was all goin' to happen some day. I . . ."

"Mellie," he said angrily, "for God's sake shut up. Has Tamara gone?"

"Yes. Only a little while ago."

"It's a trap Mellie. She's headed straight into a trap and there's nothing I can do about it. What time is it?"

She told him and he groaned. Leaning against the wall Mikel said in a despairing voice. "It's too late. The tide has turned. I couldn't get to her to stop her now. Tam . . . God, Tam. I'm sorry. But I'll get revenge, that I swear. I'll kill that dirty traitorous bastard if it's the last thing I'll ever do. They may catch you love . . . but they'll never hang you . . . never . . . hang . . ." Slowly, he sagged to the floor as the dark cloud of unconsciousness finally won the battle. The last thing he saw was Mellie's tear-stained face as she bent above him.

Steffan walked up the gangplank of the *Cecile*. Tom was there waiting for him. "I was wondering just how you'd get away."

"No need to worry, Tom. Tamara got a message from a friend who needed her help. She's spending the night there."

"Lady luck must love you," Tom laughed. "I hope she loves me enough to find and capture my lady pirate. Once I get her clapped in the brig, all my troubles will be over."

"The *Cecile's* ready. By the time the sun comes up we shall be right at the spot to catch our pirate red handed, and this time we'll be prepared for that second ship."

"How so?"

"Jaspar sent a message. The *Eagle*, his sister ship will be standing off to help us if we need it."

"We don't need his help. Taken by surprise like this, she doesn't stand a chance."

Steffan laughed.

"What's so funny?" Tom questioned.

"I'd like to see our lady pirate's face when we swoop down on her unexpectedly. I'll bet it will be the most memorable day of her life."

Steffan had no way of knowing, as he and Tom laughed together, that it would also be one of the most memorable and heartbreaking days of his life also.

Twenty-seven

Mikel groaned as the excruciating pain struck him again and again. He wove in and out of consciousness on a sea of agony. Someone lifted him and deposited him on something soft. So soft, he wanted to sink into it and let the black release roll over him, but someone wouldn't let him. Hands kept at him. Touching the burning blinding source of the pain until he could hardly bear it. He tried to strike out against it but he was too weak, then the welcome blackness came again and he welcomed the dark clouds as they rolled over him and took with them the pain.

Andrew stood over the bed and looked down at Mikel's fevered body. He didn't really know if he wanted to kill or cure him. At the moment, he was more frightened and angry than he had ever been before.

When Mikel had collapsed at Mellie's feet, she was so frightened and confused, she didn't know what to do. She knew she could not handle Mikel's body herself for he was twice as big as she. She needed help and the only person her blank mind could conjure up was Andrew. Tamara's father would be furious at all that was going on, but he would be able to do something; he had to, or Mikel would die.

She ran downstairs and knocked on Andrew's study door. When he called for her to come in, she literally threw the door open. One look at her tear-stained face, her wide frightened eyes, and Andrew knew something was seriously wrong. He rose and crossed the floor to her, because his mind envisioned Tamara hurt or worse.

"Mellie, what is the matter?"

"Oh, Mr. Marriott, please come with me as quick as you can, there's been an accident."

"An accident!" he said, his alarm rising. "Tamara! Tamara, is she all right? What kind of accident?"

"It isn't Tamara, sir . . . it's Mikel."

"Mikel . . . what happened?"

"Oh, sir," Mellie moaned, "don't ask me questions now, I don't know, and I'm so scared I can't think. Please come with me. You've got to do something. He might die."

"All right. Where is he?"

She gulped. "Upstairs, sir . . . in Tamara's room."

"In Tamara's room! How . . .?" he began, but he didn't finish as fresh tears clouded Mellie's eyes. "Come along Mellie, lead the way. We'll find out later."

In relief, Mellie ran ahead of him to Tamara's room. She ran again to Mikel's side. He was still unconscious and a stain of blood on the floor told her he was bleeding badly. Andrew knelt beside him. In one glance, he knew Mikel had been shot, but by whom and, worse yet, why did he run to Tamara's room? As gently as he could, he lifted Mikel's body from the floor and carried him to Tamara's bed. He heard him mutter feverishly and the words froze his heart.

"Tam" he muttered. "Got to get to Tamara . . . got to warn her . . . trap, it's a trap . . . he'll kill her . . . Tam . . . Tam."

A million questions formed in his mind, but there was no way Mikel was rational enough to answer them, then he looked at Mellie's face again and saw the horror there at Mikel's words.

"Mellie," he said, his voice much more calm and subdued than he felt, "you must tell me what you know of what's going on."

Eased by the gentleness of his voice, Mellie knew she had to tell him what she knew, but she was also aware that she didn't know enough to help Tamara. Once she began the whole story poured out. Andrew's face became pale, but he held himself under rigid control until Mellie finished.

"Where has she gone tonight, Mellie?"

"I don't know, sir."

"Where does she keep her ship?"

"I . . . don't know, sir."

"God," he cursed, "do you know who the 'he' is that Mikel keeps mumbling about. Who has set some kind of trap?"

"No sir," Mellie sobbed. "I don't know . . . I don't know. Oh, Mr. Marriott, what are we going to do?" she cried wringing her hands in distress.

"Well, first," Andrew said firmly, "you go and get some hot water and something I can use as bandages. If I'm going to find out what's going on, I've got to get this boy cared for."

"Yes, sir," Mellie said, a little relieved that someone was doing something. She went to the door.

"Mellie?"

"Yes, sir?"

"Have one of the men send a message to the *Cecile*. Steffan will want to know that Tamara is in some kind of danger. He'll want to be there to help. See that the message gets sent immediately, then hurry with that water and bandages."

Mellie ran down the steps, and went to the back of the house to the servants' quarters. Wakening one of the stableboys, she told him of Andrew's message to Steffan and sent him on his way, then she heated some water after she had thrown several pieces of wood into the open fireplace. Gathering all the cloths she could find, she took the bucket of water and went up the stairs as fast as she could.

Andrew had stripped away Mikel's clothes and covered the lower half of his body with the sheet. Mikel was turned on his side and Mellie gasped at the wound in his back, just under his right arm. To her, it looked so very deadly. This and the fact that Mikel's face was so white, terrorized her anew.

"Is . . . is he going to die, sir?"

"Not if you get over here with that water," Andrew replied. She set the bucket down beside him. Quickly Andrew took a piece of cloth and wet it in the hot water. Sponging the wound clean he examined it closely.

"Mellie, run back down to the kitchen and fetch me the smallest sharpest knife you can find. The ball is still in there. It's broken a couple of ribs, but I don't think it's hit the lung. Hurry child, we've got to get that ball out of there."

Again, Mellie ran as fast as she could, returning with the knife.

"Mellie, go on the other side of the bed. You have got to hold him as motionless as you can." She obeyed, but she doubted very much that she would be able to hold Mikel's strong body still if he decided to move.

Suddenly, Andrew noticed Mikel's eyelids flutter.

"Mikel," he said firmly, "I have to dig that ball out of you before it begins to fester. Do you understand?"

Mikel hovered near unconsciousness again, but Andrew's words echoed somewhere in his mind and he gasped out a ragged, "yes."

"You have got to hold as still as you can. Do you hear me, Mikel? Your life depends on how much of this you can bear and remain still." Mikel tried to whisper yes, but only a mumbled sound emitted. Andrew understood that he had reached Mikel's mind. Again, he swabbed the wound clean, then he picked up the knife. The moaning sound of pain came from Mikel's lips, but his body remained rigidly still. Sweat ran from him and his hand clenched Mellie's until she almost cried out. Andrew cursed under his breath and wiped quickly at the sweat that trickled into his eyes. After what seemed to Mellie to be hours of probing with the bloody knife, Andrew gave a satisfied grunt as he dropped the ball into the pail of water. Quickly, he cleaned the wound, made a pad of some of the cloth and bound Mikel tightly. He stood up and looked down at the boy on the bed. "He'll be all right, Mellie. Soon, he'll waken, then we'll get to the bottom of this mystery."

It was over five hours later that Mikel's eyes fluttered open and he looked about him. Mellie sat beside the bed watching for the first sign of movement. When she saw him begin to waken, she rose and went to him.

"Where . . . where am I?" he muttered.

"You're in Miss Tamara's bed," Mellie answered. At that everything flooded back into Mikel's memory.

"Tamara!" he gasped and tried to move, but deep, stabbing pain told him quickly this was impossible. "Mellie, for God's sake, help me. I have to get to Tamara!"

"You can't move. Don't worry Mikel, Mr. Marriott has sent for Steffan. You tell him where Miss Tamara is and they'll go after her."

"Steffan!" Mikel cried. "No! No! Get her father for me. Hurry, Mellie, hurry."

Mellie ran from the room. She was half way down the steps when she saw Andrew at the door speaking to someone. When he turned and saw Mellie he had a frown on his face.

"The *Cecile* is gone, Mellie. The boy asked around a while. Steffan took the *Cecile* out right after he left here. Something about this whole story is strange."

"Mikel's awake, sir. He wants to see you. He said to hurry."

They went back up to find Mikel beside himself with anxiety. "All right, Mikel, tell me what happened to you and why."

Mikel began speaking rapidly. He told Andrew exactly what he and Tamara had been doing. He told him of the trap that was set to capture Tamara . . . then he told him who had set it.

"The rotten . . ." Andrew's eyes flashed fire. "To cold bloodedly tell her he loves her then set a trap to hang her. My

God, has the man no conscience at all?''

"We've got to stop her, sir. Maybe we can head her off."

"Mikel," Andrew exclaimed. "You tell me she uses the dawn to strike in."

"Yes. If that ship comes at you out of the early morning sun, you can't see her until she is upon you."

"Do you know what time it is?"

Mikel looked at Andrew blankly, then toward the windows that were already beginning to brighten with the first rays of dawn.

"We're too late," Andrew said as Mikel's silent agonized gaze met his, "but if what you say is true, Steffan Devers will regret the day he ever saw this island, and if he harms one hair on my daughter's head he had best wish himself dead, for my revenge will be much worse."

The three of them were silent, unable to think of where Tamara was at that moment and what would happen to her. All three were startled when someone rapped on the bedroom door.

Mellie went to answer and stood talking for a few minutes when she returned, she went to Andrew's side.

"There is an officer downstairs. He says he wants to talk to you, sir."

"Mikel," Andrew said quickly, "they have no way of knowing you are here. We've got to keep your presence a secret until we find out exactly what is going on. I'll go down and talk to them."

Both Mellie and Mikel were silent for a few minutes after Andrew left, then Mikel began to slowly and painfully rise from the bed.

"Mikel, what are you doing!" Mellie cried as she ran to him.

"Mellie, don't be a fool. No matter what Andrew thinks, they will search, they will expect me to have come here to warn Tamara. I've got to get out of here and you've got to cover up any evidence that I've ever been here."

"But you can't" she said miserably. "You don't have the strength."

"I've got to," he gasped as he clung to the bed post. "Help me, Mellie, before it's too late."

Andrew walked slowly down the steps and across the foyer to the door of his study. There he stopped and looked across the room at the tall, handsome and very arrogant officer. His eyes took in quickly the three men who were with him.

"I'm Andrew Marriott. You wanted to see me."

316

"I'm sure this visit comes as no surprise to you, Mr. Marriott. Surely word has reached you by now that the little game you people have been playing with His Majesty's Navy has been uncovered. You, sir," Jaspar smiled, "are under arrest. You will be held until we bring your daughter here and recapture your other pirate. Then we will take the three of you back to England . . . to be hanged like the criminals you are."

In a voice just as politely cool as Jaspar's, Andrew replied, "I sir, know nothing of what you are talking about and I want you out of my house. What right do you have to come here making such outrageous accusations without proof?"

"Soon there will be plenty of proof, and you will confess to everything . . . unless it is your goal to see your daughter hang in your place. Who's to blame, Mr. Marriott, you . . . or your daughter?"

"What do you want, captain . . ."

"Sinclair, Captain Jaspar Sinclair of His Majesty's Navy, and I have everything I want. Your daughter will be brought here when she so foolishly attacks the *Peacock*. I have you, and you will tell me just where Mikel Robbins is. We wounded him, I'm sure, and I'm just as sure he will try to find his way here. First to try to warn your daughter, and second to get some medical help. In fact, I'm sure if I search now, I will find him somewhere in this house."

Andrew stiffened, then protested against Jaspar's high handed actions.

"You've no right to search my home."

"Oh, but I have all the authority I need, my friend." He waved his hand toward his men. "Superior forces." He chuckled, then his face became serious. "Come, show me the other rooms in this house."

Again Andrew was about to protest, but a nudge from the gun of one of Jaspar's men told him that Jaspar was in a postition to have him shot where he stood. He turned and walked from the room with Jaspar and his men on his heels.

Andrew made his way to every room except Tamara's, but at the last, there was nothing he could do but open the door that would put a wounded helpless Mikel in the hands of a man he felt to be heartlessly brutal. "Forgive me, Mikel," he thought to himself, then he opened the door.

No one was more surprised than Andrew to find the room empty and tidy, as though no one had been in it for hours. The bed was without a wrinkle and all signs of blood and bandages were gone. He didn't know how Mikel and Mellie had done it, but for now, he did not question, just breathed a sigh of relief.

"Damn him," Jaspar cursed. "Where have you hidden him, Marriott?"

"I told you," Andrew said coolly, "I have no idea what you are talking about. No matter what else you may have, you have no proof of your charges against me."

"No matter. Your daughter will be in our hands soon. Will you let her go back to stand trial alone or will you admit to the truth?"

Andrew kept his head. If Tamara were captured she would need him and Mikel free. With Andrew's wealth and friends, it might be possible to win her freedom.

"I cannot admit to something I know nothing about."

Jaspar's face became stiff with the inner rage he controlled. To have forced Andrew to admit some part of this would have taken the matter out of Steffan's hands for his orders were only to capture the pirate ship. Andrew would be Jaspar's prisoner, along with Mikel. They forced Andrew back down the stairs and into the study again.

"Make yourself comfortable," Jaspar said smugly. "The day is almost upon us. Steffan should be coming with your daughter soon, unless, of course," Jaspar watched Andrew closely, "he decides to stop along the way to sample some, ah . . . pleasures."

Andrew looked into Jaspar's eyes and for a minute Jaspar could see and feel the murderous rage there. It shook his nerve and he found himself being grateful for the men he had brought with him.

"I," Andrew said coldly, "will prove my innocence and then I will get my daughter free. When I do, you and your friend, Captain Devers, had best find some small corner of the world to hide in, for if he or any other man harms one hair of her head, he shall pay for his stupidity with his life."

"We know all what is about to happen. There is no way to get your daughter free. She will hang, and we will also find her accomplice before we leave and he will hang. How do you think you can stop it if they are caught red handed? Steffan has taken the time to make very sure before he strikes."

"Steffan Devers," Andrew spat angrily, "shall wish he had never seen this island. What he has done to my daughter is unforgivably cruel and unnecessary. Why did you do this?" Andrew challenged. "Were you not men enough or sailors enough to protect your ships that a woman could take them away from you? What kind of man is Steffan that he had to reduce himself to this filthy and unforgivable thing."

"Steffan," Jaspar chuckled. He was enjoying the fact that he was damning Steffan with every word he spoke. "He has a way with women, he enjoys seducing them and walking away. We would have arrested you sooner, but he ordered us to wait. The challenge of your daughter's charms was too much for him to leave untasted. I'm sure he made it as enjoyable for her as it obviously was for him. Now that he has acquired what he wanted, we can finish up this dirty little business. There is very nearly a war between the Colonies and England. In fact, I would not be surprised that it had already begun by the time we get back. If so, what was an act of piracy by your daughter will become a much more serious act . . . an act of treason."

Andrew found himself so angry that he did not dare move or speak again or he would have thrown himself at Jaspar and twisted his hands about his neck until that smug smile disappeared and death claimed him. He sat down, remaining silent, but praying that maybe his daughter could escape their snare and wondering, above all, just where a badly wounded Mikel was at the moment.

Mikel made his way to the windows that led to the balcony with Mellie's aid. There he leaned against the frame of the window panting. "Mellie, make the bed and clean up any signs of our being here. I'd help you if I could, but I'm going to need every ounce of strength to get out of here."

Mellie spread the covers on the bed smoothly, then she gathered all the bloody rags and water. The water she threw out, then she hid the other evidence in the closet, covering them with clothes. She went back to Mikel whose face was alarmingly white and whose body trembled like a leaf in a storm.

"Mellie, is there any way you can get me to a boat?"

"If I could get you down to Bryant's Cove, I could go home and get my brother's boat."

"Good girl."

"You," Mellie's voice broke in fear, "you'll never make it."

"Mellie, hate is a strong medicine. I'll make it. I'll stay alive and I'll get well, and when I do, I shall hunt down the great Captain Devers and kill him like the dog he is."

Mellie put her arm about his waist and they slowly worked their way down the steps and across the garden. Once on the beach, Mikel had to rest several times but by the time the sun was completely up he was lying on the sand at Bryant's Cove waiting for Mellie to bring the boat.

He could see Tamara's face before him, shining with the love she felt for Steffan. He cursed him again and again, then he cursed fate that would not let him be by her side when she needed him.

It was almost the middle of the day when Mellie maneuvered the small boat ashore and helped a half conscious Mikel into it.

"Where are we going," Mellie questioned preparing to head the boat from the cove.

"I'll take her. Where we're going takes some expert maneuvering."

Reluctantly, she let him have control, then sat and watched, knowing that it was only grim determination that kept Mikel conscious. Mellie's eyes widened when they neared the huge rock.

"We'll be killed if we go too close to it," she shouted.

"We're not going close right now," Mikel replied, "We'll sit here until the tide goes in again."

Mellie had no idea what he was talking about and she began to wonder about his sanity. That huge monstrous rock would smash their small boat to nothing, not to mention their bodies. She found herself wishing Mikel would faint so she could take over the boat and get away from here.

Mellie who had been accustomed to boats all her life, felt the shift of the tide and knew when she felt the current that they were no longer able to pull themselves away from the rock. She closed her eyes in sheer terror and prayed silently that death would come quickly. The roar of the waves was deafening and hot tears fell on her cheeks as she clutched her hands together. Then suddenly it was quiet. Slowly, she opened her eyes and stared in wonder about her. Looking back, she could see the entrance. Quick of mind, she realized this must be the secret hiding place of Tamara's ship. The place was so beautiful, she could not believe it was real and wondered for one minute if she had died and gone to heaven. She turned again to speak to Mikel and found him unconscious in the bottom of the boat, fresh blood staining his shirt.

Mellie moved Mikel over just enough so she could get control of the boat. Expertly, she maneuvered it to the dock. There were only the few men of Mikel's crew there and they helped her tie the boat, then they spotted Mikel.

"It's Mr. Robbins," one of them shouted.

"Lift him easy, please," Mellie cried, "he's been shot."

Two of them jumped down into the boat and helped lift Mikel gently up on to the dock.

"What happened?" one of them questioned her.

"I'll explain it all to you later. Now we've got to care for him or he will die."

"You're right, miss. We'll carry him down to his bunk and have the doctor look at him. He'll be all right."

"Good" Mellie replied. "Please, please be careful with him."

"You look exhausted too, miss, best you come on board and get somethin' to eat and some sleep. Then you can tell us how this came about."

Mellie agreed, for after a sleepless night watching Mikel, then the dash to this place and the terrible fear, she felt completely exhausted.

She went with them to see that Mikel was put to bed safely. Once the doctor had examined him and told her that he would be all right, that he was now in a deep and healing sleep, she took a blanket from his bunk and curled up in a chair close to him. After a few minutes, she fell into a deep restful sleep.

Once she was wakened by the sound of a voice near her and found that Mikel was crying out in his sleep. Tamara's name was repeated over and over in a hoarse grief-filled voice. That did not alarm her until his voice turned hard. Through clenched teeth, she heard Steffan's name cursed. She wondered how a man could have treated a woman so gently and lovingly and then turn on her like a vicious animal and attack her so ruthlessly. Was everything the way they thought it was, she wondered, or was there another story to this they did not know? Somewhere deep inside, Mellie did not believe Steffan was as evil as he had been painted. She would try to talk to Mikel as he got well, try to make him understand that there might be more than he knew. Maybe she could get him to talk to Steffan first.

She wondered where Steffan was at the moment, and where was Tamara? Would Steffan be brutal to her, would he hurt her? Worse yet, she thought in absolute misery, would Steffan be the one to take her back to England and calmly hand her over to a ruthless justice that would hang her like a common criminal? She closed her eyes again to sleep with the one thought in her mind. Could Tamara, by some chance of fate, have escaped?

Twenty-eight

Tamara held the black mask in her hand. The ship was ready, the tide had turned, and they had to leave now. Dressed in the familiar black pants and red shirt with her hair bound and completely covered, Tamara was prepared to go after a ship for the first time without Mikel's help. Everyone awaited her orders, and she herself could not understand her hesitation. Some vague feeling of unrest nagged at her spirit, with it came the worry of what could have happened to Mikel. She watched the entrance to the cave, waiting for the exact moment. "We're ready," she called. Her acting first mate shouted the orders to hoist the sails. Already she missed Mikel. They moved toward the cave. With a suddenness she could never quite become accustomed to, they were swept into the darkness of the cave by the tremendous current. When they hit the open sea, all the sails unfurled caught the crisp early morning breeze, lifting the ship and pushing it along swiftly. She watched their position carefully, timing the proper moment. Aware each minute of where the *Peacock* would cross her path. The first gray light of dawn was behind her. The sun's rays had not yet touched the sky. If her calculations were correct, by the time the sun appeared over the horizon, they should be sighting the *Peacock*.

Just over the crest of the horizon, another ship awaited. Other calculations had been made, and Steffan was timing everything as closely as he could. He remembered all too well his meeting with the lady pirate. She would not catch him unprepared again. He could barely stand the tension of waiting and watching the pale gray clouds on the horizon. Slowly they began to widen as the first rays of sun touched the sky. Tom stood by his side and they spoke in whispers because both of them were aware that voices carried a long distance over water.

"Give me the glass, Tom."

Tom handed the telescope to Steffan who put it to his eye and scanned the water.

"Any sign of either of them?"

"No. But the *Peacock* should be coming soon."

"Our lady has to come from over there," Tom pointed, "if she wants to catch the morning sun."

"Right . . . any minute now, Tom . . . any minute."

The ship rocked gently. Steffan had given orders for no lights and absolute silence. Again, he raised the glass to his eye. He stood quietly, then his body tensed.

"Something?" Tom whispered.

"The *Peacock*," Steffan grinned. "Right on time. My calculations are right. Now, let's see if our lady is just as punctual."

The bright globe of the sun rimmed the horizon and Steffan watched in breathless expectation. His heart leapt to his throat when he saw the vague outline of red sails against the sunlight.

"And there she comes, straight into our trap," Steffan laughed. "Come on, my lady," he whispered. "Just a little closer."

Tamara's attention, and everyone else's on the ship was locked on their quarry. None of them thought to look for another ship. Closer and closer they came, then it began to be obvious to everyone on the *Butterfly* that the *Peacock* had spotted her. She was heavy laden and slow and Tamara laughed as the *Peacock* raised all her sails in a vain effort to get away. The speed of her ship could not be matched by the *Peacock*. Quickly, she came abreast and fired a shot across her bow, just close enough to show the angry captain she meant business. She hailed him, as was her usual procedure, and when he refused to come about, she fired again, this time letting her shots rip through the rigging. The captain of the *Peacock* knew his ship was outclassed and outgunned. To prevent it from being sunk, he hauled down the sails and allowed the *Scarlet Butterfly* to close in on her for the kill. It was at that moment, when Tamara laughed with the intoxicating excitement, that Steffan struck. The sound of cannon fire and the whistling balls ripping through her rigging caused Tamara to spin about in surprise.

"A ship closing in on us," her first mate shouted. "She's fast and well armed."

"How . . . ?" Tamara began, then her eyes made out the ship and with a leaping heart, she recognized the *Cecile*.

"Steffan," she murmured, then she smiled. "Don't resist, James. This is a man who will join us as soon as he finds out who I am. He's a privateer looking for profit. Let him board us, when

323

he knows who I am, it will be all right."

No one was more surprised than Steffan and Tom when the *Scarlet Butterfly* made no effort either to escape or fight them off. They looked at each other in shock, then Steffan gave the orders that would bring the two ships together and allow them to board her. Tom, Steffan and all their crew were in full uniform when they boarded the *Scarlet Butterfly*. Tamara's men and her first mate looked toward Tamara with questioning eyes, wondering why men in the uniform of His Majesty's Navy could be considered friends, but depending on Tamara's word, they found suddenly that they had surrendered to the English Navy without any kind of fight of protecting their ship or their beloved captain.

As Steffan stepped on board, his immaculate uniform damning him, Tamara stood stunned. With disbelieving eyes, she watched him walk toward her. All the pieces seemed to fall into place. And the realism of what he truly was came through to her. A deep and piercing pain twisted within her until she could not bear it. She wanted to scream out her agony, yet found no words for it. He stood in front of her, the beloved half amused smile on his face and the taunting laughter in his golden eyes.

"Well, well, my lady. Are you surprised? I told you we would meet again. I never break a promise to a lovely lady."

She could not speak, the choking misery filled her throat. Tom stood beside him a pleased smile on his face.

"You didn't give us much of a battle. You weren't so obliging last time we met. Did we frighten you, Madam Pirate?"

Steffan chuckled and Tamara could feel the hot tears of shame. She did not care so much for herself, but her ship and the loyal men who had laid their arms down so easily at her word, broke her heart.

"Shall we see behind the mask?" Steffan laughed and reached for the mask that covered her face. Anger filled her and she slapped his hand away. Steffan laughed again and reached. This time, she struck his face with every bit of strength she possessed. It jarred him and he stepped back a step. Then hot anger filled his eyes. "Take her aboard the *Cecile* and put her in my cabin. Put a prize crew aboard this ship and bring her back to port, Tom. I'll take the *Cecile* back to port. See that all her men are locked below deck."

"Yes sir," Tom said.

Tamara found each arm gripped by one of Steffan's men. Mask intact, she was dragged aboard the *Cecile* and shoved into

324

Steffan's cabin. She faced the door as they closed it behind her and she heard the key turn in the lock. Slowly, she sat down on the edge of his bunk, her mind numb with the pain and shock of what she had done. Blindly, trustingly, she had turned her ship and her men over to the enemy. "Steffan," she thought . . . "the enemy."

On the deck, Steffan was giving brisk orders for the care of the men of the *Scarlet Butterfly,* the beautiful ship. He questioned several of the men, but could get no answers about the home port of the *Scarlet Butterfly.* None of the men would betray the woman who led them and whom most of them had loved since she was a child. They glared at Steffan in open defiance and refused to give voice to any answers.

"Tom," Steffan said in exasperation, "we'll get no satisfaction here. Take them aboard the ship. Once you get them safely locked away, take the red ship in. I'm going to board the *Cecile* and question our lady friend."

"All right, Steffan, but . . ." His words stopped as his attention was drawn elsewhere. Steffan turned to see another ship approaching.

"It's the *Eagle* . . . Jaspar . . . what the hell is one of his ships doing here?" Steffan growled.

"Trying to be a step ahead of you, I imagine."

"You go ahead. I'll make it clear to them we need no help."

Tom nodded. Quickly, he had the men in the *Scarlet Butterfly* safely locked in the hold of the *Cecile.* With a few chosen men, he took possession of the *Scarlet Butterfly* and turned it toward Marriott Island. Steffan signalled the captain of the *Eagle* who within minutes came aboard the *Cecile* and then Steffan told him to return to Jaspar.

"Tell him I need no help to carry out my orders. And I don't want him interfering in my business again."

"All right," Captain Clayton said. He had known Steffan a long time. "Steffan . . ." he began.

"What?"

"Steffan, I think it's best you know a bit more before you head back to the island."

"Tell me, Clayton."

Clayton told him about the questioning and killing of Dundee, about the death of Mikel Robbins, then the fact that Jaspar was already at the Marriott home putting Andrew Marriott under arrest.

"Andrew Marriot," Steffan said in disbelief. "Why?"

"My God, Steffan, of course since you've captured his daughter, you should know the father would be arrested also."

"His dau . . ." Steffan's face went pale and he stared at Clayton. The words echoed in his mind but somehow, he could not seem to grasp the impact of what he was being told. Clayton looked at him blankly as if he had been sure that Steffan had known all the time the captain of the *Scarlet Butterfly* was Tamara Marriott.

"Clayton," Steffan said hoarsely, "get back to the island."

"All right, Steffan, what are you going to do?"

Steffan shrugged. He really did not know what he was going to do, he only knew the last thing he wanted to do was to go to his cabin and remove the mask from the face of the woman who waited there.

He stood at the rail and watched both the *Eagle* and the *Scarlet Butterfly* disappear. His second mate stood beside him and waited in silence for his orders. It was several minutes before Steffan really became aware of him. In a voice strangely still, the second mate heard his orders.

"Take the *Cecile* back, Sam," he sighed deeply, and turned away. With dragging steps he walked toward his cabin. There, he paused at the door for a minute, then unlocked the door and then he stepped inside. Closing the door behind him, he leaned against it and looked across the room at the slender masked figure that rose from his bunk. They stood, watching each other . . . and waiting.

"Tam," he said slowly. "Why? . . . In God's name, why?"

Realizing now that he knew who she was, she reached up and pulled off the mask and scarf, letting her hair tumble about her shoulders. Her chin lifted in stubborn pride. "I might ask you the same, Captain Steffan Devers. Why? . . . why the pretense of love. You need not have lied to me."

"I did what I did out of duty to my country. I am an officer of England. I was sent here to capture a . . . traitor. Someone who preyed on English ships."

Tears were in her voice, he could hear them, and he wanted nothing more than to hold her, tell her that everything would be all right, that they could work everything out together. But he knew they both realized the impossibility of this.

"Steffan . . . was making love to me part of your . . . duty?"

His voice was harsh with anger and his eyes glowed like molten gold.

326

"You know that's a lie, Tam. What is between us was too fine, too beautiful to have been a lie."

She turned her back to him, clasping her trembling hands in front of her, trying to control the tears that blurred her eyes and the wild, heavy beating of her heart. He crossed the room and stood behind her. Then he put his arms about her, pinning her arms to her body and binding her tightly. He felt her stiffen in his arms and heard the gasping intake of breath. There was no way her slender strength could free her from his arms and she knew it.

"Don't Steffan . . . please?" It was almost a sob. "Don't touch me, leave me be."

"I could no more do that than I could fly. Tam, remember . . . remember that day we found each other. I asked you to always keep it in your heart that I would never deliberately hurt you, that I loved you more than I have ever loved anyone before." She twisted trying to get away from that soothing voice and the strong arms that bound her, but it was useless. He merely tightened them, pulling her tense body closer to him.

"Tam, listen to me!" he said urgently. "Do you think I would have had this happen if I had known it was you?"

"Would you have helped me, Steffan?"

He was silent for a moment then his reply came firm and final. "No. But I would have found some other way to stop you. Some way that would have kept you safe."

Hope sprang up within her, hope not for herself but for Mikel and her men. She relaxed her body and turned in his arms. She looked up into his golden eyes, her eyes begging him to hear and understand. "Steffan. I understand that what I did, in your eyes, in the eyes of England, would seem an act of treason. If someone must be punished, it should be me . . . me! Let my men go. Let Mikel go, they are not guilty of anything except love and loyalty toward me. Please, if you love me, let them go. I will go with you, I will acknowledge my guilt, please, please Steffan, let Mikel and my men go."

Pain appeared in his eyes and his arms fell from her. "Dammit, Tam, you know I can't do that."

"Why? It's in your power to take them or leave them here."

"It's not that easy. I have orders to bring in the *Scarlet Butterfly*, her captain and crew. I also have orders to bring in everyone I consider an accomplice. There's no way out of it, there are too many witnesses, too many people to testify that you were all captured together . . . except Mikel."

327

"Mikel," she remained silent for a moment trying to read his face. "Steffan . . ." her voice became tight with alarm. "Where is Mikel?"

Steffan turned away from her. He could not bear, after everything else she had been through, to tell her Mikel was dead. She gripped his arm and pulled him around to face her. "Tell me," she whispered. "Where is Mikel?"

"He's dead, Tam," Steffan said gently.

Tamara shook her head negatively, refusing the words. "No . . . No, not Mikel." She looked at him, the pain and shock finally registering in her mind. A whimpered sob came from her and she clasped her arms about her body and rocked with the agony she felt. "Mikel . . . Mikel," she moaned. Steffan came to her, feeling the hurt and pain emanate from her. He put his arms about her holding her tightly against him. "I'm sorry, Tam . . . God, I'm sorry."

"I killed him," she cried.

"No, Tam . . ."

"I did . . . I did. Mikel never wanted to do this. He only went along because I asked him to. He never would have been involved if it hadn't been for me. Oh, Mikel," she sobbed. Her body trembled against him, then suddenly she was stilled. She looked up at him and he became alarmed at the cold deadness of her eyes. "If Mikel is dead, and my men cannot be set free, then there is nothing more to be done. I am not ashamed of what I have done. I would do it again. I believe in America as you believe in England. You can drag me back, and maybe they will punish me, but not before I shout my beliefs before the world."

"Tam, you can't do that," he said, his voice twisted in misery. "They will hang you. Do you think it matters that you are a woman, Tam? My father and my closest friend Mr. Gillis . . . they've a lot of influence at court. If you'll just be still, maybe they can get you set free. Tam, for God's sake, listen to me."

"Steffan, you of all people should understand that I cannot do that. What sense of honor or pride have I if I turn my back on the people I believe in. We're two different worlds, you and I. You are England, firm, strong and proud. I am America, free and determined. There is no way for either of us to cross the boundaries of what we are. I believe in what I have been doing with my whole heart, and I will deny my beliefs to no one."

"You're a fool, Tam. I love you. Doesn't that mean anything to you?"

328

"Oh, Steffan," she whispered. "You know what it meant for me. Before you say anything else, answer one question for me."

"What?"

"If I asked you, would you give up England, your career, everything you've worked for and go away with me?"

"That is ridiculous!" he said angrily. "Why should we give up anything? We can work this out if you just listen to reason. We'll go home. Together, we can clear this up. You'll just promise not to do any such things again. I'm sure they'll set you free. My family is influential. We'll marry and everything will be good for us."

"In England?"

"Of course in England."

"No," she said with finality.

"Tam, for my sake," he pleaded, "listen to me. I can't lose you, I won't. No matter what you say or do. I won't let them hang you. Some way I'll reach you, make you understand. You've got to give up this foolishness."

"It is not foolishness, Steffan. Open your stubborn eyes. Stop living with your arrogant pride. Unless you intend to set me and my men free," she said firmly, then held out her hands, clenched together, toward him, "then I consider myself your prisoner, Captain Devers, and I demand that I share the fate of my men. Bind me," she said proudly, tears in her emerald eyes, "or set me free."

"Damn you, Tam," he said. "You know I can't set you free. You have to stand trial, or I must desert everything I know. Don't do this to us."

They stood looking at each other, each of them too stubborn and proud and so sure that they were right that they could not budge.

"Tam, please," he whispered.

"Choose, Steffan," she replied.

He looked into the glistening emerald eyes and silently swore that with or without her help, he would find a way to get her out of this and safely at Devers Hall. There, he thought in his masculine arrogance, he would hold her until she no longer had such thoughts and was content to be his wife.

He reached out and took hold of her wrists, drawing her to him. When he held her hands close to his chest, he bent his head and lightly touched her lips with his.

"I love you, Tam, and I know you care for me. Unless all we

329

shared before was a lie."

"No, it was no lie, Steffan. There will never be anyone in my life I love as I do you. But I cannot give up all that I am, all that I think and feel. If I did, I would be a shadow of a woman, moving through life performing just what is expected of me. I cannot live so. I do not expect to take from you your pride, your honor, your self respect and your ability to think for yourself and if you loved me as I love you, you would not ask me to make such a sacrifice."

"Where are we, Tam. I cannot set you free, but I would die also if anything happened to you. So you see, no matter what you say, I shall fight with every means I can find to set you free."

"And if you succeed, what then?"

He put both his arms about her and held her slender length against him. "You're mine . . . I'll never let you go."

She closed her eyes, knowing that he did not understand all she had been trying to tell him, and knowing that she could not deny herself or her beliefs. No matter what Steffan said, she was lost to him. Steffan gathered her close to him. Gently, he kissed her forehead, letting his lips drift down to her cheeks, then to the tear-moistened lips that trembled, then parted under his. He kissed her deeply and passionately as though he suddenly felt that somehow, she had slipped away from him. Although, his kiss was returned with passion and her body molded against him, in sweet surrender, he still felt that some deep and very important part of her had closed itself away from him.

When the ship was safely berthed, Steffan gave orders for a close guard to be placed over her men, then he took a quiet and deceivingly subdued Tamara to Marriott Hall. When they stepped down from the buggy, Steffan took her arm and they went inside. When they walked into the study, Steffan's eyes darkened as he saw Jaspar Sinclair rise slowly from a chair and smile tauntingly at Steffan. "Well, I see you caught her. Good. Now, we can take her and her father back to England. Once they're tried and hung, this whole silly affair can be over and we can concentrate on whipping these arrogant American fools."

"Jaspar, what the hell are you doing here?" Steffan demanded angrily. "You have no orders to arrest anyone, that is my province."

"He's guilty, Steffan, one of Mr. Robbins' men told me so before he tried to escape."

"Escape?" Steffan said doubtfully.

"Yes, he got away from us. We were very surprised to find out they found him dead the next day."

"I'm sure you were, and what about the one you shot?"

"Oh . . . the Robbins fellow." Jaspar laughed. Steffan could feel Tamara's body stiffen and he gripped her arm tightly to signal her to silence.

"He attacked me, tried to kill me. One of my men shot him as he tried to escape. Regrettable, but unavoidable. Besides, we have the two who are the head of everything. That's the only thing that will show on our record, that we captured the *Scarlet Butterfly* and the captain, not to mention the man who was the brains behind it all, Andrew Marriott."

Steffan could tell by the violent reaction of Tamara's body just how angry she was at the slight against her and Jaspar's idea that only a man could have thought up such a scheme. Andrew rose from his chair, his face dark with constrained anger. "Tamara, child, are you all right?"

"Yes, Father," she smiled at him. "I'm fine." She went to his side and he slid an arm about her. She sighed as she rested against him. Steffan watched him, then a sudden answer to his problem struck him. He smiled to himself for now, he had the answer, he had the way to keep Tamara from being hung for her escapades.

"Jaspar," he said firmly, "I'll be responsible for the safe delivery of everyone responsible for this affair. We'll leave for England day after tomorrow. If I were you, I'd leave tomorrow. There's nothing more here for you to do."

There was no argument Jaspar could present, and it made him furious. Then, he decided if he did get home a day before Steffan some of the glory could be channeled in his direction. He rose, his face flushed with anger, and his eyes cursing Steffan. Still, he motioned his men to follow him and he left the room. Steffan had been watching him, then he turned and met the angry unforgiving eyes of Andrew Marriott.

"Tamara," Steffan said firmly, "this house is watched closely so you cannot escape. It would be best if you had Mellie pack some of your things and have them taken to the *Cecile*. We'll be leaving day after tomorrow. In the meantime, it might be best you get some rest."

"You deceiving bastard!" Andrew shouted. "How can you so cold-bloodedly take a child like this, that you swore you loved, take her back to England to a fate you know is waiting. Leave her here. Take me. I will confess to whatever you want."

"No, Father!" Tamara said. "We were caught red-handed at sea. There is no way you can confess to that. It's all right, Papa. I'm not afraid."

"I am," Steffan thought, but he said, "Tam, get your things ready."

Quietly, Tamara left the room. Andrew and Steffan stood looking at each other across the room. Steffan could actually feel, like a live thing, the anger and hatred that emanated from Andrew.

"You'd best sit down, Mr. Marriott."

"You, damned blackguard, I'll see you dead if you harm one hair of her head."

"Mr. Marriott, if you will sit down," Steffan said calmly, "I will tell you just how you and I are going to save Tamara's life."

Andrew stood silently looking at Steffan's smiling face, then he sat down in his chair. Steffan pulled a chair up next to him and began to speak in a quiet, urgent voice.

Twenty-nine

Tamara walked up the stairs to her room. Her mind was frantically reaching for some way to convince her father to remain out of this. She knew he would be searching for every way to get her free. If he did something foolish to try and get her free, he would only incriminate himself, and she would die before she let him take the blame and the punishment for what she had done. There must be some way she thought, but what?

Her room was empty and she called for Mellie whose room connected with hers. Receiving no answer, she went to Mellie's door and pushed it open. It was empty. It was surprising for Mellie seemed always to know the comings and goings of the family and was always near when Tamara wanted her. She shrugged, it was unimportant. She needed no help to dress or to pack a few belongings. She would, in all probability, not be allowed to take Mellie with her. So she thought it might be best, for Mellie's tears would not make parting any easier. Thoughts of Mellie, a very dear friend, opened the doors to thoughts of Mikel. "Oh, Mikel," she whispered, leaning her forehead against the post of her bed, she closed her eyes and wept for him. Mikel, who had grown as dear to her as a brother, Mikel who had followed her, out of love, to his death. "I'm so sorry, Mikel, so very, very sorry. You have paid for my cause and I shall never forget you. You are the only thing I truly regret. If you know, wherever you are, I know you understand that I would gladly trade my life for yours. Forgive me, Mikel," she cried softly. "Forgive me!"

She straightened, with considerable effort, got her tears under control. With fingers that were stiff with strained nerves, she changed from her black pants and red shirt, to a deep green dress. It was a demure and girlish dress chosen by her for that very reason. Tamara was about to start on the most important campaign in her life. In the next forty-eight hours, she had to convince Steffan Devers that her father was not guilty and that the men who had followed her should be left free on Marriott Island.

She packed what she considered necessary, then she put the case by her bed and went again in a quick search for Mellie. Now, she became truly curious. It was not like Mellie not to be here when she was needed. Her search proved fruitless. Returning to her room, she went to the closet to get a cloak. Opening the closet door, she again received a surprise. Mellie was extremely neat, both with her own clothes and with Tamara's, so the small pile of clothes in the corner, including the cloak for which she was searching, came as a shock to her. She bent and picked up a few of them and when she stood up her eye was caught by a bundle of cloth underneath that seemed to be stained with something. Again she bent and pulled the pile of cloth away. A bucket . . . filled with bundles of white cloth that were saturated with . . . blood! Someone had been badly hurt, and cared for here in her room. Her mind grasped the implication. Only one person had been hurt who would have come here to her room . . . Mikel! Mikel had made his way here! He was not dead, at least he was not when he had gotten here or there would have been no need for care. He had come to warn her, but . . . where was he now, and where was Mellie?

Andrew looked at Steffan with combined anger and surprise. "I don't believe what I hear you saying."

"It's the only way. The one way I can practically guarantee her safety." Steffan leaned forward in his seat; he was doing everything in his power to convince Andrew he was right. What he planned was the only way out for all of them. "My father and Mr. Gillis carry a lot of weight both at court and with the naval authorities. That and your name and some well-placed wealth would help me get her free, but you know the circumstances. There is only one way I can do this. She has got to be my wife before she leaves this island. You know she won't do that unless she has no other way to fight."

"But . . . blackmail . . . force . . . I just can't let that kind of thing happen to her."

"Let me tell you something," Steffan said firmly. "I love Tamara, probably more than she'll ever believe now, and I will use any means I can find to keep her safe. I've thought of every way out and this is the only thing that will work."

"She'll fight you every inch of the way."

"I know that."

"Steffan," Andrew said slowly, "I know now just how you

feel about her, but . . . she'll hate you.''

Steffan's face became bleak, but he replied firmly, ''If hating me will save her life and keep her safe, then it will have to be.''

The sound of approaching footsteps brought an end to their conversation except for the final words. ''Mr. Marriott!''

''I agree,'' Andrew replied. ''You do what needs to be done, boy, I'll play along with your game. Someday, we'll be able to tell her the truth.''

Tamara came into the room and went straight to her father. ''Papa?''

''I'm fine, child. How are you my dear?''

''I'm fine, Papa. Whatever happens, Papa, I want you to know I don't regret what I did. I did what I felt was right, and I'm ready to take any punishment. You taught me well, I'm just like you and I intend to stand for my beliefs.''

''Tam . . .''

''Mr. Marriott,'' Steffan interrupted, letting a cool arrogant tone creep into his voice. ''If you would be so kind as to leave us alone for a while, I should like to talk to my prisoner for a few minutes.''

Tamara looked at Steffan in surprise, but she was even more surprised when Andrew inclined his head in a short bow and with a quick kiss on her cheek and a reassuring pat on her hand, he left the room.

''Steffan?'' she said.

''I've come to the conclusion that Jaspar is right for once, your father is decidedly guilty.''

Steffan had struck the exact spot he intended to. Danger to her father had caused Tamara to forget herself and think of him. He added a blow he thought would be enough to cause her to snap up the bait he would dangle in front of her. ''I suspect that most of your men will be convicted of treason and either hung or conscripted into the English Navy, that is if we can get the traitorous scum to work.''

Tamara's anger blazed. ''My father had nothing to do with this. You cannot charge him with treason, he is innocent. Steffan, listen to me, this whole idea was mine and mine alone.'' She went to him , her wide green eyes gazing up at him filled with pleading. She would never know how hard it was for him to retain the cool arrogant look and not take her in his arms to comfort her. ''Steffan,'' she pleaded, ''It's up to you. You can leave my father and my men here under guard and take me back with you. I'll face my punishment but please, in God's name, don't let me carry all my men's deaths on my conscience. Please, Steffan, I'll do anything . . . anything, only let my father and my men stay here.''

"Anything?" he said quietly.

"Anything! I'll shout my guilt from the rooftops. Only let them free.''

"All right, Tam . . . I'll take your offer.''

"Offer?"

"Yes. It's good for the career of a naval officer if he has a rich and beautiful wife. In return for my considering your plea, you . . . are going to marry me immediately . . . tonight.''

"What!''

"If,'' he said clearly and coldly, as if he were explaining something to a child, "you want the safety of your father and your men, you are going to become my wife . . . here . . . now.''

"You . . . I don't understand.''

"It's quite simple. I will leave your father here and your men in return for . . . you. When we're married, I'm sure your father will not be selfish with his wealth when it comes to protecting you. He'll pay and pay well just to make sure I keep you safe. It will work out well all around.''

"But what about my trial?''

"Ah,'' he laughed. "A few well-greased palms and you will find yourself free as a bird . . . except for me, of course.''

Tamara's anger blazed, and Steffan was pleased. He didn't want her rational enough to think. He wanted her off balance just long enough to get her married to him.

"You . . . You! . . . arrogant English bastard!''

"Tut, tut,'' he grinned. "Such language for a lady. I'm only making you a fair exchange. You . . . in return for the lives of your father and your men. Of course,'' he shrugged nonchalantly, "if you don't care if they hang, it's perfectly all right with me. They're guilty as hell anyway. It should be quite a circus . . . the hanging I mean. I imagine it will draw quite a crowd to see the great Andrew Marriott dance a jig at the end of a rope. With this on my record, I should get a fair promotion.''

Fury, black raging fury overcame her every rational thought. "I'll never marry you!'' she almost shouted.

His eyes glimmered a gold amber, within them again was the teasing laughter that had set her teeth on edge when she first met him.

336

"Oh, but you will, love," he said gently, "if you want to keep your father safe, you will marry me."

"You said you loved me, Steffan. How could you do this to me? If you loved me you would let my father go. He's not guilty, you know he's not."

"What I know and what can be proven in an English court of law are quite different. I do care for you, Tam, but I also know you. You will take the blame for this. I don't want you slipping out of my hands and," he shrugged, "since this is the only way I have to get you, then it's the means I will have to take."

"I don't believe you're saying this. Does my father's wealth mean so much to you? Does your career mean that much that you would hang an innocent man?"

"There is no need for your father to hang. All you have to do is come to your senses. Marry me now; we will leave your father here. Maybe his purse will be a little lighter, but it's not much to sacrifice, he's very rich. I will lubricate a few palms with some of the money and soon you will be free. Then you will remain in England as my wife and you father will be safe . . . safe," he added, "as long as you remain a docile and obedient wife. Try anything foolish and you will put the noose about your father's neck as sure as there is a God."

Tamara looked closely at Steffan. Something about all he was saying did not ring true. She had thought she knew him so well. Was he really so hard? To demand that she give herself over to him, be obedient to him, forget everything she knew and loved. Telling her that it was really her father's money and his future career was most important. She knew her father would pay anything to keep her safe. She could hardly match this hard grasping opportunist to the Steffan who had made sweet and passionate love to her. She was confused and some idea kept slipping away from her. She was too worried about Mikel and Mellie, and too frighteened for her father to realize Steffan was fighting desperately to save only her. Steffan knew that as Tamara Marriott, it could be possible that the courts could sentence her to hang, but as Tamara Devers, backed by one of the richest, most politically powerful men in England, and aided by Mr. Gillis who, it seemed to Steffan, knew every important man in the English Navy, she would have a much better chance of being sternly lectured and scolded, maybe even fined, but her life would be safe, and at this moment, that was the most important thing in his mind. He was determined to see her safe if he had to force her

337

to marry him, drag her to England and keep her under lock and key. It wouldn't be the kind of marriage he wanted to have with her, but he had to see to her safety first. Maybe someday he could make her understand just how much he loved her.

"Steffan . . . my men . . ."

"Kept here under guard. We'll work it out so that we can get them free."

"My . . . my father?"

"Held here, safely, under my guard. Completely free, unless . . . unless you decide to do something very foolish like running away from me after I get you to England and work out your freedom. In that case, we would come to this island and your father would pay the price of your mistake."

"My father will never let this happen."

"You're not going to tell him what is happening. You are going to tell him you are marrying me of your own free will and that you have complete faith in me and my ability to get you free of these charges. You will calm his fears and make him believe you are content."

"I don't know you," she said. "The Steffan I love is gone. Was he ever really here? I don't know what is real. I agree to your demands as you knew I would. But only to keep my father safe. This marriage will give you no pleasure, that I swear. You may possess access to my father's money, and you may have complete power over all our lives, but you will never have me. If the day ever comes and your hold is loosened, I will be gone."

The pain on her face and the words she spoke hurt Steffan more than he had ever known, yet he knew for the sake of her life, he could not let her know. The only way he could fight the pain and keep himself from going to her, telling her the truth, telling her how much he loved and wanted her was to resort to this teasing humor.

"Now, now, Tam," he laughed. "Don't be sure it's going to be as bad as that. I remember some very warm, beautiful moments. It might be amusing to try again; why, you might even find you enjoy being my wife. At least you led me to think so one starry night when I held a pretty, wild beauty in my arms and made her mine."

Her cheeks flushed and she glared at him. "That was a lie. You were not making love to me, but to my father's wealth. I feel ashamed now that I let you touch me. I will not be so foolish as to fall for any of your sweet lies again. Do I have your permission," she said coldly, "to go to my room. I'm sure you can make all the preparations for our wedding without me."

"Come here, Tam," he said firmly.

She lifted her chin in stubborn defiance.

"We are not safely married yet. Don't make the mistake of pushing me or I might change my mind. Come here, Tam."

She swallowed the thick lump of anger that threatened to choke her, and walked to him. No matter how angry she was, his nearness unsettled her. She had to look up at him and his immense size crowded her senses, the strong masculinity of him and the remembrance of his gentleness left her trembling and close to tears. Tears she refused to let him see.

"We've made an agreement, we are going to be married. I think we should seal the agreement."

Their eyes holding, he put his hands about her waist and slowly drew her close to him. He had to hold her, if only for a moment, and even though it was against her will. His need to feel her safe and close to him was so urgent at the moment he could not stop himself.

Despite the fact that she was hurt and angry with him, some deep inner part of her could not deny the magic he held for her. She was mesmerized by his overwhelming aura of strength, and she wanted to curl against him and cry, letting his strength surround her and hold her.

Slowly, he bent his head and took her mouth with his, searching, looking for an answer to the burning need that coursed through him. His arms closed about her and he felt the warm, softly rounded length of her pressed against him. Warm remembrances flowed through her and for that one moment she was lost. A brief second of surrender before she stiffened in his arms and her lips changed from soft, moist giving to firm, cold denial. But it was a moment he sensed. He released her slowly and she stepped back from him, her eyes sparkling with brave defiance. Wordlessly, she turned and walked from the room. He watched her walk away and he knew that if it took the balance of his life, he would make her his again one day, that he could not spend the rest of his life without her.

Steffan made the arrangements for the wedding to be held. While he did so, Tamara slipped quietly from her room to her father's. She had to talk to him. Andrew watched her as she closed the door and came to him. He knew he would do whatever was necessary to protect her. He would go along with Steffan's plans to make sure she was kept safe. "Papa," she said quietly. "I have to talk to you."

Sure that her father did not know what was going on between her and Steffan, Tamara had to find a way to explain that she was going to marry Steffan and go back to England, leaving her father on the island. Unsure of how to go about telling him, she first asked him of another thing that was pressing on her mind.

"Do you know if Mikel is alive, if he came here? Do you know if he is safe or where he is now?"

At her father's surprised look, she hastily explained the finding of the blood-soaked rags.

"He was alive when he got here," Andrew began; then he went on to explain what had happened and how Jaspar started to search, and how both Mellie and Mikel had disappeared. "They've searched the island completely. I don't know where they could be hiding, but it must be an excellent hiding place."

Tamara smiled to herself. She knew where they were. She also knew when Mikel found out she had been captured, it would not take him long to slip back and find out all that had happened. Maybe, she thought, she could leave some kind of message for Mikel. If he could get her father safely away from the island, possibly to America, she would be free. "Then," she thought angrily, "we shall see the end of the oh so arrogant Captain Devers."

"Father, I must explain something to you."

"Yes?"

"In a short while, I shall be marrying Steffan."

"I don't understand," he said swiftly, trying to show the appropriate amount of alarm. "He is the one who captured you. Surely he is not forcing you—." Alarm filled his voice accompanied by anger.

"No, Father," she replied quickly. "I'm going to marry Steffan because . . . because I want to . . . because I . . . I love him."

He went to her and took her shoulders in his hands. "Are you sure? You are not doing this to protect me?"

"Don't be silly, Father. If you must know, it is more to protect myself; I think he will find it difficult not to protect me. It would be hard for him to put his own wife on trial for her life. Don't worry, Father. You remain here and I will go back to England with Steffan. Once I have freed myself from these charges, I will return. Then everything will be over and we will be happy as we were before."

340

Andrew, who knew her as no other did, heard the false bravado in her voice and knew the heartbreak she was feeling. He wanted to tell her that he was safe, that Steffan had no intention of harming him, but he also knew that under those circumstances, she would refuse to marry Steffan and the journey back to England would be to her death. Despite what she had done, Andrew knew that Tamara was completely innocent of the evils that existed in the world. Both he and Steffan would join forces to make sure it did not touch her. "But," he thought, "Heaven help us both Steffan, when she finds out the truth. I wouldn't be in your shoes when she finds out, and she will soon, that you tricked her into marrying you for her protection and not mine."

"The wedding will be tonight. Steffan is already making the preparations. Tomorrow, he will be making his ship ready; by dawn the day after tomorrow, we will be on our way to England. You will not be able to come with us, Father, you will be left on the island under guard until my fate is decided. Father, if Mikel should make his way back here, tell him not to try to come after me until he has gotten you away from your guards and safely hidden, then to send me a message. Tell him," she stopped and thought deeply for a moment, then she smiled, "tell him to take you to the rock. If he sends me such a message, it won't be long until I join you there."

"And then what child? We will be exiles from our home. What do we do then?"

"We have no choice, Father. We will go to America and pray we have made the right choice. If England wins, we will remain exiles the rest of our lives. If America wins, we will be free to come home."

"If I had it to do over again, I would never have taken you to America in the first place. If I hadn't you and I would still be happy here and none of this would have happened."

She went to him and kissed him. "Don't let's think of the past, Father. We'll look ahead to a future, together, happy again on our island."

"And Steffan?" he looked at her solemnly. "What of the man who is soon to be your husband."

Tamara was silent for several moments, then she said thoughtfully, "I don't know, Father . . . I just don't know."

There was a light rap on the door and when Andrew called for them to enter, both Steffan and Tom came in. That Tom was uncomfortable under Tamara's gaze was obvious.

Steffan had sent for him immediately, first because he wanted him to be best man at his wedding and second because he wanted to explain to Tom what was going on. Tom had stared at him in open-mouthed amazement.

"Marrying you! I would have thought she would rather murder you instead!"

Steffan chuckled mirthlessly. "I imagine she would." He went on to explain the situation to Tom.

"So she doesn't know that her men would not be punished anyway, and that we have no way to connect her father to this?"

"No. If she did, she would never consent to this wedding, instead, she would be making plans to escape. If she thinks her father's life hangs in the balance, then I can keep her safe and protect her."

"Steff . . ."

"Don't say anything, Tom. I know all the questions and none of the answers. I only know that I love her, and I have to do everything in my power to keep her safe."

They walked into Andrew's room. Tamara looked at them both with a look so frigid they could feel it.

"I've sent for the Reverend," Steffan said to her. "He'll be here any minute in case you would care to change or . . . anything."

Tamara gave a slight nod of her head and left the room. She waited until she closed her door behind her before she gave in to tears, then she threw herself across the bed and succumbed to her misery. This was her wedding day. Her mother dead, her father's life in grave danger, and being forced into a hasty marriage to a man who stood against all she believed in.

Andrew watched her close the door behind her, and he felt deep sympathy for her, but her life was more important at the moment.

Slowly she sat up and brushed the tears from her eyes. The Marriott pride lifted her once again. She stood up and walked to a huge wooden chest that sat in the corner. Kneeling in front of it, she opened the lid. Gently, almost reverently, she unfolded the wrappings from the gown that lay there. She would show Steffan Devers! There was no one who would defeat her. If this was to be her wedding day, then she would show him just what he could see but never again possess. She reached into the chest and withdrew her mother's wedding gown, which had been carefully packed

342

away for this day.

It was a lovely ivory gown, its long, lace sleeves fitted and the lace neckline high about the neck. The narrow pleats of satin that covered the bodice, then the full shirt made of layer upon layer of fine lace. She took off the dress she wore and slipped the gown over her head. It fitted her perfectly. She stood in front of the mirror. The gown was so very lovely it was a shame that it could not have been worn under happier circumstances. She coiled her hair on top of her head, then lifted the long lace veil from the chest. A beautiful tiara of diamonds glittered as she placed it on top of her head and let the fine veil of lace fall about her. Again she reached into the chest and took out the white satin Bible that had also belonged to Joanna. She stood in front of the mirror, a beautiful vision in clouds of white.

"Mother," she whispered, "help me, I'm . . . I'm frightened." There was a quiet knock on the door. It opened and her father walked in, then stopped, struck still by the beauty of his daughter and the memories of the lovely dress she was wearing.

"You are as beautiful as she was on our wedding day," he said sadly. "She would be so very proud of you, as I am. You are all we had ever hoped you would be. Tam?"

"Yes, Father?"

"Don't make a farce out of your wedding. Give him a chance. He might make you a good husband. The vows you take are very serious and binding." She could not tell him that the whole thing was a charade, that she was being forced into it for his sake. Instead she went to him and kissed him.

"Shall we go, Father?"

Andrew sighed, then he held out his arm and she took it. Together, they walked down the stairs to Steffan and her future.

The Reverend stood directly under the huge portrait of Joanna and as she entered the room, Tamara smiled for she thought it was a sign that her mother was watching.

Steffan turned as the door opened and his breath caught in his throat. She was so lovely he could not believe his eyes. She stopped beside him, her face expressionless. Not prepared for her startlingly beautiful appearance, he was spellbound. Together, they turned to face the Reverend. The words were repeated by her firmly and clearly. Strangely, it was Steffan who stumbled over them and he could feel his hands shake as he took her cool hand in his and slipped the plain gold band on her finger.

"You may kiss the bride," the Reverend beamed. Steffan took Tamara in his arms and she lifted her cool lips for his kiss.

Once the Reverend had gone, there was silence in the room. Andrew poured them each a glass of wine. "Shall we drink a toast to the bride and groom, Tom?"

"Yes, sir," Tom said with much more enthusiasm than he felt. Andrew handed the glasses around. "To a long and happy life," Andrew said reassuringly, as he looked into his daughter's troubled green eyes. He added the words in his mind, "He loves you, my child, may you find the happiness your mother and I shared. Open your heart, Tamara and find peace and contentment."

After several more minutes, Tom and Andrew made hasty excuses and left. Steffan stood alone with Tamara, watching his beautiful wife, whom he loved more than anything in his world, look at him across an ocean that separated them. He walked to her side.

"Tam, would you believe me if I told you that I'm sorry for the way things worked out. That I really do love you."

"Don't tell me any more lies, Steffan. You and I are married. We made a bargain. I expect you to keep your end of it and I shall keep mine. I want you to remember one promise. If ever my father is safe, is out of your reach, I will be gone."

"Is there nothing we can salvage from all the beauty we shared? I take my vows very seriously, Tam. I will never let you go."

"I told you once we were two different worlds, Steffan. Maybe if this had been another time, another place, things might have been different. Now . . . we are enemies."

"Never. Leave the rest of the world out of our lives, Tam. Forget what happened before. Let's try to start a life together."

She stepped back from him. "Are you planning on claiming your marital rights? Do you claim my body as well as my life?"

Steffan felt as if she had struck him. Wearily, he turned his back on her. "Not if you don't want me. If I ever touch you again it will be if you come to me." His voice was quiet and filled with pain. "You have one day at home, then we leave for England; you had best get some rest."

She heard the pain in his voice and suddenly, she wanted to reach out and touch him. Resolutely, she held herself still, then she turned and left the room. He heard the soft click of the door.

"I love you, Tam," he whispered. "God help me, I love you."

344

Thirty

The early morning breeze caught the white sails of the *Cecile* and she moved majestically toward the open sea. Andrew stood and watched until the ship disappeared over the horizon. He prayed that what he was doing was the right thing.

The day before they left had been a difficult one for all of them. When he had walked past his daughter's room, he had heard her softly crying. He knew that Steffan had spent their wedding night aboard the *Cecile*, that he had kept himself busy with nonexistent duties aboard ship. Both Tom and Steffan had been at the table for dinner the last night which had been a quiet, uncomfortable affair for all.

After dinner, both Steffan and Tom had returned to the *Cecile*.

"We leave at dawn tomorrow," Steffan said to Tamara before they left. "Do you want me to put your things aboard tonight?"

"Yes, I've a few things ready," Tamara replied. "I'll see they get brought down to the docks."

Steffan nodded. That he wanted to say much more to her was obvious, but there was no response in her expressionless face. He left any other words unspoken and he and Tom left.

Tamara and her father were alone together for the last time before she was to be taken to England. Strangely, Tamara felt very calm and unafraid of her future; she pushed aside the idea the knowledge that Steffan would face it with her, fight for her, made everything seem more in control and secure.

Andrew sat down beside her and took her hand in his. "What are you thinking, Tamara, are you afraid?"

"No, Father, not really."

"Are you regretting all this?"

"No, what I have done I would do again, and if the opportunity comes I will."

"Once you're in England, there will be no opportunities."

Tamara smiled, for she knew that if Mikel were alive and well, he would soon be finding out all that happened. If he came to her father and received the message she had left, Mikel would find some way to elude the men Steffan was leaving to guard the ship, its crew and Andrew. If Mikel could get Andrew safely to the rock, then she would be free. Then, she vowed to herself, there would be no power on earth that would keep her chained to Steffan in England. She would find a way to get free. Andrew knew she was thinking of Mikel, and he wondered himself if Mikel was still alive, and where the rock Tamara had referred to actually was. He also had been turning over in his mind just what he was going to say to Mikel when he came back that would stop him from running to Tamara, and give Steffan the time to work things out between himself and Tamara. That Tamara still loved Steffan was clear to Andrew, but that she would surrender to him in any way was doubtful. Andrew knew now the whole problem was down to a matter of pride. Forced into a marriage, forced to let Steffan protect her had gone against everything Tamara knew. It was also against everything he knew and felt and except for one thing, he would never have let it happen. The love he felt for Tamara would have let him accept any circumstances that would keep her safe. In the hands of anyone but Steffan, Andrew knew what her fate would be. He knew Steffan loved her enough that he would do anything in his power, make any sacrifice necessary for Tamara's welfare.

When Tamara's baggage had been brought to the dock, one of the sailors carried it aboard. Tom was about to order him to put the baggage in his cabin and he would share a room with the second mate, but before he could speak, Steffan's voice came from behind him. "Put it in my cabin."

Tom turned around, but the firm look on Steffan's face told him he was not in the mood for interference. He closed his mouth until the sailor went below with the baggage.

"Steff . . ."

"You have something to say about my wife sharing my quarters, Tom?" he said, amused.

"Not me, I just think your wife will be very verbal about it and I don't want to be in cross fire."

"Get about your duties, Mr. Braydon," Steffan grinned. "And I suggest you stay out of the vicinity of my cabin for a few days. For I agree there will be some fireworks."

"What are you doing, Steff?"

"Well, Tom," Steffan said, the grin fading from his face. "I'm going to spend the next two weeks of the voyage trying to

346

put the pieces of what could have been a good marriage back together."

"After what we've pulled do you think you stand a chance?"

"I don't know, I only know that I have to keep her from finding out the truth, keep them from punishing her, and try to make her understand how much I love her before it's too late for either of us."

A harsh expulsion of breath, and Tom said, "God, I wouldn't be in your shoes for all the tea in China. I'm glad your sister is the warm, affectionate, loving woman she is; I don't think I'd be able to handle the hurricane you've chosen to navigate. Good luck, friend, I hope it all works out for the best. If ever there is any way Cecile and I can help the situation, don't hesitate to let us know. We'd do anything in our power to help."

"For now, Tom, I guess it would be best if you just stay out of her way for a while."

"That's going to be hard to do on a ship, but," he laughed, "I assure you, I'm coward enough to do my best to try."

The next morning, as dawn was breaking, Andrew helped Tamara down from the carriage. Steffan stood on the quarterdeck and watched them walk up the gangplank. He was grateful for duties that required his attention. He watched Andrew kiss his daughter a reluctant farewell, then leave the ship, standing on the dock to wave goodbye. Behind Tamara's back, Steffan raised his hand in a wave to make Andrew know he would surely take care of everything from then on.

Tamara stood at the rail as the ship moved slowly away. She stood so until land had faded completely from sight. Tears stung her eyes and the hands that gripped the rail trembled. The deep ache of loneliness struck her. Separated for God knew how long from everyone and everything she knew and loved. Taken against her will in a marriage to a man she did not really understand or know, to a land of which she knew absolutely nothing except it existed in her mind as the enemy.

"Father," she thought, in wracking pain, "I love you so much. I will survive this and I'll be back to my island. We will live again in happiness . . . one day . . . soon."

"Mrs. Devers?" came a quiet voice from her side. She turned and looked questioningly at the young sailor. It suddenly occurred to her he was really addressing her. "Mrs. Devers," she thought and for the first time since the ceremony, it really broke through her consciousness that she was now Captain Steffan

Devers' wife.

"Yes."

"I'll take you to your cabin, Ma'am."

"Thank you." She followed him, knowing ships as she did, she realized immediately it was the captain's cabin to which she was being escorted. She closed the cabin door behind her, and her first inclination was to lock it. She reached, only to find that it had no bolt. Steffan made no appearance all morning and she began to believe he had made plans for other quarters. Relieved, she unpacked a few of her clothes. By the time she was done, it was not yet noon. She did not know truthfully if she were to be treated as prisoner or guest. She sat down on the edge of Steffan's bunk and for the first time looked carefully about the room. It spoke of him. It was plain and extremely neat. Everything seemed to have its place. Through the closet door, which stood ajar, she could see his clothes hanging neatly. The heavy desk, bolted to the floor, had few things on its glossy surface. Behind it sat a large, high-backed chair made of some soft leathery material. She had a feeling it would not only be quite comfortable but that he spent many hours in it. A lamp hung over the desk. In one end of the room stood a large chest covered with a quilt. It was a beautiful piece of work and she wondered if someone special had made it for him. There was as deep an air of masculinity about the room as there was about Steffan himself. Behind the desk was a bookcase filled with books. She went over and removed one. It was a book of poetry and gave all appearances of being handled often. She opened the book. Several poems were marked.

> Out of the rolling ocean
> The crowd came a drop gently to me,
> Whispering, I love you, before long I die,
> I have travel'd a long way merely to look on you
>   to touch you,
> For I could not die till I once look'd on you,
> For fear'd I might afterwards lose you.
> Now we have met, we have look'd, we are safe,
> Return in peace to the ocean, my love,
> I too am part of that ocean, my love,
> We are not so much separated,
> Behold, the great Rondure, the Cohesion of all,
>   how perfect!

But as for me, for you, the irresistible
  sea is to separate us,
As for an hour carrying us diverse,
Yet cannot carry us diverse forever:
Be not impatient—a little space—
Know you I salute the air, the ocean and the land,
Every day at sundown for your dear sake, my love.

It caught her unaware, that he felt the same about the sea as she. Again she turned a page. Another short poem, well marked and fairly obvious that he had enjoyed it often.

My true love hath my heart, and I have hers
By just exchange one for another given;
I hold hers dear, and mine she cannot miss,
There never was a better bargain driven:
  My true love hath my heart, and I have hers.

Her heart in me keeps her and she in one
My heart in hers, her thoughts and senses guides;
She loves my heart, for once it was her own,
I cherish her because in me it abides:
  My true love hath my heart, and I have hers.

She closed the book and returned it to its place, aware that there were many things about Steffan she did not know. "And now," she thought, "I will never know, for there is no future for us. Too many things stand in the way. All our beliefs are so very different."

There was a quick rap on the door. "Yes?" she called.

The door opened and two sailors came in. One carried a small table and two chairs, the other a large tray of food.

"Cap'n thought you might be hungry by now, Mrs. Devers. Told us to bring you a tray for lunch. Jocko fixed it up personal. Said you was the only person on board this ship outside the cap'n who ever really appreciated his cookin'."

She smiled, remembering the little man who had made her welcome before and cooked such a fine lunch. "Tell Jocko I thank him and I'm sure I shall enjoy every bite."

Both men smiled. They liked the captain's pretty wife, but both of them wondered about the rumors they had heard that she was a very reluctant bride . . . almost a prisoner. They set the table down and put the tray on it. It was then she noticed the two chairs. Her heart skipped a beat. Obviously, Steffan meant to share lunch with her. After the two sailors had left, she stood in silence waiting for the door to open again, prepared to do battle with him. He had sworn, she thought in panic, that he would not touch me again until I came to him. She refused to admit that the strangling panic she felt was more fear of what she would do than fear of him. Suddenly she wanted nothing more than the safety of her home and her father's protection. She heard the sound of approaching footsteps. They stopped in front of the door. The silence was a heavy thing that caused her to hold her breath in expectation.

Steffan paused for a moment outside his cabin door, then resolutely he turned the knob and walked in. The look on Tamara's face made him stop just inside the door. Whether she knew it or not at the moment he walked in her emotions were reflected clearly in her eyes before she veiled them from him.

"Oh, I see Jocko has sent our lunch. I'm sure in your honor, he's cooked up something special and I'm starved," he said with a grin. Rubbing his hands together, he walked to the table nonchalantly and pulled out first her chair, then his own. "Aren't you hungry?"

"Steffan."

"Come and sit with me at least," he laughed. "I've got enough of an appetite for the both of us."

"Steffan, please."

Knowing he was unable to change what she was going to say, he leaned back in his chair and the smile faded.

"What is it, Tam?"

"We . . . we have to talk."

"Talk about what?"

"This . . . this situation."

"What situation is that?"

"Dammit, don't play with me!" she shouted angrily. Steffan stood up slowly and walked to her. He stood close and looked down into her anxious green eyes.

"This is not a game for me, Tam. On this ship there are over one hundred men, all of whom think you are my wife. Would we want any of them talking to the wrong people, saying anything that might make someone believe anything else?"

"You . . . you're going to stay here?" she said, her voice cracking in alarm.

"Why not? This is my cabin . . . you are my wife."

"But you can't."

He raised one eyebrow and his lips twisted in an amused grin. "Why can't I?"

Tamara stood silent for a moment. Suddenly she again realized that she was completely at his mercy. That he could do anything to her he chose to do and her only way out was to let her father hang for her crimes. Steffan knew exactly what she was thinking and it distressed him that she thought he was cruel enough to take advantage of her vulnerable situation. But there was no way he was going to allow her to know, not only that she could hurt him so but that he would never resort to rape. If she would come to him, he would love her with passion and gratitude. If she did not, he would continue to try to win her love, but under no circumstances would he let her believe he was weak, for he knew she was quick enough and a strong enough person to take every advantage he would give.

"You . . . You said . . ."

"I said I would never take you if you didn't want me, but," he stepped so close their bodies almost touched, "I never said I would not try everything in my power to make you want me."

She gulped with relief; then she saw that same deep warm gaze that reached for her. Out of self-preservation, she stepped back and her eyes fled from his.

"We are going to spend a lot of time together, Tam. We'd best understand each other. Relax, sit and eat, we'll talk." She went to the chair and sat while he walked around the table and sat opposite. Truthfully, he did have a rousing appetite and he began to eat. Soon she joined him, reluctantly drawn into his light conversation. He began to talk, of his boyhood, his friends, his family. Telling her amusing stories of his time in the Military Academy, drawing her out by asking questions of her.

Once he had finished eating, he rose from the table. "I've a lot of work to do. I'm sure you know as much about ships as I. Why don't you make yourself at home. Move about, enjoy what a beautiful day it is and the beauty you are sailing on."

"Since," she laughed reluctantly, "you know there's no way I can get away."

"No," he replied, "because I think you're honorable enough to keep a bargain once you've committed yourself to one."

She looked up into his eyes, searching for that teasing humor; instead, she found warmth and sincerity.

351

He walked to the door and she remained quietly watching as he closed the door behind him. She was confused. Confused and frightened. For the first time in her life, she would admit to herself and herself alone, that she was more afraid of Steffan's gentleness, understanding and consideration than she had ever been in her life.

She changed her dress to the more comfortable faded dress, then went on deck. In no time, it was obvious that every man on board the ship not only admired her beauty but was determined to please the captain's wife in any way possible.

Steffan, keeping one eye on the workings of his ship and the other on a laughing Tamara who was enjoying animated conversation with one of the men, stood on the quarterdeck.

That Tamara admired the beauty of the *Cecile* endeared her to the hearts of the men, and even more so when they engaged her in conversation and found she knew as much about the workings of a ship as they did.

No matter how he tried to avoid it, it was unavoidable that Tom was in the same place at the same time as Tamara. Now that she had thought it over, Tamara became amused at Tom's deliberately misleading her about the two Ceciles and decided to have some conversation with him. Slyly keeping an eye on his movements, she placed herself at the open companionway and the next time Tom reappeared, she was there to waylay him. He did not see her until it was too late to retreat.

"Good afternoon, Tom," she said, her face a mask.

"Tamara," he replied unsure of what to say to her. "I'm sorry things had to work out the way they have."

"So am I, Tom," she replied. "I'm sorry for all the lies and pretenses. There could have been a good future for Steffan and me had not his lies come between us."

"Don't you think you have things a little backwards, Tamara? Aren't you being a little extra hard on Steff and just a little easy on yourself?"

Tamara remained silent; she had no answer for this so obvious truth. Then she said, "Whatever my lies were, I never used Steffan."

"You think he's using you?"

"For his own gain, both in prestige, wealth and his career. Oh, he told me Tom, just how much my father's money means to him and how much good it would do his career to capture the pirate. I don't like to be forced into doing something. Forcing me to choose between marriage and sacrificing my father and all the others was just a little unfair, don't you think?"

Tom fought the words that were on his lips. Combined with the unfairness of the situation, her words drove him to the brink of telling her the real truth, that her father was in no danger of hanging because they could not prove his connection to her, and the worst that could befall her men was that they would be enlisted in the English Navy. The real danger was only to her, and the only one that stood between her and a horrible death at the end of a rope was Steffan and his family's influence. That Steffan truly loved her, he knew she would never believe, and to keep her life safe, no one else could tell her. He choked back the words on his lips. "Sometimes . . . sometimes things aren't always the way they seem," he said, "and the day has come when a spoiled little girl should grow up. Everything's not always black and white and it's easy to misunderstand what you think you know."

"I know," she said, stung by his reference to her being a spoiled child, "that every word you both said, every thing you did was deceit. Even your little joke to rouse my jealousy. I can just imagine the laugh you and Steffan had over that. You're right, Tom Braydon, perhaps it is time I grew up. Time I learned that the only way to get what you want in the world is to take it . . . at anyone's expense."

She spun on her heel and went back to the cabin where she got some pleasure in slamming the door behind her.

Tom sighed deeply and returned to his work; he was unhappy that Tamara felt the way she did about both him and Steffan, but he knew Steffan would never let the truth be told while her life was in danger.

Tamara calmed herself down determinedly. The time would come when she could return to Steffan and Tom what was due them. In the meantime, she would wait for the word she knew would one day come from Mikel. She had to remain docile until her father was safe. "Then," she thought, "then my time will come."

She whiled away the hours reading one of the books that Steffan had. Curled up on the bunk, she dozed off into a light sleep. A knock on the door roused her. She could tell by the darkening room that the sun was setting. Rising from the bunk, she went and opened the door.

The same two sailors who had brought her lunch stood waiting outside her door. When she questioned their reasons for being there, they replied, "Cap'n says to tell you, Ma'am, we have a big barrel of fresh rain water on the deck and a nice wooden tub. Jocko says he'll heat the water up if you'd like to take a bath."

"Oh, that sounds wonderful, thank you, and please thank Jocko for me."

"Yes, Ma'am. It should take a little while to get all that water hot. In the meantime, Cap'n Devers wants you to have dinner with him and Mr. Braydon. They're waitin' on you now, Ma'am."

"All right," Tamara replied. "Tell them I'll be there in just a few minutes."

Closing the door, Tamara changed her clothes, laughing all the while in secret amusement. She had stubbornly brought along the pirate outfit. Quickly, she slipped out of her dress and into the black pants and red shirt. It would make them all remember just who she was and why she was here. She wondered gleefully just how angry Steffan would be when he saw her. Quickly, she made her way to the small room near the kitchen where all the men ate. She ignored the stares and whispers of the sailors she passed on the way.

There were three long tables in the room, with benches on both sides, each bolted to the floor. Another small table with several chairs sat in the corner of the room. This was the captain's table.

There were several men seated at the long table; they remained silent, watching both her and their captain.

Tom, Steffan and Steffan's two ranking officers rose slowly from their seats as she approached.

"Gentlemen," she said, sweetly smiling, "Good evening."

Her eyes met Steffan's across the table challenging him. She could see the anger in his eyes, but he gritted a smile. "Mr. Kent, Mr. Javins, this is my wife, Tamara Marriott-Devers. Tamara, this is my second mate, Mr. Joseph Kent and my navigator, Mr. Anthony Javins."

"Pleased to meet you, Mrs. Devers," Joseph Kent smiled. She could see his smile was genuine and the mischievous glitter in his eyes appreciated her rebellious gesture. Anthony Javins' gaze was another matter. His look told her he appreciated more than her gesture. Combined with Steffan's cold anger, she began to wonder if her little joke was not more dangerous than she thought.

The supper was pleasant as long as she did not meet Steffan's eyes across the table, yet she was glad when it was over and she

354

could escape to her room and the promised bath.

She left the four men and made her way back to the cabin. There she found the tub in the middle of the floor filled with warm water. Beside it, on the floor, was a bar of soap, a luxury she did not know existed on board ship. Quickly, she pinned her hair up on her head and stripped off the trouble-making clothes. She eased herself down into the tub with a sigh of pleasure.

She lathered her body with the sweet smelling soap, humming softly to herself. She was remembering the anger in Steffan's eyes and she laughed lightly. It will teach him not to be so arrogant, she thought. It would also put him on edge wondering what I will do next. Reluctantly, when she opened the door to thoughts of him, other, more piercing memories came flowing behind them. For one moment, she opened her mind to all they had shared before, but then she quickly smothered those memories. She would not believe that lying touch, those tender deceiving kisses, no; she would allow herself to remember only that she was his prisoner and that her life and her father's lay in the palm of his hand.

Stepping out of the tub, she reached for the large towel that hung on the chair beside her. It was at this moment the door was thrown open, Steffan stepped inside and slammed it firmly behind him.

She froze as a surprised gasp came unbidden. His angry gaze raked insolently over her wet, naked body. She stood trembling, aware for the first time that her gentle Steffan could be roused to a terrible anger. She tried to meet his gaze and defy him as he slowly walked toward her.

Holding the towel against her, she backed up a step, but he reached out and took hold of her shoulders. He shook her until the towel slipped from her fingers and her teeth rattled. Then, suddenly, she was pulled against his body and his arms bound her helplessly against his chest. His mouth swept down and took hers in a kiss so demanding that she became dizzy from the force of it. He parted her lips in fierce angry possession. Her knees became weak and only the strength of his arms kept her erect. She was bound so tightly against him she could barely breathe and his kiss assaulted her senses and blindly she felt herself weaken and cease to resist. Her lips became soft and pliant and her body moved against his. When he felt her resistance leave her, he held her away from him, looking down into her confused eyes. "Don't push me, Tamara. You might find that no matter what I said to you, there will come a time when those words will not protect you. If I wanted to take you, I would and there is nothing you could do to stop me. Be careful, my dear.''

He turned and walked away, slamming the door behind him. She was left weakly shaken by his attack and now fully aware that he was right. She also became aware of another blinding thought. She wanted him, needed him, and would never be able to deny the truth to herself again, that despite all that had happened, she still loved Steffan Devers.

Thirty-one

Tamara donned her nightgown and robe, then sat curled up in the chair wondering if Steffan planned to return. After a while, men came to remove the tub of water, then the cabin became still and quiet. She became drowsy and reluctantly went to the bunk. Removing her robe, she slipped under the covers. She moved close to the wall and lay curled into a ball, tensely listening for every sound. The muffled sound of the keel cutting the water slowly relaxed her and after a while, she drifted off into a sleep.

It was in the wee hours of the morning that the door opened and Steffan came in. He closed the door quietly, not wanting to waken her. Silently, he walked to the bunk and looked down on her. In the pale moonlight, her hair spilled across his pillow in burnished confusion. She lay relaxed and breathing deeply in sleep, yet even in that sleep, she kept herself as far away from his side of the bunk as she possibly could. Steffan was exhausted, and most certainly in no mood to have conflict with her again. He was upset with himself at his own loss of control that afternoon, and it was clear to him just how close he had come to throwing her on the bunk and possessing her.

He had been not only angry at her act of defiance, but jealous of the hungry look of his two officers. That, combined with the fact that he wanted her beyond reason had fired his temper. He had meant only to tell her to be careful, but he had not been prepared for her wet, slender nakedness and her completely defenseless look when he had come in. His own anger had been his only defense and he had attacked her helplessness to keep himself from raping her. Then the feel of her warm wet body in his arms and the soft giving of her lips had completely undone him. He had warned her . . . then had run like a coward, he thought.

Without making a sound he took off his clothes and slipped into the bed beside her, making absolutely sure he did not touch her. Resolutely, he turned his back to her and sought sleep. It came, and with it came dreams that were unwelcome and frustrating.

Time ticked slowly by in the quiet cabin. Both Steffan and Tamara slept. The night chilled and in unknowing sleep, she sought his warmth. Slowly she moved toward him, allowing her body to curve to his, her cold feet to entangle with his, and her arm crept about his waist. She slept soundly then, her cheek pressed against his back and his warmth easing her to relaxed comfort.

They stirred restlessly, then he turned toward her. In sleep, they clung together contentedly, a thing they could not do awake.

It was almost dawn when Tamara stirred awake. She lay very still because she had suddenly realized the position she was in. Her nightgown had crept up about her and her bare leg was lying across his. Her head was in the curve of his shoulder and his arm about her held her close. She could hear the relaxed, steady beat of his heart and she knew he was sleeping. She tried to move away without waking him, but discovered her hair was caught beneath him. There was no way she could get it free without waking him and at the moment, in her position it was the last thing she wanted to do. She stopped moving and relaxed against him.

Steffan came drifting up from a dream-filled sleep. In his dream, he was holding her, feeling her unresisting body cling to him and the softness of her hair against his cheek. Then suddenly, he realized he was not dreaming, she was there, warm and real in his arms. With it came the knowledge that she was asleep and had only sought his warm body for comfort. No matter, he thought, he would enjoy her for as long as he could before she wakened. Very gently he tightened his arm about her, pressing her softly curved body more against him. She stirred, put her arm possessively across his chest and snuggled against him. They lay still and he allowed himself the dubious pleasure of holding her knowing it would soon be over. He lay still thinking of the night they had spent together on the beach. Allowing himself to enjoy every touch, every kiss again. Suddenly he was brought to total awareness that the feel of her body in his arms was somehow different. He raised his head slightly and looked down into her wide open green eyes.

He refused to move. He had told her he would never take her against her will, but now it was up to her. If she moved away, he would let her go, if not . . . unaware that his love and desire for her showed plainly in his eyes, he looked down at her. Then very slowly, very gently, she raised her hand to his cheek, touched it gently, then slid her fingers into his hair twining them there and slowly drawing his head down to hers. His lips met hers and they parted under his seeking kiss, then returned the fire and the need with a possessive demand of their own. He kissed her again and again, covering her eyes, cheeks with soft gentle kisses returning again to her lips to drink the sweet honeyed taste of them. His arms surrounded her, pulling her body together against him. His lips drifted down her neck until it met the obstacle of her nightgown. The obstacle barred him only for a moment, urgent seeking hands found the neck line and separated the front of the gown with a quick tearing sound. His lips traced a line of kisses across her heated skin finding one rosy tipped breast, he tasted again, suckling each gently, while his hands moved over her slender body until they cupped her hips and he pulled her body up to meet his. He felt the urgent need burning within her too and he gloried in it. Wanting her to need him as he needed her, wanting her completely and finally.

For Tamara the burning need for him filled her with a white hot explosion, numbing her to everything but Steffan. Steffan with the magic hands that seemed to reach within her soul and touch a place that no other could, Steffan whose fiery kisses raised her to a plane of ecstasy as she had never even dreamed of.

She cried out as her writhing body tried to draw him closer. He wanted to prolong the sweet agony as long as possible. He held her immobile against the bed as his mouth began to journey along the curves and planes of her body. Fiery kisses that left her moaning and gasping out her need for him. Still, he held her while his hands followed the pattern set by his lips and found the pulsing center of her need. She could bear the sweet agony no longer. She reached for him.

"Steffan," she moaned softly, "Please . . . love me . . . love me."

"God," he gasped, "I do, Tam, I do!" He rose above her, then suddenly he was filling her, drawing from her the depth of a love so brilliant that she could not control her sobs of pleasure. He moved slowly, drawing out each stroke until he drove her frantic. He felt her body writhing beneath him as she twined her long slender legs about him and lifted to meet him, with each move she drew him deeper and deeper within her, until they blended in one rhythmic moving entity. Together they climbed a burning pathway toward the stars, then burst among them and tumbled down clinging to each other among the glittering fiery diamonds.

They lay still, their sweat-slicked bodies entwined, neither of them wanting to do anything to separate from this glorious beauty. Daylight was turning the room into a shadowed place. Steffan sat up and looked down at the woman he loved with every fiber of his being. She lay still, their eyes held for a moment, then he reached out and gently brushed a few strands of her hair from her face.

"Steffan," she whispered.

"Shh, love," he said tenderly, "don't let's talk, for now let's just accept this beautiful thing we share."

"But, Steff," she said softly, "there's tomorrow . . . and there is yesterday."

"Tam, can you deny that you love me as much as I love you?"

"No, but is it enough? Steffan, so many things have come between us."

"We won't let it happen, Tam," he replied firmly.

"We will cast out every memory of yesterday. We will remember for all the tomorrows that come that we love each other. Together we can defeat whatever problems threaten to separate us, Tam," he said, his voice filled with a pleading urgency. "Don't let anything separate us. Trust me, Tam, trust me."

"Oh, Steffan," she cried. "What is going to become of us. I cannot turn my back on my father, my obligations, and you . . . you cannot turn your back on your duties. I've given myself in return for the freedom of my father. You've given yourself to a duty and a country I do not know or understand. Steffan, look at me clearly. Understand me. I have to be free. I belong to the cause of another country. If you pin me down in England, rob me of my freedom, I will die, worse, our love will die. Let me go, Steffan," she whispered, the pain was a deep thing that turned within him. He tried to make her know that he did understand how she felt.

"Tam, do you think I don't know how you feel about your father, your men, your ship and your adopted country? I do, but try to see it from my side. If I let you go, I make it possible for them to hang . . . your father or your men or worse even you. I love you, and I'll protect you, but for God's sake, don't ask me to let you go. You might just as well ask me to tear out my heart. Give us some time, Tam. Stay with me in England until the charges against your father and you are cleared away."

"Steff . . . would you . . . would you turn my father over to the authorities if I didn't agree?"

The time had come when he was faced with a choice. No matter what he felt, he had to have the power of keeping her, holding her until he got her free and could explain the truth. "Yes, Tam," he said wearily, "I would. If it's the only way I can hold you, yes. Now, you tell me. If I set you free, would you promise not to run to America? Would you promise to return to the island and not do anything until this is over?"

"Oh, Steffan," she cried, "you know I cannot make that promise."

"Then what do you expect me to do? I love you. I want you to be safe, and I will hold you by any means I can. I'm not going to let you sacrifice your life and our future."

"What are we going to do?" she sobbed as she turned from him and buried her face in the pillow. He lay down and drew her body into her arms.

"Tam," he said miserably. "Can't we have a bargain for a little while? We have several days before we dock." He tipped her face up and held her tear-filled eyes with his. "Stay with me, trust me for a while, and I'll do everything in my power to make everything work out right . . . trust me, Tam, just for a little while."

"A bargain has two sides, Steffan."

"All right. What do you want?"

"I'll stay with you, I'll trust you to find some way to clear my father's name, but . . ."

"But?"

"If war is declared between our two countries, you will freely let me go."

"Tam, don't you love me?"

"I do Steffan."

"Then how can you ask me to let you go so easily?"

"Because we both understand duty to others. You who have loyalty to your people, your country. Would you deny me the same loyalties just because I am a woman? You who put honor so high would deny me mine. If you love me as you say you do, and if you want me it must be because I am free to come to you, not because you bind me with the lives of those I love."

"Would you then come to me?"

"When we have done what needs to be done, when we're both free, when no others can be sacrificed for our love, Steffan, don't

361

doubt that my body, my heart, my soul calls to you, that I love you more than any other for I do. But we can't build our lives on the lives of others and we cannot turn our backs on what is demanded of us.''

Steffan knew he would agree, for it meant she would remain until he could get her name cleared and, he hoped, by that time, he might be able to convince her to stay with him always and forget her silly notions about fighting for a country he knew could never win.

He chuckled. "Tam," he bantered. "If war is never declared between our two countries, I'll hold you to your bargain. You'll never leave me.''

She laughed in response. "I may have to declare war myself.''

"I don't put it past you, little gypsy. I think it would be best if I took you home and chained you to my bed. That way, I know there would only be one kind of mischief you'd be mixed up in.''

"Why, you brute," she laughed. "Would you treat your new bride like that; after forcing her to marry you, you could at least be considerate.''

"Tam, forcing you to marry me was not exactly what I wanted, it was just that I saw you being taken away from me maybe to die, and it was the only way I could think of. Tell me, would you have married me right away if your father's life hadn't been in danger?''

"If my father's life hadn't been in the balance," she replied, "to be honest, Steffan, I would have found the means to get away. Where I have hidden my ship is impregnable and neither you nor your friend Captain Sinclair would have found me.''

My God, he thought. If she finds out that her father's life was never in jeopardy, she will kill me.

"You wouldn't," he laughed, "want to tell me where it is, would you?''

"Not on your life. Someday, when this is all over, I'll take you there. You'll not only be amazed, you will love it as I do.''

"We have a bargain then, Tam? All battles between us are over and you'll cooperate with me in the fight to get you free.''

"Yes, but if war is declared you'll set me free without punishing my father?''

"If you still want to go, I won't stop you, but I warn you, I'm going to do everything in my power to make you want to stay.''

"Agreed.''

"Then," he said tenderly as his hands began to rove searching-

362

ly over her again, "suppose we start our honeymoon again . . . properly."

He heard her soft laugh of pleasure as her arms encircled his neck and she surrendered again to the exhilarating power of his love.

Tom paced the quarterdeck, occasionally drawing his watch from his pocket. Each time he did, his frown deepened. It wasn't like Steffan to be late for duty. He knew Steffan had been coldly angry last night and Tom had stood his watch worrying about what Steffan could have done. Tamara had thrown her identity in his face in front of everyone and Steffan might have been angry enough to try to show her who was master last night. And, he thought, Tamara was stubborn enough and proud enough to fight him every inch of the way. "She loves him, dammit," he muttered, "and he loves her. Why the hell can't those two put everything else aside and be happy." He knew the answer before the words left his mind. They were identical, each with an unsurmountable pride and honor. Neither of them would step away from what they felt was their obligation or duty. Again he took the watch from his pocket. "Past noon," he muttered. "If she hasn't killed him, I'm going to push him overboard for making me worry so."

He looked up to see Joseph Kent headed toward him with a broad grin on his face. When he reached Tom, he said, "Captain Devers and his wife would like you to come down and have breakfast with them. I'll stand in for his duty."

"Breakfast!"

"That's what the captain said . . . breakfast."

Tom chuckled, then saw the answering glitter of amusement in Joseph's eyes and laughed aloud. In a minute, Joseph joined him.

"Do you think we can look forward to our captain being in better humor today?" he asked.

"Seems that way," Tom said happily. "Breakfast . . . at half past noon, with a man who's never been late for duty in his life. Joseph, it looks as though the rest of this trip is going to be fine."

Joseph's laughter followed him as he went toward Steffan's cabin. He gave a quick rap on the door. "Come in," Steffan called.

He went in and closed the door behind him searching both faces for his answer. What he saw pleased him immensely, Tamara, seated on the edge of Steffan's bunk, her hair about her in tangled confusion, her cheeks pink and her eyes shining in friendly welcome. She was dressed in an old robe of Steffan's with the sleeves rolled above her elbows and the belt cinched tightly about her slender waist. Tom's quick knowing eyes saw the torn discarded nightgown that both Tamara and Steffan had forgotten about. As for Steffan, the old bright humor lit the golden eyes and Tom saw again the quick smile and easy manner of the old Steffan. Of course, they weren't going to tell him what had happened last night, but putting the obvious two and two together, he came up with the logical four. It made him happy to see the two people he cared for so content with each other instead of locking horns every time they spoke.

"Good morning, Tom," Steffan grinned. "Breakfast will be here in a few minutes."

"Breakfast," Tom replied, his twinkling eyes catching Tamara's flushed cheeks. "Do either of you know what time it is? I'll have you know, Cap'n Devers, that I expect a reward of some sort for standing double duty for a friend."

Tamara laughed and rising from the bunk, she went to Tom. Rising on tiptoe, she kissed his cheek and smiled up at him. "Thank you, Tom."

"Well," Tom replied happily, "if I had known I would be rewarded like that I would have taken an extra round of duty long ago."

They laughed together. A few minutes later, breakfast was brought and they spent an enjoyable hour eating and talking. When breakfast was finished, Steffan rose from the table.

"Come on, Tom, I think it's time I get to work." He turned to Tamara. "I'll send someone to take the tray. After you're dressed, why don't you come on deck and enjoy yourself. The *Cecile* should be like a second home for you."

"Thank you, I will," Tamara replied. Steffan slid his arm about her waist and kissed her. "Not in that outfit you wore last night, love. I don't want anyone sharing the prize I've got. To please me, how about wearing something a little more . . ." he shrugged and Tamara laughed again. There was a bright mischievous glitter in her eyes and Steffan frowned menacingly down on her. "Tamara, I don't like the look in your eyes. Keep in mind that wasn't an order, but a very polite . . . no, practically a begging request. I would hate to have to keel-haul one of my men for your mischief."

"Steffan," she purred, "I shall be a very good little girl and dress like the captain's wife."

Steffan cocked an eyebrow doubtfully at her, then he squeezed her tightly against him until she gasped; then he quickly brushed another swift kiss across her lips and he and Tom left.

Tom walked along the deck with Steffan who was absently whistling lightly. "So everything worked out all right. She understood when you told her that you were only protecting her, keeping her out of trouble until this is all over and her father is completely safe."

The whistling stopped and they walked along a few more steps before Steffan said. "I didn't exactly tell her that."

"You what?"

"I said . . ."

"I heard what you said, I just don't believe it. I thought the lies were over. She's still under the impression that if she steps out of line, her father faces the consequences."

"We have sort of . . . ah . . . an arrangement."

"Arrangement?"

"Yes." Steffan proceeded to tell him.

"Boy, when you compound a felony, you really do the job right, don't you? Steff, what is it with you? I've never seen you like this, and worst of all, lying and then building lies on the lies, it just isn't like you."

"Tom, I'm in over my head. If she finds out now, there's no way of holding her. Wouldn't Jaspar love to get his hands on her, and won't he be trying to do just that as soon as we reach England. Until her trial is over, until I've got her free, there's no way I can tell her. By the time it's all over, I hope she'll want to stay of her own free will."

"Time is supposed to cure everything?"

"I hope so."

"And if there's a war?"

"No, come on, Tom," Steffan laughed. "You know there's no chance of a war with the Colonies. They can't be that stupid. There's no way they could win one."

"I'm not too sure now."

"What? , . . . you . . ."

"I honestly believe there is going to be a war. On the island, I associated with a lot of men who not only believe there is going to be one, but that the Colonies have the determination to win. At first it was hard to believe, but after listening to them for a while, you begin to recognize some . . . spark . . . some special thing. The kind of spirit it takes to win wars."

Steffan stopped now and was looking at Tom, a deep frown on his face.

"Steff, there's no need to look at me like that. I can't help telling you what I honestly think. If you've got the courage to listen, try and ask Tamara just why she feels as she does. Let her tell you what's going on over there. When I put everything together, what I feel and the fact that it has drawn men like Horatio Nelson, Captain Pierce, and yes, Mr. Gillis, too, I wonder . . . well, maybe, I'm kind of having second thoughts on joining Nelson if he goes."

"What about Cecile, your family, everything you've known, everything you've worked for?"

"Steff, Cecile's my wife, she'll go with me wherever I go, and you know my family would give me their blessings in anything I do. As for what I've worked for, well, you've hit the nail on the head. I worked for it, it wasn't handed to me. The only person I'm grateful to in this world are you and Mr. Gillis for opening doors. I'm a friend, Steff, and you know that, so I'll tell you something straight. You've had everything you've ever wanted all your life. Now that I think of it, I really don't envy you that. You have no idea how hard it is to pull yourself up by your bootstraps. I can probably sympathize with the Colonies' cause better than you. You only know one way of life. Ask your wife, and if you're not too hard-headed, listen to her with an open mind. You might hear things you've never thought of before. Your mind might begin to work on a whole new principle, that a man can make his future for himself and not live easy on the laurels of his family."

"Is that all I've done?"

"Isn't it?"

"I don't know, I guess maybe you're right. I never thought of it that way."

"In the back of your mind, Steff, don't you ever wonder just how it would be to be on your own, away from everything you've know? Away from the doors your family's wealth can open. I kind of admire Tamara; I guess I have since from the beginning. She chose independence and she had the courage to stand up and fight for it."

"She's not turning on her country."

"She's English born, her father English raised. I wonder just how he's going to decide to go when it happens. I'd stake my life he goes to the Colonies' side and stands beside his daughter."

366

"And you think I should go too."

"As it's always been, the choice is still up to you, but I'll tell you what I would do. If Cecile chose Tamara's path, I'd be right beside her to share it. After all, what does a man acquire in this world of real genuine worth than a woman like Tamara or Cecile to share it with him, give them children. There's a whole new future out there and when I get home I'm going to ask Cecile to go with me; and I'm going to make myself a good productive life for me, for her and for my child, whatever it is."

"When did you decide this?"

"I've been thinking about it ever since the night we met Nelson. Everything we've been involved in since then has only made it stronger. Then this whole business with Tamara—well—I like her. I told you so before. She's the kind of person I'd like to have as a friend. I like the things she believes in and the loyalty she gives it. You've got the best in the world there, Steff. If you don't tell her the truth, stand with her, you might find yourself standing all alone some day and regretting every minute of it."

Tom walked away leaving Steffan watching the rolling blue-green ocean with unseeing eyes, his thoughts on the woman he had just left and the kind of future they might have. He stood in thought for a long while and was suddenly brought back from thoughts when Tamara slipped her arm through his and stood leaning against him.

He thought of Tom's words as he looked down into his wife's smiling eyes. To share a new, free life with her, maybe to have children, to make a whole new beginning in a new place where all the old problems that would ever stand between them were gone.

"What's bothering you, Steffan?"

"Me . . . nothing . . . why?"

"You're so preoccupied."

"Going to be a busybody wife?" he grinned.

"Wherever you're concerned," she said seriously. "I intend to be. I want to be part of your life, too, Steffan. I love you. What hurts you, hurts me also."

"Tam," he said seriously, holding her eyes with his. "Talk to me. Explain to me why you did what you did. Tell me of your reasons, help me to understand you." He held her face between his hands. "I want to know you, how you feel and think. Tam, I need desperately to understand. Help me. Without either of us thinking about what we are or where we are. Without being afraid that either of us will ever use what we know against each

367

other. Open your heart to me as I will to you.''

"Steffan, what is it?" she questioned worriedly.

"It's only a need, Tam, I need you. Do you believe that?''

She could see the truth of it in his face and she could not understand the strange urgency in his voice. "Over the next few days, I want to try to understand. Maybe then, we can make a new beginning for you and me. When we reach England, there are a lot of choices and changes to be made. Without you, I don't know if I can make them.''

"Steffan, this doesn't sound like you. You are a strong . . .''

"Strong,'' he laughed harshly. "Good old Steffan, always upright and strong in his beliefs. If he starts anything he does it, and,'' he said almost angrily, "if he needs it, there is always someone there to open a door and make it possible. Tam, I don't want to be that kind of man.''

"What do you want, Steffan?''

"I don't know, I'm not sure. But whatever my future is, I want it to consist of two things. First you, because without you, there is no kind of future at all and second, I want to be responsible for my own future, build it myself with my own strength. Stand or fall by what kind of man I am and what I'm capable of, not what someone hands me.''

Tamara smiled and lifted her arms about his neck, pleased with the way he held her tightly against him.

"Whatever you want, Steff, I'll tell you about me, about what I believe if that's what you want to know. But I'll tell you this first, you laughed when I said you were strong, but you are, Steff, strong enough to know what you want and you are capable of getting it. Without any help from anyone. Yes, I'll tell you everything for I love you, I am your wife. We have no more secrets between us.''

Steffan held her close to him promising himself that no matter what the cost, he would tell her the truth and soon. "But,'' he prayed fervently, "don't leave me, Tam. It would be a dark and lonely world without you.''

Thirty-two

The days fell into a relaxed order. Tamara and Steffan spent every possible moment together. When he had duties to attend to, Tom would sit and talk with Tamara. Often they would walk the deck at night for a short time before they went to bed. As the sparkling blue days passed, Tamara slowly began to acquaint Steffan with what she was doing and her reasons for doing them. Slowly the story of the Colonies' search for independence was drawn out in front of him. With vibrant enthusiasm, she tried her best to explain, sometimes in the words of Thomas Jefferson and others she had met.

The days for Steffan were bright and informative, the nights were beyond anything he had ever dreamed. He thought of Tom's words in reference to Tamara, she's the type who gives her whole heart to anything. They were so true, for she made their shared nights together a joy that he would never forget.

They were only a day away from English shores. The night before their arrival, Steffan and Tamara strolled hand in hand on the deck of the *Cecile* in silence.

"What are you thinking, love?" he asked.

"That tomorrow sometime, we'll see the shores of England. Oh, Steff, I wish we could stay here on the *Cecile* and sail away to some far off place and just be together the rest of our lives."

He drew her against him knowing her thoughts were the same as his. The desire to take her somewhere where they could live together in peace. "I know," he whispered against her hair.

"What's going to happen now?"

"Are you afraid?"

"No, not with you."

He tightened his arms about her, crushing her to him. "It will be hard for you, Tam, the trial I mean, but remember, I'm here. I won't let anything happen to you."

She silently lifted her lips and he touched them lightly with his. They went back to his cabin to share this last night together and share their strength for whatever might be coming.

Steffan stood on the precipice of understanding without knowing. There were forces gathering now that would push him over the edge.

The *Stewart* had already docked by this time, and while Steffan and Tamara were sharing the joy of their love, Jaspar Sinclair was on his way to meet another who shared his hatred of Steffan. They would join forces and the combination would create a whole new world for the two lovers.

Another scene was unfolding in a small secret lagoon miles away, as Mikel Robbins stood on his feet for the first time. Grimly determined, he looked toward England. His wound was healing, but his hatred festered within. In a matter of a day or two, he would take his ship from the hidden harbor and head for those shores. One way or another, he vowed two things, to free Tamara . . . and to kill Steffan.

When the *Cecile* entered the harbor, the original Cecile, Maxwell and Ellen Devers were waiting impatiently. The days had been long since they had seen Steffan and Tom. Cecile bubbled with barely restrained excitement. When the ship reached the dock, she was the first to step down from the carriage.

"Cecile," her mother cautioned, "please be careful, you will hurt yourself."

Cecile bloomed, her black hair braided about her head. She wore enough petticoats so that the small rounded signs of her pregnancy could barely be seen. She looked up when someone called her name to see Tom at the rail impatiently waiting for the gangplank to be lowered. As it met the dock, Cecile ran forward and in a moment, he caught her up in his arms and was kissing her hungrily.

"Cecile, Cecile," he said against her hair. "God, how much I've missed you."

Her laughing, happy tears were kissed away and again his mouth found hers. He stood her back on her feet and held her a little away from him his eyes examining her closely. "You are the most beautiful woman in the world, my little mother to be. Has my son been behaving?"

"He's fine, and I'm fine, and oh, Tom, I'm so very glad you're home," she cried.

They were laughing and holding each other while Steffan and a suddenly nervous Tamara walked slowly down the gangplank to meet his parents.

Steffan held his mother for a moment and kissed her, then he held out his hand to his father who ignored it and embraced a son he had missed so badly.

"Welcome home, son."

"Thank you, Father," Steffan turned and took Tamara's hand and drew her forward. Placing a reassuring arm about her shoulder, he said, "Mother, Father, I want you to meet Tamara Marriott-Devers . . . my wife."

For a moment, both Ellen and Maxwell were stunned. Ellen, the first to regain her thoughts, smiled at Tamara and held out her arms to a very grateful Tamara. Then Maxwell held her for a moment in a firm embrace and kissed each cheek. "I'm sorry if we seem a little surprised," he laughed, "we should have known better than to be surprised by now at our son's excellent taste. He's done well with his life and you, my girl, are the crowning jewel to prove it."

Cecile had cast a quick look at Tom's face when she heard Steffan introduce Tamara. Knowing her husband the way she did, she immediately sensed there was something here that was being left unspoken. Tom gave a quick negative shake of his head to warn her to keep from asking questions until they could talk. For Cecile, who remained silent, this was the most difficult thing in the world.

"Tamara," Steffan said with a broad grin as he reached for his sister's hand. "This is Cecile . . . my sister and Tom's wife."

Tamara's flushed embarrassment was only understood by Tom and Steffan who both knew the cause.

"I'm so happy to meet you, Cecile."

"Finally," Steffan added.

"Finally?" Cecile questioned puzzled by both Steffan and Tom's obvious amusement and Tamara's laughing embarrassment.

"It's a long story, Cecile," Steffan replied. "Maybe some day Tamara can tell you about it."

"In the meantime," Tom said, his arm tightening about Cecile's waist, "I think we should be on our way. I've seen enough of this place and that ship for a while. I'm anxious to be home."

"Right you are, my boy. The carriage is just over there. Will you be coming on with us to Devers Hall or would you like us to drop you at your parents' home?"

"I would like to see my family for a few minutes. I'm sure my father will give us a carriage and we'll be along later."

"You and Cecile will be looking for a house nearby now that you're home, won't you, Tom?" Ellen said.

Tom looked at Cecile for a moment, then he and Steffan exchanged an unreadable look. "We'll think about that later," Tom replied. "When Cecile and I have a chance to talk."

Cecile watched Tom's face. There was something new, something different about him. That and the mystery surrounding Tamara and Steffan were two things she could hardly wait to find out about.

"We'll be having a big welcome-home supper; we would be pleased if you and Cecile would bring your parents and share it with us," Maxwell offered.

"Thank you, sir, I'll ask them."

Ellen insisted Tamara sit beside her, and on the way home, she chatted with her, putting her at ease with her friendly open smile and her sincere welcoming conversation.

By the time they reached Devers Hall, Tamara was laughing with them and feeling completely at ease.

Maxwell stepped down from the carriage and assisted Ellen. Steffan, smiling at Tamara's contained lady-like manner, took her hand in his as she stepped down. But when they reached the door, Steffan stopped and turned to Tamara. "Old family custom, love," he grinned, and before Tamara could say another word, he swept her up in his arms. "Can't cross the threshold without carrying the bride."

Amid laughter and pleased looks from his parents, once they were inside Steffan held her close to him for a moment then let her feet slide slowly to touch the floor keeping his arm about her waist.

"Well Tam, this is it, this is home."

"It is so lovely, Steffan, what a wonderful life you must have led here as a child."

"I did. There's a lot of things I would like to show you." Steffan turned to his father. "Where's Mr. Gillis?"

"He should be returning from London soon. Steffan, I'm sure he wants to talk something over with you. He's been impatient for your return before he leaves."

"Leaves? Where is he going?"

"Maybe it is best that he explain to you."

Steffan had a feeling he knew where Martin was going, the thing that shook him was the reason why he might be leaving.

The dreaded thought of war and what it would do to him and Tamara caused him to tighten his arm about her waist. She looked up at him, feeling the change and wondering why.

"I'll take the baggage up and show Tamara our room."

Maxwell and Ellen watched Steffan and Tamara go up the stairs until they heard the closing of the door.

"Maxwell, there has been quite a change in our son," Ellen said quietly. "And a wife. She's a very beautiful girl. I cannot wait for him to explain all that has happened to him since he's left."

"I would say a lot has happened. Both Steffan and Tom seem much more . . . subdued . . . preoccupied as if they had something weighing heavily on their minds. I have a strange feeling Ellen, that something's going to happen in this family and I fear it's something we are not going to like."

"What, Maxwell?"

"Maybe it's best we don't jump to conclusions," he said, "I could be wrong, at least, I hope so. Come on, my dear. Let's not be upset over something that has not happened. Let's make our new daughter welcome and make our son's homecoming pleasant." He put his arm about her and kissed her quickly. Ellen smiled, but she too sensed that some great change was coming.

Steffan kicked the door closed behind him and Tamara. After dropping the cases he was carrying on the floor, he pulled Tamara into his arms, holding her against him and kissing her soundly.

"Welcome home! Devers Hall is much more beautiful now that you are here. Besides," he laughed, "my bed has never been as warm and comfortable as it's going to be now."

Tamara's laughter blended with his as he lifted her off her feet, carried her to his bed then dumped her unceremoniously in the center of it. He stood by the bed smiling down at her.

Tamara looked up into those honey gold laughing eyes and as always, she felt the warm center of her melt under that deep intense loving look.

"Steffan," she said as she slid off the bed. "Who is Mr. Gillis?"

"Oh, hadn't I mentioned him before?"

"If you did, I don't remember. Is he part of the family?"

"By blood no, but in love and respect yes. He's been my tutor and close friend from the time I was ten. I can't wait for you two to meet."

"Why?"

"Because, I have the deep suspicion, you two have a lot in common. If I don't miss my guess, he's as much an American patriot as you are."

"Really!" Tamara said, suddenly excited to think of a compatriot in this new place. "How very wonderful!"

"I thought you'd think so. He's also a good friend of several of my instructors at the Academy. Especially Commander Pierce."

"Who?" she said softly, her eyes widening in surprise and an elated feeling she tried to control.

"Commander Pierce. He's one of the best . . ."

Steffan continued to talk but Tamara turned her back to him pretending she was occupied. She didn't want him to see the excitement on her face. Commander Pierce! . . . the man whose messages came to her and Mikel. The man who was one of the links in their chain. Her heart thudded painfully with the wonderful realization that he might also be a link to her freedom.

". . . Tamara?"

"What?" she said as she turned about realizing Steffan asked her something.

"I said, would you like to freshen up before dinner? I can have some warm water brought. Much as I would like to stay and watch," he smiled, "you can take your bath alone. I've got to talk to my father for a while."

"Yes," she managed to reply.

He brushed her lips with a quick kiss and left the room. Slowly, Tamara sagged back down on the bed. She remembered the first time she had heard of Commander Pierce. It had been Mikel who had gone to England and with the help of some men from America he had made all the necessary contacts in the Colonies. Although they had not always discussed the people who were involved, Mikel had found it amusing that they could count among their friends a commander in the English Naval Academy itself and a man with a great deal of information at his fingertips. The name, known only to a few people, would not have even been known by Tamara had not Mikel once said "Commander Pierce should be pleased with this little gift to his friends in the Colonies."

It was the one and only time she had heard his name, but she had remembered it. She was grateful now that she had for at the first opportunity she would either talk to him or send him a message. The bath water arrived and she bathed quickly. Then she drew her hair back from her face and held the wayward curls in place with a comb, letting the loose curls fall over her shoulders to her waist. She put on the many petticoats she hated, then donned a pale green gown trimmed in dark green velvet with a wide green velvet band across the waist. She was just finishing the touches on her toilette when Steffan returned to take her down to dinner. Steffan seemed quiet and contemplative, but she had no time to question him before dinner.

Steffan had gone down to his father's study. Welcomed inside, he had sat in the large overstuffed chair opposite his father's desk with the amusing thought that both pieces of furniture had overwhelmed him as a child. He watched his father pour them both a drink. He handed Steffan his and they silently toasted each other; then Maxwell set his glass down. He sat behind his desk, leaned back in his chair and said seriously, "All right, Steffan, suppose you tell me what is bothering you and if I can do anything to help you."

Steffan took another drink, then he looked levelly at his father. "Maybe it would be best if I started at the beginning. You know all about the mission we were on. My job was to find a pirate who had been waylaying English arms ships headed for the English army in the Colonies. They sent them to the Colonies all right—only to the Colonial Army."

Maxwell nodded, but remained silent. Steffan continued the story telling his father everything that had happened. When he came to the *Scarlet Butterfly* waylaying his ship, his father muttered, "Confounded gall. The man must have had a tremendous amount of courage and audacity."

Then he told his father about the *Scarlet Butterfly* and the fact that his pirate was a woman. "A woman! Astounding!" The story continued, then suddenly Maxwell's eyes narrowed as Steffan told him about Andrew, his island and his beautiful daughter whom Steffan had fallen in love with almost from the beginning. He began then the last of his story. The capture of his lady pirate.

"Why so unhappy! A beautiful wife and a mission accomplished as ordered. You should be proud."

"It's not quite that simple."

"What is the problem?"

"I have to report to Commander Pierce tomorrow. At that time I have to hand over the lady pirate and the red ship to him."

"Simple enough."

375

"No, sir."

"Why?"

"The lady pirate . . . is Tamara Marriott-Devers."

"What!" Maxwell said, startled completely.

"She is Tamara, my wife."

"My god, Steffan!"

"That's not all," Steffan said grimly. Then he told the story of how he had forced Tamara to marry him ostensibly to protect her father, yet knowing that there was no danger to her father or her men. "I love her. It was the only way I could see to try to save her."

"What are we going to do?"

"We?" Steffan smiled.

"Why, Steffan," his father returned the smile. "Tamara is my son's wife, the future mother of my grandchildren. Do you think I could stand by and let anything take her from us?"

"To be honest with you, sir," Steffan chuckled, "I had counted on something like that."

Maxwell laughed. "Martin knows about every man of influence at the Academy, maybe in the English Navy. I, I am proud to say, have quite a bit of influence at court. Put those two forces together and we might just make this whole episode a tempest in a teapot."

"I would be grateful for any help. The thought of turning Tamara over to the courts, maybe to be locked away or . . . worse, hung. God! The thought gives me nightmares."

"Martin should be home tonight. We'll talk to him then and see what can be done." He rose from his chair and came around the desk. Steffan stood and his father clapped him on the shoulder. "We'll find a way."

"I'm grateful, sir, you have no idea how grateful." *

"No? Do you think I'm blind, son? I've got a good look at the lady. I suspect if I were in your shoes, I would do anything to hold on to a woman as lovely and charming as she seems to be."

They laughed together, the old camaraderie lived between them again.

"She is, Father. Wait until you know her a little better. You've got a great experience in store for you. She's not like any other woman in the world."

"Funny," Maxwell laughed. "But I can remember saying the same thing to my father about your mother and you know, son, I think we were both right."

There was a soft rap on the door, then Ellen opened it and came in. "Dinner will be in a few minutes, if you two are through with your conference. Mr. and Mrs. Braydon can't come, they have guests tonight. Tom and Cecile sent a message that they will have dinner with his parents and come home later."

"All right. I'll go get Tamara. Be right down," he said as he closed the door behind him.

Dinner turned into a quiet affair for just the four of them, but it was a relaxing thing for Tamara who found Steffan's parents all he had told her they would be. By the time they moved to the firelit drawing room, Tamara felt as though she had come home, and Steffan smiled when he saw her relax and open herself to his family.

For Tom, homecoming was a much more frustrating affair. Not having a home of their own except for the small cottage at the Academy, they had no place to go for privacy. The Braydon home, as usual was overrun with laughing family, at the moment a little too much family for Tom. Not only were all the big and little Braydons present, but an aunt and uncle were visiting.

Cecile suppressed her teasing laughter at Tom's so obvious misery and as soon as feasibly possible, she allowed Tom to claim that she wanted very desperately to see her brother soon.

When the dinner, of which Tom ate very little, was over they had his father's carriage harnessed. Tom insisted on driving himself. They were just out of the driveway when Cecile's laughter rang out and she threw her arms about Tom's neck kissing him soundly causing him a great deal of trouble controlling the horse.

It was a long quiet road between Tom's house and Devers Hall. Over halfway there, Tom spotted a small side road. He drove down this road a way until he came to a secluded spot with overhanging trees. There, he stopped the horses, tied the reins securely then turned to Cecile with a half smile on his face.

"Now how about kissing your lonesome, hungry husband a proper hello."

The gay laughing look vanished from her eyes and the well remembered amber glow of love reappeared as she slid toward him and put her arms about his neck.

"Oh, Tom, my darling, you are so welcome. I have been so empty, so lost since you've been gone." His arms enfolded her gently and she lay against him, his mouth hovered near hers, first for a gentle touch of a kiss then he took her mouth with his. A soft moan of pleasure escaped her as her lips parted moist and trembling under his.

"God, I've missed you, Cecile."

"I wish we had a place of our own. Somewhere that we could go. Tom . . ."

"Remember," he said gently, "the first time I went away? Remember the fisherman's cabin. Cecile . . . ?"

"Yes, Tom . . . yes."

Tom took up the reins again and went to the small deserted cabin where they had found each other for the first time. Inside they stood looking at each other for a moment, then without a word, Tom began to undress her with tender and infinite care. He dropped the last of her clothes on the floor and again he stood for a moment, his eyes seeming to memorize every beautiful line and curve. He stood close to her and gently laid his hand on the soft rounded belly where his child lay. Her eyes filled with tears when she saw the depth and tenderness of the love he felt for her.

"Do you know I dream of you night after night just like this, all soft and beautiful?"

Gently he pulled the pins from her hair pulling it loose and free; he twined his fingers in it and slowly drew her against him. Eagerly, his mouth closed over hers. Slowly, blissfully, the kiss became deeper . . . hungrier . . . more searching. As he released her lips, he lifted her from the floor and carried her to the bed, laying her upon it as though she were very fragile. Then he hastily removed his clothes and eased himself down beside her on the bed.

That his wanting of her was a blazing urgent demand she could tell by the heat of his body as he drew her to him, but he remained gentle, caressing her body letting his kisses rove down her throat touching each rigid nipple with his mouth. Then he bent his head and gently kissed again and again the soft rounded flesh of her belly. His hands searched for all the remembered beauty he had known. He was rewarded by the touch of slender fingers that sought him with the same need as his. Lying back on the bed, he lifted her slender body in his hands and drew her over him, afraid his weight or his urgent need would hurt her or harm the child. Slowly, with a deep sobbing moan, he joined their bodies together and eased himself into the warmth and depth of the woman who was the other half of him. She clung to him, her soft lips touching with fire, branding him with the hot need that exploded within her. Their bodies moved together in a rhythm as

378

old as time and as beautiful as forever.

They rose beyond anything they had ever felt before and clung to each other, swirling in the torrent of love that spun about them like a million fiery stars.

She lay against him now and he held her in silence. There were no words in existence to tell her at that moment just how much he loved her and how complete and perfect she had made everything in his life. Her head nestled in the curve of his shoulder; he tightened his arm about her to keep her close. Her other hand caressed his chest.

"Cold?"

"No, I'm warm for the first time in a long time."

"Cecile, I need to talk to you and now is probably one of the few times we'll get to be alone before we go back to London to report."

"What is it, Tom? I've sensed something has been bothering you since you came home. Does it all have something to do with Steffan being married so suddenly?"

"Yes, that and another thing. Let me tell you the whole story. Then, I have to ask you something . . . something that will change our lives. I want you to tell me exactly how you feel."

"All right," she replied, then waited for him to begin. Speaking quietly, he told her all that had transpired from the day they left until the moment they had returned. She asked no questions, just listened until he was finished.

"Oh, poor Steffan," she said quietly. "And poor Tamara. Tom, what will happen? Steffan should know that he can't build anything on a lie. What is he going to do?"

"As far as the trial is concerned, I think he stands a good chance of getting her free. It's after that I'm worried about. Cecile, I think Steffan is walking a tightrope between England and the Colonies, and loving Tamara as he does might be the thing that pushes him over. But, no matter what way he decides to go . . . I want to go. I think it's right and I think it's good for me. I know what it would mean for you so I want you to think about it for a while. I want to be with Steffan and Tamara through all this. By the time it's over, you will know everything to make a decision on. When it is over, I'll ask you again."

"And . . . if I decide not to go?"

"Then . . ." he replied slowly, "we won't go."

"But you'd be disappointed."

He rose on one elbow and looked down into her eyes. "Cecile,

I think it offers me the kind of future I've always dreamed of, but more important than that is you. Do you think I would force you to do something that would make you unhappy? No, you wait and when you know what you want, you tell me; but remember, to me, you are the only really important thing."

"All right, Tom. I'll go to the trial, I'll talk to Steffan, and yes, I'll listen to and talk to Tamara. The answer I give you will be as honest as it can be."

He kissed her again, then he groaned and rolled away from her, getting to his feet.

"Whether we like it or not, we've got to get you home. Everyone will be wondering where we are."

"Tom," she said in a hushed voice. He looked down at her. "You've been gone for a long time," she raised her hand to him. "Let them wonder for a little while longer."

The soft, pleased laugh was cut short as he went back to the bed, took his warm and willing wife into his arms and held her against him.

Earlier that day, in London, another scene was transpiring. Commander Pierce sat at his desk silently watching the man who sat opposite him. He had watched Jaspar Sinclair's life for as long as he had known Steffan and he probably knew more about Jaspar than Jaspar realized. He listened and heard, no matter how Jaspar tried to disguise it, the envy and hatred in the man's voice. What had stunned him most was finding out the lady pirate had been captured. He had warned her to stay away from the *Cecile*. There was no reason for this to have happened. Now that the day was coming soon that they all could leave for the Colonies, why had she done something directly against his orders?

"I still think the father was guilty, sir."

"Was there any proof? Did he sail with her?"

"No . . . but . . ."

"Captain Sinclair, how can we prove the man guilty if he was sitting comfortably at home when she was captured?"

Jaspar knew he was defeated on that point and it infuriated him but he smiled grimly. "Anyway, the lady pirate has been captured. All we need is a quick trial; then we can hang her and get on with the more important business."

"She will get a trial," Pierce replied. He rose and turned his back on Jaspar and stood looking out the window of his office across the grounds of the Academy. "You needn't worry, Captain Sinclair, the lady will get all that she deserves. You had best

380

return to your quarters. I imagine you will be needed at the trial."

"Yes, sir," Jaspar stood and waited. Pierce turned to face him; Jaspar saluted, and when Pierce responded, he turned on his heels and left. Pierce watched from his window as Jaspar walked across the grounds to his quarters.

"Damned arrogant fool," he muttered. Quickly, he left his office and went directly to Martin Gillis' room. When Martin let him in, he said bluntly and quickly:

"She's been captured, our pirate friend. Steffan caught her and brought both her and the ship home."

"My God. I thought you warned her not to touch the *Cecile*."

"I don't know what happened. From what I understand, Steffan is on his way here. He stopped at home first."

"Where is she?"

"He must be holding her in the brig on his ship until he can bring her in. Martin, will you leave now and go to Devers Hall. Maybe there is some way you can get aboard his ship. Talk to her, tell her to be silent and we will somehow get her out of this."

"Of course, I'll leave at once."

Martin began to gather a few things together; in a few minutes, he was ready to leave. Pierce walked with him to his buggy.

"God speed, Martin," he said grimly, then he stood and watched until the buggy was out of sight.

As Jaspar cut across the grounds and headed toward his quarters, a small boy approached him. "Captain Sinclair, sir?"

"Yes."

He handed Jaspar a folded piece of paper. "I was told to deliver this to you, sir."

Jaspar flipped the boy a small coin and the child grasped it gratefully and ran. Unfolding the note, Jaspar read it and smiled. He went to the stables, had his horse saddled and rode into town. He rode to the back gate of a huge and wealthy home. Dismounting, he walked to the gate and pushed it open. Walking across the garden, he went to a door that led to a set of back stairs. Unhesitatingly, he opened the door and went inside. He climbed the stairs and walked down a hall to a room he had been in many times before.

He opened the door and stepped inside. The room was a small sitting room; the fire in the fireplace had been lit and was burning brightly. Through another half open door, he could see the small bedroom, a bedroom whose bed had been a source of deep pleasure for him.

"Sit and have a drink," came a sweet voice from within. "The wine is poured."

Jaspar removed his jacket and sat in a comfortable chair by the fireplace. He took a glass of wine from the table next to him and sipped it meditatively.

In a few minutes the door to the bedroom swung open and the woman walked into the room. Jaspar stood up and she came into his arms. He kissed her with hungry devouring kisses and crushed her body against his. He heard the soft deep throaty laugh that told of her pleasure. He held her away from him and smiled down into the eyes of the most beautiful woman he had ever seen. Into the eyes of Morgana Kyle.

Thirty-three

It was late at night when Martin guided his carriage up the drive to Devers Hall. The family, after Tom and Cecile's return, had long since retired for the night. He came into the house quietly cautioning the sleepy-eyed maid who had unlocked the door, not to waken any of the family.

"I'll see them in the morning," he smiled, "get back to bed, my girl, and get some sleep."

"Thank you, sir," she smiled and bobbed a curtsy. Martin climbed the stairs to his room as quietly as possible. He closed the door behind him and sighed tiredly as he removed his jacket. Pouring himself a glass of brandy, he sat down to think over what he would say tomorrow and how he would handle the situation with Steffan.

For Steffan, he had the affection of a father toward a son. But now he was faced with his beliefs in this new country. He was obligated to many and could not turn his back on them. He wanted to talk to Steffan alone, try one more time to show him how he felt. He could not decide for Steffan, but he silently prayed something would happen to change his mind. Tomorrow, he would try to find a way to speak to Steffan's prisoner alone. Let her know she had friends about her. What excuse he would make to Steffan he did not know, but something would occur to him.

In a few weeks, he and Pierce, accompanied by Jeff Sables who was planning on resigning his commission and accepting one with the Colonial Navy, would be sailing for the Colonies. Jeff, he knew, was searching for Brandy Maguire and the son he had never seen. That his two friends Lang and Bright had chosen to go too had pleased both Martin and Pierce.

"Well," he thought, "tomorrow I will find a way to talk to her. For tonight, I'll get some rest. I may need it in the days to come."

He went to his bed and almost immediately drifted into sleep.

The house was quiet and remained so until the soft bright rays of the sun just began to crest the horizon.

Tamara lay awake, listening to the slow steady breathing of Steffan who slept beside her. Today they must go to the authorities at the naval installation where they would be forced to surrender her for trial. No matter what she pretended, the trial filled her with a strange shivering fear. She knew that Steffan and his father would leave no stone unturned in an effort to help her, just as she knew there was an unknown friend who would also try. But, what if they both failed? She wondered just what Steffan would do should they sentence her to hang. The fear struck her again and she shivered uncontrollably. Suddenly, she felt the arm about her tighten.

"Don't be afraid, love," he whispered against her hair. "I would die before I let them take you from me. One way or another, together we will face this."

"You knew?"

"That you were frightened? Don't you know by now that I feel everything you feel. I can touch you and know," he drew her more tightly into his arms. The comfort and warmth of his hard lean body and the strength of the arms that held her, filled her now with a sense of peace and contentment. No matter what happened, she had been gifted with a sweet and beautiful love. It would be a strong thing to hold to in the hard days to come. Warm and seeking lips found hers in the gray half-light of dawn and again she felt the magic of the man who held her. She knew beyond a doubt it would always be this way between them, for Steffan not only took her love with gentleness and gratitude, but she could feel the sweet giving of a love deep and fulfilling.

Martin Gillis was the first to come down to breakfast, followed in a few minutes by Ellen and Maxwell.

"Martin, good morning," Maxwell said. "You must have come home late last night."

"Yes, very. I didn't want to waken anyone."

"Martin, you should have," Ellen said, "you must have been hungry."

"No, not really. Sleep was all I needed last night, thank you, Ellen. Maxwell, I hear that Steffan and Tom came home last night."

"Yes, Steffan intends to report this morning."

"Before he leaves, I would like to talk to him if you don't mind. There are a few questions I would like to ask."

"Steffan has brought us home quite a lovely surprise," Ellen laughed. "He's come home with a wife."

"A wife!"

"Yes, a truly lovely girl he met and married on this trip. It came as quite a surprise to us. It seems she's the daughter of the man who owns the island they visited. Andrew Marriott. Her name is Tamara."

Martin sat quite still, watching Maxwell who remained quiet while Ellen spoke of Steffan's bride and her uncommon beauty. When Maxwell's eyes rose to meet Martin's, he knew instantly that Maxwell knew everything. Before he could speak another voice interrupted.

"Good morning," Cecile said brightly, as she and Tom came into the room. "Are we late?"

"No," Ellen laughed. "Steffan and Tamara have not come down yet, and we have just sat down."

Martin and Maxwell exchanged knowledgeable glances, then Martin rose from his chair. "If you would excuse us just for a minute, Ellen. I have something I had forgotten and I must talk to Maxwell alone for a moment."

"Of course," Ellen replied, but her sharp eyes had already taken notice of the unspoken words that hung in the air. She watched Maxwell and Martin walk from the room. Later, she promised herself, whether he wanted to or not, she was determined Maxwell would tell her what was going on for she had a deep feeling her son was in some kind of difficulty and she wanted to know just what it was. As Maxwell and Martin walked across the foyer toward the study, Martin was hailed from the top of the steps and Steffan came smiling toward him with Tamara's hand in his.

"Mr. Gillis, I'm glad you're back. I have someone I'd like to introduce you to."

Martin watched them approach. That she was truly a lovely woman was beyond question. That her life and Steffan's happiness was in his and Pierce's hands was all too clear to him.

"Tamara," Steffan grinned proudly, "this is my dearest friend and teacher, Mr. Gillis; this is my wife Tamara."

Tamara extended her hand to him, her eyes glowed with friendliness. "I've heard so very much about you, Mr. Gillis, and I've been so anxious to meet you."

"It is my pleasure my dear, I assure you. So you and this young man are married? He is quite a lucky boy."

385

"Boy!" Steffan laughed. "Mr. Gillis, will you always consider me one of your students? I'm certainly a boy no longer."

"Hmmm," Martin said seriously. "Maybe I should take the lady aside and warn her of your ways."

"Good God, no!" Steffan chuckled. "I want to keep her deceived about what a fine upstanding man I am and how lucky she is to get me."

"Nevertheless, I would like to have you join me for a walk in the garden after breakfast. I'd like to find out how this young man has gotten so lucky."

"I would be pleased," Tamara replied. "And I wouldn't mind hearing a few things about Steffan."

"Tam," Steffan said, his smile fading, "we've only a short time after breakfast, then we have to go."

"I know Steffan," she said, "until then, can't I pretend this could last for a long time?"

Steffan nodded and Martin was aware of a deep misery that lurked in his eyes and his sympathy went out to him.

"I will join you right after breakfast," Tamara told Martin. "There is something I would like to ask you."

"Good, my dear, good," he nodded and watched Steffan and Tamara go toward the dining room.

"Martin?"

"Never mind, Maxwell. We know there is no need to talk now. I understand. Poor Steffan. I will try to do my best to help him as much as I can."

"We both will," Maxwell replied. They went back to the dining room. The breakfast progressed with a strange heavy silence hovering over them. Then when the meal was done, Martin rose and asked Tamara if she would join him for that walk she had promised. She agreed and they left with Steffan's disturbed look following them. Tamara's arm in his, she and Martin walked for a few minutes before he spoke softly. "So you are our lovely lady pirate?" She looked up at him thinking it strange that she was not the least bit surprised at his words.

"Yes."

"I have word for you."

She stopped and watched him.

"From Commander Pierce. He says to tell you to take heart. You are not alone or forgotten. He's going to try to bring you in front of a naval board instead of making it a civil case. That way, with the influence he has, he'll be able to get you put in Maxwell

Devers custody.''

"I'm so grateful," Tamara said, relieved, "to be fortunate enough to find such friends so quickly. What . . . what if they cannot keep it a naval case?''

"Take heart, my dear. Maxwell and I have many friends. One way or another we will get you out of this country safely.''

"I cannot go.''

"You cannot?''

"I've made a bargain with Steffan,'' Tamara began, then she continued to explain all that had happened, all that had led to her capture and after. After she had finished, he remained quiet for a moment, then he smiled. "Maybe,'' he said slowly, "maybe Steffan will go with you.''

"Oh, Mr. Gillis. If I thought that were possible, I would go through anything.''

"It's not all a bargain, or blackmail, then. You love the boy?''

"As you do,'' she smiled.

"Yes, if I had ever had a son, Steffan would be what I would have wanted him to be like. Tamara, he is a magnificent man and I am very proud of him. One day soon, you will see. The kind of man he is belongs in the new country of ours.''

"Will he understand some day?''

"He understands now, it is only his damnable sense of honor that keeps him tied here.''

"Damnable honor?'' she laughed, and he laughed with her.

"I spent years teaching it to him, and I know it is one quality our new country needs, but sometimes, just sometimes,'' he cautioned, "I wish he had just a little less of it. It keeps him from being able to bend. You, I think, are the answer. If ever Steffan would listen it would be for the love of you.''

"I wish it so. I am torn, I love him, and I know what I have to do. If Steffan were with me, everything would be so perfect.''

"Well, there is yet time. First things first. Let us do away with this trial, then we can face whatever else has to be done.''

Tamara was about to reply when she saw Steffan walking purposefully in her direction. She smiled and extended her hand to him. He took it, drawing her close to him. "It's time to go, Tam.''

"I'm ready.''

The three of them walked back to the house together.

Within the hour, Steffan and Tamara were on their way toward

London and her uncertain fate.

Pierce waited in his office, thinking of how he would handle the situation. If he could keep it a naval affair all would be well, for the men on the board were his close friends, and some like himself very sympathetic to the Colonial cause. No, if he kept the affair within their ranks, in a few hours it would be over and she would be safe. He was anxious to meet her and wondered just what kind of woman she was. He pictured a woman who was master of her own ship as a mannish woman with no redeeming feminine characteristics. Although she had been a necessary link in their endeavor, he felt he would find it difficult to deal with the kind of woman he pictured.

Steffan and Tamara were announced, and Pierce rose to meet them. When the door opened, his jaw dropped in amazement at the lovely vision who walked in on Steffan's arm. Dressed in a white dress trimmed in wine colored lace with her bright red-gold curls gathered atop her head, Tamara was delicately beautiful. "Captain Devers," he said quickly to hide his surprise, "welcome home. I hear your mission has been a success. The red ship is safely in the harbor. Where have you incarcerated our infamous woman?"

"Thank you, Commander. I wish to introduce several people to you."

"Several?"

"Yes," Steffan grinned. "First I want you to meet Andrew Marriott's daughter and the 'infamous' woman."

Pierce looked at a smiling Tamara in what was now complete amazement.

"And sir," Steffan added, "also my wife, Mrs. Steffan Devers."

Pierce sat down quickly, for the moment finding it difficult to accept all he was hearing. Then just as suddenly all the ramifications came clear to him. Good God, he thought wildly, he's married to the girl.

"Your wife?"

"Yes, sir, my wife."

"And how did this come about?"

"I imagine," Steffan laughed, "the way all marriages do, sir. I met her, fell in love with her, swept her off her feet and had her married to me before she knew what was happening."

Tamara's tinkling laughter and Pierce's disbelieving gaze were enjoyed by Steffan for only a moment.

"Captain Devers, if you will wait outside, I would like to speak to the prisoner alone."

"Sir?" Steffan said, surprise in his voice.

"That is a direct order, captain."

"Yes, sir," Steffan said, but it was very obvious he didn't want to leave Tamara alone.

"Captain," Pierce said in an amused voice, "I do not intend her harm. She'll be safe with me, I promise you."

Steffan flushed, then giving Tamara's hand a reassuring squeeze, he reluctantly left the room.

"So," Pierce said, "we finally meet. It is a pleasure to meet you although it is under the strangest circumstances I could imagine."

"Commander Pierce, may I explain to you how all this came about?"

"Most assuredly. I find I can't imagine what has transpired. Would you please enlighten me? This promises to be one of the most interesting stories I have ever heard."

Tamara explained all that had happened and Pierce did not interrupt until she had finished. Then he sat back in his chair.

"Did you not get my message warning you not to touch the *Cecile* or any other ship until we sent you word?"

"No, I did not."

"No, of course you couldn't have or all this would not have come about," he said annoyed at his own question.

"Commander, what is to happen now?"

"I and several of my friends are doing our best to channel all this and keep it a naval affair. If we are successful, I guarantee you within weeks, you will be free."

"In the meantime?"

"In the meantime, I'm afraid I shall have to hold you. There is no other way. I don't want any suspicion on us until the time is ripe."

"You believe it will be soon?"

"Very soon. Things in the Colonies are a veritable cauldron of boiling sentiment. I would not be afraid to say that within six months war will be declared. By that time, we want to have all of this cleared away, for just before that I intend to resign my post here. Martin Gillis, myself, and a few of my friends are joining Horatio Nelson. If we don't have this cleared away war will make it a civil offense—treason. For which you could be hanged." He saw Tamara's shiver. "There is no way we will let that happen.

389

None of the civil authorities or the court of His Majesty know about your capture. We intend to have it all done before they find out."

"I am grateful to you, commander, but I doubt if my husband will feel the same when he finds out you have to hold me."

"It cannot be helped. If we create a controversy over this, we may attract the wrong attention. You will have to be kept a prisoner, but I assure you, I will make you as confortable as I can. Now," he said as he stood up, "it is time to face your husband."

Pierce went to the door and opened it. "Captain Devers?"

Steffan was beside her so quickly that Tamara surmised he must have been right outside the door.

"I'm afraid, captain," Pierce said firmly, "your wife cannot return home with you."

"Sir!"

"She is under arrest for crimes against the English Navy. She will of course stand trial before a board of your superiors. In the meantime, I'm afraid she will have to be held."

"You can't hold her in a common jail!" Steffan said alarm deep in his voice. "Let me take her home. You have our guarantee she'll be here for the trial when necessary."

"Impossible. I shall give her a cell of her own but she must be kept here."

"But sir . . ."

"Steffan," Tamara said. "I'll be all right. You are near. That's all I need to know. We will survive whatever is necessary."

"I shall leave you two alone for a minute," Pierce said, "but it must be quick. I will send someone for her."

He left the room. Steffan took Tamara in his arms. She would have given her life to reassure him that she was among friends who would not let anything happen to her.

"Tam, my God, I can't go home and leave you here, I can't."

"Steffan, we both can do what we must do. I dread the thought of being away from you for even one night. Soon, maybe we will be together for always."

"I won't leave here until I know where they are going to put you," he said determinedly. Before he could say anything else, the door swung open and two men stood waiting.

"I'll go with you," Steffan said.

Since they had no orders concerning him, and he was a ranking officer, they did not argue. One of them stepped forward to take hold of Tamara.

"Leave her be," Steffan said sharply. "Lead the way, we'll follow."

They obeyed, leading them from Commander Pierce's quarters, down the hall to a flight of stairs that led outside. They crossed a wide square of cobblestones to a large square stone house. The bars on the windows marked it as a jail and Steffan stiffened when he saw it.

A door was thrown open to a small square room about eight feet wide and about the same in width. The room was furnished sparingly with a small bed and a stand that held a pitcher of water and a bowl for washing. Other than these, the room was empty. There was no sign of any touch to make it comfortable. The bars on the one window and the heavy lock on the door made it clear exactly what the room was. Steffan turned to the two men.

"Wait outside . . . and close the door after you."

They obeyed. Steffan's face was dark with his rage. To lock her up in a place like this was something he could not bear. He was angered first by the fact that it was he who had put her here and that at the moment he could do nothing about it. It was probably at that moment that thoughts of helping her escape came creeping into his subconscious mind.

"Steffan?" Tamara questioned his silence as she came to him and put her arms about his waist.

"All this time," he said angrily, "I didn't realize what I was subjecting you to. I thought, since you were my wife, since I was an officer they would trust me, that they would let me care for you until the board convened." He looked down at her and put his arms about her. "Tam, I'm sorry . . . for this, and for everything. My hard-headed obedience to duty has put you here, and by damn, I'll see it gets you out."

"Everyone is trying to help, Steffan. It will be over soon."

"I . . . I just can't walk out and leave you here."

"I'll be all right, Steffan. I have the strength of knowing you and your family are doing all you can for me. If it had not been for you this would be a terror for me. Now, I have our love to lean on. I'll be all right."

He kissed her, binding her to him in an agony of need. "I'll come back and bring you things to at least make this hole more comfortable. Don't be frightened, love, I won't let you be here any longer than is absolutely necessary."

"Steff, would you do one thing for me?"

"Of course."

"Would you think over all the things I told you on the ship? Would you try to understand? It would make me feel better to know that you knew the reasons for the way I feel."

"All right. I promise. If you need me, tell the guard to send for me. In the meantime, I'm going to see what can be done to get you out of here and back home as fast as possible."

He kissed her again, and reluctantly, she moved away from him.

"Go Steffan, before I cry and make it even harder for us."

He looked into her eyes, brushed her lips with another light kiss then turned and left the room without looking back. The harsh clang of the heavy door closing and the sharp sound of the lock did more to frighten Tamara than anything had done before. Suddenly she felt very alone . . . and very afraid. She sat on the edge of the bed and felt the hot tears in her eyes. Angrily, she shook them away. Everything will be all right, she thought. Steffan's family and her friends would not fail her. Somewhere in the back of her mind, Mikel hovered alive and well. He, too, would help her. Why then, with all these people working for her did she suddenly sense an impending disaster she had no way of foreseeing and no way to stop.

Steffan stood outside the stone prison for a few minutes. He was so angry he did not even notice the man walking toward him.

"Steff!"

Steffan looked at him in surprise. "Jeff!" he exclaimed happily holding out his hand. "It's good to see you."

"I've heard everything that's happened. There's a lot of wild publicity about your daring capture of the *Scarlet Butterfly.*"

"Daring!" Steffan said in angry disgust.

"I've been hearing a few other stories too, something about your getting married. Why don't you buy an old friend a drink and tell him the truth about what happened."

"Good, but I've got a better idea. Come home with me and I'll explain. I have to get some of Tamara's things. I can't let her spend a night in this hole without something to make it a little easier."

"Tamara?"

"It's a long story, Jeff. Come on, let's go home."

On the way home, Steffan told Jeff all that had happened. Jeff listened sympathetically, his forced separation from Brandy and the son he had never seen making it easy to understand Steffan's misery. Soon, though, Jeff knew he would be resigning his commission and going to the Colonies to find his family and, he knew, to fight for them if necessary.

When they arrived at Devers Hall, Steffan sent one of the maids for a long list of things he had prepared and while she packed them, he and Jeff shared a drink. Eventually, Martin Gillis joined them, listening, but offering no information.

When the trunk was ready, Steffan put it in the buggy and he and Jeff returned to the prison. Jeff helped him carry the trunk in and was very much surprised at his first look at the lady pirate.

Another very difficult goodbye from Tamara, and they left for the last time that day. When they were outside again, Steffan and Jeff went to the small tavern where Brandy used to work and where they had spent many happy hours together. Steffan began to talk, when his tongue was loosened by the drinks, of all that Tamara had told him. It was only then that Jeff told him what he planned to do.

"I'm going for a lot of reasons, Steff. One is, I admire a land that will let each man live his own life and not judge him by what he or she is. For another, I love Brandy and I want to see my son. They are enough reasons alone to do it. Finally, I'm beginning to understand how Nelson feels and I want to fight alongside a man of his caliber. If he thinks the cause is just, then I believe it, too."

"Jeff, have you had a chance to talk to Tom, yet?"

"No, why?"

"I think he feels as you do. He and Cecile might be going too."

"Lang and Bright are going with me."

"What about Mack, have you talked to him?"

"Yes. He's resigning his commission and going with us."

"And that leaves me," Steffan said grimly.

"What are you going to do, Steff?"

Steffan contemplated his words for a few moments, then he said calmly and coolly, "I'll tell you what I'm going to do. I'm going to watch and wait for a little while to see what Mr. Gillis and my father can do, but either way, I'm going to take Tamara from that miserable place and I'm going to take her to the Colonies. There we're going to share a long and happy life together."

"And if they can't do anything to help her?"

Steffan's eyes glowed a dark angry amber. "Then I will take her by whatever means necessary, and don't doubt me for a minute, one way or the other we'll be free."

Jeff smiled and extended his hand to Steffan who took it firmly. "Most likely they'll find a way to shuffle this about and get her out of there."

"I hope you're right, but in case there is a war, if they do try to harm her in any way, it is a move they'll regret."

Many miles away, across an ocean, in a small town with the remote name of Concord, a shot was fired, a shot heard for hundreds of miles. A shot that would alter the course of the lives of many people and begin the fight for freedom of a new country and the people who would defend her.

Thirty-four

The ship moved before a crisp breeze that filled her white sails and sent her skimming across an azure blue ocean. The man who stood at the wheel was shirtless, his bronzed, muscular body glistening in the sun; it reflected also from his sun-bleached blond hair and the cold blue of his eyes. Around his body was a wide swath of bandages, but he moved as though the wound was old and did not hurt. Shading his eyes, he looked up at the sails and shouted an order that gave them a fuller grasp of the breeze. The man knew his ship and the art of sailing her.

He watched as a man came up from below deck and made his way toward him, "Food's warm, sir, I'll be takin' her while you get something to eat."

"Keep her ahead of this wind, Rob. I don't want to waste a minute. A life can be depending on our speed."

"Miss Tamara?"

"That's right."

"Don't worry, sir, I'll keep her movin' at top speed."

"Good, I'll check back with you a couple of hours from now. Oh, by the way, Rob, how's the girl?"

"She's still a little green around the gills, sir, but I got to give her credit, the little gal's got a lot of spunk. She fightin' hard."

"Has she tried eating anything?"

"I tried, sir," Rob grinned, "but she cussed me out sumpthin' awful, then threw the dish at me."

"Well," the man laughed, "Maybe I'll go see if I have a little better luck. She's got to at least drink or she'll be dying on us."

"Maybe you could scare her with that idea, sir, might make her swallow a few bites. I kind of feel sorry for her. She's a pretty little thing to be takin' this voyage just out of loyalty to her mistress."

"Her mistress is the kind of lady who would do the same for her," came the crisp reply.

Mikel walked to the companionway and went below to the

door of his cabin, which he had turned over to Mellie for this trip. No matter what he had said, what arguments he had used, Mellie insisted she was going with him. First to care for the wound in his side which she insisted was not healed enough and second because she loved Miss Tamara and wanted to be sure she was safe. He knocked on the door and at the muffled answer, he went inside. Mellie lay curled up on his bunk.

"Rob told me you became violent when he wanted you to eat a bite."

"He," Mellie groaned, "should not have tried to make me eat. I'm dying and all he wants to do is make me eat."

Mikel laughed. "You're not dying Mellie, and if you would try to get some food down or at least some liquids, you would feel better. It's a beautiful day outside and you're missing it all."

"I should know if I'm sick or not," she complained.

"Of course you should, but I'd hate to be slipping you overboard for the sharks to feed on. You know Tamara would never forgive me."

Mellie forced herself into a sitting position.

"Good start, now try getting on your feet."

Laboriously, she climbed to her feet swaying with the movements of the ship.

"Come on, Mellie, you can do it. The longer you stay up and move around the better you'll be. I'll go and get you something and just as a favor to me, you try to force it down."

"I'll try," she gasped. "But I won't be responsible for the mess I'll make," she warned.

Mikel left the cabin and went to see the cook, ordering him to fix something that he thought Mellie would be able to hold down. Then with the tray in his hand, he returned to Mellie's side. Trying valiantly, Mellie was pacing the cabin.

"You'll get your sea legs soon," Mikel said encouragingly. "Here, try to eat some of this and drink some of that strong tea."

"Talk to me while I try. Maybe if I keep my mind off the food, I can get it down."

"All right," he said pleasantly. Drawing up a chair, he sat opposite her, "What do you want me to talk about?"

Mellie looked at him closely, "Mikel, what are you going to do when we get to England?"

Mikel's grin faded and his eyes turned cold and hard. "I told you before, Mellie. There are only two things I'm going to do. First is to find out where Tamara is and get her safely out of there."

"And the second is to kill Steffan Devers?"

"Yes. The traitor deserves killing."

"Mikel, you don't know if what that man was saying was the truth or not. I told you to stop and see Tamara's father first."

"There is no time for that. If Tamara is accused of treason, they would hang her. Would you like to be a day too late?"

"No," Mellie said slowly, "It's just that . . ."

"That what?"

"That I'm not sure he's guilty of any such thing. I think that man didn't like Steffan, I think Steffan really and truly loves Miss Tamara."

"I don't want to hear what you think, Mellie," he said as he rose impatiently from his chair. "I let you come along because you love her and were worried about her, but not to lecture me on what I'm doing. Know this, I'm going to kill that man and make him suffer as much as possible in the bargain, and if Tamara's been harmed in any way . . . I intend to make him wish he had never been born."

"But Mikel . . ."

Mikel walked to the door. "I'm going to get something to eat, Mellie. For the rest of this trip, I don't want his name mentioned again, is that understood?"

"Yes" Mellie said weakly. After the door closed behind Mikel, Mellie closed her eyes for a moment praying that for the rest of this trip her uncontrollable mouth would not let the fact slip that she had sent a long and detailed message to Tamara's father before they left.

Andrew had received the message. If Mikel had stopped to see him first, he would have explained about Steffan, but now Mikel was on his way to kill the one man who would stand between Tamara and all harm. Angrily, he destroyed the note and set his mind to devising a way to slip away from his guards and get to England as rapidly as possible. He knew that there was more than one fast ship in the harbor beginning with the *Sea Borne* and the *Adventurer* but . . . how to get one and get it free of the harbor was another question. The few men who were left to guard him found Andrew a gentleman and a most pleasant host. He invited them to stay in his home and share his meals and he politely ignored the fact that they bolted his door and placed a guard outside it when he retired for the night.

Only one time did he go to the door to test and see if it were locked. Finding it so, he knew it would be from then on so he did not try again. It was two days after Andrew received the note that he managed to accomplish his first feat. To get a message to the first mate of the *Sea Borne* with detailed instructions. That same night he invited the guards to share a meal with him. They agreed when he laughingly informed them it was his birthday and he did not want to celebrate alone. After the sumptuous meal, he escorted them all to his study where he offered them expensive cigars, good whiskey and amusing anecdotes to pass the time. None of them had the least suspicion that the drinks were heavily loaded with a potent drug. Within an hour after having the drinks, all of the men who guarded Andrew Marriott were completely unconscious. Quickly, Andrew changed clothes. He left the house by the back door, cut across the garden, down the steps to the beach. He could see the *Sea Borne* and the small boat she was sending to get him. Another hour and her sails were full and Andrew was in a race not only to rescue his daughter, but to prevent the murder of the man who held her prisoner.

As the two ships raced toward England, a ship left the Colonial shores taking the message to its native land that war between the Colonies and the mother country had begun.

A boy of about five with large intelligent gray blue eyes and a thick mass of unruly black hair stood holding his mother's hand while they watched the ship leave.

Brandy knelt in front of her son and smiled as she brushed the hair from his eyes. "Jeff, you must never come to the docks again without Mommy. Do you understand?"

"Jonah brought me, Mama. I wanted to see the big ship leave," his eyes were lit with excitement. "Someday, Mama, I'm going to sail on it."

"Jonah should have known better than to bring you without permission. You have a long time before you grow up, Jeff. Maybe by that time you'll want to be something else."

He shook his head rebelliously. Brandy rose with a sigh and took his hand. "So like his father," she thought. The resemblance between father and son was phenomenal; one could have looked at the two and known. It was a thing that kept Jeff Sables alive in Brandy's memory. Each day that she looked at her son, as she watched him grow, she could see again the man who had held all her thoughts, all her love. It was the thing that kept Brandy from seeking love elsewhere. There were many opportunities for her. When her indenture was over, she had taken her small hoard of laboriously saved money and opened a small dressmaking shop. With her skill, she became quite popular with the women of the town and her small shop prospered. She made enough money to keep herself and Jeff comfortable. Brandy had put all her past behind her and built a whole new life. In the process, she had gained a self respect and pride that made her rare beauty even more captivating. That she had changed from a pretty girl to a remarkably beautiful woman was a thing to which she paid no attention, but several bachelors of the town had.

She took his hand and prepared to leave, but Jeff pulled on it. "Jonah told me to wait for him here, Mama. He just had to run an errand for Aunt Marthie. If I'm not here when he gets back, he'll be mad."

"Heaven help me," she said, exasperated; then she laughed at the situation. "He takes you to the docks without my permission and you're worried about his being angry if I take you home," she looked down into her son's distress filled eyes. Again the poignant resemblance made her smile. Sweet and considerate of others, she thought. His father's son. "All right, Jeff, we'll wait for Jonah."

They walked slowly along the docks. Brandy as well as her son enjoyed watching the tall-masted ships that rocked in the harbor and the vibrant enthusiasm that lingered in the activity around them. She was letting her mind drift backward in time when she was brought, startled, back to the present when her son's voice, calm and quiet, asked her curiously, "Mama, what's a bastard?"

"Jeff! Where did you hear such a thing?"

"Robbie said I was a bastard and Jonah punched him in the nose . . . hard, Mommy. I bled all over the place. Jonah said if he ever heard Robbie say that to anyone he'd beat him up. Is it a bad word, Mommy?"

"It surely is, Jeff," Brandy replied angrily, "and Jonah did exactly the right thing."

"But what is it, Mommy?"

"Jeff, I'll explain it to you when you are a little older and better able to understand. In the meantime, don't pay any attention to anyone who uses such language."

Jeff laughed gleefully. "He won't say it again, Mommy, he's afraid of Jonah, Jonah'll smash him."

"I'm sure he will," Brandy replied wryly.

"There comes Jonah, Mommy," Jeff pointed toward a young man who was making his way through the crowd toward them.

The young man pushing his way toward him was a slender young man with pale blond hair and a face that was usually covered with a broad smile. Jonah Price was the nineteen-year-old son of Brandy's dearest and closest friend, Marthie Price.

When Brandy had first opened her shop and was trying to clean and make comfortable the two rooms above it in which she and Jeff would live, Marthie was the only person in the slightly shabby neighborhood who had come and willingly offered to help. Marthie was a widow and lived next door to Brandy's shop with her son, Jonah. Marthie was several years older than Brandy; in fact Jonah was not too many years younger than Brandy's twenty-four. It did not take long for Jonah to take Jeff under his wing like an older brother and as for Jeff, his admiration for Jonah, who worked in that so magical place, the docks, grew slowly to love for an older brother.

Marthie was the only one in whom Brandy had confided the truth of her situation. Brandy had used a small amount of her money each week for books and had worked long hard hours on educating herself. It was the one real gift besides her son that Jeff had given her and she refused to let it slip away from her. Marthie was fascinated by Brandy's determination for self-education and she was beside herself with happiness when Brandy offered to teach both her and Jonah to read and write. Jonah was an apt pupil and absorbed everything Brandy offered like a sponge. When he acquired a fragile knowledge of reading and writing, he found himself promoted to a better job. He was grateful to Brandy and the only way he could show it was through Jeff, for Brandy would take no gifts for sharing something that had been given so freely to her.

When Jonah reached her side, he said quickly, "I was coming for him, Mrs. Maguire. I was only gone for a few minutes; he was perfectly safe here, as a lot of my friends are about keeping an eye on him."

"I know, Jonah, but I wish you would tell me next time. It's frightening to look and find him gone even when I always know where he'll end up."

"Yes, Ma'am," Jonah replied. "It won't happen again. He surely does have an uncommon yen for the big sailing ships."

"Jonah . . . Jeff tells me I owe you thanks for defending his name. I'm grateful."

Jonah's face reddened. "It's all right Ma'am. Nobody will ever say anything about you or Jeff as long as I'm around." He looked at Brandy in defiance like a young knight worshipping from afar the fair lady of his dreams, who was as much out of his reach as the stars.

"Well," she smiled at him, "I thank you anyway. Come over later, Jonah; I made fresh berry pie today and I know it's your favorite. Tell Marthie to come also."

"I will," he answered, pleased she remembered what kind of pie was his favorite. To him, it was another reason to add to all the other reasons that he found Brandy and Jeff so dear to him. "Have you heard the news?"

"News? . . . What news?"

"That's why Jeff and I were watching the ship, she is carrying word. We're at war. There's going to be a war between us and England. It's about time we got out from under their thumb."

"Jonah!" Brandy gasped. Her face went pale and she gripped Jeff's hand so tight, he cried out. Visions of Jeff's father in a battle, wounded, dead, flashed across her mind leaving a trail of pain behind it so intense she could hardly bear it.

"It's true. I'm telling my mother. I'm going to enlist first chance."

"Oh, Jonah, your mother will be upset hearing you talk like that."

Jeff's eyes were moving from Jonah's excited face to his mother's distressed one. He could not figure out what could make Jonah so happy and his mother so sad at the same time. He pulled on his mother's hand again, drawing both their attentions. "What's the matter, Mommy?"

Jonah closed his mouth, upset that he had alarmed both Brandy and Jeff. Brandy smiled reassuringly down on Jeff. "It's all right, Jeff. Nothing is wrong."

The three of them went home together and later that evening Marthie and Jonah came over. Brandy poured tea and sliced the fresh pie. Jonah sat on the small sofa and soon found Jeff plunked happily at his feet. He suspected the boy was filled with questions and he was afraid to answer in the presence of his mother and Brandy.

Marthie was a tiny slender woman who gave the outward appearance of fragility, yet she possessed a vitality that was amazing. She could accomplish more in a day than Brandy with her slow contained perseverance. Her hair was a pale gold, parted in the middle and drawn to a thick heavy coil at the nape of her neck. Her eyes were large and the color of violets. Her skin was creamy and smooth and she looked many years younger than she was. Her quick friendly smile and gentle logic had been Brandy's support through many difficult hours.

"What's a war, Jonah?" was Jeff's first question.

"A war?" Jonah said nervously watching his mother's face. "It's when two countries fight each other."

"With guns?" came the wide-eyed question.

"Yes, with guns, with cannons and with ships."

"Do they kill each other, Jonah?"

"Jeff, enough questions," Brandy said sharply. "Especially about such a subject."

"Brandy," Marthie said gently, "you needn't protect me. I've heard the news, too." She looked at her son, and words she knew she would refuse to speak lingered in her eyes. She could see the pleading in his eyes not to shame him, make him less of a man in front of Jeff and Brandy. Marthie smiled at him, understanding his pride. She changed the subject, to the relief of not only Jonah but Brandy as well, for she did not want Jeff hearing any more of the disturbing thought for tonight.

Later, after she had tucked Jeff into bed and silenced his chatter for the night, she went to her small sitting room. There she sat in a chair and prayed silently, "Please, God, keep Jeff safe. He is a good strong man and I know if our two countries fight, he will be in it. Please, please keep him safe." She thought of the young son he had never held, never had the chance to love and in her worry, she promised, "Keep Jeff safe and when his son is old enough, I will give him up. Although it will tear out my heart, I will return him to his father . . . please, please God, keep him safe."

It was a rare thing for Brandy to allow herself to dwell in the past, but she did so now, when she was alone, with the fear that something might happen to Jeff and she would never know.

She knew there would never be another man in her life but Jeff Sables, and now that she would never see him again, she centered all her love on his son.

During the past years since she had left England, Brandy had tried to make a good life both for herself and her son. She had been satisfied with it until a few months ago. At that time, she had met, almost on the same day, two men both completely different in looks and in character. For the past few months, she had been plagued with the thought that maybe she should marry for the sake of giving Jeff a father. She thought of both men, kind, each in his own way. Promising a good future both for Jeff and for her. Jacob Miller was a carpenter. He had a good home and a prosperous business. She had met him at a fair and he had been a constant caller since. Richard Ayres, the son of a prosperous farmer, could offer Jeff the guidance of a good father. She was exhausted with her thoughts and the turmoil in her mind. She wanted to do what was best for little Jeff, but she could not conjure up in her mind the thought of lying again with any other man but Jeff. All men who had passed before Jeff were one thing, but there had been no man since and she found she could not bring herself to think of it. If she closed her eyes, she could still feel his lips against hers, the warm seeking touch of his hands that had opened the door to love for her. She knew there was no way to close her eyes and imagine any other man was Jeff. And she could no more forget him than she could cease to breathe.

Sleep overtook her and she promised herself as she drifted off that she would talk to Marthie tomorrow. Maybe Marthie could give her some advice as to what to do for Jeff's benefit, for in Brandy's mind, Marthie had done an excellent job of raising Jonah. "She'll know what I should do," she thought as she gave in to sleep.

She was preparing Jeff's breakfast early in the morning before she took him to Marthie who cared for him while she worked. At the beginning Marthie did it as a favor for Brandy, but as her shop began to earn her money Brandy insisted Marthie accept money for she knew that Marthie and Jonah lived on his wages which were barely enough to keep them going.

Urging Jeff to hurry, she bustled about setting the two rooms straight. When Jeff was finished, she put his coat on and took him by the hand.

They left the shop and Brandy locked the door behind her, then they walked the few feet to Marthie's. At her light rap, Marthie opened the door. Brandy was surprised to see that she had been crying. Her eyes were red and she looked as though she had not slept.

"Jeff," Brandy said quickly, "why don't you go out in the back yard and see if Soldier is all right?"

Soldier was Jonah's dog and since Jonah had to go to work, Jeff was proud that he had left him in charge of Soldier to see that he was fed, given water and taken for a short walk once a day. The walk consisted of two times around the house, but Jeff took his duties very seriously.

"All right, Mamma," he said and quickly he was running out the back door letting it slam carelessly behind him.

"Marthie, what's wrong?"

"Oh, Brandy . . . it's this terrible idea of war. Jonah and I talked last night. There's no swaying him, Brandy. He's going to join the Army," she laughed brokenly, "if you can call it an army. Brandy, we have no chance against such an army as the English have, I'm afraid. I'm afraid I'll lose my son."

"Tell me what's going on. They've made no call to arms. Where is Jonah going to enlist?"

"He's going over to Cumberledge, they've posted a call to men from there. One of Jonah's friends told him yesterday."

"When is he going?"

"Next week. Brandy, I'm going with him. I have to stay with him as long as possible. He'll need help until the men are outfitted and armed."

"Marthie, I've all my work caught up at the shop. If you would like, Jeff and I will go with you at least for a few days."

"Would you, Brandy? I would be so grateful and I'm sure Jonah would too."

"Of course we will. I need a few days away from the shop anyway and Jeff will be excited to go on a short trip with Jonah."

"You are a very kind sweet girl, Brandy. I know I sound like a baby, but Jonah . . . he's all I've got. I know you of all people understand."

"Of course I do. If you'll care for Jeff right now, I'll go along to the shop and close it up. When I come back I'll help you get Jonah a warm supper then we can begin to pack."

"I'll look after Jeff."

"Good" Brandy smiled, "and don't worry. Maybe this is all going to pass over before anything serious happens. Surely we don't really believe a small group of practically unarmed men can be turned into an army. Maybe we'll go to Cumberledge only to find out it's all a mistake."

"I hope so."

Brandy went out in the back yard and told Jeff to be good, that she would be right back. "When I come back, we are going to take a little trip with Aunt Marthie and Jonah; would you like that?"

"Oh, yes, Mama!" he said excitedly. "Is Soldier going too?"

"I don't know," laughed Brandy. "Leave it to you to be thinking of the welfare of a puppy."

"I think we'll have to ask Mr. Gibbons to keep Soldier for a few days," Marthie replied, her eyes held Brandy's. "I hope Jonah will be back and you can care for him again."

Brandy kissed Jeff quickly then she left the house. At the shop, she packed in the lower shelves and under the small counter all the bolts of material she had. The small back room entrance was covered by a heavy drape; the room held her sewing materials, standing mirrors for fittings and a small enclosed cubicle for women to change their clothing.

Making sure everything was put away, she checked the back door, then she came back to the front of the shop. Sure that everything was in order, she took a piece of paper and began making a sign for the door. Finished, she stood up and was on her way to the door when it opened from the other side. She smiled at the tall man who came in. "Good morning, Jacob."

"Good morning, Brandy. I've come over to see if you've heard the news."

"You mean about the war?"

"You've heard, then."

"Jonah Price told me. Oh, Jacob, he's on his way to Cumberledge to enlist. Maybe you could say something to stop him."

"To please you, Brandy, I'd like to do that, but I can't."

"Can't?"

"No, you see I'm going too."

"Oh, Jacob!"

"It's something that has to be done, Brandy. There's going to be an all-out war."

"But we're Englishmen."

"Brandy, did you get your best start in life in England? Did England offer you all you've found here? The day has come, my dear, when you have to choose. Are you an Englishwoman or are you an American? If you are an Englishwoman, you had best go home on the next ship. If you are a true Colonist, you'd best be ready to fight for her."

Brandy felt his words for to her they rang with a personal truth. Here, she had found pride, self respect and the ability to live a quiet life without the judgment of others binding her to a class. If she and Jeff had lived here there would have been no barrier to their love, she thought. The ideas and ideals clicked into place in her mind and she looked up at Jacob and smiled. "I'm an American, Jacob, and Jeff is an American too."

He grinned down at her. "I kind of thought you would feel that way. In fact, I staked a lot on it."

"Why?"

"Brandy, you'll never go back to England again?"

"No, most likely, I'll spend the rest of my life here."

"Then, spend it here as my wife, Brandy. I can make you happy if you only give me a chance to try. You know me well. You know I'd try to be a good father to Jeff. Marry me Brandy."

"Jacob . . . I . . . I can't make that kind of decision so quickly. You must give me a little time."

"All right. When are you coming back from Cumberledge?"

"In a few days, maybe a week."

"Will you answer me then?" he said, his eyes searching hers.

"All right, Jacob. I'll answer you then."

"Good," he said. Quickly, he brushed her lips with a light kiss. "Is there anything I can help you with?"

"No, I've everything."

"Money, do you have enough money?"

"I have my savings with me, Jacob," she smiled, "but thank you for your thoughtfulness anyway."

"I'll see you soon, Brandy. By that time I will have enlisted too, but we would still have time for a wedding. I'll be impatient until you get back. Goodbye my dear."

"Goodbye, Jacob," she smiled. Her smile faded as Jacob walked out the door, for she had the strange feeling she would never see him again.

Making her way back to Marthie's she helped her pack a few things. "I'm all packed, but I did not bring much," Brandy said. "I don't think we'll need too many things for a few days."

When Jonah came home later, they put their things in the wagon he brought and began the short journey to the nearby town of Cumberledge. But it was not going to be quite that easy. It was just past supper time when they arrived and Jonah began the search for the place he was to enlist.

"They've changed it, son," an old man told them when Jonah stopped him.

"Where?"

"Down to Braddock. If you want to sign up, you'd best go down there."

Jonah realized they would not be half way to Braddock before nightfall so they decided to stay at the inn in Cumberledge until the next day and go on then.

Early the next morning, they were on their way again, travelling slowly. It was late afternoon when they crested the hill above the small town of Braddock. Jonah slapped the reins and they went down to the town. They found quarters at a small inn and Jonah went out to find the location of enlistment.

They were settled in their rooms waiting for Jonah to return but when he did, his face was clouded.

"Mother, we have to stay here for a week."

"A week!"

"Yes, it takes at least that long to get all the men together, then we've got to get all signed up. Then," he said angrily, "we have to go back to Cumberledge where they're goin' to drill us and train us. What training does a man have to have to fight for his country? They just have to get us all together and when the British march on us we'll show 'em just how strong we are."

"Jonah," Marthie said, "if you cannot follow orders, you don't belong in the Army. It is for men, not for boys."

Jonah flushed, but he knew she was right. They decided to stay for the week.

Jeff was fascinated when drills were held on the green. Brandy took him every day to watch. He was delighted, but Brandy was frightened. To her, they all seemed to be boys playing at war. They were poorly equipped. Some even drilled with broomsticks instead of guns. She was frightened both for Jonah and for the future of all of them, for it was now in the hands of a small army of men who had never tasted military life. Most of them were farmers and shopkeepers. She did not yet feel the strong pull of courage and patriotism that would eventually draw them all together.

She would have felt much better if she could have seen the white-sailed ship that entered Boston harbor, and the tall handsome young man who left it and went to the home of Mr. and Mrs. Jeremy Whitticer requesting knowledge of a bond servant named Brandy Maguire.

Thirty-five

Tamara would never admit to Steffan that she was frightened of being locked in the cell but she felt so confined, restricted. Unable to see out the one window, which was well above eye level. Tamara who was used to the freedom of a bird, chafed at her confinement. Steffan would come at every opportunity he was permitted, and each time he left her it was harder and harder for him.

The nights at Devers Hall were difficult for Steffan too. He found it impossible to find any sleep in the big bed in his room, and after tossing and turning in it for a while, he would give up and would go down to the library, light a fire in the fireplace and pour himself a large glass of brandy. At these times, he would try to sort everything out in his mind and think over all that had happened. It was only then that he could find a balance in his mind, and he found it true that Tamara was the most important thing in his life. He was seated so one night when he looked up and found Martin Gillis at the door. "Can't sleep, Steffan?"

"I guess," Steffan laughed, "I've found the bed warmer when it's shared. It's—it's lonely without Tamara."

Martin poured a glass of brandy and sat opposite Steffan. "I was talking to Pierce today."

Steffan became suddenly alert. "And?"

"By the looks of everything, he is going to succeed in having this kept a naval affair. Day after tomorrow, the board will meet and Tamara's case will be reviewed, but he's sure they will take note of the fact that her activities have been brought to a halt."

"Then, she'll be free?"

"If nothing unforeseen happens, by the end of the week, Tamara should be returned to us."

Steffan sighed deeply, then he leaned forward in his seat; resting his elbows on his knees he spread out his huge hands before him. Both men could see them visibly trembling.

"God, I was so afraid this would become a civil case and she'd be tried for treason. I've had visions of her being dragged from that cell and hanged."

"I know, boy, it's been hard for you."

"It's been harder for her. She's amazingly strong and courageous. Do you know," Steffan said painfully, "that when I visit her, it's she who comforts me. I know her freedom-loving nature and I know how hard it must be for her. I can't stand to leave her there and hear that door close and the lock turn."

"Well, maybe now you can get some sleep."

"Mr. Gillis, Father has told me you are planning on leaving. Am I safe in saying I know where you are going?"

"Yes. Nelson leaves in a week. Pierce, right after Tamara's trial, will tender his resignation. We'll leave for the Colonies then."

"Everything's final?"

"Yes, Steffan."

"Do . . . do you in all honesty really believe we'll have a war?"

"I do . . . I shouldn't be surprised if the whole thing doesn't burst into flames soon."

Steffan ran his hands through his hair in a half angry, half frustrated gesture. Then he stood up and slowly began pacing the floor. Martin remained silent, the glitter in his eyes hidden from Steffan by his lowered lashes. Then, he heard Steffan stop and he looked up to find Steffan gazing at him, a faint half-smile on his face. "You know I've chosen to go, don't you?"

"Let us say that up until you captured Tamara, I had prayed you would choose to go. After you brought her home and I saw the love you had for each other I felt it would be a matter of time. You are wise enough to know what you have in her, and you are certainly too clever to let her slip through your fingers. I can only tell you how very pleased I am in your choice."

"Even though you never once told me you wanted me to go?"

Martin chuckled, "I've spent too many years with you not to know you cannot be pushed. You were shown the way. I would never want it to be any other way than your own choice."

"You think I've chosen right?"

"Yes, son . . . I do."

"I wonder if my parents will feel the same?" Martin rose from his chair and stood beside Steffan. A strong hand clasped Steffan's shoulder.

"You may feel now that you are coming to the end of something, Steffan, but you are not. You are coming to the beginning. Both of your parents understand that well. There are vistas in this new country beyond your imagination. There are challenges, only for the strong to carve out a future, no, a whole new way of life. Deep inside me, after knowing your father as I do, I would not be surprised someday to see him turn his eyes toward the new world. You, young and impatient, do not always see, but for the Colonies, for her future, and for the ambitious freedom-loving people all over the world, this is her time. America will gather her strength and she will dislodge the yoke of England, and we will be there to see her stand alone for the first time and maybe help guide her first unsteady steps. I believe you will never regret your decision. I also believe that someday your family will be part of the force that guides her."

Steffan smiled. "As always, I draw my strength from you; in fact now you make me a little impatient to see this country of yours. Jeff will be leaving with Nelson next week. He's already resigned. It would be best if I withheld mine until Tamara's trial is over, then we'll leave with you and Pierce."

"Excellent."

"And in the meantime, I'll talk to my parents. I want to know how they feel."

Martin nodded.

"I don't suppose Tom and Cecile will be going with us now."

"Why?"

"Why? Cecile is carrying the child and she won't want to leave home now."

"I wouldn't wager any money on that. If you know yourself, you know your sister. She will go with Tom wherever he wants to go. If I'm not mistaken your nephew or niece will be the first of the Devers family born in the new world."

"But not the last," Steffan grinned.

"No," Martin laughed in response, "I doubt very much if it will be the last. Well, I'm to bed, maybe now you can get some sleep too."

"Yes, now that I know Tamara's going to be safe, and now that the decisions are all made, I feel as if a load has been lifted from my mind."

"Good" Martin replied, then he went to the door. "Goodnight, Steffan."

"Goodnight."

Steffan watched as the door closed behind Martin. Then he tossed off the last of the brandy in a quick gulp and poured himself another. He had been given the reassurances that all was going to work out well. Why, then, he pondered, did this strange feeling haunt him? This feeling that something hovered near. Something he did not see, and something he instinctively felt, was reaching out for all the happiness he would find and destroy it.

Steffan rose early the next morning. He dressed, and had his horse saddled. He was anxious to see Tamara, to tell her everything was almost over and that she would be safe. He was also anxious to tell her that war or no war, he was not being separated from her, that they would both go together. Beside all these things, he felt the need to take her in his arms and hold her, feel her close to him.

He rode at a steady pace. Accustomed to riding, he was at ease, allowing his mind to follow the paths it would while his hands and body unconsciously controlled the horse. He arrived at the jail and was escorted to Tamara's cell by a young recruit. It still grated on Steffan's nerves that his sweet gypsy was held so. He stood and waited while the lock was removed and the bolt was pushed aside. The door was pushed open and he stepped inside, then the door was pulled shut and he heard the bolt slide again to lock him in. He realized just how Tamara must feel as the panicky feeling washed over him at being helplessly locked away from everything he knew and loved. He had done everything in his power to make the cell as comfortable as he could, but it was still a cell. She must have just risen from sleep for she was still wearing a robe. Her long hair was pulled over her shoulder and she sat brushing it. Her eyes lifted to his and her quick smile appeared. She dropped the brush and ran to him and he reached out and gathered her up in his arms, lifting her from her feet. His mouth found hers, and he savored the joy of holding her and kissing her deeply. Reluctantly, he lifted his lips from hers but still he held her against him, her feet not touching the floor so that her body rested against him and her arms clung to his neck.

"Steffan," she murmured softly as his lips touched her throat with soft gentle kisses.

"I miss you, love," he said. "I miss you more than I've ever thought I'd miss anyone in my life."

He slid her down to touch the floor and looked into her eyes. She looked so tired, as though she had not slept.

"It will be over soon, my darling, and I'll spend a lifetime making up to you for all you've suffered. I know how hard it is for you to be confined so. Commander Pierce has succeeded in keeping this a naval problem. From what I've been told, by the end of this week, you'll be home, with me, where you belong."

She clung to him, resting her head against his chest, listening to the solid beat of his heart and enjoying the feel of his arms about her, for they were the only strength she had. It was only his presence day by day that kept her from going mad, and even then, she wondered, for she would lie on the small narrow bed and close her eyes dreaming of the cliffs of Marriott Island and the joy and freedom she had known there. A wave of relief shuddered through her and he tightened his arms protectively about her.

"You must think I'm weak, Steffan, but this unbearable room, this feeling of . . . of being smothered. I sometimes think I can't bear it a moment longer."

"God, weak!" he exclaimed. "I don't think I could bear it for as long as you have. Come, sit with me. I have something to tell you that might help."

He led her to the bed where they sat side by side. Taking her hand in his, he fervently kissed her fingers.

"Tam, when this is all over, when you are free, I'm resigning my commission in the Navy and I am going to the Colonies with you."

One emotion followed another across her face, first shock, then sudden realization of the words he had spoken, then finally sheer joy as she cried out his name and threw herself into his arms. He laughed as he pulled her across his lap and enjoyed the multiple and enthusiastic kisses that were rained on him.

"Oh, Steffan, nothing you could have said or done could make me happier."

"Well, you see," he said, "I really began to suspect you might declare war yourself so I've very shrewdly taken away your last chance to get away from me."

"Don't pretend with me, Steffan. I know just how much of a sacrifice this is for you. I know you don't feel as I do, that you are giving up all for me." She kissed him again. "I will try to make you happy, Steffan. I will try to fill your life with the joy you've given me. We'll have the world, you and I. Oh, Steffan, I love you so. I don't want you to ever regret what we're doing. I want you to open your mind and your heart, and see all that we can have."

He tightened his arms about her. "I have the world, Tam," he said ardently, "right here in my arms I'm holding all the world I need. It took me a long time to understand, but now I know. You're my world, and it does not matter where we are as long as we're together."

He could see the shine of crystal tears on her lashes and the sparkle of immense love in her eyes as she reached up and pulled his head down to hers to speak the words that joined them inseparably together.

They were so engrossed in each other they did not hear the bolt of the door slide back or the door swinging open. It was only a soft amused laugh that separated them.

"Sorry if we're interrupting anything," Cecile said, but her eyes danced with wicked humor and Steffan chuckled in recognition of it. He stood up and slid Tamara's feet to the floor but continued to hold her close to him. He grinned at his sister as he spoke to Tamara, "She isn't one bit sorry," he laughed. "I didn't hear a knock, brat."

Cecile's bubbling laughter filled the room, "Steff, you wouldn't have heard me if I'd used a battering ram."

Tom stood behind her, his pleased eyes taking in Tamara's disheveled, half dressed state, her blushing cheeks and shining eyes.

"I've brought some things Tamara might need, and I thought I would stay and visit with her. Tom came to see if you would join him. From what I hear, he's gathered together all of your friends to have a drink together to celebrate your marriage."

"Tom?"

"Mack's here, Jeff, Lang and Bright. It's the first time we've all been together since the Academy. We thought you might like to join us. Besides, I'm sure Tam and Cecile would rather visit without us around."

"Go, Steffan," Tamara smiled up at him, "it would be good for you. Cecile and I can have a nice visit together."

Steffan was still reluctant to leave her but they finally convinced him. The door closed behind them and Tamara's encouraging smile faded. Cecile watched her as Tamara stubbornly regained control of herself. She could see the obstinate chin lift, the shoulders straighten. Cecile had visited often since Tamara had been here. She and Tamara had at first become tentative allies . . . then friends, . . . now the relationship was developing into something deeper. She admired Tamara's courage and had listened to her talk. Slowly, she had begun to feel the irresistible drawing to the Colonies that Tom felt.

"Has Steffan had any news, Tamara?"

"Oh, yes, Cecile, Commander Pierce has succeeded. I will face a naval board. Steffan has told me that it should only be a few days before I'm released."

"I'm glad. I can imagine how hard this has been on you. I don't think I would bear up as well in your position."

"Cecile, I want to tell you something else."

"What?"

"I . . . I appreciate how very kind you and Tom have been to me. At the risk of losing a friend, I must tell you. Steffan and I, when this trial is over, we're going to America to stay . . . to live . . . to fight if necessary."

Cecile stood and looked at her in silence, Tamara was unaware of what she was thinking, and afraid Cecile was either angry or trying to think of something to do to stop Steffan. She would have been shocked to hear the thoughts that were tumbling around in Cecile's mind.

"Cecile . . ." she began hesitantly.

"It's all right, Tamara," she said quietly, "you see . . . Tom and I are going too. He feels it is right and I want to be with him, wherever he goes. It is good to know that I will have some family there."

"Cecile," Tamara replied with a smile, then she went to her and they embraced. "We'll be together you, Tom, Steffan and I. Together, we'll present America with the first branch of the Devers-Braydon family."

They sat down together. Cecile's legs were weak for Tamara did not know she had just made up her mind at that moment to go along. She had not even told Tom yet, for she had still been unsure. It was when Tamara had told her that Steffan had chosen to go too that she had realized that she had abandoned all thought of not going. She knew Tom would be happy, but she still trembled with the fear of facing the unknown, and the thought of bearing a child in a strange country.

At the tavern, the six young men sat around a table and ordered their drinks. It was a laughing and happy group for it had been a long time since they had shared a drink together.

"Mack," Steffan said, "it's damn good to see you again. I hear you accomplished what you set out for."

"I was ordained just a few weeks ago."

"Do we have to watch our p's and q's?" Jeff laughed.

"As well as I know this group, I'd be afraid you were all

drastically ill if you did.''

They laughed together, all of them pleased that there had been no change in Mack. When their drinks arrived, Jeff rose and held up his tankard.

"To the six of us. May we always be able to reach out to each other in any time of need." His smile faded and his eyes became serious. "To five of the very best friends I've ever had. I wish you all the very best life has to offer." Silently, they all rose, touched their glasses together and drank.

"You sound a little melancholy, Jeff."

"I guess I hate goodbyes; you never know if fate intends you to meet again."

"We'll meet again," Mack replied. "I have it on the highest authority," as he spoke, he looked Heaven-ward, which broke the strain of the situation with laughter.

They enjoyed their short reunion, and it was with several too many drinks under their belts that Tom and Steffan returned to the jail, after they had promised solemnly they would be at the docks to see Jeff, Bright and Lang off to the Colonies two days later.

Although they were steady on their feet, Cecile, who knew both of them better than anyone, recognized the obvious signs of their intoxication. She smiled up into Tom's face. "I see you two have enjoyed yourselves," she said. "I'm ready to go, Tom."

"We'd best be going if we want to be home in time for dinner. Are you coming with us, Steffan?" he queried.

Steffan had stood in silence watching Tamara with an intense gaze.

"No" he said slowly, "I'm going to have some food brought and I'm spending the evening with Tamara."

For a moment, Cecile started to speak, but Tom took her arm and squeezed it gently, "Let's go home, Cecile."

She nodded, then she went to Tamara and kissed her cheek. "I can't wait for this to all be over so you can come home. I've always wanted a sister."

"Thank you, Cecile," Tamara replied. "You have made me feel so welcome, as though we've been sisters for a long time. I'm very grateful to you."

After Tom and Cecile had gone, Steffan went to Tamara. Without a word, he drew her into his arms and held her. She sighed contentedly, for she felt that he knew exactly how lost and lonely she was and somehow he wanted to shield her from it.

"I sent for some supper for us before we left the tavern."

"Will they allow . . ."

"I have some friends," he chuckled. "One of which is the one who has guard duty tonight. We might find that our guard had drifted away from door sometime during the evening. It won't be unbolted, but . . ." he said softly as his lips found hers. "No one here wants to leave."

"You'll stay with me?" she whispered hopefully.

"Until dawn, love. Just before dawn they change the guards."

The door was opened and a man came in carrying a large tray followed by a grinning young sailor.

"Captain Devers, it looks as though he brought everything edible in the tavern."

"I hope everythin' is satisfactory, sir," the tray carrier said. Then he paused, looking about him for someplace to put the tray.

"Put it on the bed," Steffan said. He set the tray down and left quickly.

"Captain Devers," the young sailor said, "I have to bolt the door from the outside, you understand that?"

"Yes, Jack," Steffan smiled, "and I'm sure you have duties that will take you to some other vicinity."

"Yes, sir," he smiled. "I'll be back here just before daylight. Couple of raps on the door and I'll let you out."

"We keep this a secret, Jack."

"You think I want word to get out? I'd be dead if they found out I was shirkin' my duties."

"Thanks, Jack."

"Don't thank me, I owe you a lot more than this. See you in the morning." He waved and left, bolting the door behind him. Steffan chuckled, "Good man."

"Steffan, where are we supposed to sit? With that huge tray on the bed, there is no place."

"Not a very romantic creature are you?" he laughed. He walked to the bed and worked the blanket out from under the tray. With a quick flip, he spread the blanket on the floor. "Have you never been on a picnic, Ma'am? With a little imagination, we are on the cliffs of Marriott Island." He went to her and took her hand in his. "And you have your beautiful hair tied in a green ribbon, a ribbon I shall promptly steal." He held out his other hand and in it rested the ribbon he had taken so many months ago.

"Steffan . . ."

"Shhh, love. Come with me, back to the cliffs of Marriott Island, back to the first time I held you and learned what happiness is. That is always what I dream of these nights, the beautiful wild little gypsy I found and loved on Marriott Island."

He carried the tray to the blanket and they sat crosslegged on the floor. He began to talk as though four walls no longer held them. Soon, they were laughing together over nonsensical things. They emptied both bottles of wine he had brought. Combined with what he had drunk before, both of them found themselves slightly tipsy. She found herself in his arms and being kissed with a fierce and passionate hunger.

"The bed?" she giggled helplessly.

"Shhh," he chuckled nibbling on her ear and tracing fiery patterns on her body with his hands. "Now, who needs a bed when we have the soft grass here on the island and can feel the warm breeze on our skin."

She laughed again. "I don't feel it."

"Maybe," he said shrewdly, "it's because you're wearing too many clothes." With those words, he began undressing her while she removed his clothes.

"Tam?"

"Oh, you impossible, beautiful, wonderful man. I do love you so very much." Her arms about his neck pulled him down to her and their lips met in a deep and surging passion.

Gone was the jail cell as they blended in the deep and fiery love they had found on Marriott Island.

Just as the first soft pale streaks of light touched the horizon Steffan heard the soft tap on the door. Tamara slept in his arms and he moved slowly to keep from waking her. He slipped into his clothes and went to the door and tapped softly on the inside. He heard the bolt slide back and the young sailor stuck his head around the door. Steffan motioned to him to wait outside for a moment. He went back to Tamara and very gently lifted her from the floor and carried her to the bed.

He covered her then brushed a light kiss on her head. Reaching into his pocket, he took a small scrap of paper and a pencil. He wrote a note and put it on the pillow near her cheek. Then he went to the door, opened it, and went out. He stood and watched the young sailor bolt the door, then he walked away.

Tamara blinked awake at the sounds of activity outside. Steffan was gone and she did not remember how she had gotten on

417

the bed, but she did remember the gentle giving love of the night before.

"Steffan," she murmured softly. It was then that she saw the note. Picking it up, she read, then smiled. Pressing it to her breast, she closed her eyes to better remember the man who wrote it.

Beloved

Our return to Marriott Island was a beauty beyond compare. I love you. Soon I'll return and take you away from all of this. Have faith my love, you'll be with me soon and we'll start a whole new life together.

You are my wife and my life. It is an empty place without you. Remember that I love you.

Steffan.

Without his strength she knew this terrible imprisonment would have been too much. Her life revolved about him. She curled on her side holding the note in her hand and returned to the beautiful dreams of the past night.

Steffan returned home, bathed and changed his clothes, then he went to Commander Pierce's office to see if Tamara's hearing could move any faster.

Thirty-six

Lord Lyle Whitfield, the left hand of the King, sat in a deep comfortable chair and looked at the woman who sat framed in the light of a huge window across the room. Lyle Whitfield was a handsome man of about forty. He was tall and well-built. His hair was a shade too light to be brown and he had a full moustache to match. His eyes were a startling cold pale blue. His features spoke of arrogance and of a man who was used to getting anything he wanted. It had not always been so. He was born to a destitute family and had risen not only by his grim determination but by his ability to do whatever he had to in any situation. He gave to any situation whatever it required to achieve a goal he wanted, whether it was suave diplomacy with the King, whose ear he held, or to cold and final brutality. No one living knew the extent to which the brutality and the long arm of Lyle Whitfield could reach. No one of course but the woman who sat watching him.

He tented his fingers together, tapping them lightly against his chin as he contemplated the woman. It was the first time in his life he had ever wanted a woman and did not have the means to get her. One way or the other, he had always had his way, sometimes by the use of his vast fortune and sometimes in ways that no other human knew about. He was frustrated and that was an alien emotion for him; it tended to whet his appetite for her to a degree he found difficult to control.

He rose slowly from his chair and walked across the room toward the woman, annoyed at the cool appraisal of her eyes and the half-smile on her lips, as if she knew he wanted her and could never have her. He stood behind her and let his hands rest gently on her shoulders. She remained still.

"Damn you," he whispered and was rewarded by a low throaty laugh. "What do you want? What?"

"A life," she said softly, "no . . . two lives."

He reached down and grasped her wrist, pulling her to her feet.

Their eyes met and held.

"Whose?"

"In a jail cell," she began, "there is a woman who has been held as a pirate."

"Of course" he replied. "Everyone knows the infamous lady. Of what importance to us?"

"Oh, my dear," she said softly as she reached up to stroke the side of his face. Satisfied with his reaction, she laughed again. "She is of great importance to me."

"It's a naval problem. I have nothing to do with it."

"But you can if you desire. I know your power. All you have to do is reach out and touch."

"I repeat, what do you want?"

"I want her trial made civil. I want her tried for treason. I want her sentenced and hung; then I want the life of the man who brought her here, Captain Steffan Devers."

"You ask much."

"Oh!" she cooed, as she put her arms about his neck. "But I am worth it." She drew his head down to hers and kissed him in a way he had never been kissed before, with an almost contained violence that gave promise of what could be. When he lifted his head, her eyes asked a silent question and his gave her the answer she wanted. He tried to kiss her again but she moved from his arms. "Can I expect your little . . . gift?"

"I'll find a way," he said in half-anger, "and you?"

"When I hear of the hanging of the lady pirate I will come to you. Together we will plan the death of Steffan Devers."

She walked slowly to the door with the grace of a sleek panther. At the door, she turned and blew him a kiss, and her soft throaty laugh drifted behind her as she closed the door between them.

He remembered the first time he had seen her. Had it only been weeks? He felt it was a lifetime. A lifetime of wanting something that remained out of his reach. He had been to a masque given by some close friends who took pleasures in ways that were unknown to most. He had felt her enter the room. It was the only word for her, an electrifying experience. She had been dressed in black, a revealing lace dress, cut so daringly low that her exceptional beauty was made obvious. She was so beautiful that every other woman faded to nothing in comparison.

That night she had intrigued him enough, for thoughts of her dwelt in his mind for the next few days. He began to investigate just who and what she was. Then he received another surprise; her past vanished and no matter how he tried, he could find out absolutely nothing. His appetite for her began to grow. A man whose jaded tastes had been catered to found something that was out of reach.

He saw her many times after that, then found that she hovered in his thoughts always, lurking just on the edge of his consciousness all the time. Each time he drew near, she would seem to fade away from him, always leaving in her wake that mysterious look in her eyes that seemed to promise things he had not yet tasted, and he began to want her.

A campaign was waged by him, but all he did seemed to fail. He tried expensive gifts, but they were all refused, and then he tried to strike fear and found to his astonishment that she was afraid of nothing and seemed to have an unlimited source of wealth to protect her. Lyle had always believed that there was no man or woman who did not have a price whether it be money, position, or fear of something. He felt if he looked hard enough and long enough, he would find hers, and so he drew nearer and nearer. The trap closed about him so delicately, so smoothly that he never even realized he was trapped until he began to think. Then, he found that he wanted her no matter what the cost, had to possess her no matter what price he had to pay for it.

The night before, they were again together at a party and he had forced the issue into the open. They were walking in the fresh air on a large stone terrace. The party inside was boisterous, but the soft night air and the presence of the beauty on his arm was, at the moment, more exciting and compelling than the celebration inside.

He stopped and looked at her. Her remarkable beauty was enhanced by pale moonlight, and he knew there was not another woman in the world he had ever wanted as he wanted this one and he became obsessed with finding a means to get her.

"What are you thinking of, Lyle, you seem so far away?"

He turned to her. "You!" he said almost in anger. "It seems I think of you most of my waking hours and dream of you when I'm asleep."

He put his hands on her soft bare shoulders and felt the tingle of desire rush through him as he drew her near. Her mouth tasted sweet and was rose petal soft to his kiss. The perfume she wore seemed to surround him and intoxicate him. And yet he knew when the kiss ended, that she was no more his than when it had started. He felt that having her was just out of reach and that if he pressed just a little harder, he would win. She stepped back a little from him. The small half-smile on her lips told him 'Try'. The glow in her violet eyes told him 'Try' and yet when he reached, she seemed to fade from him.

"I want you, you know that," he said tightly. "I generally get what I want."

"Really," she laughed, "are not some prices too high to pay to get something you want?"

Again he reached out and drew her against him. "I am a man of great wealth and great power. I have found that my wealth seems to mean nothing to you for I've tried its use. Yet, I know you want something from me. Don't try to deny it, no one knows better than I when someone is seeking something."

"You are right, of course," she smiled.

"Tell me and it's yours."

"And you," she countered, "what do you want?"

He laughed shortly. "You," he said, "and you know it."

The low throaty laugh answered his question, and he tried to draw her back into his arms but she stepped back from him. "Let me consider your offer," she said. "Tomorrow we will discuss our . . . mutual needs."

He reached out and took hold of her arm pulling her against him. His eyes glowed with the hunger for her and she trembled, not in excitement as he, but in joy that she finally had the man who could give her what she really wanted—the key to revenge against Steffan Devers.

"I will taste," he said huskily, and his mouth crushed down on hers. She responded in a way he never dreamed. Instead of fighting him, she melted against him, her arms drew him closer and her lips parted under his. He suddenly felt as though he was drowning and he tightened his arms about her feeling the curves of her body cling to him. He was consumed with a need so great that it left him shaking. No woman, and he had had many, had ever affected him like this. If he knew the irreversible effect she had on him, she knew it better, because it had been well planned by her a long time before she had arranged the meeting between herself and the man she knew had the power to do what she wanted done.

Without a word, she left him; watching her walk away from him, he knew he would give her whatever she wanted in return for what he now found he needed.

Now he began to move. First he sent out feelers for information. When he knew all that was to be known about Tamara Marriott and her captors, he made plans to move.

Two days later, Steffan, Tom and Mack stood on the edge of the dock and watched the ship that carried Jeff and his friends leave.

"Well," Tom said, as they turned to leave, "if all goes well and Tamara is freed, it won't be long before we'll be on our way."

"Steff," Mack said, "Once we resign, the *Cecile* or no other ship will be ours. Do we book passage on a ship or . . ."

"No, I've taken some money my grandmother left me and Tom's father is in the process of building now. By the time we're ready, the ship will be too. It's sort of a mutual enterprise. Tom, you and I will share her. Once the stupid affair between our two countries is over, we'll start our own shipping business."

"When is Tamara's hearing?"

"In three more days," Steffan said. "I don't know why Commander Pierce is having so much trouble getting the date set, but he assures me everything is going to be all right."

"Well," Mack said, "let me stand you two to the last drink I will ever probably buy you in England. The next time might be two thousand miles away."

They laughed and joined him.

Between visiting Tamara and making preparations the next three days were very busy for Steffan. Too busy for him to notice the fact that he was followed wherever he went.

The days flew quickly. Tamara clung to the frequent visits of Steffan's parents, Martin Gillis and Cecile, but it was Steffan whose strength carried her through the days and the dark hours of the night.

It was the day before her trial and both Tamara and Steffan were grateful that the next day would see an end to all the struggle and they would be free again, be together again and this time for always. As they shared a last few minutes of the evening together, Steffan encouraged her. "By this time tomorrow, love, it will all be over and you will be safe at Devers Hall with me."

They kissed a reluctant farewell and as the door closed behind him, Tamara shivered with a sudden premonition of fear. It closed with a solid thud and she heard the finality of it. There was no reason for her fear and she knew it, yet it existed like a heavy blanket smothering her.

It was at the moment Steffan closed the door that Lyle Whit-field stood at the shoulder of the King as he unfolded the message that heralded the beginning of a war. Lyle smiled, for it also held the answer to his search for a way to reach out into the lives of Tamara Marriott and Steffan Devers.

When he finally left the King's side, it was nearly four in the morning but he did not seek sleep yet. Instead, he called his secretary to his side and dictated several messages. Satisfied that his orders would be carried out to the letter, he went to his bed. He smiled as he lay alone for soon he would share his bed with the rare beauty of Morgana Kyle.

Before dawn, that darkest of all times, when the moon has set and the sun has not yet risen, the time when evil always chose to stalk the unwary, Tamara slept, safe in the knowledge that at the close of the next day, she would be at Devers Hall, safe in Steffan's arms.

The door opened with thunderous noise and in a few minutes, several men were in her cell. She sat up suddenly wakened, startled and unable to realize at the moment what was happening.

Heavy hands dragged her from the bed. She fought but it was a useless battle. She stood trembling between the two men, aware now of the thin nightgown and their warm gaze. Then she looked up toward the door and saw Jaspar Sinclair leaning against the doorway; his smile and the way his eyes roved over her made her weak with fear.

"I'm sorry to bring an end to your cozy little rendezvous but it seems Steffan is finally bored with his little pigeon and decided to find other fields."

"What are you talking about—what are you doing?"

He sighed deeply as though he regretted what he was being forced to say.

"Steffan's dirty work, as usual. I tried to warn you on the island of Steffan's . . . ah . . . unpredictability. I knew he'd tire of you soon and be looking about for something new."

"I don't know what you are trying to make me believe," she said, her eyes stormy and her chin lifted proudly. "But I don't believe a word you say."

He laughed. "You will soon enough." He nodded toward the two men who held her and they began dragging her toward the door.

"Where are you taking me!" she shouted at Jaspar as they

tried to drag her past him.

"Why" he smirked, "to the Tower to put you in your proper place until your . . . civil trial."

"No!" she gasped. "It's a naval trial. You've made a mistake."

"No, my dear, you made the mistake, War has been declared. You will be tried . . . tomorrow . . . for treason against the Crown, and it will be a civil trial, after which they will hang you."

"You can't do this. Where is Steffan! You have no right . . ."

"Oh, but I do. I am here under direct orders from the King to see that your treason is properly punished; as for Steffan, I imagine they will inform him . . . just before the trial."

Tamara was frightened, but she refused to give Jaspar the satisfaction of seeing it. She held herself steady as she glared at Jaspar's amused face.

"Take her along," he said coldly.

Tamara was dragged from the room and pushed roughly into a closed carriage. She was more alarmed when Jaspar joined her inside and closed the door after them. The carriage started with a jolt, then began to move rapidly. She sat in a corner as far away from Jaspar as she could, prepared to fight him with every ounce of strength she had. She was surprised when he made no overt action, but sat in silence and watched her; but it was the gleam in his eyes that told her she was in his power and he would choose his own time.

They rode along in the strained silence for what to Tamara seemed to be hours, then the carriage came to an abrupt halt. The door was pulled open and again, she was dragged from the carriage. With Jaspar following, they went through two huge iron gates then knocked on a thick wooden door. When it opened a man stood there holding a lantern aloft.

"You were expecting us," Jaspar said.

The man grunted and stepped aside to let them enter; then he walked ahead of them leading the way by holding his lantern high. The sharp click of their heels on the stone floor was the only sound. They came to the end of a long hall to find themselves at the top of a flight of steps. Pushing her along, they began to descend.

Tamara's breath caught in her throat as the way became colder, darker and more frightening. The smell of the place began to nauseate her but she refused to make a sound. There was no

425

way she intended to give them the pleasure of hearing her beg or cry.

Two flights down, then three. The chill now was penetrating her and her feet were extremely cold. At the bottom of the third flight of steps, they came to another long stone hall. Down this for forty feet and they came to the door. It was opened by the silent man who stepped aside while the two men who held her pushed Tamara inside.

Jaspar took the lantern in his hand and entered after her. He ordered the two men back to their barracks and the guard back to his post. Then he closed the door, set the lantern on the table and turned smiling to an angry Tamara who backed to a corner and glared her hatred at him.

Steffan whistled lightly as he came down the stairs. "Today," he thought joyfully, "today the formalities of the trial would be over. Today she will be free and we can begin a new life together." Cecile's laughter came to him and he looked to see her standing in the doorway of the dining room.

"Morning, brat," he grinned.

"My, you're happy today. It's the first time I've seen you so in a long, long time. I can't wait to see you when Tamara comes home."

He laughed as he went to her, hugged her lightly and kissed her soundly.

"It will be the happiest day of my life, Cecile. I've put Tamara through more than any woman should have to suffer and I'm going to try to make it up to her in every way I can."

"I'm sure she knows that, Steffan."

"Maybe we should have some kind of party, sort of a combination of all things. Tamara's release, our family reunited . . . everything."

"Sounds like a good idea, but it had better be quick."

"Oh?"

"Yes, Tom says Commander Pierce will resign today after the trial. By the end of the week, he should be ready to leave. He, you, Tamara and . . . Tom and I."

"You're sure, Cecile?"

"I've never been surer of anything in my life except my love for Tom."

"I imagine Mother will be upset?"

"I don't know," mused Cecile. "Both Mother and Father have

had a strange look in their eyes lately. I just don't think I'd be too surprised to someday see them join us."

"Mr. Gillis said something of the sort, too."

"Father and you are so alike, Steffan," she smiled fondly, "he thinks, decides, then does what he wants. You're the same. Once you've made a decision, it's final; you'll live by it."

Steffan was about to answer when voices came to them from the top of the steps. They were joined by their parents, Tom and Martin.

The breakfast was a joyous affair for Steffan's happiness was obvious. After they ate, Tom and Steffan left for the jail. Steffan wanted to be with Tamara when they came for her. They rode together happily making plans for their trip to the Colonies. When they rode through the gates and across the cobblestone square, they were both struck by the strangely unguarded look of the place. Then Steffan's smile froze as he looked toward Tamara's door to find it standing ajar. He dismounted quickly and followed by Tom, he ran to the door and pushed it open. He stopped in the center of the room. Unable to understand why it was empty. His face turned pale and a swift feeling of panic almost overcame him.

"Tamara!" he shouted. The sound of running feet across the cobblestones came to them. They whirled about to see the young friend of Steffan's who had been their absent guard a few nights earlier.

"Jack," Steffan said, "where is she?"

"They came early this morning, sir and took her away."

"Away! Away where? For Christ's sake, Jack where is she, what's going on? Her trial wasn't to be for another hour yet."

"Before God, sir, I don't know. I only know they had orders from the King himself. She's to have a civil trial in a few days, sir, and they took her somewhere else."

Steffan heard Tom's swift intake of breath and a band of iron seemed to squeeze around his chest, cutting off his breath.

"A civil trial," he breathed agonizingly. "Jack, you must have some idea where they've taken her?"

"No, sir, I don't. I only know Captain Sinclair and two men came just before daylight. They had orders straight from the King. They took her in a closed carriage."

"Jaspar," Steffan grated. A look of such hate crossed his face that Jack took a step back from him and even Tom became alarmed. He saw murder in Steffan's eyes and was quick to go after him as Steffan ran from the cell.

Tamara had watched Jaspar's cold amused eyes as they raked familiarly over her. The thin nightgown she wore was poor protection from the damp cold of the small dank cell and she shivered both at the cold and the look in Jaspar's eyes. He sat on the edge of the small table in the room and swung one glossy booted foot back and forth. "I must admit Steffan does have excellent taste in women. You are an exquisite rose. I imagine he was also right when he said you do a magnificent job of warming a bed."

"I know you for what you are," she snapped. "If you are trying to make me lose my faith in Steffan you are failing. When he finds out where I am, he will come for me, then look to yourself, for he will kill you for this."

"Tsk, tsk," Jaspar said. "You are still foolish enough to believe that? Oh, well, time will prove that you are wrong. Steffan will not come for you—in fact he will probably not even be present for your trial or your execution. He really has no stomach for those things."

"Liar!" she replied coldly, "Steffan will come for me the minute he finds out I've been taken."

Jaspar rose and walked slowly toward her. She would have died before she let him know the fear that gripped her. She lifted her chin and looked defiantly at him.

Jaspar reached out and twined his fingers in the tangled length of her hair, enjoying the silken feel of it. Tamara slapped his hand away, then suddenly bright stars exploded in her head as he slapped her hard across the face, hard enough to make her stumble backward and fall into the pile of filthy straw that was to serve as her bed. She was stunned for a minute, then pure white rage engulfed her and she scrambled quickly to her feet. Unprepared for her attack, Jaspar was unable to defend himself from the raking of her nails across his face, but he quickly reached for her. Doubled fists flailing and her feet kicking out toward vulnerable spots on his body brought a curse to his lips. Jaspar was almost as large and strong as Steffan and it did not take him long before he held her bound helplessly to him. He laughed down into her rage-filled green eyes and found he was enjoying the writhing half clad form in his arms. He kissed her brutally and yelped in surprise and almost released her as she bit his lip.

"Bastard, keep your hands to yourself," she sputtered as she

428

fought to free herself. She did not realize that her half naked form twisting in his arms did more to arouse him than anything else.

"Bitch," he gasped as one of her fists connected, "you need some taming."

"Not by you, you slimy deceitful snake," she snarled. "Keep away from me or Steffan will surely see you dead."

Completely furious now, Jaspar flung her from him so hard that she stumbled and fell. She felt him grasp her arm and yank her to her feet. His hand crashed against the side of her face and again she was almost blinded by the force of the blow. Before she could rise from her knees, he struck her again. Half conscious now, she tried to ward off the hands that reached for her, but she was ineffective against his strength. She heard his panting breath and felt him lift her by her hair. Then the sudden piercing cold touched her skin as he ripped the flimsy nightgown away from her and it finally reached her mind what he intended to do.

"No," she moaned, "Steffan . . . !"

"Steffan will never come to you again, bitch." He said harshly, his breath panting in her ear as his hands gripped her body. Still she fought with every ounce of strength she had left. One more blow and she fell again. She could feel the rough straw beneath her bare back. Helplessly, she put up her hands to stop Jaspar as he fell upon her. She felt his hands roughly gripping her breasts and sliding down to push her legs open. She began to sob helplessly as she knew his strength was so much greater than hers.

"Little whore, bitch," he grated in her ear. "I'll show you who is master here."

He rolled atop her pressing her against the straw and she felt the pain of his hard thrusting entry. She cried out as he began to move in brutal hard jerks against her. The last thing she heard was his triumphant laugh as all thought and feeling faded from her and merciful unconsciousness came.

Jaspar rose from her, and looked down on her slender body. "She is a beauty," he thought and since he was the only one who was going to have access to her, he intended to enjoy her often. The pleasure would be double. Once for the sheer beauty that she was, and again for the knowledge that he was possessing the one thing in Steffan Devers' life he loved beyond all else.

He bent down and gathered up the torn gown and smiled. From the table he took a worn blanket he had brought. He threw it down beside her and taking the gown with him, he took the lantern and left, closing and bolting the door behind him.

In the darkness, Tamara stirred awake. The pain in her body caused her to moan and she slowly sat up. Feeling around for her clothes, she found only the worn blanket, and knew he had taken the gown with him. She drew the blanket about her bruised and shivering body. For the first time real and hard terror overtook her. Would Steffan know where she was?

She began to cry, feeling the hot helpless tears that she hated slip down her face. She lay back on the straw, curled in a ball and cried helplessly, "Steffan . . . Steffan . . . Steffan."

Thirty-seven

Jaspar went home, riding slowly and enjoying the thought of how he and Morgana's plans were working out. At home, he bathed, changed into fresh clothes and had the scratches on his face cared for. Then he sat down to wait for the visit from Steffan he knew was coming.

About an hour later, he heard the approaching horse and smiled to himself. The door burst open and an angry Steffan stormed inside. His breath coming in short hard gasps and his eyes burning with rage, he stood trembling inside the door.

"Where, Jaspar? Tell me where she is and how you managed it, then you'd better pray nothing's happened to her or so help me God, you'll never see another dawn."

"Well, Steffan, I'd answer you if I knew. I was only told to deliver the papers for her arrest. They came straight from the King; what else could I do? I turned her over to the men and that's all I know."

"I don't believe you. Where is she, Jaspar, tell me?"

"There's no way I can answer that, Steffan for I don't know. It was not my job to take her anywhere. Why don't you see Lord Lyle Whitfield? That's where the orders came from and he's the only man who knows what is going to happen to her. I imagine though," Jaspar said coolly, "she'll have a civil trial sometime soon."

At that moment hoofbeats sounded a rapid tattoo in the drive and in a few seconds, Tom stood beside Steffan. "You damned rotten bastard," Steffan said, his voice calm and to Tom more terrifying than if he'd been raging. "Why, what in God's name can you get from this? Tell me where they're holding her or so help me I'll kill you, now, where you stand!"

"Steff?" Tom said.

"He says he doesn't know where she is, that he was only responsible for serving the orders."

"Do you believe him?"

"Whether he believes me or not," Jaspar said, "I can't tell you anything. Orders were sent. I carried them out. From there on, it is the responsibility of the Crown."

"If you read the orders, you have to know where they're holding her."

"I told you," Jaspar replied, in an exasperated voice, "there was nothing written on it to tell me where she was going. I simply had to turn her over to two of the King's men who took her away."

"And you didn't ask?" Tom said skeptically.

"I don't question what the King orders. I'm a loyal Englishman, not like some traitors. I did exactly as I was told. No matter what you try to do to me, there's nothing more you can learn here. As I suggested, the order came from Lord Lyle Whitfield, and I'm sure you know who he is. Why don't you ask him? Then maybe at the same time, you can explain to him why you are trying to defend a traitor to the Crown."

"Steff," Tom said, "maybe he's telling the truth. Maybe he doesn't know. We'd better be finding another way to find her."

Steffan looked at Jaspar's face. Inside he knew Jaspar was lying, just as he knew he would never be able to prove it. A violent rage tore through him and he contained it only with tremendous effort.

"Jaspar," he said, his voice cold and hard, "I'll find her. Mark my words, I'll find her, and if I find out this was all a lie no matter what they do to me, I'll kill you and if you've hurt her in any way, you had best find a far dark place to hide for there will be no such thing as mercy. I'll kill you," Steffan's voice became ominous as he added "I promise you Jaspar . . . I promise you." He turned and left the room.

"Jaspar, I know you hate Steffan," Tom said, "but to take revenge on a helpless woman is foul. If you have an idea where she is tell me."

"She's being held somewhere by the King's men for civil trial, that's all I know. I have my duties and I did them. I certainly am not to blame for what they're doing. They should have thought of that before they did what they did. Now, she will have to pay the price of her folly. I have no control over it and I don't know where she is."

Tom watched Jaspar's face. He too was sure he was lying, but there was nothing he could do about it. He saw the glow of pleasure in Jaspar's eyes and he wanted to smash him. Instead, he turned and left the house slamming the door behind him.

Jaspar watched as Tom left. He had never felt so exuberant before. His revenge on Steffan was almost complete and he was delighted with the way the well-formulated plans were working. In another day or so, days of agony for Steffan, the next part of the plan would be put in motion and after that his revenge would be complete. He chuckled as the door closed, then he poured himself a glass of whiskey and raised it in a toast toward the closed door.

"To you Steffan, may your misery be complete and absolute as I've been promised. I only wish I could watch you as you fight a losing battle for a change." He tossed off the drink. The chuckle on his lips turned to a laugh and he threw his head back and laughed uproariously at the feeling of power that rolled through him.

Steffan was already gone when Tom came outside but he had a good idea where. Jaspar had mentioned Lord Whitfield and Tom was sure he was already on his way there. He mounted his horse and kicked him into a gallop. "All Steffan needs," he thought, "is to lose his temper and attack Lord Whitfield; then he would really have a problem."

He rode directly to Lord Whitfield's and when he arrived, he saw that he had been right. Steffan's horse stood out front and Steffan was already at the door. Tom reached the door at the same time it was opened by a wizened old man. "Yes, sir?" he questioned.

"I'm Captain Steffan Devers, I would like to see Lord Whitfield."

"I'm sorry, sir, Lord Whitfield is not at home."

"Not at home?" Steffan questioned, "or not receiving any guests?"

"He's not here, sir, Lord Whitfield left last night for his summer residence. I believe he plans on being there a few days and then go on to his family's old home in Wales. I don't expect him back for some time, sir."

"Who is handling his affairs while he is gone?"

"His secretary, James Robin, sir."

"Is he here, now?"

"Yes, sir."

"Would you tell him I would like to speak to him?"

"Yes, sir, come in please."

Steffan and Tom went inside. They were shown to a large comfortable sitting room, offered drinks they both refused, and told to wait.

"Tom, there's something going on that we are not meant to know. While I talk to the secretary go and inform my father and Mr. Gillis what is happening. We have to turn this town upside down, but we've got to find Tamara. With Jaspar involved in this, I have a terrible feeling if we don't find her soon, it might be too late."

"You don't want me to wait for you?"

"No. We've got to start doing something fast. My father and Mr. Gillis might be able to dig out at least news of what's going on, and why this has suddenly become a civil trial."

Tom turned to leave when the old man returned with a tall skeletal man with a dour face and an impatient look in his watery blue eyes.

"You wanted to speak to me, captain?" he asked with ill-controlled annoyance. "I have a great deal of work to do."

"I'm sorry to inconvenience you, but I have to know what has happened to Tamara Marriott?"

"Who?"

"Tamara Marriott," Steffan replied.

"Oh," the secretary replied, "the pirate lady." He smirked at Steffan. "It is certainly an inopportune time for war to break out, at least for the . . . ah . . . lady," his voice became sneering. "But it has, and she will be tried as a traitor and I suppose hung like the criminal she is."

"War?"

"Yes, sir, England is now in the position of having to chastise the Colonies for their uprising against proper authorities. What better way to begin than to hang one of the blasted revolutionaries."

Steffan remained outwardly calm even though Tom knew his fury was burning deep within him. Through a gritted smile he asked, "Of course, Mr. . . . ?"

"Robin, sir . . . James Robin."

"Mr. Robin . . . you know where they've taken her. I should like to see a lady pirate up close."

"I'd like to accommodate you, sir," Robin laughed, "I should even like to get a good look at the woman myself, but I don't know where she's being held."

"You . . . you're Lord Whitfield's secretary, you should know where she is. Come along, man, I only want a look at her."

434

"I'm sorry, sir, truly, Lord Whitfield did not confide the information to me when he left. I suppose she's held at Newgate, sir, that is usually where they toss such riff-raff to wait for hanging."

Steffan stifled the urge to curse the man and the combined need to put his hands around his skinny throat and squeeze. "Thank you, Mr. Robin. We shall go to Newgate. Maybe we'll get a look at her after all."

They turned to leave. Robin escorted them to the door, and closed it behind them, then he turned to smile at the man who walked down the stairs.

"Commendable job, Robin," Lord Whitfield drawled. "While they go on their little wild goose chase, we shall close all other doors in their faces."

"Thank you, sir," Robin smirked.

"Carry out the rest of the orders I gave you, Robin."

"Yes, sir," Robin bowed slightly and left the room.

"And now," Lyle Whitfield thought, "Two more steps to our little plan and you belong to me, my dear." He chuckled and the gloating sound drifted down as he went back up the stairs.

At Newgate, Steffan found exactly what he had thought he would find, they had not seen nor even heard of Tamara Marriott. Tom went to Devers Hall while Steffan continued a fruitless search. It was as though the ground had opened up and swallowed Tamara and all news of her. When he dragged himself home that night, he was in a state of nervous exhaustion. He wanted to rage, to fight at something but everything was ghosts and shadows, there was nothing of substance for him to do battle with so he turned on himself, blaming himself and torturing himself with the thought that if he had not brought her here, had not calmly locked her away promising her freedom, none of this could have happened. If only she had not loved and trusted him.

Steffan's father and Martin reached out with all their power in all directions and each tentacle touched a solid closed door.

Without sleep or food, by the middle of the next day, Steffan could hardly contain the fear that ate at him, fear that was also etched on the faces of those about him.

They sat around waiting for the return of Martin. He was trying to get information from a member of the King's cabinet who was a friend of his. Steffan rose for the tenth time in the past hour and began to pace the floor, locked in grief-filled thoughts. Ellen wanted to go to him and try to comfort him somehow, but a quick negative shake of Maxwell's head kept her in her chair.

Cecile's eyes were filled with tears as she watched her beloved brother tear himself apart with anguish no one could ease.

Steffan froze in mid-stride as the door opened, but a low groan escaped him when he saw the defeat in Martin's face.

"I just don't understand this," Martin said angrily, "every door is closed to us. What kind of person wields the power to do this?"

"And," Maxwell added, "what kind of person carries the hate and malevolence to want to do this?"

Steffan sagged in his chair, his face grim. "She's somewhere near, I know it, and I will find her if I have to turn London upside down."

They all watched his face, each of them filled with the knowledge that he would do exactly what he had said. Pity was in their eyes for the pain he was suffering now. None of them, least of all Steffan, knew that the real pain was just beginning.

The day passed as they feverishly tried every way to find one scrap of news about Tamara. That night, alone in the study, after he had forced everyone else to bed to get some rest, Steffan drank himself into insensibility, the only way he knew he could close his eyes without visions of Tamara begging him to come to her. He saw her alone, frightened and needing him. He whispered her name over and over in his drunken sleep and tears that could not escape in the day slipped from under his closed lids.

Tamara refused to sleep. Fear kept her awake and alert. Fear of the soft furry things that lurked in the corners with gleaming red eyes. A small slit in the stone about twelve feet above her head let in just enough light to tell her that the daylight hours had come. She wrapped herself tight in the scrap of blanket. The penetrating cold chilled her to the bone and she curled herself tight to cling to what small warmth the blanket could give.

Today, Steffan would find she was missing. By nightfall, she would be taken from this horrible place. She knew Steffan would find her. Her body ached not only with the cold but with Jaspar's abuse. Her mouth was sore and bruised and she felt dirty. Still, her mind and heart clung desperately to Steffan. Now, she knew the difference between the gentle love she and Steffan had shared and the brutal lust of Jaspar Sinclair.

The time ticked by. She was stiff from huddling under the blanket. Forced to move, she wrapped the blanket about her and stood up. Despite the intense cold, she knew she had to keep her blood moving. She moved around as long as she could, then with her teeth chattering and hunger knotting in her stomach she huddled back on the straw. Surely they meant to feed her she thought angrily. Minutes turned to hours. The hunger she could bear, the cold she could bear, but the agony of wondering if Steffan would come for her soon was making her shiver in fear. The small ray of sunlight grew smaller and smaller.

It must have been long after the sun had set that Tamara gratefully heard the key turn in the lock and the rusty hinges squeak as the door opened. Expectation turned to trembling anger combined with fear as Jaspar appeared. He set a lantern on the table and closed the door. Alongside the lantern, he placed a small bundle. Then he turned and smiled at her.

"I thought you might be hungry," he said. Tamara held herself erect, watching him as he unbound the bundle. There was bread, cheese, a small piece of ham and a bottle of wine. Her mouth watered at the food, but she did not move. Somehow, as she watched his eyes, she felt there was more to getting the food than just taking it. At his next words, she knew she was right. "Drop that blanket on the floor and come here to me."

"Go to hell," she said stiffly.

He chuckled. "You'll learn obedience, my dear." He took a piece of the ham and chewed it thoughtfully. "If you want news of Steffan and a little food, you will drop that blanket. Then you can eat while I explain to you the amusing story of your lover."

Tamara watched him without moving. He laughed again and went to stand by the door. "If you want the food, and news, you will drop the blanket; then you can have it."

She wanted to cry, knowing he was playing with her, yet knowing she had to hear of Steffan and she had to eat if she didn't want to die. In hot anger, she dropped the blanket. She would not let him defeat her. Proudly she walked to the table and picked up the food. Locking her eyes with his, she bit off a piece of the bread and chewed. He made no move, only let his eyes devour her. Her amazing golden body held his hot penetrating gaze and he could feel the swift desire for her begin to grow, but he had time. Tonight was going to bring Tamara Marriott-Devers many surprises.

She could feel his eyes crawl over her and it made her stomach twist in anger. How she would have liked to fly at him and tear out those insolent, staring eyes. Again, she saw that he knew her thoughts and was actually enjoying them. Slowly, he stood up from the door and began to remove his jacket. He hung it on the bolt of the door and removed the cravat from his neck. He hung it with the jacket, then he unbuttoned his shirt. Battle climbed into her eyes and he licked his lips at the thought of it. Suddenly, she broke and ran for the blanket. She heard his laugh as he ran behind her, grabbed her about the waist and threw her brutally down on the straw and fell upon her. The battle was wild and furious as she fought with every ounce of strength she had. She felt him moving to a position between her legs and she writhed in his arms. No matter how she tried he pushed himself within her, enjoying her cry of combined rage and pain as he did. She could hear his panting breath in her ear and feel his heavy body pound against her until it quivered in releases. He looked down into her eyes and saw a live burning hatred there. Instead of leaving her body, he remained holding her.

"Your Steffan is at a ball tonight, dancing with a very beautiful woman named Morgana who was the first woman he ever loved, long before you. Shall I tell you about her? Shall I tell you that Steffan killed a man for her. That he loved her so much he would have given up his career and his wealth if she would have returned it."

"Liar! . . . Liar! . . . Liar!" she cried, but he felt the trembling in her body.

"Am I? Well to prove to you I am not, I'm going to bind you and take you to see for yourself."

She stared at him, disbelieving every word he said and wondering just what trick he had in store for her. He rose from her and snapped, "get up!"

She rose shakily to her feet. From the pocket of his jacket, he took a piece of rope and pulling her arms behind her he tied her wrists firmly. For a minute, he stood looking at her then he reached out, cupped her breasts in his hands then let them slide gently down over her body. He felt her stiffen. He took the blanket and wrapped it about her, then he put the rest of his clothes back on and taking hold of her arm, he drew her with him out the door. They passed no one in the hallway and up the steps. Once outside, he pushed her into a closed carriage. While they rode to their destination, he drew her onto his lap and enjoyed her frustrated tears as he fondled her body to his heart's content.

The carriage drew to a halt. Before he opened the door, he drew a handkerchief from his pocket and silenced all her protests by stuffing it in her mouth. Pulling her with him, they left the carriage. From what she could see they were in the back garden of a large estate. He drew her along with him; he entered and took her up a flight of back stairs to a small bedroom. There was no light in it, but across the room a door was ajar and through it light shone and a soft murmur of voices could be heard. "Quiet," he whispered. "If you are not, I will kill you where you stand. Do you understand?"

She nodded, unable to make a sound through the handkerchief that was almost choking her.

Drawing her with him they went to the door which stood ajar. He forced her close to the door and her eyes widened in horrified shock at what she saw. A large double bed, a woman of beautiful blonde loveliness in the arms of . . . Steffan! With a soft moaning sound of agonized pain, blackness overcame her and she collapsed in Jaspar's waiting arms.

Steffan had wakened from a dream feeling the perspiration on his body. Then he heard again the sound that had wakened him. Someone was knocking on the study door. He rose and stumbled towards it. The young maid handed him a small folded piece of paper. "A man left this for you, sir."

"A man? Did you recognize him?"

"No, sir," she said, "he just told me to give this to Captain Devers then he left."

"Thank you, Annette."

"Goodnight, sir."

"Goodnight."

He closed the door and opened the note; his heart leapt into his throat at the words.

If you want to know what has happened to your lady, you will come to this address immediately. You will come alone and not tell anyone where you are going. You will be followed so that if you tell anyone we will know. If you are not here by midnight, your lady will die without your ever seeing her again.

At the bottom of the note was an address. It was one he did not know, but at that moment he didn't care. All he knew was that no matter if it cost his life, someone knew something, had some word about Tamara and he had to find out.

He left the house immediately and cut across the gardens to the stable. There, without waking the stable boy, he saddled his own horse. The general area of the mysterious address was known to him and it did not take him more than a half hour to find the number he was searching for. He tied his horse, ran up the four steps to the door and knocked. He didn't have any idea what to expect or who. The door opened and a young girl stood before him. From the look on her face, he could see she expected him.

"I'm Steffan Devers."

"I know, sir, she's been expecting you. Will you follow me."

He walked in and closed the door, then he followed the girl up the dark winding stair. The candelabra she was carrying cast their shadows along the wall. At the top of the stairs, he could make out a length of hall. She kept walking so he continued to follow. When she stopped at the door, she turned to him.

"You're to go in here and wait, sir, my mistress will come to you soon."

"Who is your mistress? Whose house is this?"

"I can tell you nothing, sir, I have my orders to bring you here. Any other questions will be answered by my mistress . . . if she wants to."

The girl closed the door leaving Steffan alone in the room and wondering just who the mysterious woman was who had summoned him here and what and how she knew about Tamara. The room was large and very comfortable. From what he could see, the mysterious lady enjoyed the finest of luxury. It was lit by candles in such places as to give the room soft lighting . . . almost seductive he thought. The minutes ticked by and he began to wonder just how long she was going to keep him in suspense when a door in the far shadowy part of the room opened. From the lighted room he was in, to the semi-dark in which she stood all he could make out was the shadow of her figure. He heard the rustle of her gown, then she stepped into the light.

"Good evening, Steffan . . . we meet again," came the throaty well remembered voice of Morgana Kyle.

Of all the people in the world, Morgana Kyle was the last person Steffan expected. He stood in stunned silence for a moment, then bits and pieces of ideas began to move into place in his mind. Of course Morgana had no love for him, but what connection could she have to Tamara. "Morgana, where is my wife?"

"Oh, dear, how unpleasant you sound."

"Don't play with me, Morgana. I don't know how you got mixed up in our lives, but you surely don't intend to look upon this as some pleasant tete-a-tete. I want Tamara and I want her now. I don't want your reasons or excuses, I just want to find out where she is. I'll go wherever she is and take her home, we'll be out of your life and I want you to stay out of mine; you've never brought anything but grief and misery."

"You're very demanding for a man who could lose everything if he is not careful. Look at me Steffan." She held out her hand, palm up. "I hold your wife's life and maybe yours in the palm of my hand." She closed her fist and said grimly, "I could eliminate her just like this and," she smiled, "if you do not tread carefully, Steffan, I shall do just that."

"What do you want from me, Morgana? I'm not the same boy from long ago who was so easy to twist. Let me warn you too, if you so much as harm one hair of her head, I shall kill you with my bare hands if it's the last thing I ever do."

"Steffan, I brought you here because I know where she is and until you attacked me, I had the full intention of telling you where she was. Now, I must demand that we cease to attack one another. I have something you want, and you have something I want."

"What? What in God's name could I have that you want?"

"Are you willing to share a drink with me and talk of what we want or is this little meeting over?"

Steffan sighed, exasperated and angry yet knowing he was not going to get anywhere unless he played her game. He would do whatever she said until he heard the words he wanted, where Tamara was. Morgana walked to a table and poured two drinks, brought them back and handed him one. She took a small sip from hers, then laughed as he looked at his skeptically.

"Oh, Steffan, I needn't poison you. There are many ways and many times I could have had you dead if I had wanted it so. No, Steffan, I want you alive, very much alive."

He drank, then put the empty glass on the table. Without a word, Morgana refilled it. This time he did not see the passing of her hand over the glass nor the white powder that quickly dissolved in it. She handed it to him again and sat down in a chair waving him to one opposite her. "Morgana, come to the point."

"All right. Your wife is being held in the dungeon at the Tower."

Steffan's face went white. Stories of the Tower had been rampant before now. Strange terrible stories of a place so horrible strong men had died before they could be executed. "The

Tower?'' he gasped. ''Why . . . my God, that horrible place . . . why?''

''Drink and I'll tell you why.''

Steffan drank the drink in one gulp not even noticing the strange sweet taste. Within a minute she could notice the change in his eyes. He seemed to relax in his chair. With a throaty laugh, Morgana stood up and looked down on him, her face glowing with a contained excitement. Steffan seemed suddenly to feel as relaxed as if he had had a restful sleep. A feeling of well-being crept over him and his face lost the tense angry look that he had come with. Then suddenly, the room seemed to brighten, then fade away and he stood alone in a strange place surrounded by beautiful wavering colors.

It was a hallucinogenic drug she had given him, a drug she had used for the same purpose as now; for his mind was open to her controlling suggestions and she knew exactly what to suggest to him and knew that he would see, feel and know only what she told him.

''Come,'' she said in a soft melodic voice. ''It's me, Steffan, Tamara. Come to me and love me. I'm alone and I'm so frightened.''

''Tamara,'' Steffan whispered and he looked up at Morgana seeing just what her words had told him he was seeing . . . Tamara.

''Oh, Steffan,'' she crooned. ''I need you, I love you. Come to me.''

He rose from his seat reaching for her and she moved into his arms enjoying the strong feel of them as she had once before.

''Tam,'' he whispered as he held her and began to caress her. ''Tam, I love you. Stay with me.''

''I will love. I will,'' she sighed.

Within minutes, she cast aside her clothes and Steffan saw only his golden gypsy from the cliffs on Marriott Island. He lifted her and carried her to the bed. There he made wild and burning love to the one he thought was Tamara. While slanted pain-filled green eyes watched and filled with the agonizing pain of betrayal.

Thirty-eight

For the next three days, Steffan lived in a bright pleasant world where Tamara walked with him, laughed with him, and loved him, while Tamara lived in a world clouded with pain so black and devastating she could not bear it.

She had cried all the tears she had and had lain in a curled ball on the straw of the cell to which Jaspar had sent her. She was uncaring now of her future, all her mind knew was that Steffan had betrayed her in a manner so horrible that it had destroyed every other thought.

Steffan's family had instituted a search for him when they found that a note had been delivered to him, but for three days, the search was useless, for there was no sign of him anywhere. They were frantic with worry about what could have become of him. Then a message was again sent . . . one to tell them that the trial of Tamara Marriott for treason would be held the next day, and that the Devers family and Martin Gillis were forbidden access to the courtroom. They would not be permitted to either see the trial or send even a visual message of encouragement to Tamara. She now stood alone.

A man walked the streets of London for three days before the trial, he was a casually dressed young sailor, open, friendly and free with coins to buy ale for men who would sit and talk to him. He encouraged stories and rumors, especially those of the now well publicized trial of a notorious pirate lady, and the very mysterious disappearance of the man who had captured her.

Mikel found a source Martin Gillis and Maxwell could not have found with all their money. It took him much longer than he thought it would to find a substantial lead to where Tamara was being held; in fact the trial was well into its fourth day before he paid his way into the presence of one Jeb Crusten, jailor in the deep cellars of the Tower. Oiling his loose tongue well with both rum and money, Mikel received a story . . . a story that twisted his insides in black furious rage, a story of the beautiful naked girl in cell six who had become the personal property of one Captain Jaspar Sinclair.

"Mind ye," he chuckled at Mikel, "The cap'n says when he's tired of her I can taste a little myself, and she looks like a right nice morsel to taste. Only she don't seem so chipper lately, I guess the trial has taken some of the fight out of her. When the captain stripped her and threw her back in her cell the other day after the trial, she didn't even cover herself with the blanket like she used to, just lay there all curled up and cryin.' " 'course Cap'n Sinclair, don't pay no mind to her cryin'. I was watchin', and he took her right enough, you could hear him laugh because she couldn't fight him off anymore like she did the first time." He licked his dry lips and his eyes glowed with a deep insatiable hunger. "She's a pretty thing, all gold and round and soft. I aim to take my time when I get a chance at her . . . yep I aim to take my time and enjoy her. It'll be my only chance before they hang her. Shame . . . shame to waste that pretty little piece by hangin', sure is a shame . . ."

He was so drunk by this time that he did not even see the sweat on Mikel's face, the clenched teeth and the trembling fury that almost overcame him. By the time Jeb had finally collapsed, Mikel was gone. He strode the streets of London in an angry fog. Then he began to form a plan.

Tamara felt herself jerked to her feet and she looked up through dazed eyes at Jaspar who thrust a dress into her arms. "Put this on," he ordered.

Obediently, she slipped the dress over her cold naked body, and stood weaving on her feet, hunger and physical abuse numbing her even to the cold. He dragged her out of her cell and thrust her into the arms of Jeb . . . it was Jeb's job to take her to the courtroom each day.

Today would be the last day of the trial. The three judges would then decide her fate and it was obvious to the blood-thirsty crowd that packed the courtroom just what that fate would be.

The court was packed and no one noticed a roughly dressed sailor who pushed himself forward. When Tamara came in, she was held by each arm by a huge burly jailer. Mikel would not believe this was the laughing, carefree Tamara he had known as a child. He watched as her eyes searched the room in a moment of hope, and saw that hope die again when she did not find the one she sought. As the trial had gone on he could see that Tamara's defense was far less than adequate. There was no doubt in anyone's mind how it was going to end. Tamara stood still; she refused to let the crowd see her pain and she had long ago closed off the farce of a trial from her consciousness. She heard the voices drone on and one telling lie upon lie. When the day was finally over, Mikel left behind the closing words because he could not bear to see Tamara dragged away. As he turned toward the door, a huge strong hand gripped his arm and he found himself looking into the eyes of a coldly furious Andrew Marriott.

"Outside," was all Andrew said. Mikel nodded and left. He walked toward a tavern knowing Andrew would follow. He sat in a dark shadowed corner and ordered ale, in a few moments, Andrew slid onto the bench opposite him.

"Mikel, where is Steffan Devers?"

Mikel laughed harshly. "It seems the brave captain turned Tamara over to the authorities and left town. No one has seen him since just before the trial began . . . the bastard abandoned her," Mikel said furiously. "And I'll tell you just what he abandoned her to." He went on to explain all he knew and watched the rage burn in Andrew Marriott's eyes. "And I," he groaned painfully, "Came here to stop you from doing Steffan any harm. I fell for his lies too. When he took my daughter from me, I believed he loved her . . . he will die for those lies . . . die in a way he never dreamed possible." Andrew leaned forward and Mikel saw the death in his eyes. "Here are our plans, Mikel," he said. "Tamara will be out of that prison before they get a chance to do her any more harm."

"And Steffan?"

"In time one of my people will find him and tell me. When they do, Steffan Devers will begin to pay, and he will continue to pay for a long, long time."

The day that Tamara was to be sentenced found the courtroom crowded. There was a strange waiting silence when Tamara was brought forward and stood alone in the prisoners' box. For the first time in days, Tamara began to reach out from the dark place Steffan's betrayal had thrust her. She stood defiantly, chin up and quiet. Andrew and Mikel watched her with pride as she did not even flinch when the guilty verdict was given and the judge sentenced her.

"You are to be taken from here on Wednesday, the tenth day

of August and hung by the neck until dead, and may God have mercy on your soul.''

A low sigh seemed to ripple through the crowd when it was requested if she had any last words to say.

''Yes,'' she said, her voice low, yet it carried to the furthest corner of the quiet room. ''I stand here condemned of treason. I am innocent. The only guilt I carry is loyalty to the country and the people I love. I do not regret what I have done and I would do so again had I the opportunity. You did not catch me by courage, ability, or force of arms, but by the lowest grade of treachery and betrayal.'' She raised her fist toward Heaven, ''As God is my witness, I call down a curse on the Devers family whose cowardly son put me here. If it were in my power I would kill him like the animal he is. If he is an example of what you call bravery, if he is the example of the man who represents your country, then you are doomed to die. The Colonies will gain their freedom, and I pray that one of the guns that I supplied them will carry the bullet that ends the life of the inhuman monster who used lies, deceit and treachery to gain his ends. May his soul and the souls of all his family rot in eternal hell.''

Her eyes ablaze with her anger and her tangled hair flowing about her slender form, she created a picture no one in that courtroom would forget, especially the two men who loved her and watched her with deep pride.

She was dragged out of the courtroom and taken back to her cell to await the carrying out of her death sentence two days later.

Mikel and Andrew sat together for hours making plans for rescuing Tamara. ''One thing is for certain,'' Mikel said firmly.

''What?''

''Our plans include Jaspar Sinclair. We take him with us. Maybe Tamara might have some plans for him. At least he deserves to pay something for helping keep her.''

Mikel had never spoken to Andrew of Jaspar's brutal rape of Tamara. He would keep it a secret not to hurt either Tamara or Andrew; but he wanted Jaspar. Maybe, he thought, it might ease Tamara to have some way of returning what had been done to her.

''I agree, Mikel,'' Andrew said softly, for without effort, he had read between the lines and he knew all that Mikel had left unsaid. If Tamara took no revenge on Jaspar Sinclair . . . Andrew would.

''Mikel, there is someone else involved in this. Jaspar does not hold enough power to do what has been done. Maybe for a day we can follow him, try to find out who he meets. I would feel much better if we could exact some payment for the others behind this."

"All right. I'll follow him; you are too well known. It might be best if you're seen as little as possible."

It did not take Mikel long to find where Jaspar lived. He saw him come home with a group of friends, laughing and discussing the trial. The revelry inside the house went on a long time and it was well after dark when everyone but Jaspar left. Mikel remained, still and vigilant. He was rewarded when he saw a small carriage being brought around to the front door. He was not worried about being able to follow Jaspar unless he left the city. The streets of London prohibited, by their narrow and rough cobbled condition, travelling too fast.

The carriage seemed in no particular hurry and Mikel had no difficulty keeping up with it. Finally, he was rewarded when it stopped in front of a high iron gate. Beyond it, Mikel could see the huge house that stood enclosed by high stone walls.

Jaspar opened the gates himself, then the carriage rolled in and the gates clanged shut behind him. Mikel would find out as soon as he could who resided in the huge mansion behind the forbidding stone walls. Inside the house, Jaspar stood in the center of the drawing room, his hands folded behind him, rocking on his heels and a smug pleased smile on his face as he listened to the woman who stood a few feet from him. "I've given him the drug a little every day. By the time his little bride is hung, Steffan Devers will be addicted to it. He will be lost. We will then release him to his fate. He'll never be sure of what happened to him here, all he will know is the pain of being too late to help her and the burning need for the drug to keep him sane. I would say that Steffan Devers' life can be considered over, for knowing the kind of man he is, the guilt and the drug will drive him to insanity."

"The only thing I regret, Morgana, is that he will not know everything; I should like to see him crawl."

"Ah," she laughed. "That will be arranged too, my love. When the hanging is over, we will . . . neglect to give him the drug for a day or so. He will become a whimpering beggar. Then you can have the pleasure, along with me, of telling him . . . everything. Your pleasure with his wife before she died, and the fact that you and I hold the drug he will need for his very life. If it pleases you, we could even make him beg a little."

Jaspar laughed triumphantly at the thought of breaking Steffan and making him beg. He walked to Morgana's side and drew her up into his arms. Crushing her to him, he kissed her hungrily. "I want to see him."

"All right, come."

They walked up the stairs and into the small bedroom. Jaspar looked across the room toward the man who lay on the bed.

Steffan's mind drifted in a kaleidoscopic world where he wandered again with Tamara to the places he had found the warmth of love. The only thing that Morgana had not taken into consideration was the size and strength of Steffan's body. The drug she had been giving him was not enough to completely deteriorate him. Since it had been several hours since she had given him any, his mind was slowly drawn back to reality by the voices slipping through the mist of his mind.

"Is he asleep?" came a masculine voice.

"No," the low feminine reply. "He's in another world where I intend to keep him until Tamara Marriott-Devers has breathed her last. After that will come the pleasure of watching him suffer."

He strained to catch the words that seemed to waver like shadows against his consciousness. Bits and pieces of it flowed about him, but he could not put reason or thought to what he had heard. They talked for a few more minutes over him then he heard the door close and he was alone. He wanted to drift back to that sweet and warm world he'd left, but some urgency seemed to hold him. Some rational thought seemed to be tearing at his brain. He could feel the tentacles of it twist and search in his mind until suddenly with an intense touch of pain the woman's voice came to him. Morgana!

Why? he demanded mentally. Why was he with Morgana when it was Tamara he sought.

He tried to move, but it seemed as if every muscle he had was made of water. He could feel himself begin to perspire, both with an intense need for Tamara and a strange gripping need for something else. Tiny tingles of pain crept through his limbs and centered in his body like a huge monster with tearing claws. Think, think something pounded within him, but the strain of it brought such misery that again he began to let it all slip from him. Then suddenly the thought of Morgana again flushed in his mind and with it came the identity of the man . . . Jaspar Sinclair.

He could feel the hot tears of frustration as he again tried to force his mind and body to work together. Keeping his body very still, he put every ounce of concentrated though on Morgana, Jaspar and where he was, and with an effort that made him groan, the pieces began slowly to come together. Although he did not know what had been done to him, he began to remember all that had passed before.

He looked toward the windows and found them dark, but he wondered how many nights had passed since he had walked into this room to find Morgana. He had to get out of there and get to Tamara, get to her before they could try her, get to her before she could begin to think he had deceived and deserted her.

Again he tried to move. Every muscle and nerve complained, sweat stood out on his forehead and his heart began to pound so furiously that he thought it would burst and still he only moved a few inches. Inch by inch, he laboriously worked until he was sitting on the edge of the bed. Suddenly, his body was gripped in muscular convulsions that brought a cry of pain to his lips and set his teeth to chattering. The convulsions ripped his body as wave after wave of nausea and cold chills washed over him. He was naked and he wrapped his arms about his body to try to contain the reaction to the need for the drug he had been given. His clothes were nowhere in sight and he did not have the strength to search for them. He rose slowly to his feet, only sheer force of will keeping him erect. Will, and the face of Tamara that wavered in front of his eyes. He worked his way along the bed to grip the post at the foot. From there it was about six feet to the wall and he wasn't too sure he could make it. With a supreme effort, he pushed himself away from the wall and staggered forward coming up against the wall weak but grateful he had gotten this far. Slowly, step by step, he moved against the wall, working his way towards large glass doors that led out to a terrace. He hoped the terrace had some kind of exit, if not . . . he was lost, for there was no way he could hope to escape through the house.

There was a large chest between him and the windows. It stood about six feet in height and had two doors in the front. When he reached it, he opened one of the doors and sighed with his first touch of good luck in days . . . his clothes hung inside.

It took him over half an hour to get his clothes from the chest. Laboriously, he climbed into shirt and pants. The most difficult thing was to get his feet into the boots. Every time he looked down his head throbbed in sickening pain and his balance was so affected he almost fell over.

Finally he worked his way across the rest of the room to the door. He was breathing with great difficulty and sweat now soaked his body which was trembling so badly, he could hardly stand erect. The door clicked easily, and he was grateful it was not locked, then he groaned to himself bitterly, "Why should they lock it?" Drugged as he was, they felt he could not get the strength to escape.

Grimly determined now, he pushed the door open and was grateful for the chill night air that caused him to shiver but helped him to regain his wavering senses.

He moved across the dark terrace following the stone banister. He could have cried when his hand found the edge of the banister and felt it curve downward. Steps! A way out! He clung to the banister and slowly, step by step, made his way down to the bottom. He could not see in the dark garden, but he could see the shadow of a wall on the other side. With slow agonized movements, he made his way towards it.

Mikel watched Jaspar leave. He took note of the number and location of the house then followed Jaspar to his home where he remained until he was sure Jaspar had retired for the night, then he returned to his ship where Andrew Marriott waited in his cabin.

The next morning they again found the house Jaspar had visited the night before and it did not take long for Andrew Marriott to find out who owned the house. The names Lyle Whitfield and Morgana Kyle meant nothing to them at the moment, but circulating around a few taverns, Andrew and Mikel found out quickly who Lyle Whitfield was; of Morgana Kyle no one seemed to know, so Andrew and Mikel both jumped to the same conclusion, that Lyle Whitfield was the guilty one and Morgana was no one of importance except for being Lyle's current mistress.

Andrew's ship was anchored a few miles down the coast from the harbor that held Mikel's ship. When Andrew returned to his ship, it was to gather a few of his men who had known and loved his daughter. He told them all what had happened and watched the wild anger ripple over them. While he outlined plans, Mikel returned to tell Mellie all that had happened. Mellie's face was stained with tears when he finished and for the first time, she surrendered her faith in Steffan Devers.

As the last night of her life passed, Tamara sat alone in her dark cell. She prayed for herself and for her father and Mikel. She remembered every good thing and firmly closed her mind against everything else. She refused to let Steffan enter her mind for the pain was too much to bear and she knew she had to gather her strength to face what tomorrow had to bring. Sleep was an impossibility because of the intense cold, her hunger, and the fear that threatened to sneak into her dreams. "Papa," she whispered, aching for the strong arm of Andrew Marriott to hold her together. "I'm your daughter, Papa. I won't shame you. I would so like to be able to tell you just once again that I love you . . . oh, I love you, Papa." She sobbed covering her face with her hands. She did not hear the door open nor see Jaspar come inside until the light he carried penetrated her hand. She looked up at him and the satisfied, amused look in his eyes sapped all her rationality.

"Your father should be hanging beside you. If I have my way, we will return to Marriott Isalnd and dispatch him as rapidly as possible."

"Are you a beast—an animal that you cannot leave me alone now? Tomorrow, your brutality will be rewarded, that should be enough for you."

"My, my," Jaspar cautioned. "And here I was trying to keep your last night from being lonely and you do not appreciate my devotion."

"Leave me alone!"

"No, my dear," he laughed. "I'm afraid I enjoy your remarkable charms too much to do that; after all, tomorrow night and the rest of the nights I shall have to make do with second best. Why should I not enjoy the best while I have it?"

He was startled at the almost animal snarl that escaped her lips as she backed away from him, her hands stiffened into claws. She crouched and glared up at him. It startled him for a moment, for he thought she had finally lost her mind.

"I will fight you to my last breath. You will have to kill me before you can touch me again. I will not let your foulness touch me again."

He stalked her, amused at the game he knew could end only one way. She had the will, but the lack of food and sleep and Jaspar's physical abuse had weakened her. He knew it . . . and so did she. He feinted toward her several times in quick little jumps that caused her to jump away from him. He chuckled as he played her little game with her until he had her cornered then, he reached out and grasped her. She fought wildly and with every ounce of strength she had. She was choking on her own tears as she felt her body bound to him by the strength of one arm while he grasped her hair in his fist and held her head immobile, while leisurely he began to let his lips roam over her cheeks and throat.

"No," she sobbed. "Please, I beg you leave me be tonight."

"Oh, my pretty," he whispered. "No man could leave your ripe beauty alone." He twisted her in his arms until he had her back against him, both of her arms pulled behind her so she could not get free. Casually, he reached around and stripped away the front of her dress and caressed her breasts.

Suddenly it came to her that he wanted to shame her, make her beg, and a cold anger flooded her. She stopped fighting and stood still and erect. She placed her attention on the slit of window above her head and willed her mind to control her body.

He felt the change in her and slowly released her. He stepped in front of her. He admired the wild beauty that she was; her disheveled hair fell in tangled sun bronzed curls to her waist. Her half clad body glowed gold in the light of the lantern. The beauty of her face and the softness of her slender body surpassed any woman he had ever dreamed of before.

Again he reached out and ran the tips of his fingers over the smooth texture of her skin. "I wish I could take you home to my bed where you belong. To make love to a goddess like you is pure joy."

"Love!" she spat. "Do not call what you do love, it is the lust of a rabid animal."

He reached out as casually as if it were an afterthought and struck her across the face hard enough to make her stumble back a few steps. She was backed against the wall now, waiting for the attack she knew was coming. He took the three steps that separated them and with a confident laugh, he reached for her again. His hands never reached their mark for a cold voice from the door cut through every thought in his mind.

"Don't put your hands on her again."

He spun around and looked into the cold and forbidding faces of Andrew Marriott and Mikel Robbins.

Mikel had brought a bottle of wine to the door of the Tower, claiming a ribald friendship with the jailer and as a friend wanting to help relieve some of the tedious hours of his job. The man could not exactly remember the friendly young man, but he eyed the bottle of wine. Jaspar had promised him the girl to warm his bed for the balance of the night and the wine would help him enjoy her charms more. Once inside, it did not take Mikel long to overpower him and tie him securely. Then he opened the door for Andrew. They had to search through three floors of cells before they found the one that Tamara was in. They heard the voices and came to the door, pushing it open. The sight before them enraged them both. They stood between Jaspar and the door and watched him whirl about at the sound of Andrew's voice. Tamara's eyes widened in disbelieving joy. A sob escaped her as she ran to her father and he gathered her up in his arms. The feel of the safe strength of her father's arms brought the tears as nothing else had.

"Tamara," Andrew said hoarsely, "my child, are you all right?"

"Yes, Papa, yes, now you are here, I am. Oh, Father I prayed for you . . . I prayed," she cried as she collapsed against him. Gently he put his cloak about her and lifted her in his arms. Mikel stood with drawn sword, the point of which touched the flesh of Jaspar's throat and it was obvious to all three men that he would have liked nothing better than to run it through him.

"Patience, Mikel," Andrew called calmly, "our friend has a debt to pay before we dispatch him to the hell where he belongs. Bring him along."

Andrew carried Tamara out of the cell and Mikel motioned for Jaspar to follow, a slight prick of the sword hastening Jaspar's exit.

At the same moment, Lyle Whitfield stepped down from his carriage in front of his house. When the carriage had left, he walked up the steps to the door, but before he could open it, four men stepped from the darkness and attacked him so quickly and so expertly, he had no chance to resist. In a minute, he was bound and pushed down the drive to another carriage that awaited them outside the gates.

A half hour later, Tamara, Andrew, and the two men were on board the *Sea Borne* and on their way to Marriott Island. Mikel stayed behind to wait and watch for the reappearance of Steffan Devers.

At Devers Hall the stunned family tried every means to find the key to Tamara's release. Steffan seemed to have dropped from the face of the earth. Ellen had not slept for what seemed to her to be ages. She felt that her son was in need of their help, desperate and alone and they could not reach him. Tom, worried about Steffan and Tamara and frightened for a Cecile who seemed to have physically collapsed. He knew in her condition, this was dangerous but he could not find the words to help her for he was as scared as she was.

As for Martin and Maxwell, they had exhausted every means and no sign of Steffan could be found. They had heard of Tamara's last words at the trial and realized her desperate fear that Steffan seemed to have deserted her.

Ellen sat twisting her handkerchief in her lap while Cecile sat on a stool in front of the fire, a warm shawl about her and her shoulders slumped as she silently grieved for all that had happened in the past few days. Their whole world seemed to have collapsed.

"Martin," Maxwell said, "are you sure . . ."

"Maxwell, I have tried everything I know. Steffan has simply vanished."

"He's dead," Ellen said tearfully, "my son is dead."

"Ellen, no!" Maxwell said. "We must have hope. If he were dead, his body would be found. No! I'll never believe he is dead until I see his body."

Tom went and knelt by Cecile; seeing her silent tears he drew her into his arms. The room was quiet. All mourned for the two people they loved.

It was then that a loud shriek shattered the stillness. At first, they were all paralyzed with shock, then they all ran toward the source of the scream.

The front door stood open and a young maid was staring at a tall man who was half-carrying, half-dragging the half-dead body of Steffan Devers.

Thirty-nine

Jeff Sables paced the decks of the *Windswept*. He'd been doing the same thing for days, his impatience to reach the Colonial shores forbidding him to be comfortable doing anything else. Lang and Bright sat below deck playing cards in the cabin. The three of them shared a small cabin together for the ship was not a passenger packet, but a ship to be equipped for war. Nelson intended to turn it over to the Colonials in hope they would offer him her command. Nelson stopped on the quarterdeck and with a half smile on his lips, he watched the young man who walked the deck below him.

He liked Jeff Sables and considered him a bright ambitious youth who would make an excellent ally in any conflict. He had played chess in his cabin with Jeff and being an expert had been surprised when Jeff had beaten him soundly three games out of seven. It was unprecedented in Nelson's life, and he thoroughly enjoyed the challenge.

He had heard, finally, the story behind Jeff's journey to the Colonies. He hoped Jeff found his woman and his son, but he had his doubts. Brandy Maguire could be anywhere in the Colonies now, maybe even married. He prayed this was not so, for he had watched Jeff's face as he spoke of Brandy and the son he had never seen and he realized Jeff would be brokenhearted to find her in the arms of another man. He was sure of one thing; Jeff Sables would not give up his son quite that easily.

"Mr. Sables," Nelson shouted.

Jeff turned and looked up toward the quarterdeck. He could still not get used to being called Mister when he had struggled so long and so hard to be called captain. "Yes, sir?"

"Would you care to join me in my cabin for lunch?"

"Yes, sir," Jeff grinned.

"Please tell your friends they're welcome also."

Jeff nodded and headed for the companionway to tell Lang and Bright.

They sat at a table playing cards listlessly and talking quietly when the door opened. "Gentlemen," Jeff grinned as he came in, "we've been summoned to the captain's cabin for lunch."

"Good," Lang said quickly, "this gambler was taking my last farthing anyway. I'm grateful for the interruption."

"Calls me a gambler because he's a terrible player," Bright grinned amiably. "I believe my mother could whip the pants off him."

Lang chuckled. "Remind me to challenge her when we get home."

None of them spoke for a moment as they all realized that home was a place they might not be seeing for a long time. "Well, come along, get yourself all ship-shape and let's go and have lunch with Admiral Nelson. I know he's close-mouthed but maybe we can get something out of him about what ship we'll be on and what rank we'll have."

"God, I don't know about us, Jeff," Lang said, "but if they don't give you a captaincy they're making a big mistake. They'd be losing some of the best naval material that they have probably ever seen in their short history."

"Thanks, Lang, but I'd even consider it an honor to serve under a man the caliber of Nelson."

They left the cabin and in a few minutes, knocked on Admiral Nelson's door.

"Come in."

Once inside, Nelson welcomed them and offered each a drink. "Sit down gentlemen, make yourselves comfortable, please."

They sat around the square table that had been covered by a white linen cloth and set with china and crystal, a complete shock to each young man who had seldom seen such luxury at sea. Nelson sat at the head of the table.

"I believe it is time that I spoke to you gentlemen of the future. I've opened my orders. You four are to retain your ranks, and you, Captain Sables, will be offered the first available ship. In the meantime, you will be given quarters ashore and," his eyes twinkled toward Jeff, "given a short time free of duty to get yourselves settled, maybe tie up any loose ends that might need tending before you go to sea."

Jeff smiled broadly as did Lang and Bright, overjoyed at Jeff's rank and the time to find Brandy.

"Are there many ships available, sir?" Jeff said.

"No, but they're building as fast as they possibly can."

"They should have Tom Braydon here."

"They will, as soon as he and Steffan can come," Nelson said, "but why especially Tom?"

"Tom's father builds the most seaworthy ships in the world, and some of it has rubbed off on Tom. If anyone knows a quality vessel, it's Tom Braydon."

"Well, maybe when they get here, we'll find many uses for Tom Braydon."

"I know Tom would like to build ships, but if there's a war, he'll be beside Steffan as his first mate. There's no way Tom would stay ashore while Steffan takes a ship out to fight. They're not only brothers-in-law, they're damn good friends."

"And your friends, too?"

"The best, sir . . . the best. I would like nothing better than to have a man like either Steffan or Tom fight alongside me."

"Well, Sables," Nelson sighed, "I have a feeling we're all going to need all the friends we've got. This is quite a little chore we've set out for ourselves. The Navy is so small it's almost nonexistent. We'll need every man and every ship we can get."

Lang stood, humor glistening in his eyes, and raised a glass, "a toast, gentlemen, to the men who are going to prove there's truth in the old adage."

"And what's that?" Nelson laughed.

"Why," Lang said innocently, "that it's quality not quantity which wins the game."

They all laughed and drank a toast to the birth of a new nation and a new Navy. They arrived on the Colonial coast backed by a full wind that carried them gracefully into the harbor. It was still several hours before Jeff was free to go ashore. Land and Bright went to find lodgings while Jeff headed for the address he had memorized a long time ago. He stood at the door of the Whitticer residence, praying that if Brandy was not still here at least they were able to tell him where she had gone.

The door was opened by a comely young maid who smiled, then blushed prettily at Jeff's responding smile.

"Might I speak to either Mr. or Mrs. Whitticer please? My name is Captain Jeffery Sables. Would you please tell them it is very very important and I'll only take a few minutes of their time. I only have a question or two to ask."

"Please come in, Captain Sables."

She escorted him to a small sitting room and amid confused dimpled smiles, bade him wait.

Jeff's nerves were drawn to a fine point, and the few minutes wait felt like hours.

"Captain Sables?" A low voice came from the doorway. Jeff turned and looked at the woman who stood there.

Roxanne Whitticer was a woman of about fifty, he surmised. She stood stiffly erect and he noticed immediately the intelligent friendly eyes. "You do not need to tell me who you are, Captain Sables. I need only look at you to know I have seen that face before. Am I right in surmising you are looking for a young woman named Brandy?"

Jeff grinned, relieved that her attitude seemed so welcome.

"And the child . . . " he began.

"Is your son, is he not?" she smiled in return.

"Yes. Do you know where they are? Are they still here?"

"No, they are no longer here, Brandy's indenture has expired. She has taken her child and gone." If Roxanne was worried about Jeff's reason for coming here, the worry fled her mind as she saw his face go pale and the smile fade.

"Not here," he said in alarm.

"No, but don't be concerned. Brandy took what little money she had and opened a small dress shop. It's not too far from here. I should be glad to take you there if you don't mind a wait for a few minutes."

"Mrs. Whitticer . . . how is she? Is she well? Has it been hard for her? Can you tell me about little Jeff?"

"On the way, I will tell you all about him. He's a lovely, lovely child. Brandy is doing such a good job of raising him. Oh, I admit he can be a little devil at times, but both he and his mother are people to be proud of. I'm afraid you will not recognize Brandy when you meet her."

"There's . . . there's no one . . . I mean . . . she isn't . . . married or anything?"

"No," Roxanne laughed. "She is not married, but quite a few gentlemen would like to have her as their wife."

"She's mine!" Jeff said quickly, then he realized what he had said and how he had said it.

"If she's yours," Roxanne said pointedly, "why is she here?"

"Brandy left without telling me, either about herself or the child. It took me a long time to find out where she went. I'll tell you the whole story since it's obvious Brandy has not. But I don't want you to think what happened was because I didn't love Brandy. I did . . . I do, and I want to see our son."

"All right. I shall go and have our buggy harnessed and we will take you around to Brandy's little shop. I should like to be there when the two of you meet. I don't know who will be more surprised, you or Brandy, but I can't wait to see."

Jeff couldn't picture the changes he was hearing about. He held one vision in his mind of Brandy, beautiful and girlish when they met under the bridge near the Academy, and his impatient nerves began to tighten as he thought that after all this time, it was now a matter of minutes until he saw her again.

On the way to Brandy's shop, Jeff told Roxanne the entire story of what had happened between him and Brandy. She could see for herself the deep desire to find again the woman he had loved and lost and the child he had never seen.

When they stopped in front of the shop, Roxanne looked at it, surprise in her eyes. "That's funny, Brandy's shop is usually very busy at this time of day. It . . . it looks as though it's closed."

Jeff jumped down from the carriage and went to the door. He tried the knob and found it locked. It was only then that he noticed the sign in the window.

CLOSED. Will reopen August twenty fifth. Gone for personal reasons and will be back soon.

> Thank you,
> Brandy Maguire, Owner

Jeff was at first deeply disappointed, then he noticed the change in the writing compared to the last note Brandy had written him. He smiled in pleasure knowing that Brandy had continued to learn what he had begun teaching her.

"Captain Sables," Roxanne called, "is it closed?"

Jeff went back to the buggy. "It's closed. She has gone to a place named Cumberledge. Do you know where it is?"

"Yes, it's a small town not too far from here, but why in Heaven's name would she go there. I'm sure I know all her friends and acquaintances, and I know of no one from Cumberledge unless she's met someone who lives . . ." She stopped when she saw the dark look cloud Jeff's eyes. To travel as far as Cumberledge, someone would have to be important."

"I hate to impose on you, Mrs. Whitticer, but would it be possible to borrow your buggy today? I will go to Cumberledge and find her."

"Of course. Just take me home and you may use it."

459

Jeff took her home, received instructions from her husband on how to get to Cumberledge and was on his way within an hour.

It was nearing dark when he arrived and he went to the closest livery stable to have the horse fed and cared for while he began his search for Brandy. If she was not visiting a friend, then she would most certainly stay at an inn. He found there were three in the town. Luck glanced swiftly in his direction when he found the inn they had stayed at first, then he turned his head away when the innkeeper told him she had left with her friends the next day.

"Do you know where they went?"

"No, sir."

"Who were her friends?"

"Let me see . . . a Mrs. Marthie Price and her son Jonah. Nice people. I think the boy, Jonah, was on his way to join the army."

"Join the army," Jeff said, excitement stirred in him, "and just where would the boy be joining the army?"

"I don't know, sir, t'was supposed to be here, and a lot of their trainin' is goin' to be here, but where they're signing up sir, I just don't rightly know."

"Thank you, sir," Jeff smiled and rewarded the man with a coin that brought a smile to his face.

"You're quite welcome. I hope you find your friends," he called to Jeff's retreating form. Jeff waved and left the inn. Where to find someone who knew where they might have gone? Of course he chuckled, where else would men talk of war except in a tavern where their thoughts could be loosened by tankards of ale.

An hour spent in the tavern and Jeff went back to his buggy and headed it through the night toward the town of Braddock. He travelled most of the night. The sun was rising when he again left his horse and buggy in the care of a livery and went looking for his family.

He walked down the small main street to the center of the town. In the center, he found a huge grassy area about five hundred feet square. There was a small group of men in the center of it and others approaching from all directions. He casually moved about watching the slow gathering of men. Then he looked up one of the narrow side streets and saw a man and a boy approaching them. His heart froze as they drew near him for looking into the child's face was like looking into a mirror. He heard them talking as they approached him and the words made his heart begin to beat furiously.

"Now, for God's sake, Jeff, be good today and don't get into any mischief. Your mother's going to be mad enough at me lettin' you come to muster."

"I won't do anything, Jonah, honest."

"That's what you told me last time, then I found you had swiped the officer's gun and was goin' to practice with it. If your mother knew about that, I'd be skinned alive and you'd never be able to come with me again."

"You won't tell her, will you Jonah?"

"No, not if you're good, but one more bit of mischief and home you'll go."

"I'll sit on the edge of the green and be good, Jonah."

"Ummm," Jonah answered suspiciously.

"Jonah?"

"Yeah?"

"I want to fight, too."

"You're too little."

"But Mama says I'm the man of the family."

"I don't think she meant for you to go to war though, Jeff. She just meant because you ain't got no father you'll grow up to be the only man in the house."

"Oh . . . Jonah?"

"What now, Jeff?"

"Was that what Robbie meant when he said I was a bastard? Doesn't a bastard have a father? Is that why you hit him?"

"Jeff, for God's sake why do you always have to ask so many questions. I hit Robbie cause I don't like him and he's got too big a mouth."

They were just passing Jeff now and as they did, the boy looked up into Jeff's face and smiled. To Jeff it was like a physical blow. "You're my son," he wanted to shout, "You're no bastard, you're mine."

"Hello," was all he could manage.

"Hello, sir," the child replied.

"Hello," was repeated by an impatient Jonah. "Come on, Jeff, or I'll be late."

"I'm going to be sitting here watching you drill, the boy can sit with me if he pleases," Jeff smiled. "It will keep him out of trouble."

"Jeff, will you sit here on this bench where I can see you?"

"Yes, Jonah."

"All right, but remember," he said and Jeff smiled for he

461

knew the words were more for him than the boy, "I'll be watching you every minute so don't get into any trouble."

Jonah moved out on the green and Jeff and the boy sat down on the bench to watch. It was then that the wide-eyed boy took notice of Jeff's uniform. His eyes grew wide for his interest was no longer on the men who gathered before him. Jeff wore the uniform of a sea captain, a man who had the right to walk the deck of the huge, tall-masted ships that held young Jeff's mind and heart.

"Sir?" he began hesitantly, for he was quite in awe of the tall handsome man who sat beside him.

"Yes?"

"You're a captain, sir?"

"I am."

Young Jeff gulped. "You have your own ship, sir?"

"Not yet, but I will soon."

He could see a million questions that hovered on the lips of the boy and smiled at young Jeff's valiant effort to contain them, an effort he was slowly losing ground on.

"I'm going to be a sailor some day."

"Oh?"

"As soon as I get big."

"Why do you want to be a sailor? Why not a soldier like your friend over there?"

"My mother took me on board a ship once. They're so . . . so great."

"What does your mother say about your being a sailor?"

"She doesn't know yet. I'll tell her when I'm older, at least old enough to go."

"Don't you love your mother?"

Young Jeff looked up at him, absolute amazement on his face. "My mother is the prettiest and nicest mother in the whole world."

"Then why do you really want to leave her?"

"I'm going to go . . . and find my father."

Jeff was quiet. The voice of the boy told him all he wanted to know. They sat quietly watching the maneuvers ahead of them.

The maneuvers broke for a short while so that the men could rest. Jonah made his way to Jeff and his unknown companion. He had kept one eye on the two for there was something about this stranger that gave him the feeling he was not going to remain so.

462

"Quite a display; is this type of thing going on all over?"

"Yes, sir," Jonah grinned. "Give us enough time and you'll see an army that will surprise the English."

"I'm glad to hear that, for I've just become part of this country's Navy and I think we will all need each other if we intend to make this work."

Jonah laughed, "I don't believe we have much of a Navy."

"We will soon," Jeff grinned. "We brought one ship with us and the greatest admiral who has ever walked the quarterdeck of a ship, Horatio Nelson."

Jonah stood wide-eyed and respectful. "You know Admiral Nelson?"

"I crossed with him."

"I'm very pleased to meet you, sir," Jonah stretched out his hand to Jeff who took it in a hearty grip. "I have to take young Jeff home soon. Would you like to come? I'm sure my mother will have something good for lunch."

"Thank you, but I have something I have to do first."

"Sir?"

"I'll walk with you as far as young Jeff's house. I would like to speak to his mother for a few moments."

"All right. Let's go Jeff, your mother will be havin' lunch and wonderin' where you are."

They walked along together, Jonah casting an occasional quick look at Jeff. Something about him struck Jonah as familiar, yet he knew he had never met him before. It was when he smiled down at the young boy who was bubbling with questions and he saw the two of them look at one another that it came to him. The resemblance was so obvious it was hard for him to believe he had not seen it at first. He stopped in his tracks and he and Jeff's eyes met over the boy's head.

"I'd appreciate it if you would say nothing until I find out if I'm welcome or not," Jeff said. Young Jeff looked from one to the other aware that something was being said that he did not understand, something that touched him.

"All right," Jonah said authoritatively, "but if Miz Maguire says go . . . you go without hurtin' the boy."

"I'd do nothing to hurt him. If I can, I'll be staying to make both lives better."

Jonah nodded and they continued to walk in silence until they stopped in front of the inn. Jeff looked down at his son.

"Jeff," he said, "go up and give your mother a message."

"All right, sir."

"Can you remember what I tell you?"

Young Jeff looked momentarily offended then he said, "Yes, sir . . . I'm not a baby."

"Of course you're not, I'm sorry, it's just that what I want you to say is very important."

"Yes, sir."

"Tell your mother that Captain Jeffrey Sables has travelled half the world to find what he wants. Now that he's found it, he is waiting to see if it is still his."

Young Jeff moved away and went inside the inn and climbed the one flight of stairs to the room he shared with his mother, repeating the strange message over and over in his mind. He opened the door and went inside. Brandy and Marthie were sitting together at a small table having tea.

"Jeff, where have you been?"

"With Jonah, Mother, I watched them drill."

"Where's Jonah?" Marthie smiled at him.

"He's downstairs waitin' with the captain."

"Who?" Brandy questioned.

"Mother, I have to give you a message and I have to give it to you real careful. The captain said it was important."

"My goodness, who's this captain?" laughed Brandy.

"Mother?"

"All right dear. What is your message?"

Jeffery straightened his shoulders, concentrated deeply and said, "Captain Jeffery Sables has travelled half the world to find what he wants. Now that he's found it, he's waiting to see if it is still his." Jeff was proud of himself until he looked at his mother's face, which had gone white.

"Brandy?" Marthie said worriedly, but Brandy did not hear her over the heavy pounding of her heart. She rose slowly from her chair. "Where is he, Jeff?"

"Outside with Jonah, Mother."

"Brandy . . . who?" Marthie questioned.

"Jeff," Brandy murmured, then with a low cry she ran to the door, threw it open and ran down the hall.

Jeff waited in an agony of suspense. Was there someone else? Would she tell him to go? What about his son? Question after question pounded in his mind, but he stood resolutely still watching the door.

Suddenly it swung open and Brandy stood before him. The

young girl he expected did not come to him, instead a woman, beautiful beyond his wildest dreams stood in the sunlight. Her hair caught the sparkle of the early morning sun in its wine colored depths. Her slender body, rounded and softened after the birth of their son, had a ripe and voluptuous look. He could have cried in the joy of seeing her again and in that instant, he knew he was right in the choices he had made.

"Jeff," was a whispered sob.

"Brandy! I've waited so long, searched so hard. I could not bear to lose you again," he said. "I love you, Brandy, I always have, I always will. I need you."

She ran to him and he opened his arms to draw her inside and hold her against him, vowing never to let her leave them again.

Jonah, Marthie, and young Jeff arrived at the door. Young Jeff gave a cry of amazement when he saw his beloved mother swept up in the arms of the fascinating, handsome captain. His alarm grew when he saw her bound so tightly in his arms and he stepped forward prepared to attack if his mother should need him. Two pair of restraining hands held him and he looked up to see Marthie and Jonah both smiling. He relaxed; if Jonah and Marthie were not alarmed, then he guessed he should not be either.

When Jeff finally released Brandy's trembling lips, he began to feverishly kiss away the tears that washed down her cheeks. "Brandy, Brandy," he murmured, "I love you."

"Jeff," she whispered, "I don't understand. How did you know? How did you find me?"

"Did you really believe I would let the most beautiful thing in my life get away? I'm grateful, believe me I am, for what you did, you did for me. But more than anything I want us to be together, I want to make up for all the lonely days and nights we've both had. There has never been anyone for me but you. I want to know my son. Oh, Brandy love. I'm here to stay if you will have me. Marry me . . . today . . . now, so I can make sure this dream is real and not my imagination."

"Jeff . . . I don't understand. Your life, your career . . "

"Mean nothing to me without you and my son."

"But your family . . . friends."

"My friends understand and my family has been informed. I won't let you raise those kind of barriers, Brandy. I'm here in this country to stay, to fight if necessary, but to build a whole new life with the woman I've loved for so long and the son I want to know."

"To stay . . . you're not going back?"

"Never, from today on, Jeff Sables . . . and his family, are citizens of these Colonies. We'll be happy here, Brandy. Nothing in the past is half as important. If you tell me you're with me, tell me you want me to stay. Tell me," he whispered finally, "that your love for me has not changed. Say the words that will make my world whole again."

"Oh, Jeff, I never believed I would ever be this happy again. Yes, I love you and oh, my dear, I do want you to stay."

With a joyous laugh, he held her to him again and kissed her until she could barely breathe. She gasped as she stepped back from him. She half turned toward young Jeff who stood in the doorway watching with questioning eyes. She started toward him, but felt Jeff's hand close about her arm, restraining her. She looked up into his eyes and saw the gentle pleading there.

"Let me," he said with emotion, "I've been dreaming of this day for a long, long time. Let me tell him. I want him to want me too."

She smiled, then stepped back while Jeff and his son faced each other. Jeff went to his son and knelt in front of him. From the few words they had spoken, Jeff knew the boy had reached the age where he wanted the strength and guidance of a father. He had heard the longing in the boy's voice when he had told him he intended to search for his father.

"Jeff," he said gently, one hand lightly resting on the boy's shoulder, "I'm your father, Jeff. I lost you and your mother a long time ago. Now, I've found you, I want to take you to live with me as my family. Do you want to come?"

He saw the bright leap of pleasure in the boy's eyes. The longing and desire to have a father crowded his eyes with tears. To have a father such as this was more than his young heart had ever dreamed of. He had created visions in his mind of his father, but none of his wildest dreams had promised him anything as wonderful as this. Jeff could see that the boy was overpowered with all that had happened, that he wanted to reach out to this miraculous thing and was not sure how.

With a happy laugh, he drew the boy into his arms and felt the young arms hold him. His heart swelled with the agony of such pleasure as he held his son tight to him and looked over his head to the woman who stood tear-stained and smiling at the reunion of the two people she loved most in her life.

Forty

Jeff and Brandy made rapid arrangements, with Marthie and Jonah's help, for a small wedding. The pastor at the small church agreed to marry them that night. Young Jeff could not keep his admiring eyes off his new-found father. He hovered at Jeff's side and questioned him unceasingly until Jeff drew him up on his lap and concentrated his attention on trying to answer his son's multitude of questions.

Young Jeff had never seen his mother so happy, and he was fascinated now that she did not seem to be as impatient with his questions as she sometimes was.

It was also obvious to all that Jonah was mildly jealous of young Jeff's sudden transfer of hero worship from him to Jeff. It did not go unnoticed by Jeff who took the opportunity to take Jonah aside and reassure him. He knew it was just the sudden arrival of a father that had all of young Jeff's attention. Soon, the novelty would become the everyday, and Jonah would find that his place in young Jeff's heart had never been usurped.

Brandy and Jeff stood in the small church, many miles away from their homes, in a country soon to be caught in the whirlwind of war, and exchanged their vows.

Brandy had brought few clothes along, so the dress she wore was plain, made of deep green cotton with a small band of white lace at the neck and sleeves. Marthie had twisted her hair into tight curls atop her head, and as Jeff looked at her, he remembered Roxanne's words of how surprised he would be at the change in Brandy. She had changed. The Brandy whose hand he held now was a woman, proud, assured and of exceptional beauty, so very different from the illiterate bar girl who had first captured Jeff's heart.

The wedding over, the five of them shared a bright and laughing supper. Marthie had then taken young Jeff with her to share Jonah's room for the night. As the first stars twinkled in the heaven, Brandy found herself alone with a man she had not seen in years. Suddenly, she became a little frightened of whether things would be as they were before.

Jeff came to her and took both her hands in his and drew her close to him. Raising her hands, he kissed her fingers gently. She looked up into the deep gray eyes and felt the warm need within him reach out to her.

"I love you, Brandy. There has never been a minute that I've been able to forget you. The sweet taste of you," he touched her cheek. "You're so beautiful, Brandy," he whispered, "and I want you so much I can hardly bear it."

She stepped closer and slid her arms about his waist and raised her lips for the sweet, gentle touch of his. Their lips touched lightly, and the warm belonging feeling washed over her as it had always done when she and Jeff had kissed. She felt his mouth seek hers in a deep, questioning kiss and she answered him with the warm love of her response.

Jeff stepped back from her and with slow, precise movements, he withdrew the pins from her hair, letting his fingers thread through the soft strands of it. Then without taking his eyes from hers, he slowly loosened the robe she wore and let it drop to the floor.

Brandy's head bent forward and the thick mass of her hair fell over her and her hands fanned in front of her, shielding her body from his eyes.

"Brandy?"

"Oh, Jeff. I don't want you to look at me."

"Why?"

"I've changed . . . Jeff's birth . . ."

He reached down and took her hands and held both of them in one of his, then he tipped up her chin. Brushing her lips with a light kiss, he moved her hands to her sides and looked at the lovely, soft body he had known so very well. The breasts had softened, yet they were still youthful looking. His eyes skimmed down her narrow waist. Her flawless skin was marked in several places by tiny webbed lines. He placed his hand against her belly and caressed it gently.

"From carrying my child," he said affectionately, "Do you think I could find you any less beautiful? To me, Brandy, you are the most perfect, the most flawless woman in the world."

Her heart ached with the love she felt for this sensitive man and with a low, murmured sound, she reached for him and he drew her back into the warmth of his embrace.

There was no holding back for either of them, they tumbled together into the flaming cauldron of love they had shared before. He lifted her in his arms and took her to the bed, where soon, his warm, naked body slid down beside her and drew her against him, savoring the long, slender silkiness of her skin as their bodies molded themselves to each other.

"Oh, Brandy, it's like coming home," he whispered against her throat while his hands sought the places on her body that he remembered so well. "I don't know how I've survived without you."

Brandy was content in a way she had never been before as they reached a fulfillment far surpassing any they had ever found. They lay together talking and making plans for their future together. Jeff asked her hundreds of questions about his son for he was hungry to fill in the years he had missed.

"We'll have to buy a house when we get back to Boston," he said, enthused with plans. "A place with lots of room for Jeff and all his brothers and sisters to play in."

"Oh," Brandy laughed, "You have plans for a big family?"

"I've been an only child, it is not so grand, sometimes it's lonely. Jeff needs a brother to be a friend with and a sister to be protective of." He looked into her eyes, his laughter holding her. "What do you say, love. Shall we give them to him?"

"If we can," she giggled.

"If!" he said, as he drew her tighter to him. "I want you to know I'm a very persevering man."

"I know," she sighed. "Any other man would have given up on me and married one of the rich little girls I'm sure you know plenty of."

"Rich maybe," Jeff said gaily, "in Papa's money. But never as rich as you are in all the things that a man needs to make his life happy. Oh, Brandy, you'll never know how empty my life was without you. After Captain Daugherty told me you were pregnant with my child, I wanted to fly to you then, but he convinced me your sacrifice was too noble to be for nothing. He kept an eye on you for me." Jeff placed a hand on her belly. "I wanted to be with you, to watch you change as you carried my son, to be with you when he was born. I wanted to hold him first, to watch his first steps, hear his first words. I missed so much, but that will never happen again. If you'll give them to me, Brandy, I want children to share with you."

Brandy caressed the side of Jeff's face smiling up at him with eyes filled with the sweet tender love she felt for him.

"Yes, love, I want that more than anything."

He bent forward and gently touched her lips with his, and tightened his arms about her until she could barely breathe.

"You can get rid of your little shop when we go home. You're going to have your hands full just taking care of me and my son . . . or sons."

"Oh, Jeff. I worked so very hard to get that little shop started, can't I keep it, please? It means so very much to me. Believe me, I won't cheat you or little Jeff out of anything. It's just that . . . well . . . it means a lot to me." She furrowed her brow in a worried frown.

"Brandy, I'm not trying to take anything from you," he laughed. "I thought you might hate working. If you want it, keep it. I want to see you happy and any way I can make you smile, is all right with me. As long as I can hold you and know you love me, I'll never feel cheated."

"Well," she said blithely, "You could make me happy right now."

"How?"

"Stop talking and let's start working on giving little Jeff that brother or sister you've been talking about."

Jeff's laughter and the way he held her to him was reward enough for Brandy.

They stayed at Braddock for the balance of the week with Marthie and Jonah. Then they travelled back to Cumberledge where Jeff and Brandy left Marthie and Jonah and went on to Boston.

In Boston, they were greeted by a delighted Lang and Bright who even helped them find a house, and begin to get settled.

Young Jeff was in a glorious world he had never imagined, as Lang and Bright took him under their wing in an effort to give Jeff and Brandy a lot of time together. Over a month after they arrived Jeff was given command of a frigate named *Actaeon*. She had just been christened and Jeff was so overjoyed he could hardly contain his enthusiasm. His first step was to rush home and bring Brandy and Jeff down to the dock to see it. All the way to the dock, he bubbled over with information that neither little Jeff nor Brandy understood.

"It's not big, Brandy, but maneuverable. Thirty two guns! You should see the rigging! She's fast, she'll outrun anything on the ocean!" He went on and on about spars, masts, riding bitts, ports, hawse holes until Brandy laughingly begged him to stop for she had no idea what he was talking about.

Brandy and Jeff were escorted about the *Actaeon* by a pleased Lang and Bright who, to their pleasure, had been given berths as officers under Jeff. Brandy and Lang stood together and watched young Jeff and his father move about the ship, Jeff talking while his son looked up at him with rapt admiring eyes. Lang was watching Brandy as her eyes seemed to devour the scene before her.

"Have Bright and I ever told you how happy we are that Jeff found you and his son?"

Brandy turned her attention to him and smiled, "Thank you, Bright."

"You're different, you've changed a lot, Brandy. You're quite a beautiful lady. Jeff had a rough time after you left. There was a time we weren't too sure he was going to make it."

"What are you trying to tell me, Lang?"

"That I can see how fate worked things out. I don't mean to hurt you, but the way things were I don't think you and Jeff could have ever made a life together. I guess we have to suffer a bit if we want to grow into people worthy of the good things in life. You've suffered, and the growing you've done is a beautiful thing. Bright and I, we love you both, and that son of yours is something. We hope to stay friends for a long, long time."

Brandy's eyes filled with happy tears as she reached out and put her hand on Lang's arm. Words were unnecessary as with a smile, he patted her hand with his.

The days fled, turning to weeks, then to months and still Jeff had not been given any assignment. Brandy's nerves were taut as she began to think again of the battles to come.

Lang, Bright and Jeff were seated in Jeff's home after a comfortable, filling dinner. Brandy was putting a reluctant Jeff to bed.

"Jeff," Lang said, "haven't you been wondering about something?"

"What?"

"Where the hell are Steffan and Tamara? It was supposed to be a week until her trial, and they were to follow us. It's been months. Don't you wonder what's happened to them?"

"Yes, I do. I've been worried for a long time."

"Do you think Steff is coming?"

"Absolutely."

"Then I wonder why they're not here. I have a feeling things are going to being popping pretty soon."

"Steff will be here. He's committed himself to Tamara and to us. He's not a man to turn his back on something like that. If he said he'd come, believe me, he'll be here. Maybe he had a little trouble with the ship he was having built and it delayed him."

"I've got a better reason," Bright offered.

"What?"

"He's waiting on Tom and Cecile. Their baby was due and Steff wouldn't want to travel with her in that condition. I'll bet they're waiting on the baby so the four of them can come together."

"Of course," Jeff replied, "I'd forgotten about Cecile expecting. Tom would want Steffan to wait for him and they're too close for Steff to refuse."

The subject settled to their satisfaction, they shared a last drink and Lang and Bright left. Brandy and Jeff had purchased a small house at the edge of town, close enough for Brandy to walk to her shop where she went three days a week, and far enough for Jeff to have plenty of room to play.

Jeff walked up the stairs deep in thought and met Brandy just coming out of young Jeff's room.

"What's the matter darling?" she asked.

"We were just talking about Steff and Tamara."

"What about them?" she questioned. Jeff had told her all the details of Steff's and Tamara's lives together and she was not only anxious to meet Tamara but curious about the girl who had captured the heart of Steffan Devers.

"They should have been here by now. Bright thinks they were waiting for Tom and Cecile, but now that I begin to calculate, Cecile's baby should have been born over two and a half months ago, plenty of time for them to have gotten here. I've got the strangest feeling that something has gone wrong."

"What could have gone wrong?"

"I don't know."

"Maybe nothing has, Jeff, maybe some unimportant thing holds them temporarily. Maybe one of them is sick or something. They'll be here."

He grinned and put his arms about her, drawing her against him and kissing her firmly and thoroughly.

"Have I told you in the last hour or so that I love you, woman?"

"No," she laughed, "you've left me alone to carouse with

your friends. I'm beginning to feel neglected."

"Well," he chuckled, "we can't have that. I love you, Mrs. Sables," he began. "That's for this morning. I love you my sweet, sweet woman, that's for this afternoon." His eyes smiled down into hers as he again bent his head to touch her lips. "I love you my beautiful, wonderful wife, and I need you. That is for now and for all time."

She sighed as he lifted her from the floor and cradled her against him, his lips burning a fiery path down her throat. She wrapped her arms about his neck while he carried her to their room.

As the days went on, Jeff began to really worry about why Steffan and Tom had not arrived. He checked each incoming ship, but no one had news of them. He knew now it would not be long until he was given orders to take the *Actaeon* out of port for some assignment. He had hoped Steffan and Tom would come before it did, but fate did not will it so. The orders came. Within two weeks, Jeff and his ship would leave Boston harbor. Where he would be going, Jeff didn't know for the sealed orders were still in possession of his commanding officer.

Another thought had crossed Jeff's mind. No matter what was going on with Steffan and Tom, Martin Gillis and Commander Pierce should have been here. The whole thing had an uncertain feel about it. Slowly, his worry began to increase. Deep inside he knew he and his three friends felt the same. Something was drastically wrong. Something they would now never know, and something they could do nothing about if they did.

Brandy hummed lightly to herself as she held the new dress she had just finished making up to her and surveyed it in the mirror. Pleased, she laid it gently aside. It was a gown she had taken great care in making, for it was the one she would wear to the first and only ball she had ever been to.

Mr. Randolph Perry was holding a ball for all the military men stationed in Boston. It would in all probability be the last as the war built in strength. Mr. Perry was a well-known patriot and spoke out often in defense of the Colonial Army and even more so in defense of her young Navy. When the invitation had come, Brandy had seemed to Jeff to be frightened.

"Why, love, it's just a ball!"

"Jeff," she said in an agony of fear. "I . . . I've never been to a ball. I've never been among such people. You're used to this, but I'm afraid."

"Afraid?"

"Afraid I'll shame you by doing something foolish, or looking like . . . like what I am."

"What you are," Jeff said indignantly, and for the first time in their lives together she saw anger cloud his eyes. He bent down and took her hand and drew her in front of the tall mirror, then he stood behind her, his hands on her shoulders and holding her eyes in the mirror with his. "I'll tell you what you are," he began. "Look Brandy, for maybe the first time, look. Throw away the idea of what you were. Now, you are the most beautiful and sweet woman that ever existed. You are a woman any man would be pleased and proud to show to the world as his. You are a woman who has given me the greatest joy in my life. You are the mother of my son and the one thing in my life above all others that I am proud of. Had I all the women in the world to choose from today to share my life, guide my children, it would surely be you. Always and forever it would be you."

Tears fell from her eyes as she slowly turned and moved into his arms. "Never again let me hear you slight yourself. I happen to love you and I'll let nobody, even you, do anything to hurt you."

"Oh, Jeff . . ." she cried. "I don't know what I ever did in my life to deserve you."

"Well," he grinned wickedly, "why don't you show me just how much you appreciate me."

Their lovemaking was an exquisite thing that left Brandy crying in his arms, and holding him tightly against her.

Now she stared at the beautiful gown she had taken such time to make and again the warm feel of him swept over her.

Brandy went to the window for the fifth time in a half hour to see if Jeff and their son were coming. She saw them walking together down the long shaded road. The man shortening his steps to match the boy's and the boy clinging to the man's hand, his face turned up toward him with questions. She saw the smile of contentment on Jeff's face as he patiently answered the multitude of questions that were always on his son's lips. She closed her eyes, aware of her complete happiness, of her love for the two, and her prayers that nothing would happen in the hard dark days to come that would take them away from her.

She ran down the stairs as Jeff came up on the porch. He was accompanied now not only by young Jeff, but Marthie Price as well. Marthie had come back to Boston a few days before when her son had been ordered to march with the Army.

Marthie would stay the evening with young Jeff while Brandy and Jeff went to the ball.

Jeff kissed Brandy when he came in, then looked down at his son. "Scat upstairs and get washed up for supper."

"You won't leave before I get back, will you?"

"No, I won't leave."

Young Jeff ran up the stairs and Jeff laughed as he watched him go.

"I swear everything that boy has to say comes out in the form of a question. If I had a penny for every question he's asked me today, I'd have a fortune."

Brandy laughed.

"You think it's funny," Jeff grinned. "The only thing that worries me is he seems to think I have all the answers. Sometimes, I have a pretty difficult time doing so and he's just a child. What am I going to do when he's older?"

"By that time," Brandy said humorously, "you'll be an old man filled with wisdom."

Jeff laughed and slid an arm about her waist. "I've no intention of getting old with you around. He'll just have to go off and find some of his answers, like I did. Maybe if he's as lucky as his father, he'll find someone as beautiful as his mother to answer some of his questions for him."

"Jeff!" Brandy exclaimed looking from Marthie to Jeff, blushing. "He's just a baby."

"Love," Jeff laughed hilariously as he kissed her again and winked at Marthie, "I was just a baby once and some of my adventures proved rewarding." Jeff was already on his way upstairs before Brandy could answer.

Jeff dressed for the ball as elaborately and carefully as he could. When he came back down the stairs, both young Jeff's gaze of rapt hero worship and Marthie's look of admiration told him how well he looked in the new blue and white uniform of the young Colonial Navy. The white pants hugged Jeff's lithe form like a second skin and the waistcut navy blue jacket with its gold buttons, loops of gold braid at the shoulder, and the high gold trimmed collar was very complimentary to his dark hair and skin and his blue-gray eyes.

"Jeff," Marthie smiled, "you look splendid in your new uniform."

"Thank you, Marthie. Has Brandy finished dressing yet?"

"Yes, I have," came a voice from the stairs and the three of them turned to look at her.

Brandy had drawn her thick, wine colored hair to the nape of her neck in a chignon. The dress she wore was ivory satin with thick ruffles of green lace clustered at her elbows and around a neckline that was cut so the soft, round breasts swelled above it. She wore a pearl necklace Jeff had recently bought her with earrings to match. In her hand she carried an ivory lace shawl.

"God, Brandy," Jeff breathed as he went to her, "You are the most beautiful woman I've ever seen."

"Do you like it?" she said, as she turned about for him to better see the dress. When she turned back to face him, their eyes held.

"Like it," Jeff whispered, "I love it." His eyes told her the was certainly not talking about the dress.

They prepared to leave, each of them kissing young Jeff and cautioning him to not regale Aunt Marthie with too many questions and to be obedient when it was time for bed. Young Jeff agreed and watched them, his little heart swelled with pride. How very strong and handsome his father was, and how pretty his mother was. He stood at the window and watched the carriage take them away.

Jeff and Brandy rode along in silence. He held her hand in his, feeling it tremble. There was nothing he could say to make her feel any better. He was confident when she saw how her beauty affected everyone she would be able to relax and enjoy the evening as he was going to. He tucked her hand in his arm when they stepped from the carriage and they walked into Randolph Perry's beautiful home.

They were welcomed in such a friendly manner by the Perrys and with such enthusiasm by all the others present that Brandy did relax and in no time she was laughing and having a good time. It was Jeff who raised an eyebrow threateningly at several young officers and protected his rights vigorously.

It was over two hours after they had arrived that Jeff got her away from some of her admirers for a dance. They were laughing together when Brandy looked toward the door.

"Why Jeff," she said breathlessly, "what an absolutely beautiful woman."

Jeff turned toward the door, and Brandy was surprised when he stopped dancing and stood staring at the newcomers.

She had her hand tucked into David Perry's arm and stood

quietly surveying the room. Brandy was fascinated not only by her extraordinary beauty which brought a low murmur of appreciation from everyone in the room but by the fact that her husband seemed to know her.

"Who is she?" Brandy questioned, but Jeff did not seem to hear her.

"Jeff?"

"Who . . . what?"

"Who is she?"

"I don't believe is, Brandy, and I've no idea how this came about, but that beautiful woman is Tamara Marriott-Devers . . . Steffan's wife."

"Where is Steffan?"

"That," Jeff said quietly, "is what I'd like to know."

Forty-one

When Andrew lifted his daughter in his arms in the dark cell, she had reached the end of her endurance. The knowledge that she would die the following day, extreme cold and hunger and Jaspar's physical abuse had driven her to the edge. Then the shock of seeing both Mikel and Andrew when she thought she was completely lost was too much.

She laid her head against her father's shoulder and closed her eyes letting the warm strength of him seep through her consciousness. She did not care at the moment why Andrew had come, or how he had gotten free; all she knew was that he was here and she was safe.

She refused to let any other thought into her mind, for she knew if she did, she would fly to a million pieces and never be able to retrieve them again. She let welcome numbness hold her as Andrew wrapped a warm blanket around her and held her on his lap as he had when she was a child. She wanted to be a child again, to know that she would always be safe from the pain of living, to not have to reach anymore, decide anymore, feel anymore, just depend on those who loved her.

The ride to the *Sea Borne* was not long and soon she felt herself lifted again. Voices around her echoed in her mind like the tolling of a huge heavy bell. They were wordless voices, sounds that meant nothing to her.

Then she felt herself sink into something soft and warm and she let the threatening darkness roll over her.

Andrew Marriott stood by his bunk and looked down on his daughter's sleeping form. She lay curled in a self-protective ball, clinging to the blanket he had wrapped about her. Her face, even in sleep was twisted in fear and pain. Pain she would never have known had he not let Steffan take her away from him. "If I had gone with her," he thought miserably, "and not let Steffan Devers convince me that he too loved her, she would still be safe." He cursed Steffan Devers and vowed, as he stood over his daughter, that Steffan would pay a price for this that he could not even imagine.

Mikel would watch, and some day, soon, Steffan would return to his home. When he did, Mikel and the two men left with him would see that one way or another, Steffan would be brought to Andrew. When he did, Andrew would throw in his face the words he had said, then he would sentence Steffan, sentence him to exactly what Tamara had suffered. Imprisonment without help or hope for as long as Andrew cared to hold him. When he thought the time was right he would have him taken from his prison and hung.

The first three days of the voyage home, Tamara alternately slept and sat staring out the porthole. Andrew left her to herself, letting her have the time to think, to gather herself back together. After a while, she began to open up and talk, but Andrew could still see, feel, and hear the part of her that still lay wounded.

They arrived at Marriott Island. Mellie, who had made the trip back with them, was overjoyed, for she felt Tamara's healing lay on the rocks and sand of Marriott Island.

Once there, Tamara seemed to lose herself in the peace and contentment of the island. She walked the beaches of her childhood, she swam in the warm waters of the lagoons, staying away from the place where she and Steffan had swum together. Often she lay, naked and warm on the heated sand and let the place she loved close about her and heal her.

Andrew watched her closely as the days turned into weeks. He knew her body had recovered from its ordeal. Young and healthy, it did not take long for the golden glow to return.

Like a wild thing, she returned to the place where she felt safe and as it had always done, it returned the love she gave.

Her body was one thing, her mind was another. She sat on an outcropping overlooking a section of the coastline that was rocky and violent. It reflected the mood she felt; for the first time since her rescue she allowed Steffan to walk through her memory. She conjured up every memory, every thought from the first time they had met. Piece by piece she joined everything in her mind, then she added to it his strange disappearance, for her father said he had not been seen since the trial had started. She wanted to hate him, more than she had ever wanted anything in her life, but some part of her remained unsure. Some deep thing within her resisted still the idea of Steffan's treachery. No matter how she tried to fight it, the obvious was there for her to see. He had

479

simply walked away from a bad situation, one he could no longer control and left her to face her fate alone.

Her thoughts poked and prodded at the memories and she began to build into a deep urgency the need to face Steffan one day and look into those golden eyes and see for herself where treachery lay. She would know, if she saw him; she would know, then she would take her own personal revenge. She would see him suffer some way, somehow. She would see those golden eyes burn with pain, she would hear him beg for mercy as she had begged Jaspar, and in the end, it would be her hand that put an end to his life. She rose slowly from the rocks and walked toward the strip of beach that led to the steps and home.

Andrew stood at the edge of the cliffs and watched her approach. She walked slowly, her feet bare and ankle-deep in the warm surf. Her head was bowed and she seemed deep in thought and not really knowing and feeling where she was. It was unlike her and Andrew continued to watch, feeling the pain she was feeling and cursing again the name of the man who had caused it.

She came to the bottom of the steps and began to climb, still not noticing he was there. She had almost reached the top before his shadow appeared at her feet. She looked up and her eyes brightened. His heart twisted when he saw the deep love there, for he had finally made his mind up about one thing. He could not bear it on his conscience any longer and had decided to tell her the truth about how Steffan had forced her into marriage.

"Father," she smiled, "good morning."

"Good morning. Enjoying the early sun again? Is the water warm?" he questioned.

"Yes."

"It would be a good day to go for a sail."

"Would you like to go?"

"I would."

"Fine, shall we go in and have breakfast first, I'm famished."

They walked back to the house arm in arm. Breakfast was eaten rapidly and soon they were on their way to the dock. Tamara's smile faded when she saw Mikel's boat the *Tamara* swaying gently in the water. Andrew cursed; the last thing he needed at the moment was a reminder of all that had happened. He could see the turmoil in Tamara' mind and waited with bated breath for her to collect herself. She did, resolutely straightening her shoulders, she looked up at him. "Shall we take Mikel's boat? I'm sure he wouldn't mind."

He nodded. "I'm going just as a passenger. You sail, I'll talk for I have something very important to tell you. I cannot live with a thing I have done unless I explain it to you and receive your forgiveness."

"Forgiveness, Father, for what?"

"I must explain it all to you. Come on, let's take the boat out."

They climbed into the boat; Andrew relaxed and watched Tamara ease the boat from the protected harbor and out into the strong tides of the ocean.

"Tamara, I know you remember all too well what has happened and I hate to revive old painful memories, but I cannot live with the feeling of guilt for what befell you."

Her brow furrowed with concentration as she listened to him talk.

"The night that Steffan captured you. You did not know that it was impossible for him to do anything to me without proof of my guilt of which he had none." She nodded, silently watching him.

"The only excuse I have for what I did was that I loved you and trusted Steffan. He convinced me that the only way he could keep you safe was to have you marry him. I knew you would never agree to marry him as conditions were and so did he. He told me if he could use your love for me, in order to keep me safe, he would be able to protect you from harm. God, he was convincing. I thought he was sincere, was right, and so I agreed to keep my silence. I stood by and watched him take you away, thinking it was the only way to keep you from harm. I let a scoundrel walk in and take from me the most important, beloved person in my life without a fight. I let him make you suffer and did nothing to protect you. I never even knew of his perfidy until Mikel came to me. I have not slept a night since then without the guilt filling my dreams. Can you forgive me, child, can you know the pain I have suffered seeing you hurt so? Can you find it in your heart to understand?"

Tears glazed her eyes, but they were tender tears filled with the love and forgiveness he sought. "Father, I understand only, that as always, you thought you were doing what was best for me. Not for a moment in my life have I ever doubted your love for me and I do not doubt it now. If it is a question of forgiveness, then you must also forgive me for putting you in such a position. Let us both forget it if we can, for with the love we share, there is no need for forgiveness."

Andrew took her hand and kissed it gently.

"Now Father, I have something to show you."

"What?"

"You always wondered where I hid my ship."

"I was sure that Mikel had hidden it for you."

"You've blamed Mikel for many things he is not guilty of. His only guilt was loving me."

Andrew grinned. "It seems like Mikel and I have much in common. We are both captives of that same wild gypsy."

Tamara's smile faded as she recalled Steffan's voice when he had laughingly called her his wild gypsy. Andrew saw the flicker of pain cross her face and wondered what he had said to cause it.

"Tamara?" he questioned.

Her smile reappeared, somewhat unsteady but there. "It's all right, Father. Now if you are in for a big thrill I shall show you where the *Scarlet Butterfly* made her home."

"I'm ready for whatever you have."

"I doubt it," she laughed. "You'll have to put your trust in me completely. It's very frightening for anyone the first time."

"Now that you've roused my curiosity, lead on, I'm anxious now to see a place the whole English Navy could not find."

"Sit back and relax, Father. I've a surprise you will never forget."

Andrew obediently relaxed for he was enjoying the first sound of spontaneous laughter he had heard from her since their return to the island. He remained quiet for an hour watching the ease with which she handled the boat and the look of pleasure in her eyes. The roar of the heavy waves that crashed against Corvet's Rock drew attention from her.

"You'd better stay away from that monster," he shouted above the thunderous waves. "Too close and you will find yourself smashed to a million pieces upon it."

Tamara edged the boat closer and closer to the rock. "Tamara!" her father shouted, his face pale. "You're too close, I can feel the tide pulling us in. Give me the boat, maybe I can get us away."

"Father," she laughed, "you promised to trust me. How far does your faith go? Is it enough if I tell you I know what I'm doing?"

Andrew gulped and she could see the very visible effort it took him to sit down. His face was white, as were the knuckles of the hands that gripped the sides of the now swiftly moving boat. The tremendous tide lifted them and pulled them toward the huge gray rock that towered over them. He had visions of their smashing against the rock, he could see her beautiful body broken upon the rough crags. He used every ounce of strength he had to remain still as they drew nearer and nearer to the rock. Then suddenly they were swept through the dark cave. Andrew blinked as the blackness surrounded them. He was astounded. He could not believe what his eyes were telling him was true. In the darkness he could hear Tamara's joyous laughter. With a suddenness that left him stunned and gasping for breath, they shot from the cave and into the most beautiful lagoon he had ever seen. He sat still, staring about him in wonder. "I don't believe this," he said in an amazed voice. "No one would have ever found you here if they had searched for a million years."

"Yes, treachery found us, not ability."

Tamara and Andrew tied the boat to the dock and she began to escort him about her hideaway.

"How did you find it?"

She told him about the day she and Mikel had come here, how they were sure they were going to die against the rocks, then she told him of how they had built the dock and used it as a safe harbor to harass the English ships.

"All right," he chuckled, "now just how do we go about getting out of here?"

"Well for a while we don't, but don't worry, it is possible."

"Is it as menacing going out as coming in?"

"More so. You shoot out into the open sea on a tide that is frightening. Before the shock is over the sea tide lifts you. It is beyond belief. No matter how many times I've done it, it still has the power to frighten me to death."

They walked in the solitude and talked, and as they did, Andrew realized there was some part of her that no longer seemed opened to him.

"I've been holding the two responsible for your grief in the hold of my ship. I'm sure by now they are worried enough and uncomfortable enough to talk. I did not want to say anything until I was sure you were able to face it; now I must decide what to do with them."

Tamara walked beside him, but she remained silent for so long he did not think she meant to answer him at all. Then she said, "I do not know what to do, Father. When I was imprisoned in that horrible place all I could think of was revenge, of killing the one responsible for my pain, but now . . .''

"Now?"

"Now, I can think more clearly," she turned to face her father, "I cannot be what they are and neither can you. I cannot kill for the love of killing. I . . . I want to talk to each of them . . . separately . . . I have to know . . .''

"Just what the extent of Steffan's guilt really is," her father supplied.

"Yes. I have to know why."

"Do you think they can tell you why?"

"Why would a man like Lyle Whitfield want me dead? A woman he had never met, who had never done anything to him? From the way you have watched them, they obviously do not even like each other. There is something between them we don't know about. There is someone else who is a shadow we cannot see."

"Steffan?"

"I don't know," she replied. "But some way, somehow, I have to find out both who and why, and if it is Steffan, then . . . then I want one day to face him myself. I want to see him, see his face when I brand him for the cowardly liar he is."

"You have been making plans for a while haven't you?" he asked.

"Yes," she replied. "I'm going to take *The Adventurer* and I'm going to the Colonies for a while. I'm going to see David and his family. I'm going to get my strength back, renew my faith in what I was doing, and then," she looked up into her father's eyes and said firmly, "the lady pirate will be reborn. Reborn with one goal in mind. To find Steffan Devers and the ship he commands. To shame him, degrade him, sink his ship, and kill him."

"Any other man would tell me I am a fool to even think of letting you go. But I know you too well. You will go no matter what I say. All I ask is that you wait until Mikel returns and let the two of us go with you. I will not stop you from anything you want to do, but I want to be there to support you. I'm sure Mikel will feel the same."

"You're hoping that Mikel has found where Steffan went, perhaps so you can eliminate him before I have the chance."

"I gave Mikel orders to find out where he had gone and what he had done. I did not tell him to try to kill him. If possible, he might find a way to bring him here, but if not, he's to bring me

484

word and I . . . we . . . will go to him."

"Can you leave Mikel a message to follow us to the Colonies? The hostilities have begun and I want to see if I can offer some help."

"Yes, I suppose I can."

"I cannot say what it is, Father, but there is something about all that happened that has no logical sense or reason. For my own peace of mind, I have to try to find out what it is. Will you bear with me?"

"Haven't I always? Tamara, your happiness is very important to me. At the risk of making you very angry with me I'm going to say something."

"I am never that angry with you," she smiled.

"You may be this time, but angry or not, I know you will tell me the truth."

"Yes, if I can."

"No matter what you've been through, and even if your mind accepts it, your heart will still not accept the fact of Steffan's treachery. Somewhere deep inside you still love him, even if everything tells you he is guilty. Some hope seems to linger that he might not be, that some way he can explain all that has happened. Steffan was the man who took a little girl, Tamara, and changed her to a woman. Do you still remember that? Is that why your mind still clings to thoughts of facing him because the shadow of that love is haunting you?"

She looked up at him, her eyes clouded by doubt. "Maybe," she whispered, "maybe you are right, Father. I loved him so completely and he seemed to love me the same way. After all we had meant to each other can you blame me if some small doubt remains. That is why I have to find my answers. That is why, one day, I must face him again. To kill off any doubts, to smother any embers that might be left, I have to see his face. I will never be a woman for any other man if I cannot erase Steffan from that small corner of my heart he refuses to leave. If ever I am to be whole again, if ever I am to love again, I must find my answers."

"Yes, I think I've know that since we returned to the island. I knew it would come some day, I just did not know when."

"You once told me, Father, that love cannot be turned off and on at will. I know now you are right. I must let him finally kill it. Maybe then, I can turn to someone else."

He drew her into his arms and held her. "I want you to be happy again, child. I want to see you as you were before, free and loving. Whatever it takes to make you so then do it and know I'm with you."

She relaxed against him and said, "I love you, Father."

"You said you wanted to talk to Sinclair and Whitfield separately. When?"

"Tonight, if possible."

"It is," he smiled. "Now tell me what is the key to the door of this place."

"The shifting tide. We can only come and go as it does."

"Maybe some day I should widen the neck and make a channel, then we could come and go as we pleased."

"No, please. Leave it just the way it is. I love it like this. That secure feeling, that once you are inside, no one can come in. It has the peaceful solitude that I enjoy. Please leave it so, Father."

"I won't touch it," he chuckled. "It was just a thought."

"Are you hungry?"

"You have food here?" he said in surprise then he laughed, "Of course you do. If you didn't, knowing Mikel's appetite you soon would have. Lead on, milady, I'm ravenous."

Tamara took him to the edge of the cliffs; there he stood and looked up at their monstrous height. "We climb?" he asked with misgivings and was rewarded again by the tinkle of her laughter.

"We climb," she repeated, "and it might be best if you remove your boots. Barefoot is not only much easier, it is much safer."

He grunted as he leaned against the wall and began to remove his boots. "You will make a wild heathen of me, too, if I give you half a chance. I wonder what my friends would say if they could see me now. The wealthy, important Andrew Marriott climbing cliffs in his bare feet at the whim of a wild little gypsy. I'd never live it down."

"Tsk, tsk," she said in make-believe sympathy. "You poor, poor man to be so put upon. Do you want to forget it?" she challenged.

Andrew's heart leapt to see the animated sparkle in her eyes and her bright smile. She stood, hands on hips, her head tipped, watching him. The wind blew strands of her hair free of its confining ribbon and her body braced against the breeze.

"Not on your life," he chuckled.

He followed her as she climbed up the side of the cliff using a small path he could barely find. Over halfway up they came to the opening of a cave. She went inside and he followed. He could see it was dimly lit by both entrance and exit. He followed her shadowy retreating form until he could see her outlined against the exit.

When he stepped to the exit of the cave he caught his breath at the astounding beauty. They stood in the opening of the cliff at least five hundred feet above the churning ocean. He had an unobstructed view for more miles than he could imagine. Below him the waves crashed violently against the rocks and above him sea gulls soared in the blue, cloud-filled sky. He stood in silent wonder at the breathtaking beauty. "My God, I could never imagine this in my wildest dreams. It is so remarkably beautiful! I can imagine how you must have felt when you first saw it."

"I knew you would appreciate it," she said. "I have such a sense of belonging when I come here."

He turned to her and smiled, "And why not? It is so like you. Strong and intensely beautiful. Outside the freedom and the wind, inside a safe and peaceful harbor. Yes, your sanctuary is Tamara, and always shall be."

She smiled at him, joy filling her again at the way her father knew and understood her. "Come, let me feed you, then before the tide turns we can explore the rest. I'll show you my beautiful kingdom."

From the food they had stored in the caves, Tamara gathered enough for the two of them. They made their way back to the beach where they ate and laughed together. Andrew was overjoyed at the way Tamara seemed to unwind and relax. She was more herself now than she had been from the day he had brought her home.

After they had eaten, she took him on a tour of her domain. He was amazed over and over again at the multitude of caves it held. If a person had enough supplies, he could hold a fortress like this forever. "If I were a pirate," he laughed, "I could make this a fortress and no one would be able to touch me."

"Now, Father," she laughed wickedly, "don't go giving me any ideas."

"Heaven forbid," he said in mock horror. "You needn't blame me anyway. I'm sure you had your wicked ideas long before I did."

"Don't worry, Father. I'm not turning to buccaneering. I've other more important things to do."

"Good," he sighed.

"First," she added.

"Tamara!" He looked at her aghast and she laughed delightedly.

They prepared their boat, for soon the tide would turn. Andrew's stomach and nerves were doing unbelievable things at the thought of running through the dark cavern of the exit again. He promised himself to show Tamara how they could arrange lighting inside, then he changed his mind. Maybe it would be less fearsome in the dark than in the light.

As he expected, it was heart-stopping when he felt the tide lift their boat and draw it toward the mouth of the cave. Suddenly surrounded by darkness, he could feel beneath him the tremendous power that moved them forward at a speed he hated to guess. They were thrust into the even more powerful tide of the ocean like a bullet and he did not gain his breath and control until he again felt the small boat respond to their guidance.

"You have to have very strong nerves to run that gauntlet very often."

Tamara agreed for she was always unsettled when she had either come or gone from the Rock.

As the island drew near, Andrew watched her face. He was relieved to see that their day together had given her something. She seemed to be drawing on some inner strength now as they slowly made their way back to an unknown and uncertain future.

Once ashore, they walked up the beach, climbed the steps, crossed the garden and reentered the mansion.

It was a relieved Mellie who also saw the welcome change in her mistress. Tamara and her father ate their dinner and Mellie was surprised to see them again prepare to leave.

"You're going out again, Miss Tamara?" she asked.

"Yes, Mellie. Father and I are going down to the *Sea Borne*. We have some unfinished business aboard."

"Will you be home soon?"

"Yes, we'll only be gone a short while."

"What is it, Miss Tamara?" Mellie asked. "You're not going away again are you? You look so . . . so sad."

"No, Mellie, I'm not going away for a while. First I have to find out just where I begin my journey when I do go."

"Begin your journey to where, Miss Tamara?"

"Back to myself, Mellie," she whispered. "Back to my beginning . . . or my end."

Forty-two

Jaspar Sinclair and Lyle Whitfield had shared the dark dirty room in the hold of the *Sea Borne* for weeks. The food they had been served was only the barest necessity for sustaining life. Water was also rationed and their facilities for sanitation had been so slim as to be almost nonexistent. Both of them were bearded, unwashed, and beginning to grate on each other's nerves.

They had never met each other until they were tossed together in the hold of the ship. Lyle was a man of strong nerves and capable of containing himself. He was a thinking man and it did not take him long to figure out just who, how and why he was where he was. He was definitely aggravated with the fact that he had allowed a woman to draw him into something that had put him in this position. Several times in the journey he had vowed that Morgana Kyle would answer to him. He would do whatever necessary to get out of this position. When he did, he would stretch out the long arm of his power and find Morgana. When he did . . .

He sat in a small narrow bunk and silently contemplated just what he would do to her while Jaspar Sinclair sat on the other bunk across the four foot room and glared at him.

Jaspar was a completely different breed of man than Lyle. He was a man of courage only when the odds and the power were in his favor. He could be arrogant and antagonistic when he was in the right position and had men to back him up. Now was not one of those situations. Bodily comforts had always been a necessity for Jaspar and the frail nerves he had were rapidly disintegrating under the lack of them.

He knew who had captured him, and he knew why. He was afraid, and that fact stretched his nerves to the breaking point. But the thing that twisted in his mind was the calm, cool attitude of the man who sat opposite him. He wondered why Lyle had been put here with him. For a moment or so at the beginning he had thought he had been planted there to watch him, but it soon became obvious that they were both getting the same treatment.

Now, he glared at him in silence, mostly because Lyle seemed to contain himself with a kind of pride and arrogance that escaped Jaspar.

That Lyle had refused to converse with him after the first week of their imprisonment, answering only in short terse replies when Jaspar spoke, he told Jaspar exactly how he felt toward him, which did more to infuriate him than anything in his life ever had before. Because the situation was so, he made a mistake. The mistake of saying too much to the wrong person.

He stood up now and looked down at Lyle. Despite his filthy condition, Lyle still gave off an aura of the gentleman as he smiled arrogantly up at Jaspar.

"Who the hell are you and why are you here?"

"Ah, my friend," Lyle chuckled, "I might ask you the same question."

"You smooth bastard, you've been lording it around in here ever since we came. Are you Andrew Marriott's plant?"

"Plant!" Lyle actually laughed. "I, a plant!" he threw back his head and roared with laughter. Jaspar had reached the last reserve of his nerves. He reached out and grabbed Lyle by the lapel of his jacket and dragged him to his feet, but his eyes widened in fear as the sharp blade of a thin knife lay against his throat. Lyle smiled at Jaspar, but the smile reached only his lips, the eyes were hard and cold.

"I would suggest that you take your hands from me immediately before I become careless and use this little beauty to show you just how very, very foolish you are," he said mildly.

Jaspar swallowed heavily and released Lyle's lapel.

"Now," Lyle sat down. "I suggest again that you tell me just how you came here. Somehow our paths must cross and I should like to know how. I am really very choosy about the people with whom I associate and I should like to know who our . . . mutual acquaintance is."

"As far as I know, we have none."

"Don't be stupid, my friend, of course we do. Why don't you tell me how you got here."

"I'm here because I was stupid enough to listen to someone else instead of doing what I wanted."

"Oh?"

"I would have eliminated my problem simply by eliminating

490

the two people involved, but no," he sneered. "Let it be a civil trial, Jaspar Dear, let the law hang her, separate them and make her believe it's his fault."

"Civil trial?" Lyle questioned. He rose slowly and walked to Jaspar. Putting one hand on Jaspar's shoulder, he pressed him down in his seat. "Suppose," he said very softly, "you tell me the whole story, especially about your woman friend. Maybe I can find a way after that to get us both out of here."

Tamara and Andrew walked up the gangplank of the *Sea Borne*. Tamara went to Andrew's cabin and Andrew, accompanied by two of his men, went below to the hold of the ship to talk to the two men he had kept on the edge of survival for weeks.

When the door opened, both Jaspar and Lyle rose to meet him; Jaspar, his face white with fear and Lyle with the half smile of secret knowledge on his lips.

Jaspar licked his dry lips as he met the eyes of Tamara's father. Andrew motioned toward him and the two sailors went to each side of him. Jaspar whimpered in fear.

"What are you going to do with me?"

"Not what I would like to do, believe me," Andrew said as he walked to Jaspar. Standing inches from him, he spoke in a quiet voice. "If I could do what I wanted, you would have been dead long ago. Do not cause me any grief or I will do what I want no matter what."

Jaspar remained quiet. Andrew motioned to his men and they dragged a stubbornly resistant Jaspar toward Andrew's cabin.

Andrew stood calmly looking at Lyle who returned his scrutiny unblinking. "You are Tamara Marriott's father?"

"Yes, how did you know?"

"I believe I know more than it was meant for me to ever know. I believe for the first time in my life I have been taken in by a beautiful but ruthless woman. If I'm to be given a chance to talk before you kill me, I think I have something to say that might interest you."

"Sit down and tell me what you have to say; and," he paused, "you had best make it very good, my friend, for your life hangs in the balance."

They sat facing each other, and Lyle Whitfield began to talk.

Jaspar was dragged along, trembling with fear, to the door of Andrew's cabin. One of the sailors knocked, then reached out and opened the door. They then thrust Jaspar into the room and pulled the door closed after them. Jaspar stood facing Tamara who looked at him with icy green eyes and remembered the last time they had been together. Jaspar could see very clearly the remembrance in her eyes. Neither of them spoke for a moment, then Tamara said quietly, "So we meet again, in different circumstances."

"Let . . . let me talk to you, I can explain . . ."

"Can you really? That's too bad; you see, I don't care to hear any explanations. I'm here only to repay you for the kind and gentle treatment I got at your hand. You see," she came closer to him speaking very softly, "I remember every cold, hungry pain-filled moment of it. I remember crying and begging . . . yes, begging to an animal like you. But I will be fair. I shall show you all the mercy you have shown me. My father is determined you shall die very slowly, but I have pleaded for mercy for you."

A ragged sigh came from Jaspar.

"He has agreed that the hanging will be quick and simple."

"Hanging?" Jaspar choked, his face going white.

"Oh, come now," Tamara smiled, "it's not so hard to face. I'm only a woman," her smile faded, "and you let me face it for days. It will be quick—a rope around the neck," she said and snapped her fingers, "and just like that it's over."

"I . . . I know you must hate me for what I did," he began, his voice weak and shaky, "but I'm not responsible for putting you in the Tower. I'm not responsible for your trial or conviction."

Tamara was listening, so Jaspar hurried on. "How can you blame me for what Steffan and Morgana did." The words cut through Tamara like a knife. What doubts she had about Steffan's guilt began to fade away.

"Steffan and Morgana?"

"You saw them together with your own eyes. I can't be to blame for them."

"No, you can't. That is a future endeavor for me. I intend for you to be rewarded only for what you've done."

"But . . . please . . . I'm sorry for what I did to you. You're . . . you're so beautiful and I had been drinking. I got carried away. I couldn't help it. I'm sorry . . . I'm sorry if I hurt you."

Tamara sighed. She could not bear to look at him any longer. He had told her what she wanted to know. She walked to the door and opened it.

"Take him back!"

"You're not going to let them hang me?"

Tamara remained silent, her loathing for him clearly written on her face. The two men grasped him again and began to drag him out.

"Please," he pleaded. "Don't . . . I'm sorry . . . Please."

His voice was still pleading as she closed the door. She leaned against it pressing her cheek against the cool, smooth wood. In her mind rang two words over and over again. Steffan . . . Morgana . . . Steffan . . . Morgana.

Andrew stood up when Jaspar was brought back into the cell. Jaspar stood looking from Andrew to Lyle. He could not understand the cold, hard look in Lyle's eyes, but he understood the look of death that hovered in Andrew's. Andrew needed time to think, time to try to put together what Lyle had told him and all that had happened. He locked both men in again and went back to his cabin. He opened the door and found Tamara in his arms crying as she had never cried through her ordeal.

"I cannot bear it, Father. I thought I could, but I can't. I want no more of it. You can do with them whatever you want."

"And you?"

"I'm going to take the *Adventurer* and go to the Colonies. Please, Father, understand. I don't want to hear anymore. I found out all I need to know. Now I need time to pick up the pieces."

"All right, child. I'll take care of them, you take *The Adventurer* and go. When Mikel comes, we will join you there."

She nodded and kissed his cheek. They returned to the house where he helped her pack her clothes. They shared a quiet dinner, Tamara planning her trip and Andrew trying to fit the pieces of the puzzle. Somehow, he had the deep feeling that Steffan was not as guilty as he seemed, but he didn't want to say anything to Tamara until he was sure. He didn't want her hurt again but he promised himself that one way or another, he was going to find out all the truth that was so deeply hidden behind a mountain of lies.

The next morning, he took Tamara to the docks and held her close to him for a few minutes then watched her walk up the gangplank. *The Adventurer* moved away from the dock and Andrew stood and watched her sails fill. He stood so until she was a speck on the horizon. Then he went to the *Sea Borne* to care for his unfinished business.

Tamara paced the deck of the *Adventurer*. It felt good to be back on the deck of a ship again. She threw herself completely into enjoying the trip, not allowing herself to think of anything but the sea, the wind and the sheer pleasure of her ship.

When she reached Boston, she sent a message to the Perry home. In a very short while, a happy David Perry was there to greet her with a broad smile and a pleasant welcome. "Tamara, how wonderful it is to see you again."

"Thank you, David. I'm happy to see you again, too. You're looking well."

"I don't know about me, but you are extraordinarily beautiful. You're changed somehow. You were pretty before, now, you're . . . you're—"

"I'm what?"

"I can't think of the word to describe you. You're more beautiful than my dreams remembered."

"Oh, David," she laughed. "Still the romantic."

"Maybe," he chuckled, "but if I took a vote from all the young men in this town, I'm sure they would all agree."

"Tell me about everything, Dave. What is going on here."

"Well, things are not too bright. But to hear Mr. Jefferson and Mr. Washington tell it you would swear we are undefeatable."

"We are!"

"We?"

"Yes, we. If you'll have another ship and another captain."

David looked uncertain for a moment. "Another ship would be more than welcome, but . . ."

"But a woman captain is not."

"Tamara . . ."

"Never mind, David, we'll discuss it later. I should like to go and see your family again."

"Good, they're anxious to see you too."

The Perrys made Tamara even more welcome that they had the first time. In a few days, she found herself enjoying their company as they tried their best to make her comfortable. The town seemed to have almost doubled in population since she had visited before. She sat at the dinner table several nights later and listened to Jennifer and Martha giggling over all the new young men who had been coming and going in the town lately. She bit her tongue to keep back a sharp remark that might have upset both girls and she was too fond of them to do or say anything to hurt them.

Randolph sat watching her. He had felt some difference in

Tamara since the last time she had visited and he couldn't quite place what it was. Now it came to him. She had matured some way. Something had happened to her, something to take the glow of young, careless happiness away and replace it with . . . what? A look of quiet sadness, as though she had been hurt. He watched David in animated conversation with her and realized that though David may still have harbored deep feelings toward her, Tamara was as lost to him as if she were no longer there.

"Tamara," he said with a friendly smile. "David has told me you have brought us another ship. I cannot tell you how grateful we are. We have some high quality young captains who have recently joined us. There is a drastic shortage of vessels and the beauty you have brought will be more than welcome."

"Father . . ." David began nervously. He had seen the look in Tamara's eyes.

"Never mind, David," Tamara smiled. She knew how uncomfortable David was. "I'll tell him."

"Tell me what, Tamara?"

"My ship The Adventurer already has a captain."

"Has a captain?" he smiled. "That's good also. Who is he?"

"He is not a he . . . he is a she. The Adventurer is mine and mine alone. If she sails, she sails with me as her master or she does not sail at all."

Randolph sat looking at her in stunned surprise. "You . . ." he began. "You cannot mean that."

"Oh, but I do, Mr. Perry. I would put The Adventurer in no man's hands. She is mine."

"But Tamara, child. The Navy will not allow a woman captain. Why . . . it's . . . it's just an impossibility. They will not accept any ship under that condition."

"I will tell them as I will tell you," Tamara said finally as she rose to her feet. "If they can accept the use of The Adventurer with me it will be theirs. If they cannot," she paused for a moment, "then my ship will sail without the blessing of the Colonial Navy."

"That is piracy!" he muttered.

"Mr. Perry," she said, her voice barely audible. "I've been a pirate before; a pirate for the benefit of the same cause for which I want to fight now. What was the difference when I was staking my life before to get arms and ammunition for our cause or when I would like to give to my adopted country now what I can give. Was I just a woman then? Was the ship more valuable than I

495

then? No, it was not. How often I've been told how brave, how courageous, but that was when I was a pirate. Now, the Navy cannot allow me to stand as one of them because they cannot allow a woman to sail under their colors. If it has to be that way, then so be it. But *The Adventurer* goes with me whether it is as part of the Navy . . . or as a pirate." She turned and walked from the room and dead silence followed her.

Tamara climbed the stairs to her room slowly wondering if Randolph Perry would be angry enough to ask her to leave. If he did, she would merely stay aboard her ship until she found out exactly where she stood. As she closed the door, she suddenly felt a deep desolation as if she were isolated from the world. She walked slowly across the room and sat on the bed. It was so quiet and she was so engrossed in her own loneliness that the knock on the door startled her. She rose and went to the door, when she opened it, David stood looking solemnly at her. "David?"

"Can I talk to you, Tamara?"

"I won't say I'm sorry David, for I'm not."

"I'm not asking you to say anything. I just want to talk to you."

"Come in," she said. She stepped back, but left the door open.

"Tam, I want you to know I'm proud of you. Beside the fact that I love you still, I want you to know that I'm proud to know the kind of woman you are."

"And your father?"

"Now that Father is over the shock he seems to be fascinated with the idea."

"David, I really didn't mean to upset him so."

"I know," he smiled, went to her and took her hand in his; then he drew it to his lips and kissed her fingers. "I love you, Tam," he said, "more than I did before. You are a woman like no other I have ever known. You may share a beautiful world with a man but you will never belong to anyone but yourself. I would give my life to be the man you wanted to share your life with."

"David . . . I have to tell you."

"Tell me what?"

"It is a long story, David, and it begins with the fact that I am married."

"Married?"

"Sit down, David . . . let me tell you what has happened to me since I left you."

David sat on the edge of her bed; all through the story he said

496

nothing, merely watching her pace the floor as she spoke. When she finished talking, he went to her.

"It seems to have been a tragic thing for you. Stay here a while before you make a final decision on what you want to do. Your world is unbalanced right now. Regain your equilibrium before you try anything new."

"David, I'd . . . I'd like to go to Monticello, just for a few days. I would like to see Tom and Martha, talk to them for a while. Maybe I could tap some of the strength and conviction they have."

"That is a wonderful idea. If you don't mind, I would really like to go with you."

"Marvelous, shall we go soon?"

"Yes, I'll send a message today and we could be ready to leave by next week. Oh, by the way, let's try to be back by the first of the month. Father is planning a ball to welcome some of the naval officers. I'm sure you would find it interesting."

"Yes, I'd like that."

"Good, I'll make the preparations, now," he laughed, "come down and share dessert with us. I promised Father I'd ask you to forgive him for his lack of hospitality. Please come down and tell him what a good diplomat I am."

She smiled agreeably and went down with David. Randolph was pleased and despite what society had bred in him, he looked at Tamara with a new respect and no little wonder. Both his daughters looked at her differently also and wondered how soon they could get Tamara alone to answer the millions of questions they were both mentally preparing. Randolph began to ask her a few questions; at least he meant it to be a few, about the activities she had been involved in.

Tamara, leaving her association with Steffan completely out of it, told them of her escapades on *The Scarlet Butterfly*.

Jennifer's and Martha's eyes grew wide with wonder. "Weren't you frightened?" they asked.

"Sometimes," Tamara admitted.

"Where in Heaven's name did you arrive at that fascinating name?" Jennifer asked.

Tamara told her about her father's gift, and showed her the bracelet with the ship and butterfly that dangled from her wrist.

"But, Tamara," Randolph said, "where in the world did you hide a ship you had painted blood red? It would seem to me no matter where you put it near your island, it would not have been very difficult to find."

"I'm sorry, Mr. Perry. But that's one secret I cannot divulge. The hiding place of *The Scarlet Butterfly* is known only by my crew, who would die to a man before they spoke, and my Father and Mikel Robbins, my first mate and dearest friend."

Randolph was wise enough to know that there were many things that Tamara had left unsaid, and that these things were probably the reason for Tamara's change. He would never question her about them, but his eyes glowed with his admiration for what she had done and the beautiful and fascinating woman she had become.

The trip to Monticello was an exciting and pleasant thing for both Tamara and David. Tamara was enthusiastic about seeing both the lovely home he had built and Tom Jefferson. David was thoroughly enjoying Tamara's company and the fact that she was, at last, seeming to break away from the quiet loneliness and return to the laughing, happy person she had been before.

The Jeffersons met them with open hospitality; small luncheons, picnics and teas to introduce Tamara to all of their friends.

It was not the social occasions that Tamara enjoyed, it was the long quiet walks she took with Tom Jefferson. It was the men who visited his home whose depths of patriotism touched her own. She could feel herself renewed like an empty container being poured full of the glowing liquid of life.

Reluctantly, they left Monticello and went back to the Perry home in Boston. When they arrived, Tamara was told that a message awaited her. She opened it and her smile faded. Without a word, she dropped it on the table and left the room, climbing the steps and closing the door behind her.

David took the letter from the table and read it.

"What is it, David?" Randolph asked, "What has upset her so?"

"It seems the Navy is only too happy to accept *The Adventurer* or any other ship she is willing to donate to a worthy cause, but as for herself they politely believe a lady cannot captain a ship and refuse . . . gently but firmly . . . her offer of personal service. They are willing to put in command any officer of her choice."

"What will she do now, David?" his father asked worriedly.

"Well, knowing her the way I do, she'll never accept this. The Navy has denied her, and in the process it has lost itself one beautiful ship. I'm not too sure what she'll do, but I don't doubt it will be something effective and quick. Her pride has been hurt enough. I don't doubt she'll find some way to repair the damage that will not only startle the Navy but the whole confounded country."

In her room, Tamara stood at a huge chest. She opened it and took out the outfit of the lady pirate. Quickly, she slipped out of her clothes and into the shirt and pants. She stood in front of the mirror and looked at herself.

She was angry and hurt. When she had captained her own ship as a pirate for their benefit, and the Navy did not have to officially claim her, they would use her services. But when they had to claim her as one of them, they could not because she was a woman. Well, she would show them just how effective a woman could be. She would show them that it did not always take a strong back and heavy muscles to captain a ship, but intelligence and a quick mind. "The lady pirate is reborn," she said to herself, "the day after the ball, we will take *The Adventurer* back to Corvet's Rock and prepare her. Then the English Navy and the Colonial Navy will receive the shock of their lives." If they would not accept her on her terms and she could not accept them . . . then she would show them both what expert sailing could do. She would wage her own war under colors of her own.

Tamara was very quiet for the next few days, but David, who knew her so well, knew that something was brewing in her beautiful head. He knew that she took several trips alone to *The Adventurer*, and he knew the ship was slowly taking on supplies.

Tamara was polite to the officials who questioned her about their use of *The Adventurer* but she held them at bay without making a final decision.

The day of the ball was beautiful and Tamara was gone from the house before David arose. She came back late in the afternoon and David sensed a new expectant tension about her, yet she seemed for the first time to be excited about something. He cursed himself many times in the days to follow for believing that it was the ball that excited her and not something else. He, who knew Tamara so well, should have known that a party was certainly not something that would excite her as much as this.

The night of the ball he waited for her to finish dressing. His father had taken his mother and sisters and gone. David had been asked by Tamara to take her in a separate carriage so that they could stop at *The Adventurer* on the way home.

He stood now at the bottom of the stairs because he had heard her door close and the sound of footsteps as she came down the hall. He was completely unprepared for the breathtaking beauty that approached him. She had pulled her long hair atop her head in thick, heavy coils. The gown she wore was a deep green and left him hanging in breathless expectation that at each breath she took it would drop away from the lovely golden charms beneath it.

"Tamara," he said, as he took her hand in his when she reached the bottom of the stairs, "I have never seen a woman as lovely as you are tonight. A woman as beautiful as you should be kept under lock and key; we stand a risk of having a civil war when all our new officers see you tonight."

"Thank you, David," she smiled as she handed him her shawl. He draped it over her smooth, bare shoulders, having great difficulty in keeping himself from pulling her into his arms and pleading with her to stay there with him always.

He helped her into the carriage and climbed in beside her. For him, the trip from his home to the large ballroom in town his father had acquired for this special occasion was over too soon.

That Tamara'a exquisite beauty stunned all the young officers was obvious by the admiring stares of the men and the frowning glares of the young women present. David was pleased and proud that Tamara clung to his arm and resisted with a sweet smile all the advances of the others there. Then he sensed a stiffening in her body and he looked at her questioningly only to see her gaze locked with a tall, handsome, young officer across the room.

The woman with the officer was a beauty herself. The officer seemed to be shocked when he saw Tamara. David's brows furrowed in a frown as he felt Tamara tremble as the young officer and the woman with him started in their direction. When they reached them, David received another surprise as the young man said, "Hello, Tamara."

David looked at Tamara. She smiled a cool, regal smile, but David could feel her quiver with tension.

"Hello, Jeff. I'm amazed to see you here."

"I imagine you are. It was not easy for me. The thing that drew me here was my beautiful wife. I would like you to meet Brandy Sables, my wife. Brandy, this is Tamara Devers, the wife of my dearest friend."

The pieces fell into place for David and he wondered just how Tamara would handle it. "Where is Steff? Why didn't he call on us when he got here?" Jeff asked.

"I have no idea where Captain Devers is at the moment, Jeff," Tamara said, her voice remote and cold. "Nor do I care. I hope he has been justly rewarded for his treachery. I want you to know that as soon as it is legally possible, Steffan and I will be divorced. I want no contact either with him or anything that reminds my of my past mistakes. Enjoy your evening, Captain Sables,'' she smiled toward Brandy. ''Good evening, Mrs. Sables.''

With these words, she turned away from them and left Jeff staring after her in surprise.

The ball went on and on while Tamara tried to ignore Jeff's and Brandy's presence. She stayed as far from him as possible, Jeff could see, but he was determined to call on her the next day to find out what had happened.

When David and Tamara were seated in the carriage prepared to go home, Tamara turned to him.

''Take me to the dock, David.''

''The dock . . . why?''

''All my preparations have been made. I'm leaving tonight.''

''Tam!''

''David, please don't argue with me or try to change my mind. I've planned out all I'm going to do. I'm going home.''

David knew he was defeated so he did as she asked. It was an unhappy David who stood and watched *The Adventurer* leave, and an even unhappier one who tried to explain all that had happened to Jeff Sables the next day.

''Well,'' Jeff sighed, ''at least, if Steffan comes, we can tell him where she is. On Marriott Island.''

But he was wrong, for Tamara never had the intention of going home. She was not going to give anyone a base to search for her. She stood at the wheel and guided *The Adventurer* to the safe, secret haven of Corvet's Rock.

Forty-three

Lucius Clay was a pirate, a pirate who had the ability and means to find himself at home and accepted in any country. He was the owner of four ships, three under the command of men who owed their lives to him and the fourth, the *Golden Sword* under his own command. His wealth, and the wealth of men who backed him, was almost incalculable. Men of influence, whose names would have shocked the society in which they prospered, welcomed him to their shores. It was the reason he was on the streets of London, in fact making his way down a dark shadowed alley, the night an almost completely delirious and exhausted Steffan Devers literally fell into his lap.

Steffan had made his way across the dark grounds and had come to the base of the wall. To him, in his weakened condition, it seemed mountainous. He was sure he would never be able to make his way over it. Pressing his hands against the cool stone, he worked his way along the wall, his fingers searching for some way up. Nothing met his hands but cold blank wall until he felt despair tug at him. He was prepared to abandon the wall and cross the dark garden again, but he was not sure that, not having the wall to cling to, he could make it. Then his hands struck something and closed around thick heavy vines that climbed the wall.

He rested his whole body against the wall, gathering what little strength he had to try the ascent. He knew he was still under the influence of some drug, and he didn't know what to expect. Small glittering lights sparkled in front of his eyes and the wall itself seemed to waver uncertainly. Inhaling a deep ragged breath, he gripped the vine with what little strength he had and began to laboriously climb up.

To him, the wall seemed hundreds of feet high; in reality, it was a little over fifteen feet. What, a few weeks before, would have taken minutes, seemed to take hours. He was panting heavily when his hands gripped the top of the wall and he drew himself up.

He lay atop the wall for a few minutes unable to move. He could feel the perspiration soak his clothes and his chest felt as if someone were sitting on it. What was worse was a pounding headache that began between his eyes and cut through his brain like a dull knife. It began to make him nauseated. He clung to the wall desperately trying to focus his eyes and gather his strength for there was no vine on the opposite side and he knew he would have to drop to the ground.

He could not see the ground below him, but looking outward, he could tell it was a narrow alley. What he would meet when he did drop made him wonder. If it were the hard cobblestone road, he took the chance of breaking both of his legs. If it were uneven ground, he also took the chance of breaking other parts of his body as well. He wondered, if he did, if anyone would ever find him or if he would lie there and die like a wounded animal.

He could not gather his wandering mind; all he knew was that some form of death hovered near for him and he had to get away. He clung only to thoughts of home and the safety there. Grimly determined, he clenched his teeth together and swung his legs over the edge allowing his body to slide down to all the length he could. He hung by his arms for a few moments, then he let go.

What he struck came as much of a surprise to him as it did to Lucius Clay who picked a most inopportune time to walk beneath him.

When Steffan's body tumbled from above Lucius thought for one quick moment he was being attacked, but when Steffan fell away from him and dropped awkwardly on the ground, he realized there was something wrong with him.

Having been on the wrong side of the law of several countries and being chased through the dark alleys of most of them, he suspected that Steffan might be in the same position. He went to Steffan's side and knelt beside him. It was too dark to see Steffan, but he knew he was unconscious; he also realized that Steffan was a large heavily built man. Lucius was not a small man by any means, but he did not think he could carry him far. He was about to try to lift him when Steffan groaned and stirred.

"Can you make it to your feet, mate?" Lucius asked.

Steffan groaned again, but tried to push himself up. In actuality, he did not realize exactly where he was, or who was bending over him.

"Home . . ." he muttered. ". . . Have to get home . . ."

"And just where is home, mate?"

Steffan, in desperation, reached out for Lucius. His hand closed on Lucius' arm, "Help me . . . please? . . . I've got to get away."

"You in some kind of trouble? Who are you running from?"

Steffan's memory was so jumbled that rational thought escaped him. All that pounded through his head was that he had to escape something, and he was not sure what . . . or even why. What was worse was the need to get to someplace or someone he could not name.

Among all the other difficulties was his body's fierce demand for the drug he had been administered steadily for the past few days. His body alternately sweated, then shivered with shocking chills that almost convulsed him. It was then Lucius realized there was more wrong with Steffan than he had first thought. He reached down and gripped Steffan firmly drawing him to his feet. He felt the convulsive trembling in his body and could literally hear his teeth chatter and his ragged breathing.

"Come along, I'll get you to someplace where we can see just who and what you are."

He put one of Steffan's arms over his shoulder and his own about Steffan's waist. Together, they made their way to the edge of the alley; then Lucius half dragged, half led him to the coach that sat at the far end of the alley. The coach that had brought him to a rendezvous and was waiting to take him away.

It took all the strength he had to get Steffan inside; once he did, Steffan collapsed against the seat, his eyes closed. Lucius could see him clearly now. His body was wet with perspiration, his eyes were closed and his breathing labored. He climbed inside and pulled the door shut. In the half-light he looked closely at Steffan who opened his eyes and returned his gaze. One look at his eyes told him exactly what was wrong with his unknown companion.

"Whatever the hell you've been taking, my friend, it's damn near killed you. You look like a man of quality; what ever possessed you to begin taking something as deadly as that? From the looks of you, it's been a while since you've had some and you're in need, my friend." He reached over and took hold of Steffan's shoulder. "What have you been taking?"

Steffan groaned. Lucius wavered in and out of focus and his voice drummed in his head with a deep hollow, vibrating sound. Amid the pain in his body, the pressure in his head and the flickering memories that flashed in and out of his mind not long enough for him to grasp them completely, but long enough to leave a hollow misery in their wake, Steffan tried to speak. "Home . . . help me . . . I didn't take . . . Home . . . I've got to get home."

"Where is home?"

Steffan moaned again as fresh pain, fierce and quick ripped at his body. "Where is home," Lucius said again. "Come on my friend, don't pass out on me now. Tell me where home is and I'll get you there as fast as I can. I'd better, you're half dead. You need help badly . . . very badly. What's your name?" He reached out and smacked Steffan sharply across the face. "What's your name?"

"Devers . . . Steffan Devers."

"Devers," Lucius said in surprise. "Maxwell Devers' son? C'mon, boy, are you Maxwell Devers' son?"

"Yes."

"Good God," Lucius said in amazement. Then he took off his jacket and covered Steffan who was shaking so badly that his teeth clicked together and his muscles jerked spasmodically. Lucius tapped on the roof of the coach and said, "Devers Hall . . . and make it as fast as you can before we have a dead man on our hands, and this is the last one I would like to see die."

The coach rattled through the streets in a mad race to Devers Hall, and Lucius sat back in his seat looking with profound sorrow at the handsome young man across from him. When they arrived at Devers Hall its well lighted condition told him the family was still awake. Trying to hold a half-concsious Steffan erect made it impossible to knock on the door so he kicked it several times. When it was opened, a young maid gave a startled shriek as he stepped inside, dragging Steffan with him. He could hear footsteps approaching on the run and soon Maxwell and Ellen came into the hall followed by Cecile and Tom, their eyes registering the shock of what they were seeing.

"Steffan!" Ellen cried, in a moment she was at her son's side.

"He needs a place to lie down," Lucius said.

"Come," she replied, "bring him upstairs to his room."

It took the combined efforts of Maxwell and Lucius to maneuver Steffan up the steps and into his room where they laid him on his bed. Maxwell had Ellen send someone to ride for the doctor, then made up some excuse to get Cecile from the room. The three men undressed Steffan and put him to bed. Maxwell had said nothing, but Lucius knew that he also recognized the signs of the influence of a drug.

He looked across the bed toward Lucius with a question in his eyes.

"I found him just so," Lucius said, "on the street."

"He's been missing from home for days with no sign of where he's been. Do you have any idea, from where you found him, just where he might have been or how he got into the condition he is in?"

"You know?"

"That he's under the influence of drugs, yes, but I would like to find out just how and why."

He went on to explain Steffan's disappearance and the missing days.

"It seems your son has made himself a very powerful enemy. Someone who wanted him little more than dead."

"The only way we'll find out," Tom said, "is to get Steffan cured of this and rational enough to tell us what happened."

"Yes," Maxwell said agitatedly, the sorrow deep in his eyes. "But if and when we do get him well who's to tell him that it's too late to save Tamara? Who's to tell him that the day of fulfilling her sentence . . . was yesterday? I've never felt so helpless in all my life. No matter what Martin and I try to do, there is a force that closes every door in our face."

"Curing him of this is not going to be quite that easy either. Your son has obviously been taking a great deal of this drug. You can see for yourself, he's run out of it. I would say not too long ago. Look at him, it will be much worse before it can get better."

"Steffan has not been 'taking' drugs!" Maxwell said angrily. "He is not the kind of man to do that sort of thing. A few days ago, he was a happy man, quite normal and with no sign of any kind of problem like this. A few days ago, he simply vanished. Tonight is the first we have seen him since then."

"I think it would be best if you could tell me all that has happened."

"Who are you that we should explain anything?"

"I'm a man who happened along in time to save your son's life. I am also a man who has the type of contacts you never knew existed. If anyone could find out what has happened, it may just be me."

"Who are you?"

"My name, as far as the world knows is Captain Lucky Clay. My real name is Lucius Ezekiel Clay."

506

"Why is the name familiar to me?" Maxwell said.

"It is familiar because a little over fifteen years ago you saved the life of a first mate on the ship *Pelican* when she ran aground, saved his life by jeopardizing yours. Now do you remember me?"

"Be damned!" Maxwell smiled. "Yes, I remember you. Pulled you out of a stormy ocean."

"Yes, by jumping in with more courage than any other man I know. I've never forgotten you. If I can repay my debt just a little please let me try."

"What can we do?" asked Maxwell.

"It will take all of us to get your son through this. If and when we do, we'll ask him what happened. Then I can find the source of his enemies."

"I'll be eternally grateful. What do we do first?"

"Prepare ourselves for an ordeal. We've got to make sure your women do not reenter this room until Steffan is able to face them. Then we have to get ready for a war because he is going to fight, he is going to be strong, be sly, be anything he feels he needs to be to answer the needs of his body. He will threaten, beg, cry, use any means."

"God," Maxwell breathed.

Tom's face was pale, but he looked at Lucius straight. "Whatever Steff needs we'll do, but I think he is stronger than you know. The three of us will care for him, but I'll wager my life that he pulls himself out of this."

"You've got a lot of faith in him, boy."

Tom smiled. "I know him better than you do."

"Well, let's see how well you know him. I think he's stirring to life. You and I will stay with him for the first few hours while Maxwell talks to the women."

Maxwell nodded. He reached down and took his son's hand for a moment, then he laid it gently down and without a word, turned and left the room. Maxwell explained to Ellen and Cecile as hopefully as he could. Cecile began to cry, but Ellen straightened her shoulders and looked levelly at her husband "I too," she said bravely, "will help him."

"Ellen," Maxwell said miserably, "he might be dangerous."

"To me?" Ellen said calmly. "No, Maxwell, I must be with him now. He has too much pain to face when he wakes and recovers from this. I want to help him now and maybe help give him the strength for what he must face later."

"Ellen?"

"Maxwell, don't try to stop me, please," she said sharply, "I must be with him . . . he's my child, too, Maxwell."

Maxwell drew Ellen into his arms and held her for a moment.

"Mother, Father," Cecile said, "Can't I be with Steffan too . . . I love him."

"Cecile you must think of the child you carry. Do you think Steffan could ever forgive himself if he hurt either you or the child?"

Cecile nodded, then she turned away and left the room. Tonight and until he was well, she would pray for the brother she loved so dearly.

It was dawn when Steffan woke. He woke feeling sicker than he had ever felt in his life. His body felt as if it no longer belonged to him, and the sounds of the men who were talking near him came to him as an echo from a long tunnel. Slowly names attached themselves to the voices and as he swam upward through the gray shadows of his mind he heard his mother's low, comforting voice speaking to him as she had when he was a child.

The effects of the drug Morgana had given him would have done all she wanted if she had taken into consideration his tremendous size and his youthful strength. He was to face an ordeal, but it would have been an ordeal he might not have survived had she not made that one error.

The days were nothing to him as were the nights. He only knew he lived in a private, agonizing hell. Now that he was awake oftener, they began to speak to him, but he did not want to hear their voices. All he wanted was relief from the terrible bone-wracking pain. He did not know of the hours upon hours that they took turns watching him and keeping him from hurting himself. They had tied his arms to the bed, and day after day, night after night for over a week, they tried to break through the misery and pain to reach the mind beneath.

True to what Lucius had told them, Steffan became all that he said he would be. When Steffan finally digested the idea that what he craved was a deadly drug, he began to coax for it. His pleas slowly turned first to violent threats, then tearful begging.

He tried to work himself free of the bonds that held him, determined, if no one else would give him what he felt he desperately needed, he would go in search of it himself. It was the most painful thing for all of them to deny him what he thought he needed. To him, they seemed uncaring and cruel. His parents were beside themselves with anxiety and Tom, who loved him as a brother, felt defeated and afraid.

It was late one night, several days after he had come home, that Steffan lay awake and trying to fight the crawling need within him that made him want to shriek and curse the ones around him who held him prisoner. It was Tom's turn to watch him and he had sent an exhausted Maxwell and Ellen to bed, knowing they had almost reached the end of their endurance. Toward the wee hours of the morning when he thought Steffan was finally asleep, he sat in a chair and laid his head back. No matter how he tried to remain awake, he dozed. There was silence, complete and utter silence and as the time ticked by, he drifted into a deeper sleep. So deep he did not hear the click of the latch and the quiet opening of the bedroom door. The room had only the light of one flickering candle so there were deep shadows. Steffan raised his head a little from the pillow and could only see a shadowy form standing in the doorway. He was aware of everything now and he waited until the form detached itself from the shadows and came toward him. She stopped by the bed before he recognized Cecile. "Steffan," she whispered.

"Cee," he said, a thick heaviness in his throat. He wanted to reach for her but his bound arms wouldn't let him. They looked at each other across a few inches of space, then she smiled gently and without another word, she reached for the ropes that bound him.

When they were loosened, she dropped them on the floor; then she sat on the bed beside him. She gently reached out to touch him. "You've been away from us so long, Steff, now you're back, you're home, here among the people who love you. I knew you were too strong to let this kill you. I have missed you, Brother; I have needed your wisdom and support, and my child will need you too. Tom and I have decided to name him Thomas Steffan if it's a boy." She continued to speak to him affectionately as she stroked his hand tenderly.

For the first time since he had been brought home, Steffan's mind and heart began to feel, to reach. Tentatively, with trembling hands, he reached up to touch Cecile. There was a hoarse dry choking in his voice as he spoke.

"Cecile . . . I . . . I don't know."

"I know, Steff," she comforted, "but it's all right. You are back now." She took his hand and held it in both of hers. "Don't worry, Steff, rest, and know that we're here."

Something in him seemed to break and crumble away and he

lay back on the pillow. A peace touched him, and clinging to Cecile's hand, he drifted for the first time into deep and restful sleep, healing sleep that brought strength with it.

Tom blinked his eyes open, when he saw Cecile sitting on the edge of the bed, panic struck him. He rose quickly and went to her. Then he saw Steffan was untied and resting comfortably. He could hardly believe that this was the same man who had been violently fighting those bonds a few hours before.

"Cecile!"

"It's all right Tom. He has no need to be tied. He would never hurt me."

Tom was half-angry, half-frightened. He had terrible thoughts of Cecile lying hurt at Steffan's hands, or the baby hurt. "Cecile, you took a terrible chance," he said.

She rose and went to him, putting her arms about him. "Tom, Steffan would never have hurt me. Between Steffan and me there was always a strong, unbreakable tie. Even when we were very little children, he always protected me, cared for me, loved me. No matter how he was hurt or what was done to him, he would never have hurt me."

Tom sighed deeply and held her close to him.

The next morning, Steffan woke for the first time completely lucid. Although he was extremely weak he recognized everyone. His mother cried for the first time since he had come home. Maxwell laughed, his own voice shaking and thick with emotion.

"She cries now when you're safe. When you were in danger, she was calm and cool and very determined to bring you back."

"I'm home," Steffan said quietly, one hand holding his mother's while he reached for Cecile with the other.

"Now that I have you all together so that you cannot push the answers off on one another, I want you to tell me what has happened. Did you get to Tamara safely, get her out of jail? Is she all right?"

They looked at one another, none of them able to say the words that would again damn Steffan to the hell from which he had just emerged.

It was again Cecile who came to him. She sat on the edge of the bed.

"Steffan," she said as she reached out and took his hand in hers. She began to speak, and the words were chosen carefully but truly.

He made no sound, and his eyes never left hers; as though if

510

he looked away, broke the link between them, he would shatter. When she finished, there was a deep and painful silence.

"Have you been to the prison?" he asked.

"No," Maxwell said, "we . . . we thought . . ."

"Then you don't know for sure if the sentence was carried out?"

"Steffan!"

"You don't. Maybe . . . maybe something happened. Maybe the sentence was not carried out." He closed his fist and pounded it against the bed, closing his eyes and repeated over and over, "She's not dead . . . no, I'll never believe it. She's not dead."

Tears formed at the corners of his eyes. "I have to know, to see for myself."

"I'll go tomorrow," Tom said.

"No!" Steffan said. He looked at Tom. "I have to," he whispered, "I have to see for myself."

"You're not able," Maxwell said.

"Tomorrow, I'll be out of the bed. Tom will help me. I have to go to the prison . . . I have to see for myself. I'll never be able to survive in any way if I don't know for sure what I've done."

"You're not . . ." began Maxwell.

"Don't, Father," Steffan said, showing the deep feelings of guilt he felt. "I *am* to blame. In my own deep stubborn pride, I took a beautiful child, I took her from a safe and beautiful home where she was loved and protected and dragged her to her death . . . for what? To prove what a brave and noble hero I am. Hero!" He laughed painfully, "God, can you realize what your hero has done. I've killed her . . . God," he cried painfully; "Tamara . . . I've killed her and I stood there and asked her to please trust me and go to her death without causing any problems."

Martin had come into the room and had stood listening to Steffan's mournful outcry. "You should have let me die," he said in a voice that cracked with the pain. "How can I go on living with it . . . How can I go on living?"

"How can you not?" Martin said. Their eyes were all drawn to Martin, but he stood looking past them to Steffan. "How can you not go on living. Will you let all she wanted, all she believed in, all she tried so hard to fight for be for nothing?"

Steffan watched him without speaking.

"There are others who are more to blame than you. You did what you did with the thought of freeing her and being happy together. What they did with the malicious intent to destroy both you and Tamara. It will be painful to face, but if you do not . . . then who will find them? Who will keep them from succeeding in what they intended to do? If you fall now . . . they have succeeded in destroying you both. Are you going to submit to that or are you going to stop them and make what she fought for be brought to life again? The only way to make her death meaningful is for you to get up like the man you are and make her death mean something not only to you, but to both your enemies and your friends."

"Martin!" Maxwell said angrily.

"No, Father, he's right. I cannot let it all be for nothing." Steffan looked up at Martin. "And I know who my . . . our enemies are."

"Who," Tom asked?

"Jaspar Sinclair and Morgana Kyle."

"How do you know?" Cecile asked.

Steffan told them all that had happened to him from the night he got the note and then woke to find himself drugged and made his unsteady escape to tumble into the lap of Lucius Clay.

"What are you going to do, Steffan?" His mother said.

"As soon as I can get the strength to get out of this bed . . . I'm going to the prison," Steffan said in a deep, quiet voice. "My wife's body belongs here and I shall bring her home. I will then find Jaspar Sinclair and Morgana Kyle and make them pay the debt for what they have done so deliberately and cold-bloodedly both to Tamara and to me. Then I shall take the ship that I had built and I shall go to the Colonies and join in the battle in which she believed so deeply. It is so very little in return for her life, but for now it is all that I can give. Maybe after that, I can find some peace, maybe I can be able to live with the terrible thing I have done."

They knew he meant every word he said, and believed it more so when he began to gather his strength. He ate, rested and exercised with grim determination for the next few days.

It was over a week later when he came slowly down the steps and was met by Lucius Clay who had been invited to stay at Devers Hall for a while.

"Going out?"

"Yes. It's time I went to the Tower. I have to begin sooner or later and I guess now is best."

"Mind if I go along?"

"No, come if you must."

They left and rode without speaking to the Tower. Steffan stood outside looking at the cold dark building.

"What a terribly lonely cold place to die," he said softly.

"Yes," came a voice from behind him. "It is."

Steffan spun around in surprise and looked into the cold, ice blue eyes of Mikel Robbins.

Forty-four

"Mikel!" Steffan said and he was about to move toward him. It was Lucius who read the murderous look in Mikel's eyes. He stepped between the two just as Mikel drew a knife from his belt. Lucius drew his sword at the same time. He could have cut Mikel down in a moment, and he might have had not Steffan shouted for him to wait.

"No! Lucius, no! Don't kill him!"

Lucius held the point of the sword inches from Mikel who stood glaring at Steffan, the knife still held in his hand.

"Put the knife down, boy," Lucius growled.

"I'll put the knife where it belongs," Mikel snarled, "between the ribs of this treacherous murderous bastard."

"There's no way I'll let you do that, so you might as well forget it."

"Maybe not now," Mikel said, "but in time . . ."

"No" Steffan said evenly, "Mikel, listen to me."

Mikel laughed harshly. "Do you think to take me in the way you took Tamara? Do you think I'm fool enough to trust you? You must think I'm crazy. I don't want to end up the way she did."

Steffan winced, but he kept his eyes on Mikel. "I'm not guilty of what you accuse me."

Mikel made a harsh, disgusted sound. "My God, do you honestly expect me to believe you?"

"Lucius," Steffan said, "we are going to escort Mikel to the carriage," he looked at Mikel, "Come and I will tell you the truth. If after what I tell you, you still do not believe . . . Lucius will leave us and you can do as you please."

"You're crazy, Steffan," Lucius said angrily. "He doesn't want to hear the truth, he just wants to kill you."

"Mikel will listen," Steffan said, "he wants the right to kill me and now there's a small germ of thought in his mind that the truth might be different from what he believes. Listen to me for an hour Mikel. After that, if you don't believe me, Lucius will leave us together. At the moment I don't have the strength or the inclination to fight you. My life for an hour, Mikel, fair?''

"An hour and he leaves," Mikel said gesturing toward Lucius.

"Agreed!" Steffan replied.

"Not on your life," Lucius said firmly, "He intends to kill you no matter what you say. He won't even listen to you with an open mind. He'll only time an hour then plant that knife between your ribs and you're still too weak to do anything about it," Lucius said.

"Mikel?" Steffan questioned.

Mikel looked at Lucius, flashing anger clouding his blue eyes.

"I'm not a liar," he said through gritted teeth. "If I agree to listen for an hour then I will listen. What about you, can you be trusted to abide by an agreement?''

Lucius chuckled, "Boy, my word has been trusted in more countries than you've ever seen," he looked at Steffan. "Steffan are you sure of what you are doing?''

"Yes, Lucius . . . I'm sure. Mikel will make no attempt on my life for an hour. In that time he will listen. The truth is the only thing that will end all of this.''

Lucius sighed and reluctantly slid his sword back into its scabbard. He stood for another minute looking from Mikel to Steffan, then he turned and strode away.

"Shall we sit in the carriage and talk," Steffan asked.

Mikel shrugged and they walked to the carriage together. Once inside, Mikel sat back against the seat and waited for Steffan to begin.

Steffan did so, starting with his beginning enmity with Jaspar and his first meeting with Morgana Kyle. He went on to explain his mission on Marriott Island and how he had fallen in love with Tamara, not believing for a moment she was the pirate for whom he searched. He went on to explain Jaspar's interference, and Mikel began to wonder, when he remembered Jaspar's words about Steffan and his attack on him. He told Mikel of how he had convinced Andrew that he could keep Tamara safe.

"There were so many people working for her release, easing the way, that I let down my guard." He went on, explaining the note from Morgana and his late night visit to her house. His voice filled with anguish when he began to explain his enforced addiction to drugs and his escape and the good fortune of falling into

515

Lucius' hands.

"It is only this morning that I have had the strength to come here," he bent forward and rested his head on his folded hands. Thick choking tears made his last words almost unintelligible.

"God, Mikel, I loved her more than my own life. She was the one woman I would have cherished for the rest of my life as my wife. Without her my life is a dark and lonely place, but I will avenge her death, as God is my witness; the ones who took her life will pay for it. I will track them down to the ends of the earth if I must." He went on to tell Mikel what his future plans were. To fight the battle Tamara could no longer fight, to fulfill the dreams she had and could no longer do. He sat back wearily in his seat, his hands resting listlessly in his lap. His eyes moist with unshed tears and his face drawn with lines of sorrow and pain Mikel had not noticed before.

"That is the truth, Mikel. I have lost all that made my life beautiful. I will carry the guilt of what I have done the rest of my life. Maybe," he smiled grimly, "killing me might be the easy way out for me, for I cannot have a day or a night without the memories of the woman I loved . . . and killed."

Mikel continued to look at him, seeing for the first time the ravages of grief written on his face. Somehow, Mikel knew that what he had just heard was the truth. "My God . . . this whole thing is such a stupid tragedy."

"Tragedy . . . Yes . . . To lose someone like Tam after just finding her . . . to be responsible for the death of someone who trusted and loved you. Have you any idea of the terrible guilt I have to carry the rest of my life? She trusted me . . . and I . . . I," he sobbed thickly, ". . . told her to have faith, then I locked her in that place. I made it possible for someone who hated me to take out that hatred on someone so sweet, so innocent. She did not even know the reason for what was happening to her. How she must have suffered when I didn't come. She must have believed at the last that I deliberately abandoned her. I . . . I might be able to exist if I thought that she didn't believe I betrayed her, but in the end, she must have thought that I had. I would gladly give my life to undo what I have done. I would die in a moment if it would bring her back. But that can't be . . . no, instead, I must live in a dead empty world without her."

"Yes, you must live with the guilt . . . but . . . you can have a small bit of peace of mind . . . Tamara is not dead. Her father and I rescued her the day before the sentence was to be carried

516

out. We were at the trial the last few days. We took her from the jail and her father took her home."

"I . . . What! . . ." Steffan passed his hand over his stunned face. The hand was shaking and beads of perspiration covered his brow.

"Steffan?"

"I . . . I don't know if what I heard was actually something you said or if I am seeing and hearing things that are not there again. The drug . . . you understand . . . I don't always know if what I'm seeing or hearing is real or if it is just what I want so desperately."

"What I just said is true. Tamara is alive and well. She is with her father on the island. But I do not think either of them will ever let you near enough to explain or will they ever believe what you have just told me."

"But you do?"

"Yes . . . yes, I do."

"Mikel, tell me . . . when you saw her last, . . . was she truly well . . . I mean . . . was she hurt . . . was she . . . all right?"

Mikel knew that what he was going to say was going to hurt Steffan worse than he had been before, but he felt he should know everything. He began the story with his being shot by Jaspar; he told him about his recovery and his journey to England in time for the trial and to find Andrew already there. Then he told Steffan of the trial itself, the sentencing, and Tamara's curse on him and his family. Steffan bowed his head in silence while Mikel spoke, then Mikel told him of Jaspar's mistreatment of Tamara, of his attack at the very moment of her rescue. Steffan's head snapped up and the wild light of madness flashed in them.

"Jaspar Sinclair, Morgana Kyle," he said in a low angry voice, "I shall kill them both with my bare hands."

"There's a little more to the story than that. There was another man involved, a man of great power and wealth, and close to the King. Influenced by Morgana, he is the one who changed the trial and made it civil. He is the one who owned the judge who sentenced her. He is the man in whose home you were held."

"Who is he?"

"Lyle Whitfield."

"Where is he?"

"At the moment, both he and Jaspar are prisoners of Andrew Marriott on the island."

"And Morgana?"

"Has vanished. I imagine as soon as she found the three of you gone, she knew the game was up. Anyway, she can't be found. I've searched half of England. It's as if the ground opened and swallowed her."

"You say her father has them prisoner?"

"Yes."

"Then I shall go immediately to Marriott Island. I want to be the one who snuffs out the lives of those rabid animals."

"You don't believe Andrew will let you on that island, do you? He'll kill you at first sight."

"Possibly," Steffan admitted. "But I have to go anyway. Mikel, would you consider going with me? Maybe he might listen to you."

"I was about to suggest that. It's the only way to get to him without his killing you. He is angry enough to smash you like a bug. I would guess that both Jaspar and Whitfield are dead by this time, too."

"We'll take the chance. Are you with me?"

"I am."

"Good. We'll leave tomorrow."

"You still look ill. Do you think we should go now? You look as though you need a little more time to recuperate."

"The sea has always been good medicine for me. That, and the knowledge that Tamara is still alive is all that I need. Let's go home. I want my family to know what has happened. They are grieving as much for Tamara as I. They will be overjoyed to know she is alive."

When the carriage rolled to a halt at the front door, Mikel and Steffan were met by the entire family, all of them anxious about what had transpired between them. Lucius had told them that Steffan and Mikel had met and were talking. He had not told them the details of the circumstances surrounding the conversation.

Steffan and Mikel both caught the warning glance from Lucius as he stood behind the family and watched them approach. Once gathered together Steffan explained as rapidly as possible what had happened and what he was going to do.

"Steffan," Cecile said firmly, "Tom and I are going with you. First to the island, then on to the Colonies."

Everyone began to protest but Cecile silenced them. "It is no use to say anything. Tom and I decided before we were going. Things may have happened differently than we planned, but we have not changed our minds. We are going with you, Steffan. Maybe I can help make Tamara and her father understand all that has happened. Before this treachery, she and I were becoming very close. I should like it to become so again.''

"The baby, Cecile," her mother began.

"Our baby will be born in the Colonies, Mother," she said as she smiled up at Tom. "It is the place my husband wants to be. Maybe," she added with glitter in her eyes, "a grandchild might be the incentive to draw you and Father there also."

Tom smiled, too choked with pride and love to speak, but he took her hand in his and held it tightly.

"It is a right interesting place, the Colonies," Lucius said.

"You've been there?" Maxwell inquired.

"There, and just about every other place," he replied with a laugh.

"Come in, all of you," Ellen said warmly, "it is time that Lucius tells us all about the Colonies."

They all entered the house, Tom, Mikel and Steffan bringing up the rear. There was the shine of life in Steffan's eyes they had not seen in a long, long time. In fact, all of them were delighted to hear him chuckle.

"I have a feeling, Father, the Devers family may all be colonists one day soon."

Maxwell nodded laughing.

"Do you think it's going to be that easy for you?" Mikel asked Steffan.

"Mikel," Steffan said firmly, "Tamara is alive. If it takes my last breath, I will get to her. Whatever it takes, one way or the other, I shall have back what belongs to me and I will never lose it again."

They were silenced by the determined look in his eyes and the firm set of his jaw. At that moment, no one doubted that Steffan would go after what he wanted so desperately . . . in fact, no one even doubted that he would succeed in getting it . . . getting it or die in the attempt.

On Marriott Island, in a small dark cell on a ship anchored in the harbor, two men sat silent. Jaspar, hungry, cold and with the visible tension of worrying about his fate, sat in morose silence and glared at the man who sat across the room from him. Lyle was just as hungry, just as cold, but he had not allowed his mind to be locked into fear. He had a grim determination to find a way to get free of this place, back to the power and position he held and when he did, he would use that power and position to find Morgana Kyle. He had already made tentative contact with the man who brought their food and guarded them the few minutes each day they were allowed to walk on deck. He had told the man who he really was and what kind of reward he would get if he helped him escape. He could tell by the greedy glitter in the man's eye he was thinking seriously about it.

"You know," he had first said, "if I help you get away I have to go too. This ship or this island would not be safe for me."

"Help me get back to London and you will have enough to live well wherever you choose to go."

"We'll have to wait until the next ship docks. There's no other way off the island. You can't get anywhere on one of the captain's ships. As soon as they find out who you are, they will put you right back here. No, it will have to be an off island ship and they don't dock here too often."

"I'm a patient man," Lyle had said firmly, "as long as Andrew Marriott doesn't have us killed before you get the chance."

"I don't like him, but Cap'n Marriott ain't a man to have someone kill for him. If he's going to kill you, he'll do it hisself. I just think he ain't decided what he's goin' to do to you. Either that or he's waitin' for Mikel Robbins to bring him word about the other bird he wants to catch."

"How long do you think it will be before an off island ship stops here?"

"Don't know. Could be today, tomorrow or next week. I got no way of knowin'."

Lyle had waited, silent and patient. The door swung open now and the man who had been in his thoughts walked in accompanied by another carrying food.

The second man went to Jaspar and put the tray of food down. As he did, he stood between Jaspar and his view of Lyle and the first man. It was at that moment, Lyle felt a piece of paper pressed into his hand. He slid the note into his pocket in a quick deft moment.

After they had eaten, the men returned to take them on deck for a few minutes. There he would be able to move away from Jaspar. He did so, walking slowly the length of the ship. There he leaned against the rail and slid the note out of his pocket. He unfolded it and read quickly. Then he smiled and tore the message into tiny pieces and let them drop into the water. He turned and walked back. They were locked back into their cell and Lyle lay on his bed, his hands folded behind his head, knowing he would be free tomorrow.

Heavy black darkness came and Lyle lay still, remaining awake and listening with a pleased smiled to Jaspar's heavy breathing as he slept. The door was unlocked quietly, but Lyle heard the small sound and stood up. When the door was opened the man motioned to him quickly. He went to the door and slipped out without a sound and the door was locked again.

They moved silently, Lyle following carefully the man's movements. Within minutes, they were off the ship.

They boarded another ship a half hour later and as the sun began to rise on the horizon, Lyle felt the rocking movements of the ship change and he knew with feeling of joy that they had put to sea and he was safe. Safe to find the person who had caused him all this grief and discomfort and make her pay. He relaxed now and his body quickened in pleasure as he began to think of just what he would do to Morgana Kyle when he found her, and just how much pleasure he would get in doing it.

The news of the sailor's defection and Lyle's escape was brought to Andrew's attention a few hours later. That he was angry was fairly obvious, and it pushed him to the point of deciding to do something about Jaspar before he had a chance to escape also. He had wanted to wait for Mikel, hoping Mikel would find and bring back Steffan Devers. Then he could punish all three men responsible for what had happened to Tamara.

He had received a letter from Tamara telling him that she was leaving the Colonies and taking a short trip. She loved him and he should not write to her at the Perrys for she would not be there. It upset him that at no time in the letter did she mention where she was going . . . or why.

He had written then to David Perry who had replied that he and his family knew no more about Tamara's destination than he did. He had tried to stop her, but Tamara's plans had been made and she would tell him nothing more. He told him about Jeff Sables and Brandy who had come to see Tamara the day after the ball to find her gone. He had said Jeff Sables was a friend of Steffan's and had explained some things about his friend he thought Andrew should know.

Andrew cast the letter aside. At this moment, he was interrupted by the man who brought the message that Lyle Whitfield in the company of Miles Dobson had escaped. Andrew stood up.

"Bring Jaspar Sinclair here," he ordered. In a moment, the man was gone. Andrew went to his library and took from the wall a long gleaming saber. By the way he handled it, there was no doubt that Andrew was an expert with it.

A knock on the door and Andrew's reply brought two sailors with a frightened Jaspar between them. Jaspar eyed the saber in Andrew's hand and knew the time had come for Andrew's revenge. Mustering up what small amount of courage he had, he said belligerently, "Are you not going to let me defend myself."

Andrew rose from his chair and went to Jaspar; standing about a foot from him, he touched him lightly under the chin with the saber's point. "Did you let my daughter defend herself? A man should be returned exactly what he has given."

Jaspar gulped and his face whitened but he did not reply.

"Take him out on the back lawn," Andrew ordered. They dragged Jaspar away and for a few minutes, Andrew stood alone. He made an angry sound of disgust and he went to a cabinet where he withdrew another saber. Killing a man in cold blood, no matter what he had done, was a thing Andrew could not, would not do.

He walked out to the back lawn. Then he told the two sailors to withdraw a few feet and he flung the second saber at Jaspar, who caught it in surprise.

Andrew raised the point of his saber and Jaspar raised his. The two touched and for a few minutes; there was complete and utter silence. A voice spoke from the doorway to the house.

"Wait, Mr. Marriott. I think someone else has first call on this man's blood. Someone who owes him a greater debt." Mikel Robbins' voice rang out.

Both Jaspar and Andrew looked toward the door in complete surprise. A surprise that turned to other emotions when they saw who was standing there, for Mikel was not alone. With him were Steffan Devers and Tom Braydon. The men Andrew wanted more than anything in the world.

He motioned to the two men who had brought Jaspar to watch him, then he turned and with his eyes pinned on Steffan and the saber held firmly in his hand, he walked slowly toward him. Before he could get close enough, Mikel stepped between them. Andrew looked at him in angry surprise. "There are some things you need to hear first. If after that, you still want to kill him, then I will say nothing else."

Andrew nodded and looked at Steffan whose eyes were on the

sweating pale Jaspar who couldn't quite believe, after the last time he had seen Steffan, that he was really there.

The saber was removed from Jaspar's hand and he barely felt it. He was looking across the strip of lawn at death and he knew it. He closed his eyes, weaving on his feet as Steffan and Tom turned and went back into the house followed by Andrew and Mikel.

There was nothing he could do. The two men who guarded him were big burly sailors from whom he knew he could not escape.

The time seemed to slow almost to a stop. He could hear his own heart beat, feel every drop of perspiration that trickled down his body. His nerves strung to the breaking point and in despair he almost cried with the need to go somewhere and hide. It seemed to him to be a silent eternity before the door opened and Andrew reappeared. Again, he was followed by Mikel, Tom and Steffan. But what struck terror in his heart was that now . . . Steffan carried the saber. "Give him back the saber," Steffan said in a voice deceivingly mild.

The saber was thrust into Jaspar's unwilling hand. He seemed not to know he really had it. His eyes were held by the merciless gold brown eyes of Steffan who promised him just reward for all that had happened.

"Raise your saber, Jaspar," Steffan said. "It is time to be repaid for your deeds."

Trembling, Jaspar raised the saber. He knew he had to fight with everything he had.

"One of you at a time?" he asked shakily.

"No. If you get past me, you are free to leave the island," Steffan said calmly.

With this small ray of hope, Jaspar looked at Steffan, then raised his saber with just a little more assurance. What little certainty Jaspar might have had slowly disintegrated as Steffan attacked with ferocious energy. His saber seemed to Jaspar to be everywhere at once and he could do nothing but put up a defense. Another thing chilled his heart. After a few moments, it became obvious to Jaspar that Steffan did not intend to kill him quickly, but to slowly cut him to ribbons before he died.

He could feel his labored breathing and was frustrated that Steffan seemed to be so very cold and sure. He cried out in pain as Steffan's saber found its mark again and again. He was coated now in little ringlets of his own blood. The saber was like a flash of lightning. His cheek was cut by a long jagged slash, a cut appeared over his eye. His arms felt the cutting blade; small deep cuts across his chest and on his legs bled until the pain and the blood were too much. He gave a loud cry and charged at Steffan raining crashing blows against the defending saber. Steffan allowed him to fight until he was defeated in a way he had never been defeated before. When he saw the complete despair in the tears that washed down the bloody cheeks, he began a final assault that ended suddenly when the saber slipped beneath Jaspar's guard and found its way to his heart.

Steffan stood, his face showing no remorse or pity as Jaspar staggered, dropped his saber and collapsed in a heap at Steffan's feet.

"You are the first," Steffan said coldly, "but have no fear, Jaspar, there are others to follow you and they will also receive the same mercy you did. Morgana will join you soon."

He turned and wordlessly handed the blood-stained saber to Andrew.

"You've understood and I am grateful, but there is someone whose understanding and forgiveness I cannot live without. I'm leaving for the Colonies now to find Tamara."

"She is no longer there. I received a letter from her. She has left the Colonies."

"Where is she?"

"I'm not sure, but if I know my daughter, I have an idea what she's doing."

"And?"

"The Colonial government very foolishly wanted to accept *The Adventurer* but they did not want the lady captain who went with her."

Steffan lips twisted in the first grin of amusement Tom had seen on his face in a long time. There was even a quick flash of the glittering humor in his eyes as he replied, "A shame. They should have known better. I could have told them how dangerous it was to deny the lady's ability. But that doesn't tell me where she is."

"I would say," Andrew grinned, "that the *Scarlet Butterfly* is back in action and that all English ships carrying arms to the Colonies should go well armed."

Steffan chuckled and Andrew joined him. Tom smiled as he watched them and he and Mikel exchanged glances. They had a deep suspicion they were about to go hunting for a pirate lady.

Forty-five

The war between England and the Colonies began to build in intensity. Marthie Price was forced to come home when Jonah finished what little training he was to have and had gone off to join his regiment.

Both Brandy and Jeff insisted she move in with them in the large house Jeff had bought. She agreed only after many arguments on their part and little Jeff's tearful insistence that Soldier would need someone to take care of him until Jonah returned.

A friendship was forming between David Perry and Jeff and eventually the story of what had happened between Steffan and Tamara was told although Jeff did not himself know the reason for the break between them. After a short while, Jeff and the *Actaeon* were put under the command of John Paul Jones who was spending a good deal of time now in France in the hope that France would outfit him with a fleet of heavily armed ships to do battle with the British. He was convinced he would never get such a fleet if he waited around for Congress to present him with one. When he got his fleet, it was not exactly what he had wanted in terms of quantity and quality of the men under him. But he used it to good advantage.

His flagship in the beginning was *Le Duc de Duras*, a tired East Indiaman. She carried thirty six guns. Carpenters made a number of gunports on the lower deck, filling them with obsolete eighteen pounders which promptly exploded in his first battle.

Time after time, Jones was frustrated in his plans to raid sections of the British coast. When he finally spotted a fleet of British ships returning home, he attacked and used Jeff and the *Actaeon* for support. Jones captured the twenty gun guard ship and renamed her the *Bonhomme Richard*.

He was filled with praise for Jeff's seamanship and command ability. Jeff became quite the hero not only to the men under him but to the two people who meant more to him than any of the others . . . Brandy and his son.

On his arrival home, after another long, tedious and wasted trip, Jeff decided to accept an invitation from the Perrys to join them at the local playhouse for a play and a social evening together. Brandy was excited about it, but little Jeff was less so when he was told he would have to stay home with Marthie.

"Papa, can't I please go? I'll be ever so good. I won't say a word, and Papa . . . I . . . I won't ask a single question, honest."

Jeff laughed. "I'm tempted just to see if you could go for one evening without asking one."

"Jeff," Brandy suggested, "Marthie could come along and after the play, she could bring Jeff home. I'm sure she is lonely and would like to have some pleasure herself."

"Good idea," Jeff agreed. "Ask her if she would care to come."

Brandy did so and Marthie agreed readily. The carriage ride to the Perrys was not very long but it was gay, with young Jeff laboring to the best of his ability not to put everything he said in the form of a question. He was proud of the fact that his beloved Aunt Marthie had gifted him with a miniature uniform that was almost a replica of his father's with the exception of the officers rank and gold braid. He stood straight and proud as he copied his father's handling of his mother by extending his hand to help Marthie into the carriage. Doing her best to keep her quivering lips from outright laughter, Marthie took his hand and stepped up into the carriage.

When they arrived at the Perry home, they were surprised to see another carriage in front of it.

"Were the Perrys inviting other guests, Jeff?" Brandy asked.

"No, I don't think so. It must be someone unexpected." He stepped down from the carriage. "Let's go and find out."

Their knock on the door was answered by David himself. "Jeff, Brandy come in, come in."

"I hope you don't mind David, we brought Jeffie along. Marthie has graciously agreed to take him home after the play."

"Of course we don't mind. I'm sure Jeff will enjoy it, and Mrs. Price, you are always a welcome addition to any group."

"Thank you, David."

"We have some unexpected guests, Jeff. Come in and greet them. We've plenty of time before the play begins."

David escorted them to the sitting room door followed by young Jeff and Marthie. He was surprised when Jeff stopped at the doorway and stared in shock across the room. More surprises were to follow when Jeff smiled, crossed the room and he and David's guests threw their arms about each other laughing and clapping each other on the back.

"Steff! For God's sake, it's about time you got here. I never thought I'd see you again."

"Jeff, if you pound me that hard one more time I shall begin to regret coming."

They laughed together and Steffan put his hand on Jeff's shoulder.

"Jeff, this is Andrew Marriott . . . Tamara's father."

Jeff hesitated for just a moment; then, after casting a surprised look at Steffan, he held out his hand to Andrew. "I'm honored to meet you, sir."

"And I, you, young man. I've been hearing a great deal of you in the past few hours."

Jeff grinned in pleasure.

"This is Mikel Robbins. He was first mate on the *Butterfly* and is probably Tamara's closest friend."

Jeff held out his hand to Mikel, but like his son's, his eyes were filled with questions. "This all comes as a surprise to me," Jeff said, "I've a million questions to ask you, Steff."

"But Father," young Jeff interrupted, "you said no questions tonight. If you ask some . . . can I ask some, too?"

They all laughed at this and young Jeff looked from one face to the other unaware of what he had said that was so funny. He looked up at the man who stood beside his father. He had always thought his father was the biggest man he had ever seen, but the two strangers here were even larger. He had questions prepared already and was only holding them back with sheer determination and the threat of his father's heavy hand on the seat of his pants for disobedience. "Jeff," his father smiled down at him and young Jeff was relieved to see the humor and affection in his father's eyes. "This is the very closest and best friend I've ever had. This is Captain Steffan Devers and this gentleman here is Mr. Andrew Marriott. Mr. Marriott, this is my wife Brandy and my son Jeff. Next to them is Mrs. Marthie Price, she is also a dear friend of the family."

Andrew greeted them all with a friendly smile, but his eyes remained on Marthie. It was the first time since the death of Joanna that Andrew had felt the same depth of quiet beauty in another woman.

"Where's Tom?" Jeff asked Steffan.

"He's with Cecile. Her time is almost here and Tom won't let her out of his sight for a minute."

"Is she well?" Marthie asked.

"She claims she's as healthy as she ever was, but Tom isn't taking any chances."

"Steff, come over to the house tomorrow," Jeff said. "We have a lot to talk over and a lot of missing spaces to fill."

"Yes, I meant to find you when I got here; I just didn't know it would happen so fast. We only arrived today."

"Come for dinner," Brandy said.

"Thank you, Brandy, I will."

"Well," Randolph Perry said, "shall we go along; I believe the play should be starting soon."

They agreed and in a few minutes they were bundled in the carriage and on their way to the theater. All of them enjoyed young Jeff's rapt attention to the stage during the play. He behaved so well, Jeff agreed that he should go along to dinner afterwards. Andrew took the opportunity on the way home to talk to Marthie. Subtle questions to find out all about her. In no time, he had secured two things. The knowledge that she was a widow with a young son in the Army, and that there was no special man who occupied her free time.

The evening ended on a quiet, relaxed note. Jeff and Brandy returned home and put an exhausted Jeff to bed. Andrew and Steffan sat beside a red embered fire and spoke quietly since everyone was in bed.

"You're far away, Steffan," Andrew said.

"I was just wondering where she is, how she is. I can't rest until I find her. I have to let her know the truth. But where am I supposed to start looking?"

"Well, I have an idea."

"What? Anything, I'll try anything."

"How about repeating history."

"What?"

"Repeat history. How did you find the *Scarlet Butterfly* before?"

"You mean send out a ship, a merchant ship, and let her find me?"

"Right."

"What if she doesn't find me?"

"Now Steffan," Andrew laughed. "You are short-changing

my daughter again. You have the word spread that you're running arms then get yourself a big lumbering ship. The bait will be too strong for her to resist."

"Do you want to come along?"

"No. You're going to have some problems. I think she had planned on divorcing you. If that is completed you may have some trouble getting her back again. After what Jaspar told her and after whatever it was she thought she found out about you, I don't know. It seems there are a lot of things she left unsaid. Whatever it was, it was enough to make her hate you. I think I would only be a shelter for her to run to if you found her. No one can help you, Steffan, in getting Tamara back. It is something you will have to do all by yourself. I'm sorry for all that has happened, but I can't do anything."

"I'll be hunting up a good merchant ship tomorrow. In a week or so, I'll have it ready. Is there some way you can start the word in circulation that I'm shipping guns."

"I'm sure Randolph and I will be able to help you there."

"Good."

They were silent for a few moments, then Andrew rose. "Well, I'm going to bed. See you in the morning, son."

"Goodnight."

Andrew left the room and Steffan sat deep in thought. "Tam," he murmured, "where are you, my love? Wait for me . . . I need you, Tam . . . I wish I knew what you were doing now."

As Andrew climbed the stairs to his room, his thoughts were going in the same direction. "My dear child," he thought, "wherever you are, I hope you two find each other again. I'm so sorry for all that has happened. Now that I know it all I'm sorry for Steffan, too. It is the first time, daughter, I would like to see you caught."

Several things were happening at the same hour—there, in the same town as Steffan and his family; a beautiful blonde woman rented a small house and hired a closed carriage. At the same time Steffan and Andrew were contemplating the whereabouts of Tamara, Morgana was contemplating a future confrontation with both men and the possibilities of how she would destroy both of them.

Tamara paced the deck of the *Scarlet Butterfly*. She had not yet painted the ship red, but she planned to do so. The night was quiet and a soft breeze played with the curls that framed her face and blew them in careless strands across her troubled green eyes.

She had received word from one of her spies that two ships going from England to America were to pass this way soon. One, they said, carried men. She had no wish to kill anyone so this was not her target. The other ship was laden with arms. This ship was the one for which she was now on the lookout. She missed Mikel desperately. Her first mate now was a good man, a man who had served under Mikel for some time; a good man, but not Mikel. She longed for Mikel, the friend, the one she could talk to, the one who understood her.

She would not let her mind go back to the terrible nights and days in the prison, nor the painful tragedy of Steffan's betrayal. Despite what she wanted, the pain twisted within her. Firmly, she pushed it away, setting her mind on the past few days. She had found an attorney before she left England and she had requested he start the divorce proceedings. When she finished with her responsibilities, when all this was over, she had decided to return to her secret place on Corvet's Rock and spend enough time alone to collect herself. Free of Steffan and her past, she would one day start a new life. A life that did not include any man, for she felt she could never trust again, never love again.

"Sail ho!" came the shout.

Tamara lifted the telescope and found the dim outline of the sails that were headed in her direction. "Prepare to attack!"

At her command men leapt to their stations and prepared to meet the oncoming ship.

With a slow overburdened ship as a conquest, the slick speedy *Butterfly* had no trouble in taking her. She used the same procedure she always had. The angry captain watched as his ship load of arms was transferred from his ship to hers. Tamara taunted him with a request that he tell his owners to hurry with another shipment, the Colonies needed all the arms they could get.

"This is piracy!"

"Oh dear," Tamara said in mock sympathy, "it is not piracy, sir . . . it is the fortunes of war."

"What kind of woman wears a man's pants and attacks ships on the sea? You should be home where you belong."

Tamara's joyous laughter made him even angrier.

"You will regret this, you . . . you . . ."

530

"Watch what you say, sir. As a pirate, I might make you walk the plank."

The laughter of Tamara's crew sent the captain into a rage. His face became red and mottled. He watched her wave a jaunty farewell. Within minutes, she was gone.

Tamara made her way back to Corvet's Rock. There she unloaded the cargo into the caves to await the arrival of Jack Teel. He could take them to the Colonies for she did not want to return to the Colonies now.

Once again on the open sea, she began her hunt for more merchant ships. She spent two weeks in fruitless search then decided to return again to Corvet's Rock to do some minor repairs her ship needed. This was the time, she thought, to paint her as well. She had her ship worked on and painted. While this was being done, she spent most of her time in solitude. Walking the beach, swimming in the lagoon and sitting in the mouths of the caves and watching the crashing sea. The strong currents and thundering waves breaking against the rocks echoed her emotions now, for no matter how hard she tried to hate, how much she tried to exclude him from her thoughts, Steffan came again and again. As always, the pain was as deep and piercing as it was the first time. She could close her eyes and see him, in the arms of the beautiful stranger when she had needed him most. Worst of all, was the crushing knowledge that she could not stand anyone to touch her. It was the reason she had left David so quickly. The night before the ball, David had been strolling with her in the garden of the Perry home, they had talked and laughed together, then David had kissed her. She would never forget the strangling panic that had overwhelmed her. Again, she had felt Jaspar's brutal hands on her and his hungry hard mouth which had bruised and crushed her. She had wanted to scream and fight, and had held herself from doing so by sheer will. But she had known that Jaspar's brutality had ruined her for any man . . . No, she thought, it was not only Jaspar's brutality, but Steffan's treachery. Well, maybe she had Jaspar to thank. His brutality would help her to fight the thoughts of Steffan and the piercing memories that made both her sleeping and waking hours a nightmare.

At the Perry home, Mikel lay abed, unable to sleep. He was turning the same problem over and over in his mind. Was Tamara at Corvet's Rock? Should he tell Steffan about the entrance? He wondered why Andrew had not, for he knew Andrew wanted their paths to cross again.

The next day, he found Andrew alone for a few minutes and he asked him if she would tell Steffan before he left.

"No!"

"Why?"

"Mikel, I would like them to cross paths again on the open sea or on land, but, just in case Tamara does not want to be with him anymore, if she wants her freedom and if she cannot forgive him, then she has to have this place of her own. No, we will let them work out their problem one way or another, but we will not betray Tamara's trust. Until she tells us otherwise, Corvet's Rock is her secret . . . and ours."

Steffan had gone to Jeff's and Brandy's home for dinner and to fill him in on all that had happened.

"I thought there was something seriously wrong the last time I spoke to her, but I never got a chance to talk to her again. After the ball, I went to the Perry household only to find her gone."

Brandy sat quietly watching Steffan's face as they spoke. She could see instantly just how hungry Steffan was for any word of Tamara.

"What did she say, Jeff?"

"I don't remember exactly but it was something to the effect of 'I don't know where he is nor do I care.' She was cold, hurt and very angry. The rest of the night, she built a wall between us I couldn't get over. The next day . . . she was gone."

"She is so very beautiful, Steffan," Brandy said.

"Yes," he agreed, "she is. Has she changed because of all this, Jeff? Is she still the same?"

"She's changed, but for some reason she seems to have become more beautiful in an assured, mature kind of way."

At that moment young Jeff came in with a minor problem that only his father could repair. Jeff excused himself for a moment and Brandy and Steffan sat together.

"Steff, I don't mean to say anything I shouldn't, but the night of the ball, when Jeff and Tamara were talking I was watching her. When Jeff mentioned your name, I could see pain in her eyes, but I could see something else as well."

"What?"

"No matter what has happened . . . Tamara still is in love with you."

"How do you know, Brandy?" He asked hopefully.

"You might call it woman's instinct or some other foolish

thing, but the look in her eyes was defensive and hurt. She was afraid to speak of you, afraid her longing and need for you would show. She wanted to hate you, wanted to have it as a shield from any future hurt. It is the reason she ran before Jeff could talk to her again. She was afraid she could not fight the words that would bring you into her heart again.''

"When . . . if I ever find her, I wonder if it is not too late already. I hope it hasn't killed what love she had for me, because I cannot see the rest of my life without her and I cannot live with this guilt on my soul. Even . . . even if she can't love me,'' he said. "Maybe if she could forgive me for all I've done to her, it might be a beginning. With that much I would have the strength to fight for her for the rest of my life if necessary.''

"You'll find her, Steffan,'' Brandy said gently, "and with the love you have for her, you both can pick up the pieces and start over. Aren't Jeff and I the good example of that thought?''

"Yes,'' Steffan smiled, "I hope I'm as lucky as Jeff was.''

"What about Jeff?'' the man under discussion said as he walked back in the room.

"I was just telling your wife how very lucky an ugly lump like you is to get someone like her.''

"Well,'' Jeff sighed as he sat down by Brandy and took her hand in his, "I saved up my luck all my life to get the one thing that was worth it all.''

Their enjoyable evening over, Steffan went home slowly, allowing his thoughts the freedom to linger. When he rose and came down to breakfast the next morning he found that Andrew was already finished and prepared to leave.

"Going out?''

"Yes, I've asked Marthie Price if she would like to go riding today. It's a beautiful day for it. By the way, I'll stop around a few places and start the rumors rolling.''

"Yes, I'm going down to the docks today to find what I can in the way of a slow old tub. I'm going to lumber around the ocean until I find Tamara, or rather she finds me.''

"Then?''

"I don't know. I may have to kidnap her and hold her prisoner until she lets me talk to her.''

"Is that really the way?''

"No'' Steffan laughed. "It's just desperation.'' His smile faded. "I don't know what will happen when we meet. All I know is I've got to reach her. Somehow, I've got to make her understand how much I need her."

"I must admit that if Mikel had not been with you and urged me to listen I would have run you through that day in the garden. Both you and Tamara have been through a great deal. I hope your love is strong enough to weather the storm. The seas will be high and the gale furious."

"Speaking in nautical terms, sir, if I don't weather the storm, if I lose the first mate on my vessel, it would be best if my ship were to sink also. It is impossible to navigate the waters of life's ocean without her."

"I wish you good luck, boy. There are many who would like to help you, but we are all helpless. There is no way anyone can bring you two together and heal the wounds." He went on to tell Steffan of Tamara's last days on the island before she left for the Colonies, of their day spent together, excluding the secret of Corvet's Rock.

"She seemed to gather strength, and I have always had the feeling that her love for you is not dead, only wounded. She did not love easily, nor will she give up easily. She once voiced the desire to see you again, to look in your eyes and search for the truth. Maybe if you can get your paths to cross, she might find the truth she has been searching for."

"Well," Steffan said, "we will not accomplish anything if I sit here any longer. I would like to be on my way soon."

"Yes," Andrew rose and they left the house together.

Steffan went to the docks which were jammed with ships of all sizes from all countries. He asked around the docks for most of the day before he found what he wanted. It took the balance of the day to negotiate the purchase of a ship he would not even have looked at in earlier times. It was a huge cumbersome vessel, but exactly what he wanted. Even if he gave all appearance of a good fight, Tamara would have no trouble overtaking and boarding her. From that moment on, everything else rested in Tamara's hands.

Andrew and Marthie spend most of the day riding along the road that skirted the coast. The day was exceptionally warm and beautiful and they found, once they began to talk, that they had many likes and dislikes in common. She bubbled with relaxed laughter at his great sense of humor.

When he left her at home, it was with the promise from her that she would share dinner and the theater with him the following night.

Mikel too, found enjoyable ways for his spare time, but no matter how they all tried there was a state of suspended tension, a feeling of something imcomplete that hung in the air and lurked behind the words of every conversation. None of them would rest until the destined confrontation between Tamara and Steffan had taken place.

Maybe some of the tension hastened the birth of Cecile and Tom's son. It was an easy delivery for Cecile, but a very difficult one for Tom who was supported by Jeff, Andrew, Mikel and Steffan. Supported so well he was half tipsy when he stumbled into Cecile's room and looked down on the red wrinkled face of his son. He stood in silence, as if he were still amazed that the beauty he had shared with Cecile had brought forth such a miracle.

"He . . . he's so little," Tom said in wonderment.

"Little!" Cecile protested. "Tom, he's a big baby."

"He is? He looks awfully small to me."

"For a man who came from such a big family, you certainly know very little about babies."

"I never paid any attention before," Tom grinned. "None of them was as important as this one is."

He sat on the edge of the bed and took Cecile's hand in one of his while with the other he caressed the fringe of the light hair on his son's head. "But he is so very beautiful," he said admiringly, "like his mother." He lifted Cecile's hand and kissed her fingers gently while he held her smiling eyes with his. "I love you Cecile, and I'm grateful for all you have given me. Sacrificing your life in England, coming here with me, making my life a joy, and giving me a son. There is nothing more a man could ask for in the world than what I possess."

"And your son, my love," she said happily. "What shall we name him?"

"How does Thomas Steffan Braydon sound to you?"

"My child named after the two I love most in the world . . . it sounds beautiful."

Tom bent forward and kissed Cecile first, then his son. "Welcome to this topsy turvy world, Thomas Steffan Braydon," he said.

When he was finally forced from Cecile's room he went back down the stairs and he and the rest of the male family began to celebrate his son's birth. They celebrated to the extent that thay had to stumble to bed that night and wakened the next day with headaches as reward for their pleasure.

The ship Steffan had bought was finally prepared to leave. Tom wanted to go with him but Steffan refused. "I've gotten a whole new crew for her temporarily. I don't want anyone aboard Tamara recognizes. One look at you and the game will be over before I can get her in a position where she can't get away. Besides, Cecile will have my hide if I drag you away now. Don't worry, Tom, I'll be back soon."

Steffan went to Cecile and told her what was happening. He kissed and held his new nephew for a while. Then he said a fond farewell to everyone.

Andrew and Marthie insisted on taking him to the docks. Just before he was ready to walk up the gangplank, Andrew held out his hand to him and Steffan grasped it firmly. "I wish you good luck and godspeed."

"Thank you, sir."

Marthie kissed him on the cheek and in the next moment, Steffan was gone. They watched the ship move heavily toward the neck of the harbor.

"He's so unhappy," Marthie said feelingly.

"Yes," Andrew agreed. "There is only one cure for his unhappiness and my daughter's. I hope somewhere out there soon, they find each other . . . really find each other."

Marthie understood Andrew's unhappiness also. She put her hand in his and they stood and watched the ship vanish from sight.

Forty-six

Andrew and Randolph, true to their word, spread the rumor about that the *Bethany* was a conveyor of arms for the British army. Every ear that listened knew what the ship was. Of course, ears that were loyal to Tamara heard also. The leaving of a small sloop a few days after Steffan's departure, her destination, known only to her captain was a rendezvous with a notorious pirate . . . a pirate by the name of Jack Teel.

All of them, in their own separate ways wondered what the outcome would be. Although they did not speak of it, the questions in their minds were all alike. Would Tamara find the bait Steffan was dangling in front of her eyes. If so, would she try for it? What would happen between them if and when she did? Would Tamara give him an opportunity to explain and most important of all, if she did, would she believe him?

It was Andrew who had the gravest of doubts, for it was he who believed there was some unknown quantity, something that only Tamara knew, something that had crushed her completely. He knew what Jaspar had done to her, he knew her imprisonment and trial had been terrible, but he knew Tamara's strength and he felt she could survive all that. No, he thought, there was something else, something Steffan did that had taken the love and forgiveness she had and crushed it.

Yet he had always felt, as did the others, that Tamara and Steffan had shared a love few couples had and that the emotions they shared would not be destroyed easily.

Andrew found Marthie's company soothing to his troubled heart. She was a gentle creature and she would quietly listen to him and then tactfully point out what was faulty with his thinking. She also had a way of making him relax and laugh. Something he had not done in a long, long time.

He spent as much time with her as he could, taking her for rides, walks along the seashore and bright evenings of the theater and dinner. There were many evenings he spent at Jeff's home.

Marthie was an excellent cook and often would invite him for dinner. At the beginning, Jeff and Brandy were usually present, but lately it seemed that Jeff and Brandy found occasions to be elsewhere.

Jeff was awaiting orders from Jones again and as usual he found the waiting tedious. "I'm beginning to believe the privateers have the right idea," he grumbled often. "I could get a commission from the Colonies and be on my way free to attack any enemy ship that strayed into our waters. This way I have to sit here and twiddle my thumbs, constantly awaiting word to move here, move there. I cannot stand this inactivity."

"Jeff," Andrew laughed one evening. "Grumble as you may, you are a Navy man, you like things with order and dependability. If you did get commissioned as a privateer, you would then grumble at the fact that the Navy no longer wanted you."

Jeff chuckled and Brandy laughed outright.

"I suppose you're right. I wonder if I should not have joined the Army instead of the Navy. At least they seem to be doing something."

He was contrite the moment he finished speaking for Marthie's face had paled. They had received word of the latest skirmish. Jonah had participated in it. The word had come that the battle was severe and many had been killed or wounded. Since that battle, there had been no word from Jonah and Marthie lived in dread day by day.

"Marthie," Jeff said miserably, "I'm sorry. That was a stupid thing to say. Please forgive me, I didn't mean to hurt you or remind you so brutally."

"It's all right, Jeff," Marthie replied. "I have known how impatient you have been."

"Marthie," Andrew said as he rose from his chair. "That was a most excellent dinner. May I reward the chef by taking her for a nice relaxing ride through the park? I've my new buggy outside awaiting us."

"Thank you, Andrew," Marthie smiled at his efforts to comfort her. "I would enjoy that."

"Would you and Jeff care to come along, Brandy?"

Although Brandy's eyes twinkled with mischief, she refused politely. Andrew grinned at her over Marthie's head, acknowledging the fact that he knew she knew he would rather be alone with Marthie.

Marthie put a light shawl about her shoulders and they departed.

"She's good for Andrew," Brandy said. "I've not seen him seem so relaxed since we first met."

"Yes, but . . ." Jeff began, then he shook his head negatively.

"But? What Jeff?"

"Steffan has told me often about Andrew and Tamara's mother. It seems there has been no other woman in Andrew's life since Joanna. Oh, a few come and go, but it seems Andrew has had something very rare and special and he won't settle for anything less. I doubt if any other woman could fill Joanna's place in his heart."

"I would hate to see Marthie get hurt."

"So would I."

"Oh, Jeff, isn't it a shame that the lives of the people around us, the ones we love, are so jumbled and painful?" She rose and went to him and he drew her into his arms and held her. "Sometimes I feel so guilty. I have so very much that it hurts me to see the ones I love suffer."

"There's nothing we can do about it. We have had our share, too. When you left and I thought I would never see you again, I felt that my life was nothing. I hope Steff is as lucky as I have been. He's lost Tamara as I lost you. I hope he finds her and they can be as happy as we are."

Jeff tipped Brandy's face up and gently kissed her. He found her, as always, a warm harbor where he felt safe and loved. His arms tightened in a possessive grasp, for it had come to him again the misery he had felt when he was alone and Brandy was not part of his life.

She felt the tremor in his body and she tightened her arms about him to let him know she understood.

Andrew and Marthie rode along in silence for quite some time. Marthie watched his face from under lowered lashes and could see he was lost in deep thought. She knew he was worried about his daughter and Steffan but she felt it was more than that.

Andrew had been very good for Marthie. In her loneliness, with Jonah gone, she had turned to him and he had made her long days and quiet nights pleasant.

She was honest enough to admit to herself that she was very attracted to him. She knew that he was a widower and she never asked him about his wife and Andrew had never volunteered the information.

She respected his silence for she knew how she had felt when her husband had died. It had been a traumatic affair for her and she knew how the memories lingered in the depths of her soul.

It was obvious that he had loved his wife very much, just from what Mikel had told her. In the few times they had spoken together she formed a picture in her mind of what a beautiful woman Joanna Marriott was and how happy their life had been.

Mikel had told her all about Tamara's love for her mother and the tragedy of her early death.

It was the first time that Marthie felt that Andrew needed to talk, both about Tamara and about Joanna.

"Andrew?"

"Yes?"

"I've told you everything there is about Marthie Price you've wanted to know."

"I know, Marthie," he smiled at her, "and she is a very lovely woman. I've enjoyed knowing her."

"It's unfair, Andrew."

"What is?"

"That you know all about me and I know so very little about you."

He chuckled and slapped the reins against the horse's rump to move him into a light trot.

"And what would you like to know? I am forty-one years old, respectably wealthy and possess great charm and am considered quite handsome. Is that enough?" he laughed. She smiled, but she turned her head and looked at him.

"Tell me about Joanna."

His smile faded and he remained silent for a long time before he replied quietly. "What do you want to know?"

"How . . . how I could help you ease the pain of all the memories you hold inside and feel you cannot share."

"The only one I have ever been able to share that with has been Tamara. She has always known and understood."

"You don't think I would know and understand?"

"Of course you would. Who would understand better than one who has not lived through the same grief."

"Then, why don't you talk to me?"

Andrew guided the carriage beneath the shade of a huge tree. He stopped the horses and tied the reins firmly. Then he turned to Marthie, his face serious and his eyes affectionate and warm. "I didn't want sympathy from you, Marthie. I know you are a very warm and compassionate woman, but your compassion is another emotion I do not want."

Marthie reached out and put both her hands on his arm. She smiled up at him. "What is it you do want, Andrew?"

"I wanted you to know that what I feel for you is completely separate from the past. I want you to know you've opened the door to a future I never expected to find again. When I lost Joanna it was as though some part of me stopped living. It closed the way to a small corner of my heart and within it I kept all the love I'd ever known. There have been other women since Joanna, but none of them has even threatened my sanctuary. Then you came along. You crept into that quiet place and now I find you have gladly cleared it of all doubts. I'm asking you to share the rest of your life with me, Marthie. Come to my island, come to my world and let me show it to you. I think I could make you happy. At least I would try."

"I'm very flattered, Andrew. You have said to me words I have wanted to hear from you for quite some time. I have admired you, cared for you, since . . . well, almost the day we met."

"I know that now. With all the world in an uproar, with the worry about Jonah and Tamara, we will wait. We're not children, you and I. You know I want you. I want us to be together, but only if you tell me . . . do you want me, too?"

"I do, Andrew . . . yes, I do." She said it ardently, and watched with deep pleasure as his eyes warmed and smiled into hers. "Andrew, I have a small house not far from here. I only agreed to stay with Jeff and Brandy because they were afraid of my being alone . . . tonight, I won't have to be alone."

"Not tonight, or ever again," he said expectantly, as he bent his head and touched her lips with his. She sat very still, her eyes closed, savoring the firm seeking of his lips on hers and knowing this was the best thing that would ever touch her life.

He raised his head and smiled down again to reflect the soft violet eyes that mirrored his. "I'll come for you tonight. We'll have a nice dinner and a moonlight ride along the coast."

"Yes . . . yes I would like that. I'll be ready."

"Marthie . . . I do love you, you know," he added tenderly.

She laughed lightly. "I had hoped that was what you would say, but had you not, I should have come anyway, you see . . . whether or not, I love you, Andrew, . . . I love you."

He brushed another light kiss across her lips. "I think it best we move along. We will start the whole town whispering."

"We were doing nothing."

"It wasn't what we were doing, my dear," he laughed, "it's

541

what I would have done if you had kept on looking at me with those violet eyes and kissing me so. I won't be responsible if we stay here a minute longer."

They laughed happily together as Andrew lifted the reins and headed the carriage toward home. He smiled, for he suddenly felt young and filled with joy so pronounced he wanted to shout it to the world.

Both Jeff and Brandy noticed that Marthie paid special attention to preparations for the evening. She wore a gown of deep blue that accentuated her lovely eyes and the pink flush on her cheeks. Her blonde hair was drawn severely back and coiled at the nape of her neck in a thick glossy rope.

Andrew was no less nervous, but he concealed it well. He too shaved and dressed carefully. "I probably won't be returning tonight," he told Randolph and Mikel. "I've some things in my cabin on the *Sea Borne* to look into. I'll sleep there."

"Of course," Randolph said. "We'll expect you tomorrow, or would you like me to come around and pick you up tomorrow?"

"No," Andrew said hastily. "My business might take longer than I expect. I shall find my way home."

Randolph thought nothing more of it, but Mikel watched Andrew's receding figure with an amused grin. He wondered, happily, just what excuse Marthie would make to Jeff and Brandy, for he was sure the two of them would soon be together.

Marthie and Andrew shared a dinner at a quiet restaurant, then took the carriage and rode through the star-kissed moonlit night. Having kept her champagne glass continually full at dinner, Marthie was in a state of mild intoxication.

"Andrew," she giggled, "I do believe you are deliberately trying to get me inebriated."

"No, madam, you misunderstand. The warmth of a little champagne makes a beautiful night more enjoyable."

They laughed and talked together until he brought the carriage to a halt in front of her house. For a moment, they both sat quietly looking at it, then Andrew stepped down from the carriage and raised his hands to Marthie. Slowly, she stood up and bent forward and put her hands on his broad shoulders. He put his hands about her waist and gently lifted her and let her slide slowly down the length of his body.

Marthie was aware of his immense size as he seemed to overpower everything about them, and seemed to drown out every other sense she had except the sense of his masculine presence.

From her waist, he slid his arms about her and drew her close to him. He held her so for a minute then he captured her mouth in a kiss that swept her into a world that was Andrew and only Andrew. If there were any doubts in Marthie's mind they fled before the deep and possessive way that Andrew held her and expertly parted her trembling mouth with his.

The soft moist mouth that opened to his with the sweetness of a deep loving heart sent a current of desire exploding through Andrew's body. Here was a sweet giving woman—all woman, and he had all intentions of taking and keeping her forever.

He kept one arm about her waist and they slowly walked up the steps to her door, their eyes holding and saying a million soundless words.

Once inside, Marthie moved to light a lamp. "Don't," whispered Andrew.

"Why?"

"Because," she heard the laughter in his voice, "we aren't going to be down here that long."

He heard her responding chuckle as she turned and came into his arms again.

"Ummm," he said as their lips finally parted. "You are a sweet, sweet woman. Have I told you how much I love you?"

"No," she whispered, "but don't tell me . . . Andrew . . . show me."

Andrew bent and with ease lifted her from the floor. She put her arms about his neck and began to kiss him lightly—feather touches of kisses on his throat and cheeks until she felt his arms tighten about her.

She weighed little in his arms and he took the stairs with ease. He went to the first room he found, not caring if it were her bedroom or not. Inside he kicked the door shut behind him and walked to the bed. He stood her on her feet and again took possession of her lips.

He was surprised when Marthie gently pushed him away from her. He stood still, waiting to see what she wanted. Marthie turned from him and lit a small lamp that cast a pale gold glow over the room. She turned back to him and stood a few inches away. "You and I do not need the darkness to hide what we do. I am not ashamed of loving you or wanting to belong to you. I love you, Andrew," she said the words tenderly, and Andrew could feel his heart begin to thud as she slowly reached behind her, loosened the laces of the gown and let it drop to the floor.

Without hesitation, she again lifted her hands and loosened the thick coil of her hair, letting it drop about her. The balance of her clothes followed while Andrew stood in rapt pleasure at the woman he had chosen.

"You are even more desirable than I thought you would be. You're very beautiful, Marthie."

Marthie walked slowly toward him, the lamp flickering golden light across her body. When she stood by Andrew, she slowly reached up and put a hand on each side of his face, drawing his head down to hers and kissed him with a passion that was building to a violent fire. She slid her hand beneath his jacket and pushed it off his shoulders. Where it fell, he did not know, nor did he care, he was too busy tossing the rest of his clothes after it.

Her body was cool and soft against his. He sat down on the edge of the bed and pulled her onto his lap burying his face against her throat and caressing the soft round curves.

"Andrew," she murmured as his lips traced a path of kisses down her throat and touched lightly against the soft rise of her breasts. Her hands held him to her as his mouth found a hard thrusting nipple and captured it. He heard her soft gasp of surprise as he fell back onto the bed and drew her with him, sliding his hands down the rounded curve of her hips to draw her more tightly against him.

She turned then to a fury of passionate woman, matching him kiss for kiss and touch for touch until he felt he had fallen into a cauldron of fire. When the pounding need for her grew beyond anything he had felt before, when he heard her gasping moans of passion that matched him, he rolled to his side and pinned her beneath him. He began then a search of her smooth body that drove her to a frantic need for him. Her hands clung and she whispered words of love and encouragement she was not evern aware of.

When Marthie felt she would shatter into a million pieces, when the need for him completely overpowered her, when she felt there would be no more glorious sensation than this, Andrew entered her writhing body, joining them, blending them until she wanted to scream out the joy of fulfillment. He moved within her, lifting her with his huge hands to join their bodies ever closer. With slow even movements that drove her frantic, they rose to meet a completion that left them both so shaken neither could speak or move. "Oh, Andrew, Andrew," she whispered as he held her sweat-slicked body against him and caressed her gently.

"I know, my love, I know. We've been blessed with that very special thing that makes two people one."

He released her and laid her back against the pillows. He rose on one elbow and looked down on her. With a half smile, he brushed the tears from her cheeks. Then he kissed her with a gentle touch of his lips. "I've looked for you a long, long time, Marthie. I'm so very happy that I found you and you are free to come to me. When all of this is over, you will marry me, won't you? I'm sure you and Jonah will love the island just as Tamara does. I'll make you happy there. Say you'll belong to me always, Marthie . . . say it. I want to hear you say it."

"I will be the happiest woman in the world the day I become your wife. It is my greatest desire to come to your island, to share the rest of my days with you. I'm sure Jonah will be happy for us and I'm sure he will be proud to have such a stepfather as you. I only hope Tamara accepts me."

"You!" he laughed. "She will love you. How could anyone not. You are the most perfect woman in the world."

"And you are prejudiced," she laughed.

He kissed her several quick kisses. And squeezed her so tightly in his arms she cried out. "Oh, Marthie, if Steffan can bring Tamara home we can have such a happy life again. We'll have parties and balls and bring the island back to life again as it used to be . . ." He stopped and remained silent.

"As it was when Joanna was alive. Oh, Andrew, don't be afraid to say her name. Don't be hiding her somewhere in a shadowed place I can't reach. I know how much you loved her and I don't expect to replace her. I don't want the love you had for her, I want my own place in your heart. Don't ever be afraid to say her name if it's with good memories, but I will be your memories of the future. If that is true, I don't deny you your past. I love you."

"It is true, Marthie, you are my future. You are a woman among women. I thank you for understanding. I don't ever mean to hurt you. If I ever do, tell me. I don't want any ghosts of the past to come between us."

She wrapped her arms about his neck and smiled as she held him. "I will not let anything come between us. I would fight for you until I die. I have you now, Andrew Marriott, and I never intend to ever let you get away from me."

"Well," he sighed, "what can I do but submit. I'm at your command, my love," he whispered. "For the rest of my life, you need only ask."

Her eyes became deep pools of violet that swam with tears of love.

"Then," she whispered softly, "love me . . . love me."

"Can a man be commanded to do anything more wonderful? I follow your command, my love . . . gladly," he whispered as he bent his head to take her willing lips again and retrace the path of pleasure they had so recently walked.

Mikel walked along the docks the following day, keeping his ears open for rumors of any kind that might lead to word of Tamara. He became quickly aware then of the confusion at the edge of the gangplank of a ship that had recently docked. Nonchalantly, he walked over to see what was going on. He stood around the small group of men until he singled out one who seemed to know what he was talking about. "What's going on?" he inquired.

"Pirates caught her about two weeks ago, stripped her clean of all the guns she carried."

"Pirate or privateer?" Mikel asked.

"Not only a pirate, my friend . . . a lady pirate."

Mikel's heart leapt. "A lady pirate!"

"Well if the description is right, my guess is she ain't no lady. Dressed in pants like a man, wearing a red shirt, a thing to cover her hair and a black mask."

Mikel was so happy at that moment, he could have shouted. No, Tamara was not at Corvet's Rock licking her wounds and hiding in self-pity. She was on the open sea on the *Butterfly* again. And her spirit was as alive as it had ever been. He wished fervently he was with her, but he knew if he did join her, he could not help telling her of Steffan's search for her. She would be lost quickly and Steffan's search would be in vain. He knew if Steffan did not confront her personally, she would never listen to anyone else. He too felt there was more that had happened between them than any of the others knew. He wondered if Steffan would be able to cage her long enough to tell her the truth and even after he did, could things ever be the same between them.

He pushed aside his dark thoughts and went to talk to the captain, asking all the details. When he had heard all there was to know, he returned to the Perry home.

It was nearing the dinner hour when he arrived and he found the entire family just sitting down at the table. Cecile and Tom knew he had some news the minute he walked into the room. The first thing Mikel noticed was that Andrew was still not there.

"Mikel, you've heard something," Tom said quickly.

"Yes."

"You've news of Tamara?" Cecile asked.

"Yes again. A ship just came into the harbor. A couple of weeks ago, she was loaded with arms for the British stationed here and on the way she ran into a pirate . . . a lady pirate! . . . she stripped her clean, of all the guns, laughed at her captain's anger and sailed away. She calls her ship the *Scarlet Butterfly*. Sound familiar?"

Tom laughed. "I know exactly how he feels. She pulled the same stunt on us. She's quite a woman," Tom said. "Whatever has happened to her, she's landed on her feet and I'm glad. I only hope Steffan has the good fortune to run across her."

"He will," Cecile replied.

"Cecile," Tom answered with a grin. "It's a very big ocean out there. The only way Steffan will ever find her is if she wants to find him."

"Well," Randolph interjected, "we've certainly made Steffan's ship interesting bait. If all the rumors reach her, she'll think it's the ripest plum she's ever plucked."

"What does Steff plan to do if she does go after him? If he lets her board him as soon as she finds out who he is, she'll run. With all her men there to protect her, how will he ever get her alone?"

Cecile was looking at Tom with questions he could not answer.

"I don't know, Cecile. I guess Steff has worked some plan out in his mind. All we can do is wait . . . and hope."

". . . and pray," added Randolph.

The days passed slowly turning from days to weeks and there was no word from Steffan, although signs of the *Scarlet Butterfly* were seen often in the faces of angry captains and in the holds of empty ships.

Tamara was commended over many dinner tables for the contribution she was making to the Colonial cause. Much needed arms found their way from British ships to the hands of Colonial patriots. Soon, the name of the *Scarlet Butterfly* was as well known as Washington himself. It was often said by many of the young soldiers who went into battle with the brilliant leadership of their general and the strong shield of the guns the *Butterfly* had put into their hands, that America couldn't lose.

Andrew and Marthie had made it known that as soon as the

war was over and Jonah and Tamara were back, they would marry.

Everyone was happy for them, especially Mikel who had been there when Joanna had died and knew of the lost love and loneliness of Andrew.

Cecile and Tom lived in a good world filled with the joy of their young son. Tom, not being able to go with Steffan, had gone to Jeff and asked if it were possible he could find a place under his command for him. He felt the need to contribute something. He could not just sit by and let everyone else fight for a country that had given him and all of his friends so much. The only distressing thing was the silent absence of Steffan.

He watched Cecile who tried her best to keep the fear for Steffan out of her eyes when he was present. He wanted her to talk to him about it, but he knew she was keeping all her emotions, especially her fear for Steffan inside of her. Then came the night when he could stand it no longer.

Cecile sat in front of her mirror brushing her long black hair. The gold eyes were unseeingly watching herself and Tom knew she was deep in thought. He went to her and took the brush from her hand and continued the long even strokes, feeling the soft silky strands between his fingers. They smiled at each other in the mirror. "Cecile?"

"Yes, Tom?"

"We've always been able to reach out to each other, share what the other felt, be a comfort to each other."

"What are you trying to say, Tom?"

"Don't shut me out, Cecile. Remember that I, of all people, know how close you and Steffan are. I feel the same way. I just want you to know and to understand I'm here if you need me."

"Oh, Tom," Cecile cried, distress clear in her golden eyes. "I'm sorry." She reached out and put her hand on his cheek. "I never meant to shut you out. I guess I've been doing that without thinking. Spending all my free time fussing over the baby and the rest of my time thinking of other things. It's just that . . . I have so much and I can't help feeling so sorry for Steffan. I love him and I want to see him happy. Please forgive me, Tom. I never meant it. I would never shut you out. You are as much a part of me as my heart."

"I know. I've seen you suffer silently for a long time. I wanted you to reach for me."

"I'm selfish. I think only of myself."

"Now, that is not true, love. If you were selfish, you wouldn't be so frightened for your brother. And for what might happen to us all in the next few years. I won't have you talk about the woman I love like that. She's the most beautiful creature God ever created and I love her . . . I love you Cecile," he whispered as he touched her lips with his. Her arms encircled his neck and he drew her against him. Again his lips met hers but this time the kiss was deep and hungry. It was answered by warm parted lips that clung to his and a soft, whispered sound of pleasure. His tongue touched in light hot flickers that sent lightning-like streaks of pleasure through her.

He stood and pulled her up into his arms loosening her robe with a deft movement of his fingers. He put his arms about her pulling her close to him. Closing his eyes, he savored for a few minutes the feel of her in his arms, the soft scent of her that surrounded him, the texture of her silky soft hair against his cheek.

He felt her stir in his arms and he looked down into the honey gold eyes that seemed to be melting with warmth. He smiled as he lifted her in his arms. She was light and as tiny as ever. Though her slender body had rounded and softened with the birth of their son, she still felt very fragile in his arms and the same thought as always came to him. How anyone as sweet and beautiful as Cecile could love him. She gave him everything he ever needed or ever wanted and he longed for her to know the same sense of belonging as he did. He carried her to the bed they shared with deep pleasure. To love her was always a joy to him, but he wondered if he gave her as much as she gave him. It seemed to him to be impossible.

He joined her on the bed when he had hastily discarded the clothes he wore. She reached for him with the soft sigh of his name and he felt her arms twine about him and the silken length of her body against his.

His hands found the gentle curves and planes of her body while his mouth burned a path from her soft lips to the sweet taste of her skin. Then she put both her hands on his chest and slowly pushed him back. He looked at her in surprise.

"Tom," she whispered, "always you have given me the greatest joy, the greatest fulfillment any woman would ever want. To me, you have been friend, husband, lover, all wonderful, all complete. I want you to know that you have filled my life to the brim with every sense of love and belonging. I want to give to you what you have so very unselfishly given to me."

"Cecile . . ."

"Shhh, love. For tonight, let me love you."

He lay back, unmoving while her lips sought his. While her hands magically turned to fire as they strayed over his body. He saw a depth of love in Cecile he had never known existed before as with her magical touch and soft lips she turned his body into a bright golden flame. Slender legs straddled him, soft hair flowed about him and he reached for this wild, untamed creature with a need greater than he had ever known.

He groaned her name aloud as she moved like a wild abandoned gypsy above him and he clung to her as she carried him to the pinnacle of ecstasy and tumbled with him over the edge into brilliant starlit oblivion.

There were no more doubts left in Tom's mind as they lay silently together. Words were unnecessary, for the miracle they had just shared told them more than spoken words ever could.

"It will all work out, Cecile, with Steff, I mean. He is like you and Tamara will know, if she does not already know, that he's something very rare and special in her life. If she's as lucky as I am to know such an emotion, she would be a fool to deny it either to herself or to Steffan."

"I hope you're right, Tom," she sighed. "For I have one great and terrible fear."

"What?"

"If she turns away from him, if she denies her love for him, if she will not forgive him for all that happened, then . . . I'm afraid for Steffan, for something in him will die and I don't know what will remain."

They clung together, each of them praying that Steffan and Tamara would meet soon, for they could not bear the waiting without knowing what would happen when they did.

Forty-seven

Jack Teel had charm, wit, and exceptional good looks and he knew exactly all the attributes he had. He used them as any worker would use the tools of his trade. He was a pirate; he chose it as a career and he enjoyed it to the fullest. He had a way of enjoying all that the world had to offer with a laugh, an expressive shrug of his broad shoulders and a gay wink of the eyes that told the world he was probably guilty of everything their minds could conjure up.

Much of his reputation was exaggerated, but quite a bit of it was true. He was an expert seaman, he was completely loyal to his friends and he was a terrible man to have as an enemy, for he never forgot either a good act by anyone or a bad one.

Mikel and Jack had made tentative contacts several times before Tamara had ever chosen to sail the *Scarlet Butterfly*. Mikel had sought him out immediately when he and Tamara had made their plans, for he felt Jack was the best, maybe the only man he could trust to carry the guns to the Colonies without double-crossing them.

He had carried out his part of the bargain and had been rewarded well for his efforts.

During the time he had been gun-running for Tamara, he had only seen her a very few times and mostly from a distance. He had admired her audacity as a pirate and enjoyed the stories that rose about her. Of course, he had wanted to meet her and he had suggested it to Mikel only once. Mikel had tried to laugh it off and made it clear that he was the only contact he would have with Tamara. Jack had very quickly noticed the bristling in Mikel's attitude and after a few meetings, a few drinks together, and several business deals, he realized Mikel was in love with Tamara and wanted no part of the handsome Jack Teel meeting her.

Never having any trouble finding feminine company wherever he went, Jack shrugged it off with a laugh.

He knew where and how Tamara could be contacted for she

had sent a message to him as soon as she had her ship at sea again. Their relationship proved profitable once more for Jack, and although they again worked through others, they worked well. Still, he had the thought in the back of his mind now that if he was going to work with the famous lady pirate, it was time he met her. He waited for the right opportunity and it came in the form of word about the huge ship that was carrying British guns to the Colonies. He felt it was a ripe plum that Tamara could not resist plucking. Instead of sending the usual message, he went himself to the rendezvous point that had been used often by Jack and Mikel. It was a small atoll several miles away from Marriott Island, a half-mile wide deserted pile of sand and stone.

Anchoring his ship, he took the longboat and rowed himself ashore. When he stepped from the boat he looked up to the pile of rocks upon which sat the slender form of a woman. Despite the fact she wore pants and shirt, it did not take more than a quick glance to tell the observer she was a woman . . . completely woman.

Tamara stood up and watched the tall handsome man walk toward her. She knew in a moment this was no messenger, but Jack Teel himself. She smiled as he approached her and when he was a foot or so away he stopped.

"Captain Jack Teel?" she asked.

He bowed elaborately and his smile broadened. "And I am addressing the most beautiful lady pirate it's ever been my good fortune to meet."

She laughed lightly. "Probably the only lady pirate you have ever met."

He chuckled humorously. "Touché, Madam. You have me there. Yes, you are the only lady pirate I have met, but I was right about one thing. You are certainly the most beautiful woman I have ever seen."

She bowed her head toward him with a smile of polite acceptance of his compliment. "You have something you want to tell me, Captain Teel?"

"Can you not call me Jack? We have been almost partners for a long time in the past, and I hope a long time in the future."

"Jack," she said. She again laughed for she liked the man. The glitter of laughter in his eyes, the broad open smile and an overabundance of charm. "You do have a message for me, though?"

"Yes, I do. A nice juicy ship filled with guns and on its way to

552

the Colonial coast. She's big, slow and ready for the taking."

"What's her name?"

"The *Bethany*."

"Captain?"

"I hear his name is Dyke, Captain Roger Dyke."

"What do you know about her, about her route, how many men aboard, what does she carry in the way of guns, what's the reputation of her captain, will he fight or run? How much sail, how . . ."

"Please, madam," Jack laughed as he held up a hand as if to ward off her questions. "One question at a time. If you would care to sit down with me over a glass of wine and a map, I would be glad to answer every question you have."

"My ship or yours?" she asked.

"Yours," he chuckled. "I've been wanting a chance to see the famous *Butterfly* up close."

"Come along Jack. I'll have you served a good lunch, good wine and complete attention to all you have to say."

He stood up and watched her walk away from him. The enticing sway of her slender hips and the sunlight glinting on her deep red gold hair drew him along behind her like a magnet. She took him aboard the *Butterfly* and watched his eyes widen in surprise at the ship which was painted blood red from crowsnest to keel. As he walked about her, he also began to admire the ship's finer points and he knew from experience with ships what a beauty she would be to sail. He was filled with the beauty both of the ship and her captain. He also knew the ability of the captain and after one look into her slanted green eyes, he did not doubt for a moment that all the stories were true.

She had him served an excellent meal with even more excellent wine and bright conversation. When they were finished, they pored over the huge map and traced the path of the *Bethany*. By the time Jack Teel left, he was filled with two things. One, the desire to work with the notorious *Butterfly* and the other to possess the lady herself.

They met, more times than Tamara thought necessary, to follow the movements of the *Bethany* and to make plans to take her. She was a pleasure to be with; he admired the freedom of her spirit and the way she always seemed to be one with the sea and the winds. How he felt was obvious to Tamara and she was alarmed at the sudden bubble of fear that formed somewhere deep inside and threatened to burst if he came too close.

He came to her one evening with word of the *Bethany*. It was nearing dinner time so she invited him to eat with her in her cabin. They shared a delightful meal together, Jack kept her amused with stories of his misadventures about the world and kept her laughing with bright anecdotes. Over cool wine, they sat and talked. "Tamara, you know so much about me. What about you . . . Tamara Marriott?"

"What is there to know about me?"

"Oh, come now," he laughed. "A woman as young as you, to become a legend both for her astounding beauty and her prowess as a lady pirate. You say there is nothing to know. I have a multitude of questions I could ask."

She sat back in her chair and picked up her glass of wine. She took a sip then sat for a moment contemplating the wine. She then looked up at him and smiled, but her eyes were veiled and unreadable. "What is it you want to know?"

"About the little girl, about the woman, about the reasons for what you have become a pirate and how you became so."

"All right, Jack," she said quietly. "You want to know so I will tell you."

She began to speak, telling him of her childhood and her adventures on Marriott Island. She told him of her childhood friend Mikel and their decision to bring about the *Scarlet Butterfly*.

"I would wager, knowing Mikel, that the decision to create the *Butterfly* was more yours than his, am I right?"

"Well, yes, maybe you are, Mikel and I had always done so much together. It is difficult today to sail the *Butterfly* without him."

"The first *Butterfly,* where is she?"

"Held in London harbor."

"What happened? How did she ever get captured?"

Tamara rose from her chair and walked to look out over the soft, rolling ocean. How could she tell him all that had happened without resurrecting the memories of Steffan, memories she had put away in a dark place and tried to ignore. Jack rose from his seat and walked over to stand by her. She turned and looked up into eyes as green as her own. She might have resisted had they not been filled with compassion.

"I'm a friend, Tamara. Put aside the fact that I care for you very much. I'd like to be a friend to you. A shoulder you could lean on if the need should ever arise."

The always present need to have someone to confide in, the loneliness both for Mikel and her father, combined with the wine and the half-lighted atmosphere caused her to do what she had sworn she would never do. She began to speak slowly as though the words were coming of their own volition. She told him of Steffan and Tom. Their arrival on her island. Of falling so deeply in love with the handsome Captain Devers only to have him betray her in the arms of another woman after he had tricked her shamelessly into surrendering to him.

She spoke agonizingly of the night she had stood bound and gagged and watched her betrayer make love to another woman while she was being sentenced to die for what she had done.

The pain in her voice constricted her words so that they were barely audible. When the words died, they both remained silent for some time.

Then in a pained, cracked whisper she told him of her days in the Tower and the nights with Jaspar Sinclair. She was suffering, he could obviously see, but he saw more clearly that she would never admit what the real source of her agony was. He inhaled a deep breath and set about convincing her of what she felt, but would never admit.

He took hold of her shoulders and drew her into his arms and his mouth swept down and took fierce demanding possession of hers.

The fierce knot of terror exploded within her. Again she felt Jaspar's brutal hands tearing at her and his mouth voraciously raping her. She began to moan and to fight him, her fists flailed and her body twisted in his arms.

As suddenly as he had taken her he released her and watched her stumble back from him. Anger flashed from her eyes, but it was accompanied by another emotion he expected to see. Vulnerability, fear and a deep longing for something that had been taken from her by another.

There were tears in her eyes as she gasped, "A friend . . . you are a friend . . . why Jack? I should have known better than to have trusted any man. I never expected . . . go away, Jack, leave me alone . . . go away."

"I am a friend, Tamara, and I'm going to tell you just how much of a friend."

She turned, ran to the door and pulled it open; then turned to him. "Get out!"

"I will, but not until I tell you what I know is true."

555

She turned her back on him and snapped, "Whatever you want to say, say it and get out."

"You still love him, you know," he said.

"What!" she said as she spun around.

"You still love him, your Captain Devers."

"You're insane. A man who deceived me, betrayed me. Made love to another woman . . ." She stopped unable to speak any more.

"Listen to me, Tamara, you were hurt by what Jaspar did to you, you were angry at the trial and the way it came out, but the real hurt, the real thing you can't forgive is that he went to the arms of another woman. All the other obstacles you have overcome. All the other hurts have been put in the past where they belong, but you cannot forget that he held another woman. You cannot forget for you love him and you need him and you will not forget what he has done. I would wager that you dream of him, of the days and nights you spent together. And I know you will never be able to have peace or put him out of your heart until you face him and find out why, because somewhere deep inside you will not accept that he turned to another. You cannot accept that your love was unfaithful; but did it ever occur to you that what you saw might have had a story behind it that you don't know? Did it ever occur to you that a Jaspar Sinclair, who dragged you to that scene might have somehow staged it for your benefit? You have condemned the man and sentenced him to stay out of your heart without talking to him or letting him defend himself. You had a trial. Captain Devers did not. Don't you think that at least he deserves to be heard?"

The tears fell unheeded down her cheeks and she looked at Jack with the eyes of a frightened, hurt child. It made him miserable to know he was pushing her into the arms of another man he did not even know deserved her. He wanted to comfort her. To tell her to stay with him and he would try to make her life full and happy. But he had watched her for the last few weeks and he knew that she would never forget Steffan unless she found out that what she saw was the truth.

That she was half a woman now he knew, and he hated the fact that he could never be the other half to make her life complete. He went to her and gently cupped her face in his hand. "I envy him, you know," he said quietly. "I wish I could be the one to put the stars in your eyes and the smile on your lips. I'm sorry if I hurt you, Tamara. I just wanted to try to break through that shell. I just wanted you to be honest. Find out the truth. Don't condemn the man until the evidence is all in. Don't sentence him until the verdict is guilty."

He bent his head and brushed her lips with a light kiss. Then he turned and left the room. Tamara stood watching the closed door, his words echoing in her mind. Was it true that she had condemned Steffan only because of the woman in his arms? She searched her mind and the answer blazed within her.

All the things that had happened, being captured, taken to England, tried, could have been taken as the fortunes of war. No, what stayed alive in her mind was Steffan's strong arms holding the beautiful woman, Steffan's mouth tasting the one in his arms with passionate kisses.

She knew, and she hated the knowledge, but Jack was right. The only thing she really condemned Steffan for was that terrible sight. She in jealousy had pushed him out of her heart but she could never quite succeed in getting him out of her dreams. There was nothing to be done about it now. There was no way she and Steffan would ever meet again. But if they did, she wondered, could she listen to him or would she always look at him and remember. She didn't know, but Jack had succeeded in one thing, he had opened her mind to the new thought.

The next day, Jack had more intensive news of the *Bethany,* but he was not too sure just how he would be accepted in Tamara's presence. He came on board the *Butterfly* and went below to her cabin. Rapping on the door, he waited, then the door was opened by a new Tamara.

"Good morning, Jack," she said quietly.

"Am I forgiven?" he asked hopefully. "I trust I'm not to be marooned without your lovely presence."

"Come in, Jack. If you're asking whether I'm angry with you, no, I'm not. I'm grateful. I guess if I'm going to be able to live with myself, I have to know the truth. You were right, I do dream of the past. But I intend to cure that. I intend to wash him out of my mind once and for all. After we take the *Bethany,* I intend to go and find Steffan Devers."

"Good."

"You realized last night that I . . . that I can't . . ."

"Don't be foolish. After what happened with that animal you can't help it if you find it difficult to reach him again. I wish I was the one to release you, but I'm not. I think we both know who holds the key."

"We'll find out, but . . . I hope you're right, Jack."

"I am," he grinned. "Haven't I told you—ask anyone and they'll tell you I'm always right about affairs of the heart. Besides," he reached out and touched her hair lightly, "I've had more experience in mending broken hearts than you."

"Jack . . . you . . ."

"Forget it," he said firmly. "I've news of the *Bethany*. She's been in England the past two weeks loading a nice fat shipment of guns. In about two weeks she'll be right where we want her."

"Two weeks? Good. We'll be ready for her."

They laughed together, then prepared to make both ships ready for the attack and capture of the *Bethany*, her cargo . . . and her captain.

Through the entire trip from the Colonies to England, Steffan prayed his plan would work and he would again come face to face with Tamara. With no effort at all he could conjure up millions of pictures of her in his mind. The first time he had seen her, sweet and beautiful. The day she had taken him about the island and had shown him its beauty and hers. He could picture her the day she had stood on the rocks with the wind blowing her beautiful hair about her and the challenging smile on her face as she had gracefully leapt to the sea below. Then sweeter and more poignant memories came. The softness of her skin under his hands, the scent she wore that he could still smell. The way her nose crinkled when she laughed and her quiet moments, when she had reached out caressing hands to him and held him close. He allowed himself to enjoy every past moment for he did not know if there would be any future moments for them to share.

He had not yet made any real plans as to how he would hold her once he had her aboard the *Bethany*. He put all thoughts of that aside until he got to England. Once there, he sent his first mate about to bargain for what arms he could carry to the Colonies. While this was being done, he hired a buggy and went to Devers Halls to see his parents.

He was greeted warmly and tearfully by his mother and with jubilation by his father. The first news they gave him was that Martin Gillis and Commander Pierce had gone to the Colonies immediately after Steffan.

"Well, I shall see them as soon as I get back."

"I don't mean to sound as though you are not welcome, son, for you are. I just wondered what has brought you home now."

Steffan explained everything to them, told them what his plans were. "I've got to bait the trap with arms and hope she comes after them."

"Trap," Ellen said distastefully. "I hate to hear that word in connection with you and Tamara. It is an ugly word for a thing that should be beautiful."

"You're right, Mother. It is an ugly word, but if it will bring her back to me, I will call it anything necessary."

"What then, Steffan?" Maxwell asked. "What then?"

"I don't know yet. I guess I'll have to have some plan before I leave here."

"How soon do you leave?" Ellen asked. "It seems you've been gone for so long. You're here for such a short time, then you'll be gone again."

He went to his mother and put his arm about her shoulder.

"I'm sorry it has to be this way, Mother. But I can't let her go. I need her. She's a part of my life I can't afford to lose."

She looked up into his eyes and smiled. "I know, son," she said. "Forgive my selfishness. We love her too and we pray everything works out well for you both."

"Now," Steffan said with a smile, "after all the grim news, I have some wonderful news that will brighten everything."

"What?"

"You both are now grandparents of a beautiful little boy named Thomas Steffan Braydon."

"Oh, how wonderful," Ellen cried. "Cecile, how is she?"

"Fine, and very happy."

"Oh," Ellen said. "I should so love to see them."

"Well, why don't we?" Maxwell said.

"Maxwell!"

"We could leave after Steffan and," he smiled at Steffan, "be there to meet our son and his wife when they arrive."

Steffan grinned in return, pleased with his father's confidence in him. They spent over two weeks together while the *Bethany* was loaded with a cargo of guns and ammunition. Steffan enjoyed again walking the paths he so well remembered walking with Martin Gillis. He rode again the beaches and wandered among the caves of his childhood. He enjoyed it, but everything he saw and did made him want Tamara even more. After a while, he ceased to do it, for the need for her gnawed within him like a sickness.

It was just a few days before he was due to leave for the Colonies. He had made his every move clear, open and very obvious

559

to everyone who wanted to view him. He had talked openly of his dislike of the Colonials and their war and that he was taking guns to the British to help them win the war. He stood at the rail and watched the final preparations being made when he noticed the stranger who also stood observing. When the man saw that he was being surveyed, he walked slowly up the gangplank. He was stopped before he set foot on the planking of the *Bethany* and he said a few words to the man who stopped him, then he waited while the sailor walked towards Steffan.

"Cap'n, man says he has a message for you."

"From whom?"

"Won't say, sir. Says it is personal."

Steffan's curiosity was aroused. "Send him up here, Joseph."

"Aye, sir."

He went back and spoke to the man, then the stranger walked in Steffan's direction. He stopped near Steffan and queried, "Captain Steffan Devers?"

Steffan jerked alert. Who, he thought, had any idea of who he really was.

"I'm afraid you're mistaken. This is the *Bethany* under Captain Roger Dyke."

"One and the same," the man said.

He looked at the man who returned his gaze steadily. "Come below," he said quietly. Then he turned and walked toward his cabin. Inside he closed the door and turned to face the man again.

"Who are you?"

"Messenger from a friend."

"Who?"

"A friend."

"That's not good enough."

"It has to be," the man smiled now. "I have the message, and you want it. All you have to do is say if you are or aren't Steffan Devers."

"I'm Captain Roger Dyke," Steffan said.

The man shrugged expressively and turned toward the door. Steffan let him walk to the door and grasp the knob. Then it was clear to him the man fully intended to leave.

"Wait."

The man turned to face him again, but he waited for Steffan to speak first.

"Give me the message."

The man smiled, and Steffan could not help but grin in response.

"All right, I'm Captain Steffan Devers."

"Yes, I know."

"Who else knows?"

"My friend."

"Who is?"

"All I can say is what he told me to tell you. He's probably the best friend you've ever had and he hopes some day to meet the man who holds the heart of Tamara Marriott."

Steffan gave the man more attention now. He said nothing, only waited while the man removed a white envelope from his pocket and handed it to him. He took it and held it, sensing that it was the key to finding Tamara and he wondered just who his friend was.

"I must go now, Captain. Your secret is safe with me. The man who wrote you that message is my captain. I'm going to join him now. I'll see you again one day soon, Captain . . . Dyke. Goodbye and good luck."

"Thank you," Steffan replied. The man smiled, gave him a quick salute and left the room. The door closed and Steffan looked from it to the envelope in his hand wondering just who his friend was, where he got his information and how he knew what was happening. When he tore open the envelope, he read quickly. His face lost its angry look and broke into a smile as he sat down in his chair and began to read the message over again . . . slowly.

Captain Devers,

We have never met, but I think our paths will be crossing in the near future. I am the companion of someone for whom I think you are searching. If it were that you wanted to surrender her to the authorities I would see that you never found her, but I know the real reason behind your search. Were she to know now what I was doing she would feel the deepest betrayal. I do not think it is betrayal for a woman to find again the man to whom she wants to belong, for whom she waits without knowing.

I have a plan that will work well with yours, perhaps better. You expect the *Butterfly* to take the *Bethany,* then the two of you will meet again. I have a plan that is more complete.

Follow what you are doing, when the *Butterfly* takes

you, I will be aboard her. Tamara will board your vessel. See to it you are not on deck to greet her, but be in your cabin. She will come for you. At that time, I will remove the *Butterfly* from your vicinity. She will be left on board your ship, alone. The rest will be up to you.

Remember one thing, Captain Devers, I will not tolerate Tamara being hurt in any way. What I am doing I think in the future will mean her happiness. Should it work out differently, I will see you dead. My arm is long, my friends are many, and believe me, it is in my power to have you killed.

Care for her, love her honestly and well, or you will answer to an enemy the likes of which you have never seen before.

She is a hurt and lonely woman. If it were in my power, it would not be so, but it isn't. What happened to her has made her believe she is physically unable to love again. I would like to know she has found happiness again for she is a woman of great beauty and a capacity for a great deal of love.

Be prepared, be warned, be careful for there are many who would kill you should she be harmed. We will find you in our own good time, Captain. Until then . . .

Good luck.

Steffan let the letter fall from his fingers to the desk. His heart thudded fiercely and he shook with the desire to order the anchor up and be on his way immediately, but he knew he could do nothing differently from what he had planned. It would be too obvious.

He spent the next few days trying to contain his nerves and supervising the final preparations for departure. He spent much of his time with his parents, staying away from places where he might run into anyone he knew.

It was with the greatest sense of relief that the day of departure dawned. He had his last meal with his parents the night before, explaining why they could not come to the docks to see him off.

When he went back to the *Bethany* that night, he was faced with the longest night he had ever spent. Completely unable to sleep he had walked the silent decks most of the night.

Standing at the rail in the pale predawn light, he drew from his pocket a thin green ribbon and remembered the day he had taken it. If he had her on his ship where she could not run from him maybe he could make her understand.

Again he wondered just how his friend knew what had happened between him and Tamara, but reading between the lines he not only figured out what the situation was there, but all that had happened between her and Jaspar in that cold cell in the towers. Again he was glad he had killed Jaspar, only wishing he had it to do over with Tamara present.

Finally daybreak came and he gave the orders to raise the sails and take the *Bethany* from the harbor to the open sea and her destined meeting with the *Scarlet Butterfly*.

The *Bethany* was not the ship the *Cecile* was. She was slow and cumbersome. They worked their way slowly toward the Colonies with Steffan always on the watch for the ship that would be seeking them.

Day after day, night after night, he paced the deck wondering when and where she would strike. He slept in fitful naps and ate little. His nerves were stretched to the breaking point and still there was no sign of her.

Ten nights out of London harbor, Steffan walked the quiet deck of the *Bethany*. The night was clear and bright with a full white moon.

"Tamara, Tamara, where are you?"

He was tired and since the horizon was clear for miles, he went below and without removing his clothes, he lay on his bunk and almost immediately fell into a deep, sound sleep.

The first gray light of dawn touched the horizon and thin rays of the sun reached into Steffan's cabin. He woke to the persistent knocking on his door.

"What is it?" he shouted.

"Ship on the horizon, sir. Comin' fast."

Steffan leapt from his bed, flung open the door and ran up the steps and onto the deck. In minutes, he stood on the quarterdeck with a telescope to his eye and watched a blood red ship coming at him out of the early morning sun.

563

Forty-eight

It had been an accident that Jack Teel had found out just who the captain of the *Bethany* really was. His spy system was widespread, and he knew the whereabouts and destinations of every ship that would be of interest to him.

The plans to take the *Bethany* had been completed, and they had only to wait until it was loaded and on its way. He was sitting in his cabin contemplating Tamara, and what he knew she really felt about Steffan Devers. He had sent word among his network of spies to find out just where Steffan was and what he was doing. He even made it clear that he would welcome any news at all about all Steffan's past activities.

The knock that sounded on the door interrupted his thoughts.

"Come in."

His first mate opened the door and stepped inside. "McGregor has just come aboard, sir; says he has some information just passed to him that might interest you."

"Send him down."

"Aye, sir."

It was a few minutes before the second knock came and Jack called for him to enter. The man who did was a small, nondescript man who had worked for Jack Teel for many years. Jack knew just how trustworthy he was. There would be no doubt that what McGregor told him would be well checked out and perfectly true.

"What is it you've found, Mac, that is so interesting?"

"Well, captain. You've told us you and the *Butterfly* are goin' after the *Bethany*."

"That's right."

"You've also told us you're looking for a Captain Steffan Devers, and any information about him."

"Right again."

"Well, I've found out something strange that might interest you."

"What?"

"Well, Captain Steffan Devers and Captain Dyke of the *Bethany* are one and the same."

Jack looked at him, not quite believing what he said, then his mind quickly slipped the pieces of the puzzle together. Slowly a smile appeared on his face and he sat back in his chair.

"So," he said, "my work is all done at one time. Oh how very clever, Captain Devers. I must see to it that your plan succeeds."

"Sir?"

"Get yourself a good meal, Mac, I've a letter to write and I want you to deliver it."

"Yes, sir."

When Mac had closed the door behind him, Jack took paper from his desk. For a few minutes he sat in deep thought, then he began to write.

For the next few days, he began to work on the balance of his plan. He watched Tamara closely, trying to make absolutely sure that what he knew and felt was right.

The letter he wrote to Steffan was written very carefully and with much thought. He had to make him understand the whole situation in a few words. When it was completed to his satisfaction, he sent for Mac, gave it to him with explicit instructions as to his behavior and questions, then had sent him on his way to the *Bethany*.

Tamara was restless; she wanted to be about some activity, something definite that would take the edge off this terrible waiting. The words that Jack had said to her echoed in her mind, and she wondered if her path would ever cross Steffan's again and if it did, what would happen. What would she say to him or he to her. She had been honest with herself, yes, she could have forgiven him his obedience to duty; maybe even tried to understand the terrible way he had done it; and yes, she had finally admitted to herself what she could not forgive. Steffan and the beautiful blonde woman. Could she ever admit that to him or anyone else?

In her mind it was the one unforgivable betrayal. She could close her eyes and see the scene again and again. Slowly, they merged in her mind, what had happened to her with Jaspar and Steffan and the woman in his arms. She knew the combination of both had rendered her less than a woman.

She stood up from her chair and walked to the mirror. There, she stood and looked at herself. What about her was different?

Slanted green eyes contemplated her slender figure and the gold red hair. What about her had changed? Why could she not go to another man? Marry? Have children? Be happy? Why did the fear grip her, why could she only feel the terror and the darkness?

Angrily, she pushed the thoughts away. She would think only of what she had to do. She would take care of the commitments she had and when the war was over, she would be able to handle the problem. She would find someone and together they would go to England. She would face Steffan and find that this would all be for nothing, that all the pain had gone, and she would live a good full life without him.

Jack was making his plans well. He was satisfied that they would work. Slowly, he had maneuvered some of his men aboard the *Butterfly*. Innocently, he had asked Tamara for the temporary use of some of hers. When the time came that the *Butterfly* attacked the *Bethany,* he wanted as many of his own men, and men influenced by him, to be aboard. When word finally came that the *Bethany* had left England for the Colonies, Jack was pleased that he was completely prepared for what was to happen.

The day they were to leave he came to Tamara. "My dear," he smiled. "I'm requesting permission to go along with you on the *Butterfly*. My ship has developed a few minor difficulties and I will not be able to support you with her as we planned."

"What's the matter with the *Dragon*" she asked, concern in her voice.

"Nothing serious" Jack dismissed it with a wave of his hand. "It is just necessary to repair her now. May I accompany you?"

"Of course, Jack, you're quite welcome."

"Thank you," Jack went to the door. Once there, he turned and looked at Tamara. "You are so very beautiful, Tam. You don't know how much I wish you could belong to me. Knowing how impossible that is, I hope you find your way back to some happiness. I want you to remember that I always have your interests at heart. I want what will make you happy."

"Jack?"

He grinned. "Just remember, my love" he said as he left, closing the door solidly behind him. She stood looking at the door, puzzled both by his words and the strange change in him. When the sun came over the horizon, the next day, she would use its red glow to attack the *Bethany*. She stripped off the clothes she wore and donned the scarlet shirt, black pants and high boots. She left the mask lying on her bed along with the scarf that would confine her hair. About her slender waist, she buckled the scabbard and belt that held her sword at which she was more than proficient. She went on deck and joined Jack who awaited her, then she gave the order to hoist all sails. The chase was on.

It was a deep black night before they began to near the rendezvous point where the *Bethany* would cross her path. Tamara gave the order and the sails were lowered. They waited in the waters just east of the *Bethany's* path for the touch of the rising sun. She stood at the wheel when the first pale gray touch of dawn bordered the horizon. When the glow of the rising sun followed, the *Bethany* was already in sight. Red sails catching a full breeze billowed in the sun's golden glow. They bore down on an almost helpless *Bethany* which rolled heavily in the ocean and made a valiant pretense of trying to get away.

Using her usual procedure, Tamara fired the first warning shot across her bow. When she did not heave to immediately, she fired again, this time sending a shattering volley crashing through her rigging. She smiled in satisfaction as the white flag came up and the *Bethany's* sails were lowered in capitulation.

"Prepare a boarding crew," she said to Jack, who smiled.

"I already have. They're ready and waiting for you."

Excited now, Tamara paid no attention to the fact that the boarding crew were Jack's men, not hers.

Grappling hooks were thrown and the two ships were brought side by side. Accompanied by Jack's men, Tamara boarded.

"Where is your captain?" she said, angry with a man who seemed not to have the courage to defend his ship or to surrender with some dignity.

"He's below in his cabin."

"Have the cargo transferred," she said. "I will go below and bring this coward on deck where he belongs."

Steffan's men were silent, and put up no fight as Tamara started below deck. She would have been both angry and surprised if she had seen what happened when she left the deck of the *Bethany*. Jack's men made a speedy return to the *Butterfly* after they had told Steffan's first mate quickly what was happening.

"We'll be standing off a way, just in case she should need us, but Cap'n Teel doesn't want her to be able to board the *Butterfly* or get help from her men until Captain Devers has had a chance to talk to her."

"I know the whole situation," Steffan's first mate said with a smile. "Captain Devers has already given us our orders. He told us to tell both you and your captain that he is grateful and that she is completely safe with him."

"Good. I'd best get back now. We've got to pull away before she realizes what is going on."

"I would, too. If that angry lady gets hold of you when she finds out, I wouldn't want to be either in your shoes or your captain's. We were told to tell Captain Teel that Captain Devers is looking forward to meeting him in person either to thank him for helping him get his woman back or to get drunk with him to drown his troubles."

They laughed. "I'll tell him." He swung a leg over the rail and in a few minutes, the *Butterfly* pulled away from the *Bethany* and stood off about a half mile away . . . waiting.

Below, Steffan stood just inside his cabin door and listened to the approaching footsteps. His heart was pounding and he had to laugh at the fact that he was actually sweating and shaking in anticipation.

He stood behind the door when it was pushed open and Tamara was half way across the room before she heard it slam shut and the bolt pushed home to lock it. She spun around and was met by a pair of honey gold eyes that smiled at her.

"Hello, Tamara," he said. "Welcome home."

"Steffan."

"I've been looking for you for a long time, Tam."

"Why?" she said bitterly, "to finish the job you started?"

"That's not true, Tam."

"Oh, of course not. I'm to fall into your arms again like a fool while you tell me the lies."

"I've never lied to you."

"Let me pass, Steffan."

"You're not leaving this room until you listen to me, until we talk, until you understand."

"I have men on board to help me. I need only shout and you will be dead."

He shook his head. "There's no one on board. If you will look out, you will see the *Butterfly* has pulled away. You and I are alone."

Tamara ran to the porthole and looked out. True enough, the *Butterfly* was a bright red spot standing to with a half mile of ocean between them and it. She bent her head forward and rested it on her hands just for a moment.

568

"Betrayal! Is that all I'm ever to know from the men I trust? How much did you give Jack to buy my life?"

"The assurance that I love you. That all the things you think are lies. Lies that others put into motion to separate us. Lies that I can prove to be what they are if you give me a chance."

"Chance! So you call trapping me like this giving you a chance?"

"Would you have let me near enough to talk to you any other way?"

"I was thinking about it," she said, "one day. When I was sure . . ."

"Sure that you could control the fact that you want to know what really happened? Sure that you didn't still love me, too."

Quickly, Tamara pulled her sword from its scabbard and turned to face him for she had sensed the fact he was moving toward her. "I don't still love you, Steffan. I know you for what you are. I can understand your loyalty to your country, but don't expect me to be fool enough to fall for your sweet words again. The last time was much too painful to be repeated."

"I've resigned my commission in the English Navy. I intend to join Jeff, Tom, Mack and the others in the Colonies to do what I can. I couldn't do that until I had found you, made you understand what had happened. We could go then together the way we should be if you willingly listen."

"I don't believe you, and I have no intention of listening to any more lies." She moved a little forward until the point of her sword touched his broad chest, slightly nicking the skin. He did not move.

"Give your men the order to signal the *Butterfly*. I'm leaving your ship."

"I'll not give that order," he said quietly, his eyes holding hers, "and if you leave this cabin it will have to be because I'm dead. I'm going to explain all that happened. If you want to listen, listen. But if you want to leave you will have to press that sword home for I cannot lose you again. If I do, I might as well be dead."

"Let me go, Steffan."

"I can't."

"Please, let me pass."

"You can go any time you're ready to push that weapon home. In the meantime, I will tell you all I want you to know."

"I don't want to hear."

"But you will. God, I love you, Tam. You are even more beautiful than I remembered and believe me I remembered every touch, every move." He began to talk, telling her all that had happened to him from the last moment they had seen each other. He told her of the drug he had been administered and how he had made his escape. He told her of the ordeal of trying to wash his body clean of the drug. He told her of his deep grief and guilt when he thought she was dead and how he had vowed then to complete her commitment to the Colonies. He told her of meeting Mikel and joining her father who were both in the Colonies waiting for the happy news that he had found her. Finally he told her that he knew all that had happened to her and that he had gotten some small form of revenge by killing Jaspar. "We are all still searching for the others responsible. When they are found, I shall see that they pay for all you have suffered."

She felt the heat of the tears on her face and he could see that she half believed what he had just said, but still the long slender sword stood between them.

"You're my wife, Tam," he said beseechingly, "I love you more than my own life. I'll never let you go. I want to hold you, to tell you how sorry I am for all you've suffered. But we can start over. There's a whole long life for us and I can't walk through it in the dark without you. Now," he added, "if you want to kill me, you will have to." He reached out and touched the handle of the sword.

"Give me the sword . . . or push it home. For without you there is no real purpose to my life." He moved against the sword until a small trickle of blood ran down his chest, then with a soft sob, she released her hold on the sword and he took it. She turned from him and buried her face in her hands, her body trembling with her tears. "Damn you," she whispered, "after what you have done why can't I kill you as I should?"

He came to her, took her shoulders and turned her to face him, then he removed her hands from her face.

"Because deep in your heart you know that what I'm saying is true. You know that what we had was too real, too beautiful to have ever been a lie. I ask you for forgiveness, Tam, for letting you be hurt so. I would gladly give my life to have had it never happen. But it did, and I can do nothing but ask your forgiveness and tell you that I love you. I have never stopped loving and wanting you for a moment."

"And yet you do not ask forgiveness for the only real betrayal that mattered?"

He looked at her with questioning eyes unable to understand of what she spoke. He did not for a moment remember a single minute he spent with Morgana and so he had no way of telling her what had happened.

Then it was her turn to throw the angry words at him. She told him how she had faith in him no matter what they said to her. Faith, until Jaspar had dragged her to that room. Faith, until her eyes saw his betrayal. She went on to describe minutely what she had seen.

"Tam, it was the drug," he said desperately, "if I reached out for a woman it was because I thought it was you. I remember you were always in my mind. She must have suggested to me that she was you. It was always you in my mind, in my heart. Tam, I have reached out to no other woman of my own free will since that beautiful day on Marriott Island that you came to me with all the beauty and love I ever needed or ever will need for as long as I live. Please believe me, Tam, please? I love you . . . I would not betray you so."

He could see the sudden despair-filled look in her eyes and such a flush of pain crossed her face that he could almost feel it.

"It's too late, Steffan."

"No!" he said angrily, giving her shoulders a shake. "It is never too late. I won't let you go, Tam, I love you too much."

"It's too late for me," she said forlornly, "I don't know what happened to me after Jaspar. I only know that I can feel nothing, give nothing. I am dead to love. I've tried. It is no use. All I can see or feel is his brutal tearing at me . . . I cannot love," she sobbed as she pounded on his chest with her fists. "Not you, not anyone. I am half a woman. Go away, leave me alone."

Despite the fact that she fought him, he drew her into his arms and held her. His superior size and strength were more than she could do battle with. He held her a moment before he began to speak, a moment to gather the hate and anger he felt for Morgana Kyle and hold it in check while he spoke. The words were said low and soothing as he held her tight with one arm, pulled the scarf away from her hair and caressed it with his other hand.

"It's all right, Tam. I know how it must have been for you. I cannot bear to think of how you must have suffered. It is a terrible thing and it takes a long time to get over. All I'm asking is that you let me try to help. I'm not asking that you come to me, only that you let me be in your life, stay with you, be near you.

571

Some day, we can start over, when you are ready. It's enough for me just to be near you, just to share your life. Can't you see? Love, making love with you was a wonderful and beautiful experience, but my love for you goes much deeper than that. I told you once a long time ago that if I never made love to you again the memories of the times we had been together would sustain me. It's true, Tam, let me be here for you. Let me hold you, shelter you, care for you. We'll face whatever tomorrow brings together.''

"Oh, Steffan . . . I don't know if I'll ever be . . .''

"Shhh, love, don't even think about it now, just think that we have overcome everything against us and we've come out together. Now it's us against the world Tam, and we're strong enough to face anything else it may have to offer.''

She sighed and for the first time he could feel her relax against him. The desire for her flooded through him like molten flame, but he firmly held it in check. He wanted her, but he could never take her. He would wait until the wounds healed, until she could come to him with the love and freedom that was hers.

He tipped her chin up and looked into her eyes and smiled. "Say it, Tam. Say you'll make room in your life for me again. Let me walk beside you. We can start now to carry out all the plans you had. Together, we could harass the English Navy from the ocean, not to mention how many arms we could acquire for our Army.''

"Our Army?''

"Our Army, our Navy, our country . . . as long as we're together, name it anything you want.''

"All right, Steffan . . . our fight. You will be content to have the name 'pirate', after all you had hoped to be?''

"What was it the man said, 'what's in a name? A rose by any other name would smell as sweet'. Well what does it matter what the world calls me. As long as you call me friend, companion . . . maybe someday again, lover, husband. We're together, Tam and we'll stay so for as long as there's a breath in my body and the devil can take the world thinks.''

She looked up at him and his unguarded eyes let her see for that moment the raging need for her that all but consumed him. He saw the quick flicker of fear, felt the stiffening body in his arms and cursed his stupidity.

"Don't be afraid, Tam. Once I said it before in anger, this time I'll say it in love. I will not touch you unless you want me to. I do not want to take you, I want you to come to me free and loving as you always were. I'll wait and pray for that day, but in the meantime . . . don't be afraid of me; I cannot bear to see fear in your eyes."

She nodded; for the first time, she completely believed again. He smiled when he felt her relax. "Now, I think it best we signal Jack Teel before he storms aboard and kills me. I promised him I would take only an hour. After that, I would return you to him no matter what the circumstances were. Besides, I have to thank him for returning my life to me."

"I have a few words for him also," she replied in mock anger.

"Now, Madam, I shall have to defend the man; he is a friend of both of us and he really had your best interests at heart. You know he cares for you a great deal."

"Yes" she replied with a smile, "but don't you think he deserves a little roasting for his trickery. You wouldn't deny me a little bit of fun, would you?"

"Maybe a little bit," he chuckled, "but I owe the man the greatest debt of my life and besides, I don't want him regretting what he did. He might try to spirit you away."

They went on deck and Steffan's men showed the broad smiles of delight when they saw their captain in smiling company with his woman. All of them knew the story and all of them were pleased with the outcome. A signal was sent to the *Butterfly* and soon she was again alongside. In a few minutes, Jack Teel stepped aboard and stood before them.

"Well, Tamara," he began hesitantly with a rather sheepish grin on his face.

"Well, Jack?" she replied and her face showed no emotion at all.

"I'm not to be forgiven for one little indiscretion that might make you happy. I think you are being unfair."

She smiled for the first time, more at his relief and Steffan's muffled laugh than at anything else. She went to him and kissed his cheek. "You're forgiven, you scoundrel," she said.

"Thank you, my dear."

Steffan held out his hand to Jack, who took it. "I owe you a debt I shall never be able to repay. If you ever need anything you have only to call on me or any member of my family and it is yours."

"I can see the notorious pirate Jack Teel calling on Lord Maxwell Devers for a favor!"

"You might just be surprised, Jack. Any member of my family would honor my obligations as I would theirs; that's the way it has always been. Try us one day and see."

"I may just do that one day."

"Well, what is next?" Steffan said.

"Steffan, we could take this load of arms and send it where it belongs. Then, I have something to show you that might surprise you." Tamara smiled at him and he was overjoyed to see the light of wicked laughter back in her eyes again.

"All right," Steffan replied, "Jack you take the arms on board and deliver them where you always do. I will sent the *Bethany* back to the Colonies to our families with a message to tell them what has happened. Then," he turned to Tamara, "if she'll have me I will sign on board the *Scarlet Butterfly* as her most loyal crewman. I go where you command, my captain."

Jack agreed and it took them several hours to transfer the guns to his ship. Tamara went back aboard the *Butterfly*. While the guns were being transferred, Jack and Steffan had an opportunity to talk. In a voice thick with warning, Jack said, "Our little bird is still wounded. I would not want the wounds made any deeper. Are you a man of strength and patience, my friend?"

"Jack, I love her. There are no other words I can say to ease your mind except that I will never hurt her again, nor will I see anything else hurt her. I am going to try to recapture what was ours once, but it will be on her terms, not on mine. I will wait as long as necessary, but I will win her love and confidence back if it takes the balance of my life."

Jack stood for a moment looking deeply into Steffan's steady gaze. Satisfied at what he must have seen there he smiled. "I wish you the best of luck my friend, and may I say that I envy you. You have something I would give everything for. Oh, I have tried to make her love me, but it was no use. No matter what had happened, I could see her love for you beneath the surface. She would not admit it, but it was always there. It effectively kept every other man from drawing too near. Yes," he sighed, "I envy you, Steffan Devers."

"Thank you, Jack. I shall care for her and one day our paths will cross again."

"Oh, yes," Jack grinned. "After all we'll be working for the same cause now, won't we?"

"Yes, I guess you're right. Well, goodbye for now, Jack. God bless you and keep you safe until we meet again, friend."

Steffan gave the order for the *Bethany* to return to the Colonies. He wrote messages to everyone concerned and instructed what was to be done with the ship and exactly what had happened between him and Tamara and what their future plans were. Then he and Tamara stood at the rail and watched the *Bethany* and the *Dragon* disappear.

That the news was greeted with almost hysterical pleasure was an under-statement. Cecile was in delighted tears when she found that Steffan was well and had recovered his lost love. They were joyous in their celebration, Tom, Mikel, Jeff and Andrew getting resoundingly drunk in toasting both Steffan and Tamara and all the other good reasons they could think of. To them everything was well, everything was settled. Two people did not share their joy when their spies brought news to them; one was Morgana Kyle who cursed with rage and began to lay plans to destroy whatever happiness Steffan might have found, the other was Lyle Whitfield, who knew that the happiness of these two would draw into the open the one he waited and searched for . . . Morgana Kyle. He would wait, and when she reached for Steffan, he would reach for her, for now he knew her evil as few others did and he vowed it was an evil he must destroy. There was no way of knowing how or when it would happen but he had the patience of a spider. He spun his web and then sat back and waited for Morgana to make the first move. When she did, he would catch her in his web and devour her evil soul.

While these two were comtemplating their actions, Steffan and Tamara stood at the rail of the *Scarlet Butterfly,* he with an astounded look on his face and she with laughter on her lips as they looked at the huge formidable and deadly looking Corvet's Rock.

Forty-nine

"Tamara" he said, "I know you are an excellent sailor, but no one could anchor a ship near that monster. It is impossible. It would chew you and your ship up and spit it back into the ocean like so much driftwood."

"Why, Captain Devers," she said with mischievous laughter in her voice, "would you care to make a wager?"

He looked at her, her green eyes laughed up at him. In the ten days it had taken to get to Corvet's Rock, she had relaxed and reverted to her sunny, freedom-loving ways.

Steffan had occupied the first mate's cabin, and not once did he reach out to her except in laughter and sharing the feeling of being with her. He had fought more than once a battle that left the nights long and often sleepless. But this was the way he wanted to see her. Bright and glowing, carefree like the gypsy she was. He could not help the words that came.

"The last wager we made, you lost, remember?"

He expected to see her withdraw into her shell and close him away from her again, but he did not take into the account her excitement and expectation.

"I shan't lose this one," she replied.

He looked again toward the monstrous granite rock with its crashing waves and nodded his head. "You're on. There's no way anyone can get a ship anywhere near that thing without being destroyed."

"Hold on tight, Captain Devers, you are about to get the ride of your life."

As they drew nearer and nearer the rock, Steffan could feel the tug of the heavy current beneath his feet.

"Tamara!" he shouted over the crashing waves.

"What?"

"This is crazy! You'll smash us against those rocks. Get us away from here!"

"Why, Steffan," she shouted, laughter on her lips and her hair

576

blowing free about her. "Are you afraid?"

"You're damn right, I am!" he returned. "Any man in his right mind would have respect enough to be afraid of that thing!"

"Don't you have any faith in my seamanship?"

"Yes!" he shouted, "it's your mental condition I don't feel too sure of right now. Tamara, I'll admit you're the greatest sailor on the ocean today if you'll give the orders to come about before it's too late."

"Too late!" she laughed. "The current's got us now."

Steffan was aware that no one but he seemed to be alarmed and he tried to hold himself in check but the overpowering gray rock and the loud crashing waves thundering against it were enough to terrify anyone. He reached for Tamara intending to hold her if a tragedy happened. His fingers found her as they were suddenly swept into the dark tunnel. In the dark, he pulled her against him and put his arms about her.

They were standing so when the ship shot from the tunnel into the quiet beautiful lagoon. Joy streaked through Tamara at two things. The amazement on his face and the fact that she was enjoying the hard strength of his arms about her.

"My God!" Steffan said in wonder, "if I didn't see this with my own eyes, I would never believe it. You could hide here forever and no one would ever find you. No wonder we searched so hard and never found you. How did you ever find a paradise like this?"

She told him of how she and Mikel first entered into the lagoon, and of the day when she brought her father.

Steffan could sense her complete relaxation with him. There was no fear in her eyes as he picked her up from the small boat they had taken from the anchored *Butterfly,* and stood her on her feet on the sand. They were alone since Tamara had given orders for the *Butterfly* to be examined from stem to stern. He wondered if the ship really needed it or if she were giving herself the chance to be alone with him. They walked along the shore and spoke of everything except what he would really have liked to talk about.

"Would you like to see the caves? From there you can watch a whole world of ships sail by without their having any idea you are there."

"I'd love to."

"Come along, let me show you my domain." She took him up the side of the cliffs where they stood together looking out over the white-capped waves.

He stood watching her as she gazed out to sea, then slowly she turned her head to look at him and their eyes held for a breathless moment. He was unsure and afraid. Afraid if he reached for her he would again see that shadow of fear in her eyes. With one tentative hand, he reached out and captured a few strands of hair between his fingers feeling the soft silken feel of it. Neither of them moved, each was caught in a spell that slowly wove its fingers around them and drew them to one another. He let his hand drop lightly on her shoulder, then move up to the nape of her neck which he caressed gently; with the softest pressure, he began to draw her to him.

There were only inches between her lips and his, then he bent his head and lovingly touched them. They were salty and moist; he allowed his tongue the pleasure of tasting as he gently moved her lips apart. He put his hands on her waist and felt no resistance as he drew her against him. He had no idea of the violent battle that was going on inside of her. Again the black smothering feeling almost overcame her. Again she felt the violence and the pain that had come with Jaspar.

"This is Steffan," her mind shouted. "He loves you. This is Steffan, not Jaspar. Be calm, remember . . . remember."

He could now feel the quivering tension in her body and he held her away from him, his eyes searching hers. Fear was there, but it was accompanied by need. Pain was there, but it was accompanied by a warm desire. The time had come for both of them to see if the barriers were too great.

"Tam," he said with restraint, "what was between you and Jaspar was cruel and vicious. It had nothing to do with love, not love as we have known it. I would never hurt you, and I would never try to take you against your will. I just want to tell you that I cannot deny the need I have for you. It is impossible to be so close to you, touch you and not want you. Will you try to remember what we had, try to forget the ugliness that followed and think only of the first time we were together. It was the most beautiful day in my life and I would give my soul to recapture it, not only for me but for you, to help you erase the black memories you have. Tam . . ." he whispered as he drew her into his arms again.

They stood clinging to one another while the wind whipped about them. The crashing waves were only an echo of his pounding heart as he felt her lips part and accept him. Her arms lifted about his neck and for the first time he felt a warm surrender.

He knew the barriers were still there and he didn't want to move too fast and frighten her. Slowly, he drew her back into the cave. In the half dark, he drew her down beside him on the warm sandy floor. It was most certainly not the place he would have chosen, but he was afraid if he let the magic moment slip by, it might never come again.

She closed her eyes and allowed herself just to feel. Feel the tenderness in the huge hands that caressed her, feel the strength in the long muscular body that held her so close to him. The old feeling of fiery need lit her body with a sudden bright flame, a flame that remembered and exalted in the memory.

It must have struck them both at the same time that they were in the most unlikely and uncomfortable place they ever could have been. The sand was rough and grainy, the cave was more than half dark. He sat up and braced his back against the wall and drew her onto his lap. Now the situation, though urgent to both of them, suddenly became humorous.

He could feel her body shaking with half suppressed giggles and he began to laugh. Soon they were clinging to each other and laughing helplessly. In all likelihood, it was probably one of the best things that could have happened. It seemed to break any remaining barriers and draw them to each other. "This is ridiculous," he said in a half strangled voice.

"It is rather amusing."

"Amusing!" he grunted, patting the sand beside him. "Your rump isn't on this nice soft mattress."

"Well, Steffan," she said, "I know where there's a much softer one."

"Are you by chance inviting me to your cabin, captain?"

"Well," she said, "I would but I have the most ferocious husband."

"Oh," he answered, "Jealous is he?"

"Quite."

"I'm quite adept at handling a husband such as he."

"Oh?"

"Yes, I just tell him he should love a wife as beautiful or someone will come along and snatch her away. It usually opens his eyes to all he's been overlooking."

"You think I've been overlooked?"

"I think you've been completely neglected and I'm too much a connoisseur of beauty to let the situation stand."

"And my jealous husband?" she laughed.

Steffan became quiet for a moment, the laughter slipped away. "He loves you, Tam. He was fool to ever let you slip away." He tightened his arm about her. "God knows I regret every moment we were apart. If you'll give me the chance I'll do my best to make it up to you. Will you give me that chance, Tam," he said, his voice slipping to a quiet whisper.

"Oh, Steffan," she murmured as she touched her lips to his. "Yes Steffan. Let's pretend today is that day a long time ago we first spent together."

She rose and he stood up beside her, feeling the tears in her voice without seeing them. He put his arm about her and they left the cave.

They spent the balance of the day swimming in the warm water of the lagoon. When the night came, they took blankets and walked down the strip of beach, away from the *Butterfly* and her crew. She came to him then, in the soft glow of the fire he had built and together they returned again to the place that held their hearts, the memories of love on the warm sands of Marriott Island. He watched the firelight play across her golden skin as he reached for her, he felt it silky smooth against his. They lay together, not rushing, but enjoying this moment as though they were the only two people in the world. He caressed the soft valleys and rounded curves of her body with gentle hands, trying to commit to memory every inch of her flawless skin. Her warm hands found him too in a touch that turned his blood to a fiery liquid. He wanted to hold this moment forever. The star kissed night, the warm breeze and the sound of the waves kissing the shore. All these and a vibrant beautiful Tamara in his arms. Warm lips captured him, silken thighs entwined him and the murmur of love words encouraged him until the moment that he joined with her, his body and hers blending into one. One rhythmic song of love, one wordless cry to the gods of passion. They mounted the steps of Olympus together in a blending of hearts, souls and bodies and they bound themselves again to one another, this time the joining was forged by a flame so intense, so consuming that it could never be broken again by anything less than death.

They spent several happy days and beautiful nights at Corvet's Rock, but they both realized that one day the outside world would call them and they would have to put their new love to the test.

They were laughing together while they shared some wine and a small picnic. He was thoroughly enjoying the return of the wild gypsy he had first loved. A young sailor approached them.

"Captain Marriott."

"Yes," Tamara said.

"We've word of another ship just left England for the Colonies. She's carrying medical supplies."

"Good, we could use them. Is the *Butterfly* ready?"

"Yes."

"We'll join you when the tide is ready to go out."

The young man nodded and left.

"So that's how we get out of here, with the tide," Steffan said.

"That's the first time you've questioned that," she smiled down on him as he lay relaxed on a blanket, his hands folded behind his head.

"It's the first time I've given a thought to leaving," he grinned.

"Did you expect to spend your life leisurely lying on a sunny beach, drinking wine and making love?"

"Sounds good to me."

"Lazy man," she laughed. "Get up from there and come with me. We are about to acquire some medical supplies. Get up and come on, we have a lot to do before we catch the evening tide."

It was to be an adventure he would never forget. First with the exit from the rock that had his heart in his throat. He caught her excitement as they bore down on the ship from the rising sun and he shared in her laughter when the ship was captured, the supplies transferred and they made the heart stopping entrance to the Rock again.

It was one of many that were to follow in the next few months. Then he helped in the transfer of their captured goods to Jack Teel's ship.

Jack had come at Tamara's request when she felt she had enough goods to be worthwhile. He would then make two or three trips. After that, he would remain dormant for a while to make sure no one found the way to the atoll where he met Tamara.

Jack and Tamara were walking along the beach waiting for the ships to be loaded, a project Steffan was supervising.

"Are you happy, Tamara?"

"I am Jack. I don't know when I've ever been happier."

"Your Steffan gives you a great deal."

"Everything."

"It is too bad you can't give also."

She stopped, her smile fading.

"What are you talking about, Jack?"

"Steffan's happiness."

"He's happy here . . . with me."

"Of course . . . for now. But what happens, Tam, when he begins to remember that his friends are fighting and he is here . . . safe. Tam, he loves you; and to get you back, to keep you, he'd do anything. I don't want to be cruel; you know I care what happens to you two, but don't you think you are being just a little selfish? You want everything on your terms."

"That's not true."

"Isn't it?"

She remained silent realizing for the first time that Steffan had turned his back on everything, his friends, his future, everything, to do what she wanted . . . to keep her love. She had taken everything from him just to prove he loved her.

"He's a man, Tam, I must say he is a strong and able man, and one day soon, he's going to want to do what needs doing. Are you going to hold him here? Are you going to make him choose between you and everything? If you do, his choice will be you for he still feels guilt for what happened to you. But if he makes that choice I think you will be the loser."

"Why must my love always hurt," she said sadly.

He shrugged. "Love needs the test now and then. If it is real it will survive."

"Why do you tell me this now?"

"Because I've had a message from Mikel. Every fighting man is needed now. Steffan should join his friends. For what you are doing you don't really need him."

She sighed, then she stood for a while in thought. "Jack" she said quietly, "I should like to see my father again, maybe it is time for Steffan and I to make a visit home."

He watched her, then he grinned. "And when he does get home and finds how he is needed, it will make it easier for you to let him stay."

"Yes."

"I always knew you were a clever woman, I just never realized how clever. Your separation will not be easy."

"When this is over, we'll make a home together in the Colonies. It will be a time then to be with each other. Until then . . . I must learn that I cannot enjoy everything I want when others suffer."

Jack was about to answer when Steffan approached them. "She's all loaded, Jack."

"Good, I'll leave within an hour."

"How are things at home?" Steffan asked.

Tamara watched him surreptitiously while he listened to Jack. It was obvious to her that he was hungry for news of the others he loved. She realized then that Steffan would never have said a word to her about how he felt. He would have gone on missing them and wanting to be home just to stay with her. His guilt and the terrible separation had made it impossible for him to leave her again.

When Jack had gone, Tamara and Steffan walked along the beach together, his arm about her waist and her head against his shoulder. They walked in silence.

"Steff?"

"Ummm?"

"The *Butterfly* will be staying hidden for the next few weeks."

"Yes, I know. She needs a little work and a lot of cleaning up."

"I . . . I thought we might go home for a while." He walked along in silence beside her for so long she didn't know if he intended to answer at all.

"Steff?"

"I heard you," he said.

"Do you want to?"

He turned to her and put his arms about her.

"You did say we?"

"Yes. I'd like to see my father and I'm sure you would love to see your family, also."

"I would. I'm just making sure."

"Sure?"

"Sure you're not making plans that don't include me."

"Steff!"

"Tam, I know how things are. I've listened to Jack. I want you to know there will be nothing that will separate us again. No matter what happens, we are in this life together."

"We'll go home together for a while, Steffan. What we decide to do later, we'll decide together, agreed?"

"Agreed. It will be good to see Tom and Cecile again."

"Yes, and my father and Mikel. Besides, we have a lot to talk over."

"How do we get there? We certainly can't take the *Butterfly*.

I've a feeling we wouldn't get too far before we were caught and hung.''

No, we'll send a message to Jack and he will have someone come for us. We should be able to leave the Rock in a couple of weeks.''

"I guess it is time to leave our own special heaven and get back to the real world and our responsibilities.''

"It has been a beautiful time and I shall never forget a moment of it. One day we will return to Corvet's Rock and build a small hideaway. A place we can run away to when we want.''

He squeezed his arm about her, not needing to tell her how much he agreed with her words.

Now that they had decided to go home, Steffan could hardly contain his excitement and Tamara was aware of his impatience to leave.

Jack, in reply to her request, sent a small nondescript ship, a ship which would impress no one and a ship that most certainly would go unnoticed in a harbor filled with many. She had her papers registered as an English ship out of Bristol, carrying a small cargo of tea. Jack even supplied the cargo which he had just recently pirated from another English ship. The idea amused him.

The journey to Boston harbor took a few days, but they were days and nights Steffan and Tamara used to the fullest. They enjoyed every moment of their floating island.

Then in the early morning the shoreline was spotted on the horizon and in less than two hours, they entered the harbor, and eased the small ship toward the docks.

No one was more suprised than the two of them when they found the entire family there to meet them. They found themselves held, kissed, pounded upon and cried over amid joyous laughter and babbled words no one could understand or cared to.

They were swept into a carriage and taken to the Perry home where a feast had been prepared for them.

"I don't understand how you knew we were coming," Steffan said in wonderment.

"Steffan," Mikel said, "one of my best friends is a pirate friend of yours. He felt we should know you were on your way so he sent me a message."

"Ah, I see."

Steffan was also delighted that Martin Gillis was there, although Commander Pierce could not come, since he had been given a ship with a full crew of recruits to train; he sent Steffan and Tamara his best wishes.

They all sat together down the length of the Perry table. Martin Gillis rose and looked about him, then he raised his glass.

"To the return of our favorite son and his beautiful lady. Now that they have found each other may they live in peace for long and fruitful days."

"Hear, hear" cried Randolph Perry. The men rose and raised their glasses to Tamara who smiled through the happy tears in her eyes.

The next day, Tamara woke to find Steffan already gone. When she inquired, she found that Jeff and Tom had come by early and asked him to go with them. Jeff had received orders and he was on his way to find out just where he was to go. After the formalities were cared for, they had found a not too noisy tavern and had a good lunch and shared a few drinks. It was then that Jeff and Tom filled him in on all that had been happening.

"Steff, I'm sure as hell glad you're home," Jeff said.

"Why?"

"Why! Look around you. This country needs good, well trained naval officers so badly it's pitiful. The Navy, if you can call it that, consists of very, and I do mean very, few ships and absolutely no men who have any training in warfare."

"From what I can see, if I stay, there's not much chance of getting my own ship unless I supply it myself. The one I was having built at home is finished but I doubt they will let me take her out of English waters if they have a suspicion where it is going."

"What do you mean 'if'?" Tom said.

"I was giving some thought of going with Tamara. She's obtained privateers' papers for two of Jack's ships. Under those we'd be free to take any English ship we found instead of staying here twiddling our thumbs waiting for orders, as I can see from you two, that very seldom come."

"Steff . . . it's no good that way," Jeff replied.

"Why?"

"Let me tell him" Tom said. "Steff, you of all people I know should understand. This is a new country; she's forming the base for a strong power, but she can't do that on letters of privateers. She's got to have both an Army and a Navy she can point to in pride. They've got some German general who's whipping their militia into something strong. She needs men to help build her Navy too. Me, I'd kind of like to be here to give it a good start."

If they could have read Steffan's mind they would both have understood. He was torn between the desire to join them and the fear of leaving Tamara. He knew she was not a woman to stay put and wait for him. No, once he was gone, she would be on the *Butterfly* and seeking British ships before long. He also knew it would do no good to ask her to remain at the Perry home for the balance of the war. She had been too much of a patriot when he had met her and she was too much of one now.

"I'll think it over."

"I wish you would. I'm not to leave for another two weeks, then I'll be joining Jones. I'm sure with your qualifications and Pierce behind you, they'd find a command fast. Maybe you'd be coming along. I have a feeling this is going to be more than a search-and-find cruise. I think Jones and Nelson expect to meet some strong opposition."

Steffan leaned forward, his interest in Jeff's words holding his attention. They also held the attention of another man who sat quietly at another table watching the three men in conversation. When they finally ceased talking and rose to leave, he placed a few coins on the table and followed them at a discreet distance.

Tamara and Martin Gillis were seated in the Perry garden. She had told him all that had happened to her from the last time she had seen him.

"So, you both decided to return home?"

"Yes."

He remained quiet for a moment then said, "It's going to be difficult for you."

"What?"

"Deciding what you will do. If you stand your ground and decide to go back to privateering, I know Steffan will choose the same route. He lost you once; he won't take that chance again. He would choose to be a privateer with no future than to let you go and stay here to be what he should be. You hold his future in your hands, you know."

"What should I do?" she said, perplexed; but the question was more directed at herself than him.

"I have a supposition."

"It is?"

"Just suppose," he began, "a pirate ship was given to the Navy with a young English captain at her helm. Suppose the lady who owned the ship remained among her friends and the people who loved her. I know it would be the most difficult thing she has ever done, but it would be her way to give the man she loved the freedom to walk the path where he is really needed.''

"You ask me to give up my way and stand beside Steffan, to give him my ship, to stay here and worry and pray he doesn't get killed, when the both of us could sail together as privateers?''

"I ask you for nothing,'' he smiled. "Your country needs what you have to offer. But your best offer might not be your own personal fight, but the sacrifice of what you want for someone else.''

"Steffan would never accept it like that. He knows me too well.''

"Then it would be up to you to convince him you are right. It's up to you to give him the freedom to go, for you and I know he will not go without it.''

She sighed and rose from her seat; he rose too and they began to walk. He smiled when he heard her soft laugh and they looked into each other's eyes, "Steffan was very lucky with the people in his life who love him,'' she said, "but especially so with you.''

"Thank you, my dear, I've always tried to help him find the right direction. I was leading him here when your lovely person appeared. You were good for him, you are strong and courageous. He needs a woman like you to stand beside him.''

"I will think about it. I want to talk to my father first. Oh, and speaking of my father, what is there between him and Marthie Price? They seem very attracted to each other.''

"Would that upset you?''

"Heavens, no, she's a beautiful person. I would like to see him find someone to share the balance of his life with.''

"I'm sure he will tell you about her, but I'm also sure they have found great comfort and peace with each other.''

"I hope so. Father has been lonely since Mother died.''

"He's had you.''

"Yes, but a man needs a woman, and I want my father to have someone to fill his days, someone he could love as he did Mother.''

"I should like to have met her.''

"She was a beautiful lady, understanding and compassionate.''

"And her daughter is much like her.''

"Thank you.''

"Yes, that's why I believe I know exactly what you are going to do.''

"And that is?''

"Oh, no I have my own ideas. You do what you have to do.

One day I will tell you what I thought. In the meantime, I had best be on my way. I've a meeting today to see where we can acquire a few more ships. We are forming a new and formidable Navy. I wouldn't be surprised some day to see it be a considerable force on the sea, maybe a hundred ships or so.''

"Oh come now, we're too young for that."

"Now, child, now, but who knows. Anyway, I must go. I shall see you and Steffan at dinner?"

"Yes. Good bye."

She watched him walk away, a straight, admirable man and she felt the influence he must have had on a growing Steffan. She wondered too about his words to her. All her life she had been a free and independent spirit. She had done as she pleased, never allowing someone else to be in control of her thoughts and her freedom. Now, she had to choose her way with someone else's freedom in the balance, and with their future and their love in the balance. The love she and Steffan shared had always been a free and giving thing. Could she now be the one to tie him to it. Restrict his freedom to choose, make her love a prize he had to hold. "No!" she thought, but then she felt the iron hand squeeze around her heart when she realized what her choice was. She would have to give the *Butterfly* to him, she would have to remain here and wait out the long painful hours, days, weeks, months he would be gone, for she knew as surely as she breathed that if she returned to the Rock and the *Butterfly* and went on privateering, Steffan would go also and they would lose a man who could give much to the cause for which they fought.

She walked the path of the garden in deep thought. So deep she did not see Steffan walking her way for a few minutes. Then at the sound of his footsteps on the stone walk reaching her, she looked up and watched him walk toward her.

Again the overpowering sense of his immense size and controlled strength overcame her. She smiled and watched him smile in return. When he reached her side, she felt again the intense searching look in the honey gold eyes. Strong arms drew her against him and a hard possessive mouth searched hers. She sighed contentedly and at that moment made up her mind about her future.

"Did you miss me, love?"

"Always, the minute you go away."

"Good" he laughed, kissing her several more times.

"Steff, you've been with Jeff and Tom?"

"Yes, getting recruited again. It seems the Colonies are building a Navy."

"Yes, so I hear. She needs more than privateers; she needs a good, strong, proud Navy of her own and the same kind of men to lead her."

"You sound like Jeff," he laughed.

"Maybe," she said thoughtfully, maybe I feel like Jeff does."

He tightened his arms about her. "If you think you're going back to the *Butterfly* alone, you're crazy."

"I'm not."

"Tam, you've got something on your mind, what is it?"

"Steff, I'm turning the *Butterfly* over to you and the Navy. I would only give her to you and to a country I loved."

"Tam, that would mean that you . . ."

"That I will stay here and wait for the man I love to come back to me."

"Tam" he whispered, then he pulled her against him and held her in a tight embrace. "I know what a sacrifice it would be for you. I can't ask it of you."

"Oh, Steffan, I have thought about it. I would give the *Butterfly* to you with all my love. I have only one thing to ask in return."

"What?"

"Come back to me safe, love. Don't let anything happen to you. I could not bear to lose you."

He could not speak, but his love for her flowed through him like a thundering river. Their eyes held and he read her love like a sweet song. Then he enclosed her in an embrace and took her lips with his in a kiss sweeter than any others had ever been.

Fifty

It was a difficult thing for the patriots who were trying to build a navy from nothing. They accepted the repainted, refitted *Adventurer,* but not before Tamara made them extremely uncomfortable by reminding them of her refusal.

The only naval action seemed to center around Jones, who, with the help of the few ships and men he could gather ravaged the English coast.

During the next year, Tom, Jeff and Steffan were away more often than home. They took some prizes and provided a small steady flow of arms and material the army needed.

The very first beginnings of an Academy for the training of naval officers was tentatively begun. Positions were offered to most of the men who commanded ships. They were enthused, but realized all their futures depended upon the outcome of the war, a war that looked impossible, but in which Martin Gillis and John Paul Jones had explicit faith.

That Tamara was not a person for waiting was obvious and she proved her love and faith in Steffan more by holding herself in check than she could have any other way. He knew it well and appreciated her sacrifice.

The scattered days that he was home they spent enjoying each other. On those few days, the war seemed a part of another life, another place. They kept these days free of it.

Despite the fact that the war raged around them, the fact that they were all united held them. Andrew and Marthie strengthened each other while awaiting word from Jonah who had spent the winter with Washington's Army at Valley Forge. Tom, Cecile and their son spent what few days they had together also trying to ignore the inevitable call to duty.

Steffan's admiration for Jones was complete. The man fought like a tenacious tiger, often taking severe damage to his ship, but in the long run usually winning the battles. He supported Jones in enough battles to realize his genius and tried to absorb some of his ability. Horatio Nelson, true to his reputation, drew men like magnets about him.

It was a time that drew them close to one another. They all felt the fine web of patriotism that drew the American colonies together. Win or lose, there was a comradeship forged that would remain unbreakable in the years to come.

Morgana Kyle lived a luxurious life. She had bought a large house about twenty miles from the Perry home. Of course, she kept herself away from the eyes of people who would know her, but she kept a close contact on what Steffan and Tamara were doing. It pleased her that they had ceased to be on guard and she waited for the time to be ripe to strike.

Morgana Kyle never forgot. She never forgot that Steffan had walked away from her. No man, before or since had ever done so. She never forgot, and she never forgave. Her evil heart held the anger to her until it blossomed into a deep and abiding hatred. It was a hatred that no longer wanted just to see them suffer, it was a hatred that wanted to see them dead, both Steffan and Tamara. With wealth she had accumulated through many ways over the years, she could reach far. The hatred obsessed her mind now and she waited only for Steffan to return again and the time she could get him and Tamara together. She plotted their deaths in so many ways, absorbed in methods . . . and madness that would come close to success.

Steffan stood at the rail of the *Adventurer* as it glided into the harbor. He had not been home for over three months. The *Adventurer* had made quite a success of this tour of duty, bringing with her two frigates and one merchant as prizes. He had taken advantage of the *Adventurer's* tremendous speed and superior maneuverability to take all three of them. The shores of home were welcome now. He saw to the docking and gave the orders for her care, then he told them to leave a skeleton crew aboard and go ashore for some relaxation, changing the crew aboard so that all the men would get some time at home before the *Adventurer* was on its way again. Then, he walked down the gangplank, whistling gaily on his way home.

Tamara had already received news that the *Adventurer* had been spotted, and she waited impatiently for Stefan, as she always did, and as he preferred, at home.

Steffan had purchased a small house of his own not too far from Jeff's and Brandy's. After that it did not take Tom and Cecile long to be looking about for a home of their own too. It was a very small cottage for Steffan had other plans for their permanent home, but he wanted to wait until the war was over and he was home to stay.

He walked up the walk, took the steps two at a time and threw open the front door to suddenly have his arms filled with woman. He laughed in exhilaration as he swung her up in his arms and kissed her fiercely.

"God, woman," he said as he dropped her feet to the floor but continued to hold her close to him. "You get more beautiful every time I see you."

"It's only because you've been at sea too long," she laughed.

He deliberately took her shoulders and held her away from him, pretending to study her intently.

"Nope!" he said firmly, "you are more beautiful today than you were three months ago." He pulled her into his arms and held her while he whispered against her hair. "You feel good, too, all warm and soft. I've missed you, love . . . I've missed you."

They walked together into the small sitting room and it was then that Steffan's eyes fell on a thick envelope on the table. He went to reach for it, but Tamara took it first.

"It's nothing important, Steffan, I was about to throw it away."

"What is it?"

"Nothing . . . really, it's nothing."

She started to walk away but he took her by the arm and turned her to face him. Firmly he took the envelope from her.

"Steffan, please," she said. "Let me throw it away. Please?"

"You're upset over something and I'd like to know what it is."

"Oh, Steffan don't open it, please let me just throw it away."

He looked at the envelope but he did not recognize the return address upon it. Then he took the papers from the envelope and read half aloud . . . . divorce has been granted to Tamara Marriott-Devers from Steffan Devers . . ." He lifted his eyes from the papers. "Tam?"

"It was so long ago . . . so much has happened. I had forgotten it . . . Steff, please . . . I . . ."

"We're divorced" he said in a voice filled with quiet shock.

"It's not important Steffan."

He looked at her for a moment, then he smiled and a look of sheer deviltry she had not seen in a long time appeared in his eyes.

"It had better be important, love; you see you have been living with me all this time unmarried. Why, love," he chuckled, "you're living in a state of sin."

"But . . . we could get married again quietly . . . no one need know."

"Well," he said slowly as though he were giving it a lot of thought. "I just don't know."

"Steffan," she said threateningly. "You wouldn't?"

"I think it might be fun. Having a pretty little thing like you at home and still be free to roam. I think I would really be able to enjoy that."

He began to chuckle but it died as she began to move toward him slowly, a brilliant gleam of anger in her eyes. He backed away from her, hands protectively in front of him, but laughter still on his lips.

"Now, Tam, there's no sense in being violent, after all it was your idea. I'm simply being agreeable. I'd live with you under any circumstances. I'm willing to be quiet about your terrible state if you'll just be nice; you know, a little love goes a long way and if you're real good, I might think of asking you to marry me . . . someday . . . maybe."

She glared at him. "I'm going to murder you if you say one more word. You, Steffan Devers," she said firmly, "are going to marry me immediately or I shall see to it you have a mutiny on the *Adventurer* and in the process they hang you . . . high . . . and for a very long time . . . until you are very, very dead."

She punctuated each word by the firm thrust of her finger against his chest.

"My dear," he said innocently, "are you proposing to me?"

"I'm proposing that if you don't marry me I shall do you great physical harm," she almost shouted, "starting with having my father poke you full of holes with the biggest, sharpest sword he can find."

"Now, hasn't anyone ever told you, love," he said as he suddenly reached out and grabbed her holding her close to him and bound so tightly she couldn't move. "That you catch more flies with honey than with vinegar? Maybe if you give me one convincing kiss I might take your proposal under serious consideration."

"You want me to convince you?" she said, sparks in her green eyes.

"If you can," he grinned. "Try hard, love."

"Damn you, Steffan Devers, I'll show you," she put both her arms about his neck, her body pressed against him and she moved it seductively. She drew his head down to hers and her parted lips and fire kissed tongue sent burning fire through him in a blazing kiss that shook him to the core.

"God," he whispered when she withdrew her lips from his.

"Captain Devers," she said in throaty, seductive voice, "that is only a small sample. Would you be interested in a larger one?"

"Interested is not exactly the word."

He tried to kiss her again, but she pulled away from him with a smile on her lips. "Now, Captain Devers, we're not married yet. Would you try to take advantage of me? I certainly will go no further with you until I know your intentions."

"My intentions," he chuckled, "are to take you to the nearest bed and change your sample into a very large amount."

"I'm afraid not."

"Tam?"

"I'm a single woman, and I will not go to bed with a woman-chaser . . . a seducer of young innocent girls a b . . ." her last words ended in a shriek as he grabbed her up into his arms and took her mouth in a ravaging kiss.

Her laughter rang joyously through the small cottage as he carried her to the small room they shared. He then made good his promise and her sample was the beginning of the most beautiful night they had ever spent together.

Together they told her father about the divorce and what started out to be a simple remarriage, turned into a gay party. It was planned as a small party by the Perrys but Jeff and Brandy along with Tom and Cecile decided to turn it into the kind of wedding Tamara had always wanted. What made the whole thing complete for them was that Tamara convinced her father that he and Marthie should be married at the same time. It turned into a large and beautiful celebration . . . it also turned into the bright day that heralded the darkest storm and brought them close to death.

The invitations to the double wedding covered most of the town. The Perrys' home was lit with hundreds of candles and food and wine were plentiful. The war, for one beautiful night, was to be held at bay. Neither couple had any plans to leave the town for a honeymoon until the hostilities ceased. Tamara and Steffan planned only to return to their cottage and Andrew and Marthie were to return to Marthie's home.

It was late and the party had reached the height of its festivity, when the butler made his way to Randolph Perry's side. He spoke to him for a moment, then Randolph rose and accompanied him from the room. It was almost twenty minutes before he returned, but when he did, his face was aglow and he seemed hardly able to contain his pleasure. He went to the orchestra and spoke to them for a moment. Their faces were filled with curiosity as were the dancers who were surprised when the music ceased. Randolph held up his hands. "Ladies and gentlemen, I crave your indulgence for some news I know you will be overjoyed to receive. The British have surrendered at Yorktown. After a long and bloody struggle, the hostilities have ended. The Colonies are now independent from English rule and I am surely grateful for all the patriots who have given their lives and their blood for her cause. We are a free nation."

The happiness was unbelievable as people shouted with enthusiasm and grasped each other in the sheer joy.

Both couples were filled with delight at the fact that the Colonies received their independence on their wedding day.

When the party was nearing its end, Steffan, who had been trying to spirit Tamara away for quite some time finally got her safely tucked into his carriage. They rode homeward laughing and holding one another feeling now that all their troubles were behind them.

When the carriage deposited them at the door of their cottage it was with Steffan's absolute assurance that neither the carriage nor the driver would be needed at least until after dinner the next day.

At the door of the cottage, the laughing couple were making their entry rather noisily and clumsily due somewhat to the fact that both were slightly tipsy, and both were completely engrossed in each other. The cottage was dark and Steffan fumbled to light the lamp. When he did, he looked toward Tamara, and received a shock that sobered him completely. Standing next to Tamara was Morgana Kyle. A triumphant smile on her lips, hatred in her eyes and a pistol at Tamara's heart.

"Morgana!"

"My dear Steffan," she said in a cold voice. Something in her voice sent a shiver of fear down his spine, then he looked into her eyes . . . and he saw the madness there. The destructive force of insanity had been given Morgana along with gift of beauty. It was the rare joke often played by the gods. He knew that he stood facing death, yet his fear was not for himself, but for Tamara who stood watching him. Her face was still, yet he could see the trembling hands, and he knew she was as frightened for him as he was for her.

"Morgana, it's me you want, let her go."

"No, Steffan," she said in a sing-song voice. "I once asked you not to leave me, but you did. I can only return the favor with one of its own kind. She will die first Steffan, I want to watch your face when you see her life's blood flow from her and you can do nothing about it."

"Morgana, you're ill. Let us help you. There are doctors . . . hospitals . . ."

"Tsk, Steffan you're like all the others."

"The others?"

"Yes, even when I was a child, my mother wanted to take me to doctors. She said I was different. I am, you know," her blue eyes narrowed shrewdly, "I can outsmart them all. I can have anything and anyone I want. They all want to give me things just to smile at them. Wade was like that, you know." She said the words dreamily, as though she were remembering something pleasant. "Even the last night of his life, he still wanted me."

"You killed him that night?" Steffan asked.

"He had to die, Steffan. He was the only man who knew you had left, run from me," her voice was almost a caress. "You have to pay for that too, Steffan. You must die."

Steffan took a step toward her but her dreaming blue eyes snapped to alertness and she pressed the muzzle of the gun against Tamara.

"No, Steffan, don't be foolish. You could not reach me before I could kill her. Why not give her all the time you can. Soon enough I will end both of your lives."

"Steffan," Tamara whispered, her eyes pleading for him not to do anything to alarm Morgana for she too could feel the un-balanced mental state she was in. For the first time in a long time, Steffan was both afraid and completely unsure of what to do. He tried to keep her talking, playing for time, at least time to think. Steffan looked at Tamara, his eyes begging her forgiveness for a moment, then he turned to Morgana . . . and smiled.

"I was a foolish boy that night, Morgana. I have often re-gretted what I did. I came back later but you had already gone. That night at your house, when you drugged me. I'm sorry for that too. It was only that I was too foolish not to recognize your beauty."

She was listening. He prayed silently. "Morgana, you are the most beautiful woman I have ever known." She smiled, but still the pistol was pressed against Tamara. "Morgana, we could go away, you and I. Somewhere far where no one would ever find us. An island, we could take my ship and go."

The pistol wavered and turned slowly toward him. There was a bestial snarl on her lips and violent, insane hatred in her eyes. She knew he had told her the final lie. He looked at the face of death and knew there were no more words he could say, and that nothing could stop the bullet that would soon be headed for his heart.

Then, as he stiffened himself in preparation for the blow, as he felt the sweat trickle down his body he clenched his teeth wondering if, even if she shot him, he could reach her, kill her, before she turned on Tamara.

Then the dark shadow seemed to loom up behind her. A hand reached out and grasped the pistol from her grip. She was held, fighting furiously and cursing wildly the restraining arms that held her. Steffan looked over her shoulder at a man he had never seen before. He had never seen him, but Tamara had. "Lyle Whitfield!" she gasped.

"Yes, I am sorry I was not here sooner or this never would have happened. She managed to elude my men tonight and it took a little time for me to figure out where she was. Then I remembered today was your wedding day. It did not take me long then to know where she had to be."

"I'll call the authorities," Steffan said. Tamara went to him and he held her while he looked over her head at Lyle.

"No . . . no authorities."

"But she's . . ."

"Insane, yes, I know. But she is too beautiful to lock away in bedlam. I will care for her. I shall keep her locked away where she can do no harm. Is that enough for you?"

"Why?" Steffan inquired. "She's dangerous."

"Why? I don't know. I only know I cannot lock her up in a cage like an animal. I will care for her, keep her imprisoned in my country home. There is no chance she can escape from there and besides if she did, England is a long way away. She would never get far. Let it be enough, Steffan."

Morgana was strangely quiet and still, but if it was a ruse, Lyle did not succumb to it. He held her, if possible, even tighter. Steffan looked at Tamara who was gazing at Morgana with pity. He knew what her answer would be. He nodded his head. Lyle requested his help and Steffan aided him in binding Morgana's hands, aware every moment that her cold violet blue eyes had never left his face. He felt an alien emotion . . . fear. It left him weak and very anxious for Lyle to take Morgana away.

When he did, Tamara collapsed in Steffan's arms and began to cry in relief.

"It's all right, love. We'll never see either of them again." He said the words wishing he was as sure as he wanted her to believe. "Tam, look at me."

She looked up into the soothing honey gold eyes that filled her with love and assurance that she was safe.

"It's all over, Tam, everything is over. All the past is wiped clean and we can start a whole new life."

"She . . ."

"Shhh, Tam. We'll forget Morgana and her evil. It will never touch us again. Now the war is over and Morgana is gone there is nothing for us but each other and a life of being together and being happy."

"Steffan . . . let's go to Corvet's Rock. Let's build our hideaway. Let's get away from all this for a while."

"Sounds good to me. Maybe we can go as far as Marriott Island with your father and Marthie on the *Sea Borne,* then we can take a small boat from there."

"I love you, Steffan."

"And I love you, my wild little gypsy. Let me take you back where you belong. I want to see you by the sea, your hair free in the wind and your heart open and filled with love. Love as we know it together."

"Yes, Steffan . . . let's go home."

A ship left for England late that night. In one of its cabins Lyle sat looking at the haunted-eyed beauty who lay quiet and still on the bed. He loved her. He knew that, just as he knew he would never let her loose on society again for she was the wildly beautiful face of evil and death and he would guard her, because he could not kill her, he would hold her forever prisoner.

The next day, the *Sea Borne* left for Marriott Island. Once there, Steffan and Tamara took the small launch and made the familiar yet still heartstopping entrance to Corvet's Rock. There they spent days of glorious beauty, walking the beach, swimming the lagoon and reaching out to touch each other to renew the bright and glowing love they had.

The path of their lives seemed bright. The days, if glorious, were nothing compared to the star-kissed nights they spent in each other's arms on the warm sand of their paradise. They promised each other the world, and they fulfilled each other's promise with giving sweet love.

"Steffan, this is our world."

"You are my world, love. If I've told you that before it bears repeating. I love you, Tam."

"And I love you Steffan."

Their lips touched, their hearts blended, and they joined their love forever.

Epilogue

The small house on Corvet's Rock was finished and Steffan and Tamara spent many of their days there, alternating them with days on Marriott Island. Jonah had joined his mother there and Mikel had returned to his home. Returned with a sweet little bride named Marrianne whom he had met in England.

As the days passed into weeks and then into months, nothing but happiness crowned the lives of the people on Marriott Island and their friends who visited often from the new country called the United States of America.

It was with great joy that Steffan was given the news by Tamara that they were to have a child. Steffan could barely wait for the time to come, and when it did, he was there beside her bed as Tamara gave birth to a lovely little girl they named Elizabeth. It was Steffan who was first to hold her, and it was he who guided the first steps she took. It was also he who swore she was an exact duplicate of her mother when she began to show more affinity for the sea, the sand and the rocks of Marriott Island than for all the toys and pretty dolls she owned. That complete happiness reigned on Marriott Island was obvious to everyone who came there. Complete, utter happiness . . .

England, dark and stormy. A house that sat secluded in a thick woods. The sea crashed upon the nearby shore and lightning split the dark clouded sky.

Inside, a man lay across a bed, his arm hung down beside it and from the tips of his fingers slowly dripped spots of bright red blood that spattered on the floor. His sightless eyes looked unblinking at the shadow of the woman who was slowly closing the door behind her. She opened the front door and walked out in the black night; with her walked evil, death and revenge. The night swallowed her up, but not before low throaty laugh touched the darkness and the sound of one name touched her smiling lips. . . . "Steffan." The whisper came . . . "Steffan."

She vanished into the blackness of the storm. And all that was left was the sound of the mournful tears of rain and the crashing of the waves on the barren shore.

THE RICHMOND SERIES
by Elizabeth Fritch

RICHMOND #1: THE FLAME (654, $2.75)

Amidst the rage and confusion of the Civil War, Melissa Armstrong fights a personal battle for an ominous goal: to maintain loyalty to her family—without losing the man she loves!

RICHMOND #2: THE FIRE (679, $2.75)

Now, in Richmond, Melissa knows a passionate love for a Cavalry lieutenant who helps her forget the only home she's known. If only she could forget that their destinies lie on opposite sides of the flag!

RICHMOND #3: THE EMBERS (716, $2.95)

If time could heal a nation stained with the death and blood of the Civil War, perhaps Melissa's heart would mend one day also. But she never really believes it—until she rediscovers love.

RICHMOND #4: THE SPARKS (962, $3.50)

Two years had passed since the Civil War had ravaged the land, and Abby Weekly knew that Richmond was the place to begin again. But as the state of Virginia struggled for readmission into the Union, Abby found herself torn between two men: one who taught her the meaning of passion—and one who taught her the rapture of love!

Available wherever paperbacks are sold, or order direct from the Publisher. Send cover price plus 50¢ per copy for mailing and handling to Zebra Books, 475 Park Avenue South, New York, N.Y. 10016. DO NOT SEND CASH.

MORE SUSPENSEFUL GOTHICS

GOTHIC GEMS FOR ROMANTIC SUSPENSE!

THE CURSED INHERITANCE (875, $2.50)
by Lizabeth Loshry
Lovely Sara will inherit her grandfather's acres of vineyards—only on the condition that she marry a handsome—but ruthless—stranger!

THE DARK SEAS OF MALTERN MANOR (832, $2.50)
by Kay Vernon
Terror haunts lovely Lettie Ardrey until one day her nightmare comes true—and the mysterious stranger of her dreams captures her heart and soul!

THUNDER CASTLE (795, $2.95)
by Veronica Smith
Katherine is compelled to search for the ancient treasure buried deep within haunted Thunder Castle—and becomes the next victim of the castle's terrifying curse!

**THE SAVAGE SPIRITS OF
SEAHEDGE MANOR** (940, $2.95)
by Dianne Price
The shrieks of the dead are Drew's nightly lullaby at Seahedge Manor. But as time passes, she wonders what she has to fear more: the island's stormy nights or her grim, unwelcoming relatives.

THE VANDERLEIGH LEGACY (813, $2.75)
by Betty Caldwell
When Maggie visits secluded Jaeger's Nest, she's sure it will calm her nerves. But then someone turns her heavenly haven into a cursed hell—and that someone wants Maggie dead!